PENGUIN BOOKS

AUGUST 1914

Alexander Isayevich Solzhenitsyn was born at Rostov-on-Don in 1918, the son of an office worker and a schoolteacher. After graduating at Rostov University in mathematics – he took a correspondence course in literature simultaneously – he was called up for the army. He served continuously at the front as a gunner and artillery officer, was twice decorated, commanded his battery, and reached the rank of captain. In early 1945 he was arrested in an East Prussian village and charged with making derogatory remarks about Stalin. For the next eight years he was in labour camps, at first in 'general' camps along with common criminals in the Arctic and later in Beria's 'special' camps for long-term prisoners. The particular camp described in his book *One Day in the Life of Ivan Denisovich* (also available in Penguins) was in the region of Karaganda in northern Kazakhstan. Released in 1953, on Stalin's death, Solzhenitsyn had to remain in exile for three years, although his wife was allowed to join him, before returning to Russia. He settled near Ryazan and taught in a secondary school. In 1960 he submitted his novel, *One Day...*, to Alexander Tvardovsky, the poet and editor of *Novy Mir* (New World), a literary journal; it was published, on the final decision of Khrushchev himself, in the November 1962 edition of *Novy Mir*, which sold out immediately. Two further stories by him were published during 1963. In 1968 Solzhenitsyn came under attack from the Russian *Literary Gazette*, which alleged that since 1967 his aim in life had been to oppose the basic principles of Soviet literature, and accused him of being content with the role given him by ideological enemies of Russia. He was expelled from the Soviet Writers' Union in 1970. His most recent novel, *The First Circle*, is now available in English; he has also written a play, *The Love-girl and the Innocent*. His novel *Cancer Ward* is available in Penguins.

In 1970 Solzhenitsyn was awarded the Nobel Prize for Literature.

Alexander Solzhenitsyn

August 1914

Translated by Michael Glenny

Penguin Books

Penguin Books Ltd, Harmondsworth, Middlesex, England
Penguin Books Australia Ltd, Ringwood, Victoria, Australia

—

First published in English by The Bodley Head 1972
Published in Penguin Books 1974

Copyright © Alexander Solzhenitsyn, 1971
Translation copyright © Michael Glenny, 1972
Maps copyright © Arthur Banks, 1974

—

Made and printed in Great Britain by
Hazell Watson & Viney Ltd, Aylesbury, Bucks
Set in Monotype Imprint

This book is sold subject to the condition
that it shall not, by way of trade or otherwise,
be lent, re-sold, hired out, or otherwise circulated
without the publisher's prior consent in any form of
binding or cover other than that in which it is
published and without a similar condition
including this condition being imposed
on the subsequent purchaser

TRANSLATOR'S NOTE

The translator wishes to record his gratitude for the invaluable help given to him in the form of research, editorial assistance and specialist advice by Vera Belyavina-Dixon, Dr M. Lewin, Susan Henderson, Leonid Vladimirov, Jacqueline Mitchell, Archpriest Sergei Hackel and Linda Aldwinckle; as well as for the skill, support and unfailing patience of the directors and editorial staff of The Bodley Head. He is also greatly indebted to his colleagues of the Department of Russian Language and Literature and of the Centre for Russian and East European Studies, University of Birmingham, without whose sympathy and co-operation this translation could not have been made.

M.G.

The maps on pages 648-55 have been specially drawn for this edition by Arthur Banks.

PUBLISHER'S NOTE

In the 'screen' sequences in this book, the four different margins are used to represent four sets of technical instructions for the shooting of a film. These are, from left to right on the page: 1. Sound effects; 2. Camera direction; 3. Action; 4. Dialogue. The symbol = indicates 'cut to:'.

I

They left the village on a clear morning at dawn. In the early sunlight the whole of the Caucasus range, each single indentation,
could be seen, brilliantly white with deep blue hollows, apparently
so close at hand that a stranger to the region might have thought it
a mere two hours' drive away.

It towered so vast above petty human creation, so elemental in
a man-made world, that even if all the men who had lived in all the
past millennia had opened their arms as wide as they could and
carried everything they had ever created or intended to create and
piled it all up in massive heaps, they could never have raised a
mountain ridge as fantastic as the Caucasus.

All the time, from village to village, the road kept the ridge
directly in front of them, an ever-present goal with its snowy expanses, its bare crags and its shadows hinting at ravines. But with
every half-hour it seemed to melt slightly at the base and detach
itself from the earth, until it appeared to be no longer fixed but
with its upper two-thirds hanging in the sky. It became shrouded
in vapour, the gashes and ribs and mountainous features seemed
blended into vast, cloud-like white masses which were then riven
into vaporous fragments indistinguishable from real clouds. After a
while they too were wiped away and the range vanished altogether
as if it had been a celestial mirage, leaving the travellers surrounded
by a greyish sky and a pale heat-haze. They had driven without
changing direction for half a day and had covered more than thirty
miles by mid-afternoon; now it appeared as though they were no
longer faced by a gigantic mountain range but were instead hemmed in by rounded foothills: the Camel, the Bull, the bare-topped
Snake and the thickly wooded Iron Hill.

When they had set out the road was not yet dusty, the steppe still cool and wet with dew, and they had driven on through the time of day when the steppe rang with bird-song, took wing, chirped, and whistled, the grassland a-rustle. Now they were approaching the spa town of Mineralnye Vody towing a lazy cloud of dust behind them, at the hour in the afternoon when everything was at its deadest and the only clear sound was the steady wooden rattle of their gig, the noise of the horse's hooves being almost smothered by dust. With the passing hours the delicate aromas of the grassland had come and gone, leaving only the warm smell of sun mixed with dust. Their gig, the straw on the floorboards and they themselves smelled of it, but having lived in the steppe for as long as they could remember, they found the smell congenial and the heat not fatiguing.

Since their father had not felt inclined to give them his sprung four-wheeler, to save it from wear and tear, they had been shaken about so much whenever they had driven at a trot that they had come most of the way at a walk. They had driven between fields of wheat and herds of cattle, past barren salt marshes, up gently sloping hills and across steep-sided gullies, some dry, some full of water. They did not see one real river, nor any big villages, and hardly met a soul as it was Sunday and no one was about. Isaakii, who was always easy-going but who because of the object of this journey was in an especially good mood today, was not wearied by the eight-hour drive and could have gone on for twice as long, just holding the useless reins hanging limply on either side of the tattered straw hat over the horse's ears.

His youngest half-brother, Yevstrashka, who was to go through all the bouncing again that night on the return journey, at first slept on the straw behind Isaakii's back, then tossed about, stood up, gazed around at the steppeland, jumped down, ran off, and caught up with the gig again. Perpetually active, he never stopped talking or asking questions: 'If you close your eyes, why does it feel as if you're going backwards?'

Yevstrashka had just moved into the second-year class of the Pyatigorsk high school, although at first his father had only agreed to let him go, like Isaakii, to the local secondary school. The elder brothers and sisters, so the argument went, only knew about farming, cattle and sheep, yet had managed well enough. Isaakii was sent to school a year later than necessary and after high school his father had kept him back for another year before allowing himself to be persuaded that what the boy now needed was to go to university. But just as oxen do not move a heavy load with a quick jerk but with a long, steady pull, so Isaakii dealt with his father by patient insistence and without a head-on clash.

Isaakii loved his native village of Sablya and their farm six miles distant from it. He loved the work, and in the holidays, as now, he never shirked his share of the scything and threshing. As for the future, he had hoped to be able to combine the life he had known since childhood with the new outlook he was acquiring as a student. But with every year this ideal faded, for his learning estranged him irrevocably from his past, from the villagers and from his family.

There were only two students in the whole village. Their ideas and their appearance provoked the villagers to amazement and laughter, and as soon as they arrived home they would quickly change into their old clothes. But one thing pleased Isaakii: for some reason village gossip drew a distinction between the other student and himself: him they teased as a *narodnik*. No one knew who had first fixed that label on him nor why it had stuck, but now everyone amiably called him by this nickname. There had long since ceased to be any *narodniks* in Russia, but although Isaakii would never have dared to call himself a *narodnik* in public he did in fact think of himself as one, as someone who had received an education to use for the benefit of the people and who would go back to the people with the book, the word, and with love.

However, even in his own family this 'return to the people' was almost impossible. The ideals which Isaakii had acquired from the teaching of Count Tolstoy demanded truthfulness and a clear conscience; yet where his family was concerned the opposite happened: he found himself telling lies. For instance it was impossible to tell his father that a church service was a spectacle unworthy of belief in God, and under some priests actually a disgraceful scandal; that he only went to church so as not to shame his father in the village and would really much prefer not to go. And, having become a vegetarian, he was never able to explain to his father and family and the villagers that it was a matter of conscience; to maintain that one should not kill and therefore should not eat any living thing would cause ridicule and laughter at home and in the village. And so Isaakii would lie, saying that abstention from meat was the latest discovery of some German doctor and that since it guaranteed a long life he wanted to try it out. Although lying caused him agony, things would have been even worse if he had not lied.

But did his father's feelings matter? As the years went by his vigorous, possessive stepmother gradually alienated him from his father and even from the home itself: his elder brothers and sisters grew up and went away and the house was taken over by her and her children. This made Isaakii's latest decision easier to take, but even here he could not be completely frank, entangled as he was in so many previous lies. He was forced to pretend he had to return to university early for 'practical work', and even this invention had to be explained to his ingenuous father.

So far the effect on their village of three weeks of war had been nothing but two manifestoes declaring war on Germany and Austria, which were read out in church and posted up in the churchyard, followed by the call-up of two contingents of reservists, while horses for remounts were delivered separately to the district town, because the men of their village did not count as Terek Cossacks but as Great Russians: they were therefore mustered into the infantry. In all other respects the war made no impact at all—newspapers never reached the village and it was too early for letters from the army in the field. In any case there was no such thing as a 'letter'; for people to 'get letters' had always been considered ostentatious and snobbish in their village and Isaakii tried to avoid receiving them. None of the Lazhenitsyns had been called up for service: the oldest brother was well on in years, his son was already on active service, the middle brother had some fingers missing, Isaakii was still a student and his stepmother's children were too young.

Nor were any signs of war noticeable on their half-day's journey through the vast steppe.

They had crossed the bridge over the river Kum, driven over the stone viaduct across the baking hot expanse of the double-tracked railway line, and were driving along the grass-grown main street of the village once known as Kumskaya, now called Mineralnye Vody. Here too they saw no signs of war. Life, stubbornly resistant to upheaval, flowed on as sluggish and unremarkable as before.

They stopped by a well in the shade of a large elm. Yevstrashka had to halt here to water the horses and cool them down before driving back home. Isaakii had a wash, sousing himself down to the waist with two bucketfuls of water. Yevstrashka poured the icy water on to Isaakii's back out of a dirty tin mug, after which he gave himself a good dry, put on a clean white shirt tied at the waist with a belt and brushed the dust off himself. Leaving his belongings in the cart except for a small bundle, he set off for the station.

The station square in Mineralnye Vody was a typical country village square, with hens scratching about along its sides and charabancs and carts, followed by a trail of dust, driving up to the long wooden station building.

The platform, by contrast, its length shaded by a light awning supported on thin painted pillars, was airy and cool, hinting, as it did this morning, at all the charms of a mountain resort. Wild vines grew up the pillars of the awning and everything had the familiar, cheerful air of a country *dacha*, as if here too no one had heard of such a thing as war. Ladies in light-coloured coats and men in tussore suits walked along behind their porters towards the platform for trains to Kislovodsk. Ice-cream, sparkling Narzan water, coloured balloons and newspapers were on sale. Isaakii had already bought several of these papers, opening some as he walked along and the rest as he sat on a bench on the *dacha*-style platform. His face, normally gentle, pensive and kind, took on an expression of keen, tense absorption. In contrast to his usual deliberate manner he did not read each news item to the end, but skipped about from column to column, unfolding a second and then a third newspaper. Marvellous news! Major Russian victory at Gumbinnen! The enemy will be forced to evacuate the whole of Prussia ... things going well on the Austrian front too ... and the Serbs have won a victory! ...

As he sat there, radiant with emotion, forgetting even to go and buy his ticket, a girl's voice called out to him excitedly and someone touched him on the shoulder. It was Varya, an old friend from his schooldays in Pyatigorsk. An orphan, in those days her scraped-back hair had made her head look narrow and smooth, but now her hair was fluffed out on either side and she was clearly thrilled to see him.

'Sanya! You? What a coincidence! How funny, all the way from St Petersburg I was thinking I would meet *you*, of all people! I wanted to send a telegram to your village but then I remembered you don't like . . .'

She did not turn her head, so that he could not see her profile, the curve of her rather large, hawk-like nose and her assertive, masculine chin. Besides, it would be unkind to notice such things when someone greeted you so warmly.

Sanya was pleased to see her, but lost for words. They sat down side by side.

'Do you remember, Sanya, how we met by pure chance in Pyatigorsk? Are you travelling, or are you meeting somebody?'

He did not look all that young, certainly not boyish; but in his clean white shirt and with his tousled, wavy, corn-coloured hair he struck her as a typical son of the steppe, tanned and healthy, as though suffused with the sunlight. Between the triangle of his clipped, russet moustache and the shaggy growth of an immature beard his lips broke into a friendly smile and he said:

'No, I'm travelling . . .'—his eyes never could express simple, uncomplicated delight, it was always mixed with inward reservation—'. . . to Moscow.' He looked down and away from her, rather as if he felt guilty or was afraid of upsetting her. 'I'm calling in at Rostov first. I have a friend there. You know him—Kotya, Konstantin.'

'But the term doesn't start for three weeks yet! Or do you think they'll call you up,' Varya asked anxiously, 'when you're still only in your fourth year? Of course they won't! Why are you going away then? Why?'

He gave an embarrassed smile.

'Well, you know . . . I'm restless at home on the farm . . .'

It was true that they had met before by accident. A pupil of the Pyatigorsk city girls' school, she had gone out one evening on to the main street secretly hoping for something to happen, when this high-school boy three years older than herself, whom she already knew slightly, had come towards her.

Whenever they met they would have discussions. Their meetings consisted of serious, intelligent conversations which were very important to Varya. She had never, as far as she could remember, had a close friend older than herself. Even when it was dark, when they could not be seen by their teachers and it would have been all right for Sanya to have taken Varya's arm, he did not take it.

Although she respected him for his seriousness, she wished he would take her arm, even if it meant respecting him slightly less.

Later on they occasionally went to school dances and other parties, but there too they spent most of their time in discussion and never danced. Sanya said that embracing during a waltz created desires which were not founded on true emotions and that Count Tolstoy considered this a bad thing. Varya gave in to his gentle, careful reasoning and convinced herself that she did not want to dance either.

After that they kept up a correspondence for several years, during which time he wrote her sober, sensible letters. Although Varya's studies had broadened her outlook considerably and she now knew plenty of clever people, she often thought about Sanya and wanted to see him again. However, burdened with her studies, she never left St Petersburg in summer, and Sanya never went there.

Three weeks ago, when Varya had read the Tsar's manifesto stuck to an advertising pillar on Vasilevsky Island where she lived, she took a tram across the Neva and there on St Isaac's Square saw the German Embassy being sacked by patriots. Everyone was wildly excited, as though what had arrived was not a war but their own long-awaited happiness. And in that moment of violence by the brownish-black pillars of St Isaac's Cathedral, Varya had had a sudden urge to see Sanya at once, that very minute. Whenever she drove past the cathedral, in fact, she always thought of him. Disliking his own name, he used to laugh it off by saying that Peter the Great was his namesake; he too had been born on St Isaac's day, hence the name of the cathedral, the only difference being that the Tsar had had his name changed to a better-sounding one whereas he, a boy from the steppe, had not.

Without warning Varya had suddenly been summoned to Pyatigorsk—her 'guardian', the man who had donated money to enable her and many other orphans to study at the university, had fallen seriously ill. It was considered proper that she should go and see him, although he did not remember all his beneficiaries and the arrival of some unknown girl student with formal expressions of gratitude was hardly likely to improve his condition. And as she sat for four uncomfortable days in the train crossing the whole breadth of the empire, for some reason the thought of Sanya suddenly came into her head and she cried out: 'Sanya, meet me! Sanya, meet me!' as she had once done when walking down the length of the main street of Pyatigorsk in the days of her angular head and scraped-back hair.

She felt frightened and lonely. Her life had not been a particularly full one, but at least she had had a sense of belonging, of being one drop of water in the great lake which was the life of Russia. Now it was as though the bottom of that lake had opened up and the water was draining away for ever, swirling and roaring as it went. Before it dried up completely she had to hurry, hurry!

And another thing—she wanted to find out why everything had suddenly been turned upside down. What had happened? Only a month or three weeks ago no thinking Russian citizen had doubted the fact that the ruler of Russia was a despicable individual, unworthy of serious mention; no one would have dreamed of quoting him except as a joke. Yet in a matter of days everything had changed. Quite voluntarily, seemingly educated, intelligent people would gather with serious faces around the advertisement pillars, and the Tsar's long string of pompous titles, simply because they were printed on these massive, cylindrical slabs, did not strike them as ridiculous at all. Equally voluntarily, people would of their own accord read out in loud, clear voices: 'At the call to arms, Russia has risen up to meet the enemy, with iron in her hands and with the cross upon her heart, ready for a feat of valour . . . The Lord sees that we have taken up arms not from martial ambition nor for the sake of vain earthly glory, but for a just cause—to defend the integrity and safety of our divinely-protected Empire . . .'

Throughout her long journey Varya had observed the effects of war—the loading of troop-trains, the farewells. Especially at small stations, the Russian leave-taking was an almost joyous affair, with the reservists dancing away to balalaika music and raising the dust on the trampled earth of the trackside. They would call out in obviously drunken voices while their relatives made the sign of the cross over them and wept as they drew away. Whenever one string of freight-cars full of reservists passed another, a fraternal 'Hurrah!' would go up from the two trains and was prolonged in a crazy, desperate, senseless roar for the length of both.

And no one demonstrated against the Tsar.

Now Sanya was equally unable to answer her question: 'What has happened?' He too felt himself being sucked by the same whirlpool into the same bottomless pit. Had he, her faithful mentor of old, taken leave of his senses too? She was now desperate to give him back the clarity of thought and firmness of will which he had once given her, to snatch him out of the whirlpool as fast as her frail, thin arms were able. Although she had not prepared her words, the thoughts flowed spontaneously as she spoke . . . The decades of 'civic' literature, the ideals of the intelligentsia, the students' devotion to the common people—was all this to be abandoned and cast aside in a single moment? Could they simply forget it all? . . . The ideals of Lavrov, of Mikhailovsky? . . . Hadn't he himself once said . . . ? Anyone watching them might have thought that she was the militant patriot of the two, and that it was he who was gently arguing against the war. Varya became quite heated, the underlying harshness of her looks came to the fore, that tenseness which was never entirely absent from her face and tended to spoil it. She stood up and in her desperation knocked her hat crooked. It was her cheapest and least flattering hat, chosen not for its attractiveness but only to protect her from the sun.

Sanya lowered his newspapers. He was lost for words and began to justify himself with some embarrassment.

'It's not like the Japanese war. *They* attacked us. What have we done to the Germans?'

A fine thing—giving way to that reactionary sort of patriotism! It was a betrayal of all his principles! All right, so he never was a revolutionary, but he was always a pacifist.

The newspapers resting on his knees, Sanya quietly folded his arms. Unable to defend himself, he stared placidly at her and nodded his head. He felt sad.

Terrified by his silence, she guessed what was in his mind.

'You aren't going to volunteer now, are you?'

Sanya nodded. He smiled diffidently.

'I feel . . . sorry for Russia.'

The water gurgled and roared as it drained out of the lake.

'What do you mean, sorry for Russia?' asked Varya, stung to fury. 'Who are you sorry for? That fool of a Tsar? Those disgusting little shopkeepers who join the Black Hundreds and beat up the Jews? The priests in their long robes?'

Sanya did not answer—there was nothing he could say. Instead he listened. The hail of reproaches did not make him in the least resentful: it was his invariable habit to test himself against the person he was arguing with.

'Have you really got the right temperament to fight?' Varya was snatching at anything to hand. For the first time she felt cleverer than he, more mature and more critical—yet the only result was a chilling sense of loss. 'What about Tolstoy?' she said as a last resort. 'What would Lev Tolstoy say about it, have you thought of that? Where are your principles? Where's your consistency?'

Beneath Sanya's corn-coloured brows on his sunburnt forehead and above his russet moustache, the sadness and irresolution in his clear, light blue eyes were all too plain.

He could find nothing to say and merely shrugged his shoulders slightly as he whispered:

'I feel sorry for Russia . . .'

2

For Sanya it was no novelty to become entangled in contradictions between his views and his feelings. His most urgent need was to bring them into line with each other—and to do that was the hardest thing of all.

He meant it sincerely when he said that the theatre and dancing were stupid, titillating amusements, though out of curiosity he felt drawn to the theatre and especially to dances. Although his body craved meat especially after loading wheatsheaves, he strove earnestly not to eat it, and he was equally sincere about being against all forms of war. Yet all their dishes included meat: it was a daily reality, and in protest against it he was able to exercise his self-control and test the strength of his opinions every day of the month. But war was something different; no one was ever in favour of war—indeed it seemed so completely unthinkable in an age of advanced civilisation that there was no time to prepare oneself for it. There was only one accepted attitude to war—that it was a sin. It was easy enough to hold this view without putting it to the test; but now the first test had suddenly come, and in the peaceful, wide-open steppelands beneath cloudless skies it was a hard one to withstand. Sanya felt helplessly that *this* war was one he could not reject, that he would not only have to go and fight but that it would be despicable of him to avoid doing so, and, what was more, that he should volunteer at once. People in the village did not discuss the war or even think about it as an event over which anyone had any control or which ought or ought not to be allowed to happen. They accepted the war and the conscription orders issued by the District Commandant as the will of

God, something like a blizzard or a dust-storm, although they could not understand why anyone should volunteer. Even on that long journey, bumping about in the gig and scorched by the sun, Sanya had not yet finally made up his mind. After listening to Varya and subjecting himself to the first lash of anti-war arguments from an intellectual, he had found nothing convincing in them —they offered no bridge across the dark, yawning abyss which was facing Russia. He left Varya more determined to enlist as a volunteer than he had been before meeting her.

He still had to seek the advice of Konstantin, his friend in Rostov.

He continued turning it over in his mind for half the night in the Baku mail-train, as he lay on the top bunk into which he could just squeeze himself at full length. They left Mineralnye Vody late that evening, when the lamps were already lit. Because of the war the train was extremely full—almost all the wooden bunks were occupied in the third class, with only an occasional one free. The carriage was stuffy, but as Sanya had the right-hand side facing the engine, he was entitled to pull his window down for ventilation. He then lowered the network screen to stop himself from falling out. The train made frequent stops, during which people walked up and down the carriage, steadying themselves by clutching at the double-breasted student jacket in which he had wrapped himself, and talked outside on the platform. Waking up, Sanya would immediately be overcome again by a sense of impending doom. Although it was not a premonition of personal disaster, this did not make it any the less keen. He would look at the glassed-in wax candle on the partition, which lit two compartments at once, and calculate the passing of time by the amount of wax burned. The flame shook with the movement of the train, making the deep shadows cast by the bunks flicker and sway.

At times he heard the name of a station being called or peered out at it through the netting of the screen. He knew every station and could reel off their names, even the small ones, from Prokhladnaya to Rostov in both directions.

He loved all these stations; this countryside was his homeland. He had one married sister living in Nagutskaya, another in Kursavka. But in recent years his affections had been divided ever since he had discovered the forest country in the true heartland of Russia, which starts north of Voronezh.

[18]

The Lazhenitsyns came from somewhere around Voronezh, and in his free year between school and university Sanya had begged his father to let him go and visit his ancestral homeland. (In fact he had been hoping to see Lev Tolstoy as well.)

When he was alive, his grandfather Yefim used to tell him how Peter the Great had punished his great-grandfather Filipp for daring to set up house there without permission, how the Tsar had evicted him in such fury that he had set fire to the whole village. Along with several other peasants, grandfather Yefim's father had been banished from the Voronezh district to the southern steppes for rioting. Once banished, however, he and the other rebellious peasants were not manacled, sent to a military colony or made into serfs. Instead they were let loose in the wild steppe country beyond the Kum river and there they lived peaceably, with so much land apiece that they did not have to divide it into strips. They sowed where they ploughed, sheared the sheep, which they herded in fast, light carts, and put down roots.

Through the gaps in the netting everything looked dark outside; then the sky began to grow lighter and lighter, until the candle became unnecessary and the conductor came and put it out. The white sky began to turn pink and Sanya gave up trying to sleep, pulled the net screen up to the ceiling, put on his jacket whilst lying on his side and with the cold air blowing in his face waited for the dawn. The pinkness spread itself like a vast tent, picking out the small clouds against the sky and leaving a blazing trail of scarlet and crimson in its wake. Irresistibly, the sky became soaked to saturation with the sun's redness. And so the sun rose, for all to see, thrusting forth its generous radiance and pouring crimson light over the vast steppe, sparing nothing, flooding every inch to the very horizon in the west.

In the other, more northerly Russia the beauties of nature, of which there are many, are gentler, smaller in scale and given variety by woods and hills; but nowhere is the sunrise such a vivid, flamboyant, all-embracing sight as in the steppeland.

It had been not yet six o'clock, after sunrise on just such a serene morning of early August four years before, when Sanya had got out at Kozlov Zasek station on his way to see Tolstoy. The countryside was lusher and fresher than it ever was in the Kuban in summer. He asked his way at the station, then crossed a little gully, climbed a hillside and found himself in a vast forest of great thick-stemmed, mature trees—the kind of majestic, park-like forest unknown to anyone living in the South, such as Sanya had never even seen in pictures. Covered in milky dew which was turning rainbow-coloured, the forest seemed to invite one not to pass through it but to stroll about in it, to sit or lie down, to linger and never leave. Moreover, it had another special quality: it breathed the spirit of the Prophet himself. Whenever Tolstoy walked or drove to the station he could not help passing the forest, which must surely mark the beginning of his estate!

But no, the forest rose uphill towards the main road to Oryol and then stopped. Sanya saw where he had gone wrong: not until he had crossed the main road did he drop down towards the park of Yasnaya Polyana and walk alongside it. It was divided from the road by a ditch and thick undergrowth. Past a bend a little further on he saw the white stone pillars of the main gateway.

Here he was too timid to go any further. He could not summon the courage to walk through the gates and up the drive, where he might be met and questioned. It was possible, in fact it was highly likely, that they would not allow him to see the great man; it seemed easier just to jump the ditch and make his way through the thicket, simply to saunter aimlessly in the park where Tolstoy was undoubtedly in the habit of taking his walk and sitting down in some favourite spot.

In the park there were some winding lanes, a small pond, then another, bridges across stagnant water covered in duckweed, and a summer-house. There appeared to be no one about. Sanya wandered to his heart's content, occasionally sitting down and looking around in the brilliant early-morning sunlight which turned everything into fine iridescent silk. He felt he could now return home to the South and that this counted as a visit to Tolstoy.

But his path took him uphill through yet another avenue of silver birches, like a long, straight, narrow corridor. The birches changed to maples and then to lime-trees, which opened out into a space, not exactly a clearing but a little glade surrounded by a rectangle of limes and criss-crossed by paths. And then he caught a glimpse of someone walking quite briskly along one of the avenues of trees. He hid behind a thick lime-tree and when he peeped out he saw him—the grey-haired, grey-bearded Sage himself, wearing a long shirt tied at the waist. He was shorter than he had expected, but so like the pictures of him that Sanya felt like shaking his head to make sure it was not an illusion.

Tolstoy was walking with a stick and looking down at the ground. At one point he leaned on his stick, stopped and for almost a minute stared motionless at one particular spot. Then he started walking again. Sometimes his head disappeared into the dense early-morning shadows, sometimes it was in sunshine and at moments the light shining on the crown of his peaked linen cap seemed to surround his head with a halo. He walked round all four sides of the rectangle and then repeated the process, coming quite close to Sanya at one corner.

Sanya, feasting his eyes on the sight, could well have stood there for an hour, his chest pressed against the lime-tree, his fingers clutching its furrowed bark and his head peering from behind the trunk. Although he did not wish to disturb the Prophet's morning meditation, he was afraid Tolstoy might not turn in his direction the next time he came round but walk off to the house instead, or that someone else might appear and speak to him.

With beating heart he plucked up his courage, stepped out on to the path, still at some distance so that Tolstoy would not be startled by his sudden appearance, doffed his school cap (which he was still wearing that year until his father allowed him to go to university) and stood stock-still without saying a word.

Tolstoy caught sight of him, approached him and looked at the cap in his hand and his open-necked shirt. He halted. Endless problems were etched on his face, his brow still furrowed with thought. He it was, however, who took the initiative and greeted his speechless admirer.

'How do you do, boy.'

Who had come to see whom? Who was the seeker and who the sought? As though he had heard the voice of the Lord of Hosts Himself, Sanya answered weakly, his throat dry: 'How do you do, Lev Nikolaevich!'

He could not think how to go on. Tolstoy himself was obliged to tear himself away from his thoughts and think up a suitable new topic. He was, of course, used to schoolboy visitors and knew in advance what sort of questions they would ask and what he should say in reply. Although they could find it all in his books, for some reason they preferred to hear it from his lips.

'Where are you from, boy?' asked the grand old man politely, without continuing his walk.

'From Stavropol province,' said Sanya, in a voice which, though audible, was still husky. Then he took himself in hand, gave a cough and said hurriedly: 'Lev Nikolaevich, I know I'm disturbing your thoughts and your walk—please forgive me. But I've come such a long way and all I want is to hear a few words from your own mouth. Tell me if I have understood you rightly. What is the aim of man's life on earth?'

He did not say what he thought it was, but waited. Tolstoy's lips, visible despite his beard, moved effortlessly to say what he had said a thousand times before:

'To serve good and thereby to build the Kingdom of Heaven on earth.'

'Yes, I see!' said Sanya in excitement. 'But tell me, how do I serve good? Through love? Does it have to be through love?'

'Of course. Only through love.'

'Only?' This was what Sanya had come for. Now he was less constrained, spoke more fluently and felt more like his usual cool self. He had seemed to be asking a question, but the question partially contained its own answer, and, as is the way with youth, he wanted to show the great Tolstoy himself that he too had a viewpoint that deserved attention.

'Lev Nikolaevich,' he said, 'are you sure you're not exaggerating the power of love inherent in man, or at least in modern man? What if love isn't as strong as that, isn't necessarily to be found in everyone and may not prevail? Then your teaching would prove to be . . . fruitless, wouldn't it? Or very, very premature. Shouldn't one envisage a kind of intermediate stage with some less exacting demand and use *that* to awaken people to the need for universal good-will? And then, after that, through love? . . .' Before Tolstoy had time to answer he added: 'Because as far as I can see, where we are in the South there simply *isn't* any universal good-will, Lev Nikolaevich, none at all!'

His own problems had still not disappeared from the old man's furrowed brow and here was a schoolboy asking yet another burdensome question. But looking straight at Sanya from under his bushy eyebrows, the Sage replied without a moment's hesitation in words tested and matured by a lifetime:

'Only through love! Nothing else. No one will ever discover anything better.'

With that he seemed to have said his say, as though his mind had clouded over or he was resentful of the way his truth had been received. He obviously wanted to continue his walk around the oblong glade, thinking his own thoughts.

Sanya was agonised: by asking his favourite question he had upset the man he worshipped. With slightly less intensity, but still hoping for a crumb of comfort on another matter, he hurried on:

'As far as I'm concerned, that's how I should like it to be— through love! And I shall go on believing that and trying to live like that—doing good. But there's one other thing, Lev Nikolaevich. I very much want to write poetry, I do write poetry in fact. Tell me, is that all right, or does it absolutely contradict what you believe?'

The old man's expression softened, but the question did nothing to lighten his mood.

'How can you enjoy lining up words in ranks like soldiers according to their sounds? Childish nonsense! It's unnatural. The job of words is to express *thoughts*, and you don't find much thought in poetry, do you? If you read twenty poems and then try and recall what they were all about, you'll get in a fearful muddle. It's a case of "here today and gone tomorrow".' Tolstoy's brow darkened. Looking past Sanya, he said: 'There's a lot of poetry written nowadays, but there's not a scrap of good in any of it.'

He was upset and shuffled his cane.

Sanya had expected Tolstoy to say that about poetry, even though he could not understand his attitude and still remained secretly attracted to composing verses. He sometimes used to write things in girls' albums as a joke. However, by cutting down on his poetry he had not saved any significant amount of time, nor had he discovered a short answer to the question: how can one serve the Kingdom of God on earth?

As with poetry, he also felt torn by contradictions in his attitude towards women. He was not attracted to women who were kind, intelligent and modestly behaved. Take Varya, for instance: he found it easy enough to discuss philosophy with her and could guide her intellectually without much difficulty, but he rarely wrote to her and he had cut short their meeting at Mineralnye Vody for the entirely base reason that he did not want to embrace her or kiss her. On the other hand, he felt a pleasant twinge when he remembered dark-haired Lena from Kharkov, an easy girl in a certain sense, who played the guitar and sang gypsy songs, and he was not sure he had the strength of will to avoid seeing her on his journey to Moscow.

It was obvious that his noble ideals were not exactly founded on granite.

Sanya could never be absolutely sure of himself; each year something would happen to knock him off balance. On several occasions he had despaired of ever overcoming his father's obstinacy and he dreaded the thought that he was doomed to end up as a provincial ignoramus. After his visit to Tolstoy he spent the rest of that year doing farm-work and reading a little, anything that came to hand, mostly Tolstoy. At last he was allowed to go to Kharkov, but even there he was not accepted immediately. Because of his name he was taken for a Jew, and the university had already filled its quota of Jews. Isaakii was kept waiting longingly on the very threshold of the university to which he had so eagerly looked forward. He was in such despair that he rushed to fetch his birth certificate, on which his Christian baptism was recorded. No sooner was he accepted as 'pure' than his boyish delight was soured by a bitter realisation: his acceptance rested on having proved he did not belong to the nation through which Christ had come into the world. For a long time this unresolved problem weighed on his mind. Then as soon as he embarked on his course in the Faculty of History and Philology Isaakii was made aware that he was an ignorant bumpkin compared with students from the cities. He realised that his high school had not been one of the best. And after a year at Kharkov he realised that this was not the best university either, so he plucked up courage to leave and transferred himself to Moscow University, taking his friend Kotya with him.

For a long time after that he still felt backward and ignorant, incapable of thinking any problem through. He was confused by the plethora of contending truths and agonised by the fact that each of them seemed so convincing. As long as he had only had access to a few books, Isaakii had felt secure and happy and he had considered himself a Tolstoyan ever since his second year in high school. But here he was given Lavrov and Mikhailovsky—and how true they seemed to be. Then he read Plekhanov, and there was the truth again—and so beautifully consistent. Kropotkin also went straight to his heart and was no less true. And when he came to read *Vekhi* he began to shudder—it was the complete reverse of all he had read before—yet true, piercingly true!

Books no longer inspired a respectful delight in him—instead they made him terrified that he would never learn to argue back at an author, that he would always be carried away, dominated by the last book he happened to have read. He was only just beginning to dare to disagree with books when the war came. Now he would never learn, never make up the time lost.

The train was about to pull up at a big, familiar station. Sanya jumped down from his bunk into the dozing compartment and managed to wash before the toilet was closed. They stood there for twenty minutes while the engine was changed. The clean platform in the early morning looked peaceful and deserted, still undisturbed by reminders of the war. Sanya drank some hot, strong, sweet tea in the station buffet and breakfasted on the food he had brought with him in a bundle from home—his only baggage.

When they moved off again he stood on the open platform at the end of the carriage. The side of the train that was in the sun was now covered in soot from the engine, but Sanya opened the other door and leaned out. He never tired of watching the swirling, motley pattern of vast fields ripe for harvest. Each carriage threw a black, quivering, elongated shadow which seemed to plunge downward whenever it crossed a gully. Otherwise the steppe was bathed in gentle early-morning sunlight which had lost its pinkness but had not yet turned yellow. And though his body was filled with the joyous strength of youth and the promise of life, it could well be that he would never again see the Kuban steppe and the morning sun over the sea of wheat.

They went through another station. Sanya still did not go back to his compartment, but remained standing by the open door with the wind of the moving train blowing into his face, gazing out and preparing himself to bid it all farewell.

Then he caught sight of an estate, or 'economy' as they say in the northern Caucasus. In contrast to the rest of the steppe, the trees were densely and evenly planted and the growth well advanced. Loaded carts were passing along the roads and oxen were pulling a traction-engine and a threshing machine. Farmhouses and barns swirled by, and then through a gap in a row of poplars beside the track he caught sight of the upper storey of a brick house with venetian blinds at the windows. He could clearly see on a wrought-iron corner balcony the figure of a woman wearing a white dress—the gay white dress of a woman of leisure.

She was probably young and charming.

Then the poplars hid her from view. He would never see her again.

3

At the very first moment of waking, even before remembering that she was young, that it was a summer's day and that life can be happy, came the dull, chilling recollection of their quarrel.

She had been on bad terms with her husband since the previous day.

She opened her eyes. He was not in the bedroom. She was alone.

She threw open the shutters giving on to the park. It was a wonderful morning, with just a touch of coolness in the air from the shade of the Himalayan silver firs, whose branches spread to the window ledges of the first-floor rooms.

Was she happy? The entire park had grown out of the bare steppe at her wish. She could have anything she desired in the world; any dress she wanted from St Petersburg or Paris could be ordered and delivered at once.

Their last serious quarrel had lasted three days. For three days they had not spoken, had ignored each other and lived separately. Then on the Day of the Transfiguration Irina had gone into town to church with her mother-in-law. The soaring chant of the liturgy, the compassionate words of the priest's sermon, then the procession around the churchyard, the joyful ceremony of blessing the colourful piles of apples and the mead in buckets and mugs, the robes, the religious banners and polished censers resplendent in the brilliant sunshine, the wafting clouds of incense—all these put her into such an other-worldly mood that her husband's insults seemed petty and unimportant compared with God's world and God's purpose, not to mention the serious matter of the war. And so Irina not only decided to ask for forgiveness this

time, although it had not been her fault at all, but resolved that
henceforth she would allow no more quarrels to take place and that
at the slightest hint of one she would be the first to admit her guilt,
that being the only truly Christian way.

When she came home from the service, she asked for her husband's forgiveness. Roman was overjoyed at this, although he had
expected it. He immediately forgave his wife and was magnani-
mous enough to ask her forgiveness in return. However, they remained on good terms only from Wednesday to Sunday, when they
quarrelled so badly that they stopped speaking to each other again.

In the passage the chambermaid asked Irina Stepanovna in a
whisper what her orders were. There were none as yet. She went
into the red and white marble bathroom.

After that she prayed in front of an icon of the Holy Virgin, but
she felt no sense of relief or forgiveness.

As she sat looking into the mirror of her dressing-table she was
not even comforted by the sight of her naturally rosy skin, her
rounded shoulders, the hair which fell down to her hips and took
four buckets of rain-water to wash.

She moved over to the covered balcony on the sunny side of the
house and watched a passing train, which she guessed was the
Baku mail-train. The view of the railway line, which passed four
hundred yards away from the Tomchaks' house, was always full
of interest. She never tired of watching trains and following them
out of sight, or foretelling some event by counting the carriages to
see if the number was odd or even. For many of the trains running
now their destinations were summed up in one word: war.

It was the war which had sparked off yesterday's quarrel. Irina
had been too outspoken about Russia being in peril and it being the
duty of her sons to defend her. She was not referring to her husband and had never imagined he would react as he did. She was
speaking about the Teutonic threat in general. But Roman took it as
a personal slight and called her a jingoistic blockhead, a woolly-
brained monarchist just like her father, who had been an ignoramus and a petty-tyrant, adding that she had no idea how few
enlightened, enterprising people like her husband there were in
their barbaric country; why, the meanest slut would be sorry to
send her husband off to the war, whereas she . . .

All their rows were like that—almost like the quarrels between
two men: either about the Tsar, whom Roman always ridiculed, or

about religion, of which not a trace was left in him, although he concealed the fact for the sake of propriety.

It would not have been so hurtful if only Roman had not dragged in his late father-in-law. Ignoramus indeed! True, he had started off as a farm labourer, the son of a soldier under Nicholas I. Petty tyrant! Who was it that Roman had first curried favour with? Certainly not with her. And the old man had chosen Roman out of all her other suitors as the one least likely to squander the family money.

Her father had been childless for a long time and was already an old man when he paid the Bishop of Stravropol forty thousand roubles so that he could remarry. From this love-match Irina was born—Órina in the local dialect, or Orya as everyone called her. When Irina was seventeen, realising that he did not have long to live he became anxious to see her married—at once, straight from boarding-school. It was now obvious that she had married too young, and she regretted it. If only he had let her grow up a bit and enjoy a taste of life. If only he had let her choose for herself.

Still, what was done was done, and Orya did not have the heart to reproach her dead father, or even to harbour any resentment at the thought that she might have had a different lot in life. Only unbelievers, she thought, feel regret about what might have been, for a believer grounds his faith on life as it is—that is his strength.

What was done was done, and Orya humbly accepted the husband who was not of her own choosing. She gave him all the capital she had inherited, without keeping any herself and without retaining a lien on any part of it. Since all the independence they now enjoyed, their boundless wealth, their leisure, their countless trips to Moscow and Petersburg and abroad, had all been acquired from her father, not his, Roman might at least refrain from cursing him every time he mentioned him.

It was time to go down to breakfast. There was a wooden staircase leading downstairs, at the top of which was her favourite painting, a view of Tsarskoe Selo, and at the bottom a picture of Tolstoy scything hay, painted by an Italian artist brought from Rostov.

The dining-room was panelled in imitation walnut, with a huge sideboard of genuine walnut, and the furniture was upholstered in chamois leather the colour of frog's skin. Lemon-trees in tubs blocked the view of the park. In the middle of the spacious room the table, which could open out to seat twenty-four people, was folded to take twelve. However, only two places were set at the top. Her sister-in-law was still asleep, Roman himself never came down for early breakfast and his father would often get up at the crack of dawn and race off in his brake round his five and a half thousand acres of steppeland. He was away today in Ekaterinodar, as he had been for the last two days. Roman's fate hung on that journey, and although no one said anything they were all thinking about it.

Irina wished her mother-in-law good morning, bent down and kissed her on her broad, fat cheek. After fifty years Evdokia Ili- nichna's rather blowsy face had become a picture of immutable calm, as if her present worries made no impression on her and there had been no sadness in her past. Her face seemed to have ab- sorbed and smothered all experience, to be reconciled with every- thing. Yet there had been one week in her life when she had lost six children all at once from scarlet fever. Xenia, the youngest, was the only one they had managed to snatch from death, as from a fire. Roman and his elder sister were by that time grown-up. Whenever Irina had occasion to resent her mother-in-law, she remembered that week.

Before sitting down she crossed herself in front of the icon de- picting the Last Supper, which because of its subject matter had been hung in the dining-room. It was the time of fast before the Feast of the Assumption and there was no meat or milk on the table. Their coffee—without cream—was served by the parlour- maid, as the butler did not come down for this meal.

Evdokia Ilinichna was the daughter of a simple village black- smith (even now, dressed in plainer clothes, she would have looked just like an old peasant woman), and for years she had been unable to get used to the idea of sitting down at table like a lady in her lace shawl and waiting to be served. She took a delight in noticing any- thing missing and fetching it herself. Some days she would push aside the cooks and make a Ukrainian borsch in a huge saucepan. Her children, ashamed at this behaviour in front of the servants, would try to stop her, and when there was company they would make her put away her inseparable knitting and the ball of wool at her feet.

Evdokia Ilinichna endeavoured to keep a check on how much soap and charcoal was used for the laundry and gave orders that her daughter-in-law's fine underclothes should not be washed:

what was the point of wearing expensive things when no one saw them anyway? She insisted that everyone, including the old man and herself, wear coarse stuff made by the nuns. After all, she and her husband had once lived in a little adobe hut with a dozen sheep, and even in her old age she could not believe in the permanence of her husband's wealth. She never did manage to trace exactly where it was leaking away, for leak it did, on all sides: with their enormous fortune people simply borrowed, embezzled or stole from them. They had ten indoor and ten outdoor servants, not including the Cossacks and the countless other labourers and employees: clerks, stewards, overseers, storemen, grooms, herdsmen, mechanics and gardeners. Who could possibly keep an eye on all of them? And was all this waste really necessary?

However, Evdokia Ilinichna resigned herself to the flow of money in their thriving 'economy' as she did to the changes in the weather; the only control she could exercise was to keep a check on thread and material used by the seamstress who came once a year. Old Zakhar Ferapontych, her husband, was quite liable to give away his old suit to a passing tramp, but if Evdokia Ilinichna found out she sent a messenger after the tramp to get it back. On the other hand, through her sister Arkhelaya, who was a nun, other nuns, monks and mendicants came flocking to their house; for them nothing was spared and the servants had their work doubled, even on the strictest fast days, preparing separate dishes for this black-clad horde. Zakhar Ferapontych also used to dispatch food to the Teberdinsky convent on ox-carts, but here Irina had some success in persuading her father-in-law that nuns were sly, deceitful and lazy and that it would be more pleasing to God to let the estate workers benefit from the surplus produce by giving them meat four times a day in summer. This was accordingly done.

With the same incorrigible naivety her mother-in-law asked her now:

'You and Romasha didn't sleep together again last night, did you?'

Irina lowered her head, which she always held straight, and blushed, not because of the ingenuous coarseness of the question but because of the hopeless situation which had dragged on for eight years and was beginning to wear her down, in which her mother-in-law seemed entitled to be as rude as she liked and her husband had the apparent right to lose his temper with her. Her mother-in-law's peasant face above her ample shoulders and bosom expressed as much surprise as was consistent with her usual indifference.

'That a *wife* should walk out of the bedroom and sleep alone, it's unheard of . . . If *he* had kicked you out, I wouldn't have said a word to you.' This was her usual way of speaking of her son, and she always made excuses for men as opposed to women. 'This way we'll never get what we're waiting for ! . . .'

The enormous chiming grandfather clock struck and played 'How Glorious is Our Lord'. It had been bought at an auction, when the State Treasury had sold off the chattels of the extinct Riurikovich family.

'You must humble your pride, Irusha . . .'

Oh, how many times had she already humbled her pride in *that* cause! Anyway what did her mother-in-law know about pride, when her husband, if he was angry with her, would spit in her face even at table—not metaphorically but with a thick gob of spittle. Evdokia Ilinichna would not jump up or cry out but would wipe her face, quite unmoved. It was Irina who had once jumped up and shouted: 'Romasha, let's go away from here ! We can't live here any more !' Whereupon her father-in-law had hurled his fork to the floor, got up and left the room. True, the menfolk cooled down at once if their wives were submissive, and then acted as if there had been no quarrel at all. Zakhar Ferapontych soon softened and started calling her affectionate names like 'my little old woman'. But was it not too high a price to pay?

Irina herself used to pray for meekness and humility, but as soon as her mother-in-law tried to instil them into her she would become obstinate and answer her back grimly:

'Why have you spoilt him so much? Why did you idolise your son like that? And now *I*'m the one who has to live with him.'

'What's bad about him?'

She looked so surprised in her simple way, her eyes so untroubled, that Irina did not have the heart to remind her of, say, the scene outside the study in front of all the servants. It had all started from an argument about some patch of land and the question of what crop should be sown on it. 'Son of a bitch !' shouted Zakhar Ferapontych, eyes bloodshot, stamping his feet. 'Son of a bitch yourself !' Roman yelled back, whereupon his father struck him as hard as he could with his heavy walnut staff. In the same state of primitive rage as his father, Roman then pulled a revolver from his bellows pocket. Irina flung herself on her husband and pushed him out of the room shouting: 'Mama! Lock the door!' and only thus succeeded in separating them. Furious, Roman left home. Immediately his parents, thoroughly frightened, began sending him telegrams: 'Darling son, come back home!'

And now today Roman and his father had fallen out again— lately this had more often been the case than not.

Breakfast was finished. Irina got up and went out. She was wearing a linen dress, and the deportment learned at her boarding-school lent her a calm and regal air. She walked across the rectangular, golden-yellow carpet, which they did not take up for summer, past the crystal displayed in a cabinet, to the staircase, down past yet another Lev Tolstoy, this time holding a plough, and out on to the front steps.

It was Roman who had insisted on having all these pictures of Tolstoy painted. He had explained to old Tomchak that to admire Tolstoy was the done thing among educated people, that he was a count and a great national figure; personally he revered and supported Tolstoy because he had rejected confession and communion, which Roman detested.

With all its outbuildings and kitchen gardens the home farm took up fifty acres; there were many places in it for her to visit. There was the laundry, built in the German colonist style, or the cellars where she could look over the stocks with the housekeeper. She could visit the wives of the seasonal labourers in their huts, or she might go to the conservatory. But wherever she went she had the same decision to make: whether or not to make it up with Roman, whether or not to humble herself.

Irina walked across the park, forcing herself not to look back, not to lift her gaze towards the verandah of their bedroom from which *he* would most likely be looking out. He was quite capable of imprisoning himself in a sulk for the day, sometimes even for the night too, without once coming out of doors or even downstairs.

She passed beneath the Himalayan firs. There had been great anxiety lest they might not 'take'. They had been brought as mature trees from the garden of a grand-duke in the Crimea, complete with clods of soil attached to their roots in large baskets, each marked to show which side should face east when planted.

Further on there were winding avenues of lilac, horse-chestnut and walnut.

'It takes brains to turn kopecks into roubles', Zakhar Ferapontych used to say. But to spend that money well required no less brains and good taste besides. The nearby Mordorenko family were as rich as Croesus, but how did they spend their money? For years they had lived like pigs. To improve his looks Yakov Fomich had a whole set of platinum teeth put in, while his young sons played heads or tails with gold coins instead of coppers. When Tomchak and his neighbour Chepurnykh bought sixteen thousand acres of land in the Kuban from a titled family in St Petersburg, Zakhar Tomchak said expansively:

'Shall we treat the counts to a good meal? Not the mean way they do things, though. We'll show 'em!' But when he got to Palkin's restaurant he had no idea what to order and just asked for the most lavish and expensive dishes.

It was from his son and his daughter-in-law that Zakhar Ferapontych learned how to live in style. On the railway side of the house they had planted balsam poplars and pyramid poplars in avenues wide enough for two troikas to pass side by side. Towards evening, after a warm day, the balsam poplars gave off a fragrant smell and for all his coarseness the old farmer congratulated Irina: 'Well done, Irusha, well done.' Plane-trees were planted along the front drive, and Irusha had the idea of digging a pond near the house as a swimming pool, with a cement base and a supply of fresh water which could be changed. The earth that was dug out was moved away to form a mound on which a summer-house was built. Thus was created a park, the kind which made old-fashioned country estates so distinctive: the landscape was given a quality of seclusion, distinction and separateness from the surrounding district. There might be steppeland, forest or marsh all around, but here the park obeyed its own laws, as though it were another country. They planted an orchard beyond the park, to which they successfully transplanted about a couple of hundred fruit-trees from the old orchard, and beyond the orchard a vineyard. Irina instructed them to plant a formal Moorish garden around the summer-house, a sunken herb-garden and a rose-garden next to the house, and a lawn of emerald-green English rye-grass alongside the drive, to be cut with lawn-mowers.

But the two conservatories were Irina's greatest concern—a

small one for spring flowers which would be ready for cutting at Easter, even when Easter was early, and a high one for keeping oleanders in tubs through the winter, also palms, yuccas, araucarias and hundreds of flowering pot-plants which only Irina and the specially trained conservatory-keeper knew by name. All these tender creatures had to be inspected nearly every day, and most needed some kind of attention: in summer they had to be carried in and out, in winter some bloom had to be moved to the winter garden, or a wilting plant taken back to the conservatory.

Among the multitude of perfumes, colours and shapes Irina regained her self-confidence and felt protected from her husband's ill-temper.

Today she had the fantastic idea that when Roman woke up he would come in search of her, in spite of everything. Normally he would never have done this; but since it was wartime and there was a chance that they would have to part—he might, after all, be called up—perhaps he would relent.

She wanted him to come to her, not so that she could feel superior, but more for his own sake, for the good of his own heart.

4

No, there was nowhere like home. Nowhere could you find such a comfortable bed, such a sweet little blue room, still dark although the sunlight was already beating against the shutters. And all the time in the world to laze about—a day, a week, even a month!

Waking up from a good long sleep to a good long life, with a delicious yawn, a stretch, then another stretch, Xenia clenched her fists tightly above her head.

True, it was a sinfully luxurious kind of life—one to be enjoyed but not one you could afford to boast about to your friends. There was much that was bad and gross about it, but it was a good life all the same. There was an indefinable pleasure, peculiar to the place, that only you and the members of your family could understand and your friends could never share. Of course the delights of Moscow were incomparable—the dancing lessons, the theatres, the discussions and public lectures and naturally the university—all that was enough to make your head spin, but here, when you woke up in the morning, you could lie in as long as you liked. All in all it was very pleasant to be the lady of leisure occasionally.

There was a cough outside, then a knock at the door.

'Xenia, are you still asleep?'

'I haven't decided yet. What is it?'

'I must just get something from the safe. But if you want to sleep, I can come back later . . .'

It was so pleasant just lying there, not quite awake. But with this intrusion everything was spoilt.

'All right!' shouted Xenia and jumped out of bed without using her hands, with one bound of her strong legs. Stumbling in her long nightdress, she ran barefoot across to the door and undid the latch.

'Wait, don't come in yet!'

And she darted back into bed with a rustle of the net curtain and pulled the blankets over her.

'All right, come in.'

Her brother opened the door and came in out of the dim light of the passage.

'Good morning. Sure I didn't wake you up? I'm sorry, but I really had to. I can't see a thing in the dark. May I open one shutter?'

He walked carefully across the room, but still managed to hit the dressing-table, making the little glass bottles tinkle. As he opened the outside shutter the glorious daylight streamed into the room, giving Xenia a momentary pang of regret that she had not been able to lie in longer. She turned over on to her side, laid her hand under her cheek and looked at her brother.

Roman peered round in the light as if, apart from his sister, he was expecting to meet some enemy lurking in the little room. His deep-set eyes had a piercing look, his moustache, which refused to curl, sprouted like two pointed sticks. But there was no enemy, and with the keys of the wall-safe protruding from his clenched fist he strode across to open it.

'I won't be long, just a minute. I can close the shutter for you again if you like.'

When the house was being built several years ago, the room had been intended as Roman's study and a steel safe had been built into the wall. Then it was decided that Roman and his father should share a study on the ground floor and that Xenia should have the room. But they had left the safe for odd papers and money belonging to Roman. His sister was in any case only here during the vacations.

Roman had an elegant figure, wiry and agile in his tight-fitting English tweed suit, but he was not quite tall enough. He was wearing a faded brown cap to match his suit and boots.

'You're not going out in the car, are you?' Xenia hazarded a guess. 'You wouldn't like to take Orya and me for a run today, would you? Into town, or over towards the Kuban, past Hempel's place?'

Her round, shamelessly healthy, unfashionably tanned face lying on the pillow, Xenia was weighing up the pros and cons: what would she have to sacrifice in order to go for a ride in the car, what would she have to put off until tomorrow? Baron von Hempel was their proudest rival among the local landowners, and on the far side of his estate there was an ancient oak forest, a wonderful rarity in the surrounding steppelands. However, Roman's car was not just any old car but a white Rolls-Royce, of which it was said there were only nine in the whole of Russia and every one of their owners known by name. It so happened that von Hempel did not have one. Roman had been taught to drive by an Englishman and knew everything about his car. He could repair it himself, but as he did not like getting dirty in the garage pit, he kept a chauffeur.

Now he looked offended and fumbled with the broad, curved peak of his cap.

'No, I was just going along to the garage. I'll take you for a ride, but not today. I must wait to hear first whether . . .'

'Oh, of course! Romasha dear, I am sorry.'

How could she be so stupid as to forget absolutely everything overnight, that Russia was at war, that the whole world was in the grip of war? And, worse still, that her father had gone to town to do his utmost to get Romasha deferred from military service? It was simply absurd—they might even commandeer the Rolls-Royce. Obviously at a time like this her brother was in no mood for frivolous amusement: the very thought seemed like tempting fate.

Yet to tell the truth, Xenia felt that any man ought to be ashamed of dodging the call-up. Of course, if he was the sole breadwinner it was excusable, but what kind of a breadwinner was Roman? Without actually wishing him in the front line, she considered that every man should join the army as a matter of common decency.

But he must surely realise this himself, and Xenia could not bring herself to mention it to her brother, especially as their relations had become so relaxed and friendly since she had grown up.

'Where's Orya?'

'Don't know.'

Roman had opened the outer and inner doors of the safe and was bending down to look inside.

'Didn't you go down to breakfast? Haven't they stopped fasting yet?'

She gave a snort of laughter. Roman turned his head slightly as a sign of understanding, showing the end of his moustache, and his lips curled into a wry smile. His nose was like his father's—large and jutting.

With Roman she was preaching to the converted. One of the stupidest traditions in the Tomchak household was the way they kept the fasts. And there were so many! Lent was understandable—the priest was brought along and for a whole week the entire estate would attend service, abstain from food and take communion, and there was a great bustle to see that all the servants and labourers went to confession and received absolution by the start of the sowing season. During Lent Xenia was always away from home and Roman would go off to Moscow or Petersburg, returning for Easter. No sooner was Trinity Sunday past than the absurd fast of St Peter began, and by the time that was over the fast of the Assumption was already on its way. Then, before being allowed to enjoy Christmas, one had to put on a long face for the Advent fast, not to mention Wednesdays and Fridays of every week! It was no hardship to fast if you were poor, but they had so much money and such a choice of delicious things to eat—everything under the sun —that to ruin half one's life in fasting was positively uncivilised.

Xenia and Roman were brought closer together by the fact that they were the only two in the family who held 'progressive' views. All the rest were double-dyed, provincial reactionaries.

Xenia, still lying on her side, her legs tucked up, her hand clenched under her cheek, mused aloud: 'I don't know . . . It's my last chance to give up the university—now, in August, when I shall only lose a year. And I can apply to go to the school for barefoot dancers.'

Because he felt possessive about the safe and needed to concentrate, Roman felt he must not allow his sister to see what it contained or what he was doing, although Xenia understood nothing about it and had no wish to. Rustling the papers, he stooped down with his back to her.

'If you backed me up,' sighed Xenia, 'I'd throw up the university!'

Absorbed, Roman said nothing.

'I'm sure Papa wouldn't find out for another three years. I'd still be going to Moscow and it would look as if I was still going to the university. Papa might shout at me a bit and get angry for a while, but he's bound to forgive me.'

Roman was still busy, his head almost inside the safe.

'And even if he doesn't, there's nothing much he can do...' Xenia pouted and smirked as she summed up the situation. 'It surely can't be right to waste my life on this useless course in agronomy. It's a crime to bury one's talents.'

Roman stopped what he was doing and straightened up. Still facing the open safe, he turned his head.

'He'll never forgive you. In any case you're talking rubbish. It's to your advantage that you should finish the agronomy course. You will be invaluable here if you do.'

He looked at her with his sharp, calculating eyes from beneath his thick black eyebrows and English cap. Xenia shook her head and made a face which Roman pretended not to see. Whenever he had a strong conviction, nothing could stop him speaking his mind. In that case, he expressed himself with such grim severity that he made even businessmen slightly apprehensive, to say nothing of Xenia.

'The fact is you'll have to manage the estate, a quarter of which you are bound to inherit. And if Papa and I quarrel without any hope of reconciliation, then you'll get more. Do you really intend to throw everything up just to prance around the stage in bare feet? It's perfectly ridiculous. You're not a pauper, you know.'

She was still only a child, amenable to guidance, seventeen years younger than her brother, who spoke to her almost like a father. Xenia listened, although she was not convinced.

He turned back to his safe. If he had been selfish he would have encouraged his sister to go to the dancing school: all he had to do was agree to her plan and show some enthusiasm for her dancing. If Xenia married and produced a grandson for the old man, he might in a fit of fury with his son bequeath everything to his grandson. In purely rational terms it was to Roman's advantage for Xenia to join the ballet troupe and quarrel with her father. But he would never allow himself to be party to anything so dishonourable—it was quite out of keeping with the style of an English gentleman which he had adopted as his own. So he gave her sensible advice.

He took what he needed from the safe, turned two different keys twice in the locks of both the steel doors, and glanced sternly at his sister lying quietly in bed.

'And then you'll marry a landowner!'

'What? Never! Oh go away, all of you!'

Xenia jumped up as if she had been stung, tore off the ribbon she wore round her hair at night and flashed the whites of her laughing eyes like a little Negro girl. Then she burst out into a peal of mirth, raising her arm towards the ceiling with the natural grace of a dancer. Her alarm at the thought of such a marriage was overcome by a sense of absurdity. The local landowners liked their women to be so big that they needed two chairs to sit on.

'Go away, I'm going to get up!'

Scarcely had he closed the door than she leaped to her feet, flung open the shutters of the other window (oh day, oh sun, oh life!), jumped up and down on the floor, then over to the dressing-table, part of a complete suite of grey bentwood furniture given to her as a present on leaving high school. But however far she turned the revolving mirror it would not take her in full-length; it was the sight of her whole figure, especially her legs, strong, slim and agile, and her tiny feet, that made one realise that Xenia was beautiful.

She gave a leap—and again! and again!—then went up to the mirror to look at her round, healthy, swarthy face; her features were a shade coarse, like a Ukrainian's or a steppe girl's—a Pecheneg girl as Yarik, a friend of her schooldays, used to say teasingly, a remark which hurt her deeply. Although her hair was not dark, it was attractive and as she had grown older her features had fined down, taken on a more thoughtful, intellectual look. Still, her complexion was far too healthy, without a trace of fashionable pallor: she would have to cultivate that. Her round face was hopelessly countrified and unintelligent-looking, and her teeth were so even, white, and strong that they made matters even worse. With a face like that how could she prove that she was well-educated, that her appreciation of beauty was already so finely developed? How could people guess from her face all the plays she had been to, all the photographs and statuettes of her idols that adorned her rooms here and in Moscow—Leonid Andreev, several each of Geltser and Isadora Duncan? Or imagine Xenia herself, dressed in her beribboned Hungarian head-dress, boots and spurs, or barefoot and ethereal in voile with a pendant between her breasts, Xenia caught in mid-flight, her dress held out like a fan, the star dancer of Madame Kharitonova's high school, perhaps the best dancer of all the high-school girls in Rostov? How could she resist it, what other career was conceivable? What else was worth doing except dancing, dancing all her life? Her arms were graceful and not too long—and what beautiful, mature shoulders she had! If only her neck would grow just a fraction longer and slimmer! The neck was a very important part of the body; it could be so expressive in dancing.

Why bother to wash, to eat or drink? All she wanted was to be allowed to dance, dance, dance!

Through the door and on to the balcony, from the balcony into the drawing-room full of that stupid old plush furniture. Still, it would be a shame to throw it out. There was the mirror where she could see herself full-length. Humming a tune to herself, she did a *jeté*—and another! How well she did it—like a bird! Her foot was so amazingly small that a man could hold it in the palm of his hand, yet what force, what thrust it had! At the school for barefoot dancing they never wore socks, they always went about in their bare feet. What they did was more than dancing, it was 'or-chae-ist-ic illustration'. 'Look,' she could hear them saying, 'she's almost as good as Isadora . . .' 'No, she *is* as good!' And her whole life was still in front of her.

By now one of the chambermaids had started to clean the drawing-room with the electric vacuum-cleaner, while another was carrying a towel warmed in the sun for Xenia's use: so nice for drying oneself with after a bath.

While she busied herself with this and that and then had breakfast, the steppe grew blazing hot. It was so hot now that no sunhat would give enough protection. The only bearable thing was to lie in a hammock in the middle of the garden, all in white.

Scorched to exhaustion, the sky had a whitish, translucent look and even in the welcome shade one could feel the oppressive intensity of the air. The sound dulled by the heat, the puffing of traction-engines from the threshing-yard could just be heard, mingled with the whir of other engines from the farmyard and the general buzz of insects. There was not the faintest hint of a breeze.

There came a crunching sound on the gravel. Xenia twisted round and saw Irina approaching, unmistakably grave and erect in her carriage. As though stretching herself, Xenia held out her arms to embrace Irina, as they had not yet seen each other that morning. Irina stooped to kiss her. Xenia's book fell shut, slipped, and rested on the net of the hammock. Irina did not fail to notice it and shook her head reproachfully.

'Another French book?'

The book, in fact, was English, but that was not the point. Xenia threw back her loosely tied pony-tail into the taut hammock and wrinkled her nose pleadingly.

'Oh, Orenka, you don't expect me to read *The Life of St Seraphim Sarofsky*, do you?'

Orya stood with her back to the trunk of a chestnut, not touching the tree, as if she had no desire to relax her body or to take the weight off her feet. She gave Xenia a kind, rather ironic look.

'No, but you don't seem to read any Russian books at all.'

'Well, what ought I to read?' retorted Xenia with a slight hint of annoyance in her voice. 'I've read Turgenev till I'm sick to death of him. Dostoevsky makes my skin creep and my hands twitch. And we don't read Hamsun, Przybyszewski or Selma Lagerlöf, so that shouldn't worry you.'

When Irina had married into the family Xenia had been a little girl of eleven, and Irina had taken charge of her until she was thirteen, when she went to high school in Rostov. The Xenia of those days had been given a religious upbringing and knew of no greater joy than to imitate her sister-in-law in her observance of the fasts, her devoutness in prayer and her love of the old Russian traditions.

Irina's brow was furrowed as she shook her head again.

'You are deserting . . .'

'What? The Ukrainian way of life?' Her lovely brown eyes sparkled. 'I should truly love to stay a simple country girl, but how can I? All these eligible young farmers smell of tar—I can't help splitting my sides whenever I have to talk to them! Yevstignei Mordorenko!' She only had to think of this particular young man to start choking with laughter. 'How he cried when he thought he was being sent off to Paris!'

Her mirth infected Orya, whose serious, expressive face was relieved by a slightly snub nose which proclaimed her sense of humour. Her lips, too, were liable to twitch when she was amused. The faintest smile from Irina signified as much as a peal of laughter from Xenia.

Mordorenko, the bumpkin in question, owned his own racehorses, which were now promising enough to run in Moscow, but as a punishment for some offence against his father he had been sent to Paris instead of to the Moscow races. Whereupon this strapping youth, as healthy as his own horses, who had seduced every girl on the estate, including his governess, had sat down and wept for two whole days and nights, smearing his face in tears and begging his father not to send him to Paris.

'And the way they throw their women about at the local balls!' said Xenia, shaking with laughter.

Just as people are tossed in the air by friends on an anniversary, so the drunken landowners would grab their wives and fiancées at their wild parties and a dozen pairs of arms would toss them aloft, making their dresses fly up, while the men watched for a chance to grab at their thighs. Feeling superior to these louts, on such occasions Roman would escort Irina away, which greatly offended the rest of the company.

'I suppose it's my fate! Can you imagine "Xenia Zakharovna Tomchak" written on your visiting card? A name like that instantly conjures up an image of something between a haycart and a sheepskin; decent people don't want to have anything to do with you.'

'But if it weren't for all the sheep, Xenia my dear, you would never have been to high school or university.'

'I wish I never had. I would never have known what I was missing. I'd have married some red-necked clod with ten flour-mills and had my photo taken standing behind my husband's chair like a stone statue.'

'Nevertheless,' said Irina in a tone of quiet insistence, 'it would have meant keeping your links with your own people . . .'

'What? *My* people? These savages!'

'Around here,' Irina went on stubbornly, frowning, the little blue veins in her long, supple neck growing taut, 'you're much closer to the real Russian people than with your educated Kharitonovs who have no time at all for Russia.'

Xenia was starting to get heated; she was fidgeting about in the hammock, straining the net.

'My God, where on earth do you get those dreary, old-fashioned ideas from? You've never seen any of the Kharitonovs, so how can you say you can't stand them? They're all decent people who work for their living. What have they ever done to offend you?'

Xenia's jerky movements made the book fall through a gap in the netting.

Irina had behaved badly and she was regretting it. She should not have been so forthright about the Kharitonovs. After all, they were not the only ones; the whole of educated Russia was like that.

'All I meant,' she said in her most conciliatory voice, 'was that it's very easy for us to laugh. Everything seems funny to us. We see a twin-tailed comet in the sky and that's funny. There was an eclipse on Friday, and that was funny.'

By now Xenia was in no mood for argument and her anger went as quickly as it had come. She squinted up at the canopy of sunny leaves above her head and conceded:

'Well, that's true enough. There is astronomy, after all . . .'

'Call it astronomy if you like,' said Irina, quietly but firmly, 'but there was an eclipse of the sun when Prince Igor went into battle. There was one at the Battle of Kulikovo and another at the height of the war against the Swedes. Whenever Russia is put to the test of war there's always an eclipse of the sun.'

Irina was fond of portents.

Xenia bent over to snatch her book from the ground and almost tumbled out. Her hair flew free of the ribbon and an opened envelope fell out of the book.

'Oh yes, I forgot to tell you. I got a letter from Yaroslav Kharitonov. Can you imagine, they were commissioned early, on the second day of war. The letter's from the army in the field, and while it was reaching us he was fighting somewhere. It's such a happy letter, he's so contented.'

At school they had been in the same year and used to do their homework together. He had been like a favourite brother to her and Xenia remembered him with a mixture of tenderness and pride.

'Where was it franked?'

'It's marked Ostrolenka; we'll have to look it up on Romasha's map.'

Orya drew her straight eyebrows together, embarrassed but approving.

'A family like that—and their son is a patriot, an officer! I find that very significant.'

But what of her own husband? What would happen to him?

5

Zakhar Ferapontych was used to doing business in the mad, bust-
ling city of Rostov, but not this kind of business. He chiefly went
to Rostov for machinery, as all the new machines were on display
there; one could look them over and handle them and the salesmen
were good at explaining how they worked. There, ahead of all the
other landowners including Baron Hempel, he had bought disc
seed-drills from Siemens, cultivators for digging potato trenches,
and those new ploughs which were pulled on long cables between
two traction-engines. Occasionally, too, he would sign big contracts for grain and wool, dealing direct with French importers.
And he would buy food there, such as fish—where else but in
Rostov should one buy fish?—and other victuals and supplies. One
day he had gone there just to buy a pair of gloves—he fancied
chamois-leather lined with squirrel fur, which was not to be had in
any of the towns nearer home—and those cunning devils had persuaded him to buy a car as well, a 'Russo-Baltic Carriage', for
seven and a half thousand roubles. There had been a time when
he used to growl at his son's 'Thomas' car, being firmly convinced
that when this monster drove round the fields it caused the lightning to strike and flatten the crops. Now he started looking for a
chauffeur himself, and employed a local lad, the son of one of his
vine-dressers, who had learnt to drive in the army.

Zakhar Ferapontych dealt with all this buying and selling in
Rostov easily and efficiently, and he liked the hustling way the
people did their business, but he had never come across a single
high school in the city or noticed any of their sign-boards. So when
Roman and Ira persuaded him to remove Xenia from the boarding-

school in Pyatigorsk and put her into a high school in Rostov, he hesitated a long time before taking his daughter there; schools were a business of which he knew nothing and he felt sure that he would be fooled and recommended the worst one.

On that occasion he also had to pay a business call on a certain highly intelligent and respected Jew—Ilya Isakovich Arkhangorodsky. Arkhangorodsky was the leading expert on flour-milling machinery; he knew so much about the latest machines, powered by electricity or by anything else, that there was not a mill from Tsaritsyn to Baku which his firm had not installed, and when the famous Paramonov put up a five-storey mill in Rostov, it was naturally Arkhangorodsky who equipped it for him. It occurred to Tomchak that Arkhangorodsky would be bound to give him good advice, so he decided to ask him which was the best school to send his daughter to. Arkhangorodsky replied in the friendliest way that although there were the state-run Ekaterininskaya School and several others, in his opinion the best of all was Madame Kharitonova's private school, where his daughter Sonia was a pupil in the fourth class. They compared the girls' ages; both were thirteen, so they would be classmates, which was fine.

Zakhar Ferapontych liked the idea of his daughter starting with a friend, but he was even more pleased that it was a private school and not a government institution: the only well-run places were those where the owner was the boss; if the Treasury and civil servants had a hand in things, no good ever came of it.

Whenever Zakhar Ferapontych went to Rostov, he wore a suit which according to the time of year was either woollen or tussore; sometimes he put on a round billycock hat or took an umbrella for smartness, but he soon gave that up and used to stride around waving his arms as he did at home in the steppe and jump in and out of cabs wearing a waggoner's cloak and dirty boots. Recently Irina had had the notion of ordering a hundred visiting cards, thinking them essential. But they were a waste of money: among the traders and businessmen whom Tomchak used to visit in banks and on the stock exchange no one bothered to use these scraps of paper, and the whole hundred stayed in his pocket like a sealed pack of playing-cards. It was only when he drove past the old cathedral towards Madame Kharitonova's high school that he broke into the pack and handed his first card to the porter to take upstairs.

Aglaida Fedoseyevna was a judicious, dignified lady with a pince-nez; perhaps she should have worn spectacles, as the pince-nez tended to fall off her nose. It was obviously quite safe to entrust one's daughter in a distant city to such a worthy person; the girl would be unlikely to misbehave here, even though she would be away from home for six months at a time.

It never for a moment entered Zakhar Ferapontych's head that the headmistress might not like *him*. It was a characteristic of all the Tomchaks of the male line that they displayed their obstinacy, peevishness and rudeness at home, but when out visiting or receiving guests they were invariably cheerful and the best of company. There was no company, no woman either, whom Zakhar Ferapontych could not charm when he wanted to.

And indeed this coarse but picturesque Ukrainian farmer, with his craggy features, bushy eyebrows and gargoyle nose, in his comical city suit with a watch-chain displayed as prominently as possible, overwhelmed Aglaida Fedoseyevna; what's more, she was charmed by his frankness, his humour stiffened by a touch of patriarchal dignity, and above all by his impetuosity which, like a gust of wind from the steppes, almost blew the papers off her desk and made the leaf of the calendar turn over of its own accord. In the circles in which she moved there were plenty of wise and intelligent people, people who sighed and dreamed a great deal, but none of them had this energy, this passion for instant, on-the-spot action. Tomchak was simply incapable of talking in a polite murmur; in the headmistress's study he shouted almost as loudly as if farm-carts were creaking along outside, and his laughter rang out powerfully enough to be heard above the lowing and bleating of a herd. Strangely enough, although Aglaida Fedoseyevna was a high priestess of the cult of restrained manners and gentle speaking, his behaviour did not irritate her; she was, on the contrary, entranced by his spontaneity. Even when he told an obvious lie—that he had already inspected four other high schools, none of which he had liked, but that this one had taken his fancy at the very first glance, the moment he had seen the porter on the staircase—she actually found herself touched by this naive piece of cunning. And although Madame Kharitonova's second-year class was full and she was not intending to take any more pupils, least of all some obviously ill-taught country girl, within ten minutes she had agreed to accept Xenia. What's more, she not only failed to put on the practised frown which implied that other, pressing matters awaited her, but she succumbed so completely to this farmer's open-hearted joviality that she began asking him questions about himself and ordered coffee to be served.

With a welter of details and comic asides, convinced that nobody had anything better to do than listen to him, Zakhar Tomchak described how as a child he had been a simple shepherd-boy in the southern Ukraine, where he had herded other people's sheep and calves; how his family had migrated to the Caucasus to hire themselves out as day-labourers, for which in those days one received a great deal less than he now paid to the last-come casual worker on his estate, to say nothing of what he gave his permanent overseers and foremen; how it was ten years before the farmer he worked for gave him a dozen sheep, a heifer and a few piglets— the source of all his present wealth, though this had been achieved purely by his own sweat and muscle. When the headmistress asked about his education, he answered that he had had a year and a half at a parish school, where he had learnt just enough for his needs: to read the Bible and the Lives of the Saints—in Church Slavonic as well as in Russian—and to write, even if very badly; he had a natural head for figures and no one had ever cheated him on a single deal. To her enquiry about his family he told her of the great trial God had sent him, how six of his children had died within a week—half of his offspring. Here his eyes filled with tears, which he wiped away with a handkerchief. Then he told her about the estate, how they had fired a million bricks of ringing ironstone in home-made kilns, how they were still selling them and with luck would go on selling them; how he himself had planned the new house with the architect, seeing to it that there was not a single window without shutters on the outside and venetian blinds inside, so that they would never suffer from the heat; how they had laid down four separate supplies of piped water and installed their own diesel generator for electricity. Now they were laying out the park and adorning it with electric lanterns. In his enthusiasm he invited the headmistress to visit them next summer to drink *kumis*, and to bring all her family with her.

In return the headmistress told him about herself: she had recently been widowed, her husband had been an inspector of government high schools, and she had three children. One daughter had just finished high school and was now going to Moscow to study, and her eldest son Yaroslav, aged thirteen, was causing her a great deal of concern as he wanted to give up high school and join his brainless friends as an officer cadet.

She announced that the tuition fees were two hundred roubles a year; this was five times more than the fees at the state schools, because . . . Tomchak was almost offended. 'I know how much it costs. You haven't any cattle, you don't grow sunflowers to press the seeds for oil and you don't grow beans—but you've got to feed the children on something.' When she asked where the girl was going to live, Tomchak put on an act of helpless concern. 'Ah, now that's the trouble—I've just nowhere to send the poor little creature! How can I leave her in this crazy big city without someone to look after her? I suppose *you* couldn't put her up, could you?' (He had prepared this move from the moment he arrived; that was why he had been so ready to sit there spinning her a yarn and drinking her coffee, and why he had invited her out to drink *kumis* next summer, even though he had other urgent matters to attend to.)

'What on earth do you mean?' Madame Kharitonova had been ready for anything except this.

'Surely you have a little room to spare, haven't you? You told me just now that your eldest daughter had finished school and was going to Moscow. Well, take my little girl in her place. If you were to give me all three of yours I'd find room for them in no time at all!'

Brash and high-handed though the suggestion was, given the amiable and good-humoured tone of their conversation so far Aglaida Fedoseyevna felt unable to revert to the icy politeness which she could so skilfully employ as a deterrent. Instead she reasoned with Tomchak, explaining why it was impossible: it was simply not done for a pupil to live in the headmistress's quarters; she had not even taken her own daughter as a pupil but had sent her to the state high school to avoid any suspicion of favouritism. But the crafty old farmer was quite unimpressed and began deploying all his resources of charm and humour to make her change her mind. 'Where am I to send her then? I won't leave her with people I don't know. If I take her home she'll just end up herding sheep. And that would be a terrible pity because she's a clever little thing.'

'But you don't know me, do you?'

'You? Of course I know you—saw at once that you were some-one after my own heart!' Tomchak was so confident, so cheerfully insistent, that the headmistress did not even have time to wonder what on earth she could possibly have in common with this wild man of the steppes.

Tomchak was well aware that the headmistress liked him, and that she would like his daughter too, but he also knew that he must not press her too hard all at once. So he dismissed the subject jokingly, asking her only one small favour: would she by any chance be willing to put the girl up in her flat for three days, as he had several more firms to visit before his business was finished and also a trip to take to Mariupol? He could hardly leave the little girl in a hotel. When he returned he would find her some lodgings.

Without quite knowing how, the headmistress found herself being persuaded. Tomchak even kissed her hand (he didn't know how to do it properly, but he'd seen others do it) and made a triumphant exit. Even before he brought the timid little girl, in her homely check dress tied at the waist with a sash, to meet this awesomely majestic lady with the pince-nez, he had already ar-ranged for delivery at her back door (the headmistress's flat formed part of the school buildings) of a china jar of caviar, a two-foot square cake from Filippov's and various other boxes and packages. A little gift, he felt, would surely not come amiss even with this highly educated lady, for all her pince-nez. The idea that *bona fide* payment in advance was not a form of bribery was perhaps too subtle for Tomchak, but he understood instinctively that generous payment for services rendered always makes for good relations between folk.

During the three days of Tomchak's absence, Xenia proved her-self to be a clean, tidy, obedient little girl, and an experienced eye could tell at once that she was receptive to teaching and routine. As her daughter's room was indeed empty, and there was no need to move any of the boys, Aglaida Fedoseyevna decided that the arrangement actually had much to be said for it: to have a girl growing up in the household alongside her two sons would act as a good influence on them. The child was excessively devout and spent a long time both morning and evening on her knees, but this only made the prospect of taking a girl from a backward country family and turning her into a creature of 'progressive' views even more enticing. She agreed to take her on condition that Xenia went home only for the holidays and that in term-time her father was not to interfere in any way. Zakhar Ferapontych could have wished for nothing better; the headmistress was a woman of strict principles—what more could the girl need?

It never occurred to Tomchak that he was putting his daughter to a severe test by making her live with the headmistress: her classmates were bound to look upon her as a teacher's pet. However, the headmistress herself shielded her from this danger: cherishing as she did the liberal tone of her school, she never allowed herself or her staff to worm information out of pupils through secret interrogation or sneaking, and during all the years that Xenia was there she never once subjected her to such questioning. She and her late husband regarded it as the chief aim of education to bring up young people as *citizens*, that is to say as individuals with an inherent mistrust of authority.

Xenia's talents and powers of application exceeded Aglaida Fedoseyevna's expectations. It only took Xenia a minute to walk from the apartment to the school building, instead of the whole hour which all the other pupils needed, and she spent that extra hour doing homework. What was more, it was the work itself that attracted her rather than rewards and prizes. In her end-of-term marks she never got less than a 5-minus for any subject, and she excelled in foreign languages, not one of which she had known when she arrived. At Kharitonova's school two foreign languages were compulsory; when Xenia graduated at the top of her class with the gold medal, she could read three fluently. She enjoyed school so much, she was so keen not to miss a day's work, and she kept her childlike timidity for so long, that she even refused Irina's invitation to go with her and Roman on a long trip abroad.

The more languages she learnt, the more books she read. The numerous bookshelves in the Kharitonovs' apartment were crammed with them, children's and grown-ups', none of them remotely resembling those Xenia had once borrowed from her sister-in-law—except for perhaps Gogol and Dickens. If the Kharitonovs bought a new edition which from its thickness and special paper looked like the Bible, it turned out to be not the Bible, but Shakespeare, full of terrifying illustrations.

And with every term, with every month of those four high-school years, the world of Xenia's former life, which had once seemed to her so full and satisfying, faded in her eyes to a dull, obscure backwater. Even her father's easy charm made her feel embarrassed now—fancy asking the headmistress to take his daughter as a lodger! Whenever she went home for the holidays, Xenia was horrified by the primitive coarseness which reigned there. Once she brought Sonia Arkhangorodsky with her, and seeing the crudeness of her family's way of life through her friend's eyes made it seem even worse, sending her hot with shame. If she had not been offered the chance to study agronomy at Moscow, she would have signed on for any course simply to be able to live in the world of education and culture.

These days nothing remained of her assiduous devotion to morning and evening prayer on her knees. When she prayed now it was in a distracted and off-hand way and she only went to church with the rest of the family when she could not avoid it. In the congregation she stood looking bored and embarrassed, crossing herself awkwardly.

Tomchak suddenly woke up to the fact that he had forgotten to ask the headmistress one small question: with all these girls in her charge, did she believe in God?

6

Roman was never in the least bored by having to spend even up to
a week in his own company: provided all his wants were catered for
punctually, there was no one whom he found more interesting or
congenial than himself.

To the elderly bewhiskered butler he gave precise orders for
lunch for one to be served here, on the balcony, before the sun
reached it. He gave particular attention to his choice of fish. (The
Tomchaks had an arrangement whereby a fishmonger in Rostov
delivered jars or packets into the care of the guard of one of the
passenger trains; a Cossack servant would ride down to the station
and tip the guard for his trouble.) Until the old man returned, it was
only sensible to pass the time with a delicious lunch—on his own
and free of scenes and quarrels. His father would probably come
back in the late afternoon, when there were two trains from Rostov
running at a close interval. It would please the old man if his son
went to meet him at the station, but they were in the middle of a
quarrel and Roman was not one to climb down or curry favour.

Today the butler shared his particular anxiety. His brother,
Roman's chauffeur, was due to be called up, but if old Tomchak
were successful in his mission he would get the man declared
exempt from conscription.

Roman himself was what was called a 'sole breadwinner', being
the only son in the family and therefore not liable for call-up. But
rumours were going about that this exemption was to be withdrawn if the son of the house proved to be not literally a breadwinner. In the last imperial manifesto concerning army reservists,
published three days ago, there had been a vaguely worded clause

about those who had been 'overlooked' by previous conscription orders, whereupon his father had hastened off to the local District Commandant to make sure, as far as possible, of plugging this loophole.

Here, on the glassed-in verandah of his first-floor bedroom, was his favourite chaise-longue, which he had removed from Irina's room. It had an elegantly curved back-rest, so that one did not lie at full length but was supported in a half-sitting position. Thus, without pillows and without the need to get up, he could smoke or read the paper or, as he was doing now, study the map of military operations hung on the wall.

Roman had ordered by telegram from a Petersburg bookshop a selection of little flags of the belligerent states, which he had been sticking into the map to represent the front lines. He had begun to be quite excited by this, until he had become aware of the rumours of the withdrawal of his exemption. Thereupon his interest and enthusiasm for the map had evaporated like a puff of smoke; the mere sight of the zig-zagging frontiers and the circles representing towns with their strange foreign names became unbearably painful.

With his gold lighter Roman lit one of his special-sized cigarettes. During a trip to France in the first year of their marriage, Irina had given her husband a gold cigarette-case which was long and thin and did not fit Russian cigarettes. As a gentleman, Roman was bound not to reject this unique and valuable present, so he had stopped buying ordinary cigarettes, had ordered from Asmolov's factory in Rostov a hundred thousand tubes of cigarette paper which fitted the case, and had then arranged for a specially-trained girl to come from town in order to fill the whole batch with tobacco.

But even smoking gave him no pleasure today.

He sat down at a card-table, spread out the papers he had brought from the safe and tried to work at his accounts. Roman had had no more than primary schooling. Thirty years ago, when the Tomchaks were still living in the Kum steppe and had only just started to make money, it would never have occurred to them that it might be a good thing to send their son to high school. Afterwards he went to a commercial secondary school, but gave it up. However, he had a good grasp of figures. He was a very competent farm manager, but it irked him to be under the thumb of his pushing, autocratic father who brooked no argument and was unusual among the local landowners in being sharp and successful at his business. Roman was waiting for the moment to come when he would be on his own; meanwhile his wife's capital spared him the need to do any work on his father's estate. Every year he spent two months in Moscow and Petersburg and two months abroad. In Moscow he would gallop around town in fast cabs, compete with foreigners to book a *suite de luxe* at the Elite Restaurant on Petrovsky Street, and at the Bolshoi Theatre, when the whole audience was already seated, he would make a point of strolling into the front row of the stalls wearing a dinner jacket. It was when travelling that Roman's self-esteem reached its peak. He liked to dress in such a way that even his acquaintances in the pump-room at Kislovodsk took him for an Englishman. At the same time he enjoyed shocking the Europeans with a display of Russian hauteur and eccentricity. In the circular purple chamber of the Louvre where the Venus de Milo is on display, but where there is not a single chair to sit on, with an imperious gesture he would hand a ten-franc note to an attendant and say: '*La chaise*!' He would then sit down, and, while Irina wandered round with the crowd, stick a cigarette between his teeth and play with his lighter. When they moved into the next room he would point to the attendant again: 'Now—*la chaise* over there!'

Irina herself fitted the part to perfection; when she put on her wide feathered hats and glided along as unbending as a stone goddess, only her nodding bird-of-paradise plumes betrayed that she was actually moving. She would have done him credit even at Court. As for himself, he felt that he might have been two or three inches taller and would have preferred it if his hair had not been so prone to fall out, which meant that he had to have it trimmed with clippers.

It was no good; he could not concentrate on his work. He was nagged by anxiety over the outcome of his father's journey. Roman started to pace up and down the verandah, smoking a cigarette and thinking.

It was in these moods of solitary reflection that he admired himself most, that he could give full play to all his abilities—and his ambitions even extended to politics, a fact which he concealed from the rest of the family. In his view, his undoubted superiority to most of the members of the Duma lay in the brutal frankness with which he treated people. Coarse and tough though most of the

neighbouring landowners were, they all respected Roman Zakharovich; they might not like him but they respected him. He did not
merely avoid flattery; without for a moment overstepping the
bounds of politeness, he never so much as smiled at anyone even as
a gesture of hospitality; in conversation he kept an air of aloof
gravity, fixing his partner with his unwavering, penetrating gaze.
Indeed, he never prolonged a conversation for more than a minute
if he found someone tedious or irrelevant; even if the person happened to be a guest, Roman Zakharovich would openly demonstrate his boredom and retire to his rooms. What the government
lacked at the present time was men of iron character such as himself—especially at the very top.

As he paced up and down, Roman's stride grew firmer and more
decisive. On the verandah lattice-work at one end of his walk there
hung a photograph of Maxim Gorky. Roman gave a sympathetic
glance at the challenging, outthrust, flat-nosed face of the famous
writer. He was always loud in praise of Gorky's novels and plays.
He considered that they had a trait in common: never fawning on
well-wishers. He was delighted by the audacity with which
Gorky would lash out and pour scorn on the great merchants
and industrialists, the same people who frenziedly applauded him
for his frankness, spontaneity and wit.

Out there, beyond the park, lay five and a half thousand acres of
the black earth of the Kuban—which would be his, provided he
inherited them. God, how good, how splendid his life was! Yet at
any minute this rich, solid, promising life and his own enlightened
intelligence were liable to be ruined at a stroke of the pen by the
District Commandant, and he would be flung into a muddy trench
to take orders from some sergeant! What a crime!

Not a single outstanding Russian politician had come from the
Kuban; it had yet to produce a great man. Roman imagined various
ways in which he would make his career in politics, each one more
fascinating than the last. He would, of course, be far more radical
than the Constitutional Democrats. But, then, who was there to
the left of the Constitutional Democrats—the socialists? Ah, now
Gorky was a socialist.

He might even have considered going in for socialism, if it had
not been so closely akin to sheer robbery, the seizure of other
people's lawful property. His only personal connection with socialism had occurred in 1906. The incident had stuck in his gullet—it

was the most humiliating loss he had suffered in his life. It was far worse than an ordinary loss; one can reconcile oneself to losing objects, just as one accepts the consequences of thunderstorms, drought or falling prices. There is nothing humiliating in that sort of loss; it happens to everyone. But voluntarily and with his own hands to have surrendered hard-earned money to those rascally blackguards who lacked both the brains and the application to earn a twentieth of that amount by honest work! The only work they had done was to write notes in clerkish copperplate and send them round to all the rich landowners: 'Dear Zahhar Ferapontych, you have been assessed as due to contribute forty thousand roubles' (some had even been asked for fifty thousand!) 'as a contribution to the revolutionary cause; if you do not pay you will instantly be put to death. Signed: The Communist Terrorist Organisation.' Just to show they meant it, they murdered the first landowner who refused along with all his family.

What were they to do? In the aftermath of the 1905 revolution everyone was still apprehensive. The government had not regained its confidence. The feeling among educated society was that it was everyone's moral duty to aid the cause of revolution, a sacred obligation to the exploited people of Russia. If only there had been a lawful revolution to unseat the hated Tsar, he would have supported it with every means at his disposal. The estates were widely scattered and unprotected in the vast expanse of the steppe. (Since that time the Tomchaks had hired four armed Cossack guards.) There was nothing for it but for Roman, the bailiff and the accountant to take a four-wheeler and drive to meet the blackmailers. His father refused to go; he could never have given away the money with his own hands, he would have had a heart-attack parting with the first thousand roubles.

They drove out to a distant acacia plantation. It was autumn, and he well remembered the wheels crunching over the broad, lilac-coloured pods that had fallen from the trees. The other men had driven from town in a rubber-tyred phaeton; far from being plainly or roughly dressed, they were extremely smart: one even wore a morning coat with satin revers and a bow-tie. They chatted politely as they patiently counted the banknotes. As the numbers were equal—three on each side—Roman's party could easily have attacked the others and shot them, or he could have arranged to have them ambushed; he was in fact carrying a revolver in his hip pocket. But he lacked the resolution. For some reason, all Russia felt that these dangerous revolutionaries had right on their side. . . Even so, Roman could not bring himself to give them the full forty thousand; he bargained with them obstinately, as a result of which he succeeded in reducing their demand by two and a half thousand, which caused them much derisive amusement over the landowners' proverbial meanness. However, his father was very pleased with him for having saved the two and a half thousand and held it to his credit for years. Afterwards the men bowed with the utmost politeness and drove away. No one ever knew what became of the money—whether they built barricades with it or bought rifles, or whether they were simply three confidence tricksters who had pulled off a splendid coup and spent it all on prostitutes in Baku.

It was still a long wait until the evening trains, and the only way to pass the time was to read and re-read old newspapers.

*

The sons of the rich are like blue horses—
they seldom win races.

7

(A Random Selection from the Newspapers)

The man who is unaware of the magical effect
of 'Lecithal' is a ***Living Corpse*** . . .
The Stimulant which combats ***Masculine Neurasthenia*** . . .

Moscow Mutual Aid Fund for Brides . . .

Ladies' Coconut-fibre Hammocks . . .

'Click-Click'—the fragrant London perfume 'S' brand . . .

Take the Waters
at
BADEN-BADEN
75 Thousand Visitors a Year

CHANCE plus LUCK equals RICHES!
Buy a ticket in the lottery . . .

... that ethical idealism in social matters, in which the Slav soul is so rich, yet of which there is such a paucity in the advanced West ...

A Cruise
to greet the arrival of

THE PRESIDENT OF THE FRENCH REPUBLIC

has been arranged for the 7th July
aboard the First-Class Steamer

S.S. *RUSSIA*
(with orchestra)

Exclusively for Fashionable Clientèle!

... the indifference displayed by French democratic socialism parties towards the external security of their country ... triumph of the anti-patriotic parties in the French parliament ...

ATTEMPT ON THE LIFE OF
Grigory Rasputin

When questioned she would only reply: 'He is the Antichrist ...'
The assailant is Khionia Kuzminichna Gusevaya, a peasant woman, of Simbirsk Province ...
Rasputin's life is out of danger ...

International Horticultural Exhibition in the Tauride Palace ...
... removal of the ban on Jews renting stalls at the Nizhni-Novgorod Fair ...

WHY BE FAT?

Ideal Anatomical Belt against Obesity ...
Indispensable for elegant men wishing to preserve a
handsome figure and a graceful carriage ...

IF YOU DON'T MIND SPENDING
15 kopecks
on a trial bottle . . .

YOUR STOMACH'S BEST FRIEND
Saint-Raphael Wine

**Silver Wedding
of Franco-Russian Alliance**

Presence of Monsieur Poincaré at

STATE BANQUET

On Her Imperial Majesty's right . . . on the left hand of the'
Sovereign . . .

*Monsieur Poincaré
receives deputation of Russian peasants*

The leader of the deputation greeted the President and asked him
to convey to the French peasants . . .

State banquet on board the battleship *France* . . . glittering affirma-
tion of an unbreakable alliance . . . shared ideal of peace . . .

Last hours of the visit of our French guests . . . When asked
whether the alarm shown by European public opinion . . . over
events in the Balkans was justified, Viviani replied: 'It is undoubtedly exaggerated.'

The Times remarks that the superiority of the Russian over the
German army is more significant than . . .

TOOTHACHE REMEDY
of the blessed Benedictine Fathers . . .

'UNCLE KOSTYA'
Cigarettes

6 kopecks for 10

The height of elegance and taste!

Shustov's Brandy!

SHUSTOV'S INCOMPARABLE ROWANBERRY

LIQUEUR!

FOR LOVERS OF BEAUTY!

Parisian-Style Photographs

Latest Models **Taken from Nature!**
Sent in sealed plain envelope

PRACTICAL GUIDE
for Police Constables . . .

. . . Russia's love of peace is well known . . . But Russia is conscious of her historic obligations, and therefore . . .

. . . in view of the continuing strike, industrialists of the Vyborg District . . . have closed factories and mills for two weeks . . .

. . . no newspapers were published in Moscow . . . one-day strike of compositors . . .

RACING today

YAR'S RESTAURANT

PEACE OR WAR?

This morning the answer everywhere was 'peace' ... Unhappy
Serbia ... peace-loving Russia ... Austria has presented the most
humiliating demands ..... Over the head of little Serbia the
sword is pointed at mighty Russia, protectress of the inviolable
right of millions to live and work ...

... instead of depression and low spirits, an access of vigour and
faith in our own powers. This is a psychological characteristic of
all healthy peoples.

... gigantic nation, its spirit unbroken by the sternest trials, will
not shrink from a bloody passage of arms, from wheresoever the
threat may come.

WHY BE WEAK
Nervous, Tired and Somnolent
when there is
Bauer's
SANATOGEN?

MANY WOMEN
WHO HAD **LOST ALL HOPE**
found their 'joie de vivre'
completely restored
by the use of this cream ...

His Majesty the Emperor has been graciously pleased to order the
Army and the Fleet to be placed on a war footing. July 18th 1914
is named as the first day of mobilisation.

From the misty North come streaming
Vengeful warriors, near and far:
Cross in hand and armour gleaming,
Slavdom's champion girds for war.

THE GERMAN AMBASSADOR IN ST PETERSBURG
HAS DELIVERED A NOTE CONTAINING
A DECLARATION OF WAR

Resolute mood in Petersburg and Moscow ... Ban on sale of spirituous liquors in both capitals.

GOD STRIKE THE AGGRESSOR!

A crowd of a hundred thousand kneeling in front of the Winter Palace with national flags dipped in salute ...

Arise, great nation of Russia! ... great feat, before which all else pales ... sake of a bright future for all humanity ... dream of brotherhood of nations ... bring to the world the Light from the East, now or never ...

RISE IN FOOD PRICES

Extraordinary price increases in Petersburg in the past few days ... Within three days, the price of meat ... from 23 to 35 kopecks ... In Kiev a crowd of the poor set up an impromptu court to condemn traders who arbitrarily raised ...

Directive forbidding the exchange of state treasury notes for gold ... Visits to banks in the capitals today ... observe with satisfaction ... in economic terms, the war represents less of a threat to Russia than to Germany ... Strikes have immediately ceased ...

GOD STRIKE THE AGGRESSOR!

In 1812–13 we saved Germany, in 1848 Austria . . .

Portraits of our enemies: His Apostolic Majesty, Emperor of Austria, King of Hungary, Francis Joseph I . . .

26th July

TRIUMPHAL ONE-DAY SESSION
OF STATE DUMA

On this historic day, the representatives of the various nationalities and parties were moved by one thought only, one great emotion rang quivering in every voice . . . Hands off Holy Russia! We are ready to make any sacrifice to defend the honour and dignity of the one, indivisible Russian state . . .
The Lithuanian people goes to the war as in a sacred cause . . .
In defence of our homeland, we, the Jews, will . . . with a sense of profound devotion . . .
We, the German colonists in Russia, have always regarded her as our motherland . . .
We, the Poles . . .
We, the Latvians and Estonians . . .
Permit me, as the spokesman of the Tartar, Chuvash and Cheremis peoples, to state that . . . as one man . . . fight the invader . . . lay down our lives . . .
The whole country is united around its Tsar in a feeling of love . . .
In complete unity with our Autocrat . . .
All thoughts, all emotions, all enthusiasm . . .
'God, Tsar and people!'—and victory is assured . . .

THE LAST WAR IN EUROPEAN HISTORY

A European war cannot be a prolonged conflict . . . From the experience of previous wars . . . The decisive moves have always taken place no later than two months . . .

BULLETPROOF VESTS

"ARA"
Laxative Pills
A gentle, painless preparation . . .

EVERY LADY can have an IDEAL BUST,
the glory of womanhood! Take Marbor
Pills! Entirely reliable. No
disappointment.

As a result of mobilisation **many vacancies** are now open . . .

ENGLISH CLOTH—40% cheaper . . .

GUITAR LESSONS by correspondence,
free of charge. Write Afromeyev, Tyumen . . .

THE SECOND WAR FOR THE FATHERLAND

Communiqué from the General Staff: Russian detachments
have penetrated into East Prussia . . . Our bold cavalrymen . . .

Nizhni-Novgorod Fair, 1st August

All beer- and wine-shops have been closed for the past two weeks
and the Fair has taken on an unusual aspect. There are no drunkards to be seen on the streets, none of the usual gatherings of tipsy
stallholders . . . thefts by pickpockets have almost ceased . . .

To the Departing

Go, beloved ones! Fearless, brave,
Drink from the proffered cup of parting . . .

[66]

Poles! The hour has struck when the cherished dream of your fathers and forefathers ... Let the Polish people unite beneath the sceptre of the Tsar of Russia ...

BULLETPROOF VESTS

WE MUST WIN!

Never before have Russo-Polish relations attained such a degree of moral purity and sublimity ...

Czechs! The twelfth hour is almost at hand!... Your three-hundred-year-old dream of a free, independent Czech State: it is now or never!

Jewish Rights

A directive has been telegraphed to every provincial governor and mayor ordering the cessation of all mass or individual evictions of Jews ...

End of German Empire Predicted

Wilhelm II, when a student at Bonn University, once put a question to a gipsy fortune-teller ... The gipsy woman replied dispassionately: 'An evil tempest will descend upon Germany and sweep all away ...'

PETERSBURG SECURE

Rumours of a German sea-borne landing ... are completely discounted ...

IN THE LAND OF THE HUN

The land of Schiller and Goethe, of Kant and Hegel . . . Under the fist of the Iron Chancellor, to whom so many monuments have been erected . . . No one will shed any tears over the ruins of this land of falsehood and violence . . .

Military Censorship

As of 7 p.m. today, August the 3rd, Military Censorship comes into force in St Petersburg.

. . . the responsibility of keeping the public informed, within the limits imposed by security considerations, has been placed upon the Chief Directorate of the General Staff. The nation must accept the paucity of information released, content in the knowledge that this sacrifice is dictated by military necessity . . .

EMPEROR VISITS MOSCOW

Speech by the Sovereign in the Great Palace of the Kremlin . . . Their Imperial Majesties seen leaving the chapel of the Miraculous Icon of Our Lady of Iverskaya . . . Tens of thousands of loyal subjects demonstrate on Red Square . . .

> *Fraternal Serbs attend the service,*
> *The Court convenes, a brilliant throng;*
> *Past eager crowds our staunch reservists*
> *Parade to cheers both loud and long.*
> *The Sovereign's head is bowed in prayer*
> *'Midst anthems, incense, cloth of gold:*
> *To greet his people comes the Tsar*
> *Before the battle, as of old.*

WE MUST WIN!

Sighted party of twenty-two horsemen . . . Shouting a battle-cry,
attacked them fearlessly . . . cut his way through . . . lashing about
him with tigerish fury . . . Comrades galloped to his aid . . . First
St George's Cross to be awarded in this war . . .

. . . due to the cessation of exports . . . disastrous fall in the price
of wheat . . . Serious crisis in the grain trade . . .

Chaliapine Escapes!

Having successfully evaded capture by the Germans, he is now . . .

A LETTER FROM AN ENSIGN AT THE FRONT:

'Today nine Austrian spies were brought in . . . According to their
accounts, the Austrian army is in poor shape . . .'

WAR DIARY

The principal event of the day is our advance on a broad front into
East Prussian territory . . . The country is thickly wooded, but
with adequate paths . . . no obstacle to movement of cavalry and
infantry . . . 7th August brought news of the capture of Gumbinnen . . . this means that we control all East Prussia . . . The
shattered German corps are incapable . . .

. . . constructive war-aims . . .

HIS MAJESTY HAS BEEN GRACIOUSLY PLEASED
to accept into the armed forces all young men who wish to join the
Regular Army for the duration of hostilities, despite exemption
through having served their statutory term as Special Volunteers . . .

GOOD NEWS

We are informed from the most authoritative sources that in the Russian Army there is now no unit under the honorary command of any member of the ruling houses of Germany and Austria.

8

One year the Tomchaks had paid six hundred roubles to the management of the Vladikavkaz Railway for the privilege of having
express trains stop on demand at their own little station, to save
them travelling twelve miles to the nearest junction.

This year they had not paid the money, but the expresses continued to stop at their station all the same. For his return journey
today from Ekaterinodar Zakhar Ferapontych did not wait for the
mail-train but took the first main-line express. He summoned the
head conductor, put two ten-rouble notes on the table, one for the
conductor and one for the engine-driver, and explained where he
wanted to stop. Regarding it as quite natural that a businessman
should wish to save time, the conductor agreed and kept his word.
It was nearly evening, though still extremely hot, when Tomchak
got down alone from the train, watched by a row of astonished
faces thrust out of the windows, and walked across the track to the
unshaded platform of his tiny halt. Under the quivering heat the
red gravel gave off the sweetish smell of train-oil.

In the shade of a storehouse stood Tomchak's phaeton, which
had been waiting for him all day. The coachman leapt up, ran forward on legs that were stiff from so much sitting and took his
master's little suitcase; then he whipped up the horses, who had
been plagued for hours by flies.

Tomchak had long ago got rid of his 'Russo-Baltic Carriage',
whose springs, spokes and axles were exactly the same in design as
those of an ordinary cart, and had bought a 'Mercedes', but he only
used it occasionally to show off when he went visiting. As a rule he
went everywhere by horse-drawn carriage, in which he felt more at

home; when he went to church or to the station, where people might see him, he drove in the phaeton, while for business journeys he travelled by droshky or by gig (he did not care for the single-axled little local cart known as a *tyrdykalka*).

The station master came out to shake Tomchak by the hand, but he was too late in crossing the track: the phaeton had already galloped off, for Tomchak, as usual, was in a hurry, the more so as he had lost three working days on his trip into town and was itching to see to a number of neglected tasks and to check how everything had been going during his absence.

Less than half a mile away to his left he noticed the first of the new threshing machines standing in a cloud of blown chaff and would have turned the phaeton aside at once to go and inspect it, except that he did not want to look ridiculous in front of his men; first he must change into his working clothes and then drive out in a droshky.

As was his habit, he was not thinking about the business which had taken him into town and which was now completed but about various jobs around the farm which he had not been able to oversee and which might have been neglected: the threshing; the need to send a quantity of carbolic up to Lukyanov's farm, where they were about to give the merinos their second clip; whether it was time to start harvesting the maize and to store the cobs in the new eight-thousand-ton capacity barn with its louvred ventilation (the sides could either be opened to let the air through or closed to make them watertight; this method of storage, which he had copied from the German colonists, promised to be highly profitable if correctly used).

Tomchak had borrowed several ideas from these colonists and had always found them worthwhile. He greatly respected the Germans and regarded the war against Germany as sheer lunacy—as idiotic in fact as the fight which he had had in a first-class compartment of a mail-train with Afanasii Karpenko, which had started because Karpenko had called his fiancée a fool. The girl was none other than Tomchak's eldest daughter, and a fool she probably was, having been snatched away from her fourth year in school to be married to a rich man, and it was ridiculous for two intelligent men to fight over a remark like that. Russia, on the other hand, had everything to learn from Germany about running an economy. Now that the lush and prosperous years had started to come to

Russia, the last thing she needed was a war; they should have just said a requiem mass for that Archduke Franz Ferdinand, after which the three emperors of Germany, Austria and Russia should have drunk a glass of vodka at the wake and forgotten the whole affair.

Holding these views, he saw no reason to let his son or his good foremen go off to the war, nor the Cossacks who had served him faithfully as mercenaries, guarding his estate and his cash after the incident with the robbers. He had arranged for them all, all those in fact whom he wanted to keep, to be exempted from service and he was now returning with this good news. If they had come to the station to meet him, with his own son at their head, that would have been a real sign of respect for the old man and they could all have rejoiced together. His son had not come to meet him—he was a devil's brat, and no son of his, perhaps he was a bastard? To calm his indignation as he drove away from the railway station Zakhar Ferapontych started thinking about urgent matters that lay ahead and put out of his mind things that were now over and done with.

Several men were squatting by the white stone pillars at the entrance to the driveway waiting for their boss: there were two Cossacks, the diesel-engine mechanic, a gardener and Roman's chauffeur, the butler's brother. Tomchak stopped the phaeton and, as the men stood up and gathered round him, greeted them with a warmth which implied that his duty to them was as great as theirs to him.

'You're all safe, lads. And you can tell the other men, too. Keep on with your jobs and light a candle in church to thank God for His mercy.'

And he drove on amid their murmurs of gratitude. The horses' hooves rang gaily on the flagstones of the avenue. As they turned towards the main entrance, only his wife was looking out from the top storey. Roman had not put his head out.

The coachman swept round to the porch in a wide circle. Tomchak got down and strode indoors. By now he no longer wanted to meet his son.

Not a single step of the new, well-built staircase creaked under his weight; at fifty-six he could still stride up it like a young man.

On the upper landing, her arms stretched out to him weakly but hopefully, stood his barrel-shaped wife.

'Well, Father, what happened?' She hardly had the strength in her voice to ask.

He felt too irritated to reply: here, under his own roof, he felt his son's failure to meet him as a humiliation. Barely pecking his wife's forehead, he went on in silence into the bedroom. She followed him.

When Evdokia had stopped doing man's work about the farm, she had been attacked by gout and a dozen other diseases, and the more she tried to cure them the more she fell prey to new ones. 'Don't you listen to any of them damned doctors!' Old Tomchak himself wouldn't let them come near him—he knew how to look after himself better than any doctor. At first they had ordered barrels of special mud from the Crimea and a nurse had been brought out to the estate to give his wife mud baths, then they had been told they should go to various spas such as Yeisk, Goryachevodsk and Yessentuki, where she had to go everywhere in lace dresses and be driven around in carriages and where her illnesses had only plagued her more.

While her husband crossed himself in front of the icon, Evdokia sidled past him and went on into her bedroom. There she clasped him round the chest and almost without words, simply gazing at his beetle-browed, big-nosed, bewhiskered face as if he were Elijah the Prophet, she put her question: would the lightning strike or would it not?

Tomchak had no wish to talk. Let the others bustle about and bring what he wanted—he would lie down on the divan for a while and get up when he was ready. Most of all he would have liked just to drive out into the steppe without saying a word to anyone, but seeing the old woman's agony he took pity on her and barked:

'The District Commandant has promised him full exemption for the whole war.'

Evdokia went limp, flushed, turned and crossed herself towards the principal icon.

'Ah, glory be, glory be! The holy Mother of God has heard my prayers.'

'Not her,' said Zakhar, frowning as he threw down his hat and pulled off his dustcoat. 'The Mother of God's got nothing to do with it. I was the one who greased their palms so they wouldn't call him up.'

He went towards his own room, but swung round and glared at

her to make sure she was still there. The lightning flashed from under his shaggy eyebrows.

'Where are you off to, eh? Don't you go and tell him! God damn him for a pig-headed fool!'

Reddened by the winds, lined with thick, knotted, dark veins, his hand clenched into a fist and he shook it. 'Let him come himself, as he should do.'

'I wasn't going to Romasha,' said Evdokia, lying cheerfully. 'What would you like them to bring you?'

'Nothing much. I'll take a drink of balsam. I'm going for a drive in the fields directly.'

He pulled off his three-piece town suit, until he stood in only his underclothes.

The fiery Riga balsam, made from birchwood sap, had been his favourite drink since he had recently discovered it in Moscow. One shiny little jug was kept in the dining-room, and another in the bedroom, from which he poured the spirit to drink it out of a tiny silver tot-measure.

'Why not have some Lenten borsch?' his wife suggested, beaming with joy. 'Shall I heat it up?'

'Why bother to heat that stuff up when it's only made with beans and sunflower oil? Give me some cold.' And he shouted after her: 'Tell one of the Cossacks to run to Semyon and harness up the droshky.'

Zakhar's bedroom led off his wife's and did not have a separate door to the outside. 'That's so there won't be any draughts around me,' he used to say. Out on the steppes in the bad weather, in the rain and the cold, he seemed quite impervious to wind, but at home he was terrified of draughts and loved to sleep warm. Quite out of keeping with their present grand style, he had had a broad, tiled stove-couch built peasant-fashion against the large, upright stove and in winter slept on it. Here too he had had a large safe fitted into the wall, with a complex set of locks and alarm bells which rang when it was opened, yet he rarely used it and only threw things in or took them out in passing; it contained a few ledgers, but Tomchak never received his employees in the bedroom and himself had little time for figures in books. He kept hardly any money in the form of cash, as all his assets were invested in the soil, in his herds of cattle and in buildings; all the Tomchaks avoided the use of gold coin, as did everybody who handled money, including workpeople (a little gold piece easily fell out of a pocket or slipped through the lining), and in the bank one had to bribe the clerk to pay one in notes instead of gold.

In his office, too, Zakhar Tomchak never spent much time bent over rows of figures or piles of cash; he stayed there no longer than was necessary to take some decision. The real heart of his business was out on the steppes, with the machines and the flocks of sheep, and in the farmyard—*there* was the place to manage and supervise. The whole success of his estate depended on the fact that his vast steppelands were divided up into rectangular sectors by long strips of acacia plantations which acted as wind-breaks; that he used the seven-field crop rotation system in which wheat and maize alternated with alfalfa, horse-beans, sunflowers, lucerne, and esparto grass, so that each year his crops grew heavier and more lush; that he had changed the breed of his milking herds to German Holsteins which gave a daily yield of eight gallons; that they would slaughter forty boars at once and hang the meat in the smoking-shed (he employed a German colonist whose hams and sausages were every bit as good as those supplied by Eidenbach in Rostov); and it depended above all on the way in which they sheared the sheep and packed the mountainous piles of fleece into bales.

Tomchak himself never missed a chance to watch the departure by rail or long-distance road-haulage of a consignment of grain, wool or meat from his estate. It was his greatest and never-failing pleasure to see with his own eyes all that bulk and weight of his own produce being sent out into the world. He sometimes used to boast: 'I feed the whole of Russia', and he liked it when others praised him for it.

While his wife went to fetch the borsch Zakhar Ferapontych changed into a linen suit and put on a pair of boots with soft double soles ('to give my feet a rest'). Right now he would have preferred to eat a slab of pink bacon three inches thick or some hot 'shepherd's' porridge with mutton fat, but the fast of the Assumption was not yet over. Instead he took a loaf of light wheaten bread squeezed flat in three places by the baker's hand, sliced it himself from end to end with a long kitchen knife and bent his whiskers over a large bowl of cold, thick, Lenten borsch.

His wife stood facing him, her arms folded on her fat stomach, and watched him eat. He was in a hurry to finish and be off, but there was a knock at the door and Irina came in.

'What? Have you told Roman already?' Zakhar Ferapontych said suspiciously, growling from his bowl like a dog.

'No no,' his wife assured him guiltily. 'Only Ira—it's all right to tell her, isn't it?'

Irina entered unabashed, tall and erect as ever with her long neck and high, elaborate coiffure. All day long the only indication she had had that her husband had not died in his bedroom had been what she had heard from the butler: he had served him lunch and taken him fresh newspapers. She watched her father-in-law as he dipped his moustaches in the borsch and, though she did not thank him for what he had done, her silent glance was friendly and approving.

Although Zakhar Ferapontych shouted and hurled his thunder-bolts at everyone else in the house, he never aimed them at her; from the first day of her arrival she had behaved with a cool inde-pendence. True, she never did anything to cross him, never even put on her expensive clothes and her *tsatski* (diamonds) at home because he disapproved of it. Having struck the right note with him from the start, she was able to persuade him in matters where no one else could—whether it was to settle his quarrels with the servants or to let the canaries out of their cages. (They had started to keep canaries in imitation of some neighbours.) Her father-in-law used to sigh: 'Ah, you're a child of God, Irusha', and gave way. Whenever there was any political news he never listened to his son or the opinions of Roman's newspapers but always paid attention to Irina's reading of the situation from *Novoe Vremya*.

'Well, come here, come here.' He beckoned to her and kissed her proffered forehead after wiping the borsch from his mouth and moustache with a large, thick table-napkin. He did not, however, invite her to sit down and addressed no more affectionate remarks to her, but simply went on noisily eating his soup and chewing the second slice of crumbly bread which he held in his hand. In between mouthfuls he grunted angrily:

'Pity I got him his exemption . . . Should have gone to the war . . . Would have taught him a lesson . . . Devil's brat, never known a worse one . . .'

He went on eating noisily.

Calmly, Irina objected:

'How can you talk like that, Papa?'

He finished eating but still seemed to be swallowing when

[77]

there was nothing in his mouth, as though something were angering him.

'Tell him he can go and start up a business on his own. He needn't expect anything from me! I'd do better to bequeath the lot to his nephew. Because . . .' He had begun hesitantly, but while he was speaking his features hardened and he seemed to make up his mind in between two swallows. '. . . Because I'm going to take Xenia away from university right now and marry her off!'

'Papa! Papa!' Irina began, groaning, the line of her eyebrows rising. 'You're in a bad temper and you can't mean it! Why send her off to university at all if you're going to bring her home in the middle of it? Where's the sense in that?'

Once, after hearing some other landowners talk of their future plans, Zakhar Ferapontych had said: 'I've a problem on my hands and I don't know what to do. I ought to have my own agronomist. Where will I find someone who knows his job and works hard, someone I can trust and who's not a swindler?' It was at that moment that Irina and Roman had persuaded him to send Xenia to read for a degree in agronomy: there's your agronomist for you, your very own daughter! But now Tomchak was staring out from under his shaggy eyebrows with a look of cunning that had quite another purpose.

'I'll tell you what's the sense in it. In a year's time I shall have a grandson and in fifteen years an heir.'

He stopped chewing and wiped his mouth. The lower half of his face was covered by the napkin, but the upper half betrayed a look of pain.

Zakhar was unable to explain to himself, let alone to these women, the reason for his sudden outburst. It wasn't that he was afraid of losing money or of the estate going to ruin—Roman was no wastrel, but somehow he had upset the functioning of the heart, the soul of the family connection. To inherit the estate and run it properly, like had to succeed to like. And he had not brought it all to such a pitch of efficiency and prosperity just to hand it over to that quarrelsome, ungrateful son of his.

Irina put forward a woman's objection:

'How can you just marry her off without asking her? And who will you marry her to, anyway?'

Tomchak got up. The stockiness of his broad Cossack figure was particularly noticeable beside the tall, stately Irina.

'And who's she likely to marry up there in Moscow, might I ask? Some student who gets sent off to Siberia before we know where we are? I was a fool to let her go and study. Done nothing but learn all these damn foreign languages and doesn't believe in God any more. Now if she'd been a son, he could have studied till he was forty for all I cared, and nobody would have thought it strange. Ah, you old baggage!' he croaked, picking up a light walking-stick with a crook at the end, polished smooth from long use. 'Why didn't you give me another son?'

'God didn't give us one, Father,' sighed his wife, with a calm, complacent look on her placid face.

'Well, I don't know about God's will . . . but that's *my* will.'

With a firm, heavy tread he strode out, and they could hear him going down the stairs.

9

Orya loved mystery. She liked to believe that forces from another world are mysteriously at work alongside us. That was why, for instance, Halley's Comet had been seen in the year in which they had built this house and planted this park. While there was no hint of it in the Gospels, Orya was also a firm believer in the trans-migration of souls. She felt that certain concepts of eastern religion were a beautiful complement to Christian beliefs. Her mind did not regard the mixture of the two as in any way contradictory; they were merely alternative manifestations of beauty. When daydream-ing, she loved to guess who she had been in her previous incarna-tions and who she would be in later ones, and to wonder whether she would attain the astral plane before being reincarnated.

> All that here is not revealed to us,
> We shall attain to in the life beyond . . .

She loved to dream as she wandered at night under a starry sky, but most of all she indulged these fancies in the golden gleam of the sunset, in the westernmost avenue of the park, where the vineyards began and where on a fine summer evening the boundless golden afterglow would spirit her away from the park, from the house, from her husband, away from this world as she walked, bathed in sunlight, untroubled, unearthly.

Today there was just such a sunset, and she felt an urge to walk towards it, to wander like a free soul, liberated from her body and all its afflictions. But if she did not go and tell the news to Roman at once, her mother-in-law would get there first. Besides, there was nothing demeaning in being the first to make up the quarrel when she had such a good piece of news to bring him. With this to announce, she could even go in without begging his forgiveness.

Irina did not give any warning signal such as shuffling her feet, coughing, or knocking before entering. She simply walked quietly up to his room and as quietly opened the door.

Still standing in the doorway, she was suffused with a bright light of mingled amber and rose: the rays of the sunset were striking through the tops of the trees in the park, through the verandah and the french windows, into the bedroom, and bathing the walls in pale pink reflected from the rose-gold counterpanes and the gleaming bronze pillars of the two maplewood double beds. It was still light enough to read and he was sitting in a low, deep armchair with his back to her, holding an open newspaper. He had heard the door open and could not help recognising her step, but he did not turn round. He was determined to show to the bitter end how wronged he had been and how firm he was.

The way he was sitting, Irina could just see the balding crown of his head over the top of the armchair. It was those deep inroads of baldness when he was still only thirty-six, the slightly defenceless look of the familiar top of his head, that suddenly made her relent. The hesitancy which had held her back fell away.

With a confident step she went towards him, expecting his head to turn, expecting to see a mixture of resentment, uncertainty and radiance on his face, doubly shadowed as it was by being turned away from the light and, for once, unshaven.

In a steady voice she announced:

'All's well, Romasha. Papa's come to an agreement and they've promised it will be kept.'

She was now standing so close to his chair that he did not have time to rise from its enveloping depths but simply seized her hands and kissed them, murmuring something as he gasped for breath. Not a word was said about their quarrel, about whether it was his fault or hers; it was as if it had never been.

His father might never have existed either, for Roman said nothing about him, asked no questions and showed no sign of gratitude. Irina, for her part, could not bring herself to tell him how his father had abused and threatened him.

Irina's arms were uncovered above the elbow and Roman kissed the little dimples inside her elbows, and above them her pure, tender, pink, unblemished skin; beyond that her arms were covered by her tight sleeves. He turned her round, sat her on his lap and pressed his head to her breast. Again she was looking down from above on to the bald patch in the middle of his short, coarse but sparse hair. Tentatively she kissed it.

'Topper darling.'

He liked that nickname, which was a private joke between them about the fact that he was thinning on top.

Eager, excited, he began to talk. At first Irina did not quite grasp what he was trying to say. He promised her that after going to America, which he had always wanted to see since it was the most energetic, most efficient, best-run country in the world, or even before going to America—as soon as the war was over in fact —they would make the journey she had always dreamed of (once, long ago, she had mentioned it; it had been rejected and thereafter became taboo): to Jerusalem, followed by a tour of Palestine and then a visit to India. There was bound to be so much there that was curious and amusing, so many new and exotic things to eat even if he did have to spit them out in disgust!

'But will you behave yourself,' asked Irina 'when we go sight-seeing? Or will it be like Paris?'

They had been about to take the lift to the top of the Eiffel Tower:

'But aren't there so many other things we haven't seen?' He was afraid of heights.

'All right—I'll go alone!'

In that case, he would reluctantly come too.

In the Louvre it was: 'Ira, are you going to go on looking at those skulls for ever? They make me feel hungry.'

At Napoleon's tomb: 'What's Napoleon to us, anyway? We beat him! Now Suvorov—there was a genius for you!'

'No, no, you can look at everything for as long as you like,' he promised now, but he had already lifted her off his knees, reached for one of his long cigarettes and was walking out on to the verandah for a smoke, picking up a crumpled copy of the *Stock Exchange Gazette*.

'Irina darling, tell them to bring us up something nice and light for dinner, chicken perhaps. We won't go out, we'll just eat together and then go to bed.'

There was still some light on the verandah, but in the bedroom it was growing darker every minute and all the colours were blur-

ring and turning grey. Irina, however, did not turn on the electric
light. She walked away from the windows to the far corner of the
bedroom. Reluctantly she picked up the corner of the bedspread,
now colourless in the twilight, which lay over one of the enormous
beds, and found that the material felt as ponderous as iron. There
she paused, holding the raised corner of the unbearably heavy bedspread. Suddenly she wondered why it was that most people lived
out their humdrum lives behind some curtain, some impenetrable
veil which denied them the experience of that benediction which
had come upon her father in his old age, that passion which had
driven him, heedless of the world's reproach and of God's judgment, shamelessly to bribe a bishop—just so that he could marry
his mistress . . .

Irina's pity for her husband left her as quickly as it had come.
Instead she felt resentment at having had to spend the previous
night alone and even at the oppressive loneliness she had felt today,
mitigated though it was by a certain sense of freedom. It was as if
by pulling off the bedspread she would uncover a pit, a deep, dark,
dried-up well, at the bottom of which she would have to lie tonight
racked by sleeplessness. There was no rope up to safety, and no
sound would come from her throat if she cried out. And no hero
would ever come to rescue her.

For since she was nine years old she had had a secret hero: he
was Nathaniel Bumppo, Fenimore Cooper's 'Hawkeye', a noble
and fearless warrior. He was her ideal; but never in her life had she
encountered any such person or even anyone resembling him. The
only outward expression of her hidden longing was her passion for
shooting; in her handbag or in a little fretwork box she kept a small
Browning automatic, while on her wall hung an English-made
lady's gun which fired small-shot or ball with enough power to
penetrate a couple of two-inch planks. Whenever officers from the
nearby garrison headquarters were invited to the estate, a target
would be set up on two poles behind the cowsheds and Irina would
join them in shooting-practice, never missing the bull. If ever she
were to meet her hero, she would be worthy of him . . .

Meanwhile Roman, who had already spent hours idly flicking
through the newspapers, had only just woken up to the extreme
importance and interest of their contents. The newspapers had
changed so dramatically that blood was almost visibly pulsing
through the letters on the page. It was still not quite dark on the

verandah, so he went up to his map to inspect his flags lined up along the frontiers.

Ever since the East Prussian frontier had been established, forming a piece of land like the outthrust stump of an arm, simply asking to be lopped off by the Russians, it had never been put to the test. Russia and Germany had not fought each other since then, in fact for even longer—they had not fought for a hundred and fifty years, since before Germany had existed as a state. And now the first trial of strength on that frontier had come.

There was an old proverb, dating from the time of Frederick the Great: 'Russians always beat Prussians.'

This time the Russians were on the offensive. The communiqués from General Headquarters never designated the numbers of the armies, army corps and divisions, so it was impossible to know exactly where to move the little flags. Nor did the flags themselves indicate anything in particular; Roman had simply ordered as many as he thought suitable. It was entirely his responsibility whether to seize or not to seize an extra dozen or so miles of Prussian territory.

Carefully, so as not to tear the map, he now pulled out the flags by their little pins and shifted them forward two days' march.

The troops were on the move!

10

_____

Darkness had fallen, and the electric street-lamps were lit around the two-storey stone building that housed Second Army Headquarters at Ostrolenka. Smartly turned-out sentries were posted at the gates and the main entrance while two more patrolled the street, moving in and out of the shadows cast by the trees.

The army commanded by this headquarters had been advancing on the enemy for the past week; but here there were no urgent comings and goings, no horsemen galloping up or away, no rumbling of carriages, no shouting of orders, no running about, no changing of the guard: an evening calm had descended and the place had relapsed into the same drowsiness that had overtaken the rest of Ostrolenka. A few windows were lighted, but those that were dark stayed dark, adding to the sense of calm. Nor was the headquarters festooned with a network of field telephone cables; a mere couple of wires from a telegraph pole linked it to the town's telephone system.

The inhabitants were not forbidden to walk the streets around the headquarters, and young Poles dressed in white and black, and in gayer colours too, were strolling along the pavements. Since many of the young men had already been called up into the army, the girls were mostly walking with each other, though a few were with Russian officers. After a hot day, this Sunday evening was still not cool; the air was oppressive, windows were open and from far away came the sound of singing from a gramophone.

The beams from its headlamps looking strangely like two white sheaves of wheat, an automobile came swaying and rattling around the corner of the block, roared down the street in a whirl of dust and drove into the gateway past the saluting guard. The car was an open one and in it sat a small grim-looking major-general.

Quietness descended once more on the headquarters building. A fat Catholic priest in a soutane waddled down the street, the Poles greeting him with a deep bow from the waist and a sweep of the hat with outstretched arm in a manner that no Russian ever used to greet an Orthodox priest.

A cab drove up, bringing two officers to headquarters. The officers paid, jumped down and went into the building. The Headquarters Duty Officer was not in the main hall, but when they did find him the senior of the two, a colonel, handed him a paper. The paper appeared to be important. Holding his sword against his side, the Duty Officer ran upstairs to report their arrival to the Chief of Staff.

Astonished and somewhat alarmed at this news, the latter made as if to go and meet the visiting officer, then thought better of it. About to invite him up to his office, he decided against that too and instead scuttled into the office of the Army Commander, General Samsonov.

In his long years of steady, uneventful military service, first as Ataman-in-Chief of the Don Cossacks, then as Governor-General of Turkestan and Ataman of the Cossacks of Semirechiye, General-of-Cavalry Samsonov had come to treat work with sensible moderation, and he used to impress upon his subordinates that, like our Creator, each one of us can reasonably do all that he has to do in six days and can, what is more, sleep soundly for six nights, after which he may justly rest on the seventh day. Working on Sundays was no cure for fuss and inefficiency.

For the last three weeks, however, the life of the fifty-five-year-old general had been filled with exceptional activity and unaccustomed disturbance. Not only had he become unable to cope with his duties by working on Sundays as well as weekdays, but he had even lost count of the days, and only towards the previous evening had he remembered that tomorrow was Sunday. No matter what night of the week it might be, he would be waiting sleeplessly for the delayed arrival of orders from Army Group Headquarters and would then have to issue his own instructions at the most unseemly hours. He experienced a permanent buzzing sensation in his head which disturbed his thinking.

Three weeks ago, by order of His Imperial Majesty, Samsonov

had been recalled from his comfortable post in furthest Asia and transferred to the front line at the start of a European war. Once in the past, immediately after the Japanese War, he had served as Chief of Staff of the Warsaw Military District; it was on the strength of this long-ago appointment that he had now been posted here. It was an honour that His Majesty should place such confidence in him, and, as with every posting in the service, Samsonov would have liked to give a good account of himself. But he was badly out of practice; he had not been in an operational post for seven years, had not even commanded a corps in action, and now he was suddenly entrusted with an army.

He had, furthermore, long since ceased to think about the East Prussian theatre of operations; in the intervening years no one had acquainted him with the war plans for this region, nor told him how those plans had been drawn up and then changed. Now he was under orders to execute in haste a plan that was not only not of his own devising, but one that he had not even had time to study, whereby two Russian armies, one advancing westward from the River Niemen, the other northward from the Narev, were to attack Prussia with the object of encircling and destroying all enemy forces in that area.

The new commander needed a chance to analyse the situation and make his dispositions calmly and deliberately. Above all, he needed to be alone for a while, to order his thoughts, to weigh up the plan and study the maps; but for none of this was he granted the time. The new commander needed to get to know his staff and find out which of them would make good advisers and assistants; but there had been no time to spare for this either. He had, too, been treated less than fairly in the way his staff had been allotted to him: before Samsonov's arrival the headquarters staffs of both Second Army and North-Western Army Group had been formed from the staff of the Warsaw Military District; when General Oranovsky had moved to Army Group Headquarters after being Chief of Staff of the Military District he had taken all the best men with him, and in hiving off a staff to man Second Army Head-quarters had filled it with a motley collection of officers drawn from different places, officers who did not know each other and had had no opportunity to work themselves into a team. Samsonov himself would never have chosen his timid Chief of Staff or his choleric Quartermaster-General, but they had been appointed before him and had met him on his arrival. The new commander also needed to visit the regiments under his command, to get to know at least the senior officers, to have a look at the rank and file and show himself to them, to make sure that they were all ready—and only then to start advancing into a foreign country, and that gradually, conserving his troops' strength for battle and enabling the reservists to get used to soldiering. But if the Army Commander was unprepared, his corps were in a far worse state. Not a single one was up to strength, the allotted corps cavalry had not arrived, the infantry had de-trained ahead of schedule and at the wrong places and the whole army was dispersed over a territory larger than Belgium. On assuming command, Samsonov had found that the supply services were still only unloading from rail transport, that the army service depots did not have the regulation seven days' portable supplies, and, worst of all, that there was not enough transport available to ensure forward delivery along the full army frontage. Only the left flank could count on rail transportation, while the other corps had to depend on waggons, and even these were inadequate: they had been given one-horse instead of two-horse waggons, and thanks to orders issued by some unknown person in Military Communications the whole of XIII Corps' waggon-train had de-trained before reaching Bialystok and was quite unnecessarily covering the rest of the journey over sandy ground on its own wheels.

There was no time to spare; schedules were inexorably tight, telegrams exhorted: the whole world must witness the awesome advance of the Russian regiments. On August 2nd they moved, and crossed the frontier on the 6th; but they met no enemy and went on, day after day, marching into a void, wastefully leaving behind units to guard river-crossings, bridges and small towns because no second-line divisions had moved up in support of the first-line formations.

There was no fighting, but with the rear echelons in such a state of disorganisation the very speed of the advance began to have disastrous effects. It became vitally necessary to call a halt for a day or two in order to allow the supply services to catch up, to give the fighting arms the regulation day's rest, indeed simply a pause to shake down and sort themselves out. Every day Army Headquarters reported progress to Army Group Headquarters: the eighth, the ninth day of the advance; the fourth, the fifth day on Prussian territory—a deserted countryside that had been stripped of all supplies, the haystacks burned. Forage and bread had to be hauled forward over ever greater distances, with increasing difficulty and without the proper vehicles; two-thirds of the army's reserves of hard-tack was already consumed; in the heat and over sandy tracks the exhausted columns marched—into emptiness!

Yet although Zhilinsky, the Army Group Commander, sat sixty-five miles to the rear reading all the reports, he understood nothing, met none of their requests, but simply squawked parrot-fashion: 'Push on! Push on! We can only win by going faster—faster! The enemy is slipping away from you!'

There were certain bounds which General Samsonov did not allow himself to overstep, even in thought. He would never have dreamed of criticising the imperial family, hence he would say nothing against the Commander-in-Chief; nor would he have ventured to put forward his own interpretation of the higher interests of Russia. It had been made clear in a directive from General Headquarters that since the enemy had declared war on us and that our ally, France, had immediately supported us, we were bound by our obligations under the alliance to attack East Prussia as rapidly as possible. Yet although the directive had spoken of a 'steady and deliberate' advance, the staff at Army Group Headquarters greeted Samsonov's progress reports with incredulity, indeed with derision, and merely dismissed his complaints as showing lack of the necessary vigour. Samsonov was stung daily by nagging, reproachful telegrams from Zhilinsky—which even he refused to take lying down. Why should his senior commander's refusal to accept the realities of the situation be regarded as a mark of *will-power*? Why should a subordinate's report of what was actually happening be labelled weakness?

The Army Group Commander's sole task was to co-ordinate First and Second Armies; nothing more. With such a ludicrously small job to do, his heavily staffed headquarters inevitably began meddling in the dispositions of the army commanders. From the very beginning even its efforts at co-ordination had been nothing but a hindrance. Neither Army Group Headquarters, nor ground contact, nor cavalry reconnaissance provided Second Army with an inkling of the whereabouts on East Prussian soil of its right-flanking neighbour. And even though for the last three days the Army Group's general orders and the entire Russian press had been lauding First Army's victory at Gumbinnen, Samsonov's troops advancing from the south among the lakes and forests could find no trace of Rennenkampf's men advancing from the east, not even of his numerous cavalry; nor was there any sign of the Germans, who were retreating from east to west. While all Russia rejoiced at Rennenkampf's success, only his companion-in-arms in East Prussia gained nothing from that victory.

All might have been otherwise if the personalities involved had been different, but Rennenkampf and Zhilinsky were temperamentally ill-matched: both arrogant, unwilling to listen or to talk face to face. Samsonov had not been on speaking terms with Rennenkampf since the Japanese War, as the result of an ugly scene between them caused by the failure of Rennenkampf's cavalry to support Samsonov's Cossacks. In the past Samsonov had not had occasion to make the close acquaintance of Zhilinsky, and only now, on his way through Bialystok, had he been introduced to him. A few moments' conversation was sufficient, however, for Samsonov to realise that he would never get any sense out of this general. When Zhilinsky spoke to him it was not in the man-to-man fashion usual between brothers-in-arms: he talked like a bullying cattle-drover, not a colleague. He made it clear that he knew best about everything and had no intention of consulting his subordinates. In the quiet of his office he spoke with needless harshness, even cut Samsonov short, probably feeling humiliated by being so much the smaller man.

A further grievance had arisen between them since the spring, when they had been rivals for nomination to the post of Governor-General of Warsaw and Commander of the Military District. Samsonov's candidature had already been approved by the Tsar when Sukhomlinov had intervened and raised an objection, alleging that Samsonov could not speak French, which was a necessity in Warsaw (in fact Samsonov could speak French, though not very fluently). So the Tsar had then accepted Zhilinsky, who had just been dismissed from the General Staff and was in need of a job. Had Samsonov returned to the Warsaw Military District that spring he would have been able to study the situation and would have known in advance about the war plans. Thus the fate of the North-Western Front was decided by the French language.

Evil people always support each other; that is their chief strength. Samsonov knew for certain that Sukhomlinov was in-

volved with the Austrian firm of Altschuller on Morskaya Street—
and he the War Minister! He knew, too, that Sukhomlinov had an
unsavoury financial reputation; consequently his connections and
obligations were suspect too. His divorced wife spent her time
travelling round the world and demanding money from him.
Sukhomlinov backed Zhilinsky, Zhilinsky favoured Rennenkampf;
Rennenkampf's marriage had made him the brother-in-law of the
head of His Majesty's Field Chancellery, and he had as his general-
in-waiting a prince in exalted circles who was close to the imperial
couple. Zhilinsky too enjoyed access to high places—he had his
links with the household of Marya Fyodorovna, which made him
independent even of the Commander-in-Chief, the Tsar's uncle.
But here Samsonov came up against his self-imposed limits: it was
not for him to judge how far it was proper for the Dowager
Empress to influence the fate of the army.

He did not envy them all their success and promotion; he sought
no links of kinship or marriage with the Court and chose a general-
in-waiting not for his connections but for his military record.
Nevertheless he was inwardly troubled by the thought that if the
hour of trial were to come upon Russia, then it would scatter all
these brilliant intriguers to the four winds and their names would
vanish for ever. Let them rise to the top—provided they did no
harm to the nation's cause.

Samsonov would have been content to be left alone to cope with
his own problems—the take-over, the training and leading of
Second Army. But they insisted on making constant changes of
plan which foiled all his efforts. He could not even keep the same
corps in his army for two days on end: I Corps had been given to
him—but not the right to move it; he had been allotted the Guards
Corps—then three days later it was taken away again (furthermore it had been removed without his knowledge, so that for
several days he was under the impression that it was advancing
under his orders); XXIII Corps had been placed under him—
and immediately one of its infantry divisions, commanded by
General Sirelius, was transferred to the Army Group reserve, while
another, under General Mingin, was removed and posted to Novo-
Georgievsk; the corps artillery was sent to Grodno and the corps
cavalry to the South-Western Front. Then there was another sudden change of plan: Mingin's division was re-assigned to Samsonov
and was obliged to catch up with the other formations by marching

even faster than they already were. Yesterday a telegram had come from Army Group Headquarters which had really stung Samsonov: he was to transfer his right-flanking corps to Rennenkampf. This brought Rennenkampf's strength up to seven corps, while Samsonov was left with three and a half!

Even this he would have accepted calmly if there had been any reason in it. But it was wholly senseless. Despite his late arrival on the scene, despite his lack of time to consider the situation and discover what plans had been laid over the years for dealing with East Prussia, it was obvious to him from one glance at this piece of land, looking like the stump of an arm thrust into Russian territory, that the way to cut it off was by a blow under the armpit, not a jab at the elbow, and that consequently it was his southern army, the army of the Narev, which should be the stronger of the two and not Rennenkampf's eastern army.

Meanwhile the argument with Army Group Headquarters dragged on and on: how was Second Army's mission to be defined and what was to be its axis of advance? Having failed to achieve an understanding face to face, the two commanders were even less able to do so by telegraph. It was easier to catch the devil by the tail than to grasp the point of Zhilinsky's plan, which rested on the assumption that the Germans would throw all their forces eastward towards the Masurian Lakes to grapple with Rennenkampf and would simply wait for Samsonov to catch them in the rear. Therefore, Zhilinsky maintained, the best line of advance for Samsonov was diagonally north-eastward. He had made the whole Second Army de-train and concentrate much further to the *right* than was necessary, after which he only gradually allowed it to move leftward, thus causing it to get unnecessarily dispersed over the ground. One look at the map was sufficient for anyone to realise that the army should have deployed much further to the *left*—along the Novo-Georgievsk–Mlawa railway, the only one in the entire frontage of the advance; the Germans on the other hand could utilise dozens of railway lines. What did Zhilinsky think he was doing by leaving the only available railway line outside Second Army's left-flank boundary and allowing the army to slog its way forward through a sandy, marshy wasteland devoid of roads?

Although late in working out his alternative plans and movement orders, Samsonov sent Zhilinsky a counter-proposal in which he agreed that he should advance diagonally, though not in the unsuitable direction laid down by Zhilinsky and Oranovsky: he would move not on a north-eastern but on a north-western axis. He proposed not to link up with his friend Rennenkampf, but to make a rapid move and cut off the Germans by denying their withdrawal across the Vistula.

On this Samsonov would not yield; if he did, he could only regard himself as a complete fool, a mere puppet on a string. Every day Zhilinsky's directives ordered: 'Diagonally right!' while Samsonov daily requested: 'Diagonally left!' Without pulling in his right-flank boundary, he began surreptitiously moving his centre-line to the left, each order to his corps and divisions embodying a slight leftward shift by two or three villages at a time. And when they crossed the German frontier and for three whole days not a German was seen, not a shot heard or fired, this merely confirmed Zhilinsky in his assumption that the Germans had come to a standstill facing Rennenkampf and were simply waiting to be struck in the rear, that they were cornered and patiently resigned to being trapped in the area of the Masurian Lakes, which formed a slanting divide between Rennenkampf and Samsonov. It was obvious to Samsonov, on the other hand, that Zhilinsky was pushing him into a void, that the Germans were going to slip free of the Russian pincers and would escape westward; the only hope, therefore, was to widen the jaws of the pincers.

So this he did, opening out the left-hand jaw as far to the left as he could, while Zhilinsky, clinging to the right-hand jaw, refused his consent to the move. The two men put their hearts and souls into the dispute. Meanwhile the troops marched and countermarched; zigzagging, pulled hither and thither by the quarrelling generals, they wore out their feet in long, fruitless changes of direction. Samsonov felt that mileage on the soles of his men's boots as if they were his own—boots that burned and raised corns, boots whose uppers were steaming at the welts. Yet he still felt compelled to contest the idiotic orders issued by Army Group Headquarters.

A further result of this dispute was that the army's frontage was widening out like a fan: three and a half corps were spread far too thinly over forty-five miles. Zhilinsky nagged and nagged at Samsonov about the over-extension, which was doubly annoying to Samsonov because in this Zhilinsky was right.

Samsonov would have much preferred to carry out his orders

precisely as received. But what if the orders were completely senseless? What if they were obviously harmful to the national cause? In a desperate attempt to clear up the misunderstandings of communication by telegraph, on the previous day Samsonov had, as a last resort, sent Filimonov, his Quartermaster-General, to give Zhilinsky a verbal explanation and to request permission at least to be allowed to advance in a straight line directly northwards towards the Baltic Sea. He was also to insist on a day's halt, and, in exchange for the right-flank corps which had been withdrawn from Second Army, to ask for full command over the left-flanking 1 Corps which had been posted to Samsonov from General Headquarters' reserve but which he was not allowed to move.

But while the Quartermaster-General was on his way the telegraph keys had continued to tap, and they had tapped out two further directives from Zhilinsky, one of which had arrived yesterday, the other today. Yesterday's had repeated the same message as before: leave 1 Corps alone, order the other three and a half corps to keep their flanks protected ('try doing it yourself, you son of a bitch!') and advance with all speed in order to ensure that the right flank occupies, by not later than August 12th, the town of —This meant that his objective was merely to rub shoulders with Rennenkampf (if it was true that Rennenkampf really was beating back the Germans) and to take over a town already occupied by First Army. Any fool could see that this was a typical piece of staff officer's balderdash; this was no way to surround the Germans—it would simply push them back. Pointing out that Samsonov was faced by no more than an insignificant rearguard, Zhilinsky accused him of advancing too slowly to overtake the retreating enemy's main force.

This at least was true—there were no Germans in front of Samsonov (at any rate there had been none up to yesterday). The great question was—where were they? Without probing, without reconnaissance, without having sent cavalry forward, without having taken a single prisoner, how could they claim to know where the Germans were? Although in reality the Army Group staff did not know, they insisted that they did.

Filimonov achieved nothing by his personal visit, because an hour before his return the directive for the day, August 11th, arrived from Army Group Headquarters. It read: 'Having already directed your attention hereto, still strongly disapprove over-extension troops along your frontage in disregard previous orders.'

These telegraphed instructions were, of course, written by Oranovsky, a handsome man with large, limpid eyes and a curly moustache; neat, vain and more poisonous than a scorpion. He wrote them and Zhilinsky signed them—this comfortable division of labour had evolved when they were serving together at the headquarters of the Warsaw Military District.

'Strongly disapprove'! So they strongly disapproved of Samsonov's efforts at least to seize hold of the German left wing and halt it! They were insisting that he let the Germans get away intact . . .

Major-General Filimonov had now returned in the Army Commander's car and without wasting a moment, without even having a wash (only stopping to check that there would be meat pie for dinner as ordered), he avoided seeing the Chief of Staff (whom he despised as a toy soldier) and knocked on the door of Samsonov's room. On receiving permission, he entered and found the Army Commander on the divan with his boots off. Although Filimonov came to attention and saluted, he did so casually and in non-regulation style, a familiarity which Samsonov permitted in his immediate circle. Instead of making a formal report he merely said: 'I'm back, Alexander Vasilich.'

He spoke sullenly, partly out of tiredness. After standing waiting for a moment, he sat down. He suffered from his diminutive stature, which had hindered him in his career. Whenever he could, he would sit down and finger his aiguillettes. His face expressed an abundance of sombre determination, an impression increased by his hair being closely shorn with clippers, like a common soldier.

The Army Commander had lain down because he was worn out, because for however long he might stand, however much he might pace up and down, it would do nothing to ease the lot of his troops or help them to move faster. He lay on his back without his tunic, hands behind his head, his feet resting on a bolster. His heavy, broad-browed face, trained to show the dignity proper to a general, was half hidden by a beard and moustache still only partly streaked with grey; his face never revealed his feelings, never expressed vexation or displeasure. He now turned his large, tranquil eyes towards his visitor and remained lying down as though he had not been waiting impatiently to hear what news Filimonov had to deliver.

And *how* he had been waiting! But those four words: 'I'm back, Alexander Vasilich', spoken in a falling cadence by Filimonov's unexpressive voice, told him everything. With the buzzing noise in his head which no one but he could hear, he remained lying down, staring up at the moulded ceiling. His broad, domed forehead was as calm and smooth and unfurrowed as ever, his permanently wide-open eyes never frowned or squinted, no crow's-feet ran down his cheeks, his thick, immobile lips were hidden by his calm moustache and beard; but inwardly the Army Commander was being attacked by a tremor of insecurity—something which he could never bring himself to admit to anyone and which terrified him. He had had no time to develop a single one of his thoughts to a conclusion, to the degree of maturity proper to the working of a sound mind; not one of his decisions had been adequately formulated before being sent out on the telegraph tape. For the first time in all his thirty-eight years of service, right back to the days when he had commanded a half-squadron of hussars in the Turkish campaign, Samsonov felt that he was not the instigator but merely the instrument of events and that they were moving past him under their own momentum.

At one glance Filimonov read all this in the commander's face. Now if *he* had been in command, he wouldn't have talked to Zhilinsky as Samsonov had, and he wouldn't have harried his corps commanders like that. But he had not been in command. His neck throttled by his high collar, drumming his fingers on his aiguil-lettes, he stared with his hard, wolfish eyes at the commander lying stretched out beside him. Filimonov, however, did not know what had happened here while he had been away. At last they had come to grips with, or at least caught up with, the retreating enemy. They had made contact yesterday evening; the news had arrived today and the joy of it was that the contact had been made by the *left*-flanking unit of the *left*-hand corps of the centre—xv Corps—which had engaged the enemy by wheeling *left*! The action had been successful and the Germans had been forced back!

Only a few hours ago General Martos had reported the details of the successful action (by a messenger who had kept up a steady gallop all the way)—and thus for the first time Samsonov had been proved right; it was now obvious that even in this soundless void his assessment of the German dispositions had been accurate. An hour ago, in reply to Zhilinsky's insulting directive, Samsonov had shamed him by dispatching his report of the victory. In his message he had included word for word Martos' account of the valiant action fought by the Chernigov Regiment: with colours flying, Alexeyev, the regimental commander, had personally led the colour-party in a bayonet charge. He had been killed. Hand-to-hand fighting had developed around the colours, but no German had succeeded in laying hands on the standard. The standard-bearer had been wounded, the colours had been taken over by a lieutenant, who was also killed. At nightfall the Chernigov Regiment had driven off the enemy and had brought back the wounded standard-bearer together with the colours and their St George's Cross. The colours were now secured to a Cossack lance.

Having dispatched this report, Samsonov had taken off his boots and lain down. Nothing in the situation had really improved yet, but at least the Germans had shown up, and, what was more, on the left. This had made Army Group Headquarters look complete fools!

So Samsonov lay with unruffled brow gazing calmly up at the ceiling. He had no wish to hear the details from Headquarters; instead he gave an unhurried account of his own news.

But it was the commander's duty to be fully informed, and without sparing him, without attempting to tone down Zhilinsky's words, Filimonov heaped coals of fire on Samsonov's head and repeated them exactly: 'There will be no halt. Your army is in any case advancing more slowly than I had expected, and to see the enemy where there is none is cowardice, and I do not permit General Samsonov to show cowardice!'

From his moustache to his greying, combed-back hairline Samsonov's calm, heavy-browed face flushed scarlet and he swung his legs on to the floor. As though wounded he stared at his Quartermaster-General, who was swearing viciously at the 'Living Corpse'—the officers' nickname for Zhilinsky. Samsonov, however, could not swear because he was too short of breath: when excited he was prone to attacks of asthma.

He felt deeply wounded because on active service orders had to be obeyed, not as a favour but as a duty, and however stupid the next order and all subsequent orders might be one had no alternative but to carry them out; even an army commander had no more freedom than a hobbled horse. He also felt wounded because in normal times one challenged another man to a duel for a remark like that, but to do so was, alas, a thing of the past, and he could neither challenge Zhilinsky's remarks through 'the usual channels' nor attempt to justify himself. A cavalryman born and bred, he had acquitted himself bravely in the face of Turkish sabres and Japanese bullets; now the only reply he could make to this vicious insult would be to distinguish himself by a display of courage on the field of battle that would equal his twin exploits of the past. It was shameful to have to bow to Zhilinsky—yet bow he must.

Cut to the quick, crimson in the face, Samsonov sat breathing audibly, too distracted to put his feet into his slippers.

At this point Postovsky, the Chief of Staff, entered. Diffident and indecisive, this major-general had never before been on active service. Despite his rank (in which he had eight years' seniority) and his considerable height, his attitude towards his commander was as timid as though he were a newly-commissioned young officer. Having served for years on the staff, and with increasing frequency on special duties, Postovsky valued above all else an undeviating adherence to regulations, and punctuality in the receipt and dispatch of directives, instructions and reports. Only two things had ever really worried him in his military career: a failure to produce the required piece of paper and an unsatisfactory encounter with someone of influence.

Stooping, he approached Samsonov, trying not to look at his commander's sweating forehead and stockinged feet, and announced respectfully:

'Alexander Vasilich, a colonel has arrived from General Headquarters with a message from His Highness the Commander-in-Chief.'

Samsonov blinked as he took in this information. God! What now? Had someone already been sneaking about him to the Grand-Duke?

'What's in it?'

'He still has it. I didn't read it. I wasn't quite sure on what basis to deal with him.'

'You should have taken it and read it.'

The commander stared gloomily at Filimonov.

Filimonov regretted not having grabbed a portion of meat pie before coming in to see the commander; it was clear that dinner was going to be very late tonight.

Samsonov called for his boots and tunic.

I I

Expecting neither help nor enlightenment from this colonel from
General Headquarters, Samsonov thought of him as probably just
another nonentity sent to tell him the proper way to conduct the
campaign. He knew in advance that he was going to dislike the
new arrival, because all decent officers were serving in their
regiments instead of roaming about from one headquarters to
another.

When they had all moved over into the Army Commander's office,
however, Samsonov changed his mind. After requesting permission without either servility or rudeness, the new arrival entered
and advanced a few paces across the empty space in the middle of
the room, in the regulation manner yet naturally and unostenta-
tiously. Deciding that this officer, a man of about forty, looked
decent enough after all, Samsonov rose to his feet behind the large
table at which he had installed himself as an aid to dignity.

'Colonel Vorotyntsev, General Staff. From General Headquarters. A letter for your excellency.'

Deftly but without making a flourish of it, Vorotyntsev drew a
paper from his map-case and proffered it to anyone willing to take it.

Postovsky accepted it warily.

'What's it about?' Samsonov asked.

Relaxing his stance, and with a frank gaze at the Army Commander from eyes that were as large and clear as Samsonov's own,
Vorotyntsev replied:

'The Grand-Duke is disturbed at the shortage of information on
the movement of your army.'

Was this really why the Commander-in-Chief had sent an

officer direct to Second Army, by-passing Army Group Headquarters? A novice might have found this flattering; Samsonov,
however, merely said gruffly:

'I thought the Grand-Duke had more confidence in me.'

'Oh, I assure you,' the colonel hastened to reply, 'the Grand-
Duke's confidence is quite unshaken. But General Headquarters
cannot manage on so little, so *very* little information on the progress
of operations. Another officer has been sent simultaneously to
General Rennenkampf. First Army Headquarters did not report
on the battle at Gumbinnen until they were sure of their success
and all the fighting was over.'

The new arrival looked about him with a frankness and lack of
suspicion which seemed to imply that he expected news of nothing
less than an undivulged but virtually certain victory.

As it happened, Samsonov had a victory to boast of, but it would
be bad form to do so and that was not what the Commander-in-
Chief's emissary had come for. He had come on a flying visit to put
things right, to lay blame, and to teach them their job. It was impossible in a quarter of an hour to describe the complexity of the
problems that had arisen in every corps throughout the army, and
in the Army Commander's head. It was useless even to start talking
about it. The most useful thing was to go and have dinner, as
Filimonov sourly invited the colonel to do.

Wearily but politely Samsonov enquired:

'What exactly would you like to know?'

With his rapid, trained glance the colonel had taken in the whole
of the room, in which everything was arranged as comfortably and
tidily as though Second Army Headquarters was going to spend
the whole war in this house; he had also taken note of the two
generals who were supposed to personify the collective brain of the
army—the Chief of Staff and the Quartermaster-General (there
was a hoary old tradition according to which the brains of the army
were called the 'Quartermaster's Department', but by now it was
obsolete). He had then turned back to face Samsonov when the
latter spoke, as politeness required, but he was already casting
sidelong glances at the wall hung with a map of East Prussia made
up of one-inch-to-one-mile sheets joined together, which drew him
irresistibly. As the colonel's eyes moved up and down the map his
look had nothing of the idle curiosity of a bystander but shared
Samsonov's deep concern.

Suddenly, through all the anxiety caused by a disturbing feeling of having overlooked something vital, it dawned on Samsonov that in this man God had sent him the very person he lacked on his staff —someone he could talk to. (There may well have been, indeed there probably was, someone like this among the junior officers in the Operations Section, but it would have been humiliating for such a venerable figure as the Army Commander to descend to that level for advice.)

Samsonov took a pace towards the map.

Vorotyntsev took two brisk paces.

His chest bore the ribbon of the officer's grade of the St George's Cross and the graduate's badge of the General Staff Academy; as was proper on active service, he wore no other decorations. Vorotyntsev, Vorotyntsev . . .? Samsonov tried to recall the name. There were not so very many General Staff officers in Russia, but he knew hardly any of the recent graduates.

Corpulent, with a slightly protruding stomach, Samsonov moved closer to the map. In this empty room it was easy to see that his was a figure which would stand out even in front of a whole division.

Robustly built, but straight-backed and light on his feet, Vorotyntsev stepped in the same direction.

The two men now faced the map itself, well removed from Postovsky and Filimonov and with their backs to them. At the level of their stomachs a large, impressive flag had been stuck into Ostrolenka: fresh and uncreased, it was the emblem of Second Army Headquarters. Above their shoulders, at eye-level, were the five little tricolour flags representing the corps: four under command and one, on the left, detached from General Headquarters' reserve. Higher still—one had to raise one's arms to move the pins —a red silk thread curved from pin to pin, representing what was supposed to be today's position of the front line.

Higher still, the black German flags were missing altogether. There, silence reigned. Among the green stretches of forest lay the dark blue of innumerable lakes, their water seeming tangibly real and deep on a map of this scale. But of the enemy there was no sign.

Samsonov leaned against the wall with the palm of his outstretched hand. He loved big maps. He used to say that if the maps were big enough to make it difficult to draw arrows, you were more likely to remember how hard it was for the troops to cover the same distances on the ground.

He came quickly to the main point, which was to test whether his visitor differed or sympathised with him in his quarrel with Zhilinsky. This all-absorbing dispute was the touchstone by which the commander could judge whether he was talking to a friend, as his eyes had told him that he was.

Glancing frequently at the colonel to check his reactions, he began hopefully explaining to him why it was essential to advance north-westward, and how Zhilinsky was forcing him north-eastward, resulting in a northward advance and a fan-shaped front line. He described it all in detail, as though to the Grand-Duke himself—to whom Vorotyntsev would in any case be reporting tomorrow or the day after.

He spoke slowly, expounding one idea exhaustively before moving on to the next. Like all generals, he did not like being interrupted.

And Vorotyntsev did not interrupt. No hint of an objection showed in his clean-cut, rather long face, rounded off by a neatly trimmed, light-brown beard. However, his bright, mobile eyes did not look quite often enough at Samsonov and were not always directed to the same place on the map as the commander's finger.

Postovsky approached them from behind and stood in a respectful attitude without joining in. On the far side of the room Filimonov's chair creaked disapprovingly.

Samsonov was saying that according to the intelligence summary issued by North-Western Army Group, based on statements made by the local population, the enemy facing First Army was definitely in retreat . . .

'And what information have you from army reconnaissance?' Scarcely interrupting, Vorotyntsev almost whispered his remark as he frowned at the blank space on the map.

'Thus we . . . what . . . ?' Samsonov did not care to be distracted. 'Klyuev's XIII Corps still has no Cossack regiment. And the cavalry divisions have their assignments—on the flanks. So we have nothing available for reconnaissance and intelligence . . . Thus in order to be absolutely certain of cutting off the enemy it is out of the question for XIII Corps and XV Corps to advance any further to the right than this line running due north to Allenstein. And from there to the Baltic Sea it's not very far—we've already covered a greater distance since we started the advance.'

As quietly as before, out of Postovsky's hearing, Vorotyntsev asked:

'How far have you marched since deployment?'

'Well . . . between a hundred and a hundred and twenty miles . . .'

'Plus deviations in the line of march?'

'Yes, there have been deviations, because Army Group Headquarters keeps changing my orders.'

'And from *here* . . ?' Vorotyntsev pointed to the bottom of the map. 'Foot-slogging all the way too?'

He should not have used an expression like 'foot-slogging' to a full general, but as his eyes met Samsonov's they expressed neither sarcasm nor impertinence but complicity in guilt. Samsonov could only agree:

'Yes, on foot. There are no railways, you see . . .'

'Ten days,' Vorotyntsev calculated. 'What about halts?'

His casual questions were painfully to the point. Well, better for him to know the full story.

'Not one! Zhilinsky won't allow it. And I've asked often enough . . . Pyotr Ivanich, go and fetch our signals!'

Postovsky bowed and hurried out, and, as though it had suddenly occurred to him that Postovsky might not find the papers without his help, Filimonov leaped to his feet and stumped out irritably.

'What I need more than anything else now is to halt and rest,' said the commander. (It was a relief to him that someone at General Headquarters appreciated this need; normally they did nothing but drive you on.) 'But on the other hand . . . we can't afford to let the enemy get away either. If we stop, he'll give us the slip. Our brave lads . . .'

Was the colonel familiar with the plan of campaign?

Yes, he was. (Vorotyntsev nodded, though without much enthusiasm.) The plan was to outflank the Germans from both directions and to prevent them from withdrawing either across the Vistula or to Königsberg. Both men knew the plan, but every problem now seemed new and fraught with untested hypotheses.

'I did draw up a plan of my own,' said Samsonov with a smile, 'though I was rather late with it.'

'What was your plan?' the colonel enquired cautiously.

Having liked the man from the start, the general now liked him even more, and in such circumstances he was unhesitatingly frank.

'I'll show it to you if you like.' The map was not big enough. The general walked over to the left, placed another map against the lower part of the wall with both his large hands and unrolled it upwards over the painted surface. 'My plan was to push both armies forward side by side along either bank of the Vistula. Then we would have been shoulder to shoulder, and the Germans would have been unable to make use of the dense network of roads in the province. We would have kicked them out of East Prussia in no time at all.'

The colonel's eyes lit up with an air that seemed to express lively appreciation.

'Good! Very daring!' Then, straightening up, he said thoughtfully: 'But it would never have been approved. It would have meant leaving Vilna and Riga undefended.'

'No, they wouldn't have approved it,' Samsonov sighed.

'And another thing,' the colonel could not help adding. 'Aren't you pushing yourself rather far into the Polish salient? Supposing they struck at you *there*—and with your rear uncovered? It would need *very* decisive action to make the plan feasible.'

'I didn't submit it,' said Samsonov, waving it aside. 'I only sent in a proposal about the direction of advance. Addressed to the Commander-in-Chief, on July 29th. But they never replied. I suppose you couldn't find out why?'

'Yes, I will find out. You may depend on it.'

The two men found that talking to each other was becoming progressively easier. Ah, yes—there was one thing the colonel still did not know: contact had at last been made with the enemy! Yesterday. Where? *On the left!* At Orlau—look, there . . . strength about two divisions. Samsonov stuck xv Corps' flag more firmly into the map, although it was already pinned quite well enough. 'Our Martos kept his head, deployed from the line of march and gave battle. The fighting was fierce, battlefield strewn with corpses. We lost two and a half thousand men but we won. The Germans withdrew this morning.'

'Congratulations.' But then came the awkward question: 'Did Martos pursue and follow up the victory?'

'Couldn't,' said Samsonov with a sigh. 'His men could hardly stay on their feet.'

This seemed the appropriate moment to tell the story of the Chernigov Regiment's colours, decorated with the St George's Cross for 1812 and for Sebastopol. The regimental commander, Alexeyev, colours flying . . . Now they were fastened to a Cossack lance.

Samsonov saw the scene vividly in his mind's eye and as he re-told the story it thrilled him: he admired the simple bravery of the action. Vorotyntsev, however, showed no surprise and only nodded a few times as though he had known of the incident for a long time and now could merely register approval.

'I see.' And he turned back to look at the map. 'So you've found the enemy. I suppose that means he's not retreating?'

'What I say is,' boomed Samsonov, 'if the enemy's been con-tacted on the left, if he's withdrawing leftward, which a child can see he is—then why have they ordered Blagoveshchensky to take Bischofsburg with his corps tomorrow? Look where it is—right over there! This means that just to please Zhilinsky we have to detach a corps and send it chasing away on its own over to the right . . . What will happen? Secure this town, secure that town—but what about the advance?'

'If you've found the enemy on the left you ought to advance to the left. If it's a screening force, shouldn't you probe it?'

'Yes, but what do we advance *with*? Two and a half corps?'

'Two and a *half*?'

'Well, there's Klyuev and Martos; XXIII Corps has been taken away from me, and Kondratovich is somewhere out there trying to collect his units together.'

While Samsonov was speaking, Vorotyntsev squatted down on his young legs, spread out two fingers as a crude pair of compasses along the scale marked at the bottom of the map, straightened up again and began measuring off the distance from stomach to eye-level, from Ostrolenka to the corps in the front line. He appeared to do this casually, for his own information, not ostentatiously or as though pointing a lesson, but Samsonov faltered, stopped talking and mentally counted the distance as the colonel measured it.

He blushed.

Six whole lengths of the makeshift pair of compasses lay between Ostrolenka and XIII Corps. He was being taught a lesson . . .

But no, it was not meant as a lesson. When Vorotyntsev turned to the general he did not look triumphant or superior but commiserating. He was not accusing him but anxious to find out *why*. Why wasn't Samsonov's headquarters advancing to keep close behind the corps?

'Well . . . communications from here to Bialystok are good,' said Samsonov. 'And with this argument going on between us all the time . . . Then we have to tackle the supply problem,' said Samsonov. 'From here it's easier to push the commissariat waggons forward . . .' said Samsonov.

But he could feel the colour deepening on his cheeks and forehead. Zhilinsky had had no right to insult him and had acted out of pure spite in calling him a coward, but this colonel from General Headquarters had every right to think him one now.

How had it happened? The Army Commander could not understand it. How was it that it had never occurred to him to make that simple measurement of six days' march with his own fingers? It was obvious, after all . . . He wasn't to blame, though, by all that was holy! He had never been afraid to go forward with his troops. But he had been badgered and hemmed in, events had pressed upon him faster than his brain could digest them, the whole absurd business had held him helpless in its grip night and day.

Meanwhile the troops were marching on and on—away from him.

Vorotyntsev did not accept the commander's reply and his burning look remained fixed on Samsonov. He noticed that the lower part of Samsonov's face, with its moustache and beard, was exactly like the Tsar's—had indeed been modelled on the Tsar—as were the lips, half-hidden and apparently firm but in reality betraying a deep lack of self-confidence. Above them, his other features were firmer—the nose, the eyes and particularly the forehead and the greying hairline; all appeared set in immutable calm. Yet beneath the immobile exterior lay the rot of inner anxiety.

Suddenly remembering, Samsonov burst out: 'But of course! I'm blaming myself quite unnecessarily . . . The real reason why we're still here is the order issued by Army Group: the location of Army Headquarters is to be changed less frequently and then only with their permission. That's another matter you ought to thrash out with them.'

'How are your communications with the Corps Headquarters?'

The colonel did all he could to make it sound like a friendly enquiry and not an official question put by an inspector; but Samsonov scowled.

'Bad. Mounted dispatch-riders riding at a canter can hardly make it in a day. Sand's deep, cars stuck.'

This colonel, of course, fancied himself cleverer than everybody else, here or at General Headquarters. He was probably thinking *he* ought to be in command! He would never conceivably understand how one could be so caught up by the whirlwind of events that there was no time to notice that headquarters was six days' march behind the front line.

'Aviation?'

'Either out of fuel or broken down.'

'No telegraph link with any of the corps?'

'No.' Samsonov clicked his tongue regretfully. 'The wires break, and there's not enough equipment. To be honest, Neidenburg was captured on the 9th, and I didn't know about it until the 10th. The fighting around Orlau started on the 10th and it was the 11th before I knew. How can I find out about the Germans when I don't even know what my own troops are doing?'

Postovsky alone, without Filimonov, brought in the signals file in two cardboard folders.

Every day reports arrived written the previous day, describing what, in effect, the corps had been doing two days ago; every evening orders were written for the following day which none of the corps would be able to carry out until the day after tomorrow.

'Ah, here we are!' Samsonov seized the folders and began searching among the papers himself. 'You asked about our request for a day's halt . . .'

'What about wireless?' Vorotyntsev insisted on adding.

'Ah, yes—we have managed to get wireless telegraphy working,' Postovsky announced with satisfaction. 'Admittedly only since yesterday, but we're already transmitting.'

That, at least, was something.

'For instance, a wireless signal has come in from XIII Corps,' said Postovsky, trying to be helpful to his chief. 'The advance guard has already pushed forward as far as Lake Omulefoffen and there's still no sign of the enemy.'

Yet the thread on their map still ran to the south of Lake Omulefoffen; they had not brought it up to date.

'There!' Samsonov found the signal he was looking for. 'I made a point of requesting a day's halt for the day before yesterday, so that all the corps could stop and straighten themselves out. And here's Zhilinsky's telegram to me: "Commander-in-chief"—not he, but the Commander-in-Chief, if you please!—"demands formations Second Army advance energetically and non-stop. This necessary not only due situation North-Western Front but also *general situation* . . .".'

Holding his finger on the spot where he had stopped reading, Samsonov looked at Vorotyntsev.

So what else, my dear fellow, could I have done? Can you suggest a better alternative? Has that taken the wind out of your sails?

It had. Vorotyntsev bit his lip, looked down at his boots, then up at the map again. There are certain words and turns of phrase which, no matter in what situation they may find you, have to be accepted uncomplainingly, like a cloudburst. *The general situation.* This means that it is not for you or me, not for a general, not for Zhilinsky, not even for the Commander-in-Chief to reason why. It is a matter reserved for the judgment of the Sovereign. We must simply obey.

' ". . . Regard your disposition August 9th", ' Samsonov went on reading, ' "extremely insecure and demand . . .".'

In silence Vorotyntsev turned his head to look up at the blank space representing the extensive territory of East Prussia.

Handing back the folders, Samsonov stared in the same direction. He, at least, never grew tired. Postovsky lacked the stamina of a seasoned campaigner. He took the folders and retreated to a distant armchair.

What they did not know was that Vorotyntsev had gone behind their backs. While waiting to be received he had not spent his time idling in the hallway, but had made straight for the Operations Room, where he had found a captain whom he knew and spent ten minutes in whispered conversation with him behind a pillar—the younger General Staffers of recent vintage all knew each other and stuck together like members of a secret order. Almost everything that Vorotyntsev heard in answer to his questions in the Army Commander's office he already knew from the captain; the only satisfaction he derived from this was a liking for Samsonov, because he had not lied or tried to embellish the facts.

From the helpful captain and now from the Army Commander's

map Vorotyntsev soaked up all there was to know about the operational situation. It was as if he had not just arrived but had spent at least three weeks here absorbed in the problem—nay more, as though his whole life, his entire military career had been nothing but a period of training for this one operation.

Everything that had been said or indicated, even if only once, during the past hour had been marked by Vorotyntsev with an imaginary pencil as squares, triangles, curves and arrows on the almost empty map and absorbed with professional ease. The blame or praise due to the various generals no longer mattered and even the main problem, namely the exhausted state of the army—the hard-tack, the heat, no rest, the lack of horses, the bad communications, the inefficiency of the staff—had faded before the overriding problem: to find the invisible Germans, to divine their plan, to feel the prick of their bayonets with his own ribs long before the thrust came, to hear their first round of artillery-fire long before the shell exploded with a crump high in the air. Just as the sensitive body of a beautiful woman can sense men's glances behind her back without turning round, so Vorotyntsev could physically feel those hungry waves of the enemy flowing towards Second Army from the blank part of the map. He was already totally absorbed into the flesh and blood of Second Army; his empty chair at General Headquarters meant nothing to him and the paper signed by the Grand-Duke was a mere cypher, as it did not entitle him to order the move of a single soldier in this army. The obsession which throbbed within him was to solve a *riddle*; his destiny was to take a *decision*; and his tact must be used to make it seem to the Army Commander that it was Samsonov himself who had made it.

The clock of fate was suspended above the whole of East Prussia, and its six-mile-long pendulum was ticking audibly as it swung from the German to the Russian side and back again.

Suddenly, raising his arm at an acute angle to his body as though in the ancient Roman salute and aiming it to the left of the map, Vorotyntsev rotated his wrist like a paddle-blade, slowly swung it in the arc made by the full length of his arm and back again, then stopped with his palm pointing from the west towards Soldau and Neidenburg. Holding it on the map, aimed like a dagger at Soldau, he turned his head towards the Army Commander.

'There, your excellency—isn't that what you expect to happen?'
Samsonov's large head with its massive brow had followed him

intently, watching the whole sweeping gesture, the broad-bladed dagger of his palm. He blinked.

'Now if only I could make use of 1 Corps, Artamonov's corps, I would order it to Soldau—if only it were taken out of General Headquarters' reserve and put under my command! But they won't give it to me!'

'Won't give it to you? But it's yours now . . .'

'They won't give it to me, I tell you! I asked—and they refused! It's not to be moved beyond Soldau.'

'But no, sir!' Vorotyntsev released his hand from its role of dagger and placed it on his breast. 'I assure you, I was present myself when the Grand-Duke signed the order: you are "given permission to include 1 Corps in active operations on Second Army's front".'

'Include?'

'. . . In active operations.'

'And can I move it beyond Soldau?'

'Well, if it says "on Second Army's front" then presumably you can even transfer it to the right if necessary. That is how I interpret the order.'

'And they won't take it away from me—like the others? Like the Guards Corps? First the orders were "not to move it beyond Warsaw", then they simply removed it altogether.'

'On the contrary—you are to "include it in active operations"!'

Samsonov's shoulders appeared to expand. He threw his chest out, beamed, rocked on his heels and said:

'When . . . was it signed?'

'When? Why—*the day before yesterday*. On the evening of the eighth.'

'What? Three days ago!' roared Samsonov. 'Pyotr Ivanich!' Postovsky stood up.

'Did you hear that? Have we had this order about 1 Corps?'

'No, Alexander Vasilich. Our last request was refused.'

'So North-Western has been keeping it from me!' Samsonov bellowed. And, overstepping the bounds of service convention: 'Tell me, Colonel, why was the North-Western Army Group ever hung round our necks at all? Just to run two armies?'

Unembarrassed, Vorotyntsev raised his eyebrows.

'Why do two divisions need a corps headquarters over them? Why are there two brigades in a division? Aren't there too many generals in a division?'

He was right—it was the same all down the line. The army was top-heavy with staffs and senior officers.

Yes, God Himself had sent this colonel. Not only did he understand everything, not only was he efficient and fast-thinking—he had simply pulled an army corps out of his pocket and handed it to him!

Samsonov strode firmly up to him. 'My dear fellow!' Putting both bear-like paws on Vorotyntsev's shoulders: 'Allow me to . . .' he gave him a hairy kiss.

The towering Samsonov continued to hold him clasped in his embrace as he said:

'I'll have to get confirmation, though . . .'

'Of course—check it! Quote me, and refer to the order of August 8th.'

Vorotyntsev gently eased himself out of the bear-hug and turned again to the map.

'Even so, how are we to interpret "include in active operations"?' Postovsky enquired grumpily. 'We must query that.'

'No need to query it! Interpret it as it suits you—all you have to do is give your orders. Well, if you like, don't tell them to *move* north of Soldau—tell them to *position themselves* north of Soldau, that'll avoid the problem.'

'But how could he delay the passing of that order for three whole days, the blackguard?' the commander said angrily.

'How? Well, I suppose he felt like keeping control of a spare formation. To relinquish it reduces the Army Group Commander's importance.' Vorotyntsev threw out the remark casually, but as usual he was thinking ahead. He went on to say: 'Look—don't bother to get confirmation. Just write out an order to Artamonov and I'll take it to him myself.'

Another amazing suggestion!

'Take it yourself? But . . . aren't you going back to General Headquarters?'

'I've brought a lieutenant with me and I'll send him back to General Headquarters with my report. So I can . . .'

Vorotyntsev had foreseen this eventuality too. No one, in fact, from the Commander-in-Chief downwards, realised that Vorotyntsev himself had dreamed up this trip and had sold the idea to his colleagues. It had sickened him to languish at General Headquarters as a kind of superior clerk with nothing to do but listen to the rustle of maps and signals that arrived forty-eight hours late, or to stare out of the window like Mengden, the Chevalier Guards officer, who, although he was the most active of the Commander-in-Chief's six lazy aides-de-camp, spent his time whistling at pigeons in case they were going to land on the carrier-pigeons' dovecote situated beneath the windows of the grand-ducal train; the other ADCs did even less. Sitting at General Headquarters as a pen-pusher was enough to make one die of suffocation at a time when a hazardous manoeuvre of the utmost boldness was being put into effect in Prussia: a converging advance by two armies with un-secured flanks.

So far, Vorotyntsev had not learned enough at Second Army Headquarters to be able to report back to the Commander-in-Chief. There was an extremely dangerous threat from the extreme left flank; he must go there too.

'. . . Regard me, your excellency, as a supernumerary staff officer of your headquarters, attached to you for operational purposes.'

Samsonov looked at him with the warmest approval.

As though deferring to Samsonov's judgment, Vorotyntsev added:

'And if asked why I have to go to 1 Corps in particular, then I shall say it's because that's where things are most likely to start happening.'

Yes, he was right—that was the place! Samsonov had realised the implication of what Vorotyntsev was saying. 'Go there, my dear fellow—and help me bring 1 Corps into line.'

'Is there anyone from your staff at 1 Corps through whom I can keep in touch with you?'

'Colonel Krymov, my personal liaison officer.'

'Ah—is Krymov there?' Vorotyntsev's attitude cooled. 'He was in Turkestan with you, wasn't he?'

'Only for six months. But I got to like him—he's intelligent, and he's a soldier.'

(Krymov was, in fact, the only officer on his staff whom he felt he could confide in.)

Vorotyntsev hesitated.

'Very well, then. Address the order to him. Only . . . why bother with a written order when I could . . . I suppose you couldn't give me an aeroplane?'

'They're all under repair,' said Postovsky apologetically.

'We only have two cars, and Krymov has one of them.' Samsonov spread his hands.

'As the crow flies, as the crow flies . . .' Vorotyntsev measured the distance '. . . it's sixty miles, across country. And by road—eighty.'

'Your best way is to go by train via Warsaw,' Postovsky advised cautiously. 'From there to Mlawa it's only a single-track line, but you'd be there by Wednesday and you'd be rested when you arrived.'

Vorotyntsev weighed it up.

'No. No, give me a good horse, better still a second horse and an orderly, and I'll ride there.'

'But what's the point?' Postovsky said in bewilderment. 'You'll arrive no sooner and you won't have had any sleep.'

'No.' Vorotyntsev shook his head resolutely. 'There's bound to be some hold-up if I try going by train, and if I go on horseback I can have a good look at the ground.'

Preparations were begun. An order was written to Artamonov. (It was extremely difficult to phrase it properly: how was one to 'include 1 Corps in active operations' without it being fully under command?) Vorotyntsev himself wrote out a signal to General Headquarters, explaining the situation to his lieutenant. Two extra sheets were glued to Vorotyntsev's map. This was done in the Operations Room, in the presence of Filimonov, from whom Vorotyntsev had asked for a copy of the wireless code used for transmission to 1 Corps. Filimonov knitted his brow. What code? They didn't use code. Vorotyntsev went to Postovsky. The Chief of Staff was already tired of him, because he was keeping him from his dinner.

'So we don't use code—what of it? That code's enough to tie anyone in knots, my friend. Do you suppose our wireless operators have been to high school? They'd simply mix everything up, get the signals all wrong, and there'd be more chaos than there is already.'

'What?' Vorotyntsev could not credit it. 'Do you mean to say you transmit corps dispositions *en clair*?'

'Well, the Germans don't know the exact times of our transmissions, do they?' Postovsky was losing his temper. (This interloper had no business to poke his nose into *that* sort of detail!) 'You don't suppose they're listening out for us all round the clock, do you? And anyway maybe their wireless isn't working or something . . . Besides, God helps the bold.'

They assembled for dinner. Samsonov sighed and agreed that it was bad about the code; they should work one out and put it into operation. It was the direct responsibility of the Quartermaster-General. But it would take three whole days to do it. In any case, they had only been transmitting by wireless since yesterday, so it couldn't have done much harm yet.

Vorotyntsev looked at Filimonov, energetic but bad-tempered, and at the ugly Postovsky—all three of them united at that moment by ravenous hunger. Did Samsonov realise how he had been cheated in being given a staff like this? The job of a proper staff was to sift through the swirling mass of conjecture and lay down a solid roadbed on which sound decisions could march forward, to send out officers to check dubious reports on the spot, to be ruthlessly selective and to see that the really important information was not swamped by a flood of trivia. A staff's job was not to replace the commander's will, but to help it reveal itself. This staff was a hindrance.

Vorotyntsev was invited to choose their best soldier as his orderly, but he merely took the first available man, intending to send him back (on the principle that it was a waste of time looking for a *good* soldier at an army headquarters; better to look for one in a regiment). He declined to sit out their elaborately served, time-wasting formal dinner; instead he ate quickly and drank nothing but some strong tea. He remained at table for as long as politeness demanded, not sharing their appreciation of the meat pie, his thoughts far away.

'But you should stay until tomorrow morning, my dear fellow!' Samsonov insisted genially. 'You don't mean to say you're leaving right away without resting for a while? That's no way to fight a war! Do stay for a bit—we'll sit and have a talk.'

He very much wanted Vorotyntsev to stay; it seemed rude of him to be in such a hurry to go. However, Samsonov got up and saw the colonel off, promising him that before lunch tomorrow he would move his headquarters forward to Neidenburg.

Exactly what had been agreed between the two men was not quite clear, nor how they would keep in touch with each other from now on. Something of the dangers and risks that lay ahead had remained unspoken between them, but this was out of a superstition that such things were best left unsaid. They would be clear enough up at the front line.

When the generals returned to their dinner, Postovsky and Filimonov tactfully suggested to the Army Commander that it was out of the question to move the headquarters tomorrow; it would mean the staff having to operate in makeshift fashion, and subjecting themselves to unnecessary hardship was not going to help the troops in the front line. It was all very well for this colonel from General Headquarters to descend on them, sweep through and ride off again, but they still had to notify Army Group Headquarters, they had to request permission, await instructions and convert them into suitable orders for their corps.

At this point a new order arrived from Zhilinsky: previous orders were rescinded and the commander of Second Army was permitted to adopt a northward axis of advance, but to ensure cover of his right flank he was to keep General Blagoveshchensky's VI Corps on the previous axis, and in order to secure the left flank he was not to move I Corps forward.

Only that morning Zhilinsky had forbidden Samsonov to overextend his frontage. Now he was recommending him to widen it. He intended to be right in any eventuality . . . However, he had given way on the *axis of advance*. Thank God for that, at least. And he must be made to stick to it.

By the time the directive had been redrafted to order the new corps dispositions, it was late at night. Some of the telephones and telegraph lines were out of order, others were lacking altogether. In order not to delay the troops' marching orders for tomorrow, they were sent by wireless, uncoded.

The Germans probably wouldn't intercept them—surely they couldn't stay awake listening all night.

12

Vorotyntsev was given a good bay stallion and as escort a sergeant on a mare. Finding the right road out of a town always needs careful enquiry, but the sergeant knew his way. Weighed down in the warm, still night air by his greatcoat and field-knapsack, Vorotyntsev strapped them to his saddle and rode light.

He had not expected to find much to hearten him at Second Army Headquarters but he now felt that things might not be too bad after all. Although it was by now so familiar that he ought to have taken it for granted, Vorotyntsev was still depressed whenever experience confirmed the invariable rule that every headquarters (and the higher the headquarters the more marked the phenomenon) was staffed by people who were selfish, rank-conscious, hidebound and slack, whose only concern was to eat and drink their fill. They regarded the army as a convenient, highly polished and well carpeted staircase, upon whose steps medals and badges of rank were handed out. It never occurred to them that this staircase involved obligations rather than rewards, that there was such a thing as military science, whose techniques altered every decade or so, and that therefore officers ought to study constantly and keep abreast of change. If the War Minister himself boasted that he had not read a single military textbook in the thirty-five years since he had left university, why should anyone else bother to exert himself? Once you had spent long enough in the service to earn a general's epaulettes, what else was to be gained by a show of zeal? There was no higher to go. For the staircase was so arranged as to encourage the ascent of slow-witted men who did what they were told rather than those with brains and independence of mind.

Provided you stuck to the letter of regulations, orders and directives, you could make as many blunders as you liked; you could be defeated, you could retreat, be routed, run away—no one would ever blame you and you would not even be called upon to investigate the cause of your failure. But woe to you if you once diverged from the letter, if you ever thought for yourself or acted on your own initiative; then you would not even be forgiven your successes, and if you failed, you would be eaten alive.

The ruin of the Russian army was the system of seniority: the supreme, indisputable factor was length of service and promotion by seniority. As long as you did not make a *faux pas* or arouse the ire of the powers that be, the mere passage of time would in due course elevate you to the coveted senior rank, and with the rank went a suitable command. Thus every officer accepted it as the natural order of things, as inevitable as the stately progress of the heavenly bodies, that the first question one colonel or general should ask another was not what active service he had seen but what was the year, month and date of his seniority in the rank—in other words, what stage had he reached in the due progression towards senior command. Thus if a Yanushkevich were appointed Chief of the General Staff, then a Postovsky would be made Chief of Staff of an army. In a system like this, what chance was there of such men grasping the lightning speed of modern warfare, or the need for efficient, sensitive, two-way communication?

Second Army was advancing to execute a manoeuvre worthy of Suvorov: a forced march to cut off East Prussia, a shattering blow to Germany as a start to the war. Yet it had begun the operation in a spirit of bungling amateurism. The attitude to intelligence was typical. Army Group Headquarters was expected to provide up-to-date intelligence and what did it produce? A report based on 'statements from the local population'! Samsonov had always been notoriously weak on reconnaissance: his cavalry had failed to locate the Japanese infantry at a range of twelve miles. Even the Germans knew of this by now; they had written about it in a book on the Russo-Japanese War which was already available in Petersburg in a Russian translation. Since they knew all about the man who was facing them, they were not expecting to be put under heavy pressure. Samsonov was one of the Kuropatkin school, which made a virtue of 'steadiness'. 'We belong in the

Kutuzov tradition' was their motto—'patient as donkeys, a bit slow maybe, but we win in the end by sheer tenacity . . .' And this was the man who was proposing to surround and cut off the enemy —and what an enemy!—knowing as much about how to conduct such an operation as a bear knows how to bend a bow to harness a horse. Unfortunately, if you don't know how to handle a shaft-bow, it is liable to spring back and crack you over the head.

As for the fighting at Orlau, how could anyone call it a 'victory'? They had suffered two and a half thousand casualties; they had failed to follow up and pursue; and having found the enemy where they didn't expect him, instead of changing their line of advance they had just kept plodding on in the *wrong direction*. And they thought they had won a victory! Who but Russian generals could indulge in self-deluding joy over such a trivial success?

The sergeant proved that he was no liar by leading them directly to the stone bridge over the River Narev. (Vorotyntsev noticed, however, that the man did not have a very good seat; he would not last sixty-five miles in the saddle and would have to be sent back.)

On the far side of the bridge the road had been diverted from the town centre of Ostrolenka, presumably so that the rumble of supply waggons driving from the railway station on the Janów road should not disturb Army Headquarters. Just as Vorotyntsev rode up, the head of a long waggon-train was starting to roll across the bridge. The carts all looked alike, loaded identically with sacks piled high above the sides and covered with tarpaulins. The train was clearly just starting, the drivers not yet sitting on their waggons but walking alongside them, presumably because in a headquarters town the train-leader was liable to be reprimanded by an officer for straining the horses unnecessarily if he let the drivers ride. A few of them were walking along in couples, some smoking, some cursing cheerfully, and they were all in an obviously hearty mood. They were even looking forward on this still, moonless night to a long journey which they would hardly have relished in times of peace. Their horses fed and watered, having eaten well themselves, with no prospect of danger for several days to come (it was still a forty-eight-hour drive to the frontier), tough and healthy enough to have been good material for the infantry, they swung their arms needlessly high as they marched, and one of them even contrived to bounce along the cobbled road in a squatting Russian dance, to the amusement of his comrades.

'Didn't have time to finish dancing with your little Polish girl, though, did you?'

'Just my luck,' said the dancer, though without a trace of complaint in his voice. 'Tonight was going to be the night—and they have to come and drag me away.'

'Tell you what,' a third driver advised him in a deep bass rumble. 'That chestnut of yours'll pull the waggon on her own, she only has to follow mine, so why don't you unhitch the bay, get leave from the sergeant-major, ride back on her and finish the job, eh? You can catch us up again by morning and you'll have another kid to look after you in your old age . . .'

There was a roar of laughter, which was immediately silenced as the men noticed an officer mounted on a thoroughbred stallion overtaking them on the bridge.

Soldiers' jokes are the slowest things to change in an army—they change more slowly than the weapons, the uniforms or the regulations. Vorotyntsev had heard the same kind of jokes in the Japanese War, they had probably been bandied about in the Crimean War, and in the seventeenth century the men of Pozharsky's militia had no doubt cracked them too. It was not the jokes themselves which made them laugh so much as the liberating, uninhibited bawdiness. To Vorotyntsev, in his depressed mood, the relaxed and self-confident ribaldry of the drivers came as a tonic when he most needed it. Having crossed the bridge, he stopped and for no particular reason called out to the sergeant-major, who was marching briskly beside the train and swearing at the leading waggon. Glancing around as he strode along, the sergeant discerned in the faint starlight reflected from the river that this was a staff officer. Turning sharply on his heel, he stamped up to Vorotyntsev with such keenness and halted at the regulation distance with such precision that he gave the impression of having marched all the way just for this.

'Whose waggon-train is this?'

'Thirteenth Army Corps, your honour.'

'How far have you come from your railhead?'

'Five days' drive, your honour.'

'What are you carrying?'

'Hard-tack, buckwheat, oil, your honour.'

'No bread?'

'No, your honour.'

These clumsy, obligatory 'your honours' wasted an intolerable amount of a soldier's time in twentieth-century warfare, but Vorotyntsev was powerless to have them abolished. He touched his horse and moved on, followed by his escorting NCO. The sergeant-major did a smart about-turn, then broke into a waddling run, bellowing loudly at the leading waggon.

Ostrolenka station was only half a mile away, yet the waggon-train had already been five days on the road, with another six-day drive ahead of it. Even that would be an excessive strain because there was not enough corps transport to rest the horses, and Army Headquarters had no transport at all. However many divisions the staff might move around by drawing arrows on maps, the forgotten deciding factor in the battle would be these waggon-wheels.

Yet these tough, cheerful drivers, graded unfit for front-line service, the smart sergeant-major, the sturdy horses, the tarpaulins stretched to keep out the rain, and the well-shod stallion beneath him baring its teeth when his escort's mare lagged behind—all combined to put Vorotyntsev in a better, calmer mood than when he had left headquarters. Russia was inexhaustibly strong, even if she was governed by a pack of fools. Sensing that strength, he took heart.

Immediately after the bridge the cobbled surface came to an end, but this at once made the roadway better for horses' hooves. Gleaming very faintly in the starlight, clearly marked by the verges on either side, the road wound its way ahead in gentle curves, now climbing a little, now running downhill across the silent, sleeping landscape whose last lights were flickering out, leaving houses and cottages on either side as dark, enigmatic shapes. There was no need to stop and ask the way. They rode at a good trot but never faster, lest the horses became exhausted by the morning. Stimulated by the ride through the warm, dark, still countryside, Vorotyntsev soon experienced the wonderful sense of buoyancy familiar to every officer (soldiers in the ranks seldom know it; it is chiefly felt by officers, whose whole life is devoted to war), when the flimsy threads which bind one to a settled existence are snapped clean, when one's body is fighting fit, one's hands are free, one feels the satisfying tug of a weapon at one's side and one's mind is wholly concentrated on the task in hand. Vorotyntsev recognised and loved this exaltation, and only when it visited him could he feel that he was really fighting. He had been created for moments like this; he lived for them.

The real reason why he had refused to go via Warsaw was that he could not properly appreciate the problems unless he himself had physically traversed the ground the troops had marched over, because for a good officer it is not enough to be bold, decisive and quick-thinking: he must also be in continual contact with the hard-ships of the rank and file; his shoulders, too, must ache until the last one of his men has thrown off his pack to bed down for the night; neither food nor water must pass his lips as long as a single company in a division has still not been given food and drink.

Vorotyntsev felt the need for this physical contact because the searing experience of the Japanese War had tormented him un-relentingly for ten long years. Those Russians who had been so insane as to rejoice over that defeat were like children who thought-lessly delight at being ill, because it means that they may not have to do something unpleasant or eat something they dislike today, without realising that the disease may cripple them for life. Russian society might rejoice and throw all the blame on the Tsar or the tsarist system, but for true patriots it could be nothing but a cause for grief. It only needed two or three such defeats in succession for the backbone of the country to be put out of joint for ever and for a thousand-year-old nation to be utterly destroyed. There had already been two successive defeats—the Crimean War and the Russo-Japanese War—only slightly mitigated by the rela-tively minor and none too glorious Turkish campaign. For that reason the present war might either herald a great rebirth of Russia or be the end of her altogether; that was why the mistakes com-mitted in the Japanese War were a matter of such anxiety to all loyal Russian officers, and why such men strained every sinew to ensure that they were not repeated.

In particular Vorotyntsev felt a need for day-by-day and hour-by-hour involvement with the action in East Prussia because he was one of the few General Staff officers who was cleared for access both to the discussion of strategic plans and to the drafting of specific tactical projects, anonymous documents which then spent year after year being endlessly signed and countersigned by generals and grand-dukes, after which they were published as 'Study Papers' in a few numbered copies, locked away in safes and only made available to an authorised handful of people.

Within the army, smarting from defeat in the Japanese War, there blazed up a brief 'military renaissance', headed in the General Staff by General Palitsyn and in the Council of Defence by the Grand-Duke Nikolai Nikolaevich. Inside the General Staff Academy a small, tightly-knit group of officers was formed who intuitively understood the military realities of the twentieth century, in which regimental battle-standards dating back to Peter the Great or the glory won by Suvorov could no longer protect or help Russia; what Russia needed was modern technology, modern organisation and alert, active minds.

Only that closed fraternity of General Staff officers, and perhaps a handful of engineers as well, were conscious of the fact that the world, and Russia with it, was moving invisibly, inaudibly and imperceptibly into a new era; that the entire atmosphere of the planet —its oxygen content, its rate of combustion, the mainspring pressure in all its clocks—had somehow changed. All Russia, from the imperial family down to the revolutionaries, naively thought that they were still breathing the same old air and living on familiar ground; only a handful of engineers and officers was gifted with the perception to sense that the stars themselves had moved into new conjunctions.

Whilst the politicians and intellectuals spent their time building barricades, summoning and dissolving sessions of the Duma, issuing emergency laws and seeking mystical paths to the other world, this little group of captains and colonels, jokingly called 'the Young Turks' (also, perhaps with a faint allusion to that other band of officer-revolutionaries, the 'Decembrists'), became conscious of their identity, read textbooks by German generals and gathered their strength. They were not persecuted, but nor was any attention paid to them after the dismissal of Palitsyn and the removal of the Grand-Duke in 1908. The group broke up almost as soon as it had formed, because its members could not stay on indefinitely at the Academy. No single staff was created specifically for them; they were obliged to disperse to their individual garrison postings, with the likelihood that they would never see each other again, although wherever they were they could at least feel they were parts of a whole, cells of the Russian military brain. A nucleus of 'Young Turks' did remain in the form of Professor Golovin's class of pupils, but in the following year the devious General Yanushkevich was made commandant of the Academy and these last few intractable enthusiasts were dispersed. None of them was placed in a position of effective power, or even given a division (Golovin, a strategist equal to any in Europe, was banished to command a regiment of dragoons), because there was a long queue of officers who were ahead of them by virtue of seniority, influence at Court and proved incompetence. But in their own eyes the 'Young Turks' felt themselves responsible for the future of the Russian army, and since most of them were posted to the Operations Sections of various headquarters, they counted on being able to direct the army along the right lines by the precision of their staff-work and the convincing logic of their proposals.

It was these men, deprived of effective command and with no special status, who picked up the gauntlet flung down by Kaiser Wilhelm; they, and not the Baltic barons, not the Tsarina's favourites, not the generals festooned with medals from neck to navel, they were the ones who really knew their enemy—and admired him! They knew that the German army was the most powerful army in the modern world; that it was an army inspired by a common patriotism at every level; that it had a superb command structure and that it combined the incompatibles—faultless Prussian discipline and a lively European spirit of initiative. The type of German officer equivalent to the handful of General Staffers in the Russian army was not only in a majority, it was to be found well placed in positions of real power, even at the level of army commander. Their chiefs of staff were not constantly being changed, as in the Russian army, where over nine years the post had been filled by six different men in a perpetual game of leapfrog; in Germany had been held by only four men in fifty years, and this not by replacement but by succession, Moltke junior succeeding to Moltke senior. Their 'Field Service Regulations' were not approved on July 16th 1914, a mere two days before general mobilisation; they did not start a seven-year rearmament programme three weeks before the outbreak of war.

Naturally it would have been much more pleasant to have been in a state of 'eternal alliance' with Germany, as Dostoevsky had advocated with such fervour. If only the Russian nation had been able to develop and grow in strength as Germany had! But fate decreed that the two nations should make war upon each other, and the élite of the Russian General Staff prided itself that it would acquit itself worthily in the fight.

This meant not merely being able to grasp the immediate short-term objective and carry it out to the best of one's ability, but to assess correctly the fundamentals of a situation: to ask not only whether this was the right place to attack, but whether it was right to attack at all.

It was the principle of the German General Staff to take the offensive at all costs, and Germany, in her position, had good reason to adopt it. She might be attacked from either side by Russia or France, so—forward! Ever forward! What an attractive idea—one that even a lightweight like Sukhomlinov could grasp. However, in military science there is a principle more important than 'Forward': it is that the task should be proportionate to the means.

According to her treaty with France, Russia was free to choose her own operational axes of advance. Years of consideration were given to the two most obvious alternatives: an advance directed against Austria, or an advance directed against Germany. The Austrian frontier would be an easy objective, whereas the Prussian lakes were highly suitable for defence and an obstacle to advance. To penetrate Germany would require large forces and offered little hope of success, whereas to attack Austria was likely to be very rewarding; the destruction of her army and probably of the state itself would produce a shift in the balance of power of half Europe. Meanwhile Russia could defend herself against Germany with a minimum expenditure of force, thanks to the lack of roads in her frontier territories and, above all, her broad-gauge railway track. So this alternative was chosen, and Palitsyn made his defence plans accordingly: a chain of fortresses on the line Kovno–Grodno–Osovets–Novo-Georgievsk (a strategy which was now affecting Vorotyntsev's horse, as it felt the going getting heavier and heavier on the sandy tracks; it was for exactly this reason that the region had been left without a single metalled road).

At this point Sukhomlinov, with the irresponsible ignorance so easily mistaken for decisiveness, had come to the General Staff and 'reconciled' the contending factions. 'We shall,' he declared, 'advance on Germany and Austria simultaneously!' Of the available alternatives he made the worst possible choice: to attack both at once. The following year Zhilinsky, who replaced him, made a personal commitment to the French, which was also binding on Russia even though it exceeded her treaty obligations, that the Russians would definitely advance on Germany as well as on

Austria—either into Prussia or towards Berlin. And now, of course, Russia was in honour bound not to disappoint her allies.

And, knowing all this, one was still expected to fight *worthily* for one's country . . .

But the Russian mind hates being faced with an 'either-or' situation such as whether to attack Prussia or Berlin, so what easier solution than to do both at once? Thus at the same time as First and Second Armies were just beginning their advance into East Prussia and all the fighting still lay ahead of them, Tenth Army was being scraped together on paper at General Headquarters in order to march on Berlin. And that was why the wretched Samsonov (although he did not know it) was deprived of the Guards Corps, and why Artamonov was forbidden to move beyond Soldau.

Yet all this was a trifle compared to the fact that Zhilinsky had given his promise to Joffre the year before and had brought forward the date of the attack so generously at Russia's expense: totally unprepared as they were, the Russians had been committed to moving forward on the *fifteenth* day after mobilisation instead of the sixtieth. Her ally France was in trouble, and Russia was ready to crawl through the mire for her while waiting for the English to get themselves across the Straits of Dover. However, just as in private life friendship should not be carried to the point of self-immolation, for which no amount of gratitude can ever compensate, the same principle applies with even greater force in international politics. How long would France remember Russia's sacrifice?

But still one must fight the good fight . . .

Beyond the hundred-odd miles ahead of him, beyond the dark night, beyond terrain which he had never seen except on a map, beyond the nodding rhythm of his stallion's powerful head, across a whole degree of latitude of the curved earth, Vorotyntsev imagined, sensed, and in his mind's eye actually saw dozens of other General Staff officers like himself—except that they were Germans and were driving through the night in motor-cars along firm, well-made roads; that they were all efficiently linked by telegraph; that they had precise intelligence data pinned alongside their map-boards, on which neat arrows showed the exact movements of their troops; that they were serving under keen-minded generals who made rationally based decisions in five minutes. Whereas behind Vorotyntsev were Zhilinsky with his jutting chin and drooping moustache, Postovsky with his files of three-days-old reports,

Filimonov with his futile, wolfish energy, incapable of team-work, and the ponderous, baffled Samsonov. Ahead of him were the army corps, lost among the lakes and sandy terrain. As he drew nearer to the terrible impending conflict, all that Vorotyntsev himself could do was to study the map in the light of memory and spur on his stallion, though not too hard for fear of overtiring the beast.

Speed, of course, was essential in this operation, but de-training the troops at Bialystok and making them march forward from there on foot was no way to achieve it. Speed was required, but not speed of the kind shown by a clown tumbling into the circus-ring; instead of entering the arena without one's trousers and boots, one should first put on a belt and tie one's bootlaces. The result of starting the two halves of the operation a week apart, of sending Rennenkampf into action before Samsonov was ready, was to throw the whole operation out of balance and so render it pointless.

There was no time to spare for talking to his escort sergeant. When they passed through villages they sometimes found a person who could tell them the name of the place, at other times Vorotyntsev simply shone his flashlight on the map and worked it out for himself. For a couple of hours his mind functioned with intense concentration, then rather more disjointedly. He wondered why Blagoveshchensky's corps had managed to shift itself so far over to the right that it seemed to be aiming to join up with Rennenkampf; to judge by the surnames of its generals—von Torklus, Baron Vietinghof, Richter, Stempel, Mingin, Sirelius, Ropp—one might be forgiven for thinking that Second Army was not a Russian force at all, particularly in view of the fact that in the spring of 1914 the man appointed to command it had rejoiced in the name of Rausch von Traubenberg. Vorotyntsev turned to thinking about the general who did at least have a Russian name, Artamonov, to whom he was now on his way and on whom tomorrow the whole honour of Russia might depend. Artamonov was the same age as Samsonov, which made him an unwilling subordinate. He had spent long years serving in staff appointments, as general-in-waiting and as honorary aide-de-camp; for some reason, although an army officer, he had also been commandant of the naval fortress of Kronstadt and even Director-General of Fortifications. Now here he was in command of an army corps. The Germans must have recorded all this in their files, and it doubtless caused them much amusement that the Russian General Staff was so ignorant of the concept of military specialisation. To the Russians, anything that wasn't cavalry or artillery was simply infantry . . .

Vorotyntsev also thought about the other General Staff officer, Colonel Krymov, who had gone to I Corps ahead of him as Liaison Officer from Second Army Headquarters. He might already be putting matters straight there; on the other hand, if he lacked the necessary insight, he might be making things worse. The two men had never met, but on his journey from General Headquarters Vorotyntsev had made use of the Army List to check the service record of every colonel and general he was likely to encounter on his mission. Krymov was five years older than Vorotyntsev, and was senior to him as a colonel by the same number of years. The record showed him to have had a somewhat uneven career. After a series of dull posts in the late 'nineties, he had managed to be a battery quartermaster for eighteen months, but his subsequent postings had given evidence of no great ambition. However, he had succeeded in passing into the General Staff Academy, whence he had graduated before the Japanese War. He had obviously fought bravely in the field, having been decorated in several engagements. Then he had spent five somnolent years as executive officer and section chief in the Mobilisation Branch of the General Staff. There he appeared to have written some studies on the Reserve Forces, no doubt necessary work in a large army; yet somehow the details of the record did not add up to a coherent portrait.

His ride through the chill, starry night stretched on and on. Sometimes the road was tree-lined, sometimes bare; it was sandy all the way. He passed the dim, black outlines of farmhouses, well-heads, tall roadside calvaries. Northern Poland lay calmly and peacefully asleep, wholly unwarlike. True, in a couple of villages some army waggons were halted for the night and their sentries could be heard calling to each other; but no one overtook him and he met no one riding towards him from the opposite direction. The horses began to tire, and the sergeant was growing more and more saddle-sore and bad-tempered. Vorotyntsev decided that before dawn they would stop, feed the horses and sleep for two hours, after which he would send the sergeant back and go on alone.

Gradually his thoughts grew less hectic and urgent, ceasing to jostle each other in the forefront of his mind. Fresh ideas began to occur to him, and he found it a pleasure to clarify and analyse them to the soothing rhythm of the long night ride.

The sleepless night caused Vorotyntsev no distress at all, neither did the prospect of another long day's journey ahead of him nor the likelihood of a week of feverish, dangerous action—for such the battle of East Prussia promised to be. There was also the possibility of death. Such was his lot. It was also to be the climax of his life— the moment for which every regular officer's training is a preparation. Not only was he not downcast, he felt an uplifting sense of buoyancy, and whether he slept or not, ate or not, was a matter of no significance to him.

13

If the truth were told, there was also another reason for his present buoyant mood. The sense of ease and freedom as he rode to the front came from the fact that he was going away from his wife.

At first he could not credit himself with feeling any such thing; never before had he known joy or relief at parting. Three weeks ago, however, when the staff of the Moscow Military District had received the order for general mobilisation and his whole heart and mind had been absorbed by the great event, Vorotyntsev had noticed that between the boulders of war a thought had darted out like a little rainbow-coloured lizard—that he would now have a perfect excuse for getting away from his wife and for taking a rest from her company.

Leave his beloved wife? The idea was incredible. Eight years ago he had stood at the altar beside a miraculous vision in white and his only fear had been that she might suddenly change her mind at the last minute. The idea was quite incredible!

He had met her immediately after his return from the Japanese campaign, in the peculiar mood of post-war elation induced by the mere fact of having survived. I'm alive, I've a long life in front of me and now I intend to be happy—now's the time to get married! From the moment when he had first stepped up to her to kiss her hand, from the first word she had spoken to him, he had made up his mind that she and she alone was the one for him. It was pointless to look further, to contrast or compare her with other women. She was the best, the only woman on earth, created specially for him. She had not understood this at first when he confessed to loving her and had hesitated before accepting his proposal. But he had known it at once.

Their first years of marriage had coincided with the strain of studying at the Academy. All his time and mental resources had been absorbed by the unbelievably full programme of studies that was crammed into each year: in addition to all the military subjects there were several branches of mathematics, two languages, military and civil law, three history subjects, even Slavonic philology and geology, not to mention three dissertations to write. It so happened that these were also the best years of the Academy, when the dead wood was cleared out (though not all of it, and not for long), when the legend of innate Russian invincibility gave way to concentration on unremitting hard work.

With so much of his energy taken up by the Academy, they were only too happy to spend the evenings together quietly in their two small rooms alongside the Ekaterinsky Canal. On his Academy pay of eighty roubles a month there was seldom enough money for theatres or concerts, and as there was practically never any time to spare either, they stayed at home. What could have been more delightful? They were years of utter happiness, of fusion and mutual comprehension: when one would start a sentence the other would instinctively finish it, or both would say the same thing at once; years of constant, unshakable, everyday happiness without quarrels or disagreements, both having found their heart's desire. While he was at his desk and she sat in the next room at the piano or lay on the couch, their private world gave them a calm and a stability which spared them from the distraction of emotional upsets in an otherwise unsettling time. Their first child miscarried, and they had no more children, but even that cast no cloud over their marriage. Georgii and Alina were convinced, so they told each other, that their love was preordained in heaven and was eternal.

Theirs, it seemed, was a love which was wholly independent of the kind of life they led or of the demands of his profession, a love unaffected by whether they lived in Petersburg or in some dreary provincial garrison. But at some point after the dissolution of Golovin's band of pupils at the Academy, perhaps after one of their changes of garrison or perhaps during the new style of life when they moved to Moscow, Vorotyntsev began gradually to sense, without being able to put his finger on it, that something had gone out of their life.

What had happened? Why did one's skin somehow seem to have hardened and shrivelled, to have ceased to register the passing touch of the least little hair? Why did they no longer begin their sentences together, why did one of them no longer finish saying what the other had started? Where was the thrill of excitement at the sight of her soft, light, scented clothes? Why, instead, were those clothes now merely objects hanging up or lying about the room? Why, when they kissed, was the touch of their lips less tender and urgent and a peck on the cheek more suitable?

Even the ritual in bed, he noticed with amazement, had turned into a mechanical activity that had lost its old freshness and savour. What did it mean? Had he no physical and emotional needs at all? Was he ageing already—and not yet forty? He would go through the same unromantic routine of washing himself, and then, too quickly, without even bothering to observe a tactful pause for contemplation, his wife would ask him to take his weight off her or would start talking in a workaday voice about domestic matters in case she forgot them later. Then she had bought herself an ugly, thick flannel nightdress. 'I don't like it.' 'Well, I don't care, it keeps me warm.'

Every plant, every tree, suffers the same fate—it hardens and grows a bark. Just as inevitably, a kind of bark grows and thickens on every love, and every marriage begins to petrify. It seems to be a natural law that as the years go by the urgency and desire of love must weaken. Hence the proverb: eat when you're hungry, love when you're young. But an ambitious young man has no time for love, life and work are calling him, and it was this that had made Georgii break off his first schoolboy love affair. And by the time one is nearing forty there is plenty more to occupy the mind and the senses: the morning dew smells as fresh as when one was young, one leaps into the saddle with as much pleasure as one did at twenty, and there is excitement in annotating the margins of a book by Schlieffen, whether in agreement or indignant rejection.

Alina still wanted him to tell her about everything—about his brother-officers, about his reading and his thoughts. She would sit down on the couch and he had to sit down beside her and recount it all. But the sheer number of new names, books and ideas was like a snowball, always growing as it rolled onward as unceasingly as the earth itself. Even Vorotyntsev's trained mind could hardly keep pace, and Alina's memory was unretentive. She would forget names, forget what he had already told her and ask him to repeat it for the second and third time, until he found it a boring waste of time which was slowing down the tempo of his mind. Finally, beginning to feel that really she was bored by it too, he stopped telling her about his doings, whereupon she pouted.

One source of dissatisfaction led to another and then to others. She noticed new, unpleasant traits in his character: he never had time for other people, he was moody, he was wholly wrapped up in himself and his own affairs. Feeling justifiably aggrieved, she took him firmly and even quite sharply to task. Admitting that perhaps she was right, that perhaps he was getting to be like that, Georgii promised to keep a check on himself. But after every one of their rows there was an aftermath of resentment and depression.

Now as he rode further and further away from his wife how much more carefree, how much more liberated and relaxed he felt! Long might it last. He felt no need for letters from her, no need for news of the trivia of domestic life in Moscow. It was not that he could find anything bad in Alina, he was not disappointed in her; he simply felt a need for separateness, to be apart. Every woman naturally tends to lay too many claims on 'her' man and never lets a day pass without somehow extending her hold over him if she can. At one time he had found this a pleasure, or at least tolerable; now it had become irksome.

In any case, women and poets exaggerated the whole business of love, with its thrills and agonies and its banal little personal dramas. The only emotions truly worthy of a man were civic duty, patriotism, a concern for all mankind.

Or perhaps he had just grown stale. Family life was no life for a soldier. He needed fresh air.

On and on he rode through the night. Strong and sure-footed, his stallion measured out the long miles of that fatal six-day journey between Army Headquarters and the front line.

This was no way to fight a war. They had fought like this in the past, but this time they would not be given a second chance . . . And the enemy had vanished. Why?

With a flash he suddenly remembered those uncoded wireless messages. How in God's name could they do such a thing? They would have been better off with no equipment at all rather than putting it into the hands of those clumsy, incompetent fools.

Far outstripping any horseman, those vulnerable, invisible radio-waves in the impenetrable darkness of enemy territory were sapping the strength of Second Army.

14

That summer Yaroslav Kharitonov was to have graduated from the Alexander Military Academy, an event which should have taken place in the following sequence: first a spell at their summer camp, then the solemn passing-out parade, followed by a month's leave at home in Rostov before joining his regiment. Countless delights awaited him in Rostov. His brother Yurik would jump for joy, his mother would fuss over him, he would rediscover the familiar rooms of his childhood, see his old school friends; but best of all he and Yurik, who was now twelve, and one other friend, would get into their sailing boat, which was all ready, provisioned and fitted out, to sail down the Don on a trip to the Cossack villages and see how these people lived. He had been meaning to do this for a long time; it was after all shameful to have been born and to have grown up in the Land of the Don Cossack Host and to know nothing about the Cossacks except that they dispersed demonstrations with whips. Yet they were a brave, strong and agile race of people, one of the most vigorous branches of the Russian tree.

But joining the army did not take place as scheduled; instead, as unexpected and terrifying as a whirlwind, there came the very thing for which armies exist—war. As early as July 19th his graduating class put on the coveted epaulettes with their stars. Far from being able to go home to say goodbye to their parents, they did not even have time to have their first photographs taken as officers, but were all drafted to immediate postings, Yaroslav to the Narva Regiment in the XIII Army Corps.

He joined his regiment at Oryol, where part of it was being loaded into troop-trains and part had still not been mustered. Although the four regiments of their division bore the first four numbers in the whole Russian army, they lacked permanent cadres. Only now were the lower ranks being brought up to complement, at a rate of three reservists to one regular soldier. Yaroslav himself arrived in time to meet these men, who came in their grey-black peasant clothes, with the remains of their food brought from home tied up in white bundles like Easter-cakes being taken to church to be blessed. He had to march the men to the bath-house, then to change into grey-green breeches and tunics, to be issued with rifles, packs and ammunition pouches, and finally to be loaded into freight-cars. Not only was there a shortage of regular private soldiers, for some reason there were not enough NCOs and officers either, although it seemed extraordinary that a country like Russia with her long military tradition should be unprepared. Companies had to make do with three or four officers each, and although as a newly commissioned officer Kharitonov was only put in command of his own platoon, more experienced officers were given two platoons and one of them was commanded by a mere sub-ensign.

For Yaroslav, who strode around straight-backed with a firm, jaunty step, it was all thrilling. He even enjoyed the three days of bustle and confusion in Oryol issuing uniforms to these country bumpkins, but best of all was the journey itself. Yaroslav did not go in the officers' coach, but stayed in the freight-car with his own, his very own men—the forty peasants who had been entrusted to him. At the head of the train of thirty freight-cars the engine hooted, the buffers clanked and squeezed each other, the couplings tautened and creaked and the whole train moved off.

People talked a great deal about loving the peasants; in the Kharitonov family the talk had been of nothing else; what was there to live for if not the welfare of the peasants? Yet somehow they never actually saw the peasants, one was not even allowed to go to the nearby market without permission from one's parents and afterwards one had to wash one's hands and change one's shirt. There was no way of coming into contact with the peasants, no common ground on which to talk with them, because one would be embarrassed and not know what to say. Yet now it seemed perfectly natural that the nineteen-year-old Yaroslav should be almost a father to these bearded muzhiks, that they should seek him out to ask questions, make requests and reports. What he had to do in return was to fulfil the role which is the most satisfying of all jobs in the service—namely to keep his eyes and ears open and to remember the men's names, where they came from and what they did at home. There was one man called Vyushkov who was a great talker and it was a pleasure to hear him describe their villages when the train passed through familiar country: over there on that high hill was the district town of Novosil, this bit of country was full of gullies, there was High Peak Farm where the best pasturage was, and the nightingales sang in that wood over there. Yaroslav longed to see it all for himself, realising that he had been nowhere and seen nothing. He was thrilled because this was the fulfilment of all his wishes—to be at one with these men, to be in their midst in the same freight-car and listen to the strumming of their bala-laika (what a marvellous instrument it was, how naturally and poetically they sang to it!), to stand beside them all day long leaning on the long bar which held the door open, while others sat under-neath it on the floor with their legs dangling outside, to lie awake at night listening to their singing and chatter and to watch the glow of their home-made cigarettes. Although they could hardly expect war itself to be fun, the journey was exhilarating, and not only for Yaroslav: the troops too were obviously in a cheerful mood, always joking, sometimes dancing and wrestling. When the train stopped at junctions they were met by crowds with bands, flags, speeches and gifts. It was in this mood that Yaroslav wrote his first letters home to his mother, to Yurik, to Oxana the Pecheneg servant-girl, and to his beloved 'adopted' sister, Xenia, who was like a real sister to him. Since his sister Zhenya had married and had a child she had turned into a younger edition of their mother and had grown away from him. He wrote that this was what he had been longing and striving for all his life: to be with the people and living a manly life to the full.

Before long, however, things became less cheerful and there was a great deal of confusion and muddle. They were suddenly ordered out of the train, although the train itself went on, and almost as though it were done on purpose as a punishment, they were made to march practically alongside the railway track as far as Ostro-lenka. They marched like this for several days and the raw reserv-ists found the going very hard in boots that were not worn in, in new and unfamiliar clothes and weighed down with packs and pouches. They could not understand why they had to do it and there was no one to ask. Probably it was because their corps had an unlucky number. A general rode by in a motor-car and said to them: 'The Germans can go by train if they like, but we Russians are tough—we can travel on our own two feet and still beat 'em! Isn't that right, lads?' And they shouted back at him: 'Right, sir!' (Yaroslav shouted too.)

The adjutant of their battalion, Staff-Captain Grokholets, a small, dapper man with two sharp, upturned ends to his moustache, a soldier to his fingertips whom Yaroslav tried to imitate, doubled himself up with laughter as he shouted to the men in the column: 'Hey, you bunch of pilgrims! Where do you think you're going—Jerusalem?' It was so funny and so apt, Yaroslav thought as he smiled; only a real soldier could have made a joke like that. The reservists dragged their rifles along as though they were heavy, useless sticks they were chained to. Their stiff new boots slowed them down and when the officers were not looking the men pulled them off, slung them round their necks on a piece of twine and marched on barefoot. The battalion was strung out over more than half a mile, the whole regiment was straggling badly, officers were losing the raw troops from their units and spent their time sorting out strays from other battalions and sending them back. Waggon-trains and herds of cows being driven along by the Supply Corps to provide fresh food for their division became entangled in the ragged column of men.

If only there had been time to train them, to organise refresher courses and to give them some arms-drill, these reservists might still have been made into first-class soldiers. Yaroslav could see this from his own men, even from someone like Private Kramchatkin, a man who had not been outside his own village for fifteen years, who was already grey-haired and who had, as the other men said of him, 'done his bit'. Nevertheless Yaroslav was amazed at how well he remembered his drill, as though he had come straight from a barrack square and had done nothing all his life but march up to an officer, salute and shout in the regulation style: 'Private Kramchatkin reporting for duty, your honour!' He looked the complete soldier, his eyes alert and wide-open like saucers, his moustaches bristling—but he was totally incapable of shooting (a fact which he concealed and which was only found out by chance).

So far, every action in this great war, Second Lieutenant Kharitonov's first war, had been conducted in a manner which in the military academy would have earned several days' confinement in the guardhouse for inefficiency. As though it were all a grim joke, the entire operation was taking place in defiance of regulations. It was as if in their keen young squad at the academy, with their snappy arms-drill, the brisk, clear way they were instructed to make reports, the barked words of command and the spirited way they sang on the march, they had been purposely shown how things never were, never would or could be done in the army. Everything which the young officers had been taught was discarded or neglected: there was no reconnaissance, no liaison with flanking units, they were bewildered by countermanded orders, and whole brigades in column of march were stopped by galloping dispatch-riders and turned around.

For two weeks they were not given their regulation day's halt. In the morning the battalions would get up at first light and were usually ready to move off in reasonably good time; then they were made to sit down and wait in the stupefyingly hot morning sunshine until orders arrived from division or brigade for the day's march. Sometimes the staffs did not even get things organised by noon and when the dispatch-rider did bring the order it stated that the battalion was to move off not later than 0800 hours, as a result of which they were then made to march all day without halt in order to make up for lost time. They would suddenly have to stop in order to clear a waggon-train which was blocking the route, or hold up their field kitchens to allow the lagging advance guard to move forward. Then they would be driven on again. They marched until sunset, until twilight and until dark, sometimes even until midnight. Sometimes their billeting officers, who had been sent on ahead, could not be found in the dark, and no one knew where they were to be quartered; at other times the senior officers would quarrel amongst themselves as to where the various units should spend the night, while the men simply hung around and lit camp fires or brewed tea over little fires of burning twigs, quite unconcerned that they were giving away their position to the enemy. The field kitchens had to work after dark by the light of kerosene flares, which threw out showers of sparks. At other times the field kitchens would be missing altogether and the men lay down hungry at midnight (like the troops, the officers froze on the ground with nothing to sleep in but their greatcoats), to be woken up at dawn to eat the supper which they should have had the night before.

As a result the nights were too short and they did not have enough sleep.

The men would ask: 'When are we going to get some proper bread, your honour? We've had hard-tack for two weeks now and it makes your guts ache!' And there was no reasonable way of explaining to them why it was that in Bialystok, where there was ample bread, their division had not been given any because the Supply Corps was too inefficient; why it was that at the very start of the war, even before reaching the German frontier, before a single shell had exploded or a single bullet had whistled through the air, the men had been issued with nothing for ten days except hard-tack that was stale and smelt of mice, biscuits that had been stored for years, or why the supply services were so erratic that the troops only rarely had salt in their soup.

Up to Ostrolenka there was only one road they could take and their route was therefore quite clear. But after Ostrolenka, where they were not even allowed a day's rest, the corps split up into divisional columns, and then, after crossing the German frontier, into brigade columns. It was here that the staff started to get particularly slow with the orders and began to muddle them up, sending one regiment or another trailing off on a useless six-mile march by mistake. This seemed to pass unnoticed by anyone up above—with the exception of the German aviators, who had been flying over the Russian columns even while they were still in Poland. No Russian aircraft were flying, however; they were being kept, so it was said, for when they were really needed. After crossing the German frontier some units were lucky enough to have firm, metalled roads to march on, but even on these the mass of boots and hooves raised thick clouds of dust, so that you could feel the grit on your teeth; and sooner or later the roads petered out or led in the wrong direction, or there were no roads at all, and the men not only had to march but to pull waggons and guns through thick dust and clogging sand in heat which never lessened for a single day, being only interrupted by one fall of rain at night—and this in country where wells were few and far between and they often had to march for hours without water. Then the terrain would change completely and they would find themselves bogged down in winding, marshy watercourses, following routes that seemed purposely chosen as impassable. Soon horses, men, and officers could only think of the one thing for which they longed so painfully—rest! The regimental standards had long ago been wound round their shafts and were dragged along like so many useless poles, the drums had been piled on to the waggons, no more orders were given to sing, companies were losing men from exhaustion and the troops only kept going by dreaming that to-morrow somebody would give the order to halt and rest.

The heat was killing the men on their feet, but evidently the plan was far too important to allow them a day's rest. With the same relentless speed they were driven forward by forced marches, even though they had not seen a single live German since entering German territory.

During a short break for a smoke, Staff-Captain Grokholets, slim as a boy despite his balding head, joked to the other officers:

'This isn't war, this is just manoeuvres. There's a dispatch-rider from Army Headquarters who's been looking for us for four days now to tell us to stop and he can't find us. We've just strayed into German territory by mistake. Now they'll have to send off a note apologising to Vasil Fyodorich.'

'Vasil Fyodorich' was for some obscure reason the nickname they used for Kaiser Wilhelm. These jokes made life a little easier to bear.

Ever since they had crossed the frontier at Chorzele (or 'Khorz-heléy' as they all called it in the regiment) they had been expecting action, in the form of artillery or rifle fire. But neither then nor during the next several days did they hear a single shot, see a single German soldier or civilian, or any sign of a living creature. Here and there barbed wire obstacles had been thrown across the path and left unmanned. In some places the Germans had started digging trenches across the road at the edge of a village and had left them half dug, and the Russians filled them in in order to let a machine-gun troop or other mounted units pass through. In one village a barricade made of carts and furniture had been set up across the street; it was also unmanned. 'Things must be going badly for the Germans!' said Second Lieutenant Kozieko. This was the first cheerful remark that this otherwise permanently dejected, whining officer had made. In the next village somebody found a bicycle and wheeled it out, and the whole battalion crowded round to watch. Many of them had never seen such a marvel in their lives. One of the sergeants demonstrated how to ride it to the noisy encouragement of a crowd of soldiers.

But the uncanniest thing of all to these hot, sleepless, stupefied Russian soldiers was the fact that Germany proved to be deserted.

Germany had turned out to be an unusual country, utterly unlike anything that Yaroslav had imagined from picture books. It was not only the strange roofs, pitched so steeply that they took up half the height of the house, which immediately gave the place such a foreign look. Even more amazing was the sight of villages made up of two-storey brick houses, stone pig-sties, concreted wellheads, electric lighting (even in Rostov they only had this in a few streets). To think that there were farms supplied with electricity and telephones, and that even in this hot weather there were no flies and no stink of manure! Nowhere had anything been abandoned, scattered or thrown down at random—and the Prussian peasants were hardly likely to have left their farms in paradeground order just because the Russian troops were coming! The bearded peasant soldiers were amazed. How, they asked, could the Germans keep their farms so tidy that there were no traces of work to be seen, everything put away in its place, ready for use? How could they live in such inhuman cleanliness, where you couldn't even throw your coat down? And with so rich a country as this, what on earth could have induced Kaiser Wilhelm to make a bid to conquer and seize filthy, backward Russia? Poland, poor and ragged as it was, had seemed familiar enough to them, but when they had crossed the German frontier it was as though they had passed through some magic barrier: the crops, the roads and the buildings—everything was eerily different.

This un-Russian tidiness was, however, the only thing which aroused their respectful awe. The fact that the countryside was deserted, a piece of lifeless, ominously forsaken booty, produced a sense of unease, rather as though the Russians were a gang of cheeky little boys who had broken into someone else's silent, empty house and would sooner or later, inevitably, be caught and punished.

Even where there was an opportunity to plunder, the troops had no time to stop and loot the houses. In any case they had no kitbags in which to carry away booty, and when you may be marching to your death it is no time to weigh yourself down with extra lumber.

The first inhabitants they found who had not run away were not Germans, but German Poles, who somehow managed to make themselves understood in broken Russian. Far from trusting them, the Russians treated them with suspicion and Kozieko's platoon was ordered to make a thorough search of the farm. As he set off for this operation, Kozieko said to Kharitonov: 'Somebody wants to get me killed. I bet there's a cellarful of Prussian soldiers in that place.' They met no opposition, made a careful search of the house and found a trumpet which looked rather like a French horn, a bicycle in the hayloft, and in the bath-house two rounds of Russian rifle ammunition and a pair of boots with spurs. Things looked bad for the Poles and the general opinion was that they should be shot. They were sent back to regimental headquarters under escort; one of them was aged about fifty and the other two were lads of about sixteen or seventeen. As they were led past the battalion they begged every officer and NCO they saw: 'Spare us! Spare us!' But the sergeant from Kozieko's platoon, who was leading them, only shouted cheerfully: 'Go on, keep moving. Moscow doesn't believe in your tears!' The soldiers crowded round to look: 'They're the ones who shoot at us from ambush. It's their sort who go round the paths in the forest on bicycles watching for us, and then tell the Germans where we are.'

There was even some shooting that day. Once a German aeroplane flew overhead and all the men started vigorously firing at it, but without scoring a hit. Later they noticed three men running out of a farm into the forest dressed in civilian clothes, shot at them and hit one. On another occasion a Cossack galloped up, saying that he had been fired on from a wood three miles away by a cavalry patrol, and at once half a company was detached to comb the wood. Cursing the Cossack and their own bad luck, the troops set off on the mission, but found nobody.

But Kozieko approved of the operation: 'Our chief danger at the moment is that we may be shot at from the rear.' The two second lieutenants could not avoid talking to each other as they had been posted to neighbouring platoons in the same company at Bialystok. Kozieko never spoke to the other officers; he was afraid of the battalion commander, did not like the company commander and avoided Grokholets whenever he could, because the adjutant was too prone to make fun of him. Kozieko poured all his observations and his urge for self-expression into his diary, which for lack of other paper he wrote in his officer's field message-pad. During every free moment he scribbled a few more lines, always noting down the exact time of the entry. 'What a feat!' Grokholets sighed in mock admiration. 'If no one else writes our regimental history, when the war ends we'll order your book to be bound in gold and sent to headquarters.'

'You can't do that!' said Kozieko indignantly. 'My diary is private, and it's my own property.'

'You're wrong there, Lieutenant, that's government property,' said Grokholets, rolling his eyes; 'the sheets of a field message-pad belong to headquarters.'

Kozieko was older than Yaroslav and had already served his two years as an officer before the outbreak of war, but all the same Yaroslav found his attitude completely unacceptable.

'You really can't behave like this when we're fighting a war. Instead of cursing it, we ought to be thinking the whole time of how we can win. In any case, how can a great people avoid wars?'

'Ah!' Kozieko winced as though he had toothache and looked round to see whether anyone could hear them. 'But that's just it! They all dodge fighting if they can! Look at Miloshevich who arranged to have himself posted to a soft job, look at Nikodimov who got himself sent away to buy cattle. Nobody with any intelligence stays in the battalion if he can help it, don't you worry.'

'In that case I can't understand,' Yaroslav protested, 'why you ever became a regular officer if you think like that.'

Frowning unhappily, Kozieko sighed as he bent over his diary. 'It's a secret. If only I could be sitting in the sunshine in my own little home . . . I know it sounds unpatriotic, but I can't live without my wife. That's why I want the war to end.'

Everything about their life made Kozieko miserable—either there was nowhere to wash his hands, or he found it impossible to eat without first having washed, or he hated having to go to sleep in his clothes. What was more, the battalion was growing increasingly dispirited and hopeless as it slogged onward unopposed. Yaroslav had always imagined that an advancing army would be cheerful: we are pushing forward, we are going to take prisoners, we are seizing territory—we are the stronger! Armies were after all created to take the offensive, and officers were trained for it. But they were growing dejected after advancing for two weeks without a single engagement, without seeing one German, without one man being wounded, while at night, to right and left, could be seen the dull red glow of mysterious fires. What had become of the lighthearted joy which not only he but apparently all of them, rank and file included, had felt when they were on the way to the front in the jolting freight-cars, with the warm summer breezes blowing past them? Private Kramchatkin was still acting the old soldier, not slouching as he marched, still looking his platoon commander keenly in the eye, but Vyushkov now looked the other way and his garrulous flow of stories had dried up. No one in the battalion sang any longer, and the bearded soldiers avoided shouting and reduced their conversation to essentials as though superstitiously afraid of angering God with idle chatter.

Even the countryside became more obstructive as the forests closed in on them. At first platoons or half-companies were sent ahead as scouts to clear the edges of the woods, then the entire regiment would simply pour into the forest and be swallowed up by it. The forest was nothing like a Russian one; there were no rotting branches or dead wood on the ground, no fallen tree-trunks. It looked as though it had just been swept, the brushwood tied up in neat bundles and the rides and fire-breaks clean, straight corridors. A number of roads cut through it in various directions, and except where they had recently been churned up or rutted they were well kept.

Although every officer was supposed to have a map of the area on his map-board, none of them in their company had a map, and Grokholets was the only officer in the battalion to possess one. Even this was a reprint of a German map; the place-names were barely legible and it was inaccurate. Among the platoon commanders, Yaroslav was the one who hovered closest to Grokholets in order to seize every opportunity for a look at his map. The Germans had burnt all the sign-posts and as the names of villages were passed verbally from officer to officer they became more and more distorted and incorrect: 'We've just passed through a place called Saddek, this is Kaltenborn and we're to spend the night in Omulefoffen.' The forest they were in, with its fifty- and seventy-foot pine-trees, was called Grünfliess Forest.

From midday on August 10th the whole forest began to echo with the sound of artillery fire coming from the west at a distance of about ten miles to their left. It was real sustained firing and it meant that the first battle had begun. But the regiments of XIII Army Corps paid no attention to it and marched on through the forest to the north, where it was silent and deserted. They spent the night in Omulefoffen.

Next morning, after rising in the dark and for the first time getting no hard-tack for breakfast, they went through the usual interminable movements of forming up and dressing in regimental and then in brigade columns, with the guns and supply waggons in their places. The columns were drawn up to march northward out of Omulefoffen, as they had to make a wide detour round a broad arm of Lake Omulefoffen.

The forming-up drill went on for a long time, the usual prayer was read, they were ready to move and the exhausting heat of late morning had already set in when a dispatch-rider from Divisional Headquarters galloped up and handed an envelope to the brigade commander. At once the brigade commander summoned the regimental commanders and orders were given to the Narva and Kopor regiments to change places. They were not allowed to do this by the quickest means of simply turning round on the spot, but were made to keep to the regulation order of march for a brigade column, only in this case with the head of the column pointing westward along another street. The August sun was now blazing down in full strength, and their dawn breakfast, which without hard-tack had been even less satisfying than usual, was forgotten by the time the regiments set off in the new direction. They had marched little more than a mile when at a road junction they encountered the Sofia Regiment marching in the same direction. It was not long before they caught sight of the distant mounted figure of the dashing Colonel Pervushin, known to everyone as the commander of the Neva Regiment. This meant that the entire division was converging on one point. Down the long forest path between colonnades of tall, mast-like pines they first of all marched back to Kaltenborn, which they had passed through yesterday, and then turned westward towards Grünfliess. Once more a rumble of gunfire could be heard ahead of them, but it was not as loud as yesterday, perhaps because the sound did not carry so well in the heat, perhaps because the firing was dying down. The fact that they were now marching towards the sound of the guns was somewhat heartening; at least they knew they were going somewhere for a purpose instead of milling about in a deserted forest. Kozieko prayed to God that the fighting would all be over by the time they arrived.

They came to a crossroads of two forest paths where they had to change direction. It was deep in powdery sand and on a slope, and the horses of the gun-teams, also exhausted and inadequately fed, could not pull the guns forward; the wheels were embedded in the sand, and even the added muscle-power of the gun-crews was not enough to shift them. Yaroslav ordered his men to go to the help of a cheerful, bullet-headed sergeant-major and managed to push two of his guns clear, but the sergeant-major had to harness eight horses instead of six to each of the others, and the column was delayed still longer.

As they marched on, the sound of gunfire ahead of them stopped altogether, to Kozieko's delight. After covering ten miles since morning, when the sun was already declining from the meridian, the whole column stopped on a path in the middle of the forest and the men threw themselves down to rest in the shade.

Worried-looking officers on horseback galloped back and forth for an hour, though neither the troops nor the junior officers were told anything. Finally the regimental commander called for the senior officers, and once again, with much creaking, shouting, confusion and lashing of the horses in the gun-teams, the entire divisional column turned round and marched back to where it had come from.

Stomachs were rumbling, the soles of the men's feet were burning hot, the sun was already setting behind the trees and it was well past the time when they should have bivouacked for the night and started cooking supper. But no, back the division marched over the same crossroads and through the same stretch of forest. The peasants in uniform grew sullen and began muttering that their senior officers were all Germans and were purposely driving the troops to exhaustion and despair before they had even started fighting. They did not halt even when the sun set in a yellow ball, promising a morrow as bright, hot and dusty as today. They did not stop at twilight, but obediently retraced their steps, and the stars were out when they returned to the village of Omulefoffen and lit their field kitchens in the same places as the day before. It was well after midnight before supper began to cook, and almost cock-crow before they went to sleep.

Their limbs felt like lead as they got up and, although none of them felt hungry yet, they gulped down their morning porridge because they knew they would have no more that day. They were at least issued with two days' rations of hard-tack. The troops fell in, dressed into line and formed up to march out of Omulefoffen by the same route as yesterday. Grumbling, the men predicted that they would be made to turn round again. Himself suffering from lack of sleep, Yaroslav tried to cheer them up by laughing at them: 'Of course not! Not today!' Then as though the prophets of doom had cast a spell, the column was made to stand there motionless for hour after hour without being allowed to fall out and sleep. Finally when the sun had reached its zenith and the troops were dripping with sweat, those invisible Germans on the staff (even Yaroslav could think of no better explanation!) gave the order for the whole column to turn round again and form up on yet a third road, which led out of the village in between the other two.

Once more a whole hour was spent in redeployment.

They set off. The day was unbearably hot, and feet and wheels dragged in the sand more than ever. This time the road was narrower and in a much worse state, the bridges along it were all blown up, and the strength of the Russian troops was drained away as they made detours, each time hauling themselves up the steep embankments on to the road again. The latest novelty was that the Germans had filled all the wells near the road with earth, refuse and timber, so there was nowhere to get water except from the lake, and for that there was no time to spare.

Today no gunfire was heard from any direction. There was no trace of a German—no soldiers, no civilians, not even old men and women. It seemed as if the rest of the Russian army had vanished and that the only living thing was their division being driven along an unknown, deserted, forsaken road. There were not even any Cossacks to reconnoitre ahead.

Even the stupidest illiterate soldier realised that his officers had blundered hopelessly.

It was now August 12th, the fourteenth day of their uninterrupted march.

*

With cross and locket on your chest,
You may walk all night and trudge all day—
A burning wound, though, in your breast
Has sealed your fate, do what you may.

15

The square in the centre of the little town of Neidenburg, which made up for its modest size by the number of its stone-built houses, was so small as to be hardly a square at all. Three streets led from it, on the corner of one of which was a two-storey house with smashed shop windows on the ground floor and plate-glass windows on the first floor; smoke was pouring from the interior and an even thicker column of smoke was rising from the court-yard.

A half-platoon of soldiers, without over-exerting themselves, were trying to douse the smoke. Water was being carried in buckets from around the corner and through the gates into the yard, whence could be heard the sound of splintering wood and chopping axes, whilst other soldiers had formed a human chain and were passing buckets up a plank placed on the window-ledge of the first floor. Working in the sun, the soldiers had taken off their tunics, and many had removed their forage-caps and were wiping their brows. They were in no hurry, because it was oppres-sively hot, and despite the clouds of billowing smoke the fire was not a serious one. There was no excitement and no shouts of en-couragement; the men chatted among themselves as they moved about, occasionally laughing when one of them made a joke.

Having left a sergeant in charge of the operation, the platoon commander had nothing to do for a while. He was an ensign wearing the badge of a university graduate, with a slightly super-cilious but keen expression which belied his rather languid way of moving. With an air of great unconcern, he first paced up and down, then stopped and selected a patch of shade on the steps of a stone porch on the other side of the street, where a cloth painted with a red cross had been tied round one of the pillars. In front of the house stood a Medical Corps two-wheeled van without a driver, the horse in the shafts shivering occasionally.

Just then a doctor in a white coat, with a black moustache and thick black eyebrows, stepped out on to the porch wearily rubbing his head and taking in deep breaths of fresh air. This made him yawn uncontrollably, his head nodding backwards and forwards as he did so. Noticing a plank on the highly polished stone step, he immediately sat down, stretching out his legs down the steps and leaning back on his arms, as though to stop himself from falling backwards with exhaustion.

Today there was no sound of gunfire; the only noise came from the soldiers putting out the fire, the only sign of war was the flag with the red cross and the deserted German houses with their steep-pitched roofs, so un-Russian in appearance.

The ensign was left with no alternative but to sit on one of the lower steps. His features had a slightly precocious look of decisiveness, his uniform hung around him like a sack, and his expression as he stared at his troops carrying water was one of boredom. The smoke did not blow in his direction as there was no wind and it was billowing straight upwards.

Having filled his lungs and finished yawning, the doctor looked across the road to see how the soldiers were putting out the fire, then glanced sideways at the young officer.

'Don't sit on that cold stone, Ensign. There's a plank here you can sit on.'

'But the stone is quite warm.'

'No, it's not. You'll catch a chill.'

'Why should I worry about that? I'm more likely to get my head shot off.'

'Well, you'll catch a chill whether you care about it or not. Come on, come and sit up here.'

Unwillingly the ensign stood up, then moved over to sit beside the doctor. The doctor was a smooth, dignified man, with bushy moustaches and silky, black side-whiskers running down to his jaw like a dark shadow. He looked exhausted.

'What's the matter with you?'

'Been operating. Yesterday, all night, and this morning.'

'Have there been so many wounded?'

'What do you think? You ought to know. Germans as well as ours. All types of wounds ... Shrapnel wound in the abdomen with prolapsed stomach, guts and caul hanging out, and the patient still fully conscious. He's only got a few hours to live and he's asking us to put some ointment on his stomach because it hurts ... Bullet through the skull, part of the brain coming out ... Hard fighting, to judge by the type of wounds.'

'Can you tell what the fighting was like by the wounds?'

'Of course. If the wounds are predominantly internal it means heavy fighting.'

'Have you finished with them now?'

'God, there were so many!'

'Go and sleep then.'

'I have to rest and relax first. The work makes you tense.' The doctor yawned. 'It weakens you.'

'But it does you good to relax, doesn't it?'

'No, nothing does any good; you just weaken. You don't react to death or wounds, otherwise you couldn't do your job. A man's looking at you with eyes like saucers and he asks only one thing—will he live? And you must coldly count his pulse-rate and work out how you'll operate on him ... If only our transportation was any good we could save a few more of these internal cases; they ought to be operated on at base. But what sort of transport have we got? Two horse-drawn vans and a covered cart. The Germans have driven away all their carts and horses. In any case, where could we take them? Over the Narev? That's nearly seventy miles, only the first six miles of it on a metalled road, then more than sixty miles over Russian country roads. Sheer murder. Whereas the Germans evacuate their wounded by motor ambulance and in an hour's time they're in the finest operating theatre you could ask for.'

The ensign's face took on a severe expression as he looked at the doctor.

'And what happens if the military situation changes now?' the doctor went on indignantly. 'Supposing we withdraw? We simply have no vehicles to evacuate our wounded. The hospital would fall into German hands. And if we advance we then have the responsibility of burying the dead. When they lie out in the fields in this heat they start decomposing quickly.'

'The worse, the better,' said the ensign grimly.

'What do you mean?' The doctor did not understand him.

Until now lazily indifferent, the ensign's eyes gleamed. 'Individual instances of so-called compassion only obscure the issue and delay a general solution of the problem. For Russia, in this war, as in everything else, it is a case of the worse, the better!'

The doctor's bushy eyebrows rose in astonishment and stayed up. 'What are you talking about? You mean you don't care if the wounded are jolted about, develop fever, delirium, get infected? Let our soldiers suffer and die—you call that better?'

The ensign's keen, intelligent features became even grimmer as he warmed to his theme.

'You have to stand back and take the long-term view if you don't want to be fooled by appearances. There are more than enough people in Russia who have suffered and are still suffering. So let the suffering of the wounded be added to the suffering of the workers and peasants. It even helps if we're so inefficient that we treat the wounded badly. It brings the day of reckoning nearer. So, the worse, the better!'

The ensign's manner of holding his head slightly back made him look as though he were not talking to his companion alone but surveying a large audience and saying: 'Any more questions?'

Although the doctor was more than ready for sleep, he stared at this self-confident young officer with wide-open eyes.

'So to your way of thinking, you mean we shouldn't even operate? Shouldn't even dress their wounds? The more men die the nearer we are to liberation? We were treating the standard-bearer from your Chernigov Regiment just now. Laceration of the major vessels. The man had lain twelve hours in no-man's land before he was brought back. No more than a whisper of a pulse. So why did we bother about him? Is that what you mean by taking the "long-term view"?'

The ensign's eyes flashed like tawny fire. 'But why did they flock like sheep behind the regimental standard, that symbol of obscurantism and reaction? Now the whole regiment is bleating about how brave they were just because the standard was unfurled! Why, they play with us as if we were lead soldiers!'

Puzzled, the surgeon asked: 'Excuse me, but you're not a regular officer, are you? What are you then?'

The ensign shrugged his narrow shoulders. 'What does it matter? I'm a citizen.'

'No, I mean what's your job?'

'I'm a lawyer, if you really must know.'

'Aha, a law-yer!' The doctor understood now and nodded his head as though he might have guessed it. 'A law-yer . . .'

'And what's wrong with that?' said the ensign guardedly.

'I might have known it. A lawyer. You lawyers seem to be springing up like weeds all over Russia, if you don't mind my saying so.'

'Since the whole country is lawless through and through, if you ask me there aren't nearly enough of us.'

'Lawyers in the courts, lawyers in the Duma,' the doctor went on, disregarding him, 'lawyers in the political parties, lawyers in the press, lawyers at meetings, lawyers writing pamphlets . . .' He spread out his big hands. 'I ask you, what sort of an education is it anyway, when you train as a lawyer?'

'I am a graduate of St Petersburg University,' the ensign explained with icy politeness.

'That's no university education. Learn a dozen text-books off by heart and pass your exams—that's all your so-called education amounts to. I knew plenty of law students. They spent their four years doing nothing but fooling around—writing leaflets, speaking at conferences, upsetting people . . .'

'That's a disgraceful way to talk for an intellectual like yourself!' the ensign reproved him, his face darkening. 'You're playing *their* game for them . . .'

He was right. The doctor realised that he had overstepped the mark and that the ensign's rebuke was justified.

'What I meant,' the doctor corrected himself, 'was that you should have read medicine or engineering and then you would have known what hard work really means. When you've studied a practical subject you don't just lean back and rest on your laurels—you have to work. Russia needs workers, practical men.'

'Shame on you!' The ensign stared at him with the same look of burning reproach. 'What—and shore up the whole revolting system? It should be smashed to fragments without mercy! We should be knocking it down to let in the light!' It had obviously not occurred to the doctor that he was shoring up anything; he had thought he was learning how to heal people.

'I suppose you graduated from the Army Medical Academy?' Eyes gleaming, the ensign rapped out the question.

'Yes, I did.'

'In which year?'

'1909.'

'I see.' The ensign made a quick mental calculation and the nostrils of his long, straight nose quivered. 'In other words, when the Academy was closed in 1905 because of the revolution you were dismissed, but you were re-admitted and were able to take your exams because you signed a declaration of loyalty.'

The doctor frowned with displeasure and tugged the end of his moustaches downwards, but they sprang up again of their own accord. 'Of course, that would be the first thing that would occur to you. So what if I did sign a piece of paper? What else are you to do if you want to be an army doctor and the Academy is the only one in the country? Anyway, even if we had the most democratic government in the world it would have the right to ensure that its army medical academy wasn't disrupted by seditious meetings, wouldn't it? In my opinion, what I did was perfectly justified.'

'And what about wearing uniform? And the students having to salute everybody, like private soldiers?'

'In the Army Medical Academy? I don't see anything wrong in that.'

'Huh! Playing at soldiers!' the ensign snorted. 'That's typical of the concessions we make, and then we're surprised when . . .'

'But when all is said and done—we heal wounded men.' Now the doctor was getting angry. 'You leave the wounded to me. Playing at soldiers indeed! You just wait until you're brought in here tomorrow with a smashed shoulder.'

The ensign grinned. He was not malicious but a young man with the sincerity and conviction that were the mark of the best Russian students.

'No one's against humanitarianism. Heal people as much as you like. You can look upon it as a form of mutual help. But let's have no theoretical justifications for this disgusting war!'

'But I wasn't doing anything of the sort . . . was I?' The doctor was thoroughly perplexed.

' "War of liberation"! They call it that just to work on people's emotions. "Save our brothers the Serbs from the hands of Austria!" So they're sorry for the Serbs, are they? We oppress all the non-Russian people in the empire but we don't seem to feel sorry for them.'

'All the same, Germany . . .' The doctor found himself faltering, as everyone in Russia tended to when faced by the dogmatic certainty of youth.

'If you ask me it's a great pity that Napoleon didn't beat us in 1812. His rule wouldn't have lasted long, and then we would have been free.'

And so the lawyer, dressed in hated uniform, pressed home point after point. It was hard to disagree with him, because his arguments were well thought out. In a more conciliatory tone the doctor asked him sympathetically: 'Why were you called up? Why didn't you get exemption or deferment?'

'Oh, you know how it is. I got into it without thinking . . . Right turn—as you were! Left turn—as you were! Shoulder arms—as you were! About turn! Double march! Then I passed my examination as an ensign in the reserve.'

'Well, let's get acquainted.' The doctor stretched out a fleshy but powerful hand. 'My name's Fedonin.'

He gripped the four narrow, bony fingers of the young lawyer, who said: 'Mine's Lenartovich.'

'Lenartovich, Lenartovich . . . Wait a moment, I've heard that name somewhere, haven't I?'

'It depends on where your interests lie,' Lenartovich replied in a guarded voice. 'My paternal uncle was executed after a certain political trial.'

'Ah, yes—of course, of course!' As he nodded in acknowledgement Fedonin felt guilty and displayed all the more respect, since he was still not quite sure which particular incident was referred to, whether it had been a successful assassination, a bomb that hadn't exploded or a naval mutiny. 'Yes, yes, of course . . . Your name is partly German, isn't it?'

'Yes, an ancestor of mine was German. Also an army doctor, incidentally; came here under Peter the Great. Then the name was russified.'

'Does your family live in Petersburg?'

'My mother. And my sister. She's at the Bestuzhev Academy. As it happens I got a letter from her today, and what do you think? It was posted on the fourth day after the outbreak of war, on the 23rd of July—and what's the date today? The 12th of August! What sort of a postal service is that? How do they deliver their letters—on ox-carts? I suppose it's because the censor keeps them so long.' He was growing more and more angry. 'It's the same

[153]

with the newspapers. The last one I had was dated the 1st of August! What a postal service! How can one find out what's going on in Russia, or in Germany, or in Western Europe? We know absolutely nothing! And then I read in the paper that Neidenburg was captured virtually without a fight, yet for some reason we shelled it and set fire to it and now we've got to put it out. Never mind, the good old Russian soldier will carry buckets of water if he's told to . . .'

'Come now, it was set on fire by the Germans . . .'

'Yes, the Germans set fire to the shops in the middle of the town, but it was our Cossacks who set fire to the outskirts. Fine. Meanwhile there's not a word of news from the Austrian front. The Austrians know nothing about us, and we know nothing about them. Is that any way to fight a war? We hear nothing but rumours. Some cavalry officer rides by and whispers something to somebody —and that's all we ever hear in the way of news. Who shows any respect or consideration for the army in the field? They despise us. And yet when you talk it's "Russia this" and "Germany that" . . . Some of our soldiers smashed down the doors of some abandoned German houses and grabbed a few things. That, if you please, is a stain on the honour of a Christian army and for that the men are punished and put in the guardhouse. But Lieutenant-Colonel Adamantov can pocket as many silver milk-jugs as he likes—that's all right, that doesn't matter. There's Russia for you!'

Had it not been for this filthy war young girls would not have clad themselves in white, would not have coiffed their foreheads to the eyebrows so freshly, cleanly, severely. Impersonal and anonymous, her education, social status and colour of hair unknown, a nursing sister stepped out on to the porch in her new uniform.

'What is it, Tanya?'

'The patient with the broken jaw is restless, Valerian Akimich. Could you come and see him?'

The argument on the steps ceased at once. The doctor sighed and went in, followed dutifully by the swan-white nurse, whose eyes, dimmed with unhappiness, gave Lenartovich no more than a passing glance.

The white head-dresses and white uniforms were, of course, merely the toys of the rich and privileged, an opiate for the mass of the soldiery.

Suddenly a lieutenant-colonel, mounted on a restless horse,

trotted into the square and bellowed as was his right: 'Who's the senior rank here?'

The soldiers immediately started passing the buckets faster, and Lenartovich ran down the steps with carefully moderated speed, doing his best to keep his dignity, and crossed the square. Without seeming over-keen he came to attention and saluted, although somewhat crookedly. 'Ensign Lenartovich, 29th Chernigov Regiment!'

'Are you in charge of putting this fire out?'

'Yes. I mean—yes, sir.'

'Well what the hell do you think you're doing, Ensign? Running a Christmas bazaar? Army Headquarters is coming here. It'll be billeted two houses away and you still haven't put the fire out after three days. It's enough to make a cat laugh—carrying buckets of water all that distance. Can't you find a pump somewhere?'

'Where can we get a pump, sir? Our battalion hasn't . . .'

'In that case you've got to use your brains a little, haven't you? You're not at the university now, you know! What do you mean by exhausting your men like this? Follow me, I'll show you where there's a pump and a hose. All you need to do is look around some of these backyards.'

And the lieutenant-colonel set off on his splendid horse like a victorious general.

Lenartovich trotted after him like a prisoner.

16

It took Vorotyntsev another whole day and a night to reach Soldau. He might have gone faster, as he had sent the sergeant back and was riding light, but he did not want to wear his horse out, not knowing what demands he might have to make on it in the next few days. He rode into Soldau in the early hours of August 13th, before it was really hot, having watered and fed his horse.

Soldau, like all German country towns, did not sprawl and take up good farmland as Russian towns do; it was not surrounded by a derelict belt of rubbish dumps and waste land; wherever you entered it you at once found yourself passing neat, closely-built rows of tiled, brick houses, some of them even three or four storeys high, with roofs pitched to half the height of the house. The streets in these towns, as neat as corridors, were closely paved with flat, smooth setts or flagstones, while each house had some individual feature—with one it might be the windows, with another the finials. Then close together would be found the Rathaus, the church, a tiny square, a monument to someone or other, not just one shop but a whole variety of them, beergardens, the post office, the bank, and sometimes even a toy-like park behind wrought-iron railings. Then equally suddenly the town would come to an end, the streets would stop and only a few paces beyond the last house there would be a tree-lined highroad and precise, carefully marked-out fields.

Soldau had been completely abandoned by its inhabitants and was not yet overflowing with Russian troops. Sentries had been placed outside several of the shops and warehouses—a proper measure, as two of them had been looted. Vorotyntsev inspected the town, intent on finding his own way and sizing up the situation for himself even if it meant spending a little extra time, and for this reason he did not ask the way to Corps Headquarters. Outside a little house, which, small though it was, had iron railings, a bench, a fountain and two pillars on either side of the porch, he saw a motor-car made by the Russo-Baltic Carriage Company. This did not look like Corps Headquarters; it was too deserted. But the sight of the car made Vorotyntsev wonder whether perhaps he had found the man he had to see before going to headquarters.

He dismounted and immediately the stiffness in his back made him realise how tired he was. He tethered his horse by the reins to a tree near the car and left his greatcoat strapped to the saddle; no one here paid him any attention, so there was no need to wear the full regulation dress. Bending and stretching his legs, he pushed the wrought-iron gate. It swung open, and he went in.

The basin round the fountain was still wet, so it was not long since the water had drained away. The flowers still stood undamaged in neat rows in their little parched beds. Only as he skirted a bush by the fountain did Vorotyntsev notice someone in the porch sitting on a stone bench with arm-rests carved in the shape of lions' heads—an elderly, rather stout officer, his chin covered in black stubble, his hair unbrushed, smoking a hand-rolled cigarette with a look of displeasure on his face. From his belt downwards he was the complete officer, with wide Cossack breeches, but above that he wore nothing but a shirt; however, although there was no way of telling his rank, there was a definite air of the staff officer about his face and figure. He showed little inclination to move as the colonel approached him.

Without giving a regulation salute, Vorotyntsev merely brought two fingers somewhere near the peak of his cap and enquired: 'Can you tell me, please, if this is Colonel Krymov's quarters?'

'Mm-mh.' The unshaven officer nodded without moving, but with a look of even greater displeasure.

'Are you Colonel Krymov?'

'I am.'

Since the somnolent Krymov clearly did not intend to stand on service ceremony either, the new arrival thrust out his right hand with the palm open.

'My name's Vorotyntsev. I've come to see you.'

Krymov rose just enough to satisfy the demands of politeness—

indeed, being such a ponderous man, his movement was scarcely even sufficient for that purpose—gave a sketchy handshake with his rough hand, drew it back and pointed to the bench beside him. He continued to smoke without the least apparent curiosity to hear any more, although colonels of the General Staff were not exactly frequent visitors in the streets of Soldau.

In no more than the time it took Vorotyntsev to sit down on the bench and mop his brow, he had calculated exactly what manner he should adopt with Krymov: as few words as possible and no mention of rank. He also sensed that Krymov didn't like him. However, he began at once:

'I've come to you from Alexander Vasilich. He told me about you . . .'

'I guessed you came from him.'

This surprised Vorotyntsev.

'How did you . . . ?'

Krymov gave a slight nod towards the fountain.

'Know that stallion. Rode him myself last week . . . How'd you bring him here?'

Vorotyntsev burst out laughing.

'I didn't bring him. He brought me.'

Krymov gave a disbelieving frown.

'You rode? From Ostrolenka?'

Vorotyntsev made a noise meant to convey modesty and to suggest that there was nothing special in that. All the same, his spine had taken a terrible jolting and he could hardly bend his back.

Krymov nodded approval, but his eyes were still narrow as he said:

'Good. But why didn't you come by train?'

'By train? Too dull. This is war, after all!' Vorotyntsev rejoined cheerfully, but he sensed from the slight movement of Krymov's large head that the latter had asked his question out of consideration for the horse and not the rider. 'No, I didn't wear the beast out. And I fed him just before I got here.'

'Quite right.' Krymov nodded more emphatically. 'The train's no way to travel when you're fighting a war.' He took an oilskin tobacco-pouch out of his pocket. 'Have some. It's Ussuri leaf. Good stuff.'

'No thanks, I've given it up.'

'Mistake.' Krymov's eyebrows expressed disapproval. 'Can't fight a war properly without tobacco. Wasn't yesterday, was it?'

'No, two years ago.'

'I meant, did you leave Ostrolenka yesterday?' Krymov explained.

'Oh, I see . . . Evening, the day before yesterday.'

Krymov blinked and nodded.

'And what did Alexander Vasilich say? Has he received my reports?'

'He didn't say.'

'Sent him three. I'm preparing the fourth one now. What about you?'

'I . . .' Vorotyntsev had still not got used to the laconic manner of this rough diamond with his fleshy, rather somnolent features. 'I . . .' Then he guessed what the other man wanted to know. 'I'm from General Headquarters.'

This might be taken as the worst possible recommendation, implying that he had come to check up, to snoop around; otherwise, why had he descended out of the blue?

Again Krymov frowned slightly. 'Right, wash and breakfast. Just got up myself, only came back late last night. Just woken up, sitting and thinking . . .'

'Where were you?'

'With Stempel, cavalry division.'

'Listen, are there really two cavalry divisions in this corps or not?' Vorotyntsev put in eagerly. 'What are they up to? What are they doing?'

'What are they doing? Eating hay! Lyubomirov had some hard fighting yesterday. Took a town, but lost it again.'

They went indoors. The furniture, polished to a subdued glow, the bronzes and marble would have been more in place in one of the best houses in St Petersburg than here in little Soldau. The place was, however, in some disarray: lace, ribbons, coral brooches and combs which no one had bothered to pick up were lying scattered around the floor.

The only occupants of the house were Krymov and his Cossack batman Yevstafii, who popped smartly out of the kitchen when called.

The two officers went into the kitchen. Yevstafii was a tall man, nearing middle age but agile and quick on his feet. He seemed

[159]

fascinated by the innumerable storage jars and boxes of china, tin and wood, labelled with incomprehensible names. He was just starting to cook breakfast and was sniffing and tasting the contents of each of the jars in turn, shaking his head as he did so.

Krymov ordered breakfast for two and showed Vorotyntsev the bathroom, complete with marble panels and mirror. The taps worked, male and female garments were hung up on the back of the door and everything was as tidy and peaceful as it had been when the owners had left two days ago.

'If you don't mind I'll have a shave,' said Vorotyntsev firmly.

His instinct was to shut the bathroom door behind him, but he left it open as he unbuckled his Sam Browne belt, swiftly pulled off his tunic and stood, like his host, in his shirt-sleeves. Instead of going out Krymov came into the bathroom, sat down on the edge of the bath, rolled himself a new cigarette in a single, practised movement and licked it.

Yevstafii brought in hot water. As he wielded his safety razor, Vorotyntsev gave Krymov the details of his mission, although the latter had asked no questions, and told him how he had come to be sent to 1 Army Corps. He realised as he did so that his journey was unnecessary.

He also noticed with irritation that he was not telling Krymov what was really in his mind. Sitting outside on the bench with the lion's-head arm-rests, he had spoken completely frankly, but now, while shaving, he slightly altered his tactics. When he had been told at Army Headquarters that Krymov was already out there on the left flank, he had hesitated; he saw now that he should have taken the hint and gone not to 1 Army Corps, but to General Blagoveshchensky on the right flank. But Vorotyntsev was plagued by an unfortunate trait: he was prone to make hasty decisions and then not alter them in time. Even before reaching Ostrolenka he had decided that he must go to 1 Army Corps, for it was there that he saw the key to the whole operation.

Now neither train nor horse would be of any use to him. He would need wings on his heels if he were to reach Blagoveshchensky in one hour.

He began to feel an increasing respect for Krymov, even for the fact that he was in no hurry to get dressed and don his badges of rank but just remained sitting on the edge of the bath, puffing out clouds of smoke. Any good that could be done at 1 Army Corps

Headquarters would be done by this roughneck on his own, without any help from Vorotyntsev.

Krymov listened to what his visitor had to say, then in his bluff manner said:

'Of course you're unnecessary here. And so am I. That Holy Joe, Artamonov, doesn't accept the Army Commander's authority. He knows that his corps is under the personal care of the Commander-in-Chief, and he's hoping that because the Guards Corps was removed from Samsonov's command 1 Corps will be too. When he came through Vilna on his way here he announced in the cathedral: "Have no fear! I'm going to fight for you!" He expects to spend the war like a tailor's dummy standing in a shop window until suddenly one day it's all over and they start handing out prizes.'

As Krymov sat there swinging his legs and sucking in his cheeks, the bath underneath him reminded Vorotyntsev of a boat without oars or mast. But his very inertia and the cheerless implication of what he was saying actually restored Vorotyntsev's self-confidence.

'All right, then, first of all let's give Artamonov a good fright. I've brought him a written order from Samsonov. If he kicks up a fuss we'll contact General Headquarters direct by telephone. Or rather we won't speak to the C-in-C direct; I know a good man there who will make sure the message gets through to the right quarter. He will have to go behind the backs of both Yanushkevich and Danilov and choose a suitable moment to talk to the Grand-Duke . . . There's no real team-work or clear thinking at GHQ either, you know. They were supposed to have transferred 1 Army Corps to Samsonov's command on the 8th of August, but they haven't issued a written order about it yet. Someone is scrimshanking, as usual. It's absolutely insane—an army corps at the most exposed spot on the extreme flank of the front line and it's not under anyone's command! I hear, by the way, that Artamonov has been in action. Is that right? They say he took Soldau and has pushed on.'

'Pushed on? Think I'll have a shave myself . . . Pushed on? Lying bastard!' Krymov suddenly lost his temper and went red in the face as he waddled up to the mirror and turned round to Vorotyntsev, who had sat down on a very small and ladylike chair. 'He sent a message to Army Headquarters that there was a German division in Soldau. He said that, though, without having done any reconnaissance and without knowing a word of German, even though he claimed to have got the information by tapping some telephone line.' Krymov shook his razor. 'He told that lie so as not to have to attack the town. And it turned out that the only German troops in Soldau were two regiments of *Landwehr*, and they pulled out of their own accord. He had to occupy the town whether he liked it or not, so he told another lie and said he had to fight for it!' Krymov barked angrily from behind a rich coating of lather. 'Now he's saying that the Germans evacuated Neidenburg because he, Artamonov, captured Soldau.'

'What about Usdau?'

'He didn't take Usdau, the cavalry division did. And consequently the poor fellow had to push on again.'

'I see . . . I've never met Artamonov.'

'Who has? Alexander Vasilich hasn't met him either. He was made a general and got his gold-hilted sword for beating a crowd of starving Chinese. Just like Kondratovich . . .'

'Have you met Kondratovich yet?'

'Not likely! He's way back in the rear collecting his corps together. And a good thing, too. Notorious coward.'

'Whom have you seen lately?'

'Martos.'

'Good general, I hear.'

'Good? Him? Terrified of the high-ups and keeps his own staff twitching like puppets. He's ruined the staff of xv Corps, they're all exhausted already.'

'What do you think of Blagoveshchensky?'

'Sack of shit. Dripping wet shit, too. As for Klyuev, he's not an officer, he's a doddering old woman.'

'What's the Chief of Staff like here at I Corps Headquarters?'

'Complete blockhead. Waste of time talking to him.'

Unable to restrain himself any longer, Vorotyntsev burst out laughing.

They went into breakfast. Yevstafii had placed a decanter of vodka on the table, and without asking his guest whether he wanted any Krymov filled two glasses. At the risk of spoiling the frank atmosphere of their conversation, Vorotyntsev declined. He had the un-Russian characteristic of being unable to drink before starting on a job. He only drank when work was successfully completed.

Krymov grasped his vodka-glass in his fist.

'An officer must be bold when faced by the enemy, by his superiors and by vodka. If he can't face all three he's not an officer.'

He drank alone, frowning, but this did not stop him from giving Vorotyntsev more of his views about Artamonov. The fact was that 1 Army Corps was short of two regiments, and all the other units were under strength. Artamonov's conclusion from this was that he could do no fighting at all. He talked loudly and glibly enough, saying things like: 'I shall answer attack with attack!' but he was nothing but a braggart and a liar. What could one do with a liar? Punch him on the nose? That was why Krymov had ridden over to Martos and made him agree to detach a column from his corps and attack Soldau from the east. But then the Germans had abandoned Soldau without a fight.

Vorotyntsev came back to the question of the cavalry. He thought that it was being misused; the task of the cavalry was flank protection and reconnaissance, in particular deep reconnaissance along the whole frontage, but this was not being done. Or else the entire cavalry should be concentrated on one flank to make a short, sharp surprise attack. The strange thing was that all the generals were cavalrymen: Zhilinsky, Oranovsky, Rennenkampf, Samsonov— they were all cavalrymen . . .

'Don't say a word against Samsonov!' Krymov ordered. 'And don't try arguing about the cavalry's role if you don't know anything about it!'

He drank a second glass and declared angrily that the cavalry had given a good account of itself, having been in some stiff fighting and suffered heavy losses. Just try charging at stone buildings or cycle troops! Still, they were being badly handled: their boundaries and centre-lines were always being changed; one cavalry unit had been made to cross a river three times; and they were being given the wrong objectives, such as making a raid on a railway junction somewhere in the rear which turned out to be a blunder . . .

In the end there was no avoiding the Russian ritual—starting with the third glass, Vorotyntsev had to join in the drinking. Both realised what it was that they had in common: neither of them was in this campaign for reasons of personal ambition.

From the cavalry the conversation inevitably turned to the artillery.

'Our experience in the Japanese War taught us that any future war would be won entirely on fire-power, that what we needed was heavy artillery, especially plenty of howitzers. We did nothing about it—but the Germans did. We have a hundred and eight guns

in an army corps, they have a hundred and sixty—and what guns!
In Russia there's always said to be an "extreme shortage of funds"
for the army. Yet although there's never any money for the army,
there's plenty to spare for the Court. They want victories and glory
without paying for them.'

'Yes, the Duma has been up to its dirty tricks there,' said Krymov, puffing out his cheeks and pouring out another glass. 'It's the
Duma...'

'On the contrary!' Vorotyntsev rejoined, springing warmly to
the defence of the Duma. 'The committee of the State Duma has
consistently blamed the War Ministry for not demanding *enough*
funds to be voted in military credits. The Duma has been insisting
for years that we need to increase our artillery and that we're unprepared—and yet the Ministry took eight years to work out an
arms programme. The programme was only approved this May,
and then the Germans declare war a couple of months later. The
people at the top still think that the *spirit* of the army will be the
decisive factor. Suvorov thought so, Dragomirov thought so, and
so did Tolstoy... So why spend money on guns? As for our
fortresses, they're so out of date they almost have unicorns in the
stables! They still have guns which fire black powder!'

None of these arguments had any effect on Krymov, but there
were certain questions on which Vorotyntsev felt so strongly that
he had to speak out—especially after a glass or two of vodka. So instead of going to see Artamonov...

Krymov frowned, though amiably enough; he was unaffected by
Vorotyntsev's heated arguments as he already knew them all by
heart. He merely nodded in agreement as though acknowledging a
law of nature.

Growing more and more amicable, they were soon calling each
other Alexander Mikhalich and Georgii Mikhalich, and before long
they were on first-name terms. This was a stage which Vorotyntsev
was normally in no hurry to reach, but again he bowed to Russian
custom. They put off their departure and sat for a long time over
breakfast.

The talk turned to the looting of German property by Russian
troops. Krymov thumped the table with a fist like a piece of
knotted rope. 'Field courts-martial and a few exemplary execu-
tions!' He had already proposed this to Samsonov.

His point of view was the natural one of a tough-minded,

conscientious, professional army officer. Vorotyntsev, however, put both his hands palm down on the table, stretching his fingers out as far as they would go.

'No. Say what you like, I cannot agree to shooting our own men. Just because they're poor and we've picked them up and put them down in a rich country? Just because we've never shown them anything better? Just because they're hungry and we have failed to feed them for a week?'

Krymov did not unclench his fist but tightened it and rapped on the table.

'But it's a disgrace to Russia! It means the break-up of discipline in the army! If we let that happen, we might just as well not have come here.'

'Well, perhaps . . .'

So that was what he thought. Krymov withdrew his fist.

'. . . perhaps we shouldn't have come at all.'

It struck Krymov now that Vorotyntsev had his weaknesses and his limitations. Clever though he was, he was dangerously infected by the ideas of the intelligentsia, and as far as the army was concerned he was a lost man.

'The way to tackle the problem is a directive from Army Headquarters,' he explained, 'laying down a policy of regular and orderly requisition. We need an effective, mobile supply service.'

'What do you mean—mobile?'

'I mean that it should be up here operating at regimental level. It should round up all the cattle and distribute them to the regiments. It should requisition all the local threshing machines and all the local mills and thresh, mill, and bake the flour and issue it on the spot.'

'But that's pure fantasy, Alexander Mikhalich! The Germans might do that, but we never would!'

Although he said that, secretly he nursed the proud conviction that there were some Russians like himself who had a German sense of efficiency and the Germans' power of steady application, characteristics which gave him an edge over well-meaning but impetuous and erratic men like Krymov.

It was time to finish breakfast, time to put an end to this inconclusive conversation, to go and prod Artamonov forward and make sure that his corps was fully under Samsonov's command. Vorotyntsev had been mentally working out exactly how to get the right man, a colonel, to come to the telephone if he had to speak to General Headquarters. However, Krymov seemed unwilling to get up, as though this morning's talk was all the work he needed to do for one day and it was now time to get some sleep. Of course he would go, he said, and soon. He might also lose his temper with Artamonov and punch him on the nose, no joking.

'Afterwards why don't you go and see where Mingin's division has got to? Has it joined Martos' corps yet?' Vorotyntsev asked casually, not wishing to seem to tell Krymov what he ought to do.

Krymov mumbled something which sounded like yes, but without enthusiasm. He seemed tired by his days in the saddle and obviously found it easier simply to stay where he was.

Suddenly they both heard the unmistakable sound of an artillery barrage opening up.

'Aha!'

'Aha!'

They went outside. It was coming from the north, about ten miles away. The hot air dulled the sound of the distant gunfire.

Knowing Artamonov, it couldn't be he who had opened up. So was it the Germans?

17

___

As Postovsky and Filimonov had insisted, there was no question of the Army Headquarters moving to a new location on August 12th. A whole day was spent in issuing preliminary orders, making preparations and, what was even more important, testing and checking the new telegraph line to Army Group Headquarters, which ran from Bialystok via Warsaw and Mlawa and then on to Neidenburg, using German lines. North-Western Army Group Headquarters would not allow Second Army Headquarters to move further away until it was certain that Second Army was firmly connected to a reliable wire and so always accessible for the receipt of orders and able to send back reports. The move was therefore ordered for August 13th.

The 12th was also a day of strain for Samsonov. Whereas yesterday his army corps had been six days' march away, today they had moved a further day's march forward. Once more a lengthy and detailed request was sent to Zhilinsky asking for a day's halt, which was again refused on the grounds that the enemy was moving away from them and might escape; Rennenkampf, it was pointed out, was still keeping up the pursuit. Information had come in from a reconnaissance by the left-flanking cavalry divisions that a heavy enemy concentration was building up in front of them. This confirmed Samsonov's reading of the situation that the enemy was building up to the *left*. But instead of feeling any pleasure at being proved correct, he was racked with uncertainty over what to do. Common sense suggested that he should wheel all his army corps to the left instead of continuing to push them forward in their present direction, but yesterday's taunt that he was a coward still rankled with him; worn out with quarrelling with Zhilinsky, he was keenly conscious that fighting a war was much more exhausting at headquarters than in the front line, and he was anxious to keep to the compromise solution over the line of advance which appeared to have been reached the day before. He was also much mollified by Zhilinsky's first telegram sent today, congratulating him on the successful action at Orlau; presumably, too, Army Group Headquarters must be in possession of some reliable information if it was sticking so firmly to the order to advance on the present axis, whereas the cavalry reconnaissance could easily have exaggerated the strength of the enemy. Yesterday one division of XIII Army Corps had moved leftward to link up with Martos at Orlau, but instead of staying there it had by now managed to return to its own corps and was moving northward again; psychologically it was almost unthinkable to order it to move to the left again. In any case, to make all the corps change direction was an extremely complicated manoeuvre which would mean halting the advance and might involve the corps supply-trains crossing over each other.

Meanwhile, to Samsonov's great annoyance, the English general Alfred Knox had arrived in Ostrolenka. Nobody knew why he had come; probably to show British goodwill while they spent six months getting their army over to the continent. Samsonov loathed these meetings with western Europeans, with their perfunctory, insincere bonhomie; this visit was especially inopportune, inconvenient and distracting for him. Samsonov had still not found time to sort out the welter of events, thoughts and plans in his badly confused mind; now there would be all the extra trouble of conducting a diplomatic reception.

That evening, the 12th, Samsonov excused himself from meeting Knox because of the lateness of the hour, but he could not avoid inviting him to lunch on the 13th. Before lunch, however, there came some disturbing news from Artamonov, who signalled that strong forces were concentrating in front of him. At once, on an empty stomach, Samsonov gathered several of his staff around a map and came close to taking the decision to wheel all his corps to the left. His staff, however, dissuaded him, reminding him that recently de-trained reinforcements for XXIII Army Corps were marching towards Soldau; these could be temporarily put under Artamonov's command, which would solve the problem of strengthening his corps in face of the enemy threat. Meanwhile the centre corps would continue their present advance.

It seemed a reasonable solution, and a fairly simple one, so it was agreed upon. The necessary order was written, and they went in to lunch. Samsonov had put on his gold-hilted sword. He should have left at once for the new location, but instead they had to sit through a formal lunch with wine, handshakes and speeches translated from one language into another, which made it interminably long and delayed the move. Knox, who looked like a thoroughbred horse, the product of ten generations of selective breeding, was a middle-aged man whose behaviour made him seem even younger; he drank with gusto and his manner was generally relaxed and amiable. The air of informality was helped by the British army uniform, with its open collar in which the neck could move freely and its light, unostentatious shoulder-tabs and badges of rank. Knox, in particular, treated his uniform without ceremony; the pockets of his tunic were bulging with papers and the cross of his high-ranking decoration hung slightly awry.

Samsonov hoped that he would be rid of his guest after lunch, that Knox would go straight back to Zhilinsky, to the Grand-Duke or to St Petersburg—anywhere, as long as he went. But it was not to be. Knox took his seat in Samsonov's car, carrying his waterproof cape rolled up and slung over his shoulder on a strap, leaving the rest of his luggage, as the interpreter explained, to be brought by an orderly with the headquarters baggage.

Exchanging glances with his staff officers, the Army Commander ordered Filimonov not to come in the car, but to give up his place to the British officer and his interpreter, while Postovsky sent a telegram chasing round the kingdom of Poland to Staff-Captain Ducimetière in Neidenburg, telling him to prepare a special dinner and see that it was properly served.

They drove off, leaving the rest of the staff to follow them in vans, charabancs, and on horseback. The Army Commander's open car, with its long protruding bonnet and high steering-wheel, was escorted by eight Cossacks who were far from being picked men: the crack squadrons were all needed in the front-line divisions. The chauffeur kept his speed down so that the eight Cossack lances could keep pace at a fast trot.

What Samsonov needed now was silence; to stare in silence at all these miles of road which his troops had covered on foot and which until now he had never seen: thirty miles from Ostrolenka to Chorzele, then fifteen to Janów and another six or so parallel to the German frontier, finally across the frontier and a journey of eight miles on enemy territory which his corps had won without shedding a drop of blood or firing a single shot.

The day had become stiflingly hot, like all the preceding days, but the movement of the car created a breeze which made thinking rather easier, so that for a moment it seemed possible that the drive might induce the mental clarity he longed for. He did not precisely know why his thoughts were still unclear: all the necessary orders had been issued and were being carried out, yet there was a blur, a kind of undissipated fog of overlapping, unfocused blobs that danced in front of his inward eye as though he had double vision. Samsonov was continually conscious of this and it worried him greatly.

The Army Commander arranged a large three-foot-square map-board on his knees, on which a 420,000:1-scale map of the whole theatre of operations, tightly fixed though it was, flapped slightly in the wind. He had intended to spend the journey glancing alternately at the passing countryside and at his map. Now, however, there was this inquisitive British officer sitting behind him in the back seat, also wanting to find out all he could, looking over his shoulder and even poking his finger at the map-board and demanding explanations for everything. The droning buzz of Knox's voice was added to the chattering of the car's engine and Samsonov gave up all hope of spending the journey alone in calm, constructive thought.

Knox showed particular interest in VI Army Corps on the right flank, because this corps had driven deeper than any other into enemy territory and was now not much further from the Baltic Sea than the distance which it had already covered.

Yes, VI Army Corps should have occupied Bischofsburg yesterday, and by today it was probably already further north.

It was shown on the map as being in that position and for the Englishman's sake Samsonov had to pretend that it really was there; he could not admit to his Allied colleague that Russians marked their maps with information they did not really possess, that not all radio signals reached their destination and that apart from radio there were no means of communication except dispatch-riders, who were highly insecure since they were sent out unescorted across enemy territory. Blagoveshchensky's corps had in fact strayed so far over to the right that it had ceased to act as a flank-guard at all; it was no longer performing a screening role but had become a detached, independent corps, the victim of a quarrel. Fortunately, however, this problem had been raised with Army Group Headquarters, and that morning they had been given permission to move VI Army Corps to the left and to close the gap between it and the centre corps. Yes, it was already on the move—look, there, beyond Lake Daday—and it was heading for Allenstein.

And over there—what about Rennenkampf? Was he advancing? Yes, according to their information.

And was that a cavalry division? Yes, for flank protection.

This was General Tolpygo's division, which had been pushed into the gap, but in fact that division was urgently needed close at hand. Another formation lost to Samsonov.

What could he tell this uninvited guest? That all his units were under strength, and that XXIII Army Corps was still not mustered? That the force under his command was only an army on paper, that in reality it consisted of no more than the two and a half army corps in the centre towards which he was now driving? And that he was not even sure of their positions either?

Knox was now interrogating him *ad nauseam* about the centre corps. Where were they?

Samsonov pointed at the map with his large finger. 'XIII Corps is here . . . approximately there . . . It is moving northwards in roughly this direction, between these two lakes . . .'

'Moving northward?'

'Yes, it's advancing northward . . . towards Allenstein. It should take Allenstein today.' (It should have taken it yesterday, but had been too slow.)

'And what about XV Corps?'

'Well, XV Corps should be level with XIII Corps and also moving northward. Yesterday it should have taken Hohenstein.' (Had it?)

'And today it should have moved far beyond Hohenstein.'

'XXIII Corps?'

The Army Commander should have known precisely when this corps would be fully mustered and put into the front line. As it was, Mingin's division had been exhausted by forced marching to keep up with Martos and had been thrown straight into action. 'Well, XXIII Corps . . . shouldn't be far away . . . It ought to cut this road running north-westwards from Hohenstein today.'

[171]

But what could he say if Knox were to ask him about the Germans? Where were their army corps? How many were there? Which way were they going? An empty, uninhabited expanse of lakes, forests, villages, roads and railway lines was all the information that he had about the Germans; nothing had been seen of them or was known of them except for the attractive booty which they had left behind undefended.

This was the crux of his problem. Every day he issued precise orders to his army corps; he told them where to go, which towns to take, all in conformity with the wishes of higher command. But a vital element was lacking: these orders were not welded into uniformity by a single, clear plan. He had no idea of what he was really supposed to be *doing*. Press on . . . cut roads . . . deny such-and-such objectives to the enemy . . . This was all very well, but what was the overall plan of the operation? Samsonov was just beginning to reach some conclusions in his own mind when Knox interrupted him again: 'What about 1 Army Corps? And what are these two cavalry divisions doing?'

Oh, if only the man would go away! 'They are, er . . . securing the left flank of the operation, providing a firm echellonned flank-guard.'

As a way of damming the Englishman's flow of questions above the noise of the engine, Samsonov took the map-board from his knees and leaned it against the door of the car. His strength drained by all these explanations and by the growing heat, he no longer felt a desire to reflect in private or to study the terrain; he only wanted to be able to doze in his comfortable seat.

The car's speed was kept down to the pace of the Cossack horses. At one point in the journey the escort was changed for a relief troop. Whenever they overtook supply-waggons, a mobile hospital or a squadron of remount draught-horses, they would stop and the Army Commander would listen to the men's reports. In Chorzele and Janów they inspected the town commandant's post, enquiring which units had been left behind, by which formation and with what objective. Once they got out of the car and sat in the shade by a stream. The sun was at the meridian when, with the Cossack escort riding beside them in close order, they drove cautiously and solemnly down the Polish side of a hill, across an old wooden bridge and up the slope on the Prussian side into new territory.

They passed through brick-built villages, every house of which, though solid as a fortress, had been abandoned without a shot. Soon they turned on to the excellent main road running from Willenburg to Neidenburg, which was completely undamaged. This just skirted the southernmost tip of the vast Grünfliess Forest, then it took them across open downland, swooping from hilltop to hilltop; although these did not look high, they commanded a view for miles around.

Knox derived a special pleasure from this journey in being the first Englishman to set foot on enemy soil during the war. On the way he composed several letters home which he was determined to write that evening in a German town. Meanwhile he absorbed as many impressions as possible, as it would be bad style to repeat himself from one letter to another.

Heralded by a powerful stench of burning, Neidenburg rose before them. From a considerable distance they could make out a large white clock-face with wrought-iron hands on a green church steeple, surrounded by a cluster of pink, grey and bluish houses, each with its inscription carved in stone. Before the fighting it had been a neat, well-built town, but now, although fires were no longer burning, there were many traces of damage: the charred, gaping embrasures of trenches, here and there collapsed roofs, blackened walls, fragments of broken glass on the pavement, reeking blue smoke from several unextinguished fires and a general glow from hot stone, tiles and iron which added to the oppressive warmth of the day.

As he drove into the town the Army Commander was met by an officer from the advance billeting party, who ran ahead down the street to show the way. As they turned the corner into the Rathaus square, the house selected for Army Headquarters confronted them; not only was it untouched by fire, it was flanked by undamaged houses. Down the steep steps of its porch a lieutenant-colonel ran towards them, snapped to attention in front of the car and bawled out that the building, the telegraph line, food and accommodation were all ready. He also reported that the town had been burning since the day of its capture, but that the fires were now under control thanks to the efforts of the troops allotted for the purpose. Then came a report from the town commandant, appointed three days previously by General Martos. He also introduced the large, fat burgomaster (the inhabitants, it seemed, had not left but were out of sight).

Driving into the town, they had not noticed at first a distant, incessant sound, muffled and diminished by the hot air, like the busy thump of countless sledge-hammers. Postovsky was the first to stop and listen once or twice, cocking his head to one side. 'It's near.' Too near to the site of Army Headquarters. The town commandant assured them that it was far away. Then it was heard again, this time to the left. The noise indicated heavy fighting. Who could it be? Whilst the Englishman turned away, Samsonov and Postovsky glanced at the map to orientate themselves. From this it appeared that the sound was coming from the left of Martos. Consequently the most likely victim was Mingin's division, the unfortunate half of the still unmustered XXIII Corps. Yet Mingin should have been further forward than that.

They went up the steps into the cool interior. Outwardly very modest in its dimensions, the first floor of the building was taken up by a kind of hall, with carved shields around the walls and a triple gothic window that seemed far too big for the building. Here the table was laid with antique silver and gold-crested goblets, and there was nothing further for them to do but to cross themselves and sit down to eat. (Samsonov crossed himself, although he did not oblige anyone else to do so.)

Throughout the meal blue-grey smoke drifted at ground level between the church and the Rathaus.

And the dull, distant sledge-hammers went thump, thump, thump.

The lavish choice of wine promised numerous toasts, and in pleasurable anticipation of all that were to come Knox rose to propose the first. The Army Commander's preoccupation and a look of sad resignation in his big eyes, certainly not the élan of a man who was winning, had not escaped his attention during the long hours of their drive, and the Allied general felt it his pleasant duty to do something to raise the morale of the Russian generals and tell them how well they were doing.

'You are writing a glorious page in the history of the Russian army!' he said. 'Generations to come will recall the name of Samsonov along with the name of . . . Zuvorov. Your troops are advancing magnificently and have aroused the admiration of all civilised Europe. You are doing a great service to the common cause of the Triple Entente . . . At this fateful moment when help-less Belgium is being savaged by a wild beast . . . at a moment when, not to mince words, a threat is hanging over Paris itself, your courageous attack has made the enemy tremble!'

At which they drained their glasses and from then on there was no avoiding the hail of toasts, which fell as thick and fast as a barrage of shells. To His Imperial Majesty the Tsar! To His Majesty the King of England! To the Triple Entente!

If it had not been for his distinguished foreign guest Samsonov would not have sat down to that lunch. He wanted to get the feel of the ground, to walk round the little town and inspect it on foot. He wanted to put his new location on the map and re-examine his dispositions; to see how near his formations were to him; by what routes they could be reached; which of them were linked to him by telegraph, and where the lines ran. He ought to have been making his own assessment of the heavy fighting to the north-west and have sent someone there to find out about it. He was still nagged by the urgent desire to sit down and think out his many problems and finally decide on a plan and for this he needed a clear head. All the wines he was drinking seemed tasteless. But the laws of hospitality and of courtesy to an ally obliged him to drink and although the wines he gulped had no savour they brought colour to his cheeks and made him feel calmer and slightly light-headed.

Perhaps, after all, he was wrong to see nothing but gloom in a situation where this by no means unintelligent British general was so optimistic. Hoisting his massive body to his feet, the Army Commander proposed a brief toast.

'Gentlemen, I give you the Russian soldier—the soldier of Holy Russia, to whom endurance and suffering are second nature! As the saying goes—killing a Russian soldier isn't enough, you have to knock him down as well!'

Having reported their arrival in Neidenburg to Army Group Headquarters, Postovsky tested each dish as it was carried in by the waiters from the hotel to make sure that it was not poisoned. This done, he would have been quite ready to enjoy the occasion had it not been for the gunfire, which sounded rather too close. He inspected the label of every bottle before pouring out the wines (marked with the names of the various estates, which Staff-Captain Ducimetière translated for him) and, overcoming his usual reticence, responded to the lavish praise of their guest. Yes, they had the Germans on the run all right! Yes, it certainly looked like victory! And if only First Army would advance with the same speed as Second . . .

With the arrival of two staff colonels, an argument broke out and, in the absence of a map, it was at once plain that there were several conflicting points of view. Everybody understood that Second Army was supposed to encircle and cut off the Germans, but the officers conducting the operation had different conceptions of how this ought to be done: should the left wing or the right wing swing round in the encircling movement? It seemed impossible to cut off East Prussia without making a left-flanking movement, but in that case why was their left wing required to stay in position while the right wing swung round?

General Knox, however, took up the main point in Postovsky's argument and deigning to rise (he had the trim figure of a sportsman), he announced as he proposed the next toast: 'The destruction of the army in Prussia will mean the end of Germany! All her main forces are pinned down in the west, leaving her exposed in the east. Once they have taken Prussia and forced the Vistula, the Russian armies will open up the shortest, most direct route straight to *Berlin*!'

The goblets were raised but not yet drained when the Duty Officer, a captain, entered and stood waiting for a suitable opportunity to report to the Army Commander. Nodding to him to approach, Samsonov put down his glass untouched.

'General Artamonov wishes to speak to you on the line, sir.'

Noisily pushing back his chair and forgetting to excuse himself, Samsonov stumped heavily out of the room. He had had a premonition that something was afoot.

His expression changing abruptly, the Chief of Staff followed him across the slippery parquet floor.

The silence of the telegraph room was broken only by the monotonous tapping of the Hughes teletype machine. Samsonov picked up the flimsy tape in his large, white, soft hands.

'General-of-Infantry Artamonov presents his compliments to General-of-Cavalry Samsonov.'

Compliments reciprocated.

'General Artamonov considers it his duty to inform General Samsonov that together with Colonel Vorotyntsev of the General Staff he has today had a telegraphic conversation with General

Headquarters concerning 1 Army Corps' degree of subordination to Second Army Headquarters. The matter will be cleared up at General Headquarters. The Commander-in-Chief's final decision is not yet known.'

(Still arguing about that? Someone was trying to put a spoke in the wheel.)

'General Samsonov hopes, however, that General Artamonov has carried out the request of Second Army Headquarters to position his corps firmly to the north of Soldau to ensure complete flank protection . . .'

Yes, General Artamonov had done that before being requested to. Positions north of Usdau had been occupied and were being held.

Usdau . . . (a look at the map to check).

Had any enemy opposition been encountered when carrying out this move?

No, no opposition had been met yesterday. However, the very large enemy forces which he had reported this morning . . .

'You were sent reinforcements . . .'

'Yes, yes, we have received them. The corps has today been under attack from these large forces, and it is for this reason that General Artamonov has felt it necessary to disturb General Samsonov.'

'Exactly how large are these enemy forces and what is the result of the engagement?'

'All the attacks have been beaten off, and all units have stood their ground with great gallantry. Enemy strength, as far as can be determined, is greater than one army corps, probably three divisions. This has been confirmed by aerial reconnaissance.'

The long, unbroken ribbon of tape passed from the Army Commander's fingers to Postovsky's whence it fell in coils on the floor.

Samsonov lowered his large head and stared at the ground.

Where, if East Prussia was as empty as it seemed, could such a large force have come from? Did this mean that the enemy's East Prussian army had managed to slip out of the trap prepared for it, but without retreating across the Vistula, and was not running away but starting to counter-attack on the left?

Or were these fresh forces recently brought in from Germany itself?

So should he now, this minute, make the whole corps wheel left?

He had to make the decision now.

This minute.

Perhaps, though, Artamonov was exaggerating. He was inclined to be over-excitable. Most likely he was exaggerating.

Artamonov ought to attack at once, without waiting for agreement from General Headquarters ... yet the orders were that he was to stay put, even though he now had one and a half corps.

As the machine ticked over without recording, Postovsky started picking up and straightening the tape to prevent it from getting in a muddle.

'General Samsonov earnestly requests the commander of 1 Army Corps to hold firm in his present position and not to withdraw on any account, as this will threaten the army's whole operation.'

'General Artamonov assures the Army Commander that his corps will not flinch and will not retreat one step.'

18

At about four o'clock in the afternoon Major-General Nechvolodov
was leading his detachment along a stony road towards Bischofsburg from the south. Nechvolodov, surrounded by several mounted men, was riding at a fast walk about six hundred yards ahead
of his detachment, a shamefully ill-assorted collection of units.

Theoretically Nechvolodov commanded an infantry brigade of
VI Army Corps, having held a similar appointment in various divisions for the past six years. He had always regarded this useless
post—placed over two regimental commanders and between
them and the Divisional Commander—as having been created
simply as a means of letting major-generals forget how to command troops in the field, but despite this he soldiered on to the
best of his ability. However, on being posted to VI Army Corps in
Bialystok, he was astounded to learn, only a day before the outbreak of war, that while retaining his post of brigade commander
he was also appointed commander of the 'Corps Reserve'. 'Commander of the Reserve' existed as a tactical appointment, usually
designated *ad hoc* for a particular operation when a reserve might
be created to act as a screening force for the main body in an
emergency, but this was the first time that Nechvolodov had heard
of a reserve being nominated on the very day of general mobilisation. General Blagoveshchensky had done it either because he had
too many generals in his corps and did not know what to do with
them, or because he was making preparations for a retreat before
the war had even begun.

The composition of the reserve, too, was odd in the extreme. It
was made up of the two regiments of Nechvolodov's brigade, the

Schlüsselburg and the Ladoga regiments, to which they had simply tacked on various specialist units: a mortar regiment, a pontoon battalion, a company of sappers, a signals company and seven squadrons of Don Cossacks (including the independent squadron which supplied the escort troops for Corps Headquarters, to which it was permanently attached). This was Nechvolodov's 'reserve'. It was as though Corps Headquarters regarded all these units not as essential auxiliary arms but as a hindrance, as though to Blagoveshchensky's mind they only served to confuse the simple organisation of a corps on purely infantry lines: four companies to a battalion, four battalions to a regiment, eight regiments to a corps. A further delight which awaited Blagoveshchensky on taking over VI Army Corps was something which a corps commander rarely enjoyed. This was a regiment of heavy artillery, equipped with guns of a calibre seldom seen in the Russian army—six-inch howitzers. Having not the least idea how to integrate this unexpected gift into his corps, Blagoveshchensky allotted it too to the reserve. (As an experienced old soldier, he knew that if you were entrusted with a scarce kind of ordnance you were severely taken to task if you lost it. Because machine-guns were so precious, he always tried to keep them away from the forward positions, usually at headquarters or in a mobile hospital.)

Not that Nechvolodov was ever given the chance of mustering his motley reserve force together; in any case it would have been pointless as well as physically impossible. Even the hard core of his force, the Schlüsselburg Regiment, was removed and sent forward, so that his brigade ceased to exist, while he himself was kept in the rear to protect the lines of communication. Now, feeling like a superfluous dummy, he was leading, in the wake of the main body, a detachment which consisted of his Ladoga Regiment (short of one battalion), the sappers, the pontooners and the signallers, but without cavalry or artillery. To make matters worse, Nechvolodov knew that both the divisions ahead of him were also under strength, each having lost a quarter of their effectives on the way; one was short of a complete regiment, the other had shed a dozen or so companies from various regiments.

Nechvolodov did not possess the usual grandiose attributes of a general—the puffed-out chest, the bloated face, the pompous dignity. Slim, long-legged (even mounted on a powerful stallion he wore his stirrups low), laconic, serious-looking and now deep in gloom, he looked more like a dull, unambitious officer permanently stuck in junior appointments.

Until now he had been depressed by the idiotic lines-of-communication work which had fallen to his lot and by the removal of the Schlüsselburg Regiment. Today a further cause for gloom was the behaviour of the normally sensible Corps Headquarters, which had this morning leap-frogged ahead of Nechvolodov to Bischofsburg, soon after which heavy gunfire had opened up ahead of them, indicating that the fighting was uncomfortably close. For the last two hours he had been depressed even more by what he had seen moving rearward from the front line: empty supply-waggons with terrified drivers, Medical Corps vans carrying wounded, a herd of lame draught-horses. As he went on, the wounded became more numerous, now including walking casualties from the Olonets Regiment and the Belozersk Regiment and a few from detached companies of the Ladoga Regiment, amongst them an elderly re-enlisted sergeant whom Nechvolodov personally knew well. Among the stretcher-cases were several officers. Nechvolodov stopped everyone he met and questioned them briefly, trying to piece together from their excited, fragmentary accounts a picture of the fighting which had been going on since early that morning.

As always with eye-witness reports soon after the event, drawn from different sectors and given by men who have not yet had time to compare their accounts, the story that emerged was wholly contradictory. Some said that they had unwittingly spent last night right alongside the Germans, and that the Germans had not been aware of this either. Others maintained that they had been marching along that morning, suspecting nothing, had been attacked when still on the line of march, and had come under murderous gunfire completely unprepared and without time to dig in; what was more, the Germans had fired on them from the flank and not from ahead. A third group said that they had been deployed into line of battle before the fighting began and had even had time to dig in to waist height. Some of the officers thought that they had bumped into the flanking column of some Germans retreating from the east and that we had given them more of a fright than they had given us, but then the Germans had deployed a great deal of artillery and had put down some very heavy fire. We had been expecting them from the east, and orders had been given to send out guard patrols eastward. Others contradicted this, saying that our troops had been advancing northward. The Olonets Regiment had even been deployed facing westward. But as soon as the heavy concentration of German guns had opened up ('Fifty guns' . . . 'No, a hundred!' . . . 'Two hundred!' . . .) firing shrapnel over the tightly packed Russian columns, they had immediately torn great gaps in our ranks and decimated them. At once there was panic and confusion, thousands of casualties, only a dozen or so men left in one battalion. No, said another, our men stood their ground well . . . No, our company of the Belozersk Regiment actually went into the attack . . . How could they have attacked when we were hemmed in by the lake? There had been nowhere to go, the men had thrown off their equipment, even thrown away their rifles and swum for it.

One thing was clear from the conflicting accounts: casualties had been heavy, and some battalions had been completely wiped out (in round numbers, a battalion contained a thousand men). The other fact that emerged was that after two weeks in which they had grown used to neither seeing nor hearing a trace of the enemy they had been advancing carelessly and too fast through unknown territory, without reconnaissance and in some cases without guard patrols. Thus yesterday they had advanced more than three miles beyond Bischofsburg, crossing the Germans' most important railroad, which ran in a horizontal east–west axis through East Prussia, and had marched on in the same disorderly fashion as if they had been at home somewhere in Smolensk Province, with supply-waggons mixed up in the columns of line troops, obviously not expecting to meet any but Russian soldiers in this area. As a result, when the fighting had suddenly begun there was no plan ready, no orders were given. The mass of troops had immediately sensed this and had at once broken up in disorder.

However, not one of the wounded Nechvolodov met came from his Schlüsselburg Regiment, and it was impossible to find out where the regiment was and what had become of it. It was unfortunate that the troops of Nechvolodov's detachment behind him would also meet these same wounded: even on the march they would soon learn enough of the bad news from them.

Already the rumble of gunfire could be heard from the north. In the circumstances, even though Nechvolodov was still behind Corps Headquarters, the time had come for him to send out his own guard patrols.

The heat of the day had not noticeably lessened, but the sun had now passed round his left shoulder and was burning his left ear.

Just as he caught sight of the grey and red spires and turrets of the town, which was undamaged by fire, Nechvolodov saw a cloud of dust approaching from the left along an unmetalled side-road and made out a column of infantry of more than battalion strength together with a battery of guns. They too were moving slowly and without suitable precautions.

Although he was not expecting any enemy from that direction, by rights there should have been no forces on his left at all. This was just the sort of situation in which our troops had been attacked and taken by surprise. A glance through his binoculars, however, showed Nechvolodov that these were Russian troops. The column was led by a mounted officer—a captain, to judge by his epaulettes. His horse was extremely restless, pulling sideways, trying to turn, jerking its head and baring its teeth as the rider struggled to make it obey him. Nechvolodov had already noticed a very conspicuous black and red dog, with large floppy ears, running along the verge. A dog (each company had its own) was a sure sign that this was a unit of General Richter's division.

At the speed that they were going the two men on horseback were due to meet at the crossroads at any moment. Noticing the general and the column behind him, the approaching officer turned his horse—the animal swung round more than was necessary and had to be reined back—and shouted to his men:

'Suzdal Regiment! Halt! Ten minutes' smoke-break! Fall out!'

The officer gave his commands in a cheerful voice without a trace of fatigue, but his men were very exhausted. They did no more than move off the road and, without even removing their greatcoat rolls, stopped only to pile arms before lying down on the dusty roadside grass, although there was a shady wood and clean grass no more than a hundred paces away.

The officer rode up on his restless bay horse, saluted with a flourish and reported:

'Captain Raitsev-Yartsev, your ex'ency! Battalion adjutant of the 62nd Suzdal Regiment!'

As he spoke one gold front tooth showed between his rather insolent lips. The horse rolled its eyes nervously and jerked its head.

Nechvolodov nodded at the horse.

'Not yours?'

'Captured it two hours ago, your ex'ency, not used to me yet.'

'But you're a cavalryman.'

'Was, your ex'ency, until God sent me to the infantry for my sins.'

This captain had the familiar gaiety, the devil-may-care spirit which is such an attractive characteristic of the true regular officer. 'We were born for war', it seems to say, 'and we only live when we are fighting.' The same spirit had once burned in Nechvolodov, but it had been smothered with the passing years.

'Where did you get it?'

'We passed an abandoned estate just down the road with some magnificent stables. I advise you to take a look. Just beside the lake, where it . . .'

Nechvolodov's hand was already tugging at his side and he opened his map-case.

'Aha, that's a fine map. There it is—Lake Daday.' In a whisper he added an obscene word to rhyme with 'Daday'.

Nechvolodov gave a slight smile. 'How did you happen to be there?'

'Because our division marched five miles from there . . . to there . . . We took a little walk, then we changed our mind and we walked back again!'

Nechvolodov could not help liking this cheerful fellow, but the captain's horse was dancing about so much that they found it impossible to look at the map together. In any case the heat was blistering.

'Let's go and sit in the shade,' Nechvolodov suggested.

The gold-toothed captain nodded in agreement, and they handed their horses to an orderly.

'Misha!' Nechvolodov called to his aide-de-camp, a pink, fat-cheeked lieutenant called Roshko whose skin glowed with youth and health. 'Let the column go on, and you ride ahead quickly and see if you can find a road to bypass Bischofsburg. If you can't, choose a street through the town which doesn't lead past Corps Headquarters.' Keen and intelligent, Roshko understood at once and galloped off with a small detachment.

Nechvolodov and Raitsev-Yartsev sat down cross-legged in the cool of the wood, where the general pulled his map from its case and opened it out. Clenching his hand, showing a gold ring on the fourth finger, Raitsev-Yartsev used the long, sharpened nail of his index finger as a pointer and briefly gave the general all his information.

Yesterday their division, with only three regiments instead of the usual four, had taken up front-line positions facing eastward, and the rumour was that the enemy had been boxed in there and would try and break out. However, not a shot was fired. Then they were ordered to pull back to Bischofsburg, where they had hung around waiting all morning. Just before noon the Corps Commander had ordered their division to march westward, to make a loop round the south of Lake Daday and to push on to Allenstein, a distance of nearly twenty-five miles. So without having had time to eat they had set off on their march, meeting no opposition and suffering agonies from the heat. But after they had gone about six miles and had already rounded the southern end of the lake, a dispatch-rider from Corps Headquarters galloped up with a new order from General Blagoveshchensky: they were to return immediately to Bischofsburg and take up a position to the east of the town. Being the last in the divisional column, the Suzdal Regiment had been the first to turn round and had then headed the column on its way back. Meanwhile an officer had come riding up with yet a third order: the Suzdal Regiment only, together with two batteries of guns, was to continue along this route and wait in the vicinity of Bischofsburg at the disposal of the Corps Commander. The rest of the division was ordered to turn northwards up the other side of Lake Daday and to advance beyond the end of the lake until it linked up with General Komarov's division, which was waiting on this side of the lake. It was only by sheer luck that the Suzdal Regiment had happened to be in the rear of the column; if the Uglich Regiment had been given that order it would have had to push its way back down the column past two regiments, and the Suzdal Regiment would have had to struggle on in the original direction.

Raitsev-Yartsev had begun by telling his story cheerfully, as though he had found all this confusion great fun, but Nechvolodov's deadly serious expression soon stopped the gold tooth flashing quite so gaily, and before long his only sign of animation was the pointed fingernail tapping the buckle of the general's map-case.

Their Corps Commander was proving a veritable Napoleon in

the wild abandon with which he manoeuvred. Having no wish to exercise command as though presiding over a charitable committee in the rear, he could now boldly stride about on enemy territory, criss-crossing every inch of the ground as he moved his regiments hither and thither. A quarter of his corps had been wiped out in the centre—so his answer was to send half the corps marching off to the left! He seemed quite fearless; after all, hadn't he formed his reserve even before the outbreak of war? Very well then, now let Nechvolodov get him out of trouble.

Nechvolodov's detachment was now marching past the two officers towards Bischofsburg. Raitsev-Yartsev's battalion was still lying on the grass, the guns halted on the road, while the rest of the Suzdal Regiment had not yet appeared. Nechvolodov ought to ride forward at once to find his Schlüsselburg Regiment and the Divisional Commander, but it was not so easy to re-orientate himself in view of the new information he had just been given. The previously familiar picture was now changing and threatening unexpected developments.

Units were being recklessly detached from their formations or cross-assigned, like the Suzdal Regiment, which had just been placed under the direct command of the Corps Commander. For the divisional and regimental commanders control and subordination had become hopelessly confused. Even if Richter, for instance, did manage to push his way round Lake Daday, how was he going to link up with a division which had already been attacked and dispersed? What had happened to General Tolpygo's cavalry division on the right? Its lancer regiment had already been broken up for use as corps cavalry, while the division's lines of march and objectives were constantly being changed. The Germans, who were supposed to be on the right, had long since disappeared. And what of Rennenkampf on the right? He was enjoying the fruits of victory and saw no need to hurry, especially since to advance would involve such risks. The place seemed deserted—not a sound, not a shot to be heard. And where was XIII Army Corps on the left?

Silence. Empty air.

'Well, thank you, Captain!' Nechvolodov gripped Raitsev-Yartsev's hand with a calloused palm, leapt into the saddle and trotted off with his orderly past his detachment to Bischofsburg.

The Germans had obviously prepared to defend the place. For the last few hundred yards leading into the town the bushes had been cut down on both sides of the road in order to give good observation and fields of fire, and a dozen loopholes had been knocked out of the wall of the first building on the edge of the town, a large, brick-built warehouse.

None of this had been used.

A long column of walking wounded met General Nechvolodov as he entered the town. Instead of cross-questioning them, he merely shouted: 'Hey there! Any of you from the Schlüsselburg Regiment?'

There were none.

The calm, round-faced Lieutenant Roshko was waiting for him at the warehouse. He reported that there was no road leading round the town, but he had found a suitable street and had put up signposts.

Nechvolodov rode off down the narrow, shady streets with their closely-built houses to look for Corps Headquarters.

So many white bandages were to be seen on the streets and through windows that his first impression was that the town was full of Russian wounded. But there were also some civilian inhabitants. One German civilian, by no means old, and then two more, were being led off somewhere under escort. At a street corner a lancer officer was surrounded by a number of German women, all of them urgently talking at once and one after another pointing first at his sword, then at their own breasts. Further on two German women were carrying enamelled buckets and giving the soldiers water to drink and joking with them.

Nechvolodov recognised the Corps Headquarters building by General Blagoveshchensky's car and by the Cossack escort squadron. Roshko and the others remained outside while Nechvolodov bounded vigorously up the granite steps, strode through the arcaded hallway and began looking for the Corps Commander. Everything in the headquarters was packed in boxes and on the move, either because of their recent arrival or because they were about to leave. He failed to find either Blagoveshchensky or the Chief of Staff, but eventually ran into Colonel Nippenström from the Quartermaster-General's branch.

'What are you doing here?' said Nippenström in horror. 'Haven't you joined up with Komarov yet? He's been waiting for you for a long time.'

'I couldn't go any faster,' Nechvolodov replied in a voice even

colder and slower than usual. 'I want to see the Corps Commander . . .'

Nippenström waved his arms.

'I warn you—if the Corps Commander sees you he'll wring your
neck! If I were you I should get out while the going's good.'

'But where am I to go? I haven't had any orders.'

'What? You don't know? Your orders are to muster your reserve
and cover the corps' withdrawal. You'll find them all with
Serbinovich . . .'

'Where is my reserve? Where's my artillery?'

'It's all there, just waiting for you.'

'I've got the sappers, pontooners and signallers with me . . .'

'You can leave them all here!'

'But where's my Schlüsselburg Regiment?'

'Serbinovich knows all that. Go and see him. We're pulling out.
We got too far ahead . . .'

Nippenström was in a hurry. He had to re-transmit a wireless
signal to XIII Corps saying that VI Corps had been attacked by
heavy enemy forces and could not move up to Allenstein in support
of XIII Corps. He had already sent the signal once, and XIII Corps
had acknowledged receipt of it but had sent no signal in reply. VI
Corps had no forces available for the move towards Allenstein, but
to avoid any awkward questions and to prevent Samsonov from
vetoing his decisions, Blagoveshchensky had so far told his staff
not to report this yet to Second Army Headquarters but only to
notify the flanking corps.

In the deep shadow of a pillar between two gothic windows, tall,
thin and motionless as the forsaken statue of a knight, Nechvolodov
stood drumming his fingers on the stone wall.

Some staff officers were packing a large box like a cupboard lying
on its side and pulling it away. No one paid any further attention to
Nechvolodov or questioned him. He went outside and mounted.
As he rode away he listened while Roshko reported that their detachment was already moving out on the road northward and that
the Schlüsselburg Regiment was nowhere to be found.

Just then a noise was heard outside Corps Headquarters, and
Nechvolodov looked round. The car had started up. General
Blagoveshchensky ran diagonally down the broad granite steps,
not seeing Nechvolodov or anyone else on the square. The Chief of
Staff and another officer with an armful of rolled-up maps ran after

him. They got into the car, the doors slammed and it started to turn round on the little square to drive away. Blagoveshchensky took off his cap and crossed himself with a wide, sweeping gesture. As a result of either a jerk of the car or a gust of wind the grey hairs fluttered on his old-womanish head, a head too stupid to be entrusted with the simplest task.

Nechvolodov led his staff out of the town at a fast trot.

19

Standing in the queue at a well, Yaroslav Kharitonov heard a hearty shout of 'Hey! Your honour!' and turned round towards the road.

A troop of four guns was passing and the man shouting at Yaroslav was the bullet-headed sergeant-major, his acquaintance from the incident on the march the day before yesterday (it seemed like a month ago) when Kharitonov's platoon had helped to drag these same guns out of the sand.

'Aha!' Yaroslav shouted delightedly, flinging both arms wide in a boyish and most un-officerlike greeting. 'Want some water?'

'What kind of water? Not moonshine vodka, is it?' asked the stocky, barrel-chested sergeant-major, still as cheerful as before.

'Nice and fresh—come and taste it!' said an infantryman from another regiment standing in the queue. 'They've thrown rubbish on top and there's sand at the bottom.'

The sun was already sinking towards the western horizon, but it was still hot.

'That's right—the Germans threw planks into the well but we managed to fish them out!' Yaroslav shouted. (He was ashamed of his clear, boyish voice but unable to coarsen it.) 'And the water's very decent, we're all drinking it.'

The sergeant-major took off his cap and waved to his men to stop. He had sparse, fair hair and a completely round head, rather like a Dutch cheese only bigger. It was adorned with a pair of bushy moustaches the colour of wheat, waxed at the ends into two points.

The well stood at the entrance to an abandoned farm consisting of several houses set in a large meadow. The troop parked its guns by the roadside, then the drivers fetched buckets of water for their horses while the gun-crews carried a large, tin water-can with a screw cap, evidently German.

Other troops always envied the artillery, as they could carry so much extra baggage on their limbers. Yaroslav envied them for something else. He complained to the sergeant-major.

'Your men are real soldiers, believe me. Mine have come straight from the plough to march into Germany. What can you do with them?'

The sergeant-major grinned smugly. 'Gunnery's a science. Can't use ploughboys in the artillery.'

Distinctly older than Yaroslav, the sergeant-major was such an imposing, solidly built man that the young lieutenant felt embarrassed by his badges of rank and by the fact that, though so much slighter and shorter, he was the senior of the two. He attempted to compensate for this by treating him with unmilitary politeness.

'What should I call you?'

'Why, sergeant-major!' The man smiled, wiping the sweat from his sunburnt face.

'No, I mean what is your name and patronymic?'

'You don't talk to people like that in the army.' The moustaches quivered on his cheese-like head.

'You talk to them like that in normal life.'

'Well, all my life I've just been called Terenty.'

'What's your surname?'

'Chernega.' He was just going to ask in return: 'What's yours?' but stopped as his sharp eyes and ears detected something in the farm buildings behind Yaroslav. Almost without looking for the man and without turning round he gave an order to a bombardier: 'Kolomyka! Something tells me I can hear chickens cackling in that farm. Take two of the lads and go and look for them. Take Chuval with you, he'll know how to deal with them!'

Yaroslav was surprised and annoyed that this model NCO should be sending his well-disciplined artillerymen scrounging. If they indulged in it, how could the other troops be prevented from looting? He warned them: 'The farm has been cleaned out. The inhabitants have gone and they've wrung the neck of the last cockerel. I did see some apples in the orchard, though.'

They could see from where they stood that troops were already roaming about in the orchard, and although no one had asked or been given permission, others were drifting in that direction too. None of them, however, were men from Kharitonov's platoon, who were so exhausted that they were glad enough to lie down where they were until told to move again.

But Chernega was not to be put off. 'Maybe, but I still think there's something worth scrounging on the far side of the orchard. Take a couple of buckets and see if you can't find any corn-bins. If there's any oats, give me a shout and we'll unharness the horses.'

Chernega made his arrangements confidently, without asking his officers. However, noticing the indignant look on the good-natured face of the freckled young lieutenant, he said in explanation:

'There are two things the artillery can't do without—oats and meat. Without them the horses can't pull the guns and the gunners can't pick up the shells. With a nice bit of roast goose under my belt I'll fight anybody's war!'

Having added this last remark as an afterthought, his face gleamed at the notion of roast goose, and the way he said it made the wish seem perfectly right and proper. On the other hand, if everybody took this attitude . . . The thought worried Yaroslav.

'Your soldier's as decent a man as the next, it's only his uniform that makes him into a scrounger,' Chernega added consolingly. 'They call us *light* artillery, but in battle order one of our guns weighs two tons. And a shell weighs nearly eighteen pounds—just you try slinging one of them about.'

Kozieko was sitting on a large plank on the ground with his legs tucked underneath him, scribbling on his inevitable field message-pad. Eyes and ears permanently on the alert, he gave Chernega a keen and disapproving stare.

The company commander shouted from a distance: 'Kharito-nov! Follow me—hurry up, man!' With two soldiers he galloped past the farm and round the corner at the end of the orchard, in the same direction as Chernega had sent his gunners.

Kozieko watched them go, then turned back to his message-pad. As he wrote he gnawed an apple, frowning with distaste either because it was sour or out of general disgust at what was happening.

The well was concreted and the wellhead above it threw a long shadow on the ground. Clanking and banging it inside the concrete shaft, the men raised and lowered the single bucket, turning the windlass and winding the chain on to it with a swing of their strong arms. As soon as the bucket was up they poured the water into billy-cans or buckets, jostling and hurrying, swearing at each other for clumsiness or for trying to grab a mouthful of water, upsetting buckets and splashing water until the ground was turned into mud, then pushing forward the empty billy-cans again in search of a fresh fill. The gunners carried their buckets at a run but without spilling them, to offer water to the big, soft mouths of their bridleless horses. The other soldiers complained that no well was deep enough to fill the gunners' great tin cans. To them it seemed unfair to stock up with water for future use; everyone ought to take as much as they could drink here and now and make do with that. '. . . And don't use it to wash your faces with either, you blockheads—if you want to wash, go to the lake and stick your head in there!'

With all the noise, bustle and cursing, the unceasing background rumble of gunfire to the west had become so familiar that the men no longer heard the sound of battle. The fighting was not many miles away, but they were separated from it by countless lakes. All day, as they marched, there had been lakes on their left side, big and small ones, close at hand and far away, and whatever the intentions of the higher command may have been, their line of march had been forced to veer northward, safely cutting them off from the nearby fighting.

There were also lakes to the right. An hour ago they had wound their way along a narrow, wooded, quarter-mile isthmus between two large lakes, Lake Plautziger and Lake Lansker, so wide that the unaided eye could only dimly see the far side. They had moved so rapidly down the long, deserted, wooded corridor between the two lakes that even though they were now well clear of them, their division was vulnerable only to another force making its way down the same corridor, and there was no sign of any such force.

A man brought Terenty some water to drink. It was so cold that it hurt the throat, and it was muddy, but the thirst in his gut seemed unquenchable.

Chernega sat down on the same plank, inviting Yaroslav to sit beside him. He pulled a tobacco-pouch from his pocket and untied the twin ribbons.

'When I put tobacco in my pipe I smoke away all my troubles. Don't you smoke, your honour?'

A.–9

His initials 'T.C.' were carefully emboidered in elaborate curling letters on the black silk of the tobacco-pouch.

'Sounds as if the earth's groaning, doesn't it?' Chernega remarked as he looked in the direction of the setting sun. 'Yet we march along without patrolling the woods and I bet you there are Germans sitting up in those fir-trees watching us with binoculars and passing back messages on their little telephones. Why, there's probably one sitting up there now ringing up and telling the German headquarters about us, telling them we're drinking water,' Terenty said with conviction, looking towards the edge of the forest. All the same, he seemed quite unperturbed by this alarming idea, made no effort to run to investigate and showed absolutely no signs of excitement, either from laziness or from the confidence bred of great strength.

Lieutenant Kozieko, however, raised his head with a worried look and said:

'And what about guarding the flanks? We've been moving at such a pace that it's all our flank patrols can do to keep up alongside the main column, and sometimes we even overtake our forward patrols. We could easily be enfiladed by one man with a machine-gun.'

'The worst thing,' Kharitonov added in an anxious voice, 'is not knowing anything. We've already covered ten miles today, and they say we've got to do another six by evening. The only news available is what you can pick up from the regimental commander's batman. There was a rumour going around this morning that a Japanese division was coming to reinforce us!'

'Yes, I heard that nonsense.' Chernega nodded, puffing contentedly. The overwhelming strength and confidence he exuded seemed almost excessive.

'What rubbish! How could a Japanese division get here? Perhaps they mean a Russian division posted from the Far East.'

'Others say that Kaiser Wilhelm is in command of the German army in East Prussia,' Chernega put in, apparently quite undisturbed by the thought.

Kharitonov was strongly conscious of Chernega's common sense, kindness and experience. Although an officer was not supposed to complain to a sergeant-major about the stupidity of the higher command, he could not help saying: 'And what happened the day before yesterday? They made us march twenty miles in one direction and twenty miles back again for no reason at all. I realise that the situation might have changed and we weren't needed once we got there, but they might at least have sent us back by a shorter route. Why did we have to go back all the way through Omulef-offen? We could have got here without going through Omulef-offen again, and we would have had a day's rest like the other division.'

Chernega nodded calmly and understandingly as he smoked his pipe. It was his imperturbable acceptance of everything that Yaroslav particularly wished he could acquire.

'And did you hear that rifle-fire an hour ago?' put in Kozieko. 'It could easily mean that the Germans have broken through at the rear.'

Chewing the stem of his pipe, Chernega said out of the corner of his mouth: 'What's he writing about? He's not noting down what we say, is he?'

Yaroslav laughed.

'Are you a regular?' he asked.

'No, I'm not such a fool.'

Although it was set at a very jaunty angle, his cap was firmly planted on his round head.

Yaroslav did not know how to ask what he longed to find out: what sort of a man was this sergeant-major? How was he to place him?

'Er, are you . . . from the town or the country?'

'Well . . . I suppose you'd say I come from the country . . .' Chernega answered haltingly and grudgingly.

'From which province?'

'Kursk, I suppose . . . or Kharkov.' He frowned.

Yaroslav was reluctant to leave this cheerful giant of a man, but he did not know how to talk to him properly.

'Married, children?' he enquired affably, his manner almost supplying Chernega in advance with an affirmative reply.

Chernega looked at the lieutenant and rolled his round eyes.

'Why bother to get married if your neighbour's got a wife?'

At that moment the bombardier who had been sent scrounging came running up at full tilt and reported to his sergeant-major in a whisper, so that the others should not hear:

'There's oats here! And smoked ham! And a beehive! The owner left this morning. There's only one watchman, a Pole, and he says take what you want. I've put sentries on the farmhouse. Better hurry. The infantry have already started grabbing the horses and killing the chickens.'

Instantly Chernega came to life and with a businesslike air jumped up on his short, powerful legs. This was just the news he had been waiting for. He shouted to his men: 'Come on, lads! Harness up! Look lively! Get moving!' Turning to Kolomyka, the bombardier, he said: 'You lead the troop and I'll go and tell the captain.'

Under its jaunty peaked cap Chernega's sweaty cheese of a head radiated decisiveness and self-confidence.

All pulling together, the men dragged the guns to the bend in the road by the orchard, where they stopped and hitched on the ammunition limbers.

Just then a couple of two-horse chaises and a sprung four-wheeler came trotting merrily towards them round the bend from behind the orchard. The watchful Kozieko, who never missed a thing, glanced at them from a distance, recognised them and said at once: 'There you are—first the battalion commander and now the company commanders are trotting around in chaises and the chaplain has found himself a four-wheeler. They have so many soldiers acting as coachmen that soon there won't be anybody left to do the fighting.'

'That's just fine!' said Yaroslav angrily. 'You're not much better. Why did you pinch those apples?'

'Oh, the devil led me astray,' said Kozieko throwing away his uneaten apple without regret. 'I don't need anything from Germany, except to get out of the place alive . . .'

'You'll survive, I'm sure you will!'

'Why do you think so?' Kozieko looked up hopefully from his note-pad. 'A direct hit's not very likely, of course, but all this shrapnel . . .'

'God helps those who help themselves! I expect you'll be sent off to buy cattle. Go on, put your notebook away and make your platoon fall in.'

The sun was now well down in the sky and even if they did not go into action that day they were bound to go on marching and marching until long after dark. Another battalion had come to the well, and the leading companies of theirs had already fallen in and were marching off. Yaroslav called to his platoon to fall in.

As they slogged forward the sweating, grumbling infantry were overtaken and pushed aside by several mounted staff and senior officers escorted by half a dozen Cossack cavalrymen, two of whom wore fresh bandages. The leading officer, a grim-looking, unshaven colonel, stopped his horse and looked at Kharitonov. The slim, keen young lieutenant ran up, snapped to attention and reported.

At that moment from the far side of the orchard there came the faint but distinct squeal of a pig.

'Are those your men looting, Lieutenant?'

'No, Colonel! My men are here.'

'Then why aren't you marching? Where's your company commander?'

Kharitonov turned his head, but the company commander's chaise had disappeared.

'I'll go and find him,' he said hastily.

'You'll be punished for this,' the colonel said, but automatically and without malice. 'Don't you realise that you are under orders to make a forced march? You've got to reach the railway line today and then advance a further five miles along the line to the right. And you spend your time messing around at this well. Where's the battalion commander?'

'Up ahead, sir.'

This news made no sense to Yaroslav. If the Germans were supposed to be on the left, why were we turning away to the right?

The mounted men set off again. Probably even they could make no sense of all this confused movement in the forest among the lakes.

The officers were from the headquarters of XIII Army Corps. An hour ago they had narrowly escaped death when they had come under heavy fire from their own infantry, who had mistaken them for Germans. To prevent it happening again (on the previous day one of the staff cars had also been knocked out by rifle-fire from Russian troops) they had brought an escort of six Cossacks whose cavalry lances would make them conspicuous; but in spite of this some Russian infantry had mistaken them for a German advance guard and had opened fire on them at two hundred yards' range.

They were on their way from Army Headquarters with the latest orders, which were that their corps should speed up its advance on Allenstein. But meanwhile VI Army Corps, lost far away to the right, had sent back an unexpected wireless signal, which was obviously important because it had been transmitted twice in succession. Unfortunately XIII Army Corps Headquarters had been unable to decipher it because the code did not seem to fit, so no one there knew what to make of it.

The mounted party stopped when it reached the guns, having caught up with two of the battalion commanders, to whom the colonel gave an angry lesson in how to conduct a forced march.

Two or three miles further along the forest road ahead of the regiment they came across two German civilians laid out by the wayside, who had been disfigured by blows and run through with lances.

'This is your men's work, I have no doubt,' the colonel said to the senior Cossack sergeant, who had been wounded when they were fired on by their own infantry.

The sergeant shrugged his shoulders and said nothing as his jaw was bandaged.

From a lone house nearby poured a column of thick black smoke, foretelling the imminent outbreak of fire.

20

When Nechvolodov arrived at five o'clock in the afternoon, the
Divisional Commander, General Komarov, who had been waiting
for him, directed him to take up positions and hold them, adding
that further orders would follow in writing; Komarov and his
staff then disappeared in the wake of Corps Headquarters. He did
not use a map to describe Nechvolodov's task, but simply waved
his hand through the air, saying that today's advance from the
north by the Germans was 'highly unexpected', that he was
not even certain whether this represented the main thrust and
that it might only be a wheeling movement by their flank, but
at all events the Belozersk Regiment was holding a defence
line to the north and must be relieved. He then begged Nechvolodov not to mistake half of Richter's division for Germans
and fire on them, as they were marching around Lake Daday from
the west and were due to arrive at any moment to reinforce him.
The divisional Chief of Staff, Colonel Serbinovich, was not only unable to give Nechvolodov any information on the disposition and
strength of the enemy, but could not even tell him anything of the
whereabouts and fighting strength of the remaining Russian units.
Assuring him that a heavy artillery regiment and a mortar regiment
were already in position well forward, he then announced, without
giving any reason, that he was withdrawing one battalion of the
Ladoga Regiment. Meanwhile he could say nothing definite about
the Schlüsselburg Regiment, which had been deployed eastwards
during the previous night, nor could he say exactly where the
Divisional Headquarters would next be located, promising only to
send him regular dispatch-riders.

They disappeared so quickly that Nechvolodov did not even

notice them going. A lieutenant from the Belozersk Regiment, who happened to pass by, reported that he had just seen their regimental commander getting into a car with General Komarov, and that they had driven off towards Bischofsburg. Asked about his regiment, he said that the Belozersk had suffered heavy losses that morning and had just received orders to withdraw completely; however, two of their battalions were still in their forward positions.

So Nechvolodov, left with only two battalions of the Ladoga Regiment, pushed on in search of his artillery. Cautiously, using patrols, he moved along the undamaged railway line to Rotfliess station, where a curving branch line merged smoothly with the main line and where, behind a wood, he actually saw a battery of 4·2-inch guns in firing positions, and slightly further on a battery of 6-inch howitzers. The remainder were presumably in position somewhere nearby.

The tense feeling in the general's chest relaxed.

Hardly had Nechvolodov reached the stone-built shelter on Rotfliess station than he was met by the commander of the mortar regiment, a man with curled black moustaches, and the commander of the heavy artillery regiment, Colonel Smyslovsky, who was short, with a head so bald that it shone in the sunlight, but also had a long, greyish-yellow beard like a magician's and an air of great confidence.

Nechvolodov had seen both men perhaps a couple of times in the past few weeks, but now he was particularly struck by a joyful gleam in the colonel's eyes, as though he had done nothing but wait for this opportunity to go into action and was positively beaming at the chance of firing his guns. (At least they now had the consolation that they were not going to leave their carefully prepared positions.)

'Is your regiment all here?' Nechvolodov asked, shaking him by the hand.

'All twelve guns.' Smyslovsky nodded.

'Ammunition?'

'Sixty rounds per barrel. And there's more in Bischofsburg which can be brought up.'

'Are they all in firing positions?'

'Yes, all of them. And all linked by telephone.'

The practice of linking the forward observation officers with the concealed gun positions was still something of a novelty, and not all artillery officers knew how to do it properly.

'And did you have enough telephone equipment?'

'Enough to run a line here as well. The mortar regiment helped us.'

Nechvolodov enquired no further. There was no time to go into details, but he did notice the mortar colonel stroking his curled moustaches with a satisfied expression.

'And how much ammunition do you have?'

'Seventy rounds per barrel.'

All the rest was so obvious that it was left unsaid: that they would fire, that they would not retreat without orders. Nechvolodov was greatly heartened by having such good guns, such good commanding officers—and a telephone link to boot.

The need for rapid action was now acute. Within the space of a few minutes he had to grasp the lay-out of the ground, determine the enemy's positions and his own, select a defensive line to be occupied by the Ladoga battalions, agree with the gunners on a common observation-post, pay out the telephone wires, and shoot in the guns by registration fire on fixed targets. If within those few minutes mistakes were made in organising, selecting or dispatching, and the orders were given in the wrong sequence or incorrectly, then they could not be put right within the next half hour, and if in that half hour the Germans attacked or started firing, then the men's keenness, their good telephone communications, and their sixty rounds per barrel would all be useless; they would simply have to run for it.

It was one of those moments in war when time contracts to an explosion, when action must be instantaneous and nothing can be put off.

'We must do something about the water-tower,' Smyslovsky declared. 'We shot in on all the more distant registration-points, but then the enemy moved further forward.'

Without a word Nechvolodov ducked his head under the low doorway of the shelter and went out, followed by the two artillery officers. They ran across the tracks, hot and smelling of warm train-oil.

Nechvolodov called up one of the battalion commanders (his regimental commander had left with the others, but he would have been superfluous anyway) and ordered him to move immediately to relieve the Belozersk battalion, adding that if he thought their position had been badly chosen he was to select another and dig trenches, even if only shallow ones, if he and his men wanted to stay alive.

A faint crack was heard from behind a distant wood, the sound drew nearer and a German shrapnel shell burst in a yellow cloud ahead of them, slightly above the water-tower and to the left of it.

'They've fired a few rounds in this direction already today,' Smyslovsky said approvingly. 'But we don't fire back and they soon stop.'

As they climbed up the wooden ladder inside the water-tower, Nechvolodov untangled the strap of his binoculars. At the top of the ladder there was a platform which commanded a view to the west and to the north. Some signallers with a couple of hand-cranked field telephones were already sitting there. No observation was possible at the moment through the westward-looking window as it was glazed and the yellow light of the setting sun was blinding, but there was a good view from the northward window as the panes had been smashed and there would be no flash of light from binoculars to draw the Germans' attention.

They spread out the map on top of a chest against the wall near the telephones. All they knew of the situation was what they could see with their own eyes and what they could piece together in their imagination.

The Germans lobbed over one high-explosive shell, then another —probably also registration shots. There was movement and troop concentration on the other side of the main line towards Gross-Bessau, also along the edge of the wood, but no enemy column or skirmishing line was to be seen moving in their direction. At any moment, however, they might start coming.

'Are any of our troops still left up there, towards Gross-Bessau? There's no danger of firing on our own men, is there?' said Nechvolodov.

'I am assuming that there are none,' Smyslovsky reported.

'There were—plenty,' said the moustached mortar officer in a serious voice. 'There were too many of them, that's why they had such heavy casualties.'

It was true: there had been no dead bodies on the way to Rotfliess. Plenty of Russians were lying dead between Rotfliess and Gross-Bessau, but they no longer exactly answered to the description of 'our troops'.

'The sun on our left—perfect for firing northward!' said Smyslovsky. 'There's a German trig. point on a little hill just up there. How I'd love to knock it out!'

Just then a German battery fired a few rounds from the direction of the lake to their left. This meant that there must be some German infantry there too, and therefore that General Richter's division could not get through. Nechvolodov ordered the second Ladoga battalion to take up a position facing west and to divide the regimental machine-gun detachment between its two flanks. Now he had no more men left. To the right, extending from north-east to east, a complete sector was still unmanned, but there was no one to put there. Serbinovich had removed a battalion of the Ladoga Regiment without saying why and Nechvolodov had tacitly allowed it to go. There had been a time when as a young man he had hotly contested everything, but after his long years of service, frustration had tightened the skin around his cheekbones and he had learnt to be silent—when to shut his mouth, and how to keep it shut.

Besides, the lances of Rennenkampf's cavalry might appear on the right at any moment. As in the Japanese War, however, the cavalry were doing little of the real fighting: it seemed to be the policy to conserve them, and commanders were praised when they did so. There was not a sign of life from Rennenkampf. This being so, Blagoveshchensky had probably done right by withdrawing. If Rennenkampf's army was immobile and out of touch far to the right, who was there for Blagoveshchensky to link up with?

If Second Army's advance into Prussia could be likened to the head of a bull, then this detachment at Rotfliess station was the tip of its horn: it had driven two-fifths deep into the body of East Prussia. By holding Rotfliess station they were cutting the main one of the two railway lines by which the Germans could move laterally across Prussia; obviously the station was vital to the Germans. Therefore the sensible thing would have been to send the whole of VI Army Corps here.

However, Nechvolodov and his men could at least be grateful that they were spared the intolerable interference from the pack of fools which made up the Corps Headquarters. Their tiny, vulnerable force now constituted the tip of the horn; the most they could do was see that they didn't make any stupid mistakes.

Two battery commanders appeared and began shouting orders.

If only they could find someone to man the right-hand sector they might be able to hold out until dark.

From their vantage-point they could see movement as the Belozersk Regiment pulled back, the infantry marching and horse-drawn carts moving along the edge of the wood on the far side of the station. The German gunfire had grown more intense and the retreating troops were glad to get out of an untenable position.

As Nechvolodov climbed down from the water-tower a tall officer with a desperate expression on his clean-shaven, fleshy face came bounding towards him with huge strides. His last bound brought him up short in front of the general; he flung his arm up in a sweeping salute that ended almost behind his ear and reported in a booming bass voice: 'Lieutenant-Colonel Kosachevsky, battalion commander, Belozersk Regiment, reporting, your excellency! We think it's a disgrace to leave you here. Please give us permission not to withdraw!'

Badly off balance, the colonel staggered and almost fell on top of the general, the look of desperation still flashing from beneath his spruce eyebrows.

Nechvolodov looked at him as though he did not understand. Then his mouth twisted into a harsh grimace and he growled:

'Well, hm . . . I suppose . . .'

And his long arms embraced Kosachevsky just as the man was about to fall.

The long, thin line of troops continued retreating into the distance, waggons swaying, men hobbling, limping, and marching as best they could.

Could these men really want to stay? Or was it only the officers who wanted to—perhaps only Kosachevsky himself?

'How many are you?'

'Well, we've been badly knocked about. But we still have two and a half companies.'

'Right, turn them round. I'll show you where you're to put them . . .'

Already single rounds were whistling cheerfully through the air as the Russian guns fired their registration shots, while German high-explosive shells bursting in black fountains of earth began throwing up deadly steel splinters. Soon the Germans were firing in salvoes, quickly answered by battery fire from the Russian guns—

four at a time from Smyslovsky's men and six at a time from the mortar regiment.

Rubbing his hands and dancing with joy, the bald, bearded colonel greeted Nechvolodov on top of the water-tower:

'We've hit it, General! We've knocked out their trig. point!'

But Nechvolodov did not have time to congratulate him. There was a roar like a gigantic tree falling and a hideous whistle came towards them.

The water-tower shuddered and was enveloped in a cloud of dust.

21

When the guns fire, it is obvious without reconnaissance that the enemy is not running away but is in strength. When the guns fire, the imagined strength of the enemy grows in proportion to the force and volume of the noise.

Over there, on the other side of the woods and hills, one imagines the threat of massed ground forces—a division, perhaps, or even a corps.

And then again perhaps the enemy troops are not so strong. Perhaps they are only two under-strength battalions, one of them badly knocked about, whose entrenching tools have only just started to chip the ground as the men dig themselves fox-holes.

But in order to create this effect the artillery must know its job. It must not run out of ammunition, and it must be well positioned so that the gun-pits cannot be spotted, either by smoke or flash, in sunlight or at twilight after the sun has set.

Smyslovsky and the colonel commanding the mortar regiment saw to all these things, as Nechvolodov had expected, having summed them up at first glance as born commanders. And if a man is a born commander, more than half of the success of a military operation depends on him. Nechvolodov had sensed, almost at birth, that he too had a natural gift of command. It was this which had encouraged him at the age of seventeen to leave the military academy of his own free will, to volunteer for regular service and to earn his commission from the ranks no later than his contemporaries trained in the hothouse atmosphere of the cadet school. He had then immediately started studying for entry to the General Staff Academy, from which he passed out at the age of twenty-five not only at the top of his class but having earned accelerated promotion for outstanding competence in military science.

Today fortune had happily brought these three men together, adding Lieutenant-Colonel Kosachevsky for good measure, and with their miserable little handful they had achieved the impossible: in the confined space around Rotfliess station, for a whole afternoon and evening, they had held up a powerful and growing enemy force heavily supported by artillery.

Soon after six o'clock the enemy had begun, after a short bombardment, by advancing on them from the north, not in a skirmishing line but in column of march, so confident were they after their success earlier in the day. At once, however, the two artillery regiments, all twenty-four guns having completed their registration shots, opened up with an oblique hail of shrapnel on the advancing troops from five concealed firing positions, dousing them with black fountains of high explosive and driving them back until they disappeared into the woods and behind the folds in the ground.

Meanwhile the Russian infantry battalions hurriedly dug themselves in while the Germans were halted and silenced.

The sun crawled slowly down to the horizon.

It is the natural instinct of every born commander to be prepared to hold on and not to retreat, to regard each particular engagement as the fight of his life, as the culmination of his military career. And thus they held their ground that day, forced to it by the enemy, by their disposition, by circumstances. Even so, they would greatly have preferred to have been given orders telling them how long they were to stay there, whether they were going to be reinforced and what further action they should take. No such orders came. The promised dispatch-rider never arrived; no one brought instructions or information, no one even came to see if they were still alive. Having made their hasty withdrawal, the Corps and Divisional Headquarters seemed to have forgotten about the men they had left behind as reserve—either that, or the headquarters themselves had ceased to exist.

At twenty minutes past six Nechvolodov sent a signal to the Divisional Commander asking for further instructions. Without knowing properly where to go, an orderly was sent off with the message.

The Germans spent some time observing and regrouping. They inflated and started to send up a captive observation balloon, which would undoubtedly have pinpointed all the Russian batteries, but something went wrong and it did not go up. They then opened fire from three positions simultaneously, smashed what was left of the water-tower and destroyed all the station buildings, but not before Nechvolodov and his staff had taken refuge in a solid stone cellar. Finally, the Germans cautiously started pushing out skirmishing patrols from the extreme limits of their positions, but at this the Russian batteries, still unlocated and undamaged, opened fire along the boundaries of the German position, while the mortars brought down a barrage of indirect fire on their troops concentrating out of sight behind cover.

The sun set behind the lake, whence there soon rose a delicate new moon. The Russians who observed it saw it over their left shoulder, the Germans over their right.

It grew bitterly cold as the dusk turned into a starry night. With the fall in temperature, the reek of explosives and the smell of destruction were quickly dissipated and carried upwards. Everyone put on their greatcoats.

Around eight o'clock the Germans fell silent, either from a general human inclination to regard the evening as the end of the day's efforts or because their preparations were not yet complete. Orders were at once given for everyone to be fed with a combined lunch and supper, which was already cooked and waiting. The infantry battalions were ordered to post forward pickets, and Nechvolodov climbed up on to the ruined wall of the station to catch a last look at the terrain in the final moments of grey twilight. While he could still read the face of his watch, he realised to his amazement at eight o'clock, and again at a quarter past eight, that three hours had passed and no one had come from Divisional Headquarters.

Carefully picking his way down from the ruined wall and into the cellar, where his long shadow stretched behind him to the very top of the vaulted ceiling, Nechvolodov squatted down on his haunches beside a small candle and on his knee wrote a message to the Divisional Commander:

'20.20 hrs. Rotfliess Station.

'Situation now quiet. Unable locate your position' (how else was he to imply 'you've run away' to his superior officer?). 'Holding position Rotfliess Station with two battalions Ladoga Regiment' (he could not mention Kosachevsky's battalion; the latter had disobeyed orders by not withdrawing). 'Am trying make contact with 13th, 14th and 15th regiments' (meaning, without actually saying so, with all the rest of the division). 'Await your orders.'

He went out of the cellar and while he was dispatching a runner with the message he made out the short, bearded figure of Smyslovsky striding towards him in the darkness.

They embraced. Smyslovsky's cap bumped against Nechvolodov's chin. The two men patted each other on the back.

'Not much in the way of good news, I'm afraid,' Smyslovsky said in a cheerful voice. 'We have about twenty rounds per gun left, and the same goes for the mortars. I've sent off for some more, but I can't be sure whether they'll bring them. What on earth is going on in Bischofsburg?'

Should they put the batteries into line of march? That would mean withdrawal.

However, there was something to be thankful for—both artillery regiments had only a very few wounded, and even those were light cases. Casualty returns had just come in from the infantry battalions and they too had escaped very lightly, with far fewer wounded than in the morning's fighting.

He who resists is not defeated. Defeat only happens when you start to run.

'I've been picking up some of the German shell splinters,' Smyslovsky said cheerfully. 'They were firing at us with little small-calibre mortars—twenty-one centimetres apparently. They'll never do any damage with those! All the same, I expect they'll knock out this cellar tomorrow.'

The wounded, coming in from the infantry battalions, were being treated in the blacked-out field dressing-station and sent back to Bischofsburg.

The slight creak of the ambulance waggons betrayed the movement on the road.

Staff and signals officers were walking to and fro, signallers and medical orderlies were talking, and although they kept their voices low the murmur had a healthy, confident ring about it. After their long day's march, in which they had encountered so many wounded and frightened men, all the troops in Nechvolodov's force were heartened by the feeling that they had won the day.

The silent, windless night grew colder. There was not a sound from the Germans. In the darkness the ruins were invisible and the peaceful, starlit sky, in which the young moon had already set, arched overhead like a dome.

'By nine o'clock it will have been four hours since we heard from them,' Nechvolodov said as he sat down on the sloping, curved roof of the cellar. 'Is it nearly nine o'clock?'

Smyslovsky, who had sat down beside him, looked up into the sky, shifted a little and said:

'It's just coming up to nine o'clock.'

'How can you tell?'

'From the stars.'

'But . . . so precisely?'

'One acquires the knack. I can always tell it to within a quarter of an hour.'

'Have you made a special study of astronomy?'

'A good artilleryman has to.'

Nechvolodov knew of the Smyslovksy family; there were four brothers, all four artillery officers, all competent, even learned. Somewhere he had already met one or other of the brothers.

'What is your name and patronymic?'

'Alexei Konstantinovich.'

'Where are your brothers?'

'One of them is here, in 1 Army Corps.'

Nechvolodov felt in his greatcoat pocket for an electric torch which he had forgotten until then. It was a well-made German torch, found that day and given to him as a present by a sergeant. He shone it on his watch.

It was three minutes to nine.

Without getting down from the cellar roof he quietly gave orders for a mounted dispatch-rider to get ready, shone his light on his field knapsack and began writing with an indelible pencil. Directing the spot of light across the paper, he wrote:

'To: General Blagoveshchensky. 21.00 hours, Rotfliess Station.

'My force of two battalions of the Ladoga Regiment, one mortar regiment and a heavy artillery regiment constitutes general corps reserve. Ladoga battalions have been committed to action. No orders received from Divisional Commander since 17.00 hours. Nechvolodov.'

Who else could he write to? And how else was he to tell them in military language that it was now four hours since they had run away to save their own skins, the cowards! Answer, for God's sake! We can hold out here, but where the hell are you all?'

Smyslovsky read it through, then Lieutenant Roshko handed it to the dispatch-rider, who galloped off. Nechvolodov issued further instructions that the infantry battalion were to strengthen their guard patrols.

No more was said. Pulling up his knees and clasping his arms around them, Nechvolodov sat in silence on the sloping cellar roof. He was a difficult man to talk to, although Smyslovsky knew that this general was no mere simple soldier and that he wrote books in his spare time.

'Am I disturbing you? Would you like me to go?'

'No, do stay.'

With that Nechvolodov lowered his head and lapsed into impenetrable silence.

The time dragged on. An unknown factor might easily change the situation, something stirring or moving forward in the darkness. By itself the thought of losing one's life, dying, was terrible to consider, but as long as two thousand men were forced to sit in hiding, abandoned and forgotten in the peaceful darkness among the ruins, it was somehow not so terrible.

The stillness was so deep that the violence and noise of only a short while ago seemed incredible, indeed the war itself seemed incredible. The soldiers hid themselves, concealing movements and muffling sounds; of ordinary peaceful folk there was no trace, no lights, everything dead. The lifeless earth, its features indistinguishable in the dense blackness, lay under a sky alive with movement and constantly changing, a sky in which everything had its place, knew its limits and acknowledged the laws which governed it.

Smyslovsky leaned comfortably back on the curved cellar roof, stroked his long beard and looked at the sky. In this position the jewel-like necklace of Andromeda was spread out before him, stretching towards the five, scattered, bright stars of Pegasus. Gradually this pure, eternal brilliance calmed the anxiety which had caused the colonel to come here, to insist to Nechvolodov that his fine batteries of heavy guns should not be left in firing positions without ammunition and almost without protection.

He lay there a little longer and then said:

'It's extraordinary. Here we are fighting for some place called Rotfliess station. And yet our whole planet earth . . .'

Smyslovsky had a lively, restless, well-endowed mind which could not let a moment pass without harnessing itself to a thought, and putting it into words.

'. . . is the prodigal son of the reigning luminary. It lives entirely off the light and heat given out by its father. But every year they're growing less and less, and the oxygen in the atmosphere is getting thinner. The moment will come when our warm blanket will be worn out and all life on earth will perish . . . If only everyone would bear that in mind all the time, what would East Prussia or Serbia mean to us then?'

Nechvolodov said nothing.

'And what is there inside the earth? Nothing but a molten, superheated mass trying to get out. The earth's crust is about thirty miles thick, something like the thin peel of a Sicilian orange or the skin on a saucepan of boiling milk. And the whole prosperity of mankind depends on that skin . . .'

Nechvolodov still had nothing to say.

'It happened once before, about ten thousand years ago, that nearly all life was destroyed. But it hasn't taught us anything.'

Nechvolodov continued to rest in silence.

There began between them, by tacit agreement, a long suspension of talk. Smyslovsky must have known of Nechvolodov's *Tales from Russian History* which he had written in simple language that peasants could understand, and since Smyslovsky belonged to the educated classes it was most likely that he disapproved of the book. But just as war shrinks to nullity compared with the vastness of the sky, so the difference in outlook between the two men receded that evening.

However, although it receded it did not disappear completely. Smyslovsky had mentioned Serbia just now. Serbia was being attacked by a powerful and rapacious nation and the need to defend Serbia could not be diminished even by comparisons with the stars.

'And then again—what is the origin of life on earth? When people thought that the earth was the centre of the universe it was natural enough to regard all forms of life as being confined to earthly existence. But is this view reasonable when we know, as we do now, that the earth is just a small and insignificant planet? All scholars are baffled by this dilemma . . . Life was brought to us by some unknown force; we don't know where it came from, or why . . .'

Nechvolodov found this line of thought rather more to his liking. Military life, consisting as it did of a series of unequivocal commands, allowed no scope for ambiguities. But when he was reflecting at leisure he believed in two planes of existence, which to him explained the marvels of Russian history. However, he found this a subject on which it was a great deal harder to talk than to write.

He now replied:

'Yes . . . you see everything on a vast scale . . . but I can't see further than the boundaries of Russia.'

This attitude was bad enough; it was even worse that a good general should write bad books and regard it as his vocation. In Nechvolodov's scheme of things Orthodoxy was always right as opposed to Catholicism, the Muscovite throne was justified when it fought against Novgorod, Russian morals were better and purer than those in the West. It was much easier to talk to him about cosmology.

But Nechvolodov had mounted his hobby-horse.

'The fact is that most of our people don't understand what Russia means. Nineteen out of twenty of our people have no conception of the idea of the fatherland. The soldiers simply fight for God and the Tsar and that's what holds the army together.'

But what could soldiers be expected to understand when the officers were forbidden to talk politics? There was an army order to this effect, though it was not Nechvolodov's business to criticise the order when the Tsar had personally approved it. However . . .

'So it's all the more important that the idea of the fatherland should become an emotion sincerely felt by everyone.'

He appeared to be bringing the conversation round to his book, which Smyslovsky found embarrassing as a subject for serious discussion. He, Alexei Smyslovsky, had progressed intellectually far beyond Tsar and religion, but he understood well enough what the concept of 'the fatherland' meant to him.

'Is it true what I have heard, Alexander Dmitrievich, that in the reign of Alexander III you submitted proposals for a reform of the officer corps, the Guards, the service regulations and so on?'

'Yes, I did,' Nechvolodov said glumly and apathetically.

'And what happened?'

His voice dropping to a scarcely audible murmur, he replied:

'One ends up by swimming with the stream. As they all do . . .'

He shone his torch on his watch.

Were the Germans asleep, or were they slowly filtering through the Russian lines, unnoticed by the guard patrols? Or were they outflanking our positions by another route so that they could cut us off tomorrow?

What decision was he to make? Should he act, or wait patiently? What should he do?

Nechvolodov sat motionless.

Suddenly a noise was heard nearby; there was talking and swearing, and Lieutenant Roshko escorted a dark figure up to the cellar.

'General, this clod has been looking for us for five hours. If he hasn't been asleep and he's not lying, he almost walked into the German lines.'

He handed over an envelope, which they opened. The two officers read it by torchlight.

'To Major-General Nechvolodov.

13th August, 5.30 p.m.'

They read it again and Nechvolodov even rubbed the figure with his finger. Yes, there was no doubt of it, it said 5.30 in the afternoon!

'The Divisional Commander has ordered you with the general corps reserve under your command to cover withdrawal of units of the 4th Infantry Division, which is engaged to the north of Gross-Bessau . . .'

'To the north of Gross-Bessau,' Nechvolodov repeated to Smyslovsky in a bored monotone.

To the north of Gross-Bessau! By now that area lay well beyond the area occupied not only by German infantry but by the guns which had until recently been firing on them for several hours, not to mention their captive balloon. There was no one in that area now except dead Russian soldiers who had been lying there all through the hot day after the confused fighting of the morning. What madness could have possessed anyone to write 'to the north of Gross-Bessau'?

Nechvolodov directed the fading beam back on to the paper. What was he supposed to do after Gross-Bessau?

He looked, but there was nothing more. It simply said:

'Signed: Kuznetsov, Captain.

For Divisional Chief of Staff.'

It had not been signed by the Divisional Commander nor even by the Chief of Staff; they had merely yelled something as they jumped into their car or their charabanc to drive away, leaving Captain Kuznetsov to do their work for them and chase after them as fast as he could go, whilst the messenger he had chosen to deliver the envelope could not have been more incompetent.

Nechvolodov shone the beam on his watch and wrote the time of receipt on the signal: 13th August, 21.55 hours.

The order had taken four and a half hours to reach him. In fact it might as well not have been written at all; Nechvolodov had been told almost exactly the same thing at five o'clock by General Komarov himself, and in those five hours Komarov had obviously had no time to spare to consider the fate of his reserve force.

Nechvolodov cocked his head, as though listening, but there was nothing. Only silence.

He said quietly:

'Alexei Konstantinovich, leave two howitzers in position and put the rest in line of march facing south. Tell the mortar regiment to do the same.'

More loudly, he said to Roshko:

'Misha! Ride to Bischofsburg at the gallop and find out yourself what units are there and what orders they have. Find the senior officer and see whether any ammunition is being sent up to our guns. And I want to know where the Schlüsselburg Regiment is. Come back as quickly as possible.'

Roshko repeated the orders succinctly and precisely, leaving out nothing, then ran off and called for a mounted escort. Several pairs of feet could be heard running—then the muffled clatter of hooves on the sandy road started and died away.

An hour and a half ago Smyslovsky had come to say just this— that if the guns were kept in their firing positions without ammunition they would be destroyed. Yet now that he had been given permission to pull out, he regretted having to go. Indeed, the lull provided by this quiet night was quite sufficient for the whole corps to move up here and deploy alongside them. To withdraw meant that all his shooting had been in vain, all those rounds had been fired for nothing and all those men wounded to no purpose.

And the night seemed so quiet, so safe.

After half an hour or so Smyslovsky returned to the reserve force headquarters and found Nechvolodov still sitting on top of the cellar. He leaned against the curving roof beside him.

'What about the infantry battalions, Alexander Dmitrievich?'

'I don't know. I can't make up my mind,' Nechvolodov said reluctantly.

Afterwards it would be easy enough to judge what he should have done. Of course he should have withdrawn as fast as possible! Of course he should have held on as firmly as possible! Perhaps at that very moment they were being cut off. Perhaps at that very moment reinforcements were marching the last few miles to their help. Meanwhile, abandoned by every one of his senior commanders, knowing nothing of what the army as a whole or the corps were doing, utterly uninformed about any flanking units or about the enemy, in the silent darkness, in the depths of enemy territory, he had to make a decision—and that decision had to be the right one!

Not daring to try and influence him, not wishing to hinder him from making up his mind, Smyslovsky stood in silence, leaning his shoulder on the vault of the cellar and stroking his beard.

Suddenly everything changed. The unpeopled darkness sprang to life, although there was not a sound: immensely long, thick, pale and milky, the beam of a German searchlight stabbed out from some high point behind the enemy lines and began slowly probing the positions of Nechvolodov's reserve force like some clumsy, hostile, lethal hand.

The transformation was as total as if a barrage had opened up from twelve heavy guns.

Nechvolodov sprang lithely to his feet and ran to the highest point of the cellar roof, Smyslovsky following him a few leaps behind. The beam was searching them out, moving very slowly, as if reluctant to leave each illuminated, naked spot. It started on the left, near the lake, and it did not have far to go before it reached the station.

Nechvolodov called a runner and shouted to him to give orders to the men of the infantry battalion that no one was to move when the light passed over them, and that they were to keep under cover. The man ran off to pass the message.

The searchlight had changed everything. It was now obvious that only the darkness was holding the Germans back. At dawn or sooner they would advance. If Nechvolodov was to wait until morning he would have to hold out here all next day; if he was not going to wait, then he must pull out at once.

Suddenly a second beam shone out, a short distance from the first and below it, but unexpectedly it did not sweep the same area; it was trained on Nechvolodov's right flank, the sector held by the Belozersk battalion.

How strong could one assume that the enemy forces were, gathered behind those bludgeons of light?

Nechvolodov called for more messengers, stretching out his long arm as he gave his orders.

'Tell Lieutenant-Colonel Kosachevsky that as soon as the searchlight has moved away from them he is to pull his battalion back from their positions, form up and bring them here by the road.'

He certainly could not keep them in position any longer. 'We ought to get behind the station buildings and out of sight,' Smyslovsky suggested.

It was annoying to have to waste time, and they would have liked to be able to watch, but they ran down from the top of the cellar towards the ruins of the station buildings and, with the aid of the torch, clambered over the heap of bricks towards a sloping plank along which they could walk to reach the far side of the wall.

But the sound of hooves from behind stopped them. Nechvolodov recognised Roshko's voice.

They had returned. Although he was panting, Roshko reported in his usual healthy, youthful voice, redolent of his pink-cheeked physical strength:

'There's not a single senior officer to be found in Bischofsburg. I couldn't find the forward echelon of the artillery park. All units are in complete confusion and the houses are full of wounded. No one knows where to go. Some of them have orders to withdraw, others haven't. The Schlüsselburg Regiment has turned up—it had only just arrived in Bischofsburg from the east. They have orders from Komarov to withdraw even further back than we were this morning. Tolpygo's cavalry division was just moving into the town and his orders were to turn westward. Meanwhile Richter's division is retreating from the west with all its waggon-train. The two divisions got hopelessly mixed up and it was impossible to force one's way through the crowd. They won't have sorted themselves out by morning. That's all.'

The searchlight beams slowly probed deeper into the Russian position, then they moved sideways and joined up.

It was a quarter past eleven. For the full calendar day of August 13th Nechvolodov's reserve had held the enemy south of Gross-Bessau. As there were no orders for August 14th, Nechvolodov had to make them up himself. Standing on a pile of smashed brickwork in the ruins of the station, glancing sideways at the approaching searchlight beam, he said in a quiet, almost languid voice:

'We shall withdraw. Alexei Konstantinovich! Pull out the last guns. Both regiments move to the northern outskirts of Bischofsburg. Reconnoitre the position for all eventualities and wait for me.'

'Very good,' Smyslovsky replied. '*Feci quod potui, faciant meliora potentes.*'

He left.

'Roshko! Order to Ladoga battalions: leave their line of defence without making a sound and come here.'

Everyone at the station froze as the deathly white beam of the searchlight moved nearer. Men stood or sat behind houses and trees. Hidden under cover, the horses grew nervous and began champing and pulling at their halters. Orders were given to hold them fast.

It was humiliating to sit there helplessly, without moving, under the motionless light. If the beam did not move they would have to stay there all night. But the threat was even worse when the searchlight moved on.

The beam went out. Everyone moved. Nechvolodov ran down into the cellar and wrote out his last order. Before putting out the candle he took a final, long look at the map.

VI Army Corps was rolling away like an uncontrolled billiard-ball—smooth, round, heedless and unchecked.

It was leaving Samsonov open to an unimpeded blow from the right flank.

*

There was a horn, but God knocked it off.

[*Chapter 22 is omitted at the author's request.*]

[218]

23

(*General Situation up to August 13th*)

The move which General Zhilinsky's feeble imagination had failed to grasp—that he should seize a larger area of Prussia than the region of the Masurian Lakes—would have been quite plain to any German schoolboy after one glance at a map. The entire East Prussian salient, thrust out towards Russia like the stump of an arm and gripped under the armpit by the kingdom of Poland, was exposed to a Russian attack. This situation made it obvious what the Russian plan should be: to amputate Prussia. From the river Niemen in the east, a direction in which the Germans would never dare to attack as this would mean lengthening their vulnerable 'arm', the Russians should push forward a weak diversionary screen to draw off the German forces; the main Russian blow should come northward from the river Narev in order to cut off Prussia at its 'armpit'.

As it was an outlying province, and in view of its unfortunate strategic position, it might have been feasible temporarily to abandon Prussia to the Russians; but it had a special significance: it was the homeland of the Teutonic Order and the cradle of the Prussian monarchy, and as such it would have to be held at all costs.

During the annual war-games, the future situation had more than once been adumbrated by the German high command, who had developed an effective counter-manoeuvre: by using the excellent road and rail network, which had been rapidly improved to meet just such a contingency, the 'German' army had pulled itself out of the trap in two or three days and hit back with a shattering blow at the flank of the main enemy force, knocking it off balance and, in some places, cutting it off.

Certainly, since the Russo-Japanese War the Germans had felt rather less apprehensive; in fact their manual of regulations contained a paragraph which read: 'The Russian command should not be expected either to take rapid advantage of a favourable situation or to carry out any manoeuvre with speed and precision. The movement of the Russian forces is extremely slow and there are long delays in the issue, transmission and execution of orders. When fighting the Russians, one may allow oneself to make manoeuvres which would be impermissible against any other enemy.'

However, even with this assessment in mind the Germans were amazed by the Russian moves in August 1914. The force which attacked from the east was no mere diversionary screen: it consisted of up to nine infantry divisions and five cavalry divisions, including two divisions of the Guards, the flower of St Petersburg. Yet in the south the Russians had not only failed to cross the frontier, they were nowhere near it.

A teasing enigma! Why were the Russian armies operating out of phase? Why wasn't the southern army hastening to overtake the eastern army's timetable and make the decisive encircling movement? Was this to be interpreted as a strategic innovation—were the Russians, in disregard of the fashionable theory of the pincer-movement, just going to push the Germans in front of them and shove them out of the way? Could this be merely a reflection of the simple-mindedness of the Russian national character (*das russische Gemüt*)?

At all events, the Germans must meanwhile strike back at Rennenkampf's army of the Niemen, and as quickly as possible, because a delay in operations could prove fatal. The commander of the Prussian army, General von Prittwitz, threw nearly all his forces into the eastern extremity of Prussia. And he might well have been successful: Rennenkampf, for all his cavalry, was so ignorant of the approach of the enemy that on the day they joined battle, August 7th, he gave orders to his army to take a day's rest; he himself exerted no control over the course of the battle, his cavalry took no part in it at all and each infantry division was obliged to operate independently. Yet on that day the Germans were taught a lesson for having underestimated their enemy. In listing the faults of the Russian high command, their manual of regulations had neglected to mention the staunchness of the Russian infantry and the superb standard of their rifle-fire; in this respect, at least, the Japanese War had not been lost for nothing. Despite its two-to-one superiority in artillery, von Prittwitz's army was given a thorough beating at Gumbinnen and the battle was lost.

In the evening of that unfortunate day, reports reached von Prittwitz that aerial reconnaissance had spotted large columns of Russian troops advancing from the south. Even if he had won the battle of Gumbinnen, the moment would now have come to disengage at once and pull back from a confrontation with Rennenkampf. Having lost at Gumbinnen, however, von Prittwitz was inclined to pull right back behind the Vistula and thereby give up East Prussia.

The disengagement was carried out extremely smoothly. Starting that same evening, by next morning the Germans had covered a distance equal to a daytime march, and for the next two days, August 8th and 9th, and even during the morning of the 10th, Rennenkampf—the second Russian enigma—made no attempt either to pursue, harass and destroy the enemy or to seize territory, roads and towns, but simply stood still, allowing a sixty-kilometre gap to open up between himself and the enemy, after which he started moving with the utmost caution at a rate of ten to fifteen kilometres a day (although this did have the advantage of sparing the horses from over-exertion).

Having successfully pulled his three army corps away from Rennenkampf in the space of three days, von Prittwitz decided not to retreat across the Vistula, but to regroup and wheel his forces to the right and strike at the left flank of Samsonov's army approaching from the south. For—and this was the third Russian enigma!—the southern Russian army was attempting neither to probe the opposing army corps commanded by von Scholtz (who was near the Polish frontier in a guarding position, like a diagonally placed shield) nor to outflank it, nor even to attack it head-on, but was calmly marching forward into empty territory *past* von Scholtz, exposing its flank to him as it did so.

However, the proposal which von Prittwitz himself had forwarded to his superiors the previous day, and the wave of alarm caused in Berlin by the floods of refugees from Prussia, had already set up a reaction. On August 9th the following decisions were taken at German Supreme Headquarters: von Prittwitz was to be relieved of his command, and two army corps—one a Guards corps and one a line corps—were to be withdrawn from that wing of the German advance on Paris which was now fighting the battle of the Marne. Thus the battle for Paris was abandoned, and with it the plan to deal with the French in forty days and then to turn and fight Russia.

The man appointed to be the new Chief of Staff of the German army in Prussia was Ludendorff, who had so recently won renown in Belgium. To him the Kaiser now said: 'You may be able to save the situation and avert disaster.' On the evening of the 9th he had an audience with Kaiser Wilhelm and was decorated for the capture of Liège, and during the night of the 10th his special east-bound train from Koblenz stopped to pick up the newly appointed Army Commander, Hindenburg, who had been brought out of retirement. Although they sent an order ahead of their train to regroup the army, this had already been done for them by von Prittwitz. (All the senior officers of the German army were taught a uniform system of military science. This was the legacy of the elder Moltke, who reasoned that since for a country to be endowed with a military leader of genius was a matter of luck and the fate of a nation should not be allowed to depend on chance, therefore by the application of military science it must be made possible for even mediocre men to put strategic concepts successfully into effect.)

At this point, the Russians produced their fourth enigma: unciphered radio messages! Several of these were handed to Ludendorff as he arrived, and while he was continuing his journey by car a courier in another car overtook him and handed him a further sheaf of intercepted Russian signals sent between Headquarters of Second Army and its Corps Headquarters, also a dozen radio messages from First Army sent on August 11th giving the precise dispositions of the corps, their objectives and intentions, and revealing the depth of their ignorance about the enemy, and finally the complete text of a signal sent on the morning of the 12th containing the entire set of orders for the redeployment of Second Army. It was clear that First Army was going to be no hindrance to the Germans while they attacked Second Army.

But was all this part of a deception plan? No, the information was confirmed by reports from aerial reconnaissance, from look-out posts, from auxiliary volunteers and from telephone calls made by local inhabitants. In all military history there can never have been such a well-marked map, such clear information about the enemy. For the Germans, what might have been a difficult campaign in a country dotted with lakes and enclosed by forests of sixty-foot-high pine-trees promised to be as simple as an exercise on a training-ground.

All four enigmas turned out to have a single solution: the Russians were incapable of co-ordinating the movements of large masses. Therefore, it was safe to run the risk of being outflanked and to turn the pincer-movement into an encirclement. The map itself spoke, positively shouted at them: all they had to do was give the necessary orders to stage the Cannae of the twentieth century.

It was tempting to try and encircle the whole of Samsonov's army, but it was too spread out and they might not have enough forces. Consequently it was decided merely to push back the flanking corps from Usdau and Bischofsburg, and thus to open the way for inserting the jaws of the pincer. For five days the Germans had been redeploying their forces for this purpose. General von François' army corps had been moved diagonally across the whole of East Prussia by train. The two corps commanded by von Mackensen and von Below (which Rennenkampf had reported as so badly beaten that only remnants of them had taken refuge in Königsberg) covered eighty kilometres by normal marches, were given a day's rest to prepare themselves, and then, on the morning of August 13th, delivered a shattering blow to General Komarov's division, which had been carelessly pushed too far forward.

August 13th was the day on which Samsonov finally moved his headquarters forward to Neidenburg, where he drank toasts to the capture of Berlin while sitting between the tips of the pincers already cutting into his army. The nearby rumble of gunfire came from the German artillery—seven times superior to his own—positioned near Mühlen, facing General Mingin's division. That was the day on which Martos' corps, advancing along the frontage of von Scholtz, after frequent minor brushes with the enemy turned to face him and successfully pushed him back. On the same day, too, Klyuev's corps, totally ignorant of the enemy, was pushing its way northwards through the sand into a trap, into a wolf-pit; and the price that he was to pay for every irrevocable mile that he advanced was to be a battalion of men. August 13th was also the day on which the Russian General Headquarters was working out a plan to withdraw Rennenkampf from a captured East Prussia, and on which Zhilinsky sent a telegram to Rennenkampf which read: 'Consider main objective blockade fortress Königsberg' (actually garrisoned by elderly troops of the *Landsturm*) 'and force Germans' (there were none) 'to sea in order deny them retreat to Vistula' (where they were not going).

Even so, the German command did not regard the day as successful. It was a failure in that for the past twenty-four hours not a single unciphered Russian radio signal had been intercepted, also because the disposition of the Russian forces, which had till then been so clear, had become indistinct as a result of numerous movements which the Germans had been unable to follow.

Despite their success in knocking out Komarov's division, von Mackensen's and von Below's two corps advanced past Lake Daday with a caution which they had learnt at Gumbinnen, a caution which proved justified. On the evening of the 13th, at Rotfliess station, the Russians put up a stiff resistance, evidently with considerable forces. (It was not until next morning, the 14th, that the German airmen located General Blagoveshchensky's army corps retreating in a state of disorder which they could not possibly have foreseen on the previous day.) Meanwhile the stand to the death made by two Russian regiments south of Mühlen concealed from Hindenburg the fact that the vital gap in the Russian lines already existed; in his orders he assumed that in this sector the Russians had more than a corps. Unaware of this ready-made gap, he forced open another one at Usdau.

The tips of the pincers were quivering before shutting with a snap.

The hand of Providence (*Vorsehung*) lay over that line of defence at Mühlen, over those lakeside cliffs and those cherished, centuries-old pine-trees, guardians of a land into which the Russian Second Army was advancing in all its naked vulnerability, for it was to this point that in 1410 the united Slav forces had advanced, and it was here, near the village of Tannenberg, between Hohenstein and Usdau, that they had dealt the blow which had smashed the Teutonic Order.

Five hundred years later fate had ordained that Germany should pronounce sentence in the Court of Retribution (*das Strafgericht*).

24

There is no innate gift that brings unalloyed reward: it is always a source of affliction too. But for an officer it is particularly galling to be endowed with exceptional talent. The army will gladly pay tribute to a brilliantly gifted man—but only when his hand is already grasping a field-marshal's baton. Till then, while he is still reaching for it, the army's system will subject his outstretched arm to a rain of blows. Discipline, which holds an army together, is inevitably hostile to a man of thrusting ability, and everything that is dynamic and heretical in his talent is bound to be shackled, suppressed and made to conform. Those in authority find it intolerable to have a subordinate who has a mind of his own; for that reason, an officer of outstanding ability will always be promoted more slowly, not faster, than the mediocrities.

In 1903 General von François went to East Prussia as Chief of Staff of an army corps. Ten years later, when he was nearly sixty, he was sent there again—as a mere corps commander.

It was in 1903 that Count von Schlieffen held the General Staff war-game in East Prussia, and von François was nominated to command one of the 'Russian' armies. His happened to be the army on which von Schlieffen demonstrated his tactic of the double encircling movement. The official account of the exercise contained the remark: 'Under threat of encirclement from the flank and from the rear, the Russian army laid down its arms.' To this von François objected provocatively: '*Exzellenz!* As long as I command an army, it will not lay down its arms!' Von Schlieffen smiled and substituted the words: 'Realising the hopelessness of his army's position, *its commander sought death in the front line—*

and found it there.' In real war, of course, such things do not happen.

General Hermann von François, however, was a man who would have preferred death to dishonour. He was descended from a family of Huguenot refugees who did not look upon Germany, which had sheltered them, as a mere temporary asylum. The François were used to acknowledging only one country as their homeland, and they served it faithfully; as a result, von François' great-grandfather was raised to the German nobility at a time when noblemen in France were being guillotined. His father, also a general, when mortally wounded by the French in 1870, exclaimed: 'I am happy to die at this moment, for Germany is victorious!'

When von François took over his command in East Prussia in 1913, he found that it had been given orders, in case of war, to adopt the system of 'yielding defence', which meant conducting a fighting withdrawal in the face of a numerically superior enemy. In his view, however, this was a wrong interpretation of von Schlieffen's plan. The adoption of a general defensive posture on the eastern front, until the main German forces should be released from the west, by no means implied that every sector had to employ the tactics of withdrawal. Comparing the German and Russian national characters, von François considered that speed and aggressiveness were essential qualities of the German soldier and of his military training, whereas the Russian was distinguished by such features as a disinclination to work methodically, lack of a sense of duty, fear of responsibility and a total inability to appreciate the value of time and to make proper use of it. Hence the typical traits of the Russian generals, which were: sluggishness, a tendency to work on set lines and a predilection for inaction and comfort. Therefore von François decided that in Prussia his tactics would be to use offence as a means of defence, and that wherever the Russians appeared he would attack first.

When the Great War began (great, that is, for Germany; great, too, for von François and long-awaited, for now was his only chance to show that he was the outstanding general in Germany, perhaps in all Europe), he counted on exploiting the speed of the German mobilisation; as soon as his corps was in a state of full readiness, he would cross the frontier and attack Rennenkampf's units as they converged during their far slower preparatory phase.

But now occurred an instance of how even the German army was unable to accept or acknowledge a dynamic talent. Von Prittwitz vetoed von François' plan with the pronouncement: 'We must reconcile ourselves to sacrificing part of this province.' Von François could not agree: against orders he engaged the enemy at Stallupönen, a battle which he considered he had won; but in the heat of the action a car drove up with orders from von Prittwitz: disengage and retire to Gumbinnen. Army Headquarters might have its plans, but the Corps Commander had his own, and von François replied to the messenger in a loud voice, in the presence of his officers: 'Inform General von Prittwitz that General von François will stop fighting when the Russians are beaten!' Alas, they were not beaten, and his own Chief of Staff informed on him to Army Headquarters. That evening von François was called upon to explain himself, and von Prittwitz reported his insubordination directly to the Kaiser. Von François also complained directly to the Kaiser that he would not continue fighting unless his present Chief of Staff were removed. This was taking a risk, as the Kaiser could well have lost his temper and himself relieved von François of his command, especially since he had already received frequent complaints about him and by now regarded him as a general of 'excessively independent character'. On the other hand, to have tolerated the presence of a hostile Chief of Staff would hardly have been the mark of an outstanding commander.

However much he might deny the fact or suppress it, there was still something of the turbulent Frenchman in von François.

So long as he was out of reach of his superiors, von François felt compelled to ensure that his actions would be truly weighed in the scales of justice. Every step he took, every engagement in which he was involved, had to be explained and justified to both history and his own descendants; if he did not take care of this himself, who else would? Unusually agile and energetic for his age, he was a man who fought his battles with élan and flair; he would climb up into belfries for observation, supervise the unloading of shells under fire (although they would probably have been unloaded well enough without his help) and visit every part of the battle-field by car to ensure that his orders were being carried out, some-times going for a whole day sustained by nothing but a cup of cocoa (this was for the benefit of his memoirs; he did not record the number of steaks he ate), often sleeping no more than two or three hours a night. Von François made quite sure that each of his decisions was triply recorded and commented upon: in the orders sent down to lower formations; in his reports to his superiors; and in a very detailed account prepared for the military archives (which would also be of use, if he survived, in the book he himself intended to write). In this detailed account he entered not only his actions, but his intentions, which he was not always allowed to carry out as he would have wished. Before battle he would write up his notes himself, and when the fighting began he was permanently accompanied in one of his two cars by a special aide-de-camp—his son, a lieutenant—who kept the general's war diary and recorded all his father's remarks on the spot.

Thus he ensured that the record of his conduct was always presented in his own words, believing that no one could do it better than he. He was at pains to make it clear when he was simply taking the line of least resistance and following orders to the letter, when he felt bound by a sense of responsibility higher than mere obedience and when he had the strength of will to overcome the fear of failure and, against all the advice of weaker spirits, to follow his own hunches.

Another dispute with von Prittwitz occurred during the battle of Gumbinnen. From its earliest stages, von François regarded this battle as a major success—an assessment which he reported to von Prittwitz, who in turn passed it on to Supreme Headquarters. Von François attacked vigorously, outflanked Rennenkampf (although his critics claim that he attacked Rennenkampf head-on, having misunderstood the disposition of the Russian forces), took a great number of prisoners and gave orders that evening that his corps was to go into the attack again the following day. It was then that he received the order from von Prittwitz to disengage in silence that night and to retire, along with all the other army corps, beyond the Vistula.

This was intolerable: at one stroke to have to lose everything *his* ability had gained that day, just because the neighbouring corps commander, von Mackensen, had fought badly; to have to abandon, too, the victory which his sixth sense told him he would win tomorrow; finally, knowing perfectly well that what he had done was right, to be made to cancel his own well-considered orders and to submit to another set which he regarded as unsound!

But that is the army. Still buoyed up by the martial enthusiasm bred of success, von François had to quit the field of his victory and transfer his corps by railway, through Königsberg, in a long 'castling' move right across the board.

That was the army; but that it was the German army was demonstrated by something else which occurred: on the following day, after furious efforts by the Chief of Signals to track down von François' whereabouts, his tiny command-post in distant East Prussia was connected with Koblenz, and His Majesty the Kaiser personally asked the general for his view of the situation, and whether he regarded the redeployment of his corps as correct.

This was a great honour for a Corps Commander (and an obvious slight to the Army Commander). But with his agile mind, von François did not stand on his dignity and insist that he had been right the day before: what might have been correct yesterday was not necessarily so today. As Napoleon said, a general will never be a great commander if he cannot see beyond his own map-board. Once begun, the withdrawal should be carried out to its conclusion. Now that they had disengaged from the army of the Niemen, he looked forward to demonstrating his unique talents against the army of the Narev.

It was then that somewhere, imperceptibly, amid the to-and-fro of telephone conversations, special trains and discussions between the newly appointed commanders at their headquarters (they all knew each other already; von François had once been Hindenburg's Chief of Staff when the latter was a corps commander, and at an earlier stage he had also served with Ludendorff), there was born the idea that the army of the Narev should be dealt with by a double encircling movement. Each of the three generals regarded himself as the author of the plan; the task of convincing history that *he* had thought of it first still lay ahead.

On the evening of August 11th (just as Vorotyntsev reached Samsonov's sleepy headquarters in Ostrolenka), General von François was sitting in the Hotel Kronprinz, close to the spot where the first units of his corps were de-training opposite Samsonov's left flank, and writing the following order of the day to the men of his army corps:

'... the brilliant victories achieved by our corps at Stallupönen and Gumbinnen have caused the High Command to transfer you, soldiers of 1 Army Corps, by rail to a position in which you may do battle, with your customary invincible bravery, against the new enemy coming from Russian Poland. When we have destroyed this opponent, we shall return to our previous position and settle accounts with those other Russian hordes who, in defiance of international law, are burning the towns and villages of our homeland . . .'

Foreseeing that he would inevitably return eastward to fight Rennenkampf again, he wrote these orders while sitting in the extreme left-hand corner of East Prussia, at a moment when his units were entraining in the upper right-hand corner near Königsberg and the trains were already rumbling across Prussia from its eastern to its western extremity. Apart from an initial twelve-hour delay in getting the operation started, this move was one of the miracles of German efficiency: day and night, at constant intervals of half an hour, a troop-train would set off, and even the operating regulations of the German railways were treated as something less than a law of nature. On each sector of line, the troop-trains moved at perilously close intervals; they used tracks in defiance of red signals and they discharged their load of men and were turned around within twenty-five minutes instead of the usual gap of two hours. At von François' request the trains travelled right up to the area of the impending battle, so that each battalion had to march only about five kilometres to reach its position.

But even this miracle was not appreciated by the heavy-jowled Hindenburg and Ludendorff. They arrived at von François' command-post at a time when almost all his artillery was still in transit and demanded that he should begin the eagerly awaited advance.

Although he was unaware of it and it was involuntary, von François' eyes were fixed in a permanent grimace of irony. He said:

'If I am ordered to, I will start to advance. But the troops will have to fight—and this will be awkward, I'm afraid—with the bayonet.'

A Russian might well have quoted the familiar proverb, 'the bayonet's a brave fellow but the bullet's a fool', from which it followed that the shell was even more of a fool. The pupils of von Schlieffen, however, had been taught that the coming war would be an artillery war and that the side which had superiority in artillery would win. It was all right to talk of invincible bravery when drafting orders of the day for the troops, but a general's real calculations were concerned with batteries of guns and rounds of ammunition.

Why must subordination always be graded in inverse ratio to talent? It hurt von François to have to contemplate these two men standing a yard away from him; both were taller than he and both had the same kind of harsh, flattened face, held with unnatural rigidity by a high, stiff collar above a big, stocky torso. Ludendorff was the younger; the line of his jaw had not yet completely hardened and his gaze was not quite so leaden, but he already bore a strong resemblance to his Army Commander. Hindenburg's face was positively rectangular, all his features were heavy and coarse, the bags under his eyes were enormous, his nose was flat and his ears seemed to grow straight out of his cheekbones. Could either of these men, who were about as subtle as sledge-hammers, possibly comprehend von François' intuitive assessment of gain and risk?

(Incapable as he was of mentally changing places with them, von François failed to see himself through their eyes: his lack of height, so inappropriate to a general; his darting glance, so unsuitable for a person of his age; and, above all, his bad habit of taking impulsive action, evading orders, and going behind the backs of his superiors.)

The question at issue was, where to advance. Von François disagreed with their proposal and suggested his own: that they should knock out the Russian I Army Corps by a single movement which would encircle the whole of Samsonov's army. An hour was spent arguing the point, until he was overruled and ordered to make an attack designed to separate the Russian I Army Corps from the main enemy body, which would then be encircled without von François' participation. As to when the advance should begin, von François only just managed to bargain out of them an extra half-day's delay—from dawn until noon on August 13th.

Thus when he began the battle, at a place and a time that were not of his choosing, he at first acted somewhat hesitantly, more for the record than from conviction, and merely repulsed the Russians' advance patrols—although the main Russian forces were in easily visible positions on high ground running from a hill topped by a windmill, past Usdau, and thence along a railway embankment. The capture of Usdau was to be the prelude to the operation on August 14th which would open up the way to Neidenburg.

At sunset the preliminary battle died down. During the night the corps artillery was due to arrive and move into position: guns of a calibre, firing shells of a weight, which the Russians had never before experienced. Next morning, at four o'clock, he, General von François, was to begin the battle between two armies.

'What if the Russians start first during the night, sir?' his son asked, taking notes by the gleam of a flashlight.

They were lying in a hayloft; the general did not care to sleep in a house which had been recently occupied by the Russians. Winding up his alarm clock and putting it under his pillow, he stretched out his short legs until the bones cracked, yawned, and said with a smile:

'Remember, my boy—the Russians never move on their own initiative until they have had lunch.'

*

(con moto)

> *Uncle Fritz has gone quite barmy,*
> *Wants to have a boxing-match!*
> Chorus: *Ho there, no there, ho there, no there*
> *Wants to have a boxing-match!*
>
> *So who leads the German Army?*
> *Willy Whiskers—stupid cat!*
> Chorus: *Ho there, no there, ho there, no there,*
> *Willy Whiskers—stupid cat!*

> ('Russian Soldiers' Song of 1914',
> a postcard showing our troops
> as heroes marching to a drum
> and Kaiser Wilhelm as a miserable
> tom-cat.

25

———

Everything had combined in the most untimely and unfortunate way: the war itself, which had interrupted General Artamonov's career; the dangerous westerly position of his army corps, the closest to Germany; the necessity to advance beyond Soldau; the news of a large enemy force in the offing, and now its first attack on him—on the very day that this spying colonel had arrived from General Headquarters, together with several teletype conversations which had tied the noose tighter around Artamonov's neck.

Until now, Artamonov had spent a large part of his military career at the top of the tree, endowed with general's rank and decorated with orders of the first class. True, he had not been idle and had worked zealously to earn his promotion: other officers went to one cadet school, he had graduated from two; others studied at one military academy, Artamonov had taken courses at two; indeed he had entered the academies no less than three times, having failed his examination on one occasion—that was the service for you! Sitting at a desk for long hours was harder for him than for most, as he had a powerful and active pair of legs and suffered from varicose veins if he did not get enough exercise. He had been fortunate, however, in spending a dozen or so years serving in a variety of appointments: as an officer 'in-waiting', as the senior executive officer at a military district headquarters, and finally 'on special attachment to the General Staff'. In this capacity he had dashed about the world, first to the Amur region in the far east of Siberia, then as an observer with the Boers, then to Abyssinia, after which, still camel-borne, he had hurried off to an inspection tour of Russia's eastern provinces. No, he could not be accused of being lazy. He had served honourably and to the best of his ability. The secret of his success had been movement—departure, travel, arrival, then off again—not fighting, for that involved the extra risk of forfeiting promotion if things went badly. The war against the rebellious Chinese had, however, passed off quite successfully for him and earned him a suitable decoration; likewise, in the Japanese War, he had managed to escape being cut off at the battle of Mukden, after abandoning without compunction about fifty Manchurian mud-hut villages to the tender mercies of the little yellow men.

The present war, unfortunately, had started badly for him. Airmen had reported that two enemy divisions were facing him; they had then grown to two army corps. Obviously the Germans were planning something which boded ill, but how was he to solve the riddle of their intentions and foil them? Artamonov had worn uniform all his life, but this was the first time he had been confronted by that grim predicament of war: the impossibility of guessing what the enemy proposed to do tomorrow and consequently of devising some counter-plan. As usual, his response to anxiety was movement: he either paced ceaselessly about the rooms of his headquarters or dashed all over his corps sector. Twice in one day his car had smothered the countryside in clouds of dust as he raced about, ostensibly to inspect his units and raise their morale, but in reality because his mind was in a turmoil of perplexity. He honestly could not think of anything better to do.

During the day the Germans started to attack, and in desperation Artamonov decided on his own initiative (since Samsonov was not in a position to order Artamonov into action) to mount a small counter-attack. Two regiments on his left flank advanced three miles westward and captured a large village. The question was, though—had this been a good idea and had it been necessary? It was unfitting for a corps commander to ask advice from anyone, especially a colonel sent down from General Headquarters. Artamonov realised that he had to think carefully and tread warily in order to discover just how influential this colonel was, to what extent he was in the confidence of the Commander-in-Chief, and who had intrigued to get him sent here. So instead of discussing his fears and worries with Vorotyntsev, Artamonov tried to put a good face on it with bluff, airy, man-to-man talk about generalities. 'The Germans' superiority', he would say, 'is supposed to rest on system and order, but really that's their weakness—once we start fighting them unconventionally, in a way they haven't bargained for, they're lost!'

This colonel stuck to him like a leech; when the fighting ebbed towards nightfall and the Corps Commander decided to make yet another trip round the forward positions to encourage the troops, the man insisted on accompanying him—a bad sign. And so it proved: every remark Vorotyntsev made *en route*, every question he asked, was uncomfortably pointed. As they drove out of Soldau, headlamps blazing, overtaking troops marching along the road, the colonel found some pretext to remark on the lack of any defensive ring of trenches around the town, which had been occupied by Corps Headquarters for four days—perhaps he had missed them? Discussing the day's fighting, he only confused Artamonov by remarking that a regiment had been withdrawn from the right flank, leaving a large gap in the line. No sooner had Artamonov silenced this awkward query by announcing that General Stempel's cavalry brigade had moved in to fill the gap than they drove into a village where they found Stempel bivouacked for the night with no intention of moving into position until the following morning. For this Artamonov gave Stempel a dressing-down. But of course you can always pick holes in anyone's dispositions if you make a tour of inspection and look hard enough. Finally, with what was now open disrespect, the colonel from headquarters started questioning the Corps Commander about his *plan* for the next day.

Plan! There was something so un-Russian about the word. What plan? Did he think Artamonov was quite such a fool as to talk about his plan to all comers? In actual fact, his plan was simply to extricate his corps from this situation well enough for their commander to avoid blame and be given a medal, but one could hardly admit to a plan of such stark simplicity. And now the colonel, who was obviously very well connected, was casually insinuating into the conversation what almost amounted to directives of his own. Since the forces under Artamonov's command were twice as large as any army corps, and since his over-extended left flank contained some cavalry divisions, surely he could put this flank's length and mobility to good use and deliver a stinging blow to the German flank tomorrow; there was still time to countermand his orders and redeploy accordingly. This, he maintained, would be in Artamonov's own interest.

Well, he considered that *he* was the best judge of his own interests. It was true, though, that today he had found himself saddled with a force of twice the normal size, involving twice as many problems. He had been incautious enough to raise the alarm and complain to Army Headquarters that heavy enemy forces were concentrating against him, whereupon Samsonov had telegraphed, transferring to Artamonov the two cavalry divisions and the remaining units which had arrived late to join the still unformed XXIII Army Corps—the Warsaw Guards Division and an Independent Rifle Brigade. This done, the Army Commander expressed himself 'convinced that even an enemy superior in numbers would be unable to break the fighting spirit of the glorious troops of the I Army Corps'. With equal dignity Artamonov had tapped out his thanks 'for the confidence in him shown by his distinguished commander'. In fact, the 'confidence' reduced him to cold despair: what in God's name was he to do with this massive burden?

This habit of exchanging hollow, bombastic compliments made Vorotyntsev see red. When military men forsook the crisp, sober language of their profession and began bandying expressions of mutual esteem like courtiers exchanging bows, he regarded it as a fatal sign of weakness; it could never happen in the German army. Strong enemy forces were concentrating on the left flank of Samsonov's army and there was not a moment to be lost—yet here were these two generals trading compliments.

The Kexholm Regiment of Life Guards had de-trained early in the day and was already on the march towards Neidenburg to catch up with and join XXIII Army Corps. The Lithuanian Regiment of Life Guards had also reached Mlawa by train that day and had now been placed under Artamonov's command. (Two other regiments of the Guards Division, the so-called 'Yellow Guard' of Warsaw, were nowhere to be found, and no one knew the whereabouts of their divisional commander, General Sirelius.) The 1st Rifle Brigade, however, was one of the newest and best trained units in the Russian army; the battalions of this brigade were now marching towards their forward positions, and Artamonov's car overtook them on the way.

If the left flank of Second Army had been deployed in the shape of a horn projecting forward from the army's main frontage, the past day's withdrawal would not have been too serious and there would have been no great harm in pulling it back a little further. But its situation now made it look more like a shoulder—and a bruised one at that.

By now, Artamonov's mind was muddled and dulled. Vorotyntsev's ideas and hints simply bounced off the general's hollow, domed, marble forehead. It was a waste of time trying to discuss with him such questions as how and why the German 1 Army Corps had got here so quickly from Gumbinnen. Vorotyntsev had spent all day at Corps Headquarters and had been watching this fussy general darting hither and thither. Greying temples and walrus moustaches, epaulettes and aiguillettes can make even a fool look imposing and prevent one from seeing a man as he always has been and still is—primeval Adam; but if one made the effort one could detect that here was really a private disguised as a general: put under a strict sergeant he would have made an excellent soldier, keen, fast on his feet, never idle, always willing, and probably brave under fire as well. Or he would have made a splendid deacon, tall, dignified, with a good voice, not too lazy to swing his censer in every corner of the church, a bit of an actor, and no doubt devoted to the service of God.

But why was he a general of infantry? Why had sixty thousand Russian soldiers been placed under his imprudent command?

He was now setting off to visit all his units by night. What arrangements had he made for headquarters to function in his absence? Who was in charge of intelligence? What communications were there between the artillery and the infantry? How many rounds per gun had been brought forward, and were there enough ammunition-boxes and waggons to keep the gunners supplied during the battle? He probably did not know, and was not even aware that he ought to. Why, for instance, had the relatively moderate fighting of the past day obliged his corps to withdraw quite so far in certain localities? Artamonov had made no effort to find out the reason and would not relish being told it by Vorotyntsev. And then there was his fondness for dashing about the battlefield in his car. In the hands of an intelligent general this method can be brilliantly used for pulling stray units back into line, being everywhere in time to exercise personal supervision—but to add four wheels to two active but totally brainless legs is to invite disaster!

There was no denying that Artamonov was at least outwardly firm. He was never downhearted at the problems facing him, he never sought advice, and a sensitive ear was needed to detect the ring of perplexity in his voice.

As they drove along the road at night the unnaturally white light of their headlamps gave a strange, dead look to the trunks of the roadside trees, to bushes, houses, barns, level-crossings, bridge-railings, waggons, and marching troops, whilst it blinded anyone coming towards them. Here and there troops would peer curiously at them out of the darkness and the lone soldiers they passed would either quicken their pace or whip up their horses.

If there had ever been any sense in Vorotyntsev's journey to the left flank of the army, there was none now. Among the orders given to him for his mission the highest priority had been allotted to 'staff reconnaissance', meaning that he was to acquire an accurate knowledge of the situation by personal observation which would enable General Headquarters to correct or supplement the information available to them. He had already amply fulfilled this brief, and the data he had to send to General Headquarters were now in danger of being delayed. It was his clear duty to return with all speed to Second Army Headquarters and thence back to GHQ. Vorotyntsev had not been empowered to hover over staff or regimental officers and offer advice. He might be able to influence the course of the action if he were to stick closely to Artamonov, be present whenever he took a decision and guard him against mistakes, but Artamonov was suspicious of such tutelage and would reject it. In any case, Vorotyntsev could scarcely bring himself to stay with Artamonov any longer. Everything comes, they say, to him who waits, but patience was not one of Vorotyntsev's virtues. He could not go through with the night-time tour of inspection in the general's company. It began at Usdau, whence it was fourteen miles by road to Army Headquarters; it was here that he decided to leave Artamonov.

The village of Usdau lay on the broad, flat top of a hill, whose slope had a noticeable effect on the car's progress. Kerosene lamps were burning in several of the windows, others were dark, but the number of horses and soldiers to be seen gave the impression that the whole place—houses, barns, and farmyards—was crammed full. Shielded from the enemy's view by a high wall, several field cookers were hissing away with a steady flame.

Behind the red-brick Gothic church they stopped and switched off the headlamps. They had given notice of their arrival and were met with a report on the situation from Major-General Savitsky, the 'sector commander' as he called himself to conceal the anomaly of his position: actually he was a brigade commander whose unit consisted of only one regiment, the 85th Vyborg, the other regiment of his brigade having got left behind in Warsaw. (Nor was this the only irregularity. On the left of the Vyborg Regiment was another division also short of a regiment still in Warsaw, while to the left of that were two regiments and General Dushkevich, the Divisional Commander of the division to which the Vyborg Regiment belonged. The overlapping and confusion could not have been greater had they been planned.)

Artamonov said he wanted to see the forward positions, and Savitsky led them round the village by the faint light coming from the windows. Savitsky was already grey, but held himself like a much younger man; even in the starlit darkness one could detect the sound sense in his description of the situation.

After a day of being harried by the enemy, the Vyborg Regiment was now occupying a strong key position. About two hundred yards from the village, where the hilltop began to slope down towards the enemy, there was a line of continuous trenches which the troops were still busy deepening.

The regiment was fresh; it had been brought up by rail, there had been no interruptions in its food supply, and it had suffered practically no casualties during the day's fighting. The men were working with a will, as one could tell from the busy, muffled clink of spades and pickaxes and from the jokes and laughter.

Savitsky had a clear perception of the weaknesses and dangers of his position. There was no unit to his immediate right, leaving a gap in the line; furthermore, for this vital sector he had been allotted too little artillery: a regiment of light field artillery and, almost as a bad joke, two medium howitzers. The other ten corps howitzers and the complete army heavy artillery regiment were far away on the left. Artamonov, however, had no time to intervene if he was to complete his tour of the positions that night. Breaking off his conversation with Savitsky and Vorotyntsev, he ordered a platoon to be paraded in front of him '—that one over there from the nearest trench, as they are, in working kit'. (After all, he had once been in charge of the defensive works of Kronstadt!) The platoon put down its tools, clambered out of the trench, and fell into line without arms. Artamonov strode along the ranks.

'Well, lads—are we going to beat the Germans off?'

In a mumbled, ragged chorus the men replied that they would.

'Easy job, eh?'

They agreed.

'Your regiment captured Berlin in 1813, and for that battle-honour you have a set of silver trumpets! You there,' he asked a broad-shouldered private, 'what's your name?'

'Agafon, your ex'ency,' the man replied promptly and smartly.

'Which Agafon? When's your name-day?'

'The Threshing-Floor, your ex'ency,' answered the soldier, unabashed.

'Fool! Threshing-floor indeed! Why threshing-floor?'

'Because it's the autumn one, your ex'ency! That's when we bring the stooks in from the fields and start threshing.'*

'You fool, you should know all about your saint—who he was and what he did. And you should pray to him before battle. Have you read the lives of the saints?'

'I, er . . . yes, your 'cency . . .'

'Your saint's your guardian angel, you see. He keeps you and protects you. And you don't know anything about him! When's the patronal feast in your village, then? Or don't you know that either?'

''Course I know it, your ex'ency! It's around the time of Mary Minor Day.'

'And what is Mary Minor Day?'

* In pre-revolutionary rural Russia the peasant's life was regulated by the Orthodox Church calendar; generally the peasants did not know the times of the year by month and date, but simply by saints' days, many of which marked the start or finish of phases of work in the farming cycle. Since there were often three or four saints of the same name, they were given extra distinguishing names or nicknames. There are three Saints Agafon in the Orthodox calendar; the feast of this man's patron saint—St Agafon Ogumennik (*ogumennik* = threshing-floor) —was on August 28th. Because the Orthodox Church used (and still uses) the Julian Calendar, which in the 20th Century is 13 days behind the Western (Gregorian) calendar, the equivalent date of St Agafon's feast-day is September 10th. By this date the harvest was in full swing and the sheaves of grain were being taken to be threshed on the village's communal threshing-floor.

Agafon faltered, but from behind him came a shout from another soldier, who from his way of speaking was obviously literate:

'The Nativity of the Most Pure Mother of God, your excellency!'

'Well then, pray to the Mother of God while there's life in you,' said Artamonov with finality. Missing out the third man in the rank, he asked the same question of the fourth soldier. He turned out to be named after St Methodius the Quail-Hunter* and knew nothing of the life of his saint either.

'But at least you're all wearing crosses?'

'Of course! Every one of us!' Holy Russia answered him as one man, even sounding offended that he should ask such a question.

'Well, then—pray! The enemy will start bombarding us in the morning—so if I were you I should pray!'

It might have occurred to Vorotyntsev that this performance had been staged for his benefit, but this was not so: Artamonov always behaved like that. It was impossible to tell whether he did it out of genuine conviction or because, having served for so long in the Petersburg military district, he knew how much it pleased the Grand-Duke to see an icon-lamp burning in every soldier's tent. One learned nothing from his face on these occasions: his features were a smooth, solid wall, his nose was like a false door-handle which opened nothing, and his eyes were equally blank.

Looking up into the sky, he crossed himself. Just as it was his habit to rush headlong from left to right of his corps, so he crossed himself with a hurried, sweeping gesture, tapping his forehead and chest and ending with a violent movement to his left shoulder as though brushing off a gadfly. Then he made the sign of the cross over Savitsky and embraced him, saying: 'God bless you! God bless your Vyborg Regiment!' He might have given the regiment its full title, though that would scarcely have been appropriate, since it was 'His Imperial and Royal Majesty Wilhelm the Second, Emperor of Germany and King of Prussia's Own Regiment'. The title had now fallen out of use and a new one had not been devised.

The Corps Commander drove away. Savitsky set off to the right, where his sector came to an end, to supervise the positioning of a half-company of machine-guns. Vorotyntsev went with him. He always had to have something to worry about. Now there was no

---

* This saint's feast-day is on June 20th O.S. (July 3rd N.S.).

longer any fear of the army being outflanked on the left, he was nagged by the thought that there was a yawning gap to the right of this corps.

Obviously fully aware of the position, Savitsky confined himself to remarks that were brief and to the point. But why was it that good sense and intelligence were never to be found at the very top, where they mattered most?

Passing between the village and the line of forward trenches, they walked towards the windmill. Isolated, on an exposed spot slightly higher than the village, its gigantic black bulk loomed up. Even by the faint starlight its motionless sails could be seen, looking like human arms crossed in entreaty: 'Oh, stop!' or sternly forbidding: 'You shall not pass!'

Was there an observation-post in the mill? Yes, there had been, but it had been withdrawn; it was too exposed and the Germans had begun firing in this direction before nightfall.

From where they stood, the road and the railway track ran side by side out of the village on two embankments, which then turned sharply northward, cutting across the front line. It was in that direction that Savitsky had to go to see to his machine-guns. He offered Vorotyntsev a bed for the night in the house in which he himself was billeted. It was time to retire at last. Vorotyntsev set off back along the track towards the village, and at the point where the Neidenburg road emerged from under the railway he sat down on the sparse, dry grass of the sloping embankment.

In the dark expanse, as far as he could see to the east, and from north to south, there was not a glimmer of light, except for Pegasus, the broad nebula in Andromeda, the bright pinpoint of Capella, and the dim cluster of the Pleiades. There was no sound of artillery- or rifle-fire, of hooves or wheels; the earth was as it had been on the first day of creation, still without beasts and men. A battle was imminent between two corps; on it would depend the fate of armies, perhaps even of the whole campaign; nearby, a stone's throw away, Stempel's brigade would move up at dawn. And what of the Germans? Had they guessed the true position? Were they infiltrating yet or not?

Perhaps the right course of action would be to run down the side of the embankment and set off along the road to Neidenburg, find Samsonov and warn him that there was a gap in the line far too close to his own headquarters, that the body of the army had already been split into two parts and Second Army Headquarters itself was defenceless. He could get him to write out an order to attack on the left flank, and bring the order back himself.

But he would never make it by morning. Even if he could find a two-wheeler and cover the fourteen miles flat out, he would never be able to get things moving before dawn. He might easily be shot at by a patrol. In any case, it was hopeless to expect he could wake up the ponderous Samsonov in the middle of the night, shake him, and persuade him to take such drastic measures.

He had better stay where he was. Usdau was the key to the situation. Unfortunately a colonel from GHQ had no business here; the whole point of his mission had vanished. The tens of thousands of officers and men around him were all working within the specific confines of duty; he alone had no direct concern here; yet some vague prompting of conscience made him stay. As soon as he had got out of Artamonov's car, the object of his journey to 1st Army Corps had ceased to exist and had not been replaced by any other. He had not even sent his report back to the Commander-in-Chief and he could see no way of intervening. He had begun to feel that he would have achieved more by staying at General Headquarters.

Always passionately keen to put his abilities to the best use, he had utterly failed to do so.

Ever since his youth, Vorotyntsev had been obsessed by one profound desire: to have a good influence on the history of his country, either by pushing it or pulling it—by the roots of the hair if necessary!—in the right direction. But in Russia that kind of power and influence was not granted to anyone who was not fortunate enough to be close to the throne; at whatever point Vorotyntsev attempted to exert pressure and however much he exhausted himself trying, the effort was always in vain.

Waves of sleep were washing over him, and he found himself nodding. He had, after all, spent the last two nights in the saddle. Was it really this morning that he had had breakfast with Krymov? It felt like a week ago.

It would have been quite comfortable simply to lean back a bit against the embankment and go to sleep. But the ground was already cold.

He ran down to the road and walked slowly back towards the village. He stumbled a little, his thoughts straying. He felt unable to act, make decisions, or even think. Condemning himself for having failed in his mission, despising himself for his muddled thinking, he tottered back to the house allotted for his billet.

Although it was only a country cottage, his room had a double four-poster bed on which was a light eiderdown in a pink silk cover. Ever since the Japanese War, his memories of front-line billets had mostly been of Chinese peasant huts, dugouts or tents. On the marble mantelpiece ticked a bronze clock with a top that tapered to a point. It probably had an eight-day movement and had last been wound up by its owners. It agreed almost exactly with Vorotyntsev's watch: a quarter to twelve.

The room was stuffy and made more so by the kerosene lamp, but this also made it pleasantly warm. With the last ounce of his strength Vorotyntsev pulled off his belt and boots, thrust his revolver under the down pillow, put a box of matches by his bedside, blew out the lamp and flopped down on top of the soft, yielding eiderdown, still with a sense of bitterness at his failure and stupidity. The bed embraced him as though it had been waiting for him, and the edges of his anxiety and confusion softened. The beating of his heart, which he could hear through the pillow, grew slower, and then stopped . . .

How long it was later he did not know, but he was in a room, though not the same one. There was only a faint light which did not reach to the corners; he could not see where it was coming from and it shone only in one place. Now it was shining on her face and breast.

It was *she*—he recognised her immediately, even though he had never seen her in his life. He was amazed that finding her had been so easy, for it had always seemed impossible. Although strangers, they recognised each other at once and rushed to seize each other by the arms.

There was light of a kind, and he could see, though not well enough to make out features and expression, yet he was piercingly aware that it was *she*—the one, the longed-for, the inexpressibly beloved woman, the loveliest of all beautiful women, of all the women in creation!

They embraced and spoke, yet did not speak; though not one clear word was uttered, their understanding was instant and complete. In the half-light of that room little could be seen, but the sense of touch was absolute. From her arms, his hands passed to her narrow, curving back; he pressed her to him and the feel of her was so good, so natural: the finding of what he had always sought.

No duty called him, no cares burdened him, there was only the ease and joy of her embrace. Strangely, it was as if this was not the first time they had seen each other, as if somehow, somewhere far away, this meeting had already been agreed between them. He led her confidently toward the bed, whither the light now moved.

Suddenly she faltered and stopped. Not from constraint, for their desire was already at full flood, but because—he knew at once—there was a reason why she could not turn back the covers of that bed.

In clumsy haste he bent down to do it himself and, as soon as he had drawn back the bedspread and the blankets, saw lying on the sheet, folded several times and half under the pillow, Alina's night-dress, pink and trimmed with lace. Although he could not distinguish colour in that light, not even the colour of *her* dress or *her* eyes, he recognised the pink nightdress at once.

Only then did the memory come back to him: of course—Alina! But he felt no inhibition; carelessly, without hesitation or regret, he threw away the delicate pink material, which at once melted, disappeared. The bed was ready and there was nothing else to disturb them.

Everything happened in an instant; he had no idea how they undressed or got into bed, they were simply lying tightly clasped together, warmed by the boundless joy of the discovery that never, never again would they need to look for anyone or anything else . . .

There was a roar and a crash and a tinkle of breaking glass. Georgii woke up, though at first he had not the strength to move his head. No glass was actually broken, but the first German shells were falling nearby. The room was full of the grey light of dawn. He shut his eyes again.

Parting from her was agony. He had only just drowned in complete intimacy with her and still lay helpless, powerless to move even if the world came to an end that moment. He could still feel her with such intensity that he had not yet begun to think rationally. Who was she? Had he really sought her? He could not remember ever having thought of her before—not in that way.

What astounded him was not that he should have dreamed of a woman who did not exist—it often happens after all—but the intensity of the sensual experience, something which Georgii thought had died in him or at least had long been forgotten.

He still felt her so powerfully that he could not bear to open his knees and lose her warmth; he continued to sprawl in a delicious languor from which he could not have roused himself if a shell had knocked down the wall of the house. It all began to come back to him: his wasted journey—today was the day of the battle—he was in the wrong place—he had to go somewhere: was it to Samsonov? or to Artamonov? In the dawn air he could already distinguish the separate report as each gun fired, the sound of shells in flight and then, in the village or near it, the explosions as they burst. Three-inch. Six-inch. And that one was even bigger.

He cursed the impotence of the flesh. He might be killed, the whole house might be blown up, and still he hadn't the strength to move. People compared this state of the body with death and the comparison seemed true enough.

But what about the men in the trenches? What of Agafon Ogumennik—how were things with him?

He could now make out the time by the clock on the mantel-piece: seven minutes past four. The explosions were getting nearer. The doors in the house were rattling. Then there was a knock on his door: a smart, efficient, round-faced army cook had brought him a mess-tin full of porridge, still hot although the troops had probably had theirs an hour ago. He did not know the man's name, but how he thanked him! His was one of a hundred thousand faces that one saw in Russia, faces that one endlessly saw and forgot—God grant that he at least remembered this man's for ever.

Vorotyntsev jumped out of bed; his legs were still weak for the first few steps, but the weakness soon vanished. He ate the porridge rapidly with a broad wooden spoon which forced his mouth wide open, wound up his pocket watch, put on his belt, greatcoat and binoculars and then stopped to think: where ought he to go? The window-panes rattled again, a shudder went through the whole house, but indoors, as usual, it was hard to determine from which direction the bombardment was coming.

When he had scraped every morsel out of the mess-tin, he found the cook waiting in the passage. The mess-tin was probably his own. A clap on the shoulder—'Thanks, brother'—and he ran out of the house towards the trenches, wide awake and almost cheerful.

It was a chilly morning. The low ground that skirted the village was dense with mist. A high-explosive shell burst nearby and the fragments whistled past. Having taken cover behind the brick wall of a barn, Vorotyntsev set off at a fast run to the nearest trench, which happened to be occupied by the same platoon which had been subjected to the general's ridiculous inspection last night. He jumped into the trench between two soldiers. They had made a good job of it; it was dug to the full depth complete with embrasures, and the sensible fellows had even scrounged a few benches and armchairs.

A little to the left, protected by a niche hollowed out of the parapet, its muzzle facing the enemy and its tail towards its masters in the trench, stood a toy lion about the size of a cat, with a beautiful, well-combed, tawny skin.

'What's that animal called, your honour?'

'They do say . . .'

The men all waited for his confirmation.

'A lion. Where did you get it?'

'Found it in a town we went through.'

'Is it solid or stuffed with rags?'

'It's solid.'

Although not yet very concentrated or accurate, the shells were still flying overhead, whistling with an evil glee that foretold a hard day's fighting. Had he been alone, he would already have been cowering in silence, pressing his head against the earth wall of the trench, but he was surrounded by men who were putting a cheerful face on it. And then there was the lion: Vorotyntsev liked that. His confusion and indecision of the early morning had been dissipated by this brisk start to the day.

From where he stood there was a wide view, though half of it was still wreathed in mist. Above it the flashes from the German batteries positioned on high ground could clearly be seen. Meanwhile there was a useful job he could do: spread out a sheet of paper on his map-board, take a compass bearing on the windmill, which was fully visible from this point in the long curving trench, and draw a sketch-map showing the estimated positions of the enemy batteries, calculating the range by eye and, if possible, with the aid of the ranging-graticules in the lens of his binoculars. Vorotyntsev liked artillery work, having at his own request taken a course one summer at the officers' artillery school at Luga, where he had learned a great deal.

'Hey, lads, why don't our guns shoot back at them?' one soldier asked another while glancing out of the corner of his eye at Vorotyntsev.

'So as not to give themselves away!' a tall soldier standing next to Vorotyntsev in the trench replied gravely, though his pursed lips and serious manner were jokingly assumed. He too glanced side-ways at the colonel.

Although the main weight of the German fire was obviously con-centrated on the other regiments to their left, it was now beginning to thicken around them too. The soldiers' faces tensed, and the strain put a stop to their jokes. One man was holding a prayer-book and whispering. Shells screamed overhead like steel whips, splinters whined past them. The soldier on Vorotyntsev's right hand cowered at even the most distant whistle, while the humourist on his left with the broad, flat nose, mouth agape and pendulous lower lip sticking forward, watched every squeak of the colonel's pencil. It was a very good-natured face. Though his mouth was wide open, the soldier's eyes were keenly watching the map-board, not out of idle curiosity but with absorption, as though at any moment he might attempt the job himself.

'Understand what I'm doing?' Vorotyntsev asked, as he looked alternately through his binoculars and down at the map-board. 'While they're still not hitting us too hard . . .'

'Yes, you're using the time to sort of blaze a trail.' The big-mouthed soldier nodded confidently. It was clear from his ex-pression that he had gathered that Vorotyntsev was calculating angles and distances but was not quite certain why he was doing it.

'What's your name?'

'Arsenii.'

'Surname?'

'Blagodaryov.'

A good name, and the relish with which he pronounced it con-veyed a current of warmth and sympathy. Blagodaryov! With a name like that he would be a man quick to show gratitude—in fact he seemed about to thank Vorotyntsev at this moment.*

* The name is derived from the Russian word for 'thanks, gratitude'.

Behind them dawn was breaking over the village and the mist in the valley was thickening. In an hour or so, with the sun rising behind them, their hill would darken and grow less distinct to the German batteries firing from the west, but to those positioned to the north it would become a clearer target. Already several shells were starting to fall nearby. Most of it was howitzer fire, heavy stuff too; the Germans were rightly using more high-explosive than shrapnel. He would not be able to finish his battery-locating work; what he had done would have to suffice.

Pushing past the men's backs, the company commander came down the trench.

'They haven't wounded the lion yet, have they?'

The men replied with a laugh.

'It's a pretty tight squeeze in this trench of yours!'

Vorotyntsev asked the officer to give his sheet of paper to the battalion commander, who should then pass it on to the artillery.

The company's only casualties so far were three men lightly wounded. There was a rumour that the first battalion, dug in below the windmill, had had a direct hit on a trench and that about a dozen men had been buried by the explosion.

As the morning grew warmer in the sunlight, the mist began to dissipate and one could now see the whole battlefield stretched out to the left, thick with puffs of bursting shrapnel and fountains of earth thrown up by the high-explosive shells. The barrage was moving closer and closer towards them along the six-mile frontage on which the two First Corps of their respective armies faced each other. The date was known: August 14th, 1914; so far, though, the battle had not been given a name. Would it be known as Usdau? Soldau? Even less certain was how it would be remembered in history. Would it bring glory to one side? Would it simply be forgotten by tomorrow?

After his short night's sleep, his awakening by a bombardment and the brisk, chilly start to the day, Vorotyntsev had still not started to think very coherently. What was his duty today? Surely not to sit uselessly pinned down in this trench. Nevertheless he felt a surge of vigour: now that he was seeing action, the aimless lounging about and dashing to and fro were at last over, and far from regretting his mission he was actually glad that he was not at General Headquarters, where they did not wake up until nine o'clock in the morning. Today, August 14th, 1914, was the beginning of the second war in Colonel Vorotyntsev's lifetime—a war whose duration and outcome for both the Russian army and himself were unknown. His entire career and training so far had been a preparation for this; he must not fight this war in vain.

'They're easing off a bit!' Blagodaryov announced before any of the others. He had been able to detect the crack of gunfire in between the noise of exploding shells, not just along the whole battle-front but in particular from the batteries facing their sector. He was seconds ahead of the rest, like an experienced concert-goer who starts to applaud before the last note has died away. At once the barrage directed against their regiment began to lessen.

'You've a good ear,' said Vorotyntsev approvingly. 'A pity you're not in the artillery, you could have located the targets by ear.'

Blagodaryov smirked, though with sufficient restraint not to show how pleased he was at the colonel's praise.

The men began straightening up and taking deep breaths. Some sprawled on the chairs and began rolling themselves cigarettes. The lion was examined and found to be undamaged. This caused much amusement: if the lion was all right in the open, why did they bother to crouch against the trench wall?

'When are they going to bring up the rations?' asked the soldier who had wondered why the Russian guns weren't firing.

They all rounded on him with gusto.

'Greedy bastard!'

'It'll come when it's ready and not before!'

'What are you worrying about food for? You make sure you don't get a hole through your gut, or you won't have anywhere to put your dinner!'

The fire had only been lifted from their sector to be moved on to the neighbouring regiments to the left. Centralised fire-control, thought Vorotyntsev approvingly. To have the whole corps artillery shift its target simultaneously was impossible in the Russian army: there was not enough telephone equipment and no one was trained in the technique. But why was the barrage shifting? Were they going to put in an infantry attack on Usdau? Although they were facing north-west, Vorotyntsev's binoculars were trained on the terrain to the north; as long as they didn't attack from there —that would be the point of greatest danger.

The crimson sun behind them had already climbed over the housetops, shining through the trees, and some sunlight was falling on their side of the hill. It was getting warmer. The men rolled up their greatcoats and slung them over their shoulders. Slightly crumpled, but still visible on all their shoulder-tabs, was the monogram of Wilhelm II.

The order was passed down the line for everyone to get ready to fire.

But no German attack came and not a single German put his head up. Again Blagodaryov was the first to spot what was happening.

'Look! Look!' he said, half to the colonel and half to the others, pointing his long arm over the parapet in great excitement. 'Over there! Over there!'

Vorotyntsev picked it up clearly with his binoculars: two open-topped cars driving out of a wood, each with four men in it. They were less than a mile away, and with his powerful glasses Vorotyntsev could even make out their faces and the badges on their epaulettes. Sitting in the first car was a short, active-looking general, the light flashing occasionally from the lenses of his binoculars, although as he was looking into the sun he could not get a detailed view of the Russian positions. The party was travelling from left to right on the far side of the valley, above the line of the mist. There was no one to warn them or stop them and they were rapidly approaching the Russian lines.

'It's a general! A general driving towards us!' Vorotyntsev excitedly told Blagodaryov and anybody else who was listening. 'Now if only we could give him a good fright! I wouldn't mind having a word with *him*!' It was a pity that he was standing here in the trench. If he'd been with Savitsky he could have stopped all the guns firing and turned them on the general. Could they see him from the command-post? It was already too late to run to the telephone.

'A ge-ne-ral!' roared Blagodaryov at the top of his voice, like a hunter who has spied a fine piece of game. 'Let's get him!'

Now the general's car was dipping down the slope into the mist; soon it would come up the other side, towards Usdau. But the men in the Russian outposts further down the slope, apparently unaffected by the artillery barrage, could not restrain themselves and several riflemen began firing at the cars at a range of eight hundred yards.

The German infantry returned the fire.

Suddenly, the cars took fright, stopped to turn round, and got into difficulties as they manoeuvred.

God, if only they could give them a taste of shrapnel! But first the men in the artillery observation-post would have to ring back to regimental headquarters, then the message would have to be passed to a battery and by that time . . .

Through binoculars the general could be seen leaping agilely out of his car, followed with equal alacrity by his staff, who did not bother to open the car doors but simply jumped and ran, crouching.

'If only we could bring down some fire on them!' Vorotyntsev shouted in vain. And since there was nothing he could do, he held the binoculars up to Blagodaryov's eyes. He expected him to be unfamiliar with binoculars, but the man focused them in a moment and burst into laughter, slapping his thighs and shouting so that the whole battalion could hear:

'Ah, the old devil! Look at him! Leaping about like an old goat! Get him, somebody! Ha, ha, ha!'

The cars managed to turn round, drove back up the road and stopped to wait for their passengers. But the officers had already run into the bushes by the roadside, where they had flung themselves into a ditch or the bed of a stream. The general waved to the drivers to go on without them. Then he straightened up and walked up the hill.

Only then did some Russian three-inchers start firing over their heads from behind the village, the shells bursting close to the spot where the cars had first stopped. At least they had found the target.

Who was the general? And why didn't he know that this position was strongly held by the Russians?

The incident had thoroughly amused the troops and had created a link between them and Vorotyntsev. In a voice which carried effortlessly for fifty yards, Blagodaryov now described how thanks to the binoculars he had practically been on the spot, how he had watched the general skip out of his car like a thoroughbred. The men were amazed: were there generals who behaved like that?

It was plain that Blagodaryov was a man who laughed easily. He looked as if he would be a good worker too, despite a hint of clumsiness about him—the clumsiness of almost excessive strength. He had given his age as twenty-five, but there was still something childlike in his fat-cheeked face, and that look of trustfulness which is only to be found in countrymen.

'Hold tight now, boys! And put that lion somewhere safe! That general's going to hot things up for us—he didn't come here for fun!' Vorotyntsev promised them cheerfully.

There was no fun about it; for many of them only death or wounds. But, as happens in all-male company, if one of them did long to duck and run, he concealed his feelings; they all suddenly began joking, laughing and showing off their unconcern.

'Remember, boys—a brave man only dies once, a coward dies a hundred times!'

Vorotyntsev could sense that the company had come to accept him and like him, and he was filled with modest pride that he was, after all, in the right place. He felt, too, an access of something which his years in Petersburg and Moscow had caused him to forget: the vigorous, inexhaustible spiritual strength of Russia that lay hidden under these soldiers' tunics and made them so fearless.

'Where's Ogumennik, lads? I'd like to see what he looks like by daylight!'

'Hey, Ogumennik! . . . Ogumennik! . . . Just coming, sir!—No, he's not, he's gone away to relieve himself! . . . We'll get him in a moment!'

'Well, the Quail-Hunter, then.'

The puny but cheerful soldier Methodius the Quail-Hunter turned out to have been standing only a few men away from Blago-daryov and was already pushing his way along the line to the colonel. But there was not time to have a look at him: suddenly, added to the crump and roar of the barrage to their left, a dozen or so guns of the batteries facing them opened up with a salvo of heavy shells which came screaming through the air—all in their direction.

'Remember your saints?' Vorotyntsev just had time to shout. 'Well, start praying!'

This echo of yesterday's ridiculous scene with General Artamo-nov produced a final flurry of jokes all round.

'Praise the Lord—but keep your head down!'

'St Nicholas will take care of us all!'

Blagodaryov roared:

'Goodbye sunshine—and goodbye home!' He was already crouching on the bottom of the trench, covering his head and crossing himself at the same time.

The entire sector of the line occupied by the Vyborg Regiment was engulfed by a tidal wave of German high-explosive. Instantaneously, thanks to the Germans' centralised fire-control and efficient communications, the fire-power of dozens of guns and howitzers, light, medium and heavy, was switched on to their half-mile of hillside trenches. Some of the shell-bursts were of an unprecedented force, obviously from guns of even heavier calibre than six inches.

There, right beside them, the earth was disembowelled by a massive explosion, tearing soul from body. Each shell came screaming straight at you—at the colonel, at every private soldier, every mother's son, God help us!—yet not one actually hit the trench. They were shaken, deafened, occasionally showered with earth or splinters, but there was so much noise that there was no hearing the whine of splinters. They were nauseated by the stinking, clinging reek of explosive, which even the men under fire for the first time soon instinctively associated with death.

Now there was no telling the shell-bursts apart. Everything merged into one shattering ordeal of imminent destruction.

Even Vorotyntsev had never been through such an experience in his life. The Japanese had never put down a barrage like this. When the earth was being torn apart you felt as though your own body was being lacerated, and it needed an effort of will to remind yourself that if you could hear and think it was the earth that had been hit and not you. Despite all the years he had been studying war, he realised that he had quite forgotten what it was actually like; he was experiencing everything as though for the first time. With a mental effort he recalled his military academy training and reminded himself over and over again that in theory, with a properly dug trench, even an hour-long bombardment of this force would not knock out more than a quarter of its occupants: therefore, one had a seventy-five per cent chance of staying alive.

But how long could one's mind and nerves hold out, without seeing the enemy and without fighting back, simply acting as a human target? He should have been taking compass-bearings and looking at his watch, but he found that involuntarily his eyes were tightly shut.

He forced them open. A foot away from him, halfway up the front wall of the trench and pressed hard against it, with his cap askew, was Blagodaryov's head. He too seemed to have just opened his eyes.

In the infernal noise blotting out all other sounds, cut off from the rest of the world as though they were the only two living creatures on earth, they gave each other what might be the last glance they ever exchanged with another human being.

Vorotyntsev winked at him to keep his spirits up. In reply Blagodaryov tried to stretch his lips in a crooked smile, but nothing came of it.

No one had ever told him that he had a seventy-five per cent chance . . .

Each interminable minute was sliced off with terrible slowness. Vorotyntsev's watch was hot from being clutched, but he simply had not the strength of will to keep looking at it: the second hand clicked round too slowly, each one of its revolutions encompassing avalanches of metal, thousands of shell-splinters and lumps of earth.

There was no more sun, no more morning, only black, smoking, reeking night.

The thoughts that jostled through his mind every second were as crowded and as hugger-mugger as the troops in the trench. How can we fight, when we are so unequal in artillery? The range of our guns is less than four miles while the Germans can fire up to seven —it had been the same in the Japanese War . . . In the Japanese War he had not been married—Alina would cry a little and marry again—pity they had no children—no, perhaps it was a good thing they had none—pity he had never met the woman he had dreamt about last night—what, if anything, had he made of his life?— August 14th, 1914—a professional soldier shouldn't be afraid of dying, it was his profession, but what about these wretched peasants—what would their reward be? Simply to stay alive. What had *he* to live for?

Blagodaryov was now staring with considerable interest at the colonel's watch, just as earlier he had looked at his map-board. Then he started to crawl towards him. Was he wounded? No, he was shouting in his ear:

'. . . what's it for?'

Vorotyntsev could not understand. What did he mean? What was his watch for? Surely he knew what a watch was?

'. . . threshing-floor!' Blagodaryov roared again, bursting his lungs with the effort.

For another moment Vorotyntsev still did not get it, then he suddenly understood. Like ears of wheat being battered on a threshing-floor, so the soldiers in the trenches could only cower and wait until their bodies were smashed—these bodies which were the only ones they had. Gigantic flails were lashing up and down their ranks to thresh the souls out of their bodies like little grains, to be used for some unknown purpose, and all that the victims could do was to wait their turn. Unhurt or wounded, it was all the same: the next moment might be their last.

How, Vorotyntsev wondered, did they survive this hammering? No one was screaming, no one's nerve had broken.

And still the minutes ticked on.

Five at least.

Ten.

Clutching a face streaming with blood, a soldier frenziedly pushed his way along the trench behind their backs.

Not far away one man was bandaging another's wound.

But their link in the chain of trenches was intact.

They were beginning to get used to it. Living under shellfire is a form of life like any other—sooner or later you adapt.

Vorotyntsev looked at Blagodaryov and saw clearly that he was not terrified. Naturally, like anyone else, he did not want to die; he knew that fear was inevitable, that everyone was bound to feel it in a situation like this, but of terror there was no trace in him: his face betrayed no panic, his eyes were not bulging, his mind was not clouded, his heart not racing.

It occurred to Vorotyntsev that this was the soldier he had subconsciously hoped to find when, on leaving General Headquarters, he had declined to accept as his orderly some spineless clown from the rear-echelon troops. This was a man he would gladly take with him and keep by his side until the end of the fighting.

Blagodaryov was now crouching in the trench in the way that one sits out a rainstorm under a leaking roof. He had weighed up the situation and was by now used to this form of life. Already on the look-out for souvenirs, he was digging out a shell-splinter lightly embedded in the trench wall. Then he picked up another one, which was still hot, and burnt his fingers. He threw it from hand to hand to cool it and gave it to the colonel to have a look—a jagged fragment of metal, whose warmth was ironically reminiscent of the feel of a cross one wears round one's neck.

There was in this soldier a great fund of simple humanity—a goodness that had nothing to do with rank, class or politics but was the unspoilt simplicity of Nature herself.

Just then Blagodaryov looked up beyond Vorotyntsev in amazement, as though he had been wearing bast shoes and had found himself in a palace instead of a barn. Vorotyntsev also turned round . . .

Screen

The windmill has caught fire!

The mill is burning!

The fire is easily visible in a direct line of sight above the parados of the trench, except that the view is blurred by the smoke of exploding shells, dust and lumps of earth.

The hilltop shudders under the infernal shock and noise of the bombardment.

So that the mill burns in silence.

It has not been destroyed by shells, but is completely in the grip of fire.

Crimson tongues are licking at the planking of its pyramid-shaped base,

flickering wild, scarlet.

The arms are motionless. The fire soon runs up the lower blades and spreads from the boss along the upper blades.

= Now the entire mill is burning! The whole building!

First of all the fire consumes the outer planking; the framework holds out longer.

The framework is getting brighter, more and more golden, but it has not given way yet! The cross-beams are still intact!

Now all the main timbers are on fire—the framework and the arms!

= For some reason the arms—because of a current of hot air?—still intact, start slowly,

infinitely slowly,

to turn! With no wind? It's uncanny.

The ribs of the red-gold blades are turning mysteriously
LIKE A CATHERINE-WHEEL,

And the wheel crashes
to the ground in a shower
of blazing fragments.

screen fades out

For more than an hour the Vyborg Regiment endured a bombardment which at first it had seemed no one could survive for
longer than three minutes. Wherever possible the dead were laid
out along the floor of the trench. The men dressed each other's
wounds. Evacuation of the wounded was difficult, as the trenches
were deep and to reach the village there were only two narrow
communication-trenches per battalion. As a result the wounded
stayed where they were, with muddy faces, blood spattered all
over them, hands and lips quivering. The Vyborgers were then
battered for another hour, but none of them showed any inclination to run away and it was unlikely that the idea of doing anything
except passively suffering the shellfire entered their heads. Just
as stones dragged along by a glacier survive the melting of the
glacier, survive aeons, survive whole civilisations, withstand
thunderbolts and scorching heat, simply lying where they are—so
these troops sat it out and were not dislodged. Ingrained in them
was the lesson inherited from their forefathers, the inexorable
lesson of centuries: suffering must be borne; there is no way out.

Like the others, Vorotyntsev hunched himself up. Because he
had been through this barrage of his own free will, because he
now shared a comradeship with the men of a regiment he did not
command, he would feel no regret if this proved to be his last
resting place.

There seemed no hope that it would ever stop. And then
suddenly the shellfire lessened—it was impossible to tell whether
it had stopped altogether or merely shifted elsewhere—and the
stinking black night began to clear, revealing a sun that, already
high over the hill, had moved round in the sky and was sending
its warming rays into the trench.

The men began to stretch, walk about, poke their heads up and
look around. Their voices, hoarse and high from the presence of
death, regained their normal pitch as they began talking to each
other again—yes, it was a lot worse than yesterday—look over
there on the left, they're giving them even more of a pounding than
us!

It was even a relief to see others getting it hotter. To their left, along the railway track and towards the next village, the same hail of shells was now falling, exploding, smothering the position in black smoke; from where they stood this new pounding, and their comrades' chances of survival, seemed even worse than theirs had been.

It takes a great wrench to bring oneself back from being a stone to being alive, and, what was more, there was no time to stretch limbs or stare aimlessly around: the urgent task now was for every man to find his rifle—to see whether it was jammed with dirt, whether the magazine was charged and the bayonet fixed. For the Germans had not raised the barrage out of pity; they would probably soon launch an attack.

But something seemed to have gone wrong on the German side; perhaps they had grown careless. The bombardment had stopped, but the infantry were not attacking. Because of this, the enemy lost precious minutes in which the Vyborg Regiment regained its strength and its fighting spirit.

In the valley in front of them the mist had completely vanished. Apparently the Germans were not coming. Then all at once, on the right, came a heavy burst of rifle-fire and the rattle of machine-guns.

His head still reeling in a kind of intoxication from the smoke and blast, not fully aware of his actions, Vorotyntsev seized a rifle and cartridge-pouch from a dead man and, holding his sword out of the way, began staggering and pushing his way down the trench, squeezing past the dead, the wounded and the unharmed, towards the right-flanking battalion whose trench curved around the base of the burnt-out windmill. Although his head still ached, he actually found thinking easier, if anything too easy—his thoughts were random and impulsive. The very fact of having lived through that bombardment had somehow changed the way his mind worked. No theory could justify a General Staff colonel pushing his way through to the right flank merely to help the battalion with a little extra rifle-fire, but to do so now seemed to him essential.

Yes, he could see the first advancing wave of spiked helmets.

'Oh, the fools!' Vorotyntsev shouted in encouragement to the men around him as he found himself a suitable position on the firing step. 'They're not as clever as we thought, these Germans—that's no way to fight.'

Not only had the Germans missed the psychological moment for attack by giving the Russians time to recover their nerve after the barrage and failing to advance while they were still dazed, but they were now committing an even worse mistake: as they advanced up the steep slope, instead of being widely dispersed in loose clusters they were coming in regular lines which made them perfect targets, and were even halting at intervals to fire from the shoulder. This was no way for infantry to attack: they should either move or fire, but not try to do both at once. The Russians had developed much better fire-and-movement tactics. The Japanese had taught them not to advance like that, and also how to shoot properly.

After the long agony of the bombardment in which they could not see their enemy, he was in sight at last! Here was the accursed, relentless enemy who had just put them through the ordeal of a lifetime: they had a score to pay off, and their shoulders itched for the feel of a rifle-butt. You made us huddle on the trench floor— now taste a bit of mud yourselves! Let's thin those lines out a bit!

As though completely unaffected by the bombardment, the right-flank battalion straightened up as one man and discharged a furious, rapid and accurate fusillade, revelling in the chance to punish the Germans for making them cower in their trenches for so long. Vorotyntsev stood in the line with them firing with gusto, emptying his magazine, reloading, aiming, firing, picking a new target—and when he thought he had brought a German down, croaking with delight.

The men in the ugly spiked helmets were coming nearer, firing from kneeling and standing positions. (We don't need helmets! We're all right with our caps, because Russians have thick skulls. Even so, there were men who clutched their heads and spun around.) But the Vyborgers stood and fired unwaveringly, without a sign of giving ground. Even when the *Pickelhauben* were no more than a hundred yards away, the Russians showed no fear, there was no need for anyone to give orders or make signals: the Vyborg Regiment stood and fired with a will.

Now the Germans were beginning to drop, some with cries of pain, some flung backwards as they were hit, others falling on purpose and rolling back down the hill to safety. The rest faltered, turned and ran, pursued by the unrelenting Russian fire. A few hot-headed enthusiasts leapt out of the trench with bayonets fixed to chase the retreating enemy, but a subaltern seized one of them by the scruff of the neck, pulled him back into the trench, and restrained the others. Quite correct.

Delighted at the way the troops had acquitted themselves, Vorotyntsev stopped firing. Clearly these troops had it in them to withstand anything—if necessary they would hold out until their colonel-in-chief, Kaiser Wilhelm himself, appeared! Half drunk on powder-smoke, at that moment Vorotyntsev loved these men of the Vyborg Regiment. He loved the day, too—August 14th—on which they had fought the battle of Usdau. Above all he felt a surge of respect and admiration for Savitsky and started pushing his way back down the trench to see the brigade commander. A company commander shouted in his ear and pointed out to him that General Savitsky was over there in the vaulted tunnel through which the road passed under the railway embankment. That was exactly the right place for the commander to be. It being quiet there, the sound of machine-guns could be heard better, and he was quite capable of detecting how many there were. So there was no point in going to Savitsky. Nor was there any call to go to Neidenburg. Stempel's brigade must by now be in position, so the right flank was secured and a visit there was unnecessary. There was no further reason for him to stay with the Vyborg Regiment either, so why was he here?

The German bombardment was still thundering away to the left, the black smoke of high-explosive blotting out the yellow clouds of shrapnel. The line there was held by five regiments in a row; at any point the battle might take a disastrous turn. That was where he ought to be, to ensure that the staunchness and bravery of the Vyborg Regiment should not be wasted, but should inspire the rest of the corps for the next few hours.

Stepping over corpses and bumping into the wounded, he made slow progress along the trench, although many of the men had now climbed out and were resting on the open ground. Slinging his rifle over his shoulder, Vorotyntsev jumped out and walked along the high ground above the trench. Although he was aware of the whistle of shells nearby, walking in the open was so much easier. His hearing had not recovered, and his ears were not properly taking in the sounds about him; strangely, too, he found he was not seeing everything in his field of vision: his eyes and mind were not yet fully receptive. The ground was littered with bloody strips of bandage and tourniquets. There were shrapnel balls strewn everywhere; a rifle with its breech mechanism smashed, surrounded by empty cartridge-cases gleaming in the sun; a tin can; the brass buckle of a discarded belt. There was a man crawling; another was clutching his bandaged forehead, the crown of his head bare. A soldier was sitting on the ground, pulling off his boot and pouring the blood out of it like water from a jug. A man lay staring up out of the trench with lifeless eyes, while others around him were already laughing and joking. Somehow he saw none of it, his eye and his mind refusing to register. There was a kind of cheerful carelessness about his movements, as though he were drunk, a sense of superfluous, unco-ordinated strength: his arm would lash out, his foot would stamp down or turn on its heel with unwonted force—a state in which a man can bruise or cut himself and not feel it. Yet despite his aching, dizzy head his mind went on working with a curious facility.

In going to the right-flanking battalion Vorotyntsev had completely forgotten about his neighbour Blagodaryov. Now, as he returned, he remembered that he urgently wanted to see him. Was he still alive? Or was he dead?

The Second Battalion had fought off the Germans as successfully as the First. The wounded were being helped or carried away on stretchers along the communication-trenches and above ground. The trenches themselves were being repaired and strengthened, the men shovelling out the surplus soil from shell-bursts like so many grave-diggers. Vorotyntsev found the place where he had been standing—he recognised it by the yellow tail of the toy lion sticking out of a pile of earth—and there to the right of it was Blagodaryov's splendid, intelligent face. Frowning, he was clearing out the trench, throwing away a smashed chair and empty zinc ammunition-boxes.

Vorotyntsev asked a captain for permission to take one of his men on detachment as his personal orderly and beckoned cheerfully.

'Blagodaryov! Want to come with me?'

'All right.' Blagodaryov showed no surprise, as though they had previously agreed on it. He ran his tongue round the inside of his fat cheeks, glanced around at the square yard of the trench where in the past hour he had come close to death, threw his tight greatcoat-roll over his head, took a powerful leap out of the trench and straightened up. 'Where are we going?'

He was the same height as Vorotyntsev, and from the way he

held himself he seemed to have grown in stature since his first taste of warfare.

'Give me your rifle, and your greatcoat too. That'll make it easier for you.'

He slung Vorotyntsev's greatcoat over his own, shouldered both rifles and clipped his mess-tin on to his belt by its handle. They set off.

It was half-past seven; at General Headquarters they had not yet woken up or drunk their morning tea; yet here, since dawn, nearly a thousand men had been under murderous shellfire, and there was a whole day's fighting still ahead of them.

The weather showed every indication of yet another oppressively hot summer's day.

To move faster and more easily, they walked along the railway track behind the line of trenches. From here one could see a lot that had been both hidden and inaudible in the trench: the Russian artillery was blasting away, the sweating gunners stripped to the waist as they carried up the ammunition or pulled the firing-lanyard. But the Germans were wide awake: their shrapnel was bursting here too, and a couple of times it came so close that Arsenii and his colonel had to throw themselves flat on their faces, although compared with the cannonade they had been through, this stuff was a joke.

As before, the main weight of the German fire was concentrated on the front-line regiments.

'Good! The Yenisei Regiment is holding!' Vorotyntsev rubbed his hands. 'Another hour or so, and the whole situation may change.'

Not long ago a photograph of the Yenisei Regiment had been circulated all over Russia, showing it marching at Peterhof in a ceremonial parade past President Poincaré, on its right flank, saluting with his head turned towards the guest of honour, the Grand-Duke himself, stiff as a ramrod. Now, only a month later, these same brave fellows were being butchered.

'And the Irkutsk is holding too!' The colonel was delighted. 'If we keep our heads, Arsenii, we may win the battle today.'

Much as he liked the idea, Senka would have preferred the war to end.

'What have we got to do now, your honour?'

'Nothing much for the moment, except quickly go and have a look at the left flank. If they don't hold out, we can't win.'

Senka had a stride like a long-legged crane; his colonel, he noticed, could cover the ground pretty well too, though of course he wasn't carrying anything. On the other hand, he was continually turning aside and running to ask people: 'What's your unit?' 'How many rounds do you have left?' 'What are your orders?'

Again the German barrage switched back and started to pound the wretched Vyborg Regiment once more, and their sector of the line was smothered in the smoke and flame of high-explosive shells. Arsenii was glad that they were out of it. To him a trench was a grave; once you crawled into it there was nothing to do but stand and shiver, like a sheep waiting for the pole-axe on the back of its neck. In the fields you could at least move your arms and legs and die like a free man. Out here, they had a chance of living a bit longer. Arsenii had been glad to accompany this keen, tough colonel. He would never have volunteered to be an orderly, but to set off like this as a kind of two-man team was different. The colonel was doing more than just staying alive—he was achieving something.

Vorotyntsev was on the look-out for reserve units coming up to the line. For the first mile or two, however, he found none, and even the artillery was very sparse. The only sight that surprised him was a motorised ambulance detachment belonging to the Grand-Duchess Viktoria Fyodorovna, probably the only one of its kind in the Russian army. He watched as severely wounded men were put into ambulances at a field dressing-station and driven off to Soldau.

At the curve in the railway line, where it made a sharp change of direction towards Soldau, they found the corps Mortar Regiment, minus the two howitzers which had been allocated to Savitsky. In their position, on a reverse slope, good stocks of ammunition were piled up and more were being brought forward, but the regiment had not done much firing. It was directly subordinate to General Masalsky, the corps artillery commander; he was nowhere in the vicinity, and they had been given no fire-tasks, nor told which units they were to support. The regimental commander, Lieutenant-Colonel Smyslovsky, was preparing his position for defence in case the battle took a bad turn. After some rapid talk, Vorotyntsev persuaded him to be ready to turn his guns through forty-five degrees until they faced north-westward and to put out lateral observation-posts to the west, as things were likely to start hotting up on the left at any moment. They agreed on methods of communication. Vorotyntsev was looking for the Rifle Brigade, and Smyslovsky suggested that it was probably on its way forward—over there on the far side of the railway line. Further away, in a wood, the Lithuanian Guards Regiment was waiting; fresh troops, they were standing around doing nothing, without taking up defensive positions or digging a second line of trenches.

Senka noticed that his colonel was already out of breath—surely he wasn't going all the way over to the Lithuanians? The ground between was dotted with black piles of ash: it had been a field of rye which the Germans had harvested and then burnt—every single sheaf. The colonel made up his mind, ordered Arsenii to sit where he was and said he would be back soon. Then he glanced at his watch—no, there wasn't time, they must go over to the left flank where the Rifle Brigade was.

They set off briskly. Crossing the railway track, the colonel looked round and pointed.

'There they come!'

And off he went again, forcing the pace.

'Why are they called "howitzers", your honour?'

'For God's sake don't keep saying "your honour", it wastes too much time.'

'But surely . . .'

'There's no one else about, and it's pointless anyway. You saw what those howitzers were like—they have short but wide barrels. Forty-eight lines.'*

'What does that mean—"lines"?'

The colonel sighed.

'Well, the main thing about them is that they fire very high in the air and give what is called "curtain fire". It's good for penetrating the enemy's cover.'

Senka sighed too.

'Pity I'm not in the artillery.'

'Would you like to be? If we manage to stay alive, I could arrange it for you.'

Senka nodded, but he didn't believe it. One had to have influence for that sort of thing. He might have liked a transfer earlier, in the days when he had thought of making a career in the regular army,

* In Russian artillery terminology of the time, a 'line' denoted one-tenth of an inch. Thus a '48-line' gun was equivalent in calibre to 4·8 inches.

but he didn't care much for this war and in any case he thought it would all be over by the Feast of the Intercession on October 1st.

In front of them now was an enormous field of potatoes. These Germans certainly knew how to grow potatoes! And they didn't waste land either: they even cultivated the gullies and the steep slopes, and their fields were all fenced off to keep cattle out. On the far side of the field were two houses standing in their own farmyard; they set off towards them, the potato-stalks whipping at their calves as they went. It would be nice to have a little farm like this, all your own, with your land around you in one holding.

The colonel walked at a cracking pace, and if Senka's legs had been shorter he would have had to run to keep up. As he went, Vorotyntsev kept staring ahead through his binoculars. On the edge of a village was a tall, brick-built barn, around which he could make out a large group of infantry. These were the riflemen.

'What are "riflemen", your hon . . .?' Senka enquired as they strode forward.

'They're infantry too, but they're specially selected. They have more machine-guns and their training's tougher. Good healthy lads, like you. That's why they have only two battalions in a regiment instead of four. You'll see—they'll give a good account of themselves.'

'Ah,' Senka said regretfully, 'if only we could go back to our boys and tell them how strong the reserves are. They'd be much easier in their minds then.'

They were making a turn to the left, parallel with the curve of the front line. Ahead of them was the Ruttkowitz estate, behind it a wood, and beyond that, Vorotyntsev presumed, were the Petrov and the Neishlot regiments, which had moved up to this area yesterday. There was much less noise from the German guns here. He had guessed their plan correctly: they dared not try outflanking the Russians to the right, where Stempel's cavalry was now in position; instead they intended to force a breach through Usdau. If so, all might be saved, the turning-point might be here! The question was: who would concentrate the necessary forces and how were they to be brought here? Who was in charge of those one and a half cavalry divisions which were still uncommitted?

The barn turned out to be a cowshed—by Russian standards a magnificent building. And the colonel had been right about the riflemen—they were tall, healthy, fresh troops. They were sitting down and eating their iron rations. Senka had begun to feel hungry too. He had a couple of hard-tack biscuits left in his knapsack and felt he ought to eat them before he was killed or wounded. He wondered why his stomach was rumbling loudly—he hadn't been ploughing or harvesting or doing anything that he regarded as hard work, yet there was a terrible gnawing in his gut.

The riflemen were arguing about why the cowshed had been built with so many holes in the wall in the shape of crosses. Was it because it was easier to build that way, or just for ornament? Or was it to protect the cattle from evil forces? They greatly approved of the steeply-pitched roof, from which the snow would fall by itself without having to be shovelled off.

Vorotyntsev could not find the regimental commander, who had gone off to look for someone to give him orders, anybody—the corps commander if necessary. However, the two battalion commanders and the regimental adjutant were there, and the four of them sat down on the ground. The Rifle Brigade had arrived in Soldau without its brigade commander, without the brigade headquarters and without its allotted artillery. It simply comprised four separate regiments, each of which had set off to find a task as it thought fit. Had they had no orders at all? There had been a general order from Corps Headquarters to move north-west, but nothing more precise than that: no sectors, no boundary lines between units, and no indication of which formations would be on their left and right.

'Very well, gentlemen!' Vorotyntsev fired them with his enthusiasm. 'Corps Headquarters is six miles away from here, and, as you can see, they've sent you no orders. There's a paragraph in the regulations which states that under certain circumstances what is called a "council of the senior officers present" may take command. We shall form one of these councils, even if it does only consist of regimental officers. I'll tell you the details of the situation in a moment. First of all, let's select a concentration area—for the time being I suggest we take the Ruttkowitz estate. Ah, one regiment's there already? Excellent. Your battalions can go there too and keep under cover in the woods. How are we to arrange for all four regiments to concentrate on the estate? I suggest that each one sends a senior officer to Ruttkowitz to arrange for his regiment to move there independently. As for the junior officers, can you give me two or three as liaison officers? I want one of them to go to the Lithuanian Regiment with a message; we may be able to persuade them to move further left. Another should go to Colonel Krymov at Corps Headquarters. If he can be found, Krymov will immediately move those cavalry divisions to us here—he may even have moved them already. And then another officer . . . Where's that Heavy Artillery Regiment?'

The Heavy Regiment was a mile to the rear. Through some quirk of the command structure it was not subordinate to the Corps Artillery Commander but was apparently able to do exactly what it liked.

'At this range they'll never achieve anything. They must be moved up here. I'll go and see them myself . . . No, I'd better go to Ruttkowitz. The Heavies haven't strung any telephone wires out there yet by any chance, have they? They must have an observation-post at Ruttkowitz. I'll send a message to their position too . . .' The bright flame of Vorotyntsev's self-confidence kindled the senior officers of the Rifle Brigade into life; no hardened old time-servers, they were agonised by their fruitless inactivity surrounded by the thunder of a decisive battle. On their map-boards, pencils racing in a hurried scrawl, they wrote out a series of tersely worded messages. Then, holding their stupid, useless swords to their sides, the young liaison officers ran off. With much clinking of arms and equipment the two rifle battalions got to their feet, fell into line and marched off to the Ruttkowitz estate.

Senka and his colonel were left alone at the barn, Vorotyntsev sitting with his back against the wall, still thinking or waiting for something.

In the meantime Senka had walked over to a pond where some ducks were swimming around, oblivious of the war, and scooped out a mess-tin full of water, which he brought to the colonel. His stomach was groaning, and there was almost nothing to eat. The hard-tack had probably been lying in the store for five years and without water you couldn't even get your teeth into it. It was amazing that none of the troops had thought of shooting the ducks yet. One of them would make a good meal, but it would mean getting his feet wet wading in. He glanced dubiously at the colonel —no, he'd never allow it.

'Care for a biscuit, your hon . . .?'

Vorotyntsev started, took a biscuit with a vague movement of his hand, but noticed the mess-tin and dipped it in.

'Only nine o'clock,' he said. 'Better save your rations for lunch.'
They nibbled at their biscuits.

The colonel stared at his map, then looked up at the road, where some ammunition-carts and supply-waggons were moving along on the far side of the fence. He went on nibbling.

'Are you married, Arsenii?' His voice sounded vague and distant.

'Sure I'm married! But we haven't been together a year yet. Married last Shrovetide.'

'Is she a good wife?'

'Well, the first year they're all good, aren't they?' Senka replied with a worldly air between bites at his biscuit. He said this out of politeness; it was not what he really thought.

'What's her name?'

'E-ka-te-ri-na,' Senka said as he chewed.

She had never been known as Katya. Her nickname in the village had been 'Mitten'. There was more than one unkind implication in the name: it was partly because she was small, but also because she was said to be an easy girl whom a man could pick up and drop again without much trouble. When Senka started walking out with her the boys and girls of the village laughed at him—why couldn't he find himself a big, good-looking girl who'd be a worker? What would he do with this little midget? And they teased her, saying that he would crush all her ribs. But despite the joking he trusted his instinct, because he could not help loving her—and what a warm, sweet, loving wife she made him! He knew that not only was she the best wife in their village of Kamenka, but he wouldn't find a better one in the whole of Tambov province. It was like the way you love a horse, when you never need to use the whip or the reins, or even speak to it, a thought is enough—it even seems to know before you do which way to turn and where to go. And if a woman is like that she is priceless. He never had to worry about anything at home; whenever he awoke she was already up and about; her only concern was that Senka should be well fed and his home orderly and cheerful.

But that wasn't the best thing about her: making love to her was as sweet as sucking the marrow from a bone. And the things she would think up! Joyfully he made her pregnant, and he was never tired of patting her belly and watching it swell. But he was called up before their happiness was complete.

Arsenii wiped his hand across his brow to drive away the aching thought. Every one of these soldiers waiting nervously or eagerly to go into action, he realised, had left some Katya behind him, and not a minute passed without him thinking of her. Would he himself be alive by the end of the day?

'Can you ride?'

"Course I can. We all can where I come from. There are stud farms in our district, and as for horses . . .'

The colonel leaped to his feet as though he had sat on a hot stove—'That must be the riflemen!'—and ran down the path to the main road. Senka followed him in a moment, slinging the rifles over one shoulder and the greatcoats over another before he strode off. One of the liaison officers, a lieutenant, ran up with a message that the Heavy Artillery Regiment had already moved off on its own initiative and was on the way. Vorotyntsev was delighted.

'Good, now we're really moving!'

At this point they met the men of the Rifle Brigade and set off with them to the estate, Vorotyntsev talking to the regimental commander, who leaned down from his horse. The riflemen were élite troops, smartly turned out, their ranks steady, keeping step as they marched. They questioned Senka:

'Has your colonel got some orders for us? Where are they sending us—do you know?'

'Do I know?' Senka replied importantly. 'There's plenty of hot stuff flying about where you're going! How come you're so late, though?' And he told them about the morning's bombardment.

Just before they reached the estate there was a strange noise overhead which was new to Senka. The troops all unslung their rifles and fired into the sky. Senka staggered back—ah, there it was, the devil, flying over them with black crosses on its wings. He was too encumbered to fire at it himself and stood wondering how this heathen thing managed to keep up in the air. What would happen if someone hit it? Would it come tumbling down to the ground?

It flew on.

The estate was a big one. It had an orchard of several hundred fruit-trees, but they had already been given a good shaking; most of the fruit had been stolen and many branches were lying broken. Near the orchard was a small wood of centuries-old lime-trees and oaks, beautifully kept with neat paths. Cattle, obviously high-grade pedigree beasts, were browsing under the trees. The stable doors were all open, the stalls spotlessly clean, the drinking troughs full of water, but all the horses gone. Some soldiers were dragging out of the house fringed divans and armchairs richly upholstered in red, on which they then sprawled and lit their cigarettes. As soon as the colonel appeared they leaped to their feet and vanished. Senka amused himself by sitting down on them. Vorotyntsev and two lieutenants from the rifle regiment decided to go up on to the roof for a look-out, and Senka went in to find the way up to the attic. The house was full of marvels. There had been a mirror covering the whole of one wall which had been smashed by the troops, who had picked up the pieces in order to see their reflections. Most of the furniture had been overturned or smashed. And there was the strangest billiard-table: it had no cloth and no sides, and was black and smooth and shaped like an axe. How did they stop the balls from rolling off?

'Bumpkin!' A lieutenant pushed Senka's forage cap down over his face. 'That's not a billiard-table, that's a grand piano!'

'And what's that thing they've smashed, over there on the wall?'

'That's their family tree, carved in marble. Shows who their grandfathers and great-grandfathers were.'

There was no less destruction on the next floor: lace curtains torn from the windows, cupboards rifled, a fluted, flower-painted porcelain dinner service smashed on the floor, clothes, books and papers scattered everywhere. The lieutenant picked up a book. 'Stud-book. He must have bred some good horses.'

Senka found the way to the attic and opened the window. Vorotyntsev leaned out and even before he had put the binoculars to his eyes he shouted:

'Look, over there beyond the park! It's a squadron of cavalry— tell their officers to come here.'

Senka missed his footing, fell down two stairs and landed heavily on the third. It was all very well for them—he hadn't enough time to see where he was going.

The cavalry was a squadron from the Sixth Don Cossack Regiment which had been assigned to replace the normal divisional cavalry regiment and ordered here as a reinforcement. Senka found the captain in command, and had the good sense to ask them to give him a mare, scrounged a two-wheeled cart, threw in an armful of straw and drove back, urging the mare along with the reins over a sandy path covered with branches to keep out the rain.

The colonel had a talk with the Cossack captain and gave him some written orders. Meanwhile the crash and thunder of gunfire had opened up nearby. Between the estate and the adjacent wood was a unit of light field artillery, who had opened fire at a furious rate. They were really hammering the enemy savagely; it was as if all the dogs in the village had turned on another dog and were tearing it to pieces. It seemed to be a turning-point in the battle.

There was a flurry of action all round. Clutching their swords to their sides, the lieutenants ran off to their regiments. Vorotyntsev leaped into the two-wheeler as though he had personally ordered it.

'The Petrov and Neishlot regiments have gone into the attack!' he shouted into Senka's ear. 'On their own! Without waiting for orders from Corps Headquarters! That's the way to do it! The riflemen are giving them covering fire, and the howitzers will be here in a moment to support them too.' He seemed ready to race ahead before the mare had started moving.

The squadron of Don Cossacks galloped past them towards the wood.

Now this was fun! For two pins Senka would have galloped off to chase the Germans himself, even if it had meant pulling the cart after him. This was the way to finish off the Germans quick— and then they could all go home. This was better than village fighting against village. It was thrilling to watch the way the troops went into action. Good lads—they had attacked on their own. Better than standing around while the German guns knocked you to bits. It was a splendid warm day, there was plenty of space and it was a foreign country, so it didn't matter how much they churned it up. Still, it wouldn't be so much fun if the fighting had been going on at home around Kamenka. In their part of the world, thank the Lord, there had been no fighting since anyone could remember.

The guns were right behind the estate, firing rapid, the gunners working fast and well: this was the spirit that won wars. Even in daylight the muzzle-flash showed clearly as each gun fired. After every round, one of the layers shook his fist in the direction of the forest—take that, you bastards! An artillery captain standing close to Vorotyntsev shouted to him: 'We're raising our sights!' The colonel explained to Senka that this meant our troops were moving forward. And forward they went! Surely they must win, must succeed!

But the Germans too were probing the Russian positions with gunfire, aiming not at the estate, but at these batteries. A little in front of them was a patch of open ground where a slight breeze was making the grass sway. A shell burst in the middle of it and a black column of earth flew up higher than the tallest tree, wider than the nearby clump of oaks, completely blackening the sand in the crater that it left.

The next moment one of the Russian batteries got a direct hit right between the guns and an ammunition-box blew up in a crackle of explosions. Crazed horses galloped in every direction as the splinters flew and the few surviving men crawled away. The mare shied off the path and bolted into the wood, Senka scarcely able to control her.

They turned back to another battery, where the limbers had been brought up ready for the guns to be hitched on and moved forward.

'Are they shortening the range again?'

'They're going to fire point-blank!' Vorotyntsev waved his arm in the direction of the enemy. 'Over open sights! Get your whip out, Arsenii, we must move!'

They drove at breakneck pace through a small wood, overtaking a rifle regiment—the other two were already deployed for action—and on over open fields, through a village captured the day before, past farms and towards a big, dense forest. Here, according to Vorotyntsev, they should find the Petrov Regiment. However, puffs of shrapnel were bursting all along the edge of the forest. As soon as one dispersed, it was followed by another, forming a continuous barrage aimed at hampering the advance of the Russian infantry.

'Can you hear that? Over there on the right. Howitzers! They're firing this way, over the heads of the Petrov.'

'Are those the ones we saw by the railway line?'

'Yes, that's them.'

'Well, we've come a long way since we saw them!'

With an ear-splitting roar a shell burst on the road in front of them, throwing up a black fountain as thick as the trunk of an oak. Deafened, they were just able to jump down and fling themselves to the ground by the roadside (Senka keeping hold of the reins), before a swarm of splinters went whining over their heads. It was a miracle that the horse was not hit and that they themselves were safe and sound. The cart was riddled with holes. They must turn off the road now and drive across the fields, their unsprung cart bumping and crashing as the mare set out at a trot across country, then on to a winding cart-track.

'Shall we go over there, your hon . . .? That looks like the riflemen over there on the left.'

'No, we're going right—we must try and drive round that shrapnel barrage and get to the Petrov Regiment.'

They drove past positions which the Germans had been holding that morning. German and Russian dead were lying scattered, and there were wounded men too, but there was no time to do anything for them. There had been a German battery here, some shell-cases had exploded, two guns were knocked out, and a few dead horses were lying in their harness, the rest captured and taken away.

The barrage of shrapnel was still blocking their way into the forest. They turned the cart further to the right to avoid it.

Just then two high-explosive rounds burst behind them without having passed over their heads. That meant that it was Russian artillery firing short—the clumsy devils!

On they drove at full tilt. The colonel felt his shoulder. 'I've had a scratch, Arsenii.' He unbuttoned his tunic and felt his shoulder again. It might have been a splinter from those Russian shells, but was more likely the German high-explosive which had just burst on the road in front of them; the wound had only just begun to hurt.

'Shall I bandage it, your honour?'

'Bandage, hell! Drive faster!'

The Germans had been here only half an hour ago. The place was littered with ammunition-pouches, cartridge-clips, discarded knapsacks, machine-gun belts and helmets. To one side lay a corpse without a head, and another intact (their pockets had already been rifled); nearby were rifles, some whole and some smashed, and something which looked as if it might have been food wrapped in coloured paper, but there was no time to stop and look. Just as they turned into the forest they heard a rattle of machine-gun fire nearby. Was it Russian or German?

'It's too risky to drive any further. Tie the horse up to a tree, we'll go forward on foot.'

Walking wounded were coming towards them through the wood —poor fellows, they had a long way to go. One of them waved his arm, describing excitedly how they had killed a lot of 'him', as they called the enemy, and how our men were sweeping forward. Another, his whole chest swathed in bandages, his greatcoat flung over his shoulders, croaked: 'They're hitting us hard, though.' A lieutenant, wounded in the neck, was staggering along unable to turn his head. He wept as he spoke to the colonel, but not from pain: 'We've nothing left to shoot with, we've fired off all our ammunition. Why the hell don't they bring up some more? What do those idiots think they're doing?'

'But how much ammunition was thrown away or lost?' asked Vorotyntsev.

Spitting blood, the lieutenant gestured helplessly. 'Yes, you're right; the troops are wasting their ammunition, they don't know how to conserve it.'

A little further on they reached a large clearing in the forest. Along its edge ran a ditch full of water, behind which men of the Petrov Regiment were lying, keeping their heads down, not firing. Across the clearing ran a road and moving along it, less than four hundred yards away, was an extraordinary apparition. It seemed to be on wheels, yet the wheels were not visible; it was like a great beast but without a head or a tail. On top was a rotating turret. They could hear the sound of its machine-gun firing, and it occasionally emitted a puff of smoke with a roar and a whistle.

What was it? The men were frightened: this was something they had never seen before. Could it move in the wood or only on the road?

'It's an armoured truck!' shouted the colonel. 'It'll never drive over that ditch, it'll get stuck.'

'What's that along its sides?'

'Sheets of armour plate, that's why it's heavy. It can't come here.'

'What's it firing with—that's not a cannon, is it?'

'Small-calibre quick-fire; it's meant to give you a fright more than anything else, it can't do much damage.'

'Why don't we try and capture it, sir? We could probably get it if we went at it from both sides and dug ditches, or blew it up.'

'How can we do that when you've run out of ammunition? There's a rumour they're bringing up some more. It should be here soon. In the meantime just lie low and wait.'

But before the ammunition arrived a sergeant ran up and reported that a message had just come from the Neishlot Regiment on their right: the order was for a general withdrawal. The colonel turned on him.

'I'll knock your block off for that word "withdrawal"! I'll murder you!'

'It's true, your honour, I didn't make it up. I'll take you to our battalion commander at the farm. He got a message, then he was told the same thing by telephone . . .'

'Battalion commander! Stay where you are, and don't listen to this nonsense! When they bring up the ammunition, push forward as far as you can go. Listen. Do you hear that? That's the Heavy Regiment moving forward and shooting-in. In a few minutes you'll have more artillery support than you've ever dreamed of. You come with me, Sergeant—we're going to the farm to check what you've told me, and if you're wrong I'll shoot you! Go on, you son of a bitch, tell all these men here you got it wrong!'

'You can shoot me if you like, your honour, but that message came through by telephone . . .'

'Blagodaryov, take the cart and drive back to the farm by road.'

Vorotyntsev was still in a mild state of shock from the pounding of the bombardment at Usdau. Ever since then he had been moving at a tempo unthinkable in normal life; his mind had been working furiously and he had been doing the work of three men. At the same time the smoke of countless explosions and fires seemed to be drifting through his head, and everything was still slightly blurred by a blue-grey haze.

He had studied the map carefully and understood exactly how the operation had developed; when the enemy's pressure on the left flank had weakened, the pent-up Russian forces, thirsting for action, had burst forward on their own initiative. This had not come from Divisional Headquarters—it had been a spontaneous movement at company level. (It was the immeasurable strength latent in the Russian people: these men were used to winning, that was all!) Without being ordered to, the men of the Petrov and Neishlot regiments had advanced—not without some help from Vorotyntsev, who had brought up three rifle regiments to support them, had induced them to deploy further to the left and had enlisted the help of two regiments of artillery. (He was particularly proud of having guessed, an hour before the attack, that it would begin.) With their first success, the men had lost all fear of danger and, exchanging excited glances, had pressed forward with increasing bravery. A regimental commander had shouted to one of the batteries: 'Well done—and thanks for the good work!' and the gunners, bombardiers and sergeants had shouted: 'Hurrah!', throwing their caps into the air. This successful advance, launched by the men themselves, had lasted no more than an hour, until half-past ten, but in that interminable hour Vorotyntsev had experienced the ecstacy of total fulfilment—not merely because they had gained a mile or two of ground and put the enemy to flight, but more on account of the elemental spontaneity of the attack—surely the true sign of an army destined for victory. At the same time, he managed to keep innumerable details clearly in his mind. How could he best help the attack to develop? How could he make it swing to the right, to strike at the German flank? Where could he find General Dushkevich? How could he bring the Lithuanian Guards into action?

In comparison everything else, more trivial matters, faded to a confused blur. Why had they been sitting nibbling biscuits beside a duck-pond? They had been walking to begin with—where had this two-wheeler come from? Just when had he been winged in the shoulder? And through the confused haze of battle elation Blagodaryov's face was constantly beside him: never servile, but always willing; kind to the point of indulgence; never impertinent but with an intelligent, independent personality. More than once Vorotyntsev congratulated himself on having found him.

When the sergeant had appeared with his order to withdraw, this mood had instantly collapsed as though the ground had given way under his feet. Vorotyntsev's voice rose to a shout. He really was ready to shoot the sergeant on the spot, not because he took him for a liar, but out of despair, from a premonition which he had had all morning that this might happen; the only uncertainty was how. The moment he heard the news, Vorotyntsev knew with a sinking feeling in the pit of his stomach that it was true. His fear had been realised; it was disastrously typical of the Russian army.

The Petrov Regiment had received no such order, but through Vorotyntsev the debilitating rumour spread like an electric current from the Petrov to the rifle regiments. In the Neishlot Regiment, which had already started to retreat, all Vorotyntsev's efforts to dissuade the officers were in vain; the order had been received by a telephonist, a reliable, literate Ukrainian sergeant, who repeated it verbatim from his own written notes: 'To divisional commander. Corps commander has ordered immediate withdrawal to Soldau.' The order had been given by the divisional signals officer, Lieutenant Struzer; the sergeant knew his voice well, as he was directly under Struzer's command.

On the high ground at the southern edge of the centuries-old pine forest, at the point from which the regiment had reeled out its now useless telephone line, high up in a pine-tree was a newly constructed German look-out post which had been knocked out an hour ago and was swaying precariously. Almost falling off the rickety, unfinished ladder, Vorotyntsev climbed up, and as he did so he began to feel pain in his shoulder. His head swam and he thought for a moment that he would not reach the top. Though he was not quite sure what to expect, he was determined to get an all-round view of the terrain. The look-out post was at a height of about fifty feet and had no railings; he would either have to tie himself to a branch or be left with only one free hand. He used his uninjured arm to hold on with, grasping the binoculars and moving the focusing screw with the other. He first looked to the left, towards the now familiar Usdau hill—the stone-built base of the burnt-out mill, and the trenches he had sheltered in that morning, now pockmarked with black shell-holes. Advancing down the hill in line, walking upright, opposed by neither bullet nor bayonet, came the German infantry!

That was enough. The battle was lost. The day was lost.

It meant that the Vyborg Regiment had been wiped out, and that all those men had withstood that terrible hammering in vain.

A voice shouted from below that General Dushkevich had arrived and wanted to know what could be seen. But with so many others present this was information which Vorotyntsev did not want to broadcast. He replied that he would be down soon. Then he turned his binoculars to the right and saw that the Germans were already swarming over the railway track; only where it made its sharp curve was there a Russian battalion still firing from positions on the reverse slope of the embankment. Behind it and supporting it, Smyslovsky's howitzers were firing away from their original position. Even further to the right, concealed by a fold in

the ground, the sound of guns betrayed the presence of the Heavy
Artillery Regiment identifiable by their especially rapid rate of
fire. Their shots were falling close by, just beyond the edge of the
big forest, at the point where the whole attack should have been
directed, where indeed it had already begun to advance—in vain.
Over the whole field of battle men and units were moving
back and forth at random, lacking the guidance of unified
command.

The strap of his binoculars had got caught round a branch, his
shoulder was aching, and his legs were so weak that climbing
down was difficult and again he almost fell off.

In addition he seemed to have gone deaf; he could hear neither
what he was saying to Dushkevich nor Dushkevich's reply.
Despite the deafness and a feeling in his facial muscles that he was
asleep, he realised that the division had started to withdraw as a
result of an order telephoned from Soldau which the Divisional
Commander knew nothing of. Dushkevich had come forward to
his troops, who were advancing in a double encircling movement.
But who was to cover the withdrawal? There was no mention of
this in the order. Were they simply to be left to pull back without
artillery cover? Fortunately both artillery regiments had good telephone communications; the only chance of getting out unscathed
would be with their co-operation in giving covering fire. Countless
wounded had been left lying all over the battlefield—what was to
become of them?

Dushkevich was gone, but Blagodaryov had turned up with his
cart and they raced off headlong, sometimes along roads, sometimes bumping over fields. They passed an eight-gun light field
battery which was pulling up stakes and moving; its battery commander, who seemed to have been wounded in the head, was
sitting on a stone, shaking. Waggons were rumbling along the
main road, their horses so lathered in sweat that they were
scarcely able to move. Infantry from broken, straggling units
were grumbling and cursing in the grip of that peculiar exasperation that seizes the rank and file when they know that the fault is
not theirs but the 'high-ups'.

They passed near the barn where they had held the conference
with the Rifle Brigade and met a battalion of the Lithuanian
Guards Regiment. Without official orders, at the personal request
of Colonel Krymov, the battalion commander was marching

forward to hold the line and cover the retreat. As the retreating horde streamed past them to the rear, the Guardsmen, without turning their heads, marched forward as though on parade. They seemed unconcerned, absorbed with their own thoughts and the numbered minutes of life ahead of them.

The Corps Commander, however, was nowhere to be seen. There was no sign of his ubiquitous car. This was the man Vorotyntsev was looking for with all speed, although no one could halt the German advance and save the battle now. His first impulse was to deliver a slap to that stupid, arrogant face, to spit at the man, to knock him down, to say things that Artamonov had never heard in his life and would never hear again; but the way to Soldau was a long one, the first few miles jammed with men and transport which only gradually thinned out enough to enable Blagodaryov to whip his mare along as fast as she could go. As Vorotyntsev stared at the animal's moving legs, he rehearsed everything he wanted to say to Artamonov, but as the journey wore on he grew calmer and reason prevailed. He wanted the answer only to one question from that thick-headed dummy: why had he ruined the attack which had developed with such spontaneous verve from the rank and file itself? How on earth could he have let slip the chance to shore up the collapse of the army's left flank? He did not expect a reasonable answer, but he wanted to hear what excuse the man would give for perpetrating that stroke of idiocy.

Artamonov's car was dozing peacefully in front of the head-quarters building.

Vorotyntsev flung himself out of the two-wheeler, bounded up the steps, pushed open the heavy door just as Artamonov, with his drooping moustache, his hooked nose, the blank, mindless stare beneath the resolute forehead, was emerging from the telegraph room. Chest flung out and shoulders back, he was as ready as ever to give battle, even to seek death for his God and his Tsar. Oh, to take a sword and split that sheep-like skull! His eyes misting over, all sense of rank gone, Vorotyntsev just managed to salute before shouting at the Corps Commander in a strange voice that was not his own:

'Your excellency! How could you give the order to withdraw when we were winning the battle? How could you allow those men to be destroyed—for nothing?'

He wanted to go on, but how could he find a way of saying that there was more to this battle than just saving one's own skin—there was Russia?

A dark purple flush of cowardly denial spread across Artamonov's face.

'I . . . gave no such order . . .'

Ah, you liar, you slimy eel with your fishlike moustache—I might have known you'd try to wriggle out of it! Who dreamed up that order, then—Lieutenant Struzer?

Samsonov had just been on the line, and Artamonov had reported to him: 'All attacks beaten off. Am standing firm as a rock. Will carry on until task completed.' What else could he have said without disgracing himself? It was a proud, tough, soldierly statement. After all, if the worst came to the worst he could always count on being able to pick up the pieces again somehow. Artamonov was quite used to doing this. The line to Neidenburg had been cut a moment ago, and just as well. Afterwards he could report that he had been forced to withdraw under pressure from two enemy corps—no, two and a half corps. Three hundred—no, four hundred guns. And armoured cars, equipped with cannon. Everything could eventually be hushed up and smoothed over; influential protectors would speak up for him.

Even so, things looked grim. Artamonov did not prize his life highly. He cared for his career and his reputation, but not his life. If he could save his name by dying with dignity, he would do so now.

He jumped into his car and ordered his chauffeur to drive on—anywhere, that way, forward to the troops! Finding it too airless behind the windscreen, he rose and was driven off standing up, gulping the wind in his face. The skirts of his greatcoat billowed and flapped behind him, their silk linings looking like two red flags.

He drove to meet his retreating troops, to shame them with the sight of their general fearlessly advancing towards the enemy. He had given no orders to cover the retreat, told no battery where to move to lay down defensive fire, given no new set of targets—other people were supposed to do that. He drove on simply to encourage the troops, to show himself, to fill his lungs with fresh air.

The lining of his coat flapped in the breeze, but he himself stood firm as a rock.

Document No. 1

14 AUGUST. NICHOLAS II TO SAZONOV, MINISTER OF FOREIGN AFFAIRS:

'*I have ordered the Grand-Duke Nikolai Nikolaevich to open up the road to Berlin as quickly as possible at all costs . . . above all, our aim must be the destruction of the German Army.*'

26

During the afternoon of August 14th the leading battalion of the
1st Neva (His Majesty the King of the Hellenes' Own) Regiment
was the first Russian unit to enter the town of Allenstein—without
firing a shot, indeed without even loading their rifles.

So many improbable factors had simultaneously combined to
bring this about that the town quivered like a mirage before the
eyes of the men of the Neva Regiment. Was it there or not?
Were they really marching into it or were they dreaming? For days
and days they had been slogging their way through the deserted
countryside without seeing a single inhabitant, passing only
ruined farms and the occasional abandoned forest hamlet, giving
every town a wide berth and choosing, as though on purpose, the
most overgrown woodland paths between the countless lakes. Now,
suddenly, in broad daylight, they were marching—hungry, dusty,
bedraggled—into one of the finest towns in Prussia, clean and
shiny, with all the bustle of its peaceful, ordinary, yet to Russian
eyes glittering, everyday life. It was filled not only with its normal
inhabitants but with quantities of refugees. This remarkable sight
greeted the Russians the moment they stepped out of the deserted
forest. For two weeks they had pushed ahead without fighting,
virtually without any evidence that there was a war in progress.
Now, as they entered the town, it really seemed as if there was no
war: the inhabitants were walking up and down the pavements
about their business, finding safety in their very numbers and
defencelessness; as they went in and out of the open shops with
their purchases, pushing prams, some of them looked around at
the Russian troops as they marched in, others did not even bother.

It was almost as though the battalion were returning from manoeuvres to their familiar home town of Roslavl—except that all these buildings were very different from shabby little Roslavl and the townspeople were, by comparison, extremely smartly dressed. The soldiers stared open-mouthed at them, breaking step, their ranks wavering.

Against this curiously unreal, alien setting, which seemed as if it might vanish if they reached out to touch it, one thing was solidly familiar to the men of the Neva Regiment—the sight of Colonel Pervushin, their much-loved commanding officer. There he was, marching along with his usual sprightly step, swinging his arms and glancing about him cavalierly, a knowing look on his slightly puffy features—the look of a tough, resourceful, decisive man who tries not to make it appear too obvious that he thoroughly understands his men and their needs and does everything for them with great efficiency. Having halted his battalion in a shady spot and given orders to post sentries, in particular outside the wine-shops, Pervushin announced to his officers:

'And now, gentlemen, any of you who wish to may take it in turns to go for a shave and a haircut.'

After two exhausting weeks on the march, this might have seemed like a joke—judging by the jocular roll of the colonel's eye and the grin concealed behind his bushy, uncombed moustaches—but it was no joke; the officers requested permission to leave and set off as though they were back in Smolensk or somewhere in Poland. They proffered coins embossed with the two-headed Russian eagle and the shopkeepers promptly and courteously supplied their orders. It was not long since these men had been arresting German civilians passing back messages and volunteer cyclists who were acting as scouts, but now German razors glided smoothly and innocuously over the necks of Russian officers. The moral double vision of war ended as though a twist of the knob on a pair of binoculars had abruptly brought the situation into proper focus: war was something that was waged by two different sets of uniforms—total war would have exceeded the bounds of common humanity. Outside one large house hung a notice in Russian, which read:

MENTAL HOSPITAL
PLEASE DO NOT ENTER AND DO NOT
DISTURB THE PATIENTS

No one went in and no one disturbed the patients. Finding that a passing Russian officer knew German, some women stopped to argue with him.

'What do you think you can gain? Surely you don't believe you can defeat a civilised nation like ours?'

The greatly increased size of the population had the novel effect of making it especially hard for the Russians physically to occupy Allenstein; there was simply no room to billet a single regiment, far less an entire army corps. Pervushin went off to find his Divisional Commander and the other regimental commanders, who were already in the centre of the town or on its outskirts, to suggest that they should make their units bivouac outside the town—by the lake, near the river, or on the edge of the forest from which they had emerged.

He met his friend Colonel Kabanov, commander of the Dorogobuzh Regiment, a man of few words, who agreed at once. He also found the commanding officer of the Kashira Regiment, Colonel Kakhovskoy, who had a nervous habit of holding his head in a stiffly upright position; again the two men quickly came to a decision. Without interference from higher formations, the unit commanders roughly allocated the areas to be occupied by their regiments. Under their previous Corps Commander, General Alexeyev, independent action and co-operation between regimental commanders had been encouraged and developed to a high degree; unmarred by envy and petty spite, relations between them were generally amicable and businesslike.

At a higher level, however, Pervushin was not so successful. As he was crossing the little town square, a dozen or so mounted men had halted; some were now holding the horses, others sitting on a bench near the fountain. He could hardly pretend that he had not noticed the Corps Commander, and was therefore obliged to report to him.

Far from belonging to the spoilt, privileged élite of the military caste, Pervushin was the son of an ensign, completely without private means and married to a merchant's daughter. Although he had been decorated with the order of St Vladimir and the Cross of St George after being wounded at Mukden in the Japanese War and was almost the same age as the Corps Commanders and the Army Commander, he had been passed over for promotion and had already spent eight years as a colonel. It was impossible to discover the real reason for this; no one ever spoke about it, although it had been the subject of confidential correspondence. It was, however, obvious that due to a secret directive his further promotion had been barred as a reprisal for insubordinate behaviour towards some highly placed personage. Yet in his dealings with his seniors Pervushin never allowed resentment to show and never referred to his grievance—especially not in wartime.

Unable to avoid the Corps Commander, Colonel Pervushin, whose waistline, gestures and voice were those of a man much younger than his sixty odd years, reported to his exalted contemporary, General Klyuev, about the posting of sentries and other measures that had been taken, information which might not have been considered strictly necessary for a corps commander.

Klyuev had the superficial facial characteristics of a military man; his moustaches, especially, were of the kind that were *de rigueur* for an officer. But on closer inspection it revealed itself as not only an unmilitary face, but no face at all; it lacked any personal, distinctive features. Whether they noticed this or not, all his subordinate officers had grown accustomed to seeing in Klyuev's place the plain, slightly frowning but universally beloved features of General Alexeyev, who only recently, at the outbreak of war, had been promoted to the headquarters of South-Western Army Group, and whenever they reported to their new Corps Commander, the thought that involuntarily crossed their minds was that, try as he might, Klyuev could never replace Alexeyev.

Klyuev himself could not help reading this in their expressions, for which he disliked his officers. He was particularly irked by Pervushin, above all by the relentless bravery in his eyes, whose tendency to protrude gave him an unintended look of slight insolence. This dislike had increased when, four days ago, when the sound of gunfire had broken out on their left, Colonel Pervushin had had the impertinence to appear without authorisation in the Corps Commander's tent—having gone behind the backs of both his brigade and his divisional commanders—and had requested permission 'on behalf of the officers of the regiment' to mount an attack leftwards in support of xv Army Corps. Such indiscipline General Klyuev did not expect from his subordinates, indeed it was unthinkable in the Russian army. That might have been the way things were done under Alexeyev, but it caused Klyuev's displeasure to be especially directed against Pervushin.

He had refused the request; he had not scrupled, however, to turn the idea to his own advantage by reporting to Army Headquarters that he was prepared to go into action in support of any other corps should this be required. He now listened disagreeably to Pervushin's report, trying to think how he could cause the latter some annoyance. On this occasion, too, Pervushin inevitably had a suggestion to make; he did not refer to the disposition of the regiments outside the town, knowing that this would be organised far better without Klyuev's interference, but instead asked the Corps Commander whether he would give orders, for purposes of greater security, to destroy the four railway lines which converged on Allenstein from various directions.

Klyuev replied disdainfully that this was not a matter for a regimental commander, but that if Pervushin really wanted to know, there was a directive from the Army Group Commander that the German railways were not to be destroyed but kept intact to assist the Russian advance. 'I should be obliged, Colonel,' he went on, 'if you would move one of your battalions to the north of the town—give me a map, please—to the woods known as the "*Stadtforst*" and deploy them in a broad semicircular position of defence.'

Pervushin knew that this encounter was bound to bring some kind of trouble; a chance meeting with a senior commander was always likely to be fatal, and doubly so if one tried to do his thinking for him and tell him how to do his job.

There was nothing for it but to compose his keen, if rather fat and choleric features into an expression of respect and repeat the order, his only revenge being a look which said: 'You can never be an Alexeyev!' Then after marching three brisk regulation paces away from General Klyuev, he dropped into his normal gait and set off to move the battalion which was to advance further into German territory than any other Russian unit throughout the war.

In the absence of any officers from the supply and finance branches, the officers of the operational staff sat down on a bench in the shade to calculate how much bread to order from the town's bakeries to supply the troops by evening, how much to pay for it, and how many additional provisions would have to be requested. Several units had no more hard-tack or salt, others had only enough left for one day, and none of the horses had been given any oats.

Here in the shade the heat was pleasantly tempered. The little fountain with its allegorical figures played gently. A few paces away, German women in summer dresses were passing, wheeling or carrying children; opposite, a draper's shop was open for business and a cab drove by with an elderly German couple. Apart from the random peaceful noises of a small town without trams and motor-cars, there were no other sounds to be heard; there was not even a hint of the distant rumble of gunfire, which is like the bottom of a huge tin drum being pushed in and out. After two weeks of unreal warfare, marching continually and never firing a shot, XIII Army Corps had landed up in this divinely peaceful spot, and the war seemed to have stopped altogether.

In all his nearly forty years of service General Klyuev had never once been in action; neither as a cadet, nor as an ensign, nor even as commander of the Volhynian Regiment of Life Guards, and least of all as an officer of His Imperial Majesty's personal suite. He had spent the Turkish campaign in the rear echelons as 'general-in-waiting' and the Japanese War as 'general on special duty'. Frequently decorated and recommended for promotion, by the time he was appointed Chief of Staff of a military district he hoped that he might never have to see active service. Now, however, it had come, and he had been ordered to replace Alexeyev in command of a corps.

General Klyuev had, it was true, been on manoeuvres quite often, and indeed the two weeks in which his corps had been advancing had passed off smoothly enough, very much as though they were on manoeuvres. The advance had only been complicated by inadequate ration supplies for the troops, difficulties in communications and heavy gunfire on the left. (Only that morning he had extricated himself from direct involvement in fighting by sending Martos a brigade composed of the Narva and Kopor regiments—the two units which had been assigned to him to no purpose and then recalled.) He was not responsible for events outside his corps boundaries, and in his own sector everything had so far gone tolerably well; his only fear was that through some mistake or carelessness in disposing his forces he might upset the unstable equilibrium and provoke an outbreak of real fighting. Klyuev was plagued by indecision, and he was conscious of the lack of moral support from his staff, none of whom were men of his own choice. Of the enemy he knew nothing. In Allenstein he had just given orders to select a building for his headquarters, and yet he could still hardly believe that he had captured the town and was going to spend the night there.

Suddenly (was this the start of the real fighting?) a two-wheeler came in sight. To lessen the noise of its wheels on the cobbled street and so attract less attention, it drove right across the sandy soil to where Klyuev was standing. As it drew up, an airman jumped out to report. He had just returned from a reconnaissance flight which had taken him nearly twenty miles to the east. Near Lake Daday he had seen two columns of troops—each, to judge from its size, of divisional strength—marching towards Allenstein. He had not flown low enough to distinguish whether they were Russians, but . . .

Staff officers put their heads together to discuss the report, peering at their map-boards to interpret the information. Then a map was taken to General Klyuev and General Pestich: there could be no doubt—it was Blagoveshchensky's corps moving up to support them on Samsonov's orders. The timing, direction and numbers were all right. Tomorrow a mighty striking force of two army corps would be concentrated in this locality, and if these were then to link up with Martos, their combined strength could deliver the enemy a crushing blow.

The corps Chief of Staff, General Pestich, did, it is true, suggest that they should send a senior and more experienced pilot to check the report, but Klyuev vetoed the proposal and ordered a written message to be sent immediately to General Blagoveshchensky, telling him to bring three-quarters of his corps to Allenstein where it could spend the night, there being no enemy in the area. At dawn Klyuev would move his corps to join up with Martos, leaving Allenstein to Blagoveshchensky.

Suddenly (this was it!) there came a heavy burst of rifle- and light artillery-fire from just outside the town.

Klyuev turned pale and his mouth went dry. How could the Germans have crept so close without warning, and where had they come from? This meant that they had already cut the line of advance of the approaching corps.

A mounted officer galloped off to find out what was happening.

There was a desultory exchange of shots for a few more minutes. The Germans in the street did not conceal their excitement. The firing, however, was confined to one area; it soon grew less and then died down.

Klyuev signed the message to Blagoveshchensky, sealed the envelope and handed it to the pilot with orders to land alongside one of the columns and deliver it to the first general he met.

Proud of his mission, the young airman leapt on to the two-wheeler and set off at a brisk pace back to his aeroplane.

The mounted staff officer returned. The firing had been caused by the unexpected arrival from the west of a German armoured train, which had steamed right into the outskirts of Allenstein and opened fire on the bivouac areas of the Narva and Sofia regiments. The Russian troops had kept their heads and had driven off the intruder.

'We must blow up the railway lines!' ordered Pestich.

An hour, two hours went by; night fell, and still the airman did not return.

However, no one was disturbed; these flying machines frequently broke down.

An officer's mounted reconnaissance patrol was sent out to meet the approaching column. Towards evening one of the officers came galloping back to report that they had been fired on by the troops in the column.

But this caused no alarm either, because it was quite a common occurrence in the Russian army to be fired on by one's own men.

27

General-of-Infantry Nikolai Nikolaevich Martos was, as the saying goes, a stickler for detail. He could not tolerate Russian procrastination, the attitude of 'wait and see', the tendency to sleep on a problem and trust to God for the morrow. The least sign of alarm, the slightest unexplained blemish in his plans, would at once provoke him to insist on an urgent enquiry, a decision or an answer. He could not sleep at night if the most trivial matter remained unresolved; this burning sense of responsibility meant that he got very little sleep, but smoked more and more. Because he slept so little, the staff of his Corps Headquarters hardly slept either, for he never forgave the person responsible for whatever tiny detail had kept him awake; he could never understand how it could have been overlooked, and always demanded that it be instantly put right. Every failure to carry out an order, every unresolved, unexplained problem made him sick. He would tirelessly insist that to every trivial question his subordinates should produce him an answer that was as neat and shiny as a polished silver coin. Unfortunately, his officers cursed Martos because, being Russian, they were unused to this kind of regime. It was this which Krymov found so intolerable, and consequently he too swore at Martos for chasing his staff too hard over matters of detail. To Krymov's rather sluggish mind, there was no more irritating general than Martos.

Although he had spent all his life in the army (starting with the Russo-Turkish War at the age of nineteen), Martos was utterly unlike the other imposing but slow-witted Russian generals: rather, he resembled a cleverly disguised starling—thin, active, sharp-tongued, and to complete the picture he went everywhere in a flapping, unbuttoned greatcoat, carrying a stick which he used as a pointer. Beneath his epaulettes he was less the general than the professor, constantly setting examination questions for his subordinates.

He had been in command of XV Army Corps for four years; he knew everyone in it, and the corps was up to strength except for the cavalry. As it had been stationed locally, in the Warsaw Military District, Martos had trained it in precisely this theatre of operations, and it was perhaps only right that events had taken the course they had: throughout the past two weeks, in which the rest of the army had either advanced blindly into empty space or been kept stupidly marking time, only XV Corps had headed straight for the enemy and, having started fighting on August 10th, had been in action almost every day since.

As in any complex undertaking, it is the start of a war which is hardest; but once the yoke is put on, in no time at all the wearer feels it to be the most natural form of neckwear and it no longer seems uncomfortable.

His corps had, for instance, recently been deprived of its permanent cavalry regiment. It had been replaced by a regiment of Orenburg Cossacks who were unfamiliar with field service, having been employed on police duties in Warsaw. Thanks to the cowardly behaviour of these men, who confined their reconnaissance activities to collecting rumours from the local inhabitants, Martos was deprived of intelligence about the enemy. He had expected to go into action at Neidenburg, where there had been no fighting at all, whilst at Orlau his corps had unexpectedly bumped into the enemy and had been forced into an engagement unprepared. Both the Army Group and Army Headquarters, having even less information than Martos about the Germans, imagined the enemy to be somewhere to the north and retreating, whereas he was not retreating but *waiting* in prepared positions, and not ahead, as they imagined, but on the *left* of the advancing Russians. It was Martos, brushing almost daily with the enemy on his left flank, who was the first to realise that the true position of von Scholtz's corps was in a diagonal line to his left, and it was Martos who, without waiting for orders, was the first Russian commander to start veering leftwards. He also had pilots whose aerial reconnaissance was of great value; it was they, for instance, who discovered the Germans' fortified line of defence behind Lake Mühlen.

However, the attack mounted against Mühlen on August 13th was a failure. Although Martos' left-hand division under General Mingin charged into Mühlen with great dash, it was repulsed and forced to withdraw southwards as fast as it had advanced. At the same time the centre of Martos' corps became over-extended, while his right flank advanced northwards. Martos realised that his already hard-pressed divisions could not be expected to defend such a wide frontage; they needed the help of fresh troops. These would have to be provided by Klyuev, who was still marching northwards unopposed through deserted territory. So on the evening of the 13th—bypassing the higher command, which is always the simplest method—Martos sent Klyuev a message requesting him to detach his nearest two regiments in support of xv Corps. Then, in a bold 'castling' move, he himself wheeled the frontage of his corps from a northward to a westward axis to face the Mühlen line. (This move threw the supply-trains into confusion for a long time.)

Martos was also the first of the corps commanders to spend his time not at headquarters but at a command post, in sight of the enemy and often under fire. He found it invaluable to be in a forward position, regarding every enforced absence from it as a waste of time. On the morning of the 14th, when his sector was already under bombardment from two directions, and when he calculated that even Army Headquarters was shortly due to rise from its slumbers, he sent a colonel to the telephone in the nearest village to urge Army Headquarters to transfer the whole of Klyuev's corps to Martos' sector.

Several hundred shrapnel and high-explosive shells had burst, dozens of stretcher-bearers had passed on their way, several battalions in the front line had been relieved by reserve units, several damaged batteries of guns had been pulled back, and a Russian aeroplane had been almost shot down by Russian troops, before the colonel returned from making his telephone call. By ill-luck he had been put through to Postovsky—he could hardly have insisted on speaking directly to the Army Commander—and Postovsky had refused the request on the grounds that the Army Commander did not want to interfere with General Klyuev's freedom of action.

Nothing was more calculated to make Martos writhe with fury. He dropped his binoculars, ran down from the loft where he had established his command post, through the pine-trees and up the winding path to the hilltop, cursing and swearing under his breath as he stumbled along. He was not so naive as to believe that his request had really been passed to the Army Commander, that the brain inside Samsonov's over-large head had carefully weighed the matter in all its aspects and had then decided to encourage the indecisive Klyuev's 'freedom of action'. On the contrary, he had immediately recognised the stamp of Postovsky's flabby, inky little soul: his fear of diverging from the two-days-old directives issued by Army Group Headquarters and his self-important habit of speaking with the Army Commander's authority when in fact he had never reported the matter to Samsonov at all. He was in any case most unlikely to risk agreeing to Klyuev being placed under Martos' command, since Martos had never been more than a corps commander, whereas Klyuev had only recently been Chief of Staff of a Military District where Postovsky had served under him as Quartermaster-General.

So Martos had no alternative but to leave the battle which he had been fighting since morning—at a time when his men had already crossed a fortified river-line, when they were on the point of capturing Mühlen and a German battalion had just fled in panic— and run to the rear in order to ring up and find out whether the Army Commander had woken up yet. It was at such infuriating moments as this, inevitable in military service, when one's wooden-headed superiors were apparently conspiring to do everything as badly and as disastrously as possible, that the only solution seemed to be to strip off the trappings of the military profession and, devoid of any semblance of army uniform, to drown oneself stark naked!

Soon, however, came messages, reports and questions that required his decision, followed by an answering signal from Klyuev: the Narva and Kopor regiments had been dispatched to Hohenstein. So the tireless Martos regained his equilibrium and once more directed his energy to the battle.

Installed in his forward command post, with good communications with his regiments and artillery units, smoking his way through thirty cigarettes and missing his lunch, Martos might have spent a tolerably satisfactory day. The fighting died down, some new units were brought up into the line, others changed their positions. News arrived that the regiments sent by Klyuev had reached Hohenstein, at which Martos at once ordered them to push on further. At four o'clock in the afternoon, without giving either the Germans or his own troops time to draw breath, Martos launched a new attack with all his regiments, which went well: the Russian troops surrounded Mühlen and cut it off. But Martos was not to be allowed to witness the culmination of the action: an orderly galloped up to summon him to the telephone—he was urgently wanted on the line to Army Headquarters.

This was the very moment when Martos was most needed at his command post. It was more than he could do to tear himself away to speak on the telephone, even to go and meet Klyuev himself; yet his training forbade him to disobey. Leaving everything to his chief of staff, he galloped off to the telephone, determined to return as quickly as possible.

In the large, heavy earpiece of the German civilian telephone Martos clearly recognised Postovsky's tiresome, squeaky voice. But it was not merely the man's vocal mannerisms that made him refuse to believe his ears and hop from foot to foot as though he were standing on hot bricks.

'General Martos, these are your orders,' Postovsky whined. 'You are to move your corps to Allenstein tomorrow morning to join up with XIII Corps and VI Corps. This will form a massive striking-force of three corps.'

Martos was so amazed that he said uncomprehendingly: 'You mean—Klyuev is not to come here, but I'm to go there?'

'Yes, that's right.'

Martos' narrow chest exploded as though it had received a direct hit. It was more than he could bear. That dummy Postovsky knew as much about war as a paper-weight. He was incapable of grasping that today was the most glorious day in Martos' life, in his whole military career! He did not realise that XV Corps alone was successfully waging a heated battle with the whole of the enemy forces so far seen in East Prussia, that each hour of the battle was of incalculable value to the whole army, and that all available forces should be thrown into it, not withdrawn from it. Postovsky was simply incapable of talking sense: right now he was droning on about XV Corps having *failed to carry out its orders* to advance further northward ...

'Call the Army Commander to the telephone!' Martos shouted furiously in his high-pitched, parade-ground voice. 'Call him this minute!'

Postovsky refused. It was difficult for him, after all—he would have to search from room to room and perhaps even look out on the staircase.

Why did General Martos need the Army Commander? The order was issued in Samsonov's name . . .

'No!' Martos screamed, almost suffocating with fury. 'No! Only the Army Commander will do! It is up to him to decide who is to take over XV Corps—because as far as I am concerned he can dismiss me. I refuse to serve any longer! I shall re-*sign*!'

Postovsky did not shout back (he was in any case incapable of it), but lowered his tone and said in a worried voice:

'Very well, I'll tell him. I'll bring him to the telephone in an hour's time.'

'In an hour's time—hell! If you ring then you won't get me!'

His slight, boyish figure bouncing like a ball, Martos leapt into the saddle and galloped back to the command post so fast that his aide-de-camp was hardly able to keep up with him.

After nightfall came news that Klyuev's corps in its entirety had been placed under Martos' command. Martos rushed to telephone the commander of his right-hand division, ordering him to send Klyuev an immediate message: 'Move here at once in support.'

Communications in the Russian army relied chiefly on lone dispatch-riders galloping across unknown terrain that might be patrolled by detachments of the enemy. There were telephone lines everywhere, but no technical units to maintain them.

So it was the middle of the night before the reply came back that Klyuev's corps could not possibly be moved in the darkness; it would set off in the morning of August 15th, but the transfer could only achieve its object provided that General Martos undertook to maintain his present position for a further twenty-four hours, until August 16th.

28

The arrival in Neidenburg did nothing to clarify the working of Samsonov's mind, nor did it make it any easier for him to intervene directly in events. He awoke to find an unfamiliar ceiling overhead; outside were the rooftops and spires of an ancient fortified town of the Teutonic Order, the inexplicably close sound of gunfire, the drifting smoke of unextinguished fires, and the intermingling of two forms of life in one town—that of the German civilians and that of the Russian military. Each of them followed its own laws, meaningless to the other, but the two were inevitably obliged to co-exist within the same stone walls, and this morning, before any of his staff officers came to see him, the Army Commander had agreed to receive a joint visit from the Russian town commandant and the German burgomaster. Flour had to be obtained from the town's stores to bake bread for the troops, which entailed settling accounts, dealing with objections and agreeing on terms. Was the military police service set up by the commandant likely to harm the civilian population? The Russians had taken charge of a well-equipped German hospital, but it still contained German doctors and German wounded; were the Russians justified in requisitioning a building and transportation for their military hospital, and if so on what terms?

Samsonov honestly strove to delve into these problems and to resolve the disagreements fairly and equitably for both sides. But he could not concentrate. Stirring in his mind was a dull anxiety about the invisible, intangible things happening out there in the seventy-mile radius of sand and forest, things which his staff officers were never in a hurry to report to him.

Although in the hierarchy of the army a senior commander holds complete power over his staff and they none over him, the erratic course of events often reverses this order of things: the commander depends on his staff officers for both what he is told and what he is not told, and they can determine the scope within which he may exercise his command.

The previous day, like every other day, had ended with the dispatch to all corps of the most reasonable of all possible orders, telling them what they were to do on the morrow; in the knowledge that they had done their utmost to ensure the army's well-being, Army Headquarters had then gone to bed. By morning some officers of the staff had thought of certain objections to yesterday's plans, but to report them further might run counter to the principle which they had laid down only the day before—namely that the staff must be selective in the reports that it showed to the Army Commander. Although some of yesterday's orders should perhaps have been modified, the new situation produced by this morning's fighting had already made it too late to change them. As a result the Army Commander could spend a fairly undisturbed morning on the assumption that with God's help matters would develop as he hoped—that is to say, for the best.

However, because it was under bombardment nearby, the plight of General Mingin's division could not be concealed from Samsonov. This division—which for some reason had not been transported from Nóvo-Georgievsk to Mlawa by rail, but had been made to march the sixty-five miles alongside the railway track and a further thirty after that—had yesterday been sent straight from its forced march into a full-scale divisional attack. Its right-flanking regiments had almost succeeded in taking Mühlen, while the left-hand regiments—the Reval and Estland—had also made a very successful push before being apparently met by heavy fire just short of the village of Tannenberg, where they were forced to retire. When Mingin heard that his left-hand regiments were pulling back, he also withdrew the two regiments on the right, thus breaking contact with Martos and exposing his flank. Further news was vague: it was not clear how heavy his casualties had been nor how far he had retreated. The inaccuracy of the information gave Army Headquarters a pretext to assess it in terms that were not unduly pessimistic, especially since the artillery bombardment had moved away this morning and swung over towards Martos' corps on the right.

Samsonov was shown a map and studied it intently. He issued an order naming a village about six miles from Neidenburg, beyond which no unit was to withdraw. He had a strong hope that at any moment the regiments of Sirelius' Guards Division would turn up to reinforce Mingin. Samsonov was expecting either General Sirelius himself or his Corps Commander, General Kondratovich, to arrive at Army Headquarters that morning, but neither of them appeared.

Samsonov wondered whether he had been wrong in sending an officer to clarify the news from General Mingin; perhaps he should have gone to have a look himself. But if he were to go to Mingin's division, some vital report from another sector was bound to come posting in.

Thus with no reliable information on the course of operations and therefore having no particular task to carry out, Samsonov spent the first half of the day in uncomfortable suspense. For some of the time he went for a ride with General Knox; he conferred with the supply staff; he visited the Medical Director of the hospital; then he saw Postovsky, and followed this by studying the telegrams from North-Western Army Group. It was nearly lunchtime when a Cossack patrol brought a message from Blagoveshchensky which had been dispatched at 2 a.m. that morning.

The message was so strange that Samsonov blinked, frowned and puffed with incredulity as he read it. Neither he nor his staff could make head or tail of it. Blagoveshchensky appeared to be ignorant of the order he had been given, which was to go and help Klyuev out of trouble; he did not even give any explanation or excuse for having failed to do so. His ignorance of the Germans was even greater; the only mention of them was the curious phrase: 'Reconnaissance has provided no information about the enemy'. Then came a statement that during the previous morning's fighting at Gross-Bessau (*What* fighting? *When* had he reported it?) the losses sustained by General Komarov's division had amounted to more than four thousand men. That was half a division! And after all that he had no information about the enemy! Then came mention of a point some twelve miles south of Gross-Bessau to which his corps was retreating—having clearly abandoned Bischofsburg altogether without saying a word about it. And how strong were these German forces? They were supposed to be retreating across the Vistula. If they had merely lashed out at Blagoveshchensky with a side-stroke as they retreated, how had he managed to lose four thousand men?

Somehow managing to slip away from Knox, Samsonov gripped this evasive—no, lying—report in his hand as he paced up and down the dimly lit council chamber of the *Landrat* like an angry bear, then sat down at the dark oaken table and clutched his head in his hands.

How disastrously the conditions of warfare had changed, making a commander as impotent as a rag doll! Where now was the battle-field that was no wider than one man's field of vision, across which he could gallop to a faltering commander or summon him to his side? The battlefield had already started to grow unmanage-ably large in the Japanese War—and now the situation was far worse. For a distance of forty-five miles, across enemy country, under threat of bullets or capture, those trusting Cossacks had ridden for twelve hours carrying a base, lying, treacherous docu-ment! Any attempt to get further information, to rectify the situ-ation, to put some backbone into a cowardly officer or counter-mand his orders, was impossible until the Cossacks had fed and rested their horses—and even then it would take them another twelve hours to ride back. The wireless telegraph stations were unable to make contact with each other, the aircraft either could not fly or did not return. Nor was it any solution to send his only motor-car with an answer to Blagoveshchensky: a car, too, needed a cavalry escort. And so to cover those forty-five miles—which in Kutuzov's time had been a mere three miles—the only means re-mained the same old horses' hooves, whose stride had not in-creased by an inch since Kutuzov's day. It would be the same time tomorrow before he could find out whether VI Corps had been able to rally and redeploy, or whether it had been completely knocked out of action, leaving Samsonov's army with an amputated right arm.

Feeling like a creature that has had a limb cut off or a wing smashed, Samsonov sat down to lunch. He could eat nothing and was openly disagreeable and offhand in answering Knox's questions.

In the middle of lunch, however, there came some unexpected good news: the line to I Corps, broken since morning, had been repaired, and a signal had come from Artamonov:

'Under attack since dawn by heavy enemy forces at Usdau. All attacks beaten off. Holding firm as a rock. Will carry out orders to the bitter end.'

Samsonov's high, receding brow lightened; he was rejuvenated and the gloom around the table vanished. Knox, enthusiastic as ever, pressed keenly to be told the details.

Although the army's right arm was cut off, its left arm, now the most vital, had taken on a new access of strength. Samsonov regretted having been so unfair to Artamonov recently, having thought him a careerist and a stupid ditherer. Now he was holding the most important sector in the whole army; it was unthinkable that he was exaggerating, or he would not have used such a strong, expressive phrase as 'firm as a rock'.

Lunch ended cheerfully. Samsonov would have liked to learn more details by calling up Krymov or Vorotyntsev—whichever was the nearer to the telegraph—but the line was broken again.

It was now more than ever essential to give some attention to the centre corps. And although it was only three o'clock in the afternoon, it was also clearly time to start drafting the army order for tomorrow—indeed, the earlier the better. It would, of course, have been more sensible not to issue orders for a whole day at a time, but hourly, as circumstances dictated; however, it was laid down as an established, accepted rule that orders were sent out once every twenty-four hours.

A map was spread out on an oval table in front of the Army Commander. With two colonels to hold down the corners, Samsonov and Filimonov paced up and down, bent over the map and pointed with their fingers, while Colonel Vyalov brought them up to date by reading aloud from the previous dispatches and orders.

Samsonov always treated this kind of staff-work as a ritual. The fate of battalions, even of whole regiments, might be affected by chance factors such as the lighting, the blink of an eye, whether one were standing or sitting at the table, the thickness of a finger, or a blunt pencil. As he attempted to reconcile the lines and arrows on the map with the orders from higher command and his own considerations, Samsonov strove conscientiously and to the best of his ability to arrive at a reasonable solution. Sweat dripped on to the map and Samsonov mopped his forehead with a handkerchief—

perhaps because the hot, sultry day made it stuffy in the council chamber of the *Landrat*, with its small, narrow windows.

The orders, as usual, began by recapitulating progress to date. It sounded quite good: I Corps had beaten off a German attack; Mingin's division was holding on to its designated position at all costs; XV Corps had captured Hohenstein and was on the point of taking Mühlen; XIII Corps was in Allenstein, and VI Corps . . . well, even VI Corps might still straighten itself out.

What of tomorrow? Obviously the centre corps would have to wheel further leftward; Artamonov's corps, holding fast where it stood, was to be the axis on which the whole army would turn. The order to Artamonov would have to be worded diplomatically, without actually suggesting that he advance—something on the lines of: 'Hold position *forward* of Soldau'. By this means the Commander-in-Chief's wish not to allow I Corps beyond Soldau would not be contravened. Klyuev would be ordered to link up with Martos by forced march. As for Martos . . . here Filimonov insisted on a subtle piece of phrasing: Martos was to 'side-step leftward and deliver a knock-out blow to the enemy's flank'.

There was, however, one thing they could not tell the corps commanders: the strength and dispositions of the enemy.

There, almost ready, was tomorrow's army order. Although the work of drafting it was rather like trying to find a way through the bushes in the dark, the order that resulted was an immaculate document, written out in beautiful, sloping handwriting.

Yet Samsonov was still not sure that all possible preparations had been made. He felt slightly unwell, finding it hard to breathe.

'I think, gentlemen, I shall go outside for some fresh air. There will still be time to sign the order later.'

Filimonov and Vyalov requested permission to accompany him. The Chief of Intelligence, a man with a gleaming, bald, pumpkin-shaped head, took the draft order into the next room to Postovsky, who immediately noticed that the order conflicted with the latest instructions from North-Western Army Group, which were that Second Army should continue advancing on a strictly northward axis.

'What d'you think you're doing?' he asked. 'Martos should be linking up with Klyuev, not Klyuev with Martos. Then we should form a striking-force like a great fist!'

It was by now five o'clock in the afternoon. The weather was no longer so hot, but the stones were still giving off heat and even in the street Samsonov found it hard to breathe. He took off his cap and again wiped the sweat from his brow.

'Let's walk to the end of the town, gentlemen—there'll be a wood or cemetery there, and we can find some shade.'

Although he had seen it yesterday, and it was now in hot sunlight, the Army Commander stopped in front of the monument to Bismarck. With flower-beds around its base, it was mounted on a jagged lump of natural, unworked, brown stone, from which another rock reared upwards. As though emerging from the upper third of this piece of stone, carved in harsh lines and sharp angles, was a black Bismarck wrapped in black thoughts.

The street that they had chosen led out of the town in a north-westerly direction—towards the position held by Mingin's division, a route which Samsonov might have chosen on purpose. He walked in his favourite attitude, with his hands clasped behind his back. From the front it gave him a look of earnestness, but from behind he looked more like a manacled prisoner—an effect which was increased by his bowed head. He did not talk to the other two officers, who walked to one side of him.

Samsonov sensed that he was doing something wrong or, rather, that he was failing to do something essential, but he was unable to grasp what it was, because he could not penetrate the veil that dimmed his inner eye. His urge was to gallop off somewhere and flourish his sword, but that would have been pointless and inappropriate in his position.

He was dissatisfied with himself. Filimonov was obviously displeased with him all the time; it was unlikely that the Corps Commanders harboured many kind thoughts about him either; the Army Group Commander had called him a coward, and General Headquarters disapproved of him.

Yet no one could tell him what he ought to do.

A little wood began slightly beyond the last houses in the town. Just as the three men were about to turn into it, there was a loud rumbling as a gig came in sight at full speed, followed by a two-horse supply-waggon. The drivers were lashing their horses as though escaping from pursuit, careering along with more speed and less care than was allowed in the proximity of Army Headquarters. Samsonov's companions ran to stop them, and Filimonov, tugging at his aiguillettes, marched angrily out into the middle of the road. Samsonov, who had not noticed, walked on into the wood and sat down on a bench.

The commotion in the street continued: as the first two carts stopped, others drove up. There was a babble of voices, which grew quieter as they approached. The threatening tones of Filimonov were heard as he questioned a soldier, refusing to let the man go. Having been requested by Samsonov to find out what was happening, the courteous Vyalov returned to the Army Commander hesitant and embarrassed, while Filimonov's voice could be heard from the street, growing louder as he delivered a sharp reprimand.

Vyalov explained that these men were the disorderly remnants of the Estland Regiment (which was supposed to be standing firm 'at all costs' in a position some six or seven miles away). They were retreating headlong and had reached Neidenburg, being unaware that Army Headquarters was located there. They were so demoralised that they could scarcely be stopped.

Breathing with difficulty, Samsonov stood up in alarm. Forgetting to put on his cap, which he carried in his hand, he walked out into the blazing heat of the roadway.

Several waggons, four officers standing to one side, and about a hundred and fifty men, who were being joined by new arrivals, were formed up into the semblance of a squad. They had been ordered to line up in four ranks, although they could hardly be called ranks: ragged, curving lines of men with hot, red faces, many of them bareheaded as though on a church parade, except that they were too untidy for that—some had lost their greatcoat-rolls, some still had them but unfastened and hanging down to their knees, and several of them had no rifles. The right marker, a short, dark man, was still carrying his mess-tin hooked on to his belt, although the bottom had been knocked out of it by a shell-splinter. A couple of dozen of the men were wounded; some had been bandaged by medical orderlies, some had bandaged themselves, while others exposed open, inflamed wounds. Although they had halted, they still seemed to be on the move: a force was making them bend and sway in the direction they had just been running. They had a wild look to them, and it was amazing that they were still able to keep to some kind of formation.

At the approach of the Army Commander, Filimonov barked: 'Atten-*tion*!' Samsonov ordered him to stand the men at ease, then

Filimonov reported to him—or rather let loose a blast of anger at this cowardly, unsoldierly rabble . . . Until now, Samsonov had only heard his Quartermaster-General speaking indoors, and had no idea that the man's voice was capable of such violent, resonant fury. Filimonov shouted at the troops with all the frustrated martial ambition of a staff officer and that assertiveness peculiar to small generals.

As Samsonov listened to Filimonov accusing the whole Estland Regiment of betrayal, cowardice and desertion, he noticed the desperation in the flushed faces of the troops. It was the utter desperation of men at breaking-point, of men who were deaf to any general's reprimand. The miracle was that they had allowed themselves to be brought to a halt: in the state they were in, a stone wall could not have stopped them.

Samsonov at once noticed, however, that there was a difference between this, the courage of despair, and the ugly, mutinous boldness which he had witnessed in 1905 on the Siberian railways, when the troops had staged angry meetings and formed committees, when with cries of 'Down with the war!' and 'We're going home!' they had wrecked stations, looted refreshment-rooms, and seized locomotives by force so that their train should be the first to return home from the hated war. The officers had lost all authority then, and from a hundred throats the mutinous hordes had yelled with impunity: 'Down with the war!' Their elemental fury was turned against all officers, however good they might have been: these men simply wanted what no officer could ever give them.

By contrast, the men of the Estland Regiment, who had just escaped death against all the odds, now stared at their officers with a look of agony which said: 'We've done all that men could do for you, damn you—and what have you done for us?'

Feeling that his face was reddening (although it was unlikely that anyone would notice it in the bright sunlight), Samsonov held up his hand, palm outward, and stemmed the roar of his Quartermaster-General's voice. Then he began quietly questioning the men—first the officers, only one of whom was a company commander, then the troops.

Unused as these men were to giving descriptions, their stories were fragmentary and disjointed; it was, in any case, hopeless to expect them to make any sense out of the chaos in that whistling inferno of death and the devastating fire from hundreds of guns, which they had withstood without trenches and with only the shallow furrows of sugar-beet fields for cover. The Russian artillery had either been lacking altogether or had failed to return the fire, and the few guns that did start firing were immediately located and knocked out. Even so, the Russian infantry had managed to answer the German artillery with rifle and machine-gun fire at long range. They even went into the attack and reached the German trenches; although they had fired all their ammunition, they began over-running the enemy's lines and the attack was followed up by cavalry support (this part of the story, however, was dubious). The noise of the bombardment had been worse than the Last Judgment; the old soldiers amongst them had never heard anything like it. Up to three thousand men in their regiment had been wiped out. It was indescribable . . .

It was Samsonov's fault. He had heard that firing yesterday, and this morning he had wanted to ride out to them. Why had he not done so? His guilt lay in the very fact that he had stayed in Neiden-burg until they came, instead of going out to find out if they were in trouble. Yet this was not the real cause of the disaster. In a flash of insight he now perceived the blunder he had made in the dim council chamber of the *Landrat*: yesterday he had sent them orders (on the advice of this same incompetent general who was now bawling at them) to advance and cut a certain main road; as the crow flies, the distance was no more than fourteen miles. But by doing this he had sent them straight into an inferno—to the *only* sector where the Germans had been reported in force. And this morning he had ordered the tattered fragments of these regi-ments to hold on 'at all costs'. . .

While the men were talking to Samsonov, there was a commotion at the end of the line and a regimental standard, the cross and rib-bons of the order of St George fastened to its upper shackle, marched up escorted by a party of soldiers who halted in silence on the left flank—a decimated remnant of wounded, shattered men.

Even though the calm, reasonable tone of his voice could be heard by all the men present, Samsonov raised it so as to be audible to the new arrivals and enquired:

'How many of you from the Reval Regiment?'

A sergeant barked jerkily:

'The colours. And one platoon.'

From the rear rank of the Estland Regiment came the hoarse voice of a soldier too impatient to wait to be questioned.

'Your excellency! Did you know we haven't had any hard-tack to eat for three days?'

'What?' The Army Commander swung round, more shocked and amazed than ever. 'Three days!' All day yesterday, advancing through that inferno, cut to pieces by shellfire, storming the German lines with bayonet charges, nine out of ten of them dying—all this without even hard-tack to sustain them . . . ?

'That's right—no hard-tack!' A ragged chorus confirmed the protest.

In sight of them all, the Army Commander's tall, ponderous frame swayed. An aide-de-camp ran up to support him, but Samsonov kept on his feet and straightened up without help.

It would have been a relief to him to have fallen to his knees and cried out: 'I am the culprit—I sent you to your destruction!' A weight would have fallen from his heart if he could have taken all the guilt on himself and risen to his feet no longer the army commander.

Instead he calmly gave the order:

'Feed them all at once. And send them to the rear for a rest-period.'

But his burden grew no less, and Samsonov walked back into the town, stumbling like a man under a curse.

Just as he was passing the plinth of the Bismarck monument, a party of men on horseback, led by a staff officer, came towards the Army Commander. The staff officer pointed Samsonov out to them. They dismounted and approached him on foot, with their brisk, bandy-legged cavalryman's gait.

The three men were a cavalry general, a colonel of dragoons and a Cossack sergeant-major.

There were so many generals in his army that Samsonov had to wrinkle his brow in an effort to recall the name of this one, then he remembered it—Major-General Stempel, a cavalry brigade commander in General Ropp's division. Stempel reported that he had arrived at the head of a special detachment consisting of a regiment of dragoons, three and a half squadrons of the 6th Don Cossack Regiment and a battery of horse artillery. The detachment had been formed by Colonel Krymov, acting on the Army Commander's authority, and given the task of re-establishing live communication between I Corps and XXIII Corps.

Although in his mind's eye Samsonov could still see those men of the Reval and Estland regiments, and his thoughts were still dominated by his own guilt at the disaster they had suffered, somewhere in his memory there stirred the thought that all *ad hoc* formations and special detachments, such as this one led by Stempel, were always a sign that things were going badly. But time was pressing; he must make an effort to grasp the new situation and cope with it.

'Detachment?' he said. 'Good. There does seem to have been a breakdown between these two corps . . .'

Shaking hands with the three men, he discovered that he knew the Cossack sergeant-major. A stocky, grizzled man with a simple, honest face and a bristly little grey beard, Samsonov recognised him from the days when he had served in Novocherkassk.

'Alexei Nikolayich Isayev, isn't it?'

Although he was nearly seventy, the sergeant-major replied briskly:

'That's right, your excellency!'

'But why three and a half squadrons?' Samsonov asked with a weak smile.

Glad of a chance to complain at being sent on this detachment and hoping that he might be sent back to rejoin his regiment, Isayev explained the reason, glancing somewhat strangely at Samsonov as he did so.

Stempel, too, had an odd look about him. The two men exchanged glances.

'Bad news, I fear,' said Isayev, fidgeting uncomfortably.

Samsonov's heart sank.

'What is it now?'

Thin and haggard, Stempel came to attention and handed over an envelope as though he expected to be punished for it.

'Personal dispatch from Colonel Krymov. He asked me to give it to you.'

'What's this all about?' Samsonov asked, as though hearing the news verbally would make it more bearable. But he was already unfolding the paper with its message in Krymov's elaborate handwriting:

'Your Excellency, Alexander Vasilievich!

General Artamonov is a fool, a coward and a liar. For no good reason he has issued orders to his corps as a result of which it has

been retreating in disorder since midday. This fact has been concealed from you. A brilliant counter-attack mounted by the Petrov
and Neishlot regiments and a rifle regiment has been nullified
and wasted. Usdau is lost, and it is doubtful whether Soldau can be
held till evening . . .'

If anyone else had told him this aloud, even under oath, he
would not have believed it. But when Krymov wrote something he
meant it.

Turning purple in the face, Samsonov drew himself up, shook
himself and threw out his chest. He had been walking along feeling
weak and guilty—but here was a scoundrel who was a greater
culprit than himself! Full of righteous anger, he bellowed out to
everyone standing near him at the crossroads:

'The swine! I shall dismiss him!'

Leaning with one hand against the rough stone of the monument
he went on:

'These are your orders. Re-establish immediate contact with
Soldau. General Artamonov is relieved of the command of 1 Army
Corps. General Dushkevich is appointed in his stead. Inform 1 Corps
and Army Group Headquarters.'

His army's left arm, which he thought had been supported on
solid rock, was gone.

It, too, had been amputated.

29

Throughout the previous day the Narva and Kopor regiments had
marched northwards at a killing pace; forbidden to stop for water,
they were still marching when twilight fell and had to bivouac in
the darkness. There was a rumour that when they reached Allenstein next day bread would be baked and issued to them. But on
the morning of the 14th—after the usual hold-ups, delays and
failures to issue and distribute orders, while the troops stood
around idle, knowing full well that it was they who would have
to pay for these delays later by being made to march all the faster—
the Narva and Kopor regiments were given the order to wheel left
and march back, away from Allenstein, thereby giving back to
the invisible Germans all those miles they had gained by foot-
slogging the day before. They were to move rapidly in support of
a neighbouring unit just as they had done three days ago—to no
purpose.

The brigade commander was perhaps given some explanation of
this order, some information about it might even have been passed
on to the regimental commanders, but at battalion level the officers
were told nothing, and with the best will in the world it was hard
to explain the previous day's forced march as the result of anything
other than stupidity or a malicious joke. And what must the troops
think? Where his men were concerned, Yaroslav Kharitonov felt
as ashamed about the exhausting way in which they were being
driven to and fro as if he himself had been that sinister traitor at
headquarters whom the troops suspected of being the cause of all
their troubles.

However, the two regiments were granted an unexpected reward for their tortuous, fortnight-long march on empty stomachs: at midday, with the bright sunshine tempered by a steady breeze and the sky patterned with fleecy white clouds, they saw their first town spread out before them below the heights of Griesslinnen. An hour later, they marched unopposed into the little town of Hohenstein. No more than half a mile square, it amazed them not only by the way so many neat, roomy houses with their steeply pitched roofs were packed into such a small space, but by being totally deserted. It was so empty that it was at first somewhat eerie. There were no Russian soldiers in it, no civilian inhabitants, no old men, no women, no children, not even any dogs; the only living creatures were some wary cats. Here and there were a few broken shutters, a few window-frames pulled off their hinges and some broken panes of glass. To begin with, the leading regiment could not believe their luck: expecting to fight for the town, they had deployed and sent forward a skirmishing patrol. Not far ahead of them there was the rumble of artillery and the rattle of machine-gun fire, but by the chance of war the town itself, with its steep roofs and tapered spires, was completely empty and undamaged. It was obvious that even before their arrival no one had fought over the town; if it had been captured it had fallen without a fight and been abandoned again.

As the regiments poured in along the road from Allenstein they were still keyed up for a fight, still prepared to go straight through the town and out on the other side as they had been ordered to do; but just as in the fairy tale where the hero's strength drains away as he enters the enchanted circle and he casts aside lance, sword and buckler under the magic influence, so as each battalion passed the first few houses a strange spell seemed to affect it. The men broke step, they stared from side to side, the urge to press on towards the sound of battle weakened and faded, and the cohesive power which welded them into brigades and regiments ceased to exist. No one urged them on, no dispatch-riders galloped up with fresh orders. Somehow, spontaneously, battalions began to turn aside to right and left, looking for a suitable place to camp; then even battalions began to drift apart as companies took on an independent existence, only to disintegrate in turn into platoons. Amazingly enough, no one was surprised at this, such was the debilitating effect of the town's magic spell.

Yaroslav struggled to resist this mood, telling himself that they

ought not to be behaving like this, that other regiments further forward needed their support. But his authority extended no further
than his own platoon, and shortly even platoons began silently and
imperceptibly to break up and seep away like water from a leaky
pipe seeking its own level. Kharitonov could hardly keep the good,
well-disciplined men of his platoon standing alone in marching
order under the hot sun; they too had earned the right to a
halt.

And what about food? After so many exhausting days on short
rations, it was surely not wrong if his men, too, began to slip away in
response to the insistent urge of hunger. Some of them even asked
his permission, like the exemplary Private Kramchatkin, who
marched up and snapped to attention. Eyes rolling, his stomach
at the mercy of his platoon commander, he said: 'Permission to
make a request, your honour? Permission to fall out and supplement the rations?'

Others simply vanished round the corner and were back again in
a moment carrying sugar, or biscuits in brightly-coloured packages,
which they passed hurriedly from hand to hand to hide them from
their platoon commander. Was this wrong? Should they be punished? After all, they were hungry, and if their hunger was satisfied
they would fight better. Was it really so necessary to take such care
of abandoned enemy property? He felt he should consult his fellow-
officers, but none of them seemed to be around to offer him advice.
Anyway, he was a grown man and an officer—he should be able to
decide for himself.

Some of his men had found some macaroni, which they had
never seen before in their lives. Even more miraculous to these
peasants was stewed veal preserved in glass jars. Nabyorkin, a thin,
ingratiating little man, offered some to Kharitonov, his eyes beaming with pleasure.

'Don't be shy, your honour—try some! Look at the clever way
these Germans do things!'

There really seemed nothing wrong in what these soldiers were
doing. They were acting in all innocence, and they deserved a
chance to sit down, to make a fire indoors or outside in a yard and
cook themselves a meal. Most fascinating of all, and something
which amazed even the officers, was the way the Germans preserved eggs: they put them into a white liquid which looked like
a solution of lime in water, and when the eggs were taken out they

were as fresh as if they were new-laid, even though they had been kept for months.

The padlocks that the Germans put on their store-rooms were not strong and, absurd though it was, they seemed to believe that any lock on a door, however small, was enough to prevent someone from trying to break it open. A rumour went about that there were some big store-houses in the town, but that other Russian battalions had already been there and broken into them.

No, thought Yaroslav, that's wrong. We must put a stop to this. I must parade the men at once and explain to them . . .

At that moment the platoon sergeant, a smart regular NCO on whom Yaroslav greatly depended, reported to him that there was a barracks on the edge of the town and that one of the offices in it was full of maps. Yaroslav was seized with an urge to look at these maps before the regiment moved on further. The men in his platoon were, after all, good soldiers; leaving his sergeant with strict instructions, Kharitonov ordered an unwilling private to come with him and hurried off to the barracks.

A few looters were wandering around the barrack buildings, but none of them showed much interest in stealing German uniforms or training equipment. But among the piles of paper in one of the wide-open offices was a large stock of maps of East Prussia, on a scale of one centimetre to one kilometre, beautifully printed in German and much clearer and more legible than those which were issued by the Narva Regiment at the rate of one map per battalion. Having shown the soldier how to hand them out to him and put away the ones he had looked at, Yaroslav selected a number of maps of the areas they had passed through and of those where they might be likely to go in future. Fighting a war was an entirely different matter when one had a complete set of maps. He eagerly examined the maps covering the route to the River Vistula, thrilled by the topographical details of regions where he had never been but where he would soon be going. Kharitonov gathered up a large selection for a crossing of the Vistula, together with three complete sets of the surrounding locality, one of which he intended to present to Grokholets.

But as he deftly and rapidly picked out the most essential maps, Yaroslav was even more rapidly overcome by a vague feeling of disquiet. His delight in finding the maps was somehow hollow and unreal, and a much stronger feeling of anxiety, even of fear, came over him—fear that he might be staying too long and the regiment might leave without him. Or was it? Was it not perhaps a different kind of fear, a foreboding of disaster? And although what he was doing was essential, he felt like throwing all the maps away and running back to the regiment to put his mind at rest. There was really no time to stay and inspect these German barracks, where by all appearances the rank and file lived in conditions far better than those provided for officer cadets in Russia. He felt a growing sense of unease in the pit of his stomach; losing all interest in examining and choosing the maps, his only desire now was to get back to his men as quickly as possible.

With the soldier carrying the maps tied up in a bundle, Yaroslav hurried back to his platoon. On the way, he noticed how much the town had changed in a mere hour: from being alien and unfamiliar, it had become Russianised. Untidy-looking soldiers were strolling about, looking as thoroughly at home as if they were in their own villages; since their own officers were not calling them to order, it was not up to Yaroslav to interfere. A few men were rolling a barrel of beer. Others had obviously found poultry in the town, as blood-stained feathers from a plucked chicken were being blown along a pavement by the breeze, mixed up with coloured wrapping-papers and empty cartons. Spilled sugar and shattered glass crunched underfoot. Through a broken window Yaroslav saw a ransacked home; although the careful, loving tidiness was still in evidence, wardrobes and chests of drawers had been turned out and table-cloths, women's hats and underwear were lying scattered over the floor.

His anxiety increased. Surely his platoon would not behave like this . . . ?

As though on sentry duty, two NCOs were standing in the door-way of a shop, keeping the rank and file out but making way for officers. Passing by, an officer of his acquaintance entered the shop and Yaroslav found himself following the man in. It was a draper's store. Waiting around by the front counter were a few privates, among whom Yaroslav recognised Lieutenant Kozieko's orderly, whilst at the back of the shop the fitting-rooms were full of officers undressing, changing clothes and trying on the merchandise—waterproof cloaks, knitted pullovers, woollen underwear, gaiters and gloves; the whole affair was being conducted very efficiently, without any noise and fuss, with the help of chairs to stand on and orderlies to reach for the goods. Elsewhere, officers were examining rugs and ladies' overcoats.

Kozieko appeared, wearing a pair of brownish-yellow woollen underpants. He shouted excitedly:

'Kharitonov, Kharitonov! Now's your chance to choose some warm things! It'll start getting cold soon, the nights are chilly enough already. You can't spend all your time brooding about death, you've got to look after number one sometimes.'

As the light from the only window was obscured, Yaroslav could not make out whether any of the other officers were known to him; from where he was standing in the dim room he could not even see Kozieko's sunburned face very clearly; the most striking thing about him was the warm, fleecy, yellowish pair of underpants. In a voice that was perhaps a shade too loud, he said to him:

'You ought to be ashamed of yourself.'

Argumentative as ever, Kozieko bounded up to him and grabbed the leather strap of Yaroslav's cross-belt to make him stay and hear him out.

'What's there to be ashamed of, Kharitonov? Just think for a moment. You and I haven't any warm things, and when are they likely to give us any? You know what our army supply service is like—they'll just let us freeze. We have to sleep on the ground in nothing but our greatcoats, the nights are getting colder already and we'll catch cold in no time. It's not even a matter of personal comfort, the army needs us fit so that we can fight better. Go on— get yourself a pullover!'

Yaroslav suddenly felt overcome, not so much by irritation or by his haste to see that all was well with his platoon, as by a kind of profound lassitude that was stealing over his legs, his eyes, his whole self. If only it would all vanish, if only this affluent little town could be swallowed up and disappear; he even wished they were still slogging their way through the sand. He suddenly felt a revulsion against all material things: how much easier it would be to live without possessions . . .

'Yes, but not like this,' Kharitonov said wearily, with a gesture of refusal. He tried to make Kozieko let go of his cross-belt, but the latter was not so easily shaken off.

'Well, how then? Tell me—how? Do you mean we should buy these things? We came in intending to buy them but there was no one to take our money. The owners have run away. And if we did put the money down, who do you think would pick it up? Anyway, you and I couldn't afford much on our pay, could we?'

'Well, I don't know.' Yaroslav could not think what to say. He was overcome by a curious revulsion. He pulled himself free and turned to go, but Kozieko strode after him and gripped him by the shoulder. His face crumpling as though about to burst into tears, he went on, almost whispering into Yaroslav's ear:

'All right, I agree—it's disgraceful. But when you realise that the Germans might advance and push the front line as far as my home in Vilna, might shove their snouts into my home, start wrecking the place and pawing my wife, just as our men treated the nice German homes in this town . . . And I'm not on the make—I don't want any rewards from the army—you know that!' He was pleading, almost weeping. 'But they'll never let you go, until you lose a leg or an arm. So take my advice—get yourself some warm clothes. We shall have to fight a winter campaign, you know, Kharitonov. Take some woollen underwear, and a sweater . . .'

Hurrying back to his platoon, Yaroslav still believed firmly that *his* men would not misbehave. Sickened by the thought of material possessions, he had now even ceased to feel hungry or thirsty.

His foreboding of disaster grew stronger.

Fires were burning in the town, tall, fierce flames leaping high into the air. It was pointless to order the troops to put them out. Here and there smoke was rising from the fires which they had lit in ovens and out of doors. Having collected their loot, soldiers were sprawled around their camp-fires like gipsies. How the Narva Regiment had changed in two hours!

Piled on top of other goods, including a crate of perfume, a bicycle was being loaded on to a cart. A lieutenant was stroking its nickel-plating and saying approvingly:

'Good! Now my young Borya will have something to ride on.'

It was disgraceful that the officers of the regiment should behave like this, but Yaroslav was still certain that the troops, with the peasant's firm grasp of simple moral principles, would recognise that looting was wrong; no one had told them, that was all. Yaroslav himself was guilty. It had started when he had tasted the preserved food and praised it. He hoped against hope that his platoon would behave differently, otherwise how could he maintain his authority when it came to the fighting? He felt helpless; what right had he, a beardless youth, to teach the rules of behaviour to these peasants, many of whom had sons of their own—yet it was his duty, for otherwise why was he wearing epaulettes?

Taking a wrong turning, he lost his way and did not recognise his platoon area when he reached it. Then he saw one of his men, Vyushkov, a tall, thin fellow, carrying a bundle wrapped in a sheet across his shoulder.

Surely this could not be Vyushkov? He ran to catch him up, shouting the man's name.

Anguished, his voice sounded sharp. Vyushkov dropped the bundle and started to run, but thought better of it and turned around with a hangdog expression, not daring to look his officer in the face.

Was this the man who had been so full of jokes and stories on the train journey, the smiling, delightful companion who had kept them all amused, who had told them about his home country as they passed through Oryol province? What a secretive, evasive, shifty look he had now; what a rogue he had turned out to be!

'What are you doing?' Yaroslav harangued him with all the persuasive force he could muster. 'Where are you going? Who is that stuff for? Any moment now we'll be fighting, none of us may even be alive tomorrow—have you gone out of your mind?' Then hopefully, in an agonised voice: 'What's come over you, Vyushkov?'

Still without looking up, with a sidelong, downcast glance, he replied:

'Sorry, your honour. The devil tempted me.'

'Now you come along with me!'

But Vyushkov's legs seemed to have taken root and refused to move away from the bundle.

Then Kramchatkin, the best soldier in the platoon, came towards them. But was it Kramchatkin? Why was he so red in the face, why was he staggering as he walked, half singing and half muttering to himself? But Kramchatkin it was, and as he saw his officer he pulled himself together and tried to smarten up, banging his heels down on the paving stones; and although his legs would not quite obey him and his eyes had a wild, glazed look, he managed to make a very creditable regulation salute as he said:

'Permission to report, your . . . ex . . . honour. Private Kramchatkin, Ivan Feofanovich, reporting . . .'

But the momentum of his arm as he saluted made him keel over, and his cap rolled away as he fell flat on his face on to the pavement.

And this was the pride of his platoon, the man whom Yaroslav had cherished as though he were his younger brother!

Appalled, and now getting angry, Yaroslav hurried on. They had been warned that looters would be sentenced to corporal punishment and flogged mercilessly. Yet somehow he had always thought of 'looters' as a remote category of evil-doers—not as the men of the Narva Regiment, and certainly not the men of his platoon.

He would order them to parade at once with rifles and full equipment in the blazing sun! Then he would reprimand them, give them the greatest dressing-down they had ever had. Each man would be made to give up whatever he had taken and throw it away!

There was the house. The gates were wide open, and in the little yard he could see a smoke-blackened cooking-pot suspended on a tripod of poles, its sides lapped by the heat from glowing coals. Seated around it on bricks, on boxes and on whatever else was to hand, were fifteen men of Kharitonov's platoon. Littered on the ground at their feet were empty tins and remnants of assorted food-stuffs. By now they had finished eating and were drinking something from the pot, which they scooped out with their mugs.

At first the thought flashed through Yaroslav's mind that there was some kind of liquor in the cooking-pot and that the men were drunk. But if so, why had they lit a fire under it?

The look on their faces was not intoxication but the benign good-humour of men replete with their first meal after the Lenten fast. They were chatting and joking, relaxed, smiling and convivial. Piled upright to one side, unneeded, stood their rifles.

When they saw their platoon commander they showed no signs of alarm, but jumped cheerfully to their feet and cleared a place for him.

'Come over here, your honour, come and join us!' Two men hurried forward; one rinsed his mug while the other dipped his into the pot still dirty, both competing to be the first to offer him their mugs, hot and brim-full, as though welcoming a guest to the Easter feast.

'Just try this cocoa, your honour, it's good!'

And Nabyorkin, who was quick on his feet despite being small and fat, was the first to offer his mug, adding in his squeaky voice:

'Have a drink of cocoa, your honour! It's what the Germans drink, lucky sods!'

Yaroslav could not shout at them, admonish them or give

them punishment-drill. He could not even refuse the drink offered him with such childlike enthusiasm.

A lump came into his dry throat, then he took a gulp of cocoa.

Behind the low wall at the back of the yard was an empty plot; beyond it, a two-storey house with a mansard roof was blazing. One by one the tiles on the dormer window exploded with little pops. At first thick black smoke poured out of the dormer, then all at once several broad, steady tongues of flame broke through.

No one ran to put it out.

Crackling, the smoke and flames consumed the abandoned wealth, the now useless products of German ingenuity and German labour, and the fire's voices hissed and groaned. All was now lost, they said; chaos and hatred had come; the old life was gone for ever.

PROPERTY OF
GOVERNOR SIMCOE SECONDARY SCHOOL

30

After a night spent in retreating a distance of nearly fifteen miles from Bischofsburg, screened from the Germans by a re-formed rearguard (still commanded by Nechvolodov), the shaken Blagoveshchensky halted on the morning of August 14th in the village of Mensguth. For a whole day neither he nor his staff issued any orders to VI Corps. Nechvolodov's rearguard was holding its position and would do so for as long as it was thought necessary. Various infantry and cavalry units of the corps had pulled back on their own initiative, without asking the Corps Commander's permission or informing him of their whereabouts; it was so much less trouble.

General-of-Infantry Blagoveshchensky had never commanded so much as a company in war—and now he had suddenly been given an army corps. As Chief of Military Communications he had once been in charge of all army rail movements. In the Japanese War he had served as Senior Duty Officer at General Headquarters, where he had spent his time writing out rail-travel warrants and had devised a scientific system for organising how, to whom and in what circumstances they should be issued. Yesterday he had been delivered a crushing blow; today the general's soul needed peace and quiet to pick up the pieces and stick them together again.

Most of the day was quiet. VI Corps had retreated so far the previous night that the Germans had not caught up with them. But calm is never long-lived in war, and they were not granted a full day's peace. Between five and six o'clock in the evening, sounds of fighting were heard coming from the direction of the rearguard in the north. High-explosive shells even began to fall on Mensguth from long-range German guns. Once more, alarm stirred in General Blagoveshchensky's breast and his staff looked grim.

Suddenly—this was the last straw—from quite a different direction, a Cossack galloped into Mensguth with a message from a Don Cossack squadron on flank picket duty. Everything in the message was correctly stated: the squadron had been in contact with the enemy at a point some nine miles away. But the messenger himself was bursting to tell someone that he had just been in action against the Germans. As he rode into Mensguth he saw another squadron of his own regiment, and . . .

Screen

Reining in his horse, the bold Cossack
waves the message and,
pointing over his shoulder (meaning: 'We've been in a
    fight back there!'),
shouts cheerfully to his fellow-Cossacks:
    'The Germans! The Germans!'
and gallops off again; he must not be delayed—he has a
    message for headquarters.
  = But the other Cossacks, camped in a large farmyard
    behind a fence, glance around at each other in alarm:
      *'Germans? The Germans—here? God almighty! We're
      not even saddled up!'*
They hurriedly saddle up,
lead their horses out of the stables at a run,
carry something out of the farmhouse,
tie it up with spare stirrup-leathers,
mount—
and out of the yard.
Clatter of horses' hooves.
    = Almost the whole squadron is galloping down the street.
Sound of hooves
    along the street.
    = But a Cossack lieutenant (of the same regiment, wearing
    the same epaulettes),
standing some distance away at a cross-roads, sees them and
    fails to recognise them.

≒ He turns his horse around and heads
at full speed for the nearby headquarters.
He rides up to a colonel of dragoons, who at that very moment is reading
the dispatch brought by the first Cossack.

≒ The lieutenant says:
> '*Permission to report, Colonel. German cavalry coming down the next street in squadron strength!*'

Unafraid, the lieutenant asks:
> '*Permission to deploy headquarters squadron to beat off the enemy cavalry?*'

≒ At once the colonel of dragoons roars out the order:
> '*Headquarters Duty Officer! Headquarters squadron to stand to!*'

≒ The duty captain shouts as he runs:
> '*Stand to! Stand to!*'

≒ Well trained, the infantrymen are already running out of their billets, rifles in hand.
There are two companies of them.
The officers bark out orders:
> '*By platoons—fall in!*
> *Right-dress!*'

No time to dress the ranks. The cavalry are
already galloping in twos and threes through the open gates and immediately turn

≒ in the direction where the lieutenant is pointing. Over there!

≒ The lieutenant points out to them: Over there!

≒ Indoors, the colonel of dragoons reports to
an exhausted, weakened, grey-haired general, who relapses further into helpless indecision as he hears the news:
> '*Your excellency! Enemy cavalry have broken through to Mensguth! I have taken the necessary . . .*'

What agony for the sick old man. He has been expecting some such horror. How he longs to be lying at home in safety on his big bed . . . even on top of a peasant stove would be better than this . . .

The general is ill and suffering. He should be taken to a doctor, to a hospital ward . . . His lips slacken and droop, unable to take on the form of a mouth:
> '*To Ortelsburg . . . to Ortelsburg . . .*'

= The dragoon colonel rapidly gives instructions.
= Load up! We're moving!
= Some staff officers are just about to hang up a map on
   the wall—
   good thing they don't have time to do it. Roll it up.
= The headquarters is soon on the move. Everyone knows
   what to do, what to carry.
= The general's car is ready and waiting.
= The general, too, moves as fast as he can; he is helped
   out.
   The car is full. They move off,
      escorted by mounted Cossacks and
      followed by a procession of waggons and carts,
   men clamber on any vehicle they can find—
   through the gates! Let's go! Faster!
= The main road.
   Not a road—a flood of men running away,
   though not running (too crowded), but pouring along.
      Everyone wants to save his skin, no one wants to be
      taken prisoner.
   The infantry ride
   on ammunition-limbers,
   on gun-carriages, in headlong retreat, each man insisting
      on the right to a place.
   A cook rides on a field kitchen, the chimney lowered on
      to its side.
   The waggon-drivers, above all, must get away as fast as
      they can, and a way is cleared for them.
Confused rumble of movement.
= Amidst this river of humanity
   how is the corps commander's car to get through, so that
      it can move faster than all the others, overtake them?
      He must move the fastest—his life is the most precious!
Blow the horn?
   Useless.
= Like this: the leading Cossacks of the escort
   clear the way:
      'Move over to the curb, you bastard!'
   The car glides forward through the cleared space, which
   immediately fills up again behind it.
= The general can hardly hold his head up;

[323]

nothing matters to him any more:
'*Drive on, drive on.*'
≈ The sun is setting.
In the distance
visibility is getting worse. The grey mass flows on.
Ahead something is burning.
Closer.
A huge fire.
Close-up.
It is Ortelsburg—burning.
The whole town is on fire.
Constant, frequent explosions as roof-tiles crack from heat.
At the head of the column:
≈ the town is impassable.
≈ The column comes to a halt.
≈ Only the Corps Commander's car moves on with the help
of Cossacks, waving their sabres:
'*Move over, you damn sheep!*'
The car forces its way through the last few yards of the
jammed road and turns aside to find a detour.
Lurching over bumps,
it follows a road leading round the town. The column
follows (lit by the burning town).
It is growing dark behind them.
But far to the rear—sudden movement.
It is coming towards them.
Piercing shouts:
'*Cavalry!*'
'*They're outflanking us!*'
≈ Alarm! Nowhere to turn off the road. Caught in a trap.
Fear and terror on men's faces (by the light of fires).
≈ A two-wheeler turns off the road
over the ditch, the ruts,
and overturns!
≈ Who cares? Every man for himself.
In the rear: rifle-fire.
≈ The shots are coming from the men in the column.
They are firing at pursuing cavalry, which cannot be
seen. Shadowy horsemen vanish.

[324]

= A runaway horse knocks a man down and tramples him:
      'A-a-a-hh!'
further back:
a shout of
      'Hurrah!'
Heavier firing.
= No one knows who's supposed to be firing. Random shots.
Infantry officer's word of command:
        'Company! In line—down!'
= Figures throw themselves prone on either side of the
    road.
Flashes from their rifle-muzzles close to the ground.
= Horses are wounded. A limber-team bolts, running down
    men and crushing them:
      'A-a-a-hh!'
A runaway waggon. Men leap out of its way, off the road,
    dropping everything they are carrying.
= A gun-team bolts, knocks over a waggon,
then another.
Cracking and splintering as waggon-shafts snap.
= Somebody cuts the traces. The waggon rolls on into the
    ditch, men run to catch the loose horses.
Everything is seen either by the reflected light of the burning
    town or against its background glare.
= Another runaway limber-team. Men jump out of its way.
The road clears of people,
horses trample abandoned equipment,
prance wildly about; wheels spin in the air.
Splintering sound.
= A horse-drawn ambulance at full speed.
Suddenly a wheel comes off.
The wheel rolls on ahead and overtakes the ambulance.
The wheel seems to grow bigger
and bigger
until it fills the whole screen!
THE WHEEL rolls on, lit up by fire, alone,
unstoppable,
crushing everything—
THE WHEEL!!!
Mad, tearing sound of rifle-fire, machine-gun fire, artillery fire!

Reddened by fire, THE WHEEL still rolls.
= The firelight glitters with savage joy,
= turning the wheel purple!
= Faces of little, frightened men:
  Why is it rolling by itself? Why is it so big?
= No longer. It is growing smaller.
Wheel shrinks in size.
= It is just an ordinary wheel from an ambulance waggon.
  Now it is slowing down. It falls over.
= The ambulance races on without one of its wheels,
    dragging the axle along the ground;
  behind it comes a field kitchen, its chimney broken, just
    about to drop off.
Firing.
= Line of men, prone, firing to the rear.
= Out of the murk, alongside the road, galloping horsemen:
  Cavalry attacking the column!
  It's all up—we're finished!
  The dragoons are shouting:
      'We're Russians! We're on your side, you mother-
      fuckers! What the hell are you shooting at us for?'

31

Today, something had broken through the veil which shrouded
Samsonov's mind and the buzzing sensation which had lately so
hindered his thinking. It was a completely useless thought, however; simply one sentence from a school textbook of German:
'*Es war die höchste Zeit, sich zu retten.*'* The quotation was from
a passage about Napoleon in the burning city of Moscow. He
remembered nothing else of it but that one sentence, thanks to
the unusual combination of words '*die höchste Zeit*'—which
literally means 'the highest time', implying that time can form a
peak, at the summit of which is one single moment in which to
escape. No one, perhaps, would ever know whether Napoleon had
been in such peril in Moscow, nor whether the timing of his escape
really had been such a now-or-never matter; but at this moment
Samsonov's heart was gripped by a feeling of dull, nagging unease
that the next few hours would have precisely that significance for
him: '*die höchste Zeit*'.

Unfortunately he could not see where that peak of time was nor
where he should apply a push to set things moving in the right
direction. He could not grasp the overall situation of his army
clearly, nor could he decide on a definite course of action.

Thanks to Artamonov's treacherous work, the entire left flank of
the army had been laid bare. Did this therefore mean that the daily
order to the corps of Second Army, which was already prepared,
should now be changed? And if so, what changes ought to be
made? Obviously, the centre corps should at once wheel left and
strike at the enemy. How was this to be done? Should he bring the

* It was high time to escape.

advance of the centre corps to a complete halt? This was the course most likely to get him into trouble. For the past four days Samsonov had been smarting under the slur cast upon him when Zhilinsky had called him a coward. Should he order the flanking corps to return to the attack? This would be desirable, but to do so at present was out of the question.

None of the officers of his staff produced any suggestions for a decisive change in the orders.

The telegraph apparatus was working again. Having crossed in transmission Samsonov's order dismissing Artamonov, the latter's most recent dispatch had just arrived after some delay: 'After heavy fighting and under strong enemy pressure have withdrawn to Soldau.' Since Artamonov was such a liar, it could well be that Soldau had already been given up. But this was evidently not so; throughout the evening, the telegraph line from Soldau continued to operate.

A report came from 1 Corps that General Dushkevich was in the forward positions, and that for the time being the corps Inspector of Artillery, General Prince Masalsky, would assume command.

There was also some delay before Second Army Headquarters telegraphed to Army Group Headquarters the news that Artamonov had been relieved of his command. Since 1 Corps was only partially subordinate to Second Army, the dismissal might not be confirmed. However, Zhilinsky and Oranovsky did not react to the news. They were, in fact, silent for most of the day, as though nothing was happening and no serious fighting was due to take place the next day.

Glum and scowling with the strain of concentration, the Army Commander left the headquarters to take a rest in his nearby billet. No one could have guessed it from his look, but he was perturbed by something which only he could sense: he felt as though somewhere deep in his mind two layers of consciousness, which were normally welded together, had become detached and were beginning very slowly to slide irretrievably apart.

All the time Samsonov was straining to hear the sound of that imperceptible dislocation.

His room was cool during the daytime, but now, as evening approached, it had become hot and stuffy, even though one window was open and the aperture was only covered with thin wire gauze.

Samsonov took off his boots and lay down.

Until the twilight grew too dark, he could see from his pillow a large engraving on the wall which might have been placed there to mock him: it showed Frederick the Great surrounded by his victorious generals—a gallant band of men sporting waxed moustaches.

It was strange. In the last few hours, his anger at Blagovesh-chensky and at Artamonov for his lying incompetence had evaporated. It was, after all, only as a result of pressure, bad luck and hellish enemy bombardment that they had behaved as they did. To be angry with them was unjust, irrelevant, and an evasion of the real issue: how could he blame them when he himself was quite as guilty? Putting himself in their places, Samsonov even found it possible to justify them; in this war, where the field of action was so extensive, a corps commander had too little control over events.

But having justified the mistakes of his subordinates what was there to be said for his own conduct?

In all his military career, Samsonov had never imagined that so many dire problems could combine to face him at once, as was happening now.

Just as a jar of sunflower-seed oil, shaken until it is cloudy, needs to stand a while for the dregs to settle to the bottom and for the rest to regain its sunny, transparent colour with a few bubbles floating on the top, so Samsonov longed for some peace and quiet to clarify his mind. He knew what was needed to achieve this: he must pray.

His daily morning and evening prayers, over-familiar and mumbled in haste while his thoughts raced ahead to cope with more mundane matters, were like washing one's hands fully dressed: a mite of cleanliness so small as to be almost imperceptible. But concentrated, dedicated prayer, prayer that was like a hunger that must be satisfied and for which there was no substitute—that kind of prayer, Samsonov recalled, always transformed and fortified him.

Without calling for his orderly Kupchik, he got up, fumbled for matches, lit the little wick of his cut-glass bedside lamp and shot the bolt on the door. He did not draw the curtains, as he was not overlooked from the house opposite.

He opened the little white metal, portable, folding icon and arranged its three panels so that it stood firmly on the table. He lowered himself heavily to his knees without bothering to see whether the floor was clean. Feeling satisfaction from the pain in his knees caused by the weight of his ponderous body, he stared at the crucifixion in the central panel of the icon and at the two saints on the smaller side-panels—Saint George and Saint Nicholas. He began to pray.

At first he recited in full two or three familiar prayers—'Let God arise!', 'Whoso dwelleth under the defence of the Most High' —but after that he prayed in a flow of thought that formed itself unconsciously and without spoken words, only occasionally leaning on the support of certain powerful, memorable phrases that stuck in his mind: 'Thy most radiant countenance, O Giver of Life!' ... 'O Mother of God, Thou that lovest God and art full of grace ...'. Then, in wordless prayer, he would return to the vaporous clouds, the mists swirling across the layers of his consciousness, which groaned and shifted like ice breaking up on the rivers in spring.

To express truly and completely the anguish which was burdening him, neither set prayers nor even his own words sufficed; the only means was to kneel upon aching knees (although he was now oblivious of the pain) and to gaze before him intently in silent devotion. This was the way he could lay before God the totality of his life and his present suffering. God must surely know that he had not spent his life in the service for the sake of personal glory or to wield power; the medals he wore were not mere adornments and he was praying for the success of his troops not in order to save his own reputation, but to serve the might of Russia, for much of her future destiny might depend upon this opening battle of the campaign.

He prayed that the victims of war might not die in vain; that there might be a reward for the sacrifice made by those who, struck down unawares by lead and iron, might not even have time to cross themselves before dying. He prayed for clarity to be granted to his anguished mind, so that on that crucial, topmost peak of time he might take the right decision—and thus ensure that those who gave their lives did not do so for nothing.

As he knelt, the full weight of his body pressing to the floor through his knees, he stared at the folding icon placed at the level of his eyes. Whispering, he prayed and crossed himself—and each time he did so the weight of his right arm seemed to grow less, the burden of his body seemed to lighten, and light filled his mind; soundlessly and invisibly the heaviness and darkness fell away from him, vanished, evaporated: God had taken all the burden upon Himself, for in Him lay the power to give rest to all who were heavy-laden.

Samsonov felt as though he had been freed of rank and position; he was no longer conscious of the tower of Neidenburg or of the nearby Army Headquarters, and as he prayed he seemed to float into union with the powers above and to give himself up to their will. For were not all strategy and tactics, the problems of supply, communications and intelligence, no more than the swarming of ants in the eyes of God? And if it should please the Lord to intervene in the course of the battle, as according to legend had happened more than once in days gone by, a miraculous victory would be won despite all the petty failings of sinful men.

For some time a dark, brilliantly coloured moth, so large and noisy that it might have been a bird, had been beating against the wire gauze of the window. Perhaps, with its unusual size and vaguely sinister colouring, it was an evil omen . . .

Wiping away the sweat brought on by the stuffy room, Samsonov rose from his prayers. No one had disturbed him to ask a question, or to bring either good or bad news. The wide-flung battles, in which tens of thousands of men were engaged, had been left to continue under their own momentum, uninfluenced by the Army Commander. Perhaps, though, his staff had purposely not disturbed him so that he might rest. It would look better if he went unprompted to see what was happening.

Outside it was pleasantly cool and dark (the streets were unlit, due to damage to the power-station). The noise of battle was muffled and distant as though the Russian forces were pushing the enemy back further and further. (What if a miracle had already begun to happen?)

Large numbers of kerosene lamps and candles had been brought into the headquarters building, which made the rooms even hotter and stuffier. All the staff officers were at their posts and busily at work preparing the daily report due to be sent to Army Group Headquarters.

Somewhat nervous of the irritating effect that it might have on Samsonov, the staff nevertheless handed him the latest message from Artamonov, which had arrived early in the evening:

'After heavy fighting 1 Corps has held Soldau . . . '

(The man certainly knew how to turn a cunning phrase to cover up his mistakes. He might have added that he had 'held Warsaw', in which case Samsonov would have had to recommend him for the Saint Andrew's Cross!)

'All forward communications broken. Casualties very heavy, especially officers. Troops in good heart' (were they?), 'and obeying orders . . .'

(By now they had been ordered to break away and retreat.)

'Am holding the town with an advance-guard composed of remnants of several regiments . . .'

(And he calls his rearguard an *advance*-guard! God, what cheek!)

'In order to counter-attack need reinforcements, since all those already received have suffered heavy losses. Will reorganise and re-form all units by night and then attack . . .'

Attack—even without reinforcements? The infuriating fool! Anyway, why had he signed the telegram at all? How dare he not accept his dismissal? Relying on his highly placed connections, no doubt . . .

However, Samsonov's mood prevented him from losing his temper completely. The work at headquarters was going ahead well. The Chief of Staff trotted up to him carrying the twice-redrafted text of the daily report to be telegraphed to Army Group Headquarters:

'For the second day running, Second Army has been in action along the whole front. Information from interrogated prisoners revealed . . .' (maybe it did; maybe it didn't, though.) 'On the left flank I Corps held its positions, but then abandoned them with insufficient cause' (Samsonov could not express himself too strongly in an official report), 'for which I relieved General Artamonov of command of the corps. In the centre General Mingin's division has suffered heavy casualties, but the Libau Regiment stood its ground with great gallantry. The Reval Regiment has been almost completely wiped out . . .'

'Add the following sentence,' Samsonov ordered: ' "Only the colours and one platoon survived".'

'. . . The Estland Regiment withdrew to Neidenburg in considerable disorder . . . xv Corps launched a successful attack . . . xiii Corps has captured Allenstein. According to latest information vi Corps has been engaged in stubborn fighting at Bischofsburg . . .'

All in all, the report was by no means a dismal one. It even sounded as if Second Army was winning. It was all more or less true. Even Blagoveshchensky had not retreated too precipitately; he was holding Mensguth and would shortly move on to Allenstein. So perhaps things really were not so bad after all.

Tomorrow morning Zhilinsky would learn that the Germans, far from retreating across the Vistula, had flung all their forces against Second Army.

It was half-past eleven. It only remained to sign the report and then, all being well, go to bed.

And yet . . . and yet there was surely some important change which ought to be made in tomorrow's orders. Some new, vital directive was missing; if only Samsonov could think what it was, the confusion which was clouding his brain would be resolved, and he would gain his peace of mind.

But his mind seemed to be shrouded in a kind of fog.

With head bowed, the Army Commander went off to bed.

Just before his orderly Kupchik, who had been a trumpeter in a battery of Cossack horse artillery, blew out the light, the figures of the proud paladins of Frederick the Great flickered on the wall.

Samsonov expected to go to sleep at once; it was dark and quiet, everything possible had been done and he was so very, very tired. Whenever duty obliged him to move and act, he longed to be able to lie down and relapse into oblivion. Now that he was lying un-dressed in a comfortable bed, the pillow under his head turned to stone and an urge to be in action tugged at his limbs, making him toss and turn.

The action that he craved was to do the simple, soldierly thing: to leap on to his horse, ride into the thick of the fighting and see for himself. As the man who had once been Ataman of the Don Cossacks and Ataman of the Cossacks of Semirechiye, where else should he be but on horseback?

It would be so much easier. The need to rack his brains to stupefaction for so many days on end had been intolerable. Worst of all was the nervous waiting by the telegraph apparatus while the white strip of tape crawled snake-like through his hands, not knowing when it might next bite him or humiliate him with some insult. Samsonov realised that he hated the telegraph more than anything else. The direct link with Zhilinsky was like a noose around his neck.

As always when one cannot sleep, the time fled away with merciless speed. All his problems crowded, unchanging, through his mind. Flicking open the double cover of his watch with his finger-nail, Samsonov glanced miserably at its luminous face: a quarter-past one . . . five to two . . . half-past two . . .

At four o'clock it would already begin to get light.

In an attempt to induce sleep, Samsonov again said his prayers, repeating the 'Our Father' and the 'Mother of God' many times.

He could see nothing, but he thought he could hear the sound of breathing beside him and a clear voice with a prophetic timbre:

'. . . Assume . . . assume . . .'

Then it was repeated.

Samsonov turned cold with fear. The voice sounded not only prophetic but authoritative, it might even have the power to predict the future, yet he could not understand its meaning.

'Assume command? But I am in command,' he said hopefully.

'No . . . assume . . . keeping . . .' said the inexorable voice.

'Am I sleeping?' said the man in bed.

'No, thou shalt be assumed into my keeping!' replied the angel, relentlessly.

It was completely incomprehensible. Straining to understand, Samsonov woke up with the effort.

With the curtains undrawn, it was already light in the room, and with the light the meaning of what he had heard became clear. 'Assumed' . . . the word came from 'Assumption', the name the Church gave to the death of the Virgin Mary. Therefore it meant: 'Thou shalt die.'

Wide awake, he broke into a cold sweat. Faint but resonant, the prophetic voice still echoed. When was the day of the Assumption?

He concentrated: we are in Prussia, it is August and today is the 15th.

He turned ice-cold and goose-flesh crept all over his skin. The day of the Assumption was today. The day of the death of the Virgin Mary, the patroness of Russia, was today. The Feast of the Assumption had already begun.

And he had been told that he was to die. Today.

Terrified, Samsonov sat up. Barefoot and in his underclothes, he sat on the edge of the bed with his arms crossed.

The mumble of uninterrupted gunfire could be heard in the distance. The sound of the guns gave Samsonov back his courage, and in the same moment his mind cleared.

Soldiers were dying out there—and their commander was afraid!

He banished the dream to where it belonged—in the shadows of a night that was past.

In a firm, wide-awake voice Samsonov called to Kupchik in the next room to get up. A few minutes later, awake and dressed, the orderly was bringing in a bowl and a jug of water.

Invigorated by the cold water on his face, by the bright light coming through the window and the insistent sound of gunfire, the Army Commander realised in a flash of insight what he must do: he must get out of this place and move the headquarters forward closer to the fighting troops. He must go there himself and lead the men into the attack!

How he would have loved to gallop away, leading a cavalry charge himself! To capture an enemy battery in a sudden raid! Ah, it made the blood course through your veins! That was the way to wage war! Ah, those days in the Turkish campaign . . .

He was like a bear roused from his lair. Without a shirt, his fleshy torso covered in hair, he walked over to the window, flung it wide open and took a deep breath of the delicious, cold air. The little town was swathed in mist like a bridal veil, and here and there, as if stretching up to greet the rising sun, were finials, turrets, spires and the ridge-trees of almost perpendicular roofs.

All might yet be well. What a liberation—not to have to sit cooped up indoors like a prisoner at headquarters with the telegraph apparatus, but to ride forward into action! He should have done it yesterday. The idea was gloriously simple. And at the same time he could rid himself of General Knox. Not that there was anything wrong with Knox as a man; from the way he strode about waving his swagger-cane, he might even make a good gun-crew member!

The Army Commander ordered his staff to get up. The people at Army Group Headquarters in Bialystok always slept late. By the time 'the living corpse' woke up, he would find that communications with Second Army had been broken and that Samsonov was no longer on the end of the line for him to harass.

He was free!

His staff, however, who were as slow as old women, took a further two hours to get ready to move. The staff officers needed much longer than their commander to get up and come to terms with the new situation.

The headquarters was divided into two. The administrative and supply branches were sent fifteen miles to the rear, across the Russian frontier to the safety of Janów. The operations branch, consisting of seven officers, was to ride forward with the Army Commander.

All the officers scheduled to go to the rear accepted the decision without complaint. Those selected to go forward were gloomily resentful. Having eaten scarcely anything for breakfast, invigorated by the bright morning, Samsonov strode briskly up and down, hastening them all on. His spirits were raised even higher—especially as it seemed to be a gesture of reconciliation from his ill-wishers—by a telegram sent from Bialystok at one o'clock in the morning, but only just handed to him, which read:

'To General Samsonov. The gallant troops under your command have done their duty honourably in the battles of 12th, 13th and 14th August. Have ordered General Rennenkampf to send his cavalry to make contact with you. Hoping you will today throw back the enemy by combined action centre corps. Zhilinsky.'

It appeared that his prayers were being answered. They might have had their disagreements, but he and Zhilinsky were, after all, both Russians and could make up their differences, forgive their past offences and insults. He had been right—his proper place was with the centre corps. And Rennenkampf was going to come galloping up in support today. Together, united as one, they must surely win!

In contrast to his mood, the surly attitude of all seven of the staff officers chosen to go with him was particularly annoying to Samsonov. He summoned them to a conference and addressed them standing up:

'Have you any objections or suggestions, gentlemen? If you have, please say so.'

Postovsky did not dare to speak. In his view, of course, it would have been more sensible to take the whole headquarters back to Janów and fight the battle from there, but he lacked the strength of will to argue with his Army Commander. Indeed all the officers felt themselves to be in a weak position, because when the move had been planned they had all suggested that they should go back to the rear headquarters, and not forward. So they hesitated. Glummest of all was Filimonov, who never agreed with any point of view except his own.

'Permission to speak, Alexander Vasilich. At the moment, Neidenburg is as near the front line as Nadrau, the place you are proposing to go to. The enemy is in the immediate vicinity of Neidenburg. That being so, the whole headquarters ought to move to Janów. Martos is managing perfectly well by himself—what is the point of going to join him?'

Then one of the colonels spoke.

'Your excellency! You are responsible for *all* the corps of this army, not only for the ones which happen to be bearing the brunt of the fighting at the moment. By going forward you are neglecting the army commander's duty to control the *whole* army. In breaking off communications with Army Group Headquarters, you have also cut the link to all the army corps.'

How they managed to complicate a clear, simple idea, and justify any evasion! For the first time in a week, Samsonov felt that his mind was at full pitch, his conscience clear, his mood bold, strong and decisive—and now they all wanted to tie him in knots and weaken him. But it was too late. He could not change his mind now.

'Thank you, gentlemen. In ten minutes we shall leave on horse-back for Nadrau. My car will take General Knox to Janów.'

Knox, however, had been expecting to go forward with Samsonov. He had done his morning exercises, breakfasted, and now appeared, dressed in field service order, keen to be off to the front. He agreed that his valise should be sent back to rear headquarters. But Samsonov told him to get into the car.

'Is the news bad?' Knox asked in astonishment. Taking him to one side without an interpreter, Samsonov laboriously explained in his best English:

'The situation of the army is critical. I cannot tell what may happen in the next few hours. My place is with the troops, and you must go back before it is too late.'

Eight Cossacks handed over their horses to the eight officers. The little group was to be escorted by a squadron and a half, as the situation near the front might be dangerous.

At five minutes past seven, hooves clattering over the smooth paving stones of the streets of Neidenburg, the cavalcade set off northwards at a slow trot. In bright sunlight they turned round for a last look at the old castle of the Teutonic Order.

On the Army Commander's instructions, it was not until he had left, just before the apparatus was removed at seven-fifteen a.m., that the last message was telegraphed back to Army Group Head-quarters:

'Am moving to headquarters xv Corps Nadrau to direct advance of centre corps. Am disconnecting Hughes teletype, therefore will be temporarily out of communication with you. Samsonov.'

*

Fate does not seek its victim—the victim seeks his own fate.

32

(*August 14th*)

Day after day the German 8th Army fought the battle as an integrated whole, and a break in communications with von Mackensen's flanking corps caused severe disruption for several hours; airmen were dispatched, and a search was made for secondary telephone lines in order to re-establish communications. The operational control of the Russian Second Army, on the other hand, disintegrated with every passing day and devolved more and more on to the corps; as each corps commander lost the feeling of overall direction by Army Headquarters, he conducted (or failed to conduct) his own separate campaign. At Soldau the situation was in an even more advanced state of collapse: the town was defended no longer by a corps, but merely by those units which had chosen not to withdraw.

Nevertheless the Germans gave the Russians a whole day in which to pull themselves together. Although the Russians' unexpected abandonment of Usdau enabled General von François to occupy it by midday and the road to Neidenburg lay open in front of him, he did not feel tactically justified in running the risk of having only a light screen of troops facing Usdau; by evening his corps was digging itself in, expecting a counter-attack. This course of action was also indicated to him by the army order for the following day: he was not to march on Neidenburg, but was to throw the Russians back beyond Soldau.

Hindenburg was particularly alarmed about his southern flank, because on the evening of the 14th, when he returned to Army Head-quarters after coping with an awkward situation in von Scholtz's sector, he received an unconfirmed report that von François' corps was almost totally destroyed, and that the remnants of it were arriving at a railway station twenty-five kilometres from Usdau. Hindenburg immediately asked to speak to the station commandant on the telephone, who confirmed this report. (Only during the night did it transpire that the story had been occasioned by one battalion of grenadiers which, panic-stricken by the attack of the Petrov Regiment, had fled, seized some supply waggons along the road and driven them all the way to Army Head-quarters.)

Meanwhile von Scholtz's reinforced corps, only half a division smaller than both Samsonov's centre corps put together and actually stronger in artillery, had been defending itself all that day from intense pressure by Martos on the Mühlen line. At one moment it was reported that Martos was bypassing Hohenstein, the next that he had captured Mühlen, then that he was hastily sending a division there, having withdrawn it from a counter-attack and having even ordered the troops to discard their knapsacks for greater speed, then that the division had not been needed.

In the middle of the day news also came that the Russians had captured Allenstein, so that von Below's corps, positioned on the other jaw of the pincers, had to be abruptly diverted to Allenstein—as did von Mackensen's corps, which had already started making the encircling movement down the corridor opened up for him by Blagoveshchensky —a passage twice as wide as von Mackensen actually needed.

The headquarters of the German army in East Prussia was blinded by its caution. A gap in the Russian line had already opened up to the south of von Scholtz's corps, the front there had collapsed, and one quarter of the still incomplete XXIII Corps was barely holding out, with no more than a cavalry brigade galloping back and forth acting as a screen, yet Hindenburg assumed that there were two Russian corps in this sector and failed to see that here lay the route for his encircling movement. The day's operations appeared to be unsuccessful, and far from being able to issue orders for a complete encirclement on the classic pattern of Cannae, he could not even penetrate deeply enough to outflank the Russian army. The intention of the high command in Prussia was to draw its thirteen scattered divisions closer together. In the orders issued that night for August 15th the encirclement plan had been reduced even further: the aim now was to surround only Martos' corps, the one which was being most troublesome.

The Germans still did not dare to assume that the generals of the apparently mighty Russian empire were so ossified that they were totally incompetent to lead their hundreds of thousands of men. It was taken for granted that there must be some plan behind Samsonov's strange tactic of moving his army forward like the outspread fingers of a hand. Presumably there was also a purpose behind the mysterious immobility of Rennenkampf, whose army was raised like a hammer over the head of the badly shaken German forces. Even at this stage Rennenkampf could still have intervened in the battle between the two armies and wrecked the German plans. But the Russians did not exploit the twenty-four hours which the Germans had lost.

In order to encircle Martos it was planned to strike at Hohenstein from three sides, to move around Lake Mühlen at dawn with the one full-strength division which von Scholtz still possessed, and to capture the village of Waplitz and the heights above it.

This order reached the division in question between eleven o'clock and midnight. It had been digging in for several hours on the assumption that its role was defensive; it had received its daily rations somewhat late, and the troops had just turned in. The divisional commander decided not to wait for dawn, but to exploit the surprise effect of an attack in the dark. Shortly before midnight the division was roused and began preparations to advance. The hilly locality and the unfamiliar, sandy paths made orientation difficult. Groping in search of their assembly-points, the troops lost their way. The advance guard was deflected too far to the right of the axis of advance, the head of the main body went too far to the left, and the rest took the correct route. But the division was unaware that German dragoons had already entered Waplitz unopposed and had halted near the positions held by infantry of the Poltava Regiment. The Russian patrols recognised them, and the German cavalry rode away at full gallop, pursued by a furious burst of rifle-fire. While it was still dark, Russian pickets outside Waplitz noticed an advance party

of Germans approaching, and withdrew under covering fire. Before
dawn, screened by a dense, milky fog, a German regiment deployed and
attacked Waplitz; however, it ran into very heavy rifle- and machine-
gun-fire, which is always particularly daunting and demoralising at that
time of day.

Then the artillery of both sides joined in the battle.

33

It was, on balance, somewhat unfortunate for General Martos that by nature he was easily roused and slow to calm down. The last few days had kept him constantly on the boil, but yesterday had been worst of all: the shifting pattern of the all-day battle; his arguments with Postovsky; chaos at Hohenstein instead of support from the brigade sent by Klyuev; and the strain of trying to predict what the Germans would do next.

Usually he gave way to exhaustion in the evening, went to bed and later woke up and was unable to sleep for the rest of the night. Now, though, he was thrown so badly off balance that he found he could not sleep even in the evening. The moon had set, and it was quite dark. Martos came out of the farmhouse where his headquarters was installed to sit on a bench and smoke awhile, rather as the farmers in his native province of Poltava like to take the air in the late evening seated on the low wall of earth that surrounds their cottages. The difference was that in Poltava it was still warm in September, whereas here it was already turning chilly. Martos put his greatcoat over his shoulders, but sat hatless to cool his head, which he stroked backwards from the temples with his hand in an attempt to soothe the stabbing darts of pain.

He took a pill, intending to relax by sitting for an hour or so before turning in.

Towards midnight the boom and flash of gunfire stopped altogether. Faint and soundless, the occasional flare glowed and died. The starry sky promised another fine day tomorrow, which in view of the widely scattered disposition of the army was just as well.

Throughout the recent fighting Martos had, indeed, been consistently successful: at the end of the day he had never left the field of battle to the enemy, he had everywhere unceasingly attacked and pressed the Germans, although he was noticeably weaker in artillery and his supply of ammunition was unreliable; where rations and forage were concerned, the situation was even worse. Yet Martos failed to detect any sign of a major victory resulting from his own unbroken series of local successes. All his gains seemed somehow to be won in vain.

But he contined fighting hard, just as an experienced actor goes on playing although his partners are missing their cues and fluffing their lines, the heroine's wig has come unstuck, one of the scenery-flats has fallen over, there is an intolerable draught backstage, and the audience is whispering loudly and seems to be jostling for the exits. So, like the professional he was, Martos went on playing his role: at least the show was not going to flop if he could help it, and he might even succeed in pulling the rest of the company through.

Ah! The sound of firing had started up again, coming from beyond Waplitz. There was no let-up in that sector.

Tomorrow was the 15th, always a significant date in Martos' life, as was the same figure doubled, the 30th. Many were the fateful or merely notable events, both good and bad, which had happened to him on those dates. When he had commanded a division it had been the 15th Division, and now his corps was xv Corps; as it happened, this corps also included the 30th Regiment, which by another coincidence was the Poltava Regiment, named after Martos' homeland. So tomorrow he would have to keep particularly wide awake.

The firing went on without respite. Yes, it was coming from between Waplitz and Wittmansdorf. There was a deep ravine in that stretch of country—a dangerous spot.

Great numbers of men had been killed in these last few days, and those who had survived were exhausted. How many officers had perished, Martos thought bitterly; he had known them all for years, and in one week they had all been swept away. Soon they would receive new men to replace them. But how could the army ensure that there were adequate replacements for experienced regular officers, unless they were distributed between line regiments and regiments of the reserve, instead of all being sent to the front line in the first days of war? An army could fight like that for two or three months, but supposing the war lasted longer?

The firing continued. To an untrained ear it was simply a ceaseless noise, an incident in the night, but Martos' ear could tell that this was no chance engagement. That noise betrayed the movement of large masses of men in the dark. The firing was probably coming from the Russians, and the Germans were preparing some move.

He put himself in von Scholtz's place, mentally running over the situation of the past day. Yes, von Scholtz's corps would now be facing in a suitable direction and the time was right.

Although the general's body now felt ready to drop asleep, somewhere within him a little warning light flashed. He went indoors, woke up his lazy and reluctant staff officers and called up the orderlies by telephone.

He gave orders for the corps reserve to stand to, to march to the ravine between Waplitz and Wittmansdorf and deploy across it, promising to go there soon himself. He then issued instructions to the artillery: two batteries were to change their positions, a third was to prepare new lines of fire. On the left, to the two weakened regiments that remained of Mingin's division—the Kaluga and the Libau regiments—he sent a warning to expect trouble. The commanding officer of the Poltava Regiment, in Waplitz, was ordered to prepare for a possible night attack.

By now the staff officers were on their feet, hating their gadfly general with his little wasp waist (which they suspected was not achieved without the aid of a corset). The regiments and batteries which had been made to get up and move in the dark swore even harder: the exhausted, sleepy men could only see these night-time orders as sheer, pointless harassment.

Oblivious of the ill-will that he was causing, Martos was once more smoking and striding with his springy gait through the lighted rooms, as he received reports confirming that his orders had been carried out. His foreboding might, of course, have been caused by his hypersensitive hearing and the deceptive characteristics of the terrain around Waplitz, but his corps had not spent ten days marching here and five days fighting only to be caught napping by a surprise attack. It even seemed as though the general actually wanted a German attack rather than a peaceful start to the next day.

Suddenly a barrage from several hundred guns came down like a deluge on Waplitz itself. Martos rushed up to the attic and just managed to catch sight of the flickering, dull red glow coming from Waplitz before it died down again.

So he had not been mistaken. He called for his horse and galloped off to join his reserve troops in the ravine.

The company in which Sasha Lenartovich was a platoon commander had been one of the first to enter Neidenburg. They had approached in skirmishing order, firing as they went, but there was no battle. As they were then detailed to carry out policing and sentry duties in Neidenburg, they also missed the fighting at Orlau, although they had to bury the dead there. It was only after lunch on the 14th that they caught up with their own unit again, the Chernigov Regiment, which was then immediately transferred to the corps reserve. However, until evening, the crash of gunfire was heard from every side, an endless stream of wounded walked or was carried past them, and it became obvious that they too would not escape being caught up in the slaughter on the following day. A whole war, a single campaign, a month, a week, even a day was far more than enough to cut a company or a platoon to ribbons or cripple a man for life: it needed only a quarter of an hour.

On the cold night of the 14th/15th Lenartovich's platoon slept in a hayloft, which was warm enough if one burrowed deep into the hay. The troops slept soundly and well, unconcerned about the morrow. In theory, Sasha should have approved of these thoroughly democratic sleeping quarters, but the past few days of being unable to wash or undress, and the handling of rapidly decomposing corpses, had made him feel repugnance at so much dirt and discomfort; his whole skin itched, and it was having a fraying effect on his nerves. Finding that he could only toss and turn in the hot straw, he went outside to cool down.

He was not kept awake by the possible imminence of death, but rather by the thought of how wasteful it would be. For the great, bright cause of revolution Sasha was prepared to lay down his life at any moment. Ever since childhood, his heart had beaten faster at the thought that soon that vital *something* would happen: that it would burst forth, illumine and transform life in the whole of Russia and throughout the world. He had been well into his boyhood when in 1905 revolution had indeed broken out;

the new dawn seemed to be breaking, the longed-for moment seemed to have come—but then the light was extinguished and stamped out. Since then Sasha had been ready to smash the iron chains not merely with his bare hands but, if need be, with his own head. Now the chief source of his gnawing discontent, which disturbed him much more than his dirty clothes, was the feeling that he was in the *wrong* place and that he might all too easily die a pointless death for the *wrong* cause. Nothing could possibly be worse than to die at the age of twenty-four defending autocracy. Having succeeded, while still so young, in perceiving the truth and having set out on the right road, he had no need to waste the rest of his life in fruitless searching or in Hamlet-like doubts: he could be working for the *cause*. Yet now he was likely to perish in the bloody shambles, a miserable pawn of the oppressors of the Russian people.

It was sheer bad luck that Sasha had not been imprisoned or exiled; among fellow political prisoners the goal would be clearly kept in sight, and he would have been kept safe and sound to take part in the coming revolution. All self-respecting revolutionaries were in exile or had emigrated. He had actually been arrested three times—for a student demonstration, for taking part in a banned meeting and for distributing leaflets—but each time he had been released because of his youth and thus denied the chance to prove his manhood. Still, all was not lost. If he managed to survive the next few days of chaos and butchery, he would look for a reliable way of getting out of the army; the best means was to have oneself court-martialled—not, of course, for some offence against normal military law but for political agitation.

Agitation, in fact, was the real purpose of his service in the army. He had tried to carry it out, but in vain. As though chosen on purpose, the troops of his platoon turned out not only to be oblivious of proletarian ideology but to lack even a spark of class-consciousness. Even the most elementary economic slogans, calling for changes which would be to their direct advantage seemed incapable of penetrating their thick skulls. The stupidity and submissiveness of these men were enough to make anyone despair.

And the tortuous complexity of the historical process! Instead of heading in a straight line towards revolution, it had diverged into this war—and both he and everyone else were powerless.

The gunfire had begun to lessen since nightfall, but when Sasha finally started to doze, rifle-shots kept hammering into his sleep like

nails. Then came shouts nearby, the clatter of boots, someone looking for someone else; and though he longed to be left alone, to lie
there curled up, even under a hail of bullets—anything rather than
get up—inexorably the cry reached Sasha's company: 'Stand to!
Stand to!'

Curse the army! The whole system was sheer lunacy, but there
was nothing for it; you had to obey. You had to crawl out of the
delicious warm hay and stumble out of doors into the damp and
darkness; there you not only faced the chance of a bullet while you
tripped over your useless sword, but you had to put on a bold voice
in front of the troops and pretend it was of the utmost importance
to parade the platoon in full equipment and listen to the sergeant
and the men addressing you as 'your honour' in that detestable
regulation phrase of enforced servility . . .

And then with a 'Right turn! Quick march!' they left their warm
barn, and stumbling, bumping into each other, almost having to
hold hands, they shambled off into total darkness.

The rumour was that they were going to help the Poltava
Regiment out of trouble. To hell with them—if they hadn't got
themselves into it in the first place, others wouldn't have to pull
them out.

Groping their way, they crossed a railway line, catching their
feet in the points and tripping over the rails. Then they bumped
into the wall of the abandoned Waplitz station, which they had
seen in daytime. After following a crooked, uneven path they
reached a smooth road; here Sasha carried out an order to re-form
his platoon into four ranks, as their whole battalion was now
mustered. Together with other units they formed up into a body
and set off again into the dark; now at least they were marching on
a smooth surface.

They crossed a bridge, after which the word was passed down
the line: 'Take care, ravine on the left.' It was so dark that the
ravine was invisible.

Suddenly a violent, staccato roar of rifle-fire opened up ahead. It
was the kind of barrage which would have been terrifying in daytime, and at night it was far worse. However, the fire was not
aimed at them; no one fell, no bullets whistled past them, and for
some reason the flashes could not be seen. But it was obviously not
far ahead of them and before long they were likely to be walking
into it.

The effect on the men was a strange trembling in one part of their bodies: they felt the odd sensation of their knee-caps shuddering and jumping about quite independently of their legs. If it had been light, they might have felt ashamed, but in the dark they could not even see it happening to themselves.

Loud, urgent orders were given to deploy into skirmishing order, some to the right and some to the left of the road. After stumbling down a steep roadside embankment, they found themselves squelching blindly across marshy ground, cold water pouring into their boots; after a patch of tussocks, they crossed a few shallow ditches and blundered across what seemed like a kitchen garden; by the time the order came to lie prone, the firing ahead of them had died down completely. New orders came to rejoin the road and form up in line of march. Back they stumbled once more, tripping over the ditches and wading through the same marshy ground until they clambered back on to the roadway.

And still their knee-caps quivered and jumped uncontrollably.

For a long time there was more shouting, re-forming, lining up. Then off they went again. Dark though it was, they were able to make out that the road was leading into a forest. As they marched through it, even the flashes of gunfire were blotted out.

The battalions marched on down the road until once again the men were made to slither down the embankment—this time on to the dam of a mill-pond, then across a stream. From there they trudged uphill across open fields, but on firm ground.

The heavy firing had stopped again, and once more Sasha decided that they were being sent on another exhausting wild goose chase. His knee-caps had stopped trembling. It had not been fear that had made them tremble: he was never afraid. It was just that he felt that he was doing the wrong thing in the wrong place, and that this was no place for him to die.

It seemed to be getting lighter, but the visibility did not improve: even though they were on high ground, the darkness of the night had only given way to thick mist.

They struggled onward across rough paths and open fields, where the crop, whatever it was, caught at their boots; the main feature of the ground was that it was criss-crossed with little gullies and ditches, and so dotted with potholes, mounds and rocks that the soldiers said the Devil had been playing ninepins here and left his skittles lying all over the ground.

All at once, less than a mile to their right, another fusillade from several hundred rifle-barrels and machine-guns opened up. But still no bullets came their way: the fighting was lower down and away to the right, and their orders were to get to the top of the high ground as fast as possible. Then, with a roaring and whistling, the gun-flashes flickering dimly through the mist, the Russian artillery opened up, to the delight of the advancing troops. Shrapnel shells burst with a faint glitter in the milky fog, and soon German guns began to reply, their shells falling a short distance away to the right.

Although he had no desire for victory, Lenartovich could not help noticing with satisfaction that the Russian artillery was getting the better of this duel. Although this contradicted his principle of 'the worse—the better', at least it meant that he was less likely to be riddled by shell-splinters. There was undoubtedly a kind of horrible beauty in the thunder of gunfire that was coming from one's own side.

Although it was growing lighter, it was so foggy that visibility was no more than three paces, and the gun-flashes were even harder to see than they had been in the dark. And still they were driven on through the thick, milky mist, across the treacherous gullies, rifles at the ready—faster and faster, lest they reach their objective too late. They ran panting uphill, then down a slope, up again and down again. It would have been safer to have crouched as they ran, but at that speed to run crouching was too much strain on the legs. So they ran upright. A few shells burst overhead, but so high that the shrapnel fell like a harmless shower of dried peas.

The order was given to deploy into skirmishing order and fire from the shoulder. They fired, although their target was completely invisible, and then ran onward again. No Russians fell killed or wounded. It seemed as if they were making an outflanking movement around some German position. The hillside grew steeper and steeper. Each man's heart was thumping, his lungs bursting; it was impossible to keep up this pace, all the more so in the damp, foggy air.

It was now completely light and for all they knew the sun might be out, but nothing around them could be even vaguely seen in the dense, all-enveloping fog.

Then just as the slope began to go slightly downhill, the invisible enemy struck at them, the unseen attackers. Although they could barely see his muzzle-flashes, the bullets were whistling very close; one of them struck a stone and sent up a bright spark.

They had long ago forgotten about their broken sleep, their unwilling blundering about in the dark, their wet feet and even their heaving lungs; now it was a matter of minutes—would they knock out the Germans or wouldn't they? Who would come out on top? It was touch and go. Every man understood this, every man threw himself into the spirit of the attack and Sasha with them. Their pouches crammed full with ammunition, they fired with reckless enthusiasm, deafened by the sound of their own shots, choking on their own powder-smoke as they slashed and slashed at the mist with bullets. Wherever he could, Sasha did his best to stop his platoon from firing at their own side. He suddenly noticed that he was firing his own revolver, although this was completely pointless. Then over a ditch and through a hedge they jumped, and now they were having to leap over bodies too—not Russian, but German bodies! Fear and pride gripped him at the same time: keep it up, we're doing fine—say what you like, but we know how to fight!

Now they were fighting in a village, taking cover behind houses, sticking their heads round corners, outflanking German strong-points. There was no holding the men as they charged in with fixed bayonets, and Sasha felt a strange satisfaction as he blazed away. He hit and wounded a German, who was at once taken prisoner.

All the while a yellow orb on their left had been growing brighter and brighter, until finally it burst through—the sun! Everything was still obscured in swirling mist, but it now began to thin out and everything grew clearer. They could see the heavy dew which had settled on their rifle-bolts and bayonets, some of which were streaked with blood. As they were on such high ground, the fog was rapidly dispersing in wisps and the men's faces were plain to see, panting, elated with the savage joy of battle. And Lenartovich felt the same. Blue, red and orange droplets glinted on the grass, and the sunshine of the new day was already shedding its warmth over them—the victors.

Somehow it was all over with surprising ease. This was no hollow boast, no hearsay account of other men's deeds: a guard detail drawn from men of their own battalion was escorting through the village a column of about three hundred prisoners and a handful of officers, squinting glumly into the sun, some without caps, some having lost their carbines. And after the roll-call only three men in Sasha's battalion were reported killed and a dozen or so wounded, only one of whom was from his platoon. His men had kept together and were now cheerfully strolling about and swopping stories.

Meanwhile the surrounding countryside was slowly emerging from the fog like a cunningly lit theatre set: height, depth and perspective began to fall into place. Right down into the nearby ravine everything stood precisely delineated and contrasted—things and creatures, living and dead, sunlight above and shadow in the valley, the greenery and the colours of field and garden. From the top of the slope where they stood in the village of Wittmansdorf, they could clearly see a column of several hundred spiked helmets being led away, and beyond it piles of corpses struck down by Russian case-shot.

No longer in a hurry, no longer running, no longer afraid, Sasha Lenartovich sat watching it all from a bench behind a garden fence where he had sat down to rest. Still possessed by a strange sense of triumph, he was bursting with elation at having had a part in a victory which had not been merely scored in verbal debate but won with his body, his own arms and legs. He sat there as though he was the great commander-in-chief in whose honour the defeated enemy was being led past in triumph below. The troops were given no time to rest; they had been ordered to dig in on the edge of the village. Sasha had to pass the order on to them, but he was not expected to do any digging himself and could stay sitting on his bench to admire the theatrical spectacle of the captured village and the dark blue depths of the ravine. In the silence around him (all firing in the vicinity had stopped), he was able to savour his joy and analyse his sudden, new-found emotion.

He now felt buoyed up by a surge of confidence. Hope had welled up and was spilling over: he would survive—he would survive this war! How he wanted to live! How precious life was! On a morning like this it was joy enough simply to sit and look, or walk about in the cool breeze, or take a bicycle and ride down that road between the fields until the wind whistled past him, or stuff apricots into his mouth—soft, melting, golden apricots of the south. And the books he still had to read! And the things not yet begun and not yet accomplished! But even that was not the best of all: thrusting relentlessly upward like an obelisk through the great pile of books, pamphlets and his staple diet of illegal literature which he had pored over for years in the public library, he now felt a sharp pang of regret—women! How had he managed to do without women all these years, preferring ideology and political activity? Perhaps they weren't, after all, the most important thing there was left to live for.

It was a base, unworthy thought, but there was no getting away from it: that was how it was. Half an hour ago he might have lost everything in a split second—the knowledge he had acquired, his convictions, life itself. And now the thought of the love of women seemed to be the most real, the most solid thing to have survived with him. It was somehow impervious to bullets, and the awareness of it would have made it easier to die.

At this moment he felt a joyful certainty that it would come to him. Lately Sasha had experienced this need like a searing, open wound which was always being prodded when he least expected it. He had been enthusiastically arguing with that doctor on the steps of the hospital when a nurse had come out—a hefty, big-breasted girl—who had said not a word to him, whom he would never see again, and who had then gone, leaving him with a feeling that she had flicked at his open wound with a towel. Even the most insignificant, half-forgotten memories of the past had lately started to come back to him, to crowd in on him and probe that wound.

Not so very long ago, when he had last been in Petersburg, there had been Yolya, his sister Veronika's classmate at the university. He had only seen her a few times: when she had come to visit his sister, and when a party of them had gone out on a boat-trip in midsummer to admire the midnight sun, and later at a student party. They had never once been out alone together for the evening. On the boat-trip he had been bad-tempered, irritated by their conventional enthusiasm for the 'white night', and he had snapped at everybody; Yolya, meanwhile, slim and silent, had sat in the bows of the boat like one of those figureheads with which the Scandinavians decorate the prows of their ships. At the party, however, Sasha had been in his element—quick, witty, unbeatable at repartee; they had all listened to him, Yolya with particular attention. Yet her manner was unusual for their group: all the other girls always spoke out boldly, had their own opinions and stuck up for them, whilst she simply watched with her dark eyes and sat through all their conversations and arguments in enigmatic silence. It was impossible to make out whether she agreed or disagreed or was in any way fired by their discussions. The lips in her narrow little face were set in a pout which was childish yet very memorable—once, as a joke, he had actually given her a fleeting kiss, and even now Sasha could feel those yielding, childlike lips.

However, he had never allowed his emotions to lead him on, and he made no attempt to be alone with her: there had been so much to do in those days in Petersburg, there was no sign of war and he expected his military service to be soon over. If only because of her views, which were not well received in his circle of friends, he had paid little attention to her.

But as soon as war broke out he suddenly began to see Yolya in a different light, and he pined for the aching sweetness which he had missed, regretting his own stupidity in Petersburg that June. How could he have failed to notice and be attracted by that peculiar tremulous quality about her. In a man, hesitancy is the worst of faults; in her, it was the essence of femininity: the perplexed tremor of her eyebrows, the trembling of her head and neck, the trembling of her shoulders, and above all the way her thin, finely shaped figure quivered when, as she quickened her pace, she broke into a comical little run.

Like a deceptively faint swell at sea which gently rolls up to a boat and sets it violently rocking, Yolya's tremulous quality was now stealing upon Sasha and drawing him, together with all his great plans for the future, in her wake. Now he realised that come what may he must take that shy creature in his own hands, and that to calm her trembling was the only way to achieve peace within himself.

He had not even had the sense to ask for her photograph; now when he wrote asking for it, his letters crawled through the censorship at the pace of a tortoise, and the only thing he had received from Yolya had been a couple of joking lines scrawled at the bottom of a letter from Veronika.

And now—he had to carry on and defend Russia, that damned country of his.

34

The Russian commandant of Neidenburg, Colonel Dovatur, learned only by chance from a telegraphist that Second Army Headquarters had left the town, with the exception of a small rearguard which was just about to go, and that the telegraph had been disconnected. No one had left him any instructions: they had been so busy with strategic matters that he had been forgotten. He ran to find some of the remaining staff officers, but they were busy packing the last of their boxes to be loaded on to waggons and transported to Janów, and only shrugged their shoulders.

Just then a sergeant from the 6th Don Cossack Regiment rode up with a dispatch for the Army Commander from the commander of the composite cavalry brigade. The commandant did not know where to send him, nor was he entitled to accept the dispatch himself. During the night he had happened to overhear that the brigade had been placed under the command of General Kondratovich, but no one had the least idea of the whereabouts of Kondratovich or his staff. At that point another dispatch-rider appeared: he had ridden all night from Mlawa, bringing the mail from Warsaw, among which, he insisted, was a letter for General Samsonov from his wife. To both these messengers, neither of whose missions concerned him, the commandant was incapable of giving advice, just as the staff officers were incapable of advising him.

Not until yesterday evening had the commandant and his men succeeded in extinguishing all the fires and tidying up the streets; after six days of Russian occupation the town had just begun to look normal, and the shops had started trading again. But the headquarters was now gone, and as though they had been waiting for this, waggons and troops on foot began streaming through the town from north to south—not in marching order, but in small, straggling groups, some men even on their own, and all of them asking to be told 'the way to Russia'.

The streets of Neidenburg were so narrow that it needed only two waggons abreast to block them completely, and the leading waggon-team of a column only had to stop in the *Rathaus* square for the whole town to be jammed; without officers to supervise them, the troops shouted to each other to halt, waggons were hitched together like barges, harness-ropes broke, the soldiers began fighting and behaved insolently to a polite officer who came up to sort them out. Meanwhile German women sat watching from their windows with bitter *Schadenfreude*. The wretched commandant was supposed to keep order in the town with only a depleted guard company (which was in any case dispersed on sentry-duty) and the kind co-operation of the portly burgomaster.

Using the small forces at his disposal, the commandant blocked the two northern entrances to Neidenburg and ordered the guards to make all approaching units bypass the town. This would have solved the problem, but after a visit to the divisional field hospital the commandant gave out a new set of instructions: waggons were to be searched at the road-blocks, all non-essential loads jettisoned and the waggons themselves made available for evacuating the wounded. Then he himself set off to the road-blocks, instructing a guard platoon to be ready to use armed force should the need arise.

Meanwhile in the field hospital the doctors held a conference. During the hour or two since Army Headquarters had left, there was a whiff of surrender in the air. The war had only just begun, and no one could yet know for certain how scrupulously the 1864 Geneva Convention on the treatment of the wounded would be observed. This stated that hospitals were to be regarded as neutral, that they could neither be fired upon nor captured, and were obliged to take in wounded from both sides; that hospital personnel enjoyed immunity and were at all times free to remain at their posts or to leave; that after regaining their health, the wounded themselves should be sent home, having given a solemn undertaking not to take up arms again; that a private house which took in a wounded man was also afforded the protection of the Convention. Half a century after the signature of the Convention there were as yet no grounds for assuming that warfare would become brutalised, but the newspapers were assuring their readers that the Germans were ruthless; the doctors themselves had also noticed that when there was an excess of wounded and a shortage of beds, it was impossible to behave with absolute impartiality towards their own men and the Germans. Thus, as they prepared the hospital for partial evacuation, it was impossible to predict what would happen to those who remained behind. Some doctors and nurses were picked to go, others to stay. Of the nurses, the older and more experienced ones belonging to the Red Cross Society were all selected to stay, while the young voluntary nurses, who had managed to sneak their way to the front line during the confusion of mobilisation, were sent to the rear. Although they had learned some of the rudiments of nursing by imitation—with varying degrees of success—most of them could still do nothing useful; they giggled a lot, and one practical joker among them who had been riding a bicycle along the corridor had knocked down a pharmacist. However, Dr Fedonin requested the Senior Surgeon that Tanya Belobragina, a quiet, sad girl, should definitely stay: although she had not had any real training, she was very dedicated, and besides doing normal ward-duties she had specialised in head and neck wounds. She was unlikely to ask to go.

The work of the hospital was in any case slowing down: while waiting for the order to move, and with the wards already crammed with hundreds of patients, it was impossible to operate, and treatment was confined to dressing wounds. This was a hard choice to make: even in a base hospital there were no really effective means of combating gangrene, and on a long and rough journey the risk was infinitely greater.

The staff tried to conceal the news from the patients, but the men themselves sensed it from the change in routine and began to grow uneasy. Every man who was conscious and able to move begged to go. Perhaps because they were lying together and in view of each other, they all felt ashamed at the idea of staying there to rest while their comrades were fighting.

A medical orderly reported to Fedonin that a colonel urgently wanted to see one of the doctors.

'Will you go, Valerian Akimich?' he asked.

Fedonin walked quickly to the main entrance. Empty waggons were already beginning to line up on the three-sided space in front of the hospital, almost filling it. On the stone porch, opening out his map-case, a dishevelled, sunburnt colonel, whose tunic was torn where it covered a bandaged shoulder, was interrogating a wounded sergeant. He swung round to Fedonin.

'Are you a doctor? How do you do? My name's Vorotyntsev, from General Headquarters.' He shook hands as though in a great hurry. 'Tell me, have you any wounded who have been recently admitted from forward positions and who are conscious? May I ask them some questions? Any officers?'

Doctors were used to working at speed, yet this thick-set but extremely active colonel moved unusually fast. Caught up by his sense of urgency, Fedonin quickly recollected and said:

'Yes. Some came in last night—and this morning, too. And there's a second lieutenant from XIII Corps. He was badly concussed, but he managed to get out and now he's fully conscious.'

'From XIII Corps? Interesting!' Surprised, the colonel pricked up his ears and quickened his pace even more. He was already leading Fedonin by a firm grip on his elbow. 'This hospital belongs to XV Corps—how does a man from XIII Corps come to be here?'

They had some little distance to go—up a staircase, along a corridor, through two wards—and Fedonin, too, quickened his pace.

'Tell me,' he asked, 'what is going to happen to this town?'

The colonel threw Fedonin a keen look. Only now did he stop treating him as a mere provider of information; glancing to right and left, he said quietly:

'If we manage to organise a defence we may hold out a bit longer.'

'*Organise* a defence?' Fedonin put in. 'You don't mean to say . . . What about Army Headquarters . . . ?'

In reply the colonel only pursed his lips.

'West of the town . . .'

But they were entering a ward, and for all his eagerness Vorotyntsev stopped, frowning with distaste at the thick stench of blood, medicaments and putrefaction which hit them on the threshold. In the first ward, standing by the aisle, a priest was administering extreme unction to a dying man, whose face he had covered with his stole:

'I believe, O Lord, and I confess . . .' How many, many times in the last few days he had intoned the familiar words in a low voice, yet each time with sincerity and without sounding bored.

By a window in the next ward they found the second lieutenant; Tanya Belobragina, who happened to be sitting on his bed, rose as they approached and stood against the wall between the windows, her hands behind her back, staring fixedly ahead with her sad, dark eyes.

Although his forehead was thickly bandaged, the quick, keen glance of youth had already returned to his face, and he made a special effort to look welcoming for his visitors.

Fedonin felt his cheeks and took his pulse.

'Feeling a bit better?'

'Yes, yes!' the freckled lieutenant assured him cheerfully; not knowing what was required of him, he pushed himself higher up in the bed.

'You don't find it too difficult to talk or answer questions, do you?'

Tanya said, blushing: 'We've been talking a little. It turns out that we are from the same part of the country.'

No one was likely to suspect her of talking too much.

'What is your regiment?' The colonel was already sitting on the bed and unfolding his map. 'Were you in the xv Corps sector? When did you join it? Where were your positions? Where were you wounded? Which units were on either side of you?'

Half sitting up in bed, the lieutenant stared with hero-worship at the colonel and answered him as though his questions were some delightful kind of examination; he was proud that he knew all the answers, both to the questions on the paper and to the supplementary questions thrown in at random. He was suffused by that sublime, youthful glow of virginal suffering. Although he felt dizzy and there was a noise in his ears, and although he had difficulty in speaking, he tried to overcome these handicaps and to make his answers as precise as possible. He confidently pointed out on the map how the previous evening they had been· made to march to the west towards the fighting (privately he recalled the sheer effort required to muster the regiment, call the roll, and make sure they were up to strength before marching out of the town), and how they had been brought back again (their regiment had started out without reaching the fighting many times before), for some reason making their ·way back to Hohenstein by a roundabout cross-country route (there had also been a moment of panic that evening, when they had fired at their own troops, but that was an irrelevancy). Then they had marched out of Hohenstein once more (again with considerable difficulty) in battle order to the edge of the town, and it was there that . . . (The rest he would describe to his mother but not to this colonel: the shell bursting so unbelievably close that there was only time to think 'This is it!' and cross himself—'Forgive me, Mother!'—and he did not even hear the next explosion . . .)

'What's happened to your shoulder?' Fedonin, returning, asked Vorotyntsev.

Reminded of his wound, the colonel said:

'Would you take a look at it? I think I was grazed by a splinter yesterday.'

The surgeon probed.

'Do you find it hard to move it?'

'Yes, it is rather difficult.'

'Come to my room—it's on this floor. The nurse will show you the way.' To Tanya he said:

'The Senior Surgeon has agreed to allow you to stay. You don't mind, do you? You may be stuck here for some time.'

There was no change in the nurse's fixed expression; she did not show a flicker of interest, but merely nodded.

'Why not? Of course.'

She waited to show the colonel out. Whenever he turned his head quickly, all the decisiveness in his nature seemed to be expressed in the short beard which framed his face. With a beard like that, his moustache was completely inconspicuous: it did not bristle or droop, nor were the ends twisted; one felt that he only covered his upper lip because it was not done for an officer to be clean-shaven.

The lieutenant had neither moustache nor beard, and there was as yet no character in his mouth; he was still in his earliest, unspoiled youth, with the innocence and good manners of a boy brought up by women. He knew absolutely nothing of life. Tanya was only a year older than he, but in wisdom she felt herself to be ten years his senior.

What if there was a chance of being taken prisoner? Tanya was prepared for anything. She regarded every possibility—capture, wounds, death—with complete indifference. The best thing would be if she were killed as soon as possible. It was, in fact, in the hope of killing herself without committing the sin of suicide that she had made a dash for the front. Nothing could be worse than what had happened to her: death in war would be the lesser evil.

Below the window, the narrow, crowded street was a scene of confusion. Soldiers were hurrying about, alone and in scattered, disorganised groups. They would stop for a rest in the shade, wipe away the sweat, throw anything superfluous out of their knapsacks, discard entrenching-tools, axes, ammunition-boxes and then quickly set off again. No one stopped them. Two Cossacks, by contrast, were actually busy strapping something to their saddles.

... They had gone for walks together, read books together holding hands. And as they had talked, by degrees they had trodden the path whose every inch is unique and unretraceable, its memory treasured all one's life. Their love grew like a plant, each stage in its proper season: first the leaf, then the bud, then the blossom. Could Tanya not have hastened the process a little? Impossible— woman's lot forbade her to do such a thing. And then that other woman—no better, no prettier, no kinder, no more faithful than she—had swooped, had seized and carried him off. No court of law existed to punish that sort of misdeed. Men! Firm and decisive in war they might be—but in nothing else . . .

How well the army trained its officers in two years—and how surely it ruined them in the next twenty. That total willingness, the agonised concern for the success of the whole campaign on that boyish forehead!

'Colonel!' Catching him by the sleeve, the lieutenant gazed hopefully at him; straining to overcome the difficulty he had in speaking, he went on: 'I have heard there is to be a partial evacuation. I couldn't stay—it would be too shameful! I don't want to start my life in a prisoner-of-war camp!' Tears glinted in his eyes. 'Please ask them to make sure I get out, whatever happens!'

'All right, I will.' The colonel shook the young man's hand with a powerful grip. Then impatiently:

'Nurse!'

Tanya turned sharply away from the window, leaving all her private thoughts behind her and showing to the outside world only the keen attention of one of those sensible, unspoiled faces that Russian girls so often have.

There was a latent fire in her look, a resolute expression that promised great strength as yet unrealised. Or was it simply an effect of the severe nurse's head-dress which covered her forehead, neck and ears?

'Nurse, I shall make a point of asking the doctor to see that Second Lieutenant Kharitonov is not left behind, but I also want you to make sure.' Although he could see that she looked thoroughly reliable and needed no threatening, rather to his own surprise he found himself wagging his finger at her. 'Beware—I shall find you wherever you may be! Where are you from?'

'Novocherkassk.'

'I'll even find you there!' With that he nodded and marched briskly off between the line of beds.

Each bed was a closed world, where a unique struggle was being waged in a unique body, each man asking himself the crucial question: Will I live or not? Will they leave me my arm or not? The war, the strategy of armies and army corps faded into insignificance. Here lay an elderly but sturdy little peasant—probably a reserve NCO, one of those whom in war the Russian army so wastefully employed as private soldiers—staring out at everyone from under the sheets with a sharp, suspicious look. Another man was tossing his head from side to side on the pillow and moaning hoarsely.

Vorotyntsev hurried to escape as quickly as possible from the overpowering stench of the ward before he suffocated. The nurse led the way.

When after some delay she returned to the same window, the lieutenant had sunk back into the bedclothes, pale and weakened, but he still managed a smile for Tanya.

'So you're staying, are you? Write a letter to your people at home—I'll take it with me and I promise to post it. Who is there at home?'

The skin of Tanya's face tightened as though it had been smeared with egg-white. She shook her head grimly. She would not be writing any letters to anyone.

There was no one.

After the war she would go anywhere rather than back to Novocherkassk.

Vorotyntsev would have reached Neidenburg early that morning, and might have been in time to catch Samsonov, if he had not turned aside en route to see who was holding the line. He found that there was no one. He had also chased after the elusive Kondratovich—and did not find him either. Thus he arrived too late for Samsonov.

On the left flank of the front line there was a gaping hole, which hurt Vorotyntsev as much as if it had been a wound in his own side; but no one had ordered any troops to fill it—indeed, there were no troops available to do so, apart from the Kexholm Regiment, which had relieved the Estland and Reval regiments and was under the command of General Sirelius, who was also wandering about somewhere, not having once been near the front line.

Vorotyntsev was equally aghast at Samsonov's departure. Why had he not organised a defence of the north-western approaches to Neidenburg? Why had he not contracted the army front, instead of going to where it was most extended?

The remnants of the Estland and Reval regiments and their supply trains were almost getting out of hand in Neidenburg, but Vorotyntsev had no time to deal with them. Leaving the horses to Arsenii, he spent an hour and a half scouting around various parts of the town before he was able to discover what had become of Army Headquarters. He persuaded the Cossack sergeant dispatch-rider to show him the message from the cavalry brigade, and induced him to wait awhile before riding off again. Then, from various people, mostly from the wounded, he was able to re-construct fairly accurately the situation of the army's centre corps; from Kharitonov he found out how things were going at Hohenstein, but the fate of the rest of XIII Corps remained an impenetrable enigma. Even harder to deduce was the likelihood of a supporting attack by Blagoveshchensky and Rennenkampf. He would have galloped over there to find out for himself, but the gaping hole on the left flank called more urgently for his attention. As he hurried away from the hospital, Vorotyntsev seemed already to have a plan.

Even yesterday's retreat to Soldau was not the ultimate catastrophe, provided the necessary counter-action was taken within the next few hours.

He had arranged to meet the Cossack sergeant at the monument to Bismarck, a conspicuous landmark.

It was under Bismarck that the League of the Three Emperors

had been created and Eastern Europe had enjoyed half a century of peace. Peace between Russia and Germany was far preferable to this disastrous alliance with those circus-artistes in Paris.

The horses stood tethered to a tree, and in the shade of the statue's plinth, beyond the flower-bed, sat Arsenii. He rose hastily, but remained stooping and said in a solemn, confidential tone:

'Time for a bite to eat, your honour!'

There was some concoction in his mess-tin.

'You almost ruined my stomach yesterday with your hard-tack ... Have you fed the horses?'

'Of course I have!' Arsenii was offended. His mouth, big enough already, gaped even wider. 'Found a cemetery—good grass there.'

Behind the monument were two stones designed as a bench, and a spoon-handle was sticking out of Arsenii's fist.

'What about you?'

'After you,' Arsenii demurred with studied politeness.

'No, let's eat together.'

'Very well, then.' Blagodaryov agreed, knelt down in front of the mess-tin and began eating.

Vorotyntsev spooned up the food with his left hand, hungrily yet distractedly, without looking to see what he was eating. At the same time, with his right hand he began writing a message to Samsonov, pressing against the firm, smooth leather of his map-case on his raised knee—hurriedly, so as not to delay the Cossack sergeant:

'Your excellency!

'On the left flank, under pressure but far from beaten (they won the battle at Usdau and only withdrew because of a stupid mis-understanding), is a *third* of your army. But at the moment there are *three* corps commanders in that sector (Artamonov, Masalsky, Dushkevich) and no clear leadership. If you yourself found it possible to go there (the 6th Don Cossack Regiment would escort you there safely in two or three hours), you could, by mounting a vigorous attack, save the situation for the whole army: you would halt and repulse General von François, who is now intending to *cut you off*.

'Krymov joins me in begging you urgently to adopt this course of action. Colonel Krymov has just taken over as Chief of Staff of I Corps.

'I shall be to the west of Neidenburg, where there is a gap in the line: the town is virtually undefended.

'Colonel Vorotyntsev.'

He should also have advised the Army Commander to pull back the centre corps, but he dared not make the direct suggestion—Samsonov would have to guess that for himself.

The Cossack sergeant rode up. Vorotyntsev warned him that he must burn or eat the message rather than let it fall into enemy hands.

Meanwhile the courier from Warsaw had gone astray, and Samsonov was fated never to receive the letter from his wife.

35

It was a long time since Samsonov's mind had been so clear or he
had felt so confident in his actions. At the head of the dejected
group of staff officers he rode boldly out of Neidenburg, his horse
keeping up a brisk trot beneath him. He felt fresh, despite having
slept so badly. The freshness was enhanced by the damp August
morning, in which the sun was triumphantly ripping the mist to
shreds and dispersing the haze which had veiled the sky since dawn.

How splendid it was to get up early, how well one could think
and act in the morning! How optimistic he felt about the outcome
of the fighting in the bracing chill! And there would be many
more fine mornings for a man of fifty-five to enjoy.

The route, which was not of his choosing, led in a wide eastward
loop that passed through the village of Grünfliess and a corner of
Grünfliess Forest. The commander of the Cossack escort and the
officers of the staff assured Samsonov that the shorter route to
Nadrau was unsafe; a German patrol might break through, or
they might be ambushed. And sure enough, when they were nearly
half way, cavalry was seen approaching in a cloud of dust from the
right. The escort deployed into battle order and sent out a
picket.

The cavalry turned out to be Russian—a troop of dragoons from
VI Corps, escorting dispatches. They had covered thirty miles
across the half-deserted no-man's land in enemy territory, and if
Army Headquarters had not taken this roundabout route, they
would never have found Samsonov.

It was now 8.30 a.m. and Blagoveshchensky's dispatch had been
sent off at 1.00 a.m.—just twenty-four hours after the previous

day's routine report, as though nothing important had occurred in the interval. What was Blagoveshchensky doing? Had he gone to help Klyuev? Was he covering the exposed flank of the centre corps? Or was he standing firm? Samsonov read:

'... have withdrawn to Ortelsburg...'

Without dismounting, Samsonov called for a map: yesterday Blagoveshchensky had inexplicably retreated to Mensguth, which was bad enough. If only he had stayed at Mensguth today! But no, he had retreated another twelve miles—back towards Russia, of course. The cornet of dragoons in command of the troop was obviously bursting to tell more about the retreat, but the Army Commander restrained him. He purposely spared himself any possible distress in order outwardly to maintain a solid, confident air for the benefit of those around him.

In the seven hours which the dragoons had taken to ride here, Blagoveshchensky might well have abandoned Ortelsburg as well. He might even be back in Russian territory by now...

What orders could Samsonov give him? Should he tell him to hold on to Ortelsburg at all costs? Yes... *at all costs*... 'On the staunchness of your corps depends...'

The cornet and his troop galloped off carrying the message, which they would deliver by the middle of the afternoon.

Blagoveshchensky's dispatch passed from hand to hand among the staff officers. Klyuev should be informed of VI Corps' latest withdrawal. But how? Klyuev was moving to link up with Martos, and Samsonov was on his way to join Martos.

Perhaps the best thing to do was to inform Zhilinsky of this; there was just a chance that it might, for once, galvanise him into action to save the situation. A message should be sent by dispatch-rider to Janów, whence it could be telegraphed to Zhilinsky.

His large map-board resting on his horse's head, Samsonov wrote in his scrawling hand:

'... According to an officer who was an eye-witness, VI Corps has withdrawn to the south of Ortelsburg in disorder. The corps has been physically weakened and its morale has suffered badly. I am going to Nadrau, where I shall take the necessary decision concerning the centre corps...'

He wrote 'I shall take the necessary decision' as though it had not already been taken. One set of plans having been changed for him by events, it was reasonable for him to change the rest of his plans too, despite his extreme reluctance to do so. The battered flanks of his army were collapsing; yet for Samsonov this invigorating ride to the front line was a psychological necessity. He would 'take the necessary decision' in the front line, towards which he now spurred his horse.

Grumbling, his staff rode after him. (An expert in army paperwork, Postovsky consoled himself with the thought that these few hours which he was having to spend in dangerous proximity to enemy artillery-fire would at least count favourably in his service record.)

From the top of a hill a broad, magnificent view down the oblong length of Lake Maransen spread out before them. With the sun shining from behind them, the water did not sparkle, but lay dark and calm, surrounded on all sides by dense forest. Here and there the red roof-tiles of abandoned German farmhouses could be seen on the slopes of the surrounding hills. Gladdened by the sight of that unspoiled natural beauty, Samsonov forgot his troubles for a moment and exclaimed:

'What a beautiful country, gentlemen! Did you ever see such hills, such a superb view?'

Coming towards them up the slope was a cart-load of casualties, many of them with bayonet wounds. Some of them were groaning, but others were able to talk quite coherently, especially when they saw that the party included three generals. They had been engaged in a night-time bayonet attack at a village about six miles away. They all asserted unanimously that the encounter had been won by the Russians.

Then, from nearby to their left, came the roar of gunfire.

'God and the Virgin Mary protect us!' Samsonov cried. 'Forward, gentlemen—and hurry; we must find out all we can about this battle!'

Although the location of Martos' command post was given as Nadrau, it was actually positioned in a semicircle of forest on some high ground slightly to the west of this small village—an excellent spot, commanding a wide view. As the front line had by now moved well forward of Nadrau, it was safe from shellfire, and several officers were standing in hot sunshine on the hillside, taking it in turns to look through a pair of binoculars.

Down below, along the main road leading to the railway and beyond it, a column of men—no less than a thousand prisoners—

was slowly trudging along, or rather being escorted by a cordon of Russian troops.

Martos, short and narrow-shouldered, was sitting on a chair and also peering through binoculars. Unaware that Army Headquarters was being moved, he turned round into the sunlight and at first did not recognise the approaching horsemen.

The Corps Commander bounded nimbly to his feet, changing over to his left hand the swagger-cane which he always swung as he walked. Springing to attention in front of the thick-set, mounted figure of the Army Commander, he reported, squinting into the sun:

'Your excellency! Last night the enemy in divisional strength tried to attack us in Waplitz by a concealed approach. Not only was his intention discovered and frustrated, but he lost control of the operation: at Waplitz cemetery the enemy troops were knocked out by their own artillery, which was obviously firing to a prepared plan without direct observation. The division which made the attack was dispersed and thrown back, and we have gained an important vantage-point—the Wittmansdorf heights. We have taken two thousand two hundred prisoners, including nearly a hundred officers, and have captured twelve guns. Although greatly weakened, the Kaluga and Libau regiments also contributed to the success by attacking the enemy in the rear.'

(Giving credit where it was due, Martos made a point of mentioning the part played by the two regiments from XIII Corps.)

It was all laid out before their eyes: there were the prisoners being led away, and a small group of captured officers being escorted uphill towards Corps Headquarters. This was the moment of triumph which Samsonov had envisaged: *this* was his reason for tearing away from Neidenburg that morning! He had not come in vain!

Samsonov remained in the saddle as he listened to the report, then, ponderously but confidently, he dismounted and handed over the reins. He walked straight up to Martos and, towering over him, clasped the neat, slim Corps Commander around the shoulders with his massive arms and kissed him.

'You are unique! You alone will save us, my dear fellow!'

He stepped back, looking at Martos as though about to reward him with the gift of a quarter of his kingdom, like the king in the fairy-tale. He knew which order would most suitably adorn that narrow chest—were it not for the rules which specified that decorations must go according to seniority.

Perhaps this was the moment to wheel xv Corps and deal the enemy a smashing blow in the rear, the moment to make that side-stepping attack already envisaged in the army order sent out the previous night. Who better to advise him than the victorious Corps Commander himself?

'What do you think of the idea, Nikolai Nikolaevich? I'd like your opinion.'

Looking resolutely at Samsonov, head held high, eyes flashing, Martos did not have to make a show of wrinkling his brow in thought or asking for time to consider the problem. As quick off the mark as a young subaltern, his shoulders squared, the end of his moustaches neatly curled, his reply was as crisp as his appearance:

'With your permission, we must withdraw at once!'

He had not heard the news of Artamonov's and Blagoveshchensky's precipitate retreats, but some sixth sense told him that his corps had no business to be in this exposed forward position, but should move back as quickly as possible. Just as air pressure or astral rays enable snails and birds to sense a storm before it comes, Martos felt a premonition.

Samsonov was dumbfounded. 'What? I don't understand. Why?'

Helped by a Cossack, Postovsky had cautiously dismounted. Seeing that the Army Commander disagreed with Martos, he came up and said:

'What's the matter with you? In a panic? Lost your nerve? The Kexholm Regiment will be coming up on your left at any moment, on the right you've been given a brigade from xiii Corps, and the whole of xiii Corps will be here before long . . .' He looked round, as though expecting to see the corps march out of the forest at that moment. 'And then there will be Rennenkampf's cavalry. What possible reason can you have for withdrawing?'

Martos was never indecisive. Briskly he rapped out his arguments:

'My corps has been fighting now for five out of the past six days, and for the last three days without a break. I have lost my best officers and several thousand men. The corps is weakening and is no longer fit for offensive action. I have no cavalry, so I can't reconnoitre and have to operate in the dark. Artillery ammunition is running low and no new supplies are being brought up. Our incessant attacks are not helping the army as a whole to win the battle, in fact they're only making its situation more difficult. We must withdraw—and at once.'

The inexorable logic of his conclusions dashed all the hopes Samsonov had cherished that morning into irrecoverable fragments. There was to be no exhilarating attack into which he could send his men or gallop himself. The battle had been decided without him—everything won that was to be won, all discussions and proposals already over, everything lost that was fated to be lost.

Samsonov blinked slowly, as though fighting off sleep. He took off his cap to relieve the pressure on the hair-line of his greying head, and wiped his brow.

For the first time, there was a helpless look about his great forehead: a white target above a defenceless face.

36

In the heat of the moment Vorotyntsev had made an error: having started the day looking for Kondratovich, he should not have given up the search for this evasive general, but should have tracked him down and used the prestige of General Headquarters to shame or frighten him. By this means it might have been possible to deploy to the west of Neidenburg all the remnants of XXIII Corps that were capable of fighting a defensive action.

It had been General Kondratovich's good fortune to have had his corps broken up piecemeal; he was able, on the excuse of mustering it, to spend a long time shuttling back and forth by train between Warsaw and Vilna. Although on the morning in question he was undoubtedly somewhere in the vicinity of Neidenburg, it proved impossible to locate him: first he was said to be somewhere near the front line, where he had been seen in one place an hour, in another half an hour, before Vorotyntsev arrived. But the colonel lacked the patience to keep chasing after Kondratovich, and while Vorotyntsev had been collecting information from the wounded, Kondratovich had galloped into Neidenburg and, finding no officer senior to himself, had given orders to the commanding officer of the Estland Regiment to detail six companies and a machine-gun detachment to escort him eastwards along the main road. Obviously he had calculated that since the single battered division of his unmustered corps had in any case been subordinated to Martos, since the Kexholm Regiment was already in a forward position and able to fend for itself, and since the remaining Guards regiments which should have comprised his corps were not likely to arrive, there was nothing for him, the Corps Commander, to do, and it would be safer for him to retire across the Russian frontier, where he could await the outcome of the battle.

All this Vorotyntsev learned, to his fury, after he had dispatched his message to Samsonov.

Only this morning Neidenburg had been the site of Army Headquarters, a road junction and communications centre; by midday there was not a single general left in the town, in fact no one senior to Vorotyntsev. There were no communication links either forwards to the corps or rearwards to Army Group Headquarters, and it was up to anyone who had been left behind to choose his own course of action in accordance with his conscience and abilities.

Fortunately Vorotyntsev was still in a mood of supreme energy, of utter buoyancy and freedom from dependence on the physical and psychological demands of his own organism: he was simply a mobile device for saving whatever could be saved of the situation. He felt the chill draught blowing through the gap in the army's left flank as keenly as though it were a 'stitch' in his own chest, and his overriding thought was that the gap must be plugged during the few hours needed for the Army Commander to ride over to the I Corps sector.

In the uneasy, blockaded town of Neidenburg he found Lieutenant-Colonel Dunin, who commanded a battalion of the Estland Regiment: his four severely battered surviving companies had been resting in the town since the previous day, and he was unable to decide what to do. A further five companies of the same regiment, under another lieutenant-colonel, had also come from the north; these, however, were in such a state that each was hardly bigger than a platoon. They had been in the line all night, before being relieved that morning by the Kexholm Regiment.

In a few sentences Vorotyntsev explained to the two lieutenant-colonels, and to half the surviving company commanders, the situation of the town, the position of the army, the fact that their regimental commander had retreated back to Russia along with the remaining companies of their regiment, and the job that he wanted the rest of them to do. As he spoke he looked into their faces and saw, as though in his own features, the indelible impress of a similar background: army tradition, long spells of garrison service in a world isolated from the rest of society, a sense of alienation, of being despised by that society and ridiculed by liberal writers, minds blunted or stultified by the official ban on discussing politics and political literature, a permanent shortage of money, and yet, despite it all, the knowledge that they represented, in purified and concentrated form, the vitality and courage of the whole nation. Now was the moment they had lived for, and Vorotyntsev had no doubt what their response would be.

If it must be done—it must be done, that was all. Both lieutenant-colonels agreed to place themselves under Vorotyntsev's command, but pointed out that their men might not stand and fight: they were in a state of considerable shock from bombardment by German heavy artillery endured without the protection of trenches. Vorotyntsev asked only that the men should be paraded at the western edge of the town, on the road to Usdau.

While the troops were lined up and marched out—dejected, grumbling and surly—Vorotyntsev had time to see the commandant, Colonel Dovatur, a very polite, obliging, stout little man with a paunch. They agreed on arrangements for the supply and replenishment of ammunition and fixed on a point to the west of the town to which Dovatur should send Vorotyntsev a message as soon as the town was clear of all waggons and troops retreating on foot.

The men of the Estland Regiment were drawn up in six ranks in close order; they were in the shade, and the ranks were short enough for them all to be within easy earshot. While the parade fell in, Vorotyntsev, hands behind his back and feet planted firmly apart, was able to cast an eye over this detachment, with a tall, dark, long-service soldier as its right marker, of which he now unexpectedly found himself in command.

During the two days in which their regiment had taken such a battering, the survivors had noticeably aged. They had acquired the dignified lack of haste of men condemned to death; no one made any effort to hurry, to appear keen or to put on a show of smartness in carrying out an order. There was not a carefree face or a trace of bravado among them; after such intimate contact with death, the instilled disciplines of military behaviour had begun to flake away. The process was not, however, so far advanced that they had ceased to obey orders. A command might still suffice to send them back to the firing-line, but they would probably run away as soon as they got there—and the situation demanded that they hold firm.

So what was he to say to them? Their eardrums had not yet

recovered, they had not had time to get their breath back after barely escaping from death—and now they had to be told to go back and face it all again. Who was he, anyway? In their eyes some unknown colonel who would never share the risk with them and would vanish as soon as he had ordered them into action.

There was no point in using words like 'honour'—the concept was an incomprehensible piece of aristocratic fiddle-faddle; still less would he impress them by talking about their 'obligations to Russia's allies'. Should he invite them to sacrifice themselves in the name of their Little Father, the Tsar? They understood that, and would probably respond to the notion of fighting for the name-less, faceless, timeless figurehead. But to Vorotyntsev there was no eternal, anonymous Tsar—only the real, present-day Tsar, whom he despised and who headed a system of which he felt ashamed; it would be sheer hypocrisy to invoke him.

God, then? The name of God would touch a chord in them. But in Vorotyntsev's eyes to appeal to God would be blasphemous and intolerably hollow—as though it were a matter of supreme importance to the Almighty to defend a German town against the Germans themselves. In any case, every one of these men was capable of realising that God would scarcely choose to give His exclusive support to the Russians; why treat them as if they were fools?

One last appeal remained—their fatherland. This was a concept that did mean something to Vorotyntsev, but he realised that it did not mean much to *them*—their 'fatherland' scarcely extended beyond their local district; and since he would probably be unsure of himself, his voice was bound to convey an incongruous note of falsity and sentimentality which would only make matters worse. Obviously he could not appeal to them in the name of Russia.

So he did not compose a speech. As he gazed at the rows of grim, tired, sullen faces he put himself in their place, in their sweaty greatcoat-rolls, in sweaty shirts and leather straps that cut into their shoulders, in boots hot with the reek of unwashed feet. Having called them to attention and stood them at ease, he began to address them—not in ringing, hectoring tones, but in a voice that sounded as tired and stiff as they felt, rather as though he had not yet finally made up his own mind what to do.

'Men of the Estland Regiment! You have been through more than enough in the last few days. Some of you have had time for a rest, some of you haven't. But look at it like this: the others, half your regiment, have laid down their lives. The chances are always unequal in war—that's what wars are about. And what we ought to be thinking of now is not how we can get ourselves out of this, but how we can avoid letting our comrades down.'

At this point he was very tempted to give them a straightforward, truthful account of the position, to describe the whole situation and explain the military objective; regulations forbade an officer to talk to the rank and file like that, but in reality it was the only proper way to do it. In that case he would say to them: 'The centre corps of the army are about to be smashed to pieces. The generals have bungled it—all our generals are either fools or cowards, so it's up to you peasant lads to get us out of this mess!' But again he imagined himself standing in those ranks, under that equipment and those rifle-slings.

'Brothers!' As he flung out his arms he seemed to take root in the ground, and the men saw and felt his utter sincerity. 'Isn't it selfish to save ourselves at the expense of others? We haven't far to go from here to reach Russian territory, we could easily make it—but if we did, other regiments would simply be cut to pieces. And after that the Germans would catch up with us too, and even we might not get away . . . I know it's asking a lot of you, but right here there's nothing but a gaping hole in the line—there's absolutely no one there! For just as long as it takes the waggons to get the wounded out of the town we must plug that gap. We must hold out until evening. There's no one else to do it except you.'

He was not giving them orders or threatening them—he was explaining. And in all those grim, stubborn faces the light of understanding and sympathy suddenly shone out; they almost smiled—the spontaneous smile of pity for a wounded bird. Hating the idea of going back into action, weak and reluctant, instead of giving an articulate reply in an obedient, well-drilled chorus, they responded with a warm, indistinct murmur, a confused rumble of approval.

Seeing them break out in great-hearted smiles and hearing them murmur agreement, the colonel snapped to attention, reassumed a military air and shouted in a voice of command:

'I want volunteers *only*! Front rank! Any man volunteering to go—three paces forward—march!'

The whole rank stepped forward.

[376]

More confidently, almost triumphantly, Vorotyntsev shouted:
'Second rank! Volunteers—three paces forward—march!'

The second rank stepped forward.

Then the third rank.

All six ranks stepped forward to a man, grimly, without enthusiasm—but they all took the three paces.

Although he realised that this was no occasion for rejoicing, that such a feeling was out of place, almost indecent, in spite of himself Vorotyntsev roared:

'Well done, the Estland Regiment! Mother Russia hasn't run out of good men yet!'

At that moment mention of Mother Russia *did* seem appropriate.

❋

The horseradish hates being grated, but it dances on the grater when it has to.

37

With no time to spare, Vorotyntsev hurried back to his party of
horsemen—three Cossacks on detachment from the 6th Don
Cossack Regiment and Arsenii. The Cossacks were men of just
the right type—one with a big curly forelock, one with a stolid,
sleepy face, the other with a shock of hair, all three superb horsemen. As for Arsenii . . .

'As for you, Arsenii, I am downright ashamed of you. You told
me you could ride.'

'And so I can! Only bareback, though, without a saddle. In our
village we all ride like that. A saddle's just a fancy toy for the
gentry.'

Yesterday, in his haste and enthusiasm, Arsenii had ridden with
a saddle. It had given him a sore behind, so he had thrown it away
and was now riding without stirrups. Stung by Vorotyntsev's
reproach, he had done his best to improve his seat by tying on a
down cushion with a strap passed under the horse's belly, and was
now seated cheerfully upon it, his legs dangling, as he parried the
jibes of the laughing Cossacks.

'Is this all right, yer honour?' he said, pretending to be willing
to untie the cushion at once, but making no effort to do so. 'I
could ride all the way to Turkey like this,' he growled with bravado,
puffing out his cheeks.

'Yes, with that thing, Turkey's where you belong!'

Vorotyntsev slung a rifle across his back, cavalry fashion, and
they rode off.

One problem followed on the heels of another. A moment ago,
Vorotyntsev had been worried about whether he could persuade

the troops to go back into the hell-fire of the front line. Now his concern was, having promised they would only have to stay there until evening, who was going to relieve them if it proved necessary to hold the line for longer? He even wondered whether they would stick it out until evening. And if they did, would their sacrifice have been worth while—or was he deceiving them? He had no control over what happened on the rest of the front; it was all in the lap of the gods. At his relatively minor tactical level, he had more than enough to do deciding where and how to position these five companies (which, although they had been brought almost up to strength by merging the two Estland battalions, were still weak) and how to spread the troops between the Kexholm Regiment and the Neidenburg-Usdau road. The available forces were clearly inadequate to man the frontage in strength, yet the whole point of the operation was to ensure that the line was held unbroken.

They rode out several miles north-westwards along cart-tracks, towards the region where Vorotyntsev sensed there was a gap. His hunch proved correct. The area was completely devoid of life: there were neither Russian nor German troops, no local inhabitants, no stray horses, dogs or chickens, not even corpses. It was like the eye of a cyclone: while all around was roaring, swirling darkness, here were calm and blue skies.

Here, and no further, was the place to position the Estlanders; leaving behind one Cossack as a marker, he set off with the rest to make contact with the neighbouring unit which was to be on their right flank, and then to return.

Undimmed by a single cloud, the sun poured down pure heat, scorching the deserted, open countryside, where, it seemed, not a living soul was to be found. In front of them was a hillock dotted with a sparse growth of young pine-trees, and Vorotyntsev decided to ride up there to have a look around. Their powerful horses easily took the slope in their stride, and the way through the pines provided cover and soft going. Just before reaching the top they were surprised to hear a strange, growling noise, which immediately stopped. As they rode over the brow of the hill, there in front of them were Germans! Facing them only ten paces away was a car which had obviously just been driven up and its engine switched off.

Seated in the car were four Germans, no less amazed than the four mounted Russians.

At first both sides were too nonplussed to do anything. Then with a hiss the Cossacks drew their swords.

The officer sitting behind the German general produced his revolver and flourished it. With some difficulty, the man sitting on the other side of the rear seat pulled out a light machine-gun.

Arsenii deftly unslung his rifle and pushed a round into the chamber.

They were all sufficiently keyed up for a fight to have broken out spontaneously, which would have finished them all. But the Cossacks—and the Germans even more so—were trained to wait for a word of command.

The diminutive general did not draw his revolver and gave no order. Bolt upright, sharp-eyed and unafraid, he surveyed the unusual situation with amused astonishment.

Seeing this, Vorotyntsev did no more than keep a grip on the handle of his sword. (Being unfamiliar with a rifle, it would have taken him too long to unsling it.)

As the horses did not neigh and the car's engine was no longer running, the silence on the warm hilltop was such that the only sounds to be heard in the resin-scented air were the horses' breathing and the buzzing of gadflies or mosquitoes. As the moment of sun-warmed quiet and faint humming went by without a shot being fired, the threat of death passed from all eight men.

The general ('he's the same one we saw yesterday, your honour,' Arsenii whispered), craning his head, continued to stare ahead of him with extreme curiosity, as though forbidding anyone to shoot or slash at him. His ears were flattened against his head as though in fear, although he was not in the least frightened. A trace of humour lurked in his features, perhaps in the twitch of his bushy moustache which bristled outwards to either side; at any rate he clearly had a sense of the absurd, which he showed when he said with mock severity in German:

'Colonel, I should have taken you prisoner.'

Even before he had had time to grasp the significance of the encounter and how to act for the best, Vorotyntsev caught the tone of relaxed, cheerful reproach. In the same mood, and with a shade more jocularity, he flashed his fine set of even teeth in a smile and replied in German:

'No, your excellency, I'm the one who should take you prisoner.'

Machine-gun, revolver and swords were all lowered. Reasonably enough, the general countered:

'You are, after all, on our territory.'

Entering into the spirit of the exchange, Vorotyntsev put forward an equally sound argument:

'This area is in our hands.'

(This was pure bravado, but it was a good card to play in an uncertain situation: the Russian infantry might well be lined up just over the hill.) He added in a slightly crisper tone:

'And if I may venture to give you a piece of advice, General, you would do better to leave.'

Arsenii had been right; he was the same one they had seen yesterday when he had jumped so nimbly out of his car—and he was obviously no younger than Samsonov.

However, the general, evidently not wishing to carry on this kind of conversation, asked:

'What is your name, please, Colonel?'

There being no need for secrecy over names, he answered:

'Colonel Vorotyntsev.'

Either because he felt that a colonel might be embarrassed to ask a full general for his name, or because he was enjoying the exchange, the general politely introduced himself, the same glint of humour sparkling in his eyes:

'And I am General von François.'

Aha! So he was the commander of the German 1 Corps. And almost in their hands. Perhaps they could take him prisoner . . .

Unfortunately, it was not clear who was in whose hands.

But although it was natural enough to shoot and hack at the enemy when you were strangers, it was somehow inhuman when you had made each other's acquaintance.

'Aha! I recognise you. Was it your car we fired on yesterday? Why were you trying to go to Usdau?'

The general nodded and burst out laughing.

'There was a report that my troops were already there.'

He looked up at Vorotyntsev with an approving frown. It was one of the jokes of war, which one should be able to appreciate.

The Cossacks sensed this. Grinning as they caught the mood of the conversation, the two men—Kasian Chertikhin, with the quiff and a slight squint, and the sly, shock-headed Artyukha Serga— sheathed their sabres with a satisfying rattle.

The German officer had by now put his revolver away, and only the machine-gun was just visible behind the driver's back. Arsenii, too, had slung his rifle. Now he whispered again to Vorotyntsev:

'Look, your honour . . . the lion! They've pinched our lion!'

Having kept his eyes fastened on von François and the machine-gun, Vorotyntsev had not yet noticed that there was a mascot fastened to the car's radiator: it was the toy lion which had helped to keep up everyone's spirits in their section of the trenches at Usdau—long ago, it now seemed. Amazingly, it was still completely unharmed.

At the moment when the Russians noticed the lion, the Germans had noticed something else and were whispering with amusement.

'Are you a Russian?' von François asked appraisingly. He seemed to want to continue this talk. Confident in his power to fascinate, he clearly enjoyed the idea that he could charm even the enemy.

'Yes, I'm a Russian.' Vorotyntsev smiled, not too surprised that a Western European should ask such a question.

He finally decided that they had better go. The Germans now probably believed that the Russian forces were close by. He must hurry and put the Estlanders in position. With an expression of polite regret he saluted and said:

'Excuse me, your excellency, but I'm afraid I must hurry.' Another look into the general's eyes and a fleeting glance at the machine-gun. Would the Germans shoot them in the back? No, impossible. 'Farewell, your excellency!'

With the same blend of amiable irony, this time tinged with regret, the general replied with a wave of three fingers of his hand:

'Adieu, adieu!'

The Cossacks, too, understood the meaning of the gesture and at once, following the colonel, jerked their horses round and galloped off down the hill, guffawing with amusement.

At that moment the Germans burst into a roar of laughter. Hearing it, Vorotyntsev guessed the cause, and for the first time he lost his temper with Arsenii.

'They're laughing at your cushion. You've disgraced the whole Russian army!'

Arsenii rode on with unshakable dignity, but to judge from his scowling face he was offended.

The German machine-gunner might still shoot them all down with a burst of fire. But that would be unthinkable after their civilised encounter, and utterly unseemly for a great commander who was about to take his place in history.

38

For a military commander of the superior kind, winning battles is not enough: he must also fight with panache and flair. History will not fail to record his every gesture, every detail of his method of command: if these are carefully fashioned and polished, they will create an image of perfection; if not, he will be written off as nothing more than a clumsy boor who happened to be lucky.

On the evening of August 14th, General von François could not yet issue his orders for the 15th. His instinct was tugging him towards Neidenburg, but there was a threat of a counter-attack from Soldau, and it was towards Soldau that he was being pushed by Army Headquarters. In this kind of situation a mediocre commander will torment himself and his staff all night, waiting to see what will turn up, and then in the small hours of the morning pens will start scratching as orders are written out. But Hermann von François merely issued this laconic statement: 'Divisions are to prepare to advance in their sectors. The nature and timing of the advance will be given tomorrow morning at 6.00 a.m. on Hill 202 near Usdau. Officers will kindly report there to receive orders.' Then, in one of the still undamaged houses in Usdau, the general went to sleep under an eiderdown with a pink cover. This was a calculated gesture: the commanders of divisions and subordinate units would not dare to presume that there might not be an advance or that the corps commander did not know what he was going to do tomorrow.

An important adjunct to this gesture was the choice of the site where orders would be given out. Had his troops not already advanced so far beyond it, von François would have chosen

Windmill Hill at Usdau instead of Hill 202. Windmill Hill was the most beautiful and prominent height in the vicinity; he had also felt a special link with it since the previous day, when it had still been intact and he had made his mistaken and unsuccessful but exhilarating attempt to go there. It was yesterday that half his corps artillery, working to a system of concentrated fire that was being introduced for the first time, had set about scouring the hill and annihilating the Russian troops positioned on it. In the afternoon General von François had been able to inspect the pile of dead and dying Russians in the trenches and on the slopes of the hill, the first time in his career that he had ever seen a comparable result from an artillery barrage. As he had walked up the hill, on which stood the smouldering ruins of the mill (they were not extinguished until the dew and fog settled on them that night), he realised that every step he was taking was historic. Here began the road to Neidenburg, along which he was destined to accomplish his leap into fame. It was here, too, that he had noticed a patch of yellow in the banked-up earth of the parapet of a Russian trench, and his drivers had enthusiastically dug out a beautifully made, undamaged toy lion, which had survived the murderous bombardment. Someone had then had the idea of fixing the lion to the radiator of one of the general's cars, and to mark the capture of Usdau the animal was given the rank of sergeant-major in anticipation of a long and victorious military career which would culminate in a field-marshal's baton.

It was necessary, however, to issue orders closer to the front line. A thick mist was obscuring even the high ground and blotting out detail. Arms folded on his chest, von François paced up and down, having arrived at the rendezvous ahead of the appointed time. His isolation and his importance were stressed by the fact that for the past ten days he had continued to ignore his Chief of Staff, having decided to exclude that traitor from all participation in the work of the corps.

Earlier that morning, he had made up his mind: of his three divisions, one half would begin by advancing on Soldau as the higher command required, whilst he would keep back the other half in readiness to make his secret dash for Neidenburg. For this purpose, too, he would assemble his mobile detachment—made up of motor-cyclists, bicycle troops, a regiment of uhlans and a battery of horse artillery—at the start of the Usdau–Neidenburg road. Judging by the unconcern and silence of the Russians in Soldau, he felt confident that he would not be threatened from that direction and that the Russians there were wholly preoccupied with their retreat across the river.

When a great opportunity comes and knocks at the door, its first tap may be no louder than the beating of one's heart, and only a sensitive ear can detect it. Although there was no proof that the supposed threat from Soldau was an unreal one, and although artillery-fire had broken out in von Scholtz's sector on the far side of Soldau during the night and had continued until morning, nevertheless General von François felt sure that he had heard the fateful, almost inaudible signal. On his own initiative, therefore, he launched his 'flying squad' towards Neidenburg—although not by the direct route but in a southward loop, in order to capture the Russian supply trains which would undoubtedly be pouring south. He left the main road open to be used by his main forces, and so that he could follow them into action without delay.

At Soldau things looked promising: the Russian gunfire covering their retreat was listless, and they were abandoning the town without counter-attacking. But the bombardment in von Scholtz's sector was lasting for an uncomfortably long time, and at ten o'clock in the morning von François' plans to take independent, unauthorised action were ruined at the last moment when a car drove up with an urgent order from Army Headquarters:

'A division of General von Scholtz's corps has been pushed out of the village of Waplitz by the enemy and is still in retreat. You must give it immediate support by sending the whole of your corps reserve. *This manoeuvre must take the form of an attack.* Move at once. Situation calls for speed. Report when action taken.'

To von François this proved that neither Ludendorff nor Hindenburg were born commanders. They had not heard fate knocking at the door. The least action by the enemy threw them into a panic, and they were mistaking what was no more than a shallow trickle for a deep-flowing river. What a cowardly, unimaginative order—to tell him to send his corps into a frontal counter-attack (and to make a fifteen-kilometre advance in the 'form of an attack') just when the most magnificent encircling movement was ripe for execution!

However, with his reputation for insubordination, which had

reached as far as the Kaiser himself, von François had no choice but to obey. At the same time he could not bring himself to submit entirely to the dictates of faint-hearted mediocrity.

In war, compromise proves more often to be fatal than wise. Yet the only way out of the situation was a compromise: von François sent one division of his reserve in the direction required of him, while he himself remained with a reinforced brigade at the starting-point of his proposed dash for Neidenburg. By midday, as soon as Soldau was taken, he would pull back the division from that sector and reconstitute his corps reserve.

He knew, in any case, that Ludendorff's orders never remained in force for long. Sure enough, before one o'clock in the afternoon a liaison officer appeared from Army Headquarters with a new set of instructions: he was to divert the division sent to support von Scholtz on to a more easterly axis. No, Ludendorff was no general! These fickle, womanish changes of mind were no way to run an army. His only idea of what to do was to safeguard his own prestige by avoiding every possible risk.

Regretfully, von François realised that he need not have obeyed the first order after all; it had inevitably been countermanded by Ludendorff himself. The latest order had concluded:

'. . . from now on, the whole outcome of the operation depends on your corps.'

It had, of course, depended on von François' corps from the very beginning—and would do so until the very end.

At that point he launched the brigade (reinforced by a mounted *Jäger* regiment) along the Usdau–Neidenburg road. They were to take the town and advance beyond it. Leaving behind a thin line of patrols and road-blocks, they were to push on along the same road towards Willenburg, thus extending the jaws of the pincers as fast as possible. These detachments were to be closely followed by mobile field kitchens, to keep them fed. (A good commander always remembers his soldiers' rations.)

Von François himself, who no longer felt any great need to be in telephone communication with Army Headquarters, set off with two cars to observe and direct the departing brigade.

Among some scattered pine-trees on an isolated hilltop he had an amusing encounter with a Russian patrol.

The division that had been sent to the aid of von Scholtz had become involved on its way in a fight with a Russian Guards regiment, when at three o'clock in the afternoon a third order caught up with General von François: he was to withdraw the supporting division, as it was no longer required! In the view of Army Headquarters, the task of von François' corps was now as follows: 'To block the enemy's line of retreat to the south, for which purpose you must occupy Neidenburg today and move on towards Willenburg from dawn tomorrow.'

Where would he be, von François wondered, if he always waited for those great strategists at Army Headquarters to perceive the obvious? He need not have split his forces in two this morning after all, and he could have captured many more Russian supply waggons. Compromise in war was always a mistake.

And so the long summer day passed imperceptibly in a series of orders, counter-orders, suggestions, disappointments and successes. At about five o'clock in the afternoon the mounted *Jäger* regiment entered Neidenburg without meeting resistance, where it found no Russian fighting units but only rear-echelon services and supply trains. The only defence of the town was a thin line of infantry spread out to the north of the main road (von François himself had come under fire from part of this force positioned in a potato field). The general was amazed: were the Russians really so incapable of understanding a situation that they had made no serious attempt to defend this key town? What, indeed, did they expect to gain from fighting this war at all? What had induced them to get involved in it?

The chief obstacle to the advance of von François' corps was the great number of Russian supply waggons. The mobile detachment sent off that morning had caused a complete blockage on the roads south of Neidenburg by stopping the fleeing Russian transport, whose booty had included a paymaster's cash-box containing three million roubles. The congestion caused by the Russian supply trains was even worse in the town itself: when von François and his staff drove into Neidenburg shortly before twilight, his cars had to halt and he was obliged to reach the hotel in the market-place on foot.

A military police detachment and a battalion of grenadiers (the same one which had retreated twenty-five kilometres in panic from Usdau yesterday; their commander, a major, was now showing particular zeal in an effort to redeem himself) were searching all the houses, attics and cellars in order to winkle out any hidden

Russians and remove them under escort. All this was accomplished virtually without a shot being fired.

In front of the hotel the general was introduced to two men at once: the German burgomaster and the Russian commandant. The latter reported on the completion of his duties, on the state of the hospital, on the stores of German equipment and on the arrangements made for prisoners of war. The burgomaster was full of praise for the measures which the commandant had taken to preserve order in the town and to protect the lives and property of the inhabitants. Von François thanked the commandant and asked him to choose himself a room, where he would remain under house-arrest on his word of honour. He also asked him for his surname.

'Dovatur,' said the short, stout, dark-haired colonel.

Von François' ginger eyebrows were raised expressively.

'And what is your christian name?'

'Ivan,' the colonel answered, smiling.

Hermann von François' eyebrows rose even higher, and his lips pursed in a smile of thoughtful irony.

Two far-flung descendants of the French aristocracy from two different phases of their unhappy history of political emigration— Bourbon and Huguenot—had met for a moment on the farthest fringe of Europe, one to deliver his report, the other to place him under arrest.

A room in the hotel had already been prepared for General von François. Darkness was setting in. The town hummed with voices, shouted commands, the creak of waggons and the neighing of horses. On this chaos night fell.

In the meantime the mobile brigade and mounted *Jäger* were already pushing on in the twilight, eastwards along the road from Neidenburg, to close the second half of the encircling ring.

*

O Hermann the German, you're wicked and silly!
Almost as bad as that fool Kaiser Willy!
And stupid old Fritz, always huffing and puffing,
Just wait till we catch you and knock out your stuffing!

39

On the hillside behind Martos' command post stood a neat spinney of beech and fir, and beyond that were two farmhouses; in them Samsonov's mobile headquarters and its Cossack escort squadron were temporarily installed.

If there was to be no retreat, what were they supposed to do instead? The staff officers wandered about, grumbling: deprived of telephones, telegraph, and even of dispatch-riders, they had been forced to come here without rhyme or reason, far up among the forward positions. German shells were bursting close by; they could distinctly hear the boom of the Russian artillery and the rattle of machine-guns. The Mühlen line, where the Germans had held out until yesterday, was now in Russian hands but showing signs of cracking; it was held by one of Martos' divisions, the flanks of which were exposed and which was under enemy pressure that increased hourly. At Waplitz the Poltava Regiment also seemed unlikely to hold till evening the positions it had won that morning. The Army Commander had refused a withdrawal, but he had not been able to propose any other way out of this desperate situation. A retreat had begun to flow of its own accord, as solid metal will inexorably run as soon as it reaches its melting-point.

Unable to express their complaints to the Army Commander, they were, however, sensible enough not to wait idly until Samsonov's ponderous brain assimilated the facts and he was induced to change his mind; instead they concentrated on drawing up a subtle plan of withdrawal (although, thanks to Postovsky's foresight, they refrained from calling it 'withdrawal' in case it might be held against them later). On a little table, its legs dug into the ground under an apple-tree, lay a map, to which Filimonov pointed with confident gestures as the staff officers buzzed around him. To avoid any subsequent blame, this complicated plan was designed to be an impeccable model of tactical doctrine. The system was known as the 'sliding shield': in the manner of an endless belt sliding over pulleys, a constant westward-facing defensive frontage was to be maintained by means of each unit, as it reached the rear, sliding leftwards to act as cover for the others, which would then pull back through it and perform the same function in their turn. The first to withdraw under the protection of this defensive barrier would be the supply trains, followed by XIII Corps (which unfortunately had still failed to link up with XV Corps); while this was in progress XV Corps would hold the front line (this would be its seventh day of uninterrupted fighting), together with the remnants of XXIII Corps. Then, leaving the Poltava and Chernigov regiments as a rearguard, XV Corps would sidestep leftwards. (How huge, clumsy and unmanoeuvrable an army corps seemed when it had to retreat!) As soon as XV Corps had pulled back as far as Orlau, the scene of its first successful battle, it would hold the front line again, only now on a south-westerly axis towards Neidenburg, while the remaining elements of XXIII Corps would pass across its rear. Meanwhile XIII Corps, having spent all the previous day moving rearwards (at a rate of twenty-four miles a day), would in turn take up a position even further to the left of the others, allowing them to pull back across the Russian frontier.

Under a fir-tree, alone and apart on a wide, crude peasant bench without a back-rest, sat the Army Commander; he was within sight of all the others, yet he might have been shut up inside his private study. His gold-hilted sword and his map-case lay on the bench beside him; he had taken off his cap and from time to time he wiped his bare, prominent forehead with a handkerchief, although he could hardly have felt hot in the shade of the tree, fanned by a cool, gentle August breeze. To the despair of his staff, Samsonov had sat like this for several hours—his neck rigid and strained, scarcely moving, his small eyes betraying little comprehension, his answers courteous as ever but monosyllabic. He might have been reflecting on a way out of the situation for them all, or he might equally well have forgotten that he had a whole army under his command. With his two powerful hands planted on the bench to either side of him, he would sit motionless, staring at the ground in front of him, for half an hour at a time. He took nothing to eat or drink, he was not resting, and he did not seem to be waiting for news—he was simply engaged in agonised thought, the insoluble problem bearing hard on the crown of his head like a boulder; it was this pressure which made him mop his brow.

What could he be waiting for? Was he expecting to see Klyuev's column approaching in a thick cloud of dust from the north-east, the direction in which he was staring? The lances of Rennen-kampf's cavalry, perhaps? Or could he see nothing, was he not using his eyes, but merely listening to what was happening within himself—the muffled shifting of the deepest strata of his conscious-ness, the hollow rumble as they collapsed?

In the direction he was facing, the hillside sloped away to a peat-bog, while beyond it, easily visible half a mile distant scaling another hill, the Hohenstein–Nadrau road cut across the landscape from left to right. There had not been much traffic on that road all day, except for ambulances: it was not a lateral route and therefore of little tactical use to xv Corps. But by the late afternoon the traffic down the road from Hohenstein began increasing—supply and ammunition waggons, limbers but no guns, and all in disorder; then, in twos and threes among the transport, stragglers from the infantry appeared. With the sun behind them as they watched, the staff officers could plainly see that these men were not only detached from their units, but had already lost their rifles or were throwing them away and discarding their equipment as they went.

Samsonov, motionless and apparently unseeing in his patch of shade, was one of the first to notice the rout. Abruptly standing up on his strong legs, he loudly ordered the officers of his staff to move as fast as they could to stop the men and restore order.

So they ran—the grumblers and the less critical ones, colonels and captains, some ordering Cossacks to go with them, others drawing their unused staff officers' revolvers—down the little-used grassy path, along the barbed-wire fence dividing a cattle-pasture from a stone dike that skirted a marsh, and up the hill on the far side. They could be seen brandishing their revolvers and waving their arms, causing a crowd to form and block the road; the men at the back had already thrown away their equipment, while those in front were being forced to pick it up again. Messengers galloped back and forth to report to Samsonov that the troops fleeing in disorder from Hohenstein were men of the Narva and Kopor regiments who had abandoned an artillery regiment in its positions, leaving it without infantry cover; that the machine-gun detachment had also broken and run; that the commanding officer of the Kopor Regiment had behaved disgracefully; that the retreating men had gone out of their minds and were convinced that all was lost, but that thanks to the action of the staff officers . . .

In return, the Army Commander issued his orders: the stragglers were to be sorted out into their units along the roadside; the senior officers of the two defaulting regiments were to be further interrogated as to the cause of the panic flight; and as many men as possible were to be sent back to Hohenstein, after first being paraded by battalions alongside their regimental colours.

Samsonov came to life, strode up and down and peered through his binoculars; the firm, confident frown above the hirsute lower half of his face gave promise of calm leadership and a wise solution to every problem: nothing was irretrievably lost, the Army Commander would save them all! At last the great moment had come—the very situation, perhaps, that he had been seeking when he rode here this morning. Day by day the urge to go to the forwardmost sector of the front himself had grown stronger— and now the front line had come to him, in full view and less than half a mile away.

The Army Commander's horse was already saddled and waiting for him, but the confusion was slow to be sorted out. In the time that it took the two battalions to form up on parade outside Nadrau, hundreds of shrapnel shells burst over Martos' corps, and the disposition of its units changed, undoubtedly for the worse. The sun had moved on its course from afternoon to early evening when the Army Commander was at last able to ride over to where the defaulting battalions stood on parade. He mounted easily and set off with confidence.

The two battalions were drawn up to await the general's verdict on them, the regimental colours of each unfurled on the right flank. Their commander, a mighty mounted figure of godlike superiority, his massive head planted solidly on his massive body, rode up to inspire his troops to miraculous deeds of martial valour. Without strain, in a powerful voice that had a certain affinity to the tolling of Russian churchbells, Samsonov boomed out his words over the ranks and the surrounding countryside:

'Men of the Narva Regiment, Field-Marshal Golitsyn's Own!

Men of the Kopor Regiment, General Konovnitsyn's Own! *Shame on you!* You have sworn allegiance to your colours. Look at them! Remember the famous battles in honour of which those standards were adorned with eagles and with the Cross of St George!'

This was the bitterest reproach he could make; he could not curse and swear at them—they were all Russians, honourable men, and it was to their honour that he was appealing.

Then, mysteriously, as his powerful voice floated above the soldiers' heads, Samsonov's confidence seeped out of him. A moment ago he had known exactly what words to use, known how he would work the miracle of making not only these battalions but their regiments and all the centre corps turn back and fight; now, suddenly, his memory failed him, he forgot what else he wanted to say, and into his blurred mind there drifted another incident from some vaguely remembered time in the past, when he had barely managed to halt another mob of fleeing troops, whose shirts, rifles and mess-tins had been even more ragged and battered, whose faces even more distorted and flushed than these. What had he said to them? He could not remember. . .

A speech by a general ought to be effective: military history is full of instances of a commander addressing his troops in a moment of crisis, inspiring them, so that they . . .

'So remember that you are soldiers—and soldiers are brave. Keep faith with your regimental colours and the glorious names which . . .'

No, it was gone; the vital, galvanising phrase eluded him. But he went on:

'How could you do this? How could you bring such shame . . ?'

When he makes a speech, a general has the advantage of a captive audience; his listeners cannot protest or heckle. Although Samsonov had asked them: 'How could you . . ?' he was not really expecting to be told how bad the conditions were which every officer and man standing there had endured. Certainly Staff-Captain Grokholets, whose curled moustaches made him look keen and dashing even on a punishment parade, could have given him an answer—in a sharp voice and with a snort of indignation. He could have told him how, after standing their ground for a whole night beyond Hohenstein, they had gone into the attack next morning on Martos' orders and prevented the enemy from turning the flank of xv Corps; how they had then come under the fire of more than a dozen German batteries—a barrage of a ferocity that the Army Commander himself had probably never experienced; how only three Russian batteries had replied, and even these were short of ammunition; how they had pulled back into Hohenstein and managed to hold it, but the promised help from xiii Corps had never come; how the enemy began to exert pressure on Hohenstein concentrically, from three sides at once, in an arc from the south-west to the east; how when the German cavalry broke through to cut them off, they still held their ground and when a cloud of dust was seen coming from the north-east it had been not Klyuev coming to their support, but the approaching enemy. Only then had they turned and run . . .

Lieutenant Kozieko, blinking as he stood in the rear rank, might have put his complaints to the Army Commander in slightly more personal terms. He might have pointed out how the situation at Hohenstein had been so bad that it was bound to have ended in a rout; how terrible was the thought of being covered with blood or ripped to shreds or getting a bayonet-thrust between the eyes; how his beloved little wife would suffer if he were missing or taken prisoner; how many corpses they had seen in the last few days and how little consolation it was that some of them were German; how heavy their casualties had been—and all to what end? Was such sacrifice justified?

Private Vyushkov, who could just see the general out of one eye from behind another man's head, would have said to him: 'It's your job to preach to us; but we're not stupid and we know what really happened.'

Private Nabyorkin, on his stumpy little legs, was thinking: 'Those Germans shoot hellish well, your excellency!'

And Private Kramchatkin, in the front rank right below Samsonov, was standing stiffly to attention, straining every sinew, his head held back rigidly, his protruding eyes sparkling as he stared in admiration at the general. His whole stance showed that he had done what he could—more than that was not in him.

The general could not help noticing the fine, keen soldier staring at him with faith and devotion. He experienced an access of strength from this man's trust.

'The commanding officer of the Kopor Regiment is relieved of his command! This colonel here is to be your new commander and will lead you into battle. He is a brave soldier—I know him from the Japanese War. Follow him bravely and be worthy of your traditions. . .'

A large man, well seated on a large horse, Samsonov resembled a monument. With a monumental gesture he raised his hand and pointed towards Hohenstein. At the signal, the regimental choir-leader broke into the opening lines of the regimental marching song with the thrilling sweep of a falcon rising into the air. The battalions turned about and stumbled back up the road whence they had fled. The Army Commander returned to his staff.

Yet he still felt that there was something he had failed to say. He was not satisfied with his speech; he had made better ones. Some-how the great event for which he had hoped had not taken place.

Weakened, Samsonov slumped in his saddle. As he rode up the hill and saw Martos coming out of the wood—supple as ever, though by now looking tired—in that moment Samsonov realised that Martos had been right, that he now agreed with his advice to retreat which he had rejected that morning. Ten minutes ago, as he had raised his arm in martial exhortation, he had been telling those men to do the very opposite. Yet now, in the greyish shade of the spinney, screened from the blazing sunlight, he met Martos' exhausted, reddened eyes—and changed his mind. Even before Martos had finished recounting how the troops were falling back of their own accord, how regimental command posts had inevit-ably been forced to withdraw, how one by one the telephones had stopped working, how his best officers had been killed, Samsonov concurred. He had just upbraided two battalions for retreating; now he realised that they had had no choice . . .

The greatest decision of his lifetime had been taken in a mo-ment, and it did not seem to have required any mental effort. But when had the change come about, where had the turning-point been? At what point of time had it suddenly become necessary to reverse the direction of his troops after two weeks of movement which pressing logic had decreed should be in precisely the oppo-site direction? It was as though north had become south and east west, as though the sky above those pine-trees had been turned upside down. If Samsonov had been able to define that point of time, he might have discovered when and how he had lost the battle.

His staff officers were now showing him their neat, sensible plan of the 'sliding shield'; this, like the sky, seemed to be revolving too. Clutching for solid support amidst so much movement, Samsonov put his heavy, trusting paws on the thin, sharp shoulders of the man who, though he had underestimated him at first, was now his favourite corps commander.

'Nikolai Nikolaevich! According to the plan your corps will be at Neidenburg tomorrow. Everything will be decided there. Kondratovich should be somewhere in that vicinity too, as well as the Kexholm Regiment. Give instructions now for your corps to move, and then go ahead to Neidenburg yourself to reconnoitre and choose the positions for a last-ditch defence of the town.'

In placing the main burden upon him again, the Army Commander was showing how much confidence he had in Martos. But the latter misunderstood him: did this order mean that he was being relieved of command of the corps? Otherwise why was he being asked to leave it? What could he do without his corps? To whom should he give orders? Did the Army Commander realise what he was doing?

'And hurry, my dear fellow. Remember—everything will be decided at Neidenburg tomorrow. My staff and I will go there too.'

Abandoned this morning as useless, Neidenburg was now apparently the key which would release them from danger.

In a·gesture of affection, as he said goodbye Samsonov kissed Martos. And destroyed him.

All the energy which had been boiling inside Martos suddenly cooled. In an instant he was transformed from a Toledo blade into a brittle reed. As ordered, he left his corps and went where he was told.

Darkness was coming on. The day's army order was distributed. (A captain was sent to I Corps ordering it to advance immediately to Neidenburg; as for VI Corps . . . well, there was little they could do except tell it to hold on . . . at all costs.) The staff was ready. They tried to persuade the army commander to go to Janów, but he refused to move further than Neidenburg.

The town which that morning had seemed intolerable now beckoned invitingly, even though they might have to die defending it.

More insistently this time, the staff officers succeeded in persuading Samsonov that this morning's route was now too dangerous, and that on the return journey they would have to follow an even more circuitous path. Enemy shrapnel shells were bursting almost above the headquarters itself, the jagged flashes sharply visible in the fading light, and in Nadrau, through which they would have to pass, two houses had already been set on fire by high-explosive shells. The sound of machine-gun fire could also be heard coming from the town—whose was it? All around was the seething confusion left behind by a day of disorder and defeat. In the light of the fires, men could be seen running back and forth. Or were they running away?

Then the machine-guns stopped. With no one to put them out, the glowing fires lit up the sky. Unnoticed by day, the dogs had begun to bark.

The Day of the Assumption was coming to an end, and despite his incomprehensible dream Samsonov had survived.

General Samsonov was alive; but his army was dead.

40

Who can undertake to name the decisive battle in a war that lasted four years and strained the nation's morale to breaking point? Of the countless battles, more ended with ignominy than with renown, devouring our strength and our faith in ourselves, uselessly and irretrievably snatching from us our bravest and strongest men and leaving the second-raters. Nevertheless it can be claimed that it was the *first* defeat which set the tone of the whole course of the war for Russia: having begun the first battle with incomplete forces, the Russians never subsequently managed to muster enough men in time before an engagement. Unable to discard bad habits acquired at the start, they went on throwing untrained troops into action direct from the railhead without a pause for acclimatisation, thrusting them into the line wherever there was a breach or a leak, in a series of convulsive attempts to regain lost ground, without considering whether these attempts were strategically justified, and regardless of losses. From the very first our spirits were damped, and our self-assurance was never regained; from the very first both our enemies and our allies were disappointed by our poor showing, and with the stigma of that contempt we had to battle on until we collapsed; from the very first, too, the doubt was awakened in us: did we have the right generals, did they know what they were doing?

Without allowing any more scope to one's imagination than what can be learned from precise data, preferring historians to novelists as sources, we can only spread our hands and admit it once and for all: no one would dare to write a fictional account of such unrelieved blackness; for the sake of verisimilitude a writer would

[399]

distribute the light and shade more evenly. But from the first battle onwards, a Russian general's badges of rank come to be seen as symbols of incompetence; and the further up the hierarchy, the more bungling the generals seem, until there is scarcely one from whom an author can derive any comfort. (In which case there might appear to be some consolation in Tolstoy's conviction that it is not generals who lead armies, not captains who command ships or companies of infantry, not presidents or leaders who run states or political parties, were it not that all too often the twentieth century has proved to us that it *is* such men who do these things.)

What novelist would be believed if he wrote that General Klyuev, who led the centre corps furthest of all into Prussia, had *never before fought on active service*? There are no grounds for assuming that Klyuev was stupid, nor that he was not in some respects able and adroit. In his dispatches, for instance, he was able to describe the belated, pointless dash to Orlau by one of his divisions in such terms that in the reports submitted to the Commander-in-Chief and the Tsar himself he and not Martos was represented as being the victor at Orlau who had forced the enemy to retreat by threatening to outflank him. And in his memoirs, written in captivity, he managed to slant, colour and blur his account of events so that everyone was shown to be at fault except himself. Nor have we any direct proof that Klyuev was wholly worthless; indeed, if one is to judge by many later historical instances of this kind, we do not doubt that plenty of reliable, mitigating evidence could be found to show that he was a good family man and loved children (especially his own), a delightful companion at table and perhaps an amusing raconteur. But the fact remains that these virtues do not suffice to whitewash or justify a commander who undertook to lead thousands of men on a fateful enterprise—and led them badly. We may feel pity for the novice soldier when, caught in the evil toils of war, he first faces bullets and shellfire; but the novice general, however dazed and nauseated he may have been by the fighting, we can neither pity nor excuse.

The following is an account of what General Klyuev did. While his corps spent almost the whole day of August 14th in Allenstein, the furthest point to which Samsonov's army penetrated, he made no attempt to reconnoitre the locality and discover whether the enemy was to his right, in front of him or to his left, or in what strength; instead he asked Army Headquarters in Neidenburg to provide him with all this information. On the morning of the 15th, before abandoning Allenstein as a fruitless prize, he announced his intention to do so by sending a plain-language radio signal, thus informing the enemy as well as his own side of the route, boundaries and timing of his move to support Martos. Klyuev had at his disposal six regiments, which he scattered around with prodigality. To hold Allenstein 'until Blagoveshchensky arrived', he left behind (to their destruction) two thousand men—a battalion of the Dorogobuzh Regiment and a battalion of the Mozhaisk Regiment. Soon after that, with his corps strung out in column of march along the road to Hohenstein, he left the rest of the Doro-gobuzh Regiment in a rearguard position (which was also to prove a death-trap) because he thought he was being pursued.

Acting on Klyuev's radio signal, which they intercepted at 8.00 a.m. that morning, the Germans had hastened to send troops to harry his column from the rear, unaware that, since Russians can never keep to time, when Klyuev stated he would be at a certain point by midday he would not, in fact, reach there until evening.

When Klyuev reached the Griesslinnen Heights above Hohen-stein—the key town which he was to secure in order to help Martos, and which two of his own units, the Narva and Kopor regiments, were already holding—he stopped to wait. Did he do this to allow the rest of his column to catch up with him? Or did he pause, as seems more probable, from uncertainty as to who exactly was occupying Hohenstein—a distance of two and a half miles away? (As it happened, the Narva and Kopor regiments, from the low-lying town, thought that their own corps on the heights above was a concentration of German troops.) Klyuev made no effort to prevent another—a German—detachment from deploying be-tween himself and Hohenstein. Was he waiting for the situation to clarify? Or was he waiting for new orders?

The only orders which he gave were to send his leading regiment, the Neva, out to one flank and involve it in a useless battle that lasted all day in the dense Kammerwald Forest. Without artillery and with only a machine-gun company in support, the objection-able Colonel Pervushin led his regiment into an engagement of a kind peculiar to thickly wooded country, in which visibility is no more than twenty paces in any direction, no one can tell where firing is coming from, and the crack of a shot is particularly loud and vicious. The noise of bark being ripped from trees by rifle-fire makes the bullets sound as if they are explosive, and ricochets sound like new shots; troops have to fire over the heads of their own side and are killed by their own bullets; even brave men lose their heads, and the fighting dissolves into chaos. In that battle, for hours the Neva Regiment pressed back a German force of up to divisional strength (they even scattered the remnants of a divisional headquarters, consisting of a general and eight soldiers) and pushed their way through several miles of dense forest until at twilight they emerged on the far side as victors. But though successful, the action was pointless: the forest was of no tactical value.

As late as the morning of August 13th, the progress of XIII Corps could have been regarded as a purposeful advance; but during the half day's inactivity spent without firing or moving on the Griesslinnen Heights, there came a moment when the corps imperceptibly degenerated into something about as useful as a heap of junk. At all events, it should have *moved*—either to support Martos' nearby XV Corps (from whom an officer came requesting their help), or at least to escape by withdrawing southwards without delay while the narrow isthmus between the lakes was still open. But throughout the Day of the Assumption Klyuev dithered until evening, and he was still in the same place when night fell.

During that period of inactivity the Narva and Kopor regiments abandoned Hohenstein to the Germans and retreated to the south. At the same time, the two battalions left as a rearguard in Allenstein were overwhelmed and cut to pieces by German cavalry (the civilian inhabitants joined in by firing out of windows, and a machine-gun opened up from the lunatic asylum, still hung with a notice in Russian requesting that the inmates should not be disturbed). The supply trains, which had sensibly been sent to the rear that morning by a detour, were seized and their escort killed to a man. Acting as cover for the rest of the corps while it marked time to no purpose, the Neva Regiment took a severe beating as it fought in the forest. But the unit which did most to guarantee Klyuev's security while he stood still instead of pulling out of trouble by a tactical withdrawal was the Dorogobuzh Regiment, left to fight a rearguard action six miles back.

Soon after leaving Allenstein, the Dorogobuzh Regiment, made up of three under-strength battalions, was drawn into a rearguard battle. Its commander, Colonel Kabanov, received no phased plan of withdrawal from Corps Headquarters, but was simply told to conduct a rearguard action until he was relieved. It is very probable that Colonel Kabanov's opinion of Lieutenant-General Klyuev and of his plans and dispositions was extremely unflattering, but this in no way influenced Kabanov's execution of his duty. He had one task to perform: to judge where and how he could best delay the enemy pressing forward, and then to hold him.

We, whose daily life is always governed by considerations of self-preservation, are able to ignore the enigma of the behaviour of professional officers and other people guided by a sense of duty (as if such people, trained though they are in a hard school, were not recruited from ordinary mortals like ourselves): how is it that they will unflinchingly face a premature death so fatal to the plans they have made for their lives? What makes a human being cease to shun death? In every army there is always to be found a number of outstanding officers in whom is concentrated the utmost potential of manly courage.

At a time such as that Day of the Assumption, Colonel Kabanov clearly did not pay excessive regard to doubts or dilemmas (if one is a professional soldier, it is part of one's job to die sooner or later). Obviously he would have laid down his life without hesitation if by doing so he could delay the enemy. But to achieve this effectively he would have to use all his troops, especially since the forces pressing them amounted to a whole German division. If he was troubled by a doubt, it can only have been as to whether he should try to save the main body of the corps by the sacrifice of his beloved regiment or attempt to get the regiment away to safety. For the regimental commander, the agony of his position was that he must assume the role of fate for the men under his command: it was *he* who would have to pronounce sentence of death on his regiment. Kabanov had been given no artillery support. His ammunition waggons had been unable to get through to his position, and as a result he was so short of ammunition that only one out of four of his machine-guns could operate. Before long there would be no rifle ammunition either. So in the fourteenth year of the twentieth century the only weapon left to the Dorogobuzh Regiment with which to fight against German artillery was the Russian bayonet. Evidently, the regiment was doomed to perish; but although the death sentence which he had to pronounce on every single man lay on his conscience, this did not affect the clarity with which he took the necessary decisions: where to draw his boundary-lines, where to position strong-points so that bayonet attacks could be made across the shortest possible stretches of ground, how to sell their lives most dearly and how to win as much time as possible.

One such boundary Kabanov chose at Dereuten, where the high ground was favourable; one of his flanks was secured by a large lake, the other by a chain of smaller lakes. There the Dorogobuzh Regiment stood and held its ground throughout the bright, sunny afternoon and evening. There they exhausted all their ammunition; there they counter-attacked three times with the bayonet; there, at the age of fifty-three, Colonel Kabanov was killed, and of every company less than one man in twenty was left alive.

This miracle was due to more than just the bravery of the officers. Half of the troops were reservists who a mere month ago had reported to their assembly-points wearing bast shoes, fresh from their villages, their fields, their private aspirations, and their families. They knew nothing about European politics, the war, the battle which Second Army was fighting, or the objectives of their army corps, whose number they did not even know. And yet they did not run away, they did not waver or malinger, but drew on some unknown source of strength to cross the barrier which divides a man's love of family and instinct of self-preservation from devotion to cruel duty. Three times they stood up and walked into fire with their silent bayonets. If that regiment had been put down among the booty of the empty town of Hohenstein instead of the Narva Regiment, then it too would have looted and swilled (indeed, a week previously the Dorogobuzh Regiment had broached the liquor barrels in Willenburg). And if it had been the men of the Narva Regiment that had been obliged to fight that rearguard action (though, despite Tolstoy's view, they would have needed Kabanov and his battalion commanders), they too would have attained the heights of bravery where simple peasants are transformed into heroes.

They had burned their boats. Others like them would retreat, return home; they owed such men nothing: they were not their relatives, nor their brothers—yet they would stand and die so that they might live.

Who knows what they thought that day, those doomed men, as they looked up into an alien blue sky, across alien lakes and forests? There they stayed, buried in communal Russian graves, which the Germans preserved at Dereuten until the Second World War.

What did Colonel Kabanov look like? Either because his heroism passed unnoticed or because his photograph was difficult to find, his picture never appeared in any newspaper; much less did the faces of any of the rank and file, as it was thought quite unsuitable to publish photographs of them in newspapers or journals. It was in any case impracticable, as they were so numerous; a mass, they were only of value when called upon to hold out to the death. The press did its duty by them by lumping them together under the phrase, 'the grey heroes'. But photographs there were none; and more's the pity, because since then our national make-up has changed completely. Our features have altered, and no camera-lens can ever again find those trusting, bearded men, those friendly eyes, those placid, selfless faces.

No one was sent to tell the regiment that its task was done, that it could withdraw. The Dorogobuzh Regiment perished and only a very few survived. Ten men carried away the body of their colonel and the colours. It is known for certain that the Germans who attacked them from Allenstein made no progress until far into the night, when it was time for them to halt and sleep.

It is not known how much longer Klyuev intended to stay where he was, but around midnight a rider broke through with an order from Army Headquarters:

'In order to assist in concentrating the units of Second Army and provisioning them with all types of supplies, XIII Corps must withdraw during the night to the — region, making use of the following route between the lakes . . .' (It then named a route which had been ignored the previous day and was now totally inaccessible.)

Thank God, Klyuev observed, no mention was made in the

order of all the tasks and objectives that had been given to his corps in the last few days. Coming from the hand of Postovsky, the order assumed that all was peaceful, that regular routine could take its course and that for reprovisioning purposes it would be convenient for XIII Corps to move at night over a distance of twelve miles and across seven lakes to reach a tiny village of a dozen houses—and that there all its requirements would be met.

It was certainly in need of provisions: since leaving Allenstein on the previous day, the corps had had nothing to eat.

Escape! The time had come to escape, and this order gave him a pretext to get out, as Klyuev well understood. So, by unmarked tracks and by-roads, sometimes bumping into the enemy, XIII Corps melted silently away.

It no longer even amounted to a corps; it had only three regiments, all the rest having been thrown away. A further regiment had been destroyed when Klyuev left the Kashira Regiment, with sixteen guns, to fight yet another rearguard action near Hohenstein. The Neva Regiment now had to give up the position which it had won and hack its way through the forest by night to rejoin the main body. And then there was a sapper company which Corps Headquarters simply forgot; when it woke up next morning, it was to discover that it was alone, without orders to move and surrounded by the enemy. Further adventures were to await it.

41

_____

(*August* 15*th*)

The Quartermaster-General of General Headquarters, Danilov, was
third in rank in the Russian army, but foremost in initiative. He had
spent the last few days diligently working out matters of prime importance: he had drawn up one plan for the speedy transformation of
conquered East Prussia into a separate governor-generalship, and
another for the immediate cessation of warlike operations there; the task
of Rennenkampf's army thus being completed, it would be moved forward across the Vistula for operations aimed at Berlin. As part of this
plan he had asked North-Western Army Group to have one army
corps transferred from Rennenkampf to Warsaw.

Since the Chief of Staff of North-Western Army Group, General
Oranovsky, was in no position to protest at this directive (any objection
made by a junior against an order from above always undermines his
status and prospects), he had already issued instructions for the corps in
question to be pulled back to the railhead. (Rennenkampf, having mis-
interpreted the order of the previous night instructing him to send help
to Samsonov, had pushed this corps deeper into Prussia and received a
severe reprimand for his error.) Nor did Oranovsky dare, in reporting to
his superiors, to lay much stress on the anxiety which was beginning to
make itself felt among the staff of North-Western Army Group. He
merely reported that 1 Corps had been forced to withdraw near Soldau
'in a certain amount of disorder', and that the two corps of von François
and von Mackensen, 'which have disappeared from the enemy forces

facing Rennenkampf', had suddenly shown up in front of Second Army. But General Headquarters was unperturbed by any of this, and in a long telephone conversation on the night of the 15th/16th Danilov, in pursuit of his latest plan, induced Oranovsky to effect the immediate transfer of the Guards Corps from Warsaw to the Austrian front, remarking with complete unconcern that Samsonov would have to do without the Guards—he already had nearly five corps anyway.

Zhilinsky and Oranovsky might have passed on some of the anxiety they felt that day by harrying Samsonov, but to their annoyance (and partly to their relief, because he would then be entirely to blame for anything that went wrong) Samsonov cut off communications. This absolved them of any responsibility for intervening directly to make Blagoveshchensky's VI Corps and Artamonov's former corps (I Corps) move inward to the aid of the centre corps of Second Army. To have done this would have been too much trouble for Army Group Headquarters; it would also have been beneath their dignity, since according to service practice they were not obliged to intervene.

Meanwhile Blagoveshchensky's corps was living a wholly separate existence, just as if it did not constitute the flank of Second Army and had no responsibility towards it. Uncontrolled and unstoppable, it had rolled back almost to the Russian frontier, where it was no longer in anyone's way—indeed, it was temporarily out of the war. By sheer luck, General Blagoveshchensky had avoided being suspended from command of his corps on the day before Artamonov's dismissal; this had been entirely due to the delay in communications and the adroit wording of his reports. However, after the bad fright he had had on August 13th, caused by his sudden clash with the Germans—about which the higher command had not forewarned him—after his fear of being taken prisoner at Bischofsburg and being killed at Mensguth, and after a series of nightmarish withdrawals on August 14th and at dawn on August 15th, when a wave of terror had seized his whole corps and swept it into headlong retreat, what Blagoveshchensky needed was time for his nerves to recover (the more so as he was sixty years old) and a breathing-space in which he would neither be plagued by orders from above nor be forced to spend time making them up himself. Since, thank God, no one had so far come from Army Headquarters to investigate the situation on the spot and he was cut off from all telegraph or telephone links, Blagoveshchensky himself now had time to recuperate and to let his corps recover.

Therefore he did not order them to hold on to Ortelsburg, a road and rail junction, but to bypass it as it was on fire, abandon it without a fight and retreat away from the roads into the depths of the countryside.

How Blagoveshchensky wished that the detachment of dragoons which he had sent off the previous night with a dispatch to Samsonov would never return! Of course he did not wish them killed, but merely that they might be detained at Army Headquarters and attached to some other unit. And if they did return with orders, let it not be today, but tomorrow or the day after, which would give them the chance to repair their morale by getting a good night's sleep in some quiet spot. Alas, his hopes were in vain. The tireless dragoons made their way back across thirty miles of enemy country, and at midday on August 15th arrived, bringing these lines written in Samsonov's sprawling hand:

'Hold your ground at all costs in the area of Ortelsburg. On the staunchness of your corps depends . . .'

Hopeless! Ortelsburg was fourteen miles away . . . Profoundly depressed, Blagoveshchensky read and re-read the impossible order. He summoned his staff officers and discussed with them in detail the reasons why it was out of the question to carry out these unwelcome instructions.

So Blagoveshchensky decided, for the safety and well-being of the corps entrusted to him (and to the relief of many of his subordinate officers), to revise the Army Commander's directive: not only would the corps not move that day, but he would declare the following day a rest-period. The only person to exert himself would be Blagoveshchensky himself: he would compose a carefully worded, convincing dispatch explaining why he had had no alternative but to abandon Ortelsburg: '. . . Approaching Ortelsburg, the whole town was found to be on fire, having been set alight by the inhabitants. It was, of course, a deliberate trap. Realising that it was impossible to remain on the heights above the town, I withdrew the corps southwards.' Then he added: 'The men are exhausted. I request permission to give them a rest-day.' He skilfully decided not to send the document at once (by dispatch-rider to the nearest town inside Russian territory and thence by telegraph), but to wait until the following morning, when the rest-day would have already begun.

As for 1 Corps (where Artamonov, although dismissed, was still making his presence felt to the nervous General Masalsky, who had temporarily assumed command for twenty-four hours before Dushkevich arrived and took over), lacking a guiding hand and demoralised by its retreat, it had also taken the line of least resistance and withdrawn for safety to Mlawa, across the Russian frontier. Although the frontier was not fortified, was not even a line of trenches but merely a boundary on a map, it was reassuring because it offered apparent protection from the Germans. The senior officers of 1 Corps knew that Neidenburg was already in enemy hands; yet because they had no firm instructions to take decisive action, not one of the dozen or so generals was capable of acting strongly on his own initiative.

Thus on August 15th the Russians did everything needed to ensure their opponents' triumph—the long-awaited *revanche* of Tannenberg. Only the doomed centre corps failed to behave submissively. The Kexholm Regiment, which only reached the front line at midday, had by evening lost more than half of its complement. The battle of Waplitz ruined the Germans' plan for a 'tight' encircling movement around Hohenstein. All the battles in the centre that day were either won by the Russians or at least not won by the Germans. But in the vortex of fighting, the face of war can alter so completely that what is gained by first-class regiments may be reduced to ashes by incompetent command at corps and army level. With each tactical engagement won in the centre, the Russians became increasingly the losers in the battle as a whole and plunged themselves deeper into ruin.

On the German side, however, none of this was quite so obvious. The costly attacks made by von Scholtz's divisions all seemed to end clumsily in setbacks due to failures in co-ordination. Frequently the German infantry took their own returning cavalry for Russians and subjected them to heavy fire, at times even routing them. German guns fired on their own troops; a unit was hit by sudden enfilading fire from the Russians and thrown back. After fighting all day, they hardly gained an inch. In Kammerwald Forest a whole division, including its headquarters, was cut to pieces by the Neva Regiment. Even Hindenburg and Ludendorff, in their car, were briefly caught up that day in a panic near Mühlen caused by Russian prisoners: some medical units and artillery ammunition trains had mistaken the prisoners for fighting troops and had fled with shouts of: 'The Russians are coming!'

Two German corps commanders, von Below and von Mackensen, spent the day arguing over who should advance on Hohenstein and who should move southwards. As the senior in rank, von Mackensen ordered von Below to clear the way for his corps. Von Below refused to obey. An airman was sent to Army Headquarters for a solution to the argument. Then von Mackensen stopped moving altogether and gave his corps a rest-day. It was nearly four o'clock in the afternoon before Hindenburg managed to reach von Mackensen by telephone and ordered him to advance southwards to carry out the encircling movement. Less than an hour after this telephone call, however, the encirclement plan had to be abandoned, and both von Mackensen and von Below were made to wheel and face Rennenkampf. Information (false) had been received that three of Rennenkampf's corps, together with his cavalry, were moving westwards at a moment when the German corps were in disarray and had their backs turned to this new threat. (Ludendorff wrote: 'Rennenkampf need only have closed with us and we would have been beaten.')

In actual fact, Zhilinsky's principal order to Rennenkampf that day was to tell him to advance to surround and maintain observation on Königsberg (which was garrisoned by a handful of elderly reservists and second-line troops). However, on the night of the 14th/15th, still possessed by anxiety over the incomprehensible goings-on along Samsonov's front and the appearance there of new German corps, Zhilinsky and Oranovsky sent Rennenkampf a telegram ordering him to make a left-flanking movement towards Samsonov and to push his cavalry forward in that direction. In order not to disturb General Rennenkampf's sleep, the telegram was not delivered to him until six o'clock the next morning. He issued the necessary orders, but the main cavalry force (commanded by General Khan Nakhichevansky) proved unable to get on the move until the evening of the 15th; General Gurko was nearer to the scene of the fighting, but he, too, failed to arrive.

Meanwhile, at the headquarters of the German army in Prussia, the orders for August 16th had already been altered and redrafted. Ludendorff does not mention those particular orders in his memoirs, but in Golovin's opinion they were excellently drawn up according to the very best principles of military science: with a minimum of redeployment by von Mackensen's and von Below's corps a new front was to be formed against Rennenkampf, while von François' and von Scholtz's corps, by simultaneously pursuing and enveloping Samsonov, would form a trawl-net, open at one end, which would also serve to scoop up the approaching Rennenkampf.

On the evening of that day—the very day on which German Supreme Headquarters withdrew two corps from the Marne to reinforce the army in Prussia!—Army Headquarters in East Prussia, abandoning its dream of another Cannae, reported to Supreme Headquarters: 'The battle is won. Pursuit will be resumed tomorrow. Encirclement of the northern corps probably no longer possible.'

The decision made by Hindenburg and Ludendorff was a triumph of mediocrity. The only thing it lacked was the spark of intuition.

That spark came, however, from the self-willed von François, who was probably ignorant of Tolstoy's advice: 'It is senseless to stand in the path of men who are bending all their energies to escape.' In disregard of his orders, von François drove his uhlans, his bicycle troops and his armoured cars on and on—through Neidenburg and even further eastward towards Willenburg.

And the stubborn von Mackensen, cursing at the change in orders from Army Headquarters, offended at the way his quarrel with von Below had been decided, broke off communications (allegedly *before* the rewritten orders reached him) and then, inaccessible to any further changes and counter-orders, set off hell-bent southwards—also to Willenburg!

Nor should we forget the imperturbably efficient German supply services, who saw to it that despite all the sudden changes in plan the German troops lacked for nothing.

42

To make a farewell tour of Moscow on foot, be it only of the chief
sights, is an undertaking beyond even the powers of two tireless
pairs of young legs. Where three or four roads branch out from
every crossroads, each street not chosen is a whole lost tour. They
spent the morning in the offices of the Alexandrovsky Cadet School,
where they were told to report back in the evening, then a final visit
to the University, and with that their official business was largely
done. For the rest of their time they were free to say a last, senti-
mental goodbye to the city. Although they were not born Musco-
vites but only temporary citizens by adoption, they felt a heavy pang
of regret—ah, Moscow!—and the thought of leaving it hurt them.

The traditional starting-point for anyone arriving in Moscow or
leaving it was the spacious square in front of the church of Christ
the Saviour. From there you only had to stroll a short way along
the embankment to see the vast, unique Moscow roofscape—
towering housetops, belfries, the turrets of the Kremlin. As if of
their own accord, their legs took them along the embankments—a
hundred yards wide and with a completely different set of views
from the houses on one side and the riverside parapet on the other.
The bridges invited them to cross to the far bank: over there was
the Tretyakov Gallery, and they would have liked at least to have
patted the familiar tracery on its walls, but there was no time to
spare. Instead, a look around the Kremlin—it was a unique sight, a
walk they had never taken before because they had always been
too busy, but now was just the moment to see it at last. So they
toured those cities-within-cities, the Kremlin and Kitaigorod, the
districts of the Varvarka and the Ilinka, and Nikolskaya Street—

crammed with houses adorned with carved and moulded stucco façades, with a church on every corner crowded with worshippers for the Day of the Assumption; each street, so it seemed, with at least two monasteries, with noblemen's palaces and cramped, jostling shops. Did you know that old Moscow was never built to any plan? Perhaps it was a good thing: everyone simply fenced off a piece of land wherever he thought fit, so that no one corner of the city is like another, and this is what gives Moscow its character.

There was so much else they wanted to do: see the ring-boulevards and the lakes, pay their respects to the Moscow Art Theatre, stuff themselves at the food-stalls on Okhotny Ryad and then wander down every single one of the little alleyways around the Arbat. But how would they find the time? They still had to go back to the Cadet School and collect their papers and their posting-orders. And how could they miss a visit to the Pushkin Statue on Strastnoi Boulevard? And what about a tram-ride? No, that would feel too much as if their student days were completely over and they were saying goodbye to them for ever. Of course those days were not over! Other young men might never come back from the war, but they would. Of course they would return and finish their course, take their degrees . . .

The dear old place was just the same; and now that they were taking their leave of them, the pavements and roadways somehow felt softer to walk on, as though their feet were striking the ground with less than the full force of gravity. In the two short years since Sanya and Kotya had first stepped out on to the square in front of the station in Moscow, they had not only come to know and love Moscow, but in a certain sense had already outgrown it, and with that sense of slight superiority they now felt a particularly generous affection for it.

In their tour of Moscow there was another thing they noticed: that the city did not seem very conscious of the war, did not sense it as something fateful. If one had not heard about the war and had not peered hard at the few announcements pasted up here and there, or if one had failed to notice an occasional squad of soldiers from a reserve regiment being marched to the public baths, it was quite possible to be unaware that Russia had already been at war for four weeks. The pedestrians and carriages in the Moscow streets were no fewer, the faces and the colour of people's clothes had not darkened, the shops were as cheerfully noisy, the showcases as bright as ever. There were perhaps a few more men in uniform to be seen, and a few flags and portraits of the Tsar not yet taken down after the pomp and splendour of his recent visit to Moscow.

Kotya and Sanya kept up a lively exchange of comment on all this; the sum total of it, however, aroused a hint of doubt which disturbed both of them and which neither mentioned aloud: had they not, they wondered, been too hasty and made too rash a decision to cut themselves off from this exciting, carefree, abundant life? It would have felt quite natural to leave Moscow if the city had been in a mood of grief and mourning or of anger, but were they not in a little too much of a hurry to say goodbye to a place that was so full of vitality and gaiety? However, as long as this doubt stayed deep inside them, vague and unspoken, it remained unreal. For one of them to have brought it out into the open by uttering it aloud would have meant hurting the other, and neither of them could be so unkind. Kotya in particular was incapable of mentioning it, because that would have implied a reproach to Sanya for having come to Kotya in Rostov and proposed that they should both volunteer for the army. The idea, after all, had been Sanya's in the first place. It was quite another matter that Kotya had instantly agreed: 'You're right—let's go!' To be honest, the thought had never occurred to him until Sanya had arrived, but in a second it had dawned on him that of course they should join up. His mother would object strongly, but they had to go all the same. (She objected so violently, in fact, that they had to suffer the nervous strain of twelve continuous hours of tearful entreaty, until finally Kotya left his large, powerfully-built mother prostrate in a faint.) Even this morning, in the offices of the Cadet School, it had not been too late to withdraw (although they would have been too ashamed to do so in front of each other), but now there was no going back. The two friends were more carefree than ever as they laughed and shared all their thoughts—all, that is, except one.

On their second visit to the Cadet School they were given posting-orders to the Sergievsky Heavy Artillery School, which was what they had wanted, and were told when to report there next morning and what to bring with them. The churchbells were ringing for vespers when, their feet aching pleasantly from so much walking, they crossed Arbat Square towards Nikitsky Boulevard, then walked between the showcases of Blank's Zoological Store (a magnet for small boys) and the church of St Boris and St Gleb, down an alleyway so narrow that two drunks clutching each other could hardly pass through, and along which by some amazing feat a little tramcar managed to squeeze its way. Turning into the Voz-dvizhenka, the warning clang of its bell mingled with the vaster tolling of churchbells and the general hubbub of the Arbat—the clatter of the cab-horses' hooves, the ponderous clip-clop and rumbling wheels of a dray passing over the cobbles, the shouts of newsvendors and the cries of hawkers. 'Out of my way there!' came the peremptory bark of a cab-driver to a pedestrian. 'Gid-dup!' shouted another as he whipped up his horse, one wheel of his cab scraping the kerbstone.

As evening approached, the two young men found themselves growing more sensitive to various powerful aromas wafting on the air—the smell of a pastrycook's, of a cook-shop, or of freshly baked bread—and they planned to have a bite to eat in some tavern before continuing their stroll.

Then on the Nikitsky Boulevard they saw walking in the same direction ahead of them a tall, thin, grey-haired man, carrying a pile of loose books under his arm. They recognised him almost as soon as they saw him, having once spent hours staring at his back: he was an acquaintance of theirs from the reading-room of the Rumyantsev Museum. Giving Sanya a dig in the ribs, Kotya said: 'Look—the Stargazer!' Annoyed, Sanya restrained him. Always unaware of the carrying-power of his voice, Kotya never could talk quietly; the Stargazer might overhear them and turn round, which could be very embarrassing. He was not exactly an acquain-tance, as they had never been introduced to him or talked to him. Once in the reading-room he had reduced them to silence by glancing reproachfully in their direction when they had been whispering loudly. On another occasion, in the corridor, when he had been carrying a dozen or so books under his arm, as he was now, and had dropped them, the two boys had happened to be there and had bounded over from either side and picked them up. After that, although strictly speaking still unacquainted, they would nod to him in passing and exchange half-smiles, and they frequently saw him in the reading-room. There was something distinctive about the Stargazer, even among the extremely serious, learned readers who used the library of the Rumyantsev Museum. It was partly the extreme thinness of his side view and his head, partly his dark, glittering eyes in their cavernous sockets, which gave his face such an inveterate look of profound seriousness, or it may have been his peculiar mannerism when he was deep in thought: he would lean his elbows on the table, form his long arms into the shape of a wigwam by linking his fingers and then, brushing them lightly with the tip of his beard, stare fixedly over the other readers' heads towards the topmost bookshelves and galleries. It was at one of these moments that Kotya had called him 'the Stargazer', although they had no idea what he was studying and felt too embarrassed to ask him.

Now they both said at once: 'Shall we go and talk to him?'

The mood of their farewell visit had overcome their normal inhibitions, making them eager to miss nothing and to seize every chance. Overtaking the Stargazer on either side, glancing across at each other, their friendly intonation softening the discourtesy of addressing him without a name, they said in chorus:

'How do you do?'

The old man did not start in surprise. Turning his deep-set eyes on the two young men, he looked at them (he was not as tall as they remembered; being so thin had made him appear taller than he was), recognised them and replied:

'Ah, young men! Delighted.' Arranging his pile of books with his left hand, he held out the other to them. The wrist that emerged from his cuff was thin, but his palm was as broad as a workman's. 'The name's Varsonofiev.'

They introduced themselves. For a moment they stood silent in their pale, belted linen shirts and students' caps, then Kotya took the initiative and announced loudly:

'It's our last day! Tomorrow we join the army—as volunteers.'

He was not bragging; it was simply his nature to sing out aloud whatever was on his mind. His broad face, with its high cheekbones, shone with enthusiasm, and his arms spontaneously flung themselves wide to express his zest for life.

Pavel Ivanovich Varsonofiev allowed the stiff bristles of his clipped grey beard and his thick, grey moustache to part slightly. It was obviously a smile, although his lips could hardly be seen. Staring intently at them each in turn, he said:

'Really? H'mmm.' His voice, which seemed to issue from cavernous depths, was a deep rumble. He looked at them again. 'Aren't you afraid that your friends will sneer at you as "patriots"?'

'Well, er . . .' Sanya tried to find something to say in self-justification. 'Of course, they do call us that. But then in a certain sense that's what we are . . .'

'And why shouldn't one be patriotic?' Kotya blurted out loudly and aggressively. 'After all, we didn't attack them—they attacked us. Or at any rate they attacked Serbia.'

His head bent forward, the old man gave them a searching look.

'Indeed, so it would seem. I only ask because until a few weeks ago to call someone a patriot in Russia was practically equivalent to calling him a member of the Black Hundreds.'

'What do *you* think, though?' Kotya pressed him. 'Are we doing the right thing, or not?'

This was a heaven-sent opportunity for Kotya to raise the question which had been troubling him and to test his own feelings without offending his friend. The old fellow might come out with something sensible.

Varsonofiev raised one eyebrow.

'To say whether you are doing right or wrong depends on your convictions.' Then with a sparkle in his dark, piercing eyes he enquired:

'I suppose you are socialists?'

Shyly, Sanya shook his head.

Kotya pursed his lips as though deploring the suggestion.

'What? You aren't? Then I hope you are at least anarchists?'

Neither of the boys gave an affirmative nod. They noticed that the old man did not seem to be making fun of them—or rather it was unimaginable that his deeply serious features should ever express sarcasm. Although it was hard to detect anything in the way of an expression in the slight movement of his lips between his beard and moustache, there was a faint but definite gleam in his eyes.

'Well, I for one am a Hegelian,' Kotya declared firmly and solemnly. He had a very decisive way of speaking, jaw firm and chin thrust out.

'A pure Hegelian?' said the old man in amazement. 'That's a rarity!'

'That's right—a pure Hegelian,' Kotya affirmed proudly. 'And he,' poking his finger into Sanya's chest, 'is a Tolstoyan.'

They had meanwhile started walking again, back along the Nikitsky Boulevard.

'A Tolstoyan?' The old man sounded even more surprised as he looked the shy, diffident Sanya up and down. 'Good heavens, how can you go to war, then?'

He noticed how crushing and hurtful this remark was. Sanya knew only too well that he was acting inconsistently; unable to find anything to say, looking deeply pained, he could only brush his soft, corn-coloured hair away from his forehead.

'Oh, he's serious about it all right!' Kotya groaned, feeling more and more at home with this splendid old man. 'He didn't eat meat for two years. Today in Okhotny Ryad I managed to stuff some meat pies down him for the first time. Just think how he'll manage in the army. He won't be able to pick and choose there—you all eat out of one pot.'

Sanya was not upset at this teasing between friends. He smiled gently, but still felt awkward.

Glancing kindly at them both, the old man asked:

'Well, young men, if you're not in a hurry to join some young ladies, why don't we drink a glass of beer? And I expect you're hungry, aren't you?'

No, they were not going to see any young ladies. Scarcely exchanging a glance, they accepted with delight. Getting to know the Stargazer better would be a fascinating way of spending the rest of their last day.

'Then if you wouldn't mind, just wait a moment for me here—I have to go to the chemist.'

They were standing at the side of the chemist's shop on the corner of Nikitsky Boulevard, and Varsonofiev went round the corner. He stooped slightly as he walked.

'Hell!' Kotya burst out. 'We should have offered to carry his books for him, then we could have seen what they were. We didn't think of looking when we picked them up for him that day in the library, either. Listen, don't go on about Tolstoy too much; everyone knows all about Tolstoy and Tolstoyans.'

Sanya smiled agreement.

'The best thing is to let *him* say what he thinks about us joining the army. Then we'll get him to talk about history—you know, give us his general ideas about Russia and the West, and so on . . .'

Trams passed, clanging, their pick-ups hissing along the wires; cabs trotted by, their pace brisk or leisurely according to the kind of passenger; passers-by streamed unconcernedly along the boulevard, as though oblivious of the war. A girl with long plaits carried her score to a music lesson, a scruffy waiter in a stained white bumfreezer trotted across the road with a pile of covered dishes, delivering an outside order. Beside the semicircular building at the intersection of Nikitsky Boulevard, which was enlivened by a jolly advertisement for 'Uncle Kostya' cigarettes, stood a tall policeman in his black and white uniform, observing the exemplary public order around him. Other advertisements streamed past them on billboards fixed to the tops of tramcars. The long row of shop-signs, whose attractions had brought them here, immortalised the names of countless solid tradesmen in elaborate lettering—painted and embossed, curling and straight—and affirmed the lasting material solidity of Moscow. At the same time the city was completely un-real, because tomorrow the two boys would no longer be in it. Only the Union Cinema proclaimed that it knew this:

IN DEFENCE OF OUR BROTHER-SLAVS!

Sensational Kinematic Record of the
Great Historic Events.

Meanwhile, apart from that solitary sign of the times, the city moved on and stood still, changed and stayed the same, unaware in its vast insensitivity of the special, exalted character of this, their last day, unconcerned at the braveness of the step they were taking. Whether the massive city collapsed or survived no longer mattered to them, because they had already absorbed all that was best in Moscow and would carry it away with them, locked within, to-gether with their own unique selves.

Then they did something that they called 'starting to sneeze'.

Leaning his head back slightly, Sanya narrowed his eyes and said pensively as he put his hands on his friend's shoulders:

'Listen. All this . . . all this . . .' He looked around in search of words to sum it all up, but could not find them. Anyway, they both knew what he meant—no two people understood each other better. 'We must come back here after the war. To this same spot. Shall we?'

'Yes, yes!' As a sign of agreement Kotya grasped him under the armpits and lifted him a little off the ground; he was as strong as Ivan Poddubny, the great wrestler.

Their buoyant spirits carried them high above the gleaming, clanging, clattering, seething reality around them. A force of furious joy propelled them into the future. And if disaster were to strike, or had already struck, they were convinced that they could survive unharmed, that they could savour even the fearful beauty of catastrophe.

Varsonofiev came out of the chemist's shop and waved them towards the Union Cinema. They noticed now that he did not stoop, but held his head of grey-white hair, cut *en brosse*, slightly forward, as though straining to hear or see something.

'There's a very decent beer-house under the Union, and it's usually full of interesting people.'

The old man was not so other-worldly as he had seemed; he obviously knew his way around.

As they walked in, the first thing that struck them were the smells—warm, delicious, tangy smells, mixed with an overpowering aroma of beer. The place simply consisted of three interconnecting rooms, one of them giving on to Nikitsky Boulevard and another on to an interior courtyard, and they passed through into the last room. Kotya nudged Sanya: sitting over beer and *vobla** was a famous professor from the Natural Science Faculty, surrounded by students. Here and there were army officers, and some men who looked like lawyers. There was not a single woman to be seen! The place was a haven of male leisure. One could see from the quantities of beer-bottles—left on the tables as a means of adding up the bill—that people spent hours here, talking to their hearts' content. They also read newspapers and magazines supplied by the management. As they walked through, Kotya picked up a copy of *Niva* and Sanya took *Russkoye Slovo*. They chose a table by a window, beside a huge pile of beer-crates.

'The war news is good so far,' said Sanya as he glanced through the newspaper. 'We're advancing in Austria and in Prussia. It's going well everywhere.'

'Listen to this!' Kotya exclaimed loudly. 'An order to the troops by the British War Minister Lord Kitchener: ". . . treat women with courtesy, but avoid intimacy with them"! How about that, eh? What are they worrying about?' He burst into deafening laughter; it was really very funny. The beer-house was not a quiet place: all around, people were talking noisily and laughing. By now

---

* Roach, a delicacy in Russia, eaten as a snack with drinks.

they were both extremely hungry, their appetites titillated by their sense of smell, and they were more than ready for a drink.

'Well, now, young men—what is it to be? *Solyanka*, meatballs, scrambled eggs?' said the old man invitingly. 'How do you manage about meat?' he enquired solicitously of Sanya.

'*Solyanka* for both of us!' said Kotya firmly. 'You'll just have to make a clean sweep of it, Sanya. You're going off to fight anyway, so that makes nonsense of all your Tolstoyan ideas. Just for the occasion and in honour of Pavel Ivanovich, stop fasting and eat some red meat for once!'

At that moment some *solyanka* was carried past, the thick, delicious soup giving off clouds of subtle, tantalising vapour. Sanya gave Pavel Ivanovich a defensive, guilty look, in an agony of choice. But having already eaten meat pies and being about to set off to kill people, it would be hypocritical to split hairs over a bowl of *solyanka*.

Varsonofiev ordered two.

'What about you, Pavel Ivanovich?'

The Stargazer held up one long finger, like a white candle.

'At your age, eating is a pleasure; at my age, pleasure lies in abstinence.'

'How old are you, Pavel Ivanovich?'

'A round fifty.'

From his grey hair and lined face they had expected him to be older, but fifty was still a respectable age. Having given the order, he poured out the beer and ate some salted peas with relish. To Sanya, who had, after all, chosen *solyanka* with cabbage instead of meat, he said consolingly:

'What is the hardest thing to do in life? It is to adhere to a belief in its pure form, as your friend follows Hegelianism. Eclecticism is always easier—anyone can play at it. So if you haven't any teeth you must live off *solyanka*.'

Varsonofiev discovered that they had finished their third year in the Faculty of History and Philology, that Kotya was more of a historian, Sanya more of a philologist. With polite interest he asked Kotya a more specific question:

'Might I ask which of Hegel's ideas, for instance, is your favourite? Just say the first one that comes to mind.'

As easily as it broke into laughter, Kotya's broad Slav face took on a pensive look. There was so much that he found fascinating in

Hegel—the dialectic, his defence of a principle for its undeveloped potential... But he knew which concept appealed to him most.

'The idea of advance by the "dialectical leap".'

Kotya found something very attractive in the 'dialectical leap'. Delightedly, Varsonofiev clasped his fingers on the table.

'But if you are a Hegelian, then you must affirm the existence of the state.'

'Yes ... I do,' Kotya agreed after a slight hesitation.

'But the state does not like a sharp break with the past. It favours gradualism. A sudden change, a leap forward, is destructive to the state.'

They ate, and drank the strong and perfectly cooled beer. Varsonofiev nibbled at some salted biscuits. His teeth were white, unblemished and even.

'And may one ask, Pavel Ivanovich,' Kotya boomed, 'what you do? You see, we tried to guess ...'

'Well, let me see ... I read certain books and write certain others. I read thick ones and write thin ones.'

'That's not exactly clear.'

'When things are too clear they are no longer interesting.'

Kotya's manner of blurting out his thoughts without regard for politeness made Sanya wince. In an effort to make the talk sound less like an interrogation, he asked:

'Do you really think so?'

'You see, the more important something is to us the more impenetrable it seems. Only simpletons find things absolutely clear. The best poetry of all is in riddles. Haven't you noticed what delicate complexity of thought there is in riddles?'

' "I have two ends, I have two rings, and a nail right through the middle"!' said Kotya, reciting with the snappy rhythm of an abacus, and burst into laughter. Loud though it was, his laugh was drowned by the general babble; cut off by the wall of sound around them, they could hear each other more clearly than if they had been in quieter surroundings.

'I know a better one than that,' said Varsonofiev, savouring the last of his beer and pouring out some more all round. ' "At eventide the little white hare is running free, by midnight she's served on a platter." '

He pronounced the words in a peculiar, deep, sing-song tone,

unlike his normal voice and in even greater contrast with the booming chorus of beery, guzzling men around them.

'What's the answer to that one?' asked Kotya quickly.

In the same mysterious voice came the oracular reply from between the old man's moustache and beard:

'A bride.'

'Why on a platter?'

'Because if one simply said "on a bed" there would be no riddle.
It's a poetic metaphor. She's on a platter because she has been
handed over, helpless, spreadeagled.'

Did Sanya blush slightly? No, he was thinking it over.

They ate and drank some more. Varsonofiev mentioned something to do with Tolstoyanism. Kotya, who could not tolerate the
subject, rushed to his friend's defence.

'Don't provoke him—he's not really much of a Tolstoyan, you
know. In his village, for instance, they call him a *narodnik*.'

Varsonofiev puffed out his moustache.

'Well, really, I have fallen among strange company—you seem to
profess every possible creed!' And he ordered four more bottles of
beer. 'But words get worn out and often obscure the meaning of
things after a while. What does it mean to be a *narodnik* nowadays?'

Ignoring what was on the table in front of him, Sanya concentrated his thoughts. For all its glowing health and steppeland
sunburn, which was noticeable even in the dim light cast by the
little windows of the beer-house, his face had a softness which was
quite untypical of a Kuban farmer's son; in the gentle blue eyes beneath the tousled fringe of hair one could read unceasing mental
effort. He was not very keen to talk, and when he did speak he was
always ready to make concessions to the other person.

'Well . . . it's someone who loves the people. Believes in their
spiritual strength. Places their eternal interests above his own
petty, short-term ones. Someone who doesn't live for himself, but
for the people's happiness.'

'Happiness?'

'Ye—yes, for their happiness.'

Gleaming brightly, though screened behind the broad ridge of
his eyebrows, Varsonofiev's eyes pursued their quarry.

'But for the majority of the people happiness is having enough to
eat, enough to wear—in fact prosperity and material satisfaction,

isn't it? Do you think a whole century is needed to feed and clothe them? As for their "eternal interests", presumably the obstacles to realising them are poverty, serfdom, lack of education, bad government, and to change all that and put it right, do you think the *narodniks* will need three generations?'

'Yes, possibly.'

Staring ahead, as he was able to do without blinking, Varsonofiev kept his quarry in his sights.

'And if all these *narodniks*, in trying to save nothing less than all the people, refuse to save themselves until that goal is reached? According to their creed, they are forced to do so. And they are equally forced, are they not, to regard everyone who does not sacrifice himself for the people as worthless—everyone, for instance, who is concerned with art for art's sake or with abstract speculation on the meaning of life or, worst of all, with religion—everyone, in fact, who cultivates and saves his own soul?'

Sanya listened with painful attentiveness. He raised his hand, holding up a finger to get his word in before he forgot what he wanted to say.

'But can't a soul be saved in the very process of sacrificing itself for the people?'

Varsonofiev blew through his moustache.

'But what if that sacrifice proves to have been misconceived? Don't the people have any *obligations*? Or do they only have *rights*? Are they simply meant to sit and wait while we first supply them with happiness, then provide for their "eternal interests"? And what if the people themselves aren't ready? Because if they aren't, then neither food, nor education, nor a change of institutions will be of any use.'

Sanya wiped his forehead, staring fixedly at Varsonofiev as though he could draw understanding directly from the other man's eyes.

'Not ready—but in what sense? In moral stature? In that case, who is?'

'Exactly—who is? It may be that the people were at a high level of moral development before the Mongol invasions in the Middle Ages; and we have assumed that they have retained that level ever since. But once serfdom was introduced, and tsars and revolutionaries began alternately to shackle the people and incite them to throw off their chains—starting, perhaps, with Ivan the Terrible, or, if you prefer, with Peter the Great on the one hand and the rebel Pugachyov on the other, right up to the present fumbling regime and including the 1905 revolution—who knows what happened to the Russian people? What is written on their inscrutable face now? What goes on in their heart of hearts? Look at our waiter over there—a pretty unpleasant-looking face, don't you think? Upstairs in the Union Cinema there's a pianist thumping away in the dark: what sort of an ugly mug does he have, and what lurks in *his* soul? Why should one perpetually be obliged to sacrifice oneself for his sake?'

'A cinema pianist and a waiter,' Kotya objected, 'hardly make up the people.'

'Then who does?' Varsonofiev turned his grey, bristling head towards Kotya. 'For how much longer must we always identify the people with the peasantry? Millions of peasants have left the land—what has become of them?'

'In that case we need a strictly scientific definition of what we mean by the people.'

'Yes, we all like being scientific, but the fact remains that so far no one has ever defined precisely who the people are. At all events, it does not just consist of the illiterate peasantry. Nor can you treat the intelligentsia as separate from the people.'

'So you must define the intelligentsia too!' said Kotya forcibly, as ever.

'No one can do that either. The clergy, for instance—you don't regard them as belonging to the intelligentsia, do you?' He caught a momentary snort of agreement on Kotya's part. 'And no one who holds "reactionary" views counts as one of the intelligentsia either, though he may be the most eminent philosopher. But students, of course, are automatically members of the intelligentsia, including failures and second-year blockheads who need cribs to pass their exams . . .'

Unable to keep up his earnest tone, Varsonofiev parted his bearded moustache in an unmistakable laugh. Beer-froth was sticking to his whiskers; beckoning to the unpleasant-looking waiter, he said:

'Two more bottles, please.'

The seriousness which had informed the conversation was dissipated, but Sanya was still held by it: he felt there was something in the short discussion that had been left unresolved and hanging in the air. He was not simply reflecting on their talk; he was overwhelmed by it.

'By the way, young men, if it's not an impolite question, I'd very much like to know who your parents are. What are your social backgrounds?'

Kotya blushed deeply and fell silent, as though he had choked. After a pause he said reluctantly:

'My father's dead.'

And poured himself some more beer.

Sanya knew that this was Kotya's raw spot: he was ashamed that his mother was a stall-keeper in the market, and he avoided the subject whenever possible. Tearing himself away from the problem which was still worrying him, Sanya spoke up for his friend.

'His grandfather was a fisherman on the river Don. And my parents are peasants. I'm the first person in our family to go to university.'

Gratified, Varsonofiev linked and unlinked his fingers.

'There you are—a perfect example. You are both from the land and you are both students of Moscow University. You belong both to the people and to the intelligentsia. You are *narodniks*—and you volunteer to go to war to defend the state.'

The choice was indeed difficult as well as flattering: to which category did they really belong?

Kotya slit open a fish as though cutting into his own flesh.

'I think I'm beginning to understand that you are not exactly a supporter of democracy—is that right?'

Varsonofiev made a slight affirmative inclination of his head and asked:

'How did you guess?'

'So you don't think that democracy is the highest form of government?'

'I do not,' he said quietly but firmly.

'Then what would you propose instead?' Kotya rejoined with his keen, almost childlike enthusiasm.

'Propose? I wouldn't venture to.' His dark eyes flashed from their twin caverns. 'Who is conceited enough to imagine that he can actually *devise* ideal institutions? The only people who think they can are those who believe that nothing significant was ever done before their own time, that their generation will be the first to achieve anything worth while, people who are convinced that only they and their current idols possess the truth, and that anyone who doesn't agree with them is a fool or a knave.' The old man seemed to be growing angry, but at once checked himself. 'I'm not specifically accusing the youth of Russia; it's a universal law—intolerance is the first sign of an inadequate education. An ill-educated person behaves with arrogant impatience, whereas truly profound education breeds humility.'

Sanya could hardly keep up. While listening to each new turn the conversation took, he was still mentally struggling with the previous phase—they had touched on so many things, dropped them and passed on. However, leaving the rest aside as hopeless, he seized on the last subject.

'In general, though, do you believe that it is possible to develop an ideal social order?'

Varsonofiev's resigned yet unwavering stare was capable of kindness, as was his voice, and the look which he gave Sanya was kindly. Quietly, pausing occasionally, he said:

'The word "develop" has a better and more important application—we should develop our *soul*. There is nothing more precious than the development of a man's own soul; it is more important than the well-being of countless future generations.'

That was it—that was the thought they had failed to pursue earlier! It was the need for that choice that Sanya had been groping for. The cultivation of one's own soul: wasn't that what Tolstoy had taught? But then what would become of the people's happiness? Were they incompatible?

Lines of concentration spread across Sanya's forehead. Varsonofiev went on:

'Above all, each one of us is called upon to perfect the development of his own soul.'

'What do you mean—called upon?' Kotya interrupted.

'Another riddle!' Varsonofiev held up a finger to stop him. 'It is the reason why, while you may pray for the people and sacrifice everything for their good, you must never trample your own soul underfoot—for who knows when one of you may not be fated to catch an echo of the true, the secret order of the world?'

As he spoke he looked at them both. Was this beyond them? He fell silent and drank up his beer, then, as he had done countless times that evening, wiped the froth from his moustache. Young people might well find his ideas tempting, as he could tell from the reaction in their eyes: what if he's telling the truth? what if those vague stirrings in me really are something of ultimate importance?

But the boys were still interested in their previous question.

'And what of the social order?'

'The social order?' With an evident waning of interest, Varsonofiev took a few peas. 'Obviously one kind is less evil than all the others. Perhaps there may even be a perfect one. Only remember, my friends, that the best social order is not susceptible to being arbitrarily constructed, nor even to being scientifically constructed —everything is allegedly scientific nowadays. Do not be so arrogant as to imagine that you can invent an ideal social order, because with that invention you may destroy your beloved "people". History'—his long, thin head nodded up and down—'history is not governed by reason.'

There it was again! Sanya seized on the words, clasping his hands in a gesture of urgency.

'Then what is history governed by?'

By good? By love? Pavel Ivanovich would probably reply in some such terms, which would connect with what Sanya had already heard from many other sources. How good and how simple it would be if he were to confirm it.

But Varsonofiev disappointed him. Again he sprang a surprise on them.

'History is *irrational*, young men. It has its own, and to us perhaps incomprehensible, organic structure.'

He said this with despair. Until now sitting bolt upright, he sagged and leaned against the back of his chair. He was no longer looking at them, but at the table or through the distorting green glass of the beer-bottles. Then, although he had failed to convince either Kotya or Sanya of anything, he began speaking again, this time taking care not to be vague or inconsistent; it occurred to the two boys that he must have given lectures at some time.

'History grows like a living tree. And as far as that tree is concerned, reason is an axe: you'll never make it grow better by applying reason to it. Or, if you prefer, history is a river; it has its own laws which govern its flow, its bends, the way it meanders. Then along come some clever people who say that it's a stagnant pond and must be diverted into another and better channel: all that's needed is to choose a better place and dig a new river-bed. But the course of a river can't be interrupted—block it at all and it won't flow any longer. And we're being told that the bed must be forcibly diverted by several thousand yards. The bonds between generations, bonds of institution, tradition, custom, are what hold the banks of the river-bed together and keep the stream flowing.'

'So it's impossible to propose any changes?' said Kotya, blowing out his cheeks. He was tired.

Sanya gently put his hand on Varsonofiev's sleeve.

'Where should one look for the laws that govern the flow of the river?'

'That's the riddle. It may be that they are unknowable.' The thought gave Varsonofiev no comfort, and he sighed. 'At all events, they are not to be found on the surface, where every busy little half-wit casts around for them.' Again he raised a finger as large as a candle. 'The laws of the perfect human society can only be found within the total order of things. In the purpose of the universe. And in the destiny of man.'

Silent, he relapsed into the characteristic pose he adopted in the library, his forearms forming a triangle with the table, his round, carefully trimmed beard brushing back and forth across his interwoven fingers.

Perhaps he should not have said all that. But then these two students were rather out of the ordinary.

Kotya gloomily drained his beer. A vein on his forehead was knotted from concentration.

'In that case, there is absolutely nothing to be done except to stand to one side and observe. Is that so?'

'Every *true* path is very hard to follow,' Varsonofiev replied, resting his chin on his hands. 'And virtually inaccessible.'

'But is it right to join the army and go to war?' Kotya blinked.

'I must say—yes, it is.' Varsonofiev nodded emphatically and approvingly.

'Why? How are we to know?' Kotya went on obstinately, although his posting-order was in his pocket. 'How can anyone judge?'

Varsonofiev unlocked his fingers and spread them in a gesture that embraced the two young men as his equals.

'I can't prove it, but I feel it. When the trumpet sounds, a man must be a man, even if merely for his own self-respect. This, too, is something inscrutable. For some reason it is important that Russia's backbone shouldn't be broken. And for that young men must go to war.'

[430]

Sanya appeared not to hear the last remark. He was thinking that the way ahead, or the bridge across the river, would remain invisible forever—or visible only to the unknown few. Otherwise mankind would have found and crossed that bridge long ago.

'What about justice?' he put in doggedly, sensing another idea that had been left unconsidered.

'Yes!' Varsonofiev turned his two glittering, deep-sunk eyes on him. 'But again not our own invented justice, which we have simply thought up to fit our convenient earthly paradise. There is a justice which existed before us, without us and for its own sake. And our task is to *divine* what it is!'

Kotya sighed noisily.

'You're full of riddles, Pavel Ivanovich, and they're all difficult. You should give us one that's a bit easier.'

Pavel Ivanovich gave a sly smile and said:

'Well, here's one. "If I stood up, I'd reach the sky; had I arms and legs, I'd tie up a thief; had I mouth and eyes, I would tell all."'

'No, Pavel Ivanovich,' said Kotya protesting humorously, already slightly drunk but pleased that his taste for riddles was appreciated. He tapped on his plate with the tail of a fish. 'We must leave it to you to put the most important question. Otherwise when we join the army we'll regret not having heard what it is.'

Varsonofiev relaxed and said with a tired smile:

'Important questions always have long, tortuous answers. And no one can ever answer the most important question of all.'

*

The answer to a riddle is short, but there are seven leagues of truth in it.

[431]

43

Terenty Chernega hardly remembered his father; he was brought up by his stepmother until he could fend for himself, then she married again and Terenty left home without having gained a great deal from his step-parents. Nor did he acquire much of an education from two years at a village school and a year at a commercial school. In any case, book-learning was not essential to a lad who knew how to keep his eyes and ears open. When necessary, Chernega's agile native wit enabled him to follow the talk of educated people, including officers.

Once Chernega heard the brigade commander, Colonel Khristinich, talking to his battery commander, Lieutenant-Colonel Venetsky, about the general state of affairs in the artillery. They were discussing the inefficient use of draught-horses and the amount of time wasted while guns stood idle as a consequence of there being eight guns in a battery, whereas the Germans had six- or four-gun batteries. The government lacked the necessary funds to convert six eight-gun batteries into eight of six guns; it was cheaper simply to keep the extra guns in a battery without firing them. Battery commanders, they complained, were so bogged down with administration and the task of maintaining and cleaning spare equipment that they had no time for firing-practice or for studying gunnery manuals—although these were all out of date and the latest ones did not reach them before war broke out.

This only confirmed Chernega's view that the most important man in the artillery was the sergeant-major. Who else took care of all the administration and maintenance?

During his term of military service Chernega had been promoted from trail-number to gun-layer, and then to gun-captain. Called up on the first day of the war, two days later he was posted to Smolensk, where he caught the eye of Colonel Khristinich, who glanced at Chernega in passing from under his bushy grey eyebrows and said to Venetsky:

'Pity for a good man like that to stay a sergeant. You ought to make him your battery sergeant-major.'

He was right in guessing (Chernega himself knew it already) that he would make an excellent sergeant-major. When Chernega came to know Lieutenant-Colonel Venetsky better, he realised that Khristinich would not have advised every battery commander to take a man into his battery and promote him to sergeant-major. Venetsky knew all about gun-sights, fuses and ranging, but he was too easy-going; when talking to his men he invariably used language that was above their heads and issued requests rather than orders, and no one would have kept a tight grip on the battery if Chernega had not been appointed its sergeant-major.

From his first cheerful roar of command, he fitted into his new job as to the manner born, and the whole battery accepted him. Owing to the nature of the campaign in the first fortnight of the war, the sergeant-major was plainly the mainstay of the battery. For two weeks the guns were never unlimbered, the unit never once took up a firing position, and whether the officers had mastered their gunnery manuals or not was of no consequence. Although they showed the men which route to follow, the general direction taken by the divisional column made this obvious enough; otherwise the officers did nothing but write reports. The man who actually led the battery, who saw that it was fed and watered, who organised the move to each new bivouac, who looked after the horses and ammunition, was Chernega; all the men recognised him as the boss, and the horses, by the way they pricked up their ears, sensed that he understood them. (Horses responded to Chernega from the moment he first patted them on the neck. He knew everything there was to know about horses, having bought and sold many of them—not for profit, but for love of them. He felt more passionately about horses than about women.)

At country fairs, Terenty had carried fifteen-gallon barrels of sauerkraut, bent horseshoes and ten-kopeck pieces, rung the bell with sledgehammers—had taken part, in fact, in all the favourite spare-time competitions enjoyed by strong men in Russia. He was like a barrel himself. Despite his lack of inches, his strength was prodigious; but except in fire or flood he had almost never had occasion to use it to the full. He never needed to exert more than half of it to get all he wanted in life, because he had learned many skills and trades, relying more on brains than brawn and keeping his muscle-power in reserve. Up till now, in war, Chernega had still had no cause to show his full strength. He did his job with the relaxed ease of a natural leader. The war had come as an unwelcome interruption when he was in his prime at thirty-two, at a time, as always seems to be the case, when he was finding life more interesting than ever. So he decided that though he would do his duty, he would also see to it that he did not wear himself out.

Then in the middle of one night the troops were roused to the sound of the alarm. For the past week, anxiety had been building up in the men's minds, caused by lack of information, the eerie emptiness of the countryside and the feeling that they were walking into a trap. When this mood was suddenly dispelled by a clear order—which came like a release—to get on the move with all speed, Chernega, in the space of time between two heartbeats, unleashed all the strength in him and ran to his battery commander.

'Just tell me what we have to do, your honour.'

By the light of a candle in his tent, Lieutenant-Colonel Venetsky clasped the sergeant-major by his sinewy forearm, and said:

'We must get the battery across this damned river, Chernega . . .'

A lock of white hair falling over his forehead, pointing to the map spread out on his folding camp-bed (which he was to leave here forever), he explained the situation with more than his usual rapidity and assurance.

'. . . so as to avoid moving along the main road and making a big detour. It seems the Germans are in this area. There's some kind of a bridge across this river—here. It may be damaged, it may be rotten, and the approaches to it are marshy, but we must get across it. If we do, we save six miles and we'll dodge the Germans. Then we must immediately move on and cross this causeway, called *Schlage M.*'

The map was not much help—just a series of marks in green, black and blue. Much of the area was dotted with lakes and impassable. Chernega's round eyes took it all in even quicker than was necessary. One thing puzzled him, though.

'What is *Schlage M*?'

Schlage, the officer explained, was the German word for a sledgehammer; there was a Polish saying '*Szlag trafi*' which meant roughly 'Drop dead' or 'I hope you're hit by a sledgehammer'. . .

'In this case,' he went on, 'it's obviously the German name for the dike or causeway across this stretch of water, which is either a millpond or the village pond of the hamlet of Merken. We can by-pass Merken by going this way, but we can't avoid crossing *Schlage M*. If we can get across that dike, we'll come out of this alive, whereas if we stay here . . .'

If we stay here—we're done for! Gently, so as not to crush him in his grip, Chernega clasped Venetsky by the shoulder.

'We'll do it, your honour. You just send the officers ahead to reconnoitre the route and we'll see to the gun-teams!'

'And . . . the ammunition . . . you do understand, Chernega?'

'Of course I understand!' Chernega ran out of the tent. 'We'll get the ammunition through even if we have to pull our arms off to shift it. We'll waddle along with two rounds apiece like fat old women swinging their tits!'

This was an emergency worse than a fire or a flood; at moments like this officers were useless—a sergeant-major with two brawny arms was what was needed. For all their generations of book-learning, officers could only cough apologetically when there was man's work to be done; should he leave them in the lurch and let them go to hell this time? It occurred to Chernega not to take the ammunition—they could have ordered him to take it a hundred times, and he would still have left it behind. But he was keenly aware that they were short of ammunition and that each round might save the lives of five, if not twenty, men.

Chernega roared at his men like a lion, drowning the noise of other orders being given, of grumbling, of horses neighing and the clank of equipment. Although the men of the battery thought they knew their sergeant-major, until then they had not realised the full extent of his abilities; the real war began for them that night. That leonine roar told every one of them that from now on they would have to strain every sinew, that if the horses failed the men would have to haul the guns themselves. (His roar, though loud, was not as loud as it might have been; sound carries far at night, and there was no point in telling the Germans that the battery was moving and where it was going.)

The still, fine night, lit only by starlight after the moon had set,

[435]

became a whirlwind of urgent action. The information was not announced officially, but the rumour quickly got around and was accepted by everyone as genuine that somewhere there was a bridge which they had to reach as fast as possible, and that if the Germans knocked it out they were lost. Never stopping to draw breath, Chernega ran up and down the column, always in time to sort out problems as they arose. Without pause they strained and heaved as though struggling against a violent downpour or as though under fire. The cart-track between the fields twisted and turned and was crossed by other tracks; at every intersection sign-posts awaited them, placed there by the officers' reconnaisance party. As they approached the river, Chernega carried out a personal reconnaissance, testing the ground with his foot to discover where it was boggy and how soft it was. Every man lending a hand, stumbling, sinking in, they unharnessed the limbers and man-handled the guns up to the bridge. There was more work awaiting them on the bridge itself: in the last village they had dismantled a shed and lashed the timbers to the gun-barrels; now, in the dark, they made good the bridge by replacing missing or rotten planks with sound beams. Then they watered the horses. After the bridge came a long haul over low-lying, marshy ground, and to prevent the teams from getting bogged down the guns were once more un-harnessed and pulled by hand. After this the terrain rose fairly steeply, so again the teams were harnessed up, the crews helped by heaving on the wheels, and at last they breasted the rise and drove on to firm ground. That was war: woken up at midnight, they had accomplished in the dark a feat which by day would have seemed impossible. The operation had taken up the whole of the short summer night. Leaving the bridge and the dark, rutted cart-track for the rest of the regiment behind them, the battery silently hauled itself up to the main road at first light, under cover of a wood. No one had fired at them, no one had tried to bar their way; the furious German attacks of the last few days seemed to have slackened. The night was as quiet as if there were no war.

Before reaching the road, the battery halted in the wood. They were the first to arrive, which meant that the alternative route, which the infantry were following, was a long one and that some of the regiments had probably gone astray. Although it was not yet quite daylight, visibility was much better. The village of Merken lay on high ground half a mile away to the right. Down the road to the left, at a distance of some six hundred yards, but separated from the road by the height of the embankment and a further dip in the ground, was the fateful *Schlage M*, and if the party sent out to reconnoitre it was not met by enemy fire, the whole battery could be across it in fifteen minutes. The commander of No. 1 Troop, however, had reported that three miles further on there was another, similar bottleneck. When they had made their way across that, they would then have reached the point where they had been less than three days ago.

Thus they had had to drag all their guns, ammunition, spare parts and supply waggons for three days, without firing a single round, making a twenty-five-mile loop across country simply in order to get back to the place from which they had started.

Chernega slumped down on a broad tree-stump at the edge of the wood, his arms and legs aching, hungry and longing for sleep.

They could already hear the creak of wheels and sound of voices coming from the village. This was the leading unit of the Russian column, and it meant that the battery must push forward again if it was to reach the causeway before the others.

The reconnaissance party returned: *Schlage M* was open for them to pass. Although free of obstructions, the roadway on top of it was only seven feet in width, which was dangerously narrow.

There being no longer any need to keep the noise down, the order to move off rang out in loud, resonant voices: 'Gun-teams— stand to! Drivers—mount!', and the battery swung out on to the road and started to drive down towards the *Schlage*.

Suddenly, German shells began to fall on the village, and at once a house burst into flames. Then machine-guns opened up from the German lines—although at that point it was impossible to tell exactly where the Germans were positioned. Germans and Russians seemed to be mixed up in the same area, but the Russians were in greater numbers since a whole corps of them was converging on the village. In the pale dawn light the muzzle-flashes of rifles sparked from all sides, left and right of the village and then from behind it as the fire-fight shifted. Only one spot was still absolutely safe: *Schlage M*, down there below the road embankment, was free; to reach that causeway they had struggled through the marsh, torn their fingernails until the blood ran and lashed their horses to exhaustion. If the battery could get out on to the road quick enough and drive down there, they might still make it ahead of the supply train, which at this moment was racing towards them at the gallop to escape the bombardment in Merken. The rattle of their wheels could be heard and the first infantry units were already approaching in the ditches along the roadside.

These few moments were one of those crucial turning-points when uncertainty reigns, when no voice is heard and no officer is to be seen, and when a man has to make his own decision—though decision is hardly the word since there is no time to think—and in a flash all is decided.

All the guns were on the road, and now was the moment to turn off, down the embankment and across the causeway. As they stood, they were in an ideal firing-position, but the guns would be unable to shoot from below the embankment. Chernega galloped up and with a wave of his arm, as though casting a thousand roubles to the wind, stopped the first two guns from driving down and showed them where to deploy on the other side of the road into firing-positions.

There was a chance that the troops might not obey. Why should they take orders from the sergeant-major? They could decide to wait for the troop commander. There was the causeway—the way back to Russia. They had struggled, sweated and heaved all night; they had a right to be the first to get away to safety.

But Chernega's generous spirit of self-sacrifice spread like a violent contagion, with practised skill the drivers wheeled their teams, and soon Bombardier Kolomyka, with his flat, high-cheek-boned face, was unlimbering his gun. At that moment the staff-captain came running up, waving his arms. In an instant of doubt Chernega wondered whether he was signalling to them because they had done wrong. Perhaps he should not have deployed the guns . . . Then—yes! He was right, for Christ's sake! Well done, lads!

The thin, tall Lieutenant-Colonel Verietsky came out of the wood and ran up the hillside towards the village, clutching sword and knapsack to his sides. Behind him trotted the battery signallers, reeling out their telephone-wires as they went.

Although the rising sun was still hidden below the trees behind them, it was already brilliant daylight. The sound of firing spread in all directions around the bare hillside ahead of them. They were not going to get away as had been intended last night, nor was the rest of XIII Corps either: they were caught.

Four guns of Chernega's battery deployed on the uphill side of the road, and the limbers drove back into the wood where the ammunition supplies were waiting to be brought up—an ideal position. The first of the retreating supply waggons began to appear, tangling as they tried to overtake each other in a mad, furious rush; this was risky enough here, but on the narrow causeway it could be disastrous. Blocking their path, the remaining gun-teams of the battery sprawled across the roadway as they wheeled to take up position.

Soon the first of the infantry came running down the road as fast as their legs could carry them.

'Who are you?' With his lion's roar Chernega called out from over the top of a gun-shield. 'What's your outfit? What the hell are you doing?'

'Zvenigorod Regiment!' came the reply.

Chernega's face turned purple with fury.

'Where d'you think you're going, you mother-fuckers—trying to save your own skins while we stay here firing just so you can get away? Turn around, damn you, and give us covering fire!'

The gunners around Chernega ran down the hillside to the road, and less by shouting than by using their arms and fists stopped the men of the Zvenigorod Regiment. They argued, milled about, fights broke out; then the first wave, hesitant, still prepared to start running again, turned back. Before long some of their officers appeared, and instead of urging the men towards the causeway led them off the road and showed them where to take up positions.

Before the sun had risen from behind the forest, while the first red glow was colouring the treetops, the Zvenigorod men were digging in on the slope ahead of the guns, the gunners were revetting their gun-pits with felled timber, and ammunition was being piled into a bunker dug into a small reverse slope. The defences of *Schlage M* were prepared: an operation wholly unforeseen by the Corps Commander, who was in headlong retreat.

The firing did not start at once. Nearby, to left and right, from the centre outwards and into the centre from the encircling ring, the two sides exchanged desultory rifle-shots. Then the Russians began falling back towards the right of the position, making for the road along which Chernega's battery had come. From the same spot on the edge of the forest from which the battery had emerged two battalions of the Neva Regiment came out, led by the tall, grim-looking Colonel Pervushin—a familiar figure to all the artillerymen and to everyone in the division. In a gully below the roadside they halted, took a short rest and bandaged the wounded; they described how they had made their way all night from a distant forest, how two of their battalions had fallen back towards Hohenstein and had been lost, how they had been caught and enfiladed between Russian and German fire, and how they had only just managed to get away. By now the Zvenigorod Regiment was blazing away at the enemy.

The relative positions of the two sides were now clearly defined. The Germans were pressing from the right simultaneously on this position, on the village and on the town of Hohenstein. As the sun began to climb behind the pine-trees, from the depression in which they were located the tiled rooftops and chimneys of Hohenstein came into view—the town they had been making for all the previous day and had never reached. Some Russian troops were in Hohenstein, but they were caught in a trap that was fast closing.

Then the orders began coming from Venetsky: 'No. 1 gun! Elevation . . . range . . . shrapnel . . . fuse . . . gunfire!' and, following the first gun, the whole battery belched smoke and flame.

Shrapnel is deadly against bodies of troops: fire it at a battalion in line of march, and in three minutes it will be wiped out.

The German guns opened up in reply, and the rounds began getting closer, but against the sun they were unable to locate the Russian battery.

The Sofia Regiment passed through, followed by supply waggons and ammunition trains.

The Mozhaisk Regiment passed.

The success of the action was now to be measured not in minutes, nor in rounds of gun fire, nor in wounded, but in the number of marching columns that passed. How many would succeed in scraping through? How many would be cut off?

A gun-layer was knocked out, and Chernega took over in his place.

Smoke was billowing up from several burning houses in the village—and still Russian troops were pouring out of the smoke, mounted and on foot, running and walking in an endless stream: two more battalions of the Zvenigorod Regiment, mixed stragglers from several shattered units, a handful of men from the Dorogobuzh

Regiment, and then their own brigade commander, Colonel Khristinich, together with the remaining half-battery.

He recognised them and waved. 'Well done, lads! Magnificent!' And his gunners waved back at him, shouting in reply. Khristinich leaped from his horse and embraced the battery's staff-captain. But this was no time or place for congratulations, and they both had to take cover in a ditch. The Germans had got the range of the main road, and any man who had not been hit ran off it for safety. It was over: they were cut off and no more troops would be able to get through.

Pervushin had been expecting it; he led the Neva Regiment down the embankment to the *Schlage*, now empty of fleeing troops.

The Zvenigorod Regiment, too, started to pull out of their covering positions and withdraw.

Then Khristinich himself gave the order to the battery: 'By numbers in turn—limber up!' As soon as each gun was harnessed, the team immediately set off for the *Schlage* at the canter.

What about Venetsky? the men wondered. Surely he wouldn't stay and be cut off? That would be a pity—he was a good officer and looked after his men. No, he was safe: he and his signallers came running down the hill; the Germans could pick up their telephone wires for all they cared.

Two guns were still roaring defiance.

Remember us, brothers—we did what we could for you!

But for any Russians left behind in Hohenstein it was the end.

Document No. 2

COMMUNIQUÉ FROM THE COMMANDER-IN-CHIEF, GENERAL HEADQUARTERS, AUGUST 16TH, 1914

'... *on the East Prussian front, throughout August 12th, 13th and 14th stubborn fighting has continued in the Soldau-Allenstein-Bischofsburg area, where the enemy has concentrated the Army Corps which retreated from Gumbinnen, together with fresh forces. Allenstein is held by Russian troops. The Germans suffered particularly heavy losses at Mühlen, where they are in full retreat ... Our energetic attack continues ...*'

44

The story has it that Abgar, Prince of Edessa, being covered with leprosy sores, heard of a prophet in Judaea and, believing him to be the Lord, begged him to come to his principality, where he would be welcomed; but that if he could not come, he should ask an artist to paint his picture and send the likeness instead. While Christ taught the people, the artist tried his best to record his features, but they constantly changed in so miraculous a way that he laboured in vain and let fall his hand, helpless: it was not within the power of man to make a likeness of Christ. Then Christ, seeing the artist's despair, washed His face and pressed it to the canvas— and the water was changed into paint. Thus was made the Miraculous Uncreated Image of Christ, and with that canvas Abgar was cured. Afterwards it was hung over the gate of the city, protecting it from attack, and the princes of ancient Russia adopted the Uncreated Image of the Saviour as the battle-standard of their armies.

This legend was once told to Samsonov by the dean of the Cathedral of the Cossack Host at Novocherkassk. Beginning with the little village church of his childhood in Ekaterinoslav Province, Samsonov had stood in countless churches through hundreds of vigils, liturgies, thanksgiving services and requiems; if all those hours had been put together they would have added up to months and months spent in prayer, meditation and spiritual uplift. In many churches, among the blue-grey clouds of incense, he had been granted awareness of the healing grace of the Spirit; in many churches, as he stood with head erect, there had been much for the contemplation of his inner eye. Yet nowhere had he felt so much at home, nowhere had his spirit ranged with such freedom, as in the mighty cathedral of Novocherkassk, high on its rocky crag, yet intimately linked with both the Don Cossack Host and the city. The whole of Novocherkassk, in fact, was a place after Samsonov's heart: solidly built above steep-sided ravines, spreading out spaciously from the foot of the mountainside into three avenues, each almost wider than the great avenues of Petersburg, with its covered market, too, that rivalled the Gostiny Dvor of Petersburg, and its statue of Yermak in front of the Cathedral in whose square ten regiments could march past on parade with room to spare. His two years in Novocherkassk had been among the happiest in his life, and whenever he lay awake unable to sleep, of all the memories of those years he recalled with particular nostalgia the August days spent attending service in the cathedral.

This year, at midnight—between the Assumption of the Blessed Mother of God and the Feast of the Uncreated Image of Christ which follows it—General Samsonov was in the saddle, retreating. The last minutes of the Day of the Assumption had inexorably run out, and still the Mother of God had not stretched out her compassionate hand over the Russian army. Nor was it very likely that Christ Himself would save them now.

It was as though Christ and the Virgin Mary had rejected Russia.

At the darkest hour, towards two o'clock in the morning, by a roundabout route over almost non-existent tracks, the Army Head-quarters party reached a hamlet, consisting of half a dozen houses, near Orlau—earlier the scene of Second Army's first successful battle, whose name now had the bitter ring of irony. Here, as they blundered around in confusion, groping in the dark, they learned from a squadron of the 6th Don Cossack Regiment and from supply-train drivers of the Kaluga Regiment that there was no defensive screen to the west of the army, as had been envisaged in the 'sliding shield' plan; that on the previous evening the Kaluga and Libau regiments (having held on, to the limits of human endurance) had pulled out of the position that they had been ordered to hold for the whole of the coming day; and that the front line was now somewhere out there in the darkness—only a mile away. In Orlau itself two supply trains had become entangled, and the drivers were fighting each other to clear a way.

Two army corps were still up there to the north, caught in a trap

shaped like an inverted flask of which the neck was rapidly narrow-
ing. And Neidenburg—so they all loudly agreed, as there was no
other explanation for the situation—was already in German hands.

Longing desperately to ride on as fast as possible, the staff
officers were now more than ever justified in warning Samsonov
that it was useless for them to go to Neidenburg, and that they
should push on to Janów at once. But the Army Commander, alas,
appeared not to hear or understand them: he had lost all sense of
his position and his duties. Instead of concerning himself with the
whole army, he started giving directions to battalion commanders.

Hour by hour Samsonov felt more confident and less dependent
on his advisers; it was as though in his eyes they had ceased to be a
headquarters staff and were simply an irrelevant handful of officers
who for some reason had been detached from regimental duty. By
the light of a kerosene lamp in a room cleared of other occupants,
Samsonov sat at a table, his large head bare, his forehead creased
with an expression of apparent perplexity. He summoned various
officers to him and with the aid of a map gave them instructions on
how to get the Kaluga and Libau regiments back to their positions;
he specified which artillery units should support them, which roads
and localities should be reconnoitred and cleared for the approaching supply trains of xv Corps. He gave precise explanations,
listened to all objections without giving way to bad temper and
spoke with unfailing kindness, prefacing his orders with 'my dear
fellow' and 'please'.

Dawn was beginning to whiten the sky and the morning light
was seeping in at the window, competing with the lamp. Unhurried, Samsonov remained seated over the map, slowly curling
his fingers through either side of the parting in his beard and
around his smoothly clipped side-whiskers. His large, wide-open
eyes seemed to have no need of sleep.

Surely he could now evacuate his headquarters staff? But no; he
had lost all sense of his proper function: shrugging their shoulders
and hunched with cold, the staff officers mounted their horses to
make a journey, for no apparent reason, right up to the very front
line at Orlau.

The normally untrodden forest path, shown on the map as a
dotted line, had already been driven over and rutted by a succession
of carts, two-wheelers and waggons which were bringing up rifle
and artillery ammunition needed in the area. It was enough for one

two-horse cart to come to a halt for all the rest to be forced to stop too; there was no way round the obstacle, and it was easy to imagine the chaos that would result when two army corps were trapped on paths like these. In single file the line of mounted staff officers and Cossacks, pushing aside the branches of trees, overtook the blocked supply trains.

The forest narrowed to a thin, wedge-shaped strip. Until now only the indirect light of the sun had been visible in the pine-tops, but as the path led them out into open country the semi-gloom of the forest gave way to the full blaze of the bright crimson sun, which had just risen over the top of another line of trees—the interminable, twenty-square-mile expanse of Grünfliess Forest, thick and dark, whose brooding depths lay waiting for the retreating Russian army. Four hundred yards in front of the edge of the forest the meadows sloped abruptly towards a river at the bottom of a ravine, now full of quivering mist which rose upwards in wraith-like wisps.

Shuddering, Samsonov stared at the vapour and at the sun as though seeing them for the first time. The great floating orb brought more illumination than had been vouchsafed to him in all the mental exertions of the past few days.

The cavalcade rode down through the vaporous mist, across the damaged weir of a millstream and up again towards Orlau. They were now crossing the field of the recent battle, scene of many costly attacks and of the hand-to-hand struggle for the colours of the Chernigov Regiment; if they had taken time to ride around and look, they would undoubtedly have found many fresh communal graves. But no one, apart from the Army Commander, seemed to spare a thought for the battlefield. When they reached a crossroads it was free of the long, congested lines of supply trains, but it might not be for long—a new line of waggons was already rolling in from the west.

There they spent the morning. All lines of communication were broken. In enemy country, caught in a series of desperate, unexpected situations, there were dispersed five infantry divisions, five artillery brigades, cavalry and sappers; but news, and only bad news, was brought by random individuals from all parts of the surrounding forest with a speed and accuracy that even the best signals officer could scarcely have arranged.

It was learned that Colonel Kabanov had been killed and the

Dorogobuzh Regiment wiped out, that yesterday, after being ordered back into the line near Hohenstein, the Kopor Regiment had held out for less than an hour before running away again, and that the newly appointed regimental commander, after planting the staff of the regimental colours in the ground, had knelt down beside it and shot himself. Worse still was the report that General Martos had been killed, as was reliably stated by some Cossacks of his escort.

When the news of these three deaths reached Samsonov, he took off his cap three times and crossed himself; but even this did not disturb the look of melancholy calm and new-won understanding on his face. He seemed to be listening: not to the hubbub around him, nor to the distant sound of firing, but to something beyond them.

He left his staff in Orlau and rode off with a small escort to the forward positions held by the Kaluga Regiment. There, as they rode up, they found a battalion commander in a gully using his stick to chase his men out of the bushes, where they had taken refuge from the firing-line. Turning aside from his task, which was to strengthen the position as a whole, Samsonov stopped for a personal talk with this lieutenant-colonel.

Meanwhile, not daring to leave without the Army Commander, the angry staff officers wandered around Orlau with nothing to do. Then something encouraging happened: suddenly General Pestich, Chief of Staff of XIII Corps, rode up to report and ask for further orders. The corps, it appeared, was alive and intact and marching in this direction, but it lacked news of the situation and had no orders. Furthermore, units of xv Corps were also approaching Orlau.

The staff came to life: they would resurrect their 'sliding shield' tactics, and all might yet be well. The officers sat down to compose and draft a modified plan. XIII Corps was to withdraw by forced march (it had not exactly been wasting time before!) towards ——, allowing such-and-such a period to cover the distance. xv Corps and the remnants of xxIII Corps were to hold the line at ——. The trouble was that none of the corps and divisional commanders were present; if only they could be assembled and given their instructions, the staff of Army Headquarters would have done its job and be free to withdraw to Russian territory. To deal with this problem they devised the following solution: one senior officer should be nominated to take command of all the units which were threatened with encirclement. Yesterday Martos would have been the man to do this, but Martos was dead. The next most suitable would have been Kondratovich, but no one knew where he was. The obvious candidate for leadership of the retreat was therefore Klyuev, although he was furthest away; nevertheless, Pestich himself undertook to convey the order to him. The question remained, however: would Samsonov sign an order of that kind?

All this time a field near Orlau was filling up with units, some broken up and some still intact, assembling with a growing sense of desperation as they waited to be told what to do. Supply trains and ammunition waggons drove away carrying the wounded, but the crowding grew no less. The field was without shade, the morning sun was burning hot, there was not enough water and no food. More and more soldiers swelled the numbers of what was little more than a confused, defenceless gipsy encampment.

The fighting, after five furious days, seemed to have slackened, as though the Germans had relaxed and relented and were no longer so intent on driving the Russians out.

An aeroplane flew over the horde of men, but no one bothered to fire at it.

Around noon Samsonov returned from the forward positions. However, he did not turn off at a bend in the road to the house where his staff was quartered but rode on uphill through standing crops—straight towards the dense mass of men in the field.

The muddle that reigned among this medley of units, all lacking orders, was abnormal enough; even more unusual was a general riding up to them without the usual orders to fall in, dress the ranks, look to the front and reply to his greeting with a concerted roar from several hundred throats. Oddest of all was the general himself: his cap held in his lowered hand, exposing the crown of his head to the boiling sun, his look was not one of martial command but of compassion and sorrow. It might have been a church festival, though a strange one, lacking the sound of bells and the gay kerchiefs of the womenfolk: it was as though a crowd of sullen peasants from the surrounding villages had gathered on a hillside and a mounted figure was riding round to inspect them—a landlord or a priest on horseback—and promising them land or paradise in the hereafter to make up for their sufferings in this life.

The Army Commander did not shout at the soldiers to ask why they had left the firing-line, gave them no orders to move,

demanded nothing of them. In an ordinary, kindly voice he asked
the men around him: 'What's your regiment, lads?' (They replied.)
'Have you had many casualties?' (Again they replied.) At which he
crossed himself in memory of the fallen and said: 'Thank you for
doing your duty,' and nodded to either side. The soldiers did not
know what to answer, but simply responded with a sigh or an
inarticulate groan which never quite formed itself into the
regulation reply: 'Glad to do our best, your excellency!' With that
the Army Commander rode on, repeating his remarks in a more
muffled voice: 'What's your regiment, lads?' ... 'Many casualties?' ... 'Thank you for doing your duty.'

As the general was making his farewell round of the encampment, two horsemen rode up by another track and rounded the
corner into the field: a colonel, and a private whose long legs
dangled down without stirrups. If the circumstances had been
different, the colonel had intended to present this soldier to the
Army Commander and recommend that he be awarded the St
George's Cross. As it was, he left the man on the edge of the horde
and went forward into the midst of it.

The colonel had come after hearing a rumour that the army
commander was here. He made his way through until he reached
Samsonov, and began to speak, but the general, distracted and
remote, did not notice him. The colonel rode on, keeping close
beside him.

The Army Commander's voice was kindly, and all the men, as he
passed them to say farewell and give them his thanks, followed him
with looks of equal goodwill, none with resentment. That bared
head, the expression of exalted sorrow, that unmistakable, purely
Russian face with its thick black beard and large, plain ears and
nose, those heroic shoulders weighed down by an invisible burden,
that slow, regal progress, reminiscent of the hieratic bearing of the
tsars of ancient Muscovy: where was the man who could curse him?

Only now did Vorotyntsev perceive (he wondered how he had
failed to notice it before; it could not be something just acquired)
the look of pre-ordained doom in Samsonov's face: for all his great
bulk, Samsonov was a sacrificial lamb. Looking slightly upwards
all the time, he seemed to be expecting a blow from a great club to
fall on his proffered brow. All his life, perhaps, he had been unconsciously expecting that blow and at this moment he was
entirely prepared for it.

Ever since they had last seen each other, Vorotyntsev had tried to think well of the Army Commander; much had occurred for which Samsonov was to blame, but he had always sought excuses for him, waiting anxiously for him to take action that would be decisive and timely. On that first evening he had felt that he might be able to exert a strong and positive influence over him at crucial moments. He had even hesitated whether to stay at Army Headquarters, where he was an unwanted outsider, an interloper likely to get on everyone's nerves. During the last few days he had felt an urge to see Samsonov again, to warn him, to prevent him from taking a false step—for from the very beginning Vorotyntsev had, he now realised, expected him to make that false step.

In the space of four and a half days catastrophe had overtaken Second Army—in fact, the Russian army as a whole. If only (watching Samsonov's solemn valediction), if only (sensing the instinct which had prompted this age-old Russian gesture), if only things had been otherwise . . .

He had come to tell Samsonov how, after retreating all day yesterday, the remnants of the Estland Regiment were still holding out, in open ground, with one machine-gun and the last few rounds of ammunition; but what was the use of telling him now? Why had the Army Commander not gone to I Corps? And why was this disorganised rabble gathered here, which should be a defended area? Why were the troops being allowed to trickle away in small, defenceless groups? They should at least be made to stand and fight for half a day, to be formed into a striking-force; only then would they have some chance of breaking through. But Samsonov seemed no longer to need such advice, vital though it was.

'Your excellency!'

Samsonov turned round to look at the dusty, sunburned colonel with a bandaged shoulder and a bruise on his chin, and nodded amiably, though with no sign of recognising him. He said goodbye to him, too, and thanked him for doing his duty.

'Your excellency! Did you get the message I sent you yesterday from Neidenburg?'

Vorotyntsev realised that the cloud which had been hovering over Samsonov's brow was a cloud of guilt. Perhaps unconsciously, perhaps half-aware of what he was saying, Samsonov replied:

'No, I didn't.'

What more could he do? Who now would listen to his story

of what had happened at Usdau and at Neidenburg only yesterday?

It was too late, it was no use now: Samsonov was so far above it
all that he had no need for such news. He was no longer surrounded
by an earthly foe, no longer threatened; he had risen above all
such perils. The cloud which darkened the Army Commander's
brow was not after all one of guilt but of ineffable greatness:
perhaps outwardly he had done things which were wrong by the
petty canons of strategy and tactics, but from his point of view
what he had done had been profoundly right.

'I am Colonel Vorotyntsev, from General Headquarters! I . . .'

As he floated rather than rode above that encampment, above
the whole field of battle, the Army Commander was past the need to
recall former meetings and mundane, bygone matters.

Why was he saying goodbye? Where was he going? Yesterday
morning he had ridden off to the centre corps. In whose charge
was he leaving them now? Why had he not formed a breakthrough
force? Was the magazine of his revolver loaded?

No. By virtue of his age and his many years of seniority this
general-of-cavalry was immune to good advice from a colonel, even
if he had not been in this trance-like state. His was the helplessness
of high position.

The heads of their horses were side by side. Suddenly Samsonov
smiled at Vorotyntsev and said simply:

'From now on the only thing left for me is a life like Kuropatkin's.'*

Had he recognised him?

Making no objections, he signed the army order that was handed
to him.

Suddenly he slumped and went limp. He could ride no further.
When Army Headquarters left Orlau that afternoon on horseback,
General Samsonov and General Postovsky were crammed side by
side into a small open carriage.

* General A. S. Kuropatkin (1848–1925). Russian commander-in-chief in
Manchuria at the start of the Russo-Japanese War in 1904, he suffered a series
of defeats culminating in the disaster of Mukden. He resigned in disgrace and
admitted his mistakes in his history of the war, published in 1909.

45

Sasha Lenartovich's experience of the strange, wild, brutal joy of victory (victory over whom—and what for?) did not outlast the morning. It would have taken him a long time to forgive himself for that animal feeling, if it had not spontaneously vanished after an hour or two.

What gain had the victory brought their regiment? A column of prisoners, some captured guns? In fact nothing had been gained, nor could have been; all it had done was prolong their agony and increase their casualties. The fighting had not been shortened by it, nor did it make the rest of the day any easier for them—in fact it made it much worse: the Germans subjected them to a furious bombardment all day, backing up a relentless series of counter-attacks with unremitting gunfire. The heavy calibre of the German artillery and their inexhaustible supplies of ammunition forced the victors of that morning's attack to sit there as living targets all day, constantly expecting certain death. Forced by the barrage to dig in deeper, they extended their line of trenches, while the wounded crawled, walked or were carried away.

While the general bombardment was far from mild, at times the salvoes thickened to a sudden, squall-like intensity. Physically drained, mentally exhausted, listless, self-alienated and self-hating, Sasha despaired of staying alive until evening. Hunched in a too shallow slit trench, he despised all cannon-fodder and himself especially for being cannon-fodder. It was no use blaming the illiterate and uneducated soldiery for accepting it as their lot, when he, a politically active intellectual, was incapable of devising any alternative and could only crouch in a little hole in the ground, his head bent between his knees for safety. All day long only one thought obsessed him as he waited passively, devoid even of the will to live: would he be hit or not? He tried to concentrate his mind on some interesting, rational problem, but nothing came into his head; the empty box of bone at the top of his neck simply hung down, waiting for the blow to fall.

It was, of course, obvious that, given the fact of universal military service, this senseless form of warfare was the only possible kind: the conscript troops were not required to hate the enemy; they were merely driven forcibly to fight against another anonymous and equally unfortunate mass of men. There could be no justification for wars of this kind. A war fought by volunteers was quite another matter—a war, for instance, against the true, age-old enemies of one's social class, in which one knew one's foe and chose to fight him; in that case, fortified by the will to destroy the enemy, one would feel no fear of death.

If only a tenth of their present casualties, a tenth of these men's endurance and half this number of shells were expended in a revolution—then what a wonderful new life could be built!

One such day spent under shellfire ages a man. Just let him survive this one, last day—and then something would have to be changed. Of that Sasha was firmly convinced: there must be a change. Tonight, when the bombardment died down.

But how was he to alter the situation? It was beyond his power to end the whole war, therefore he must bring his own part in it to a stop. The most sensible solution would have been to emigrate, as many others had done, but he had missed this blessed opportunity. There, in Switzerland or France, they could disregard the war and were free to carry on with party politics, discussion and active work. Here, though, in the East Prussian trenches, the only way to emigrate was through the enemy lines—in other words to surrender.

That was it! Surrender was a sensible and practical step: the important things—his life, his educated mind and his political views—would be preserved. There was nothing reprehensible in that; later he would devote these talents to the workers. But surrender, though feasible, was also difficult. It was impossible to cross no-man's land under shellfire; if he went at night he might blunder, go astray, get killed. The ideal conditions for success would be when the opposing forces were at close quarters and in confusion. What would happen, though, once he had surrendered? How could he be sure that the Germans would believe he was a socialist? Would an officer of the Kaiser's army know enough about politics to understand his motives? Besides, they might not have much sympathy for socialists—they were, after all, sending German socialists off to fight along with everyone else. They would not let him go to Switzerland, but would pack him off to a prisoner-of-war camp. Still, it would mean saving his life. But how was he to cross the lines?

With a head that felt as if it were swelling, he found it extremely difficult to follow a logical train of thought. Would the day ever end? Would the shelling ever stop? How could the Germans have quite so many guns, quite so much ammunition? How could Russia's leaders, brainless idiots that they were, have dared to go to war in such a state of military inferiority?

But mercifully the sun sank behind the German lines and at last the day, August 15th, came to an end. The firing subsided too, though not entirely; several machine-guns went hammering on long after dusk; but when night came Sasha was still alive.

Gradually the cool of the night began to be felt. The field kitchens drove up and fed them. There was plenty to be seen to in his platoon—the roll-call and casualty returns, inventories of dead men's property to be made—but all that Sasha left to his platoon sergeant. As they slowly straightened up and stretched their legs, the men began talking in louder voices. They discussed what had happened since the previous night, who had been killed and who wounded, how they felt about it, and here and there a burst of laughter could even be heard—what an incorrigibly resilient people the Russians were! They were in no hurry to go to sleep, but were relaxing and enjoying the gathering night. Officers went the rounds, visiting each other.

An hour, two hours, passed, and still Sasha had made no decision; he had eaten his supper and had then simply sat on a log beside a broken fence in a kind of lethargy. The moon was bright enough for him to go, but he stayed. It was hard to pluck up his courage and make a move. Yet all that was needed was to get up and go; dangerous it might be, but no more dangerous than going into the attack at dawn.

Having been given no orders or information, the regiment was completely ignorant of the situation. But the power of rumour was

[453]

great, and from somewhere or other the news filtered down to officers and men alike: we're starting to retreat. The Kremenchug Regiment has already been ordered ... The Murom and Nizhni-Novgorod Regiments are also preparing to ... General Martos has pulled out ... General von Torklus is nowhere to be found ... Soon it will be our turn ... our turn ...

The feeling was percolating from above that their leaders were running away. How did they know? Their leaders might well have been killed or taken prisoner. No, the rumour spread like an infection: the generals are on the run; soon we shall be running too. Sasha's heart beat faster. This was the moment—now! He should not wait until the regiment was ordered to withdraw; even if they withdrew, they would still be subjected to an equally ferocious bombardment in the next village. He must get away. If General von Torklus could save his skin, why shouldn't he? If he were caught, he could easily invent some pretext in the general chaos of a retreat.

It did not occur to him to take anyone with him. Lenartovich hardly made use of his orderly, and in general his platoon were frightened, silent men with whom he had no real contact. Even if he were to approach some of the more articulate ones and suggest, as though jokingly, that they might get their own back on the generals by deserting, the most that he could expect would be tight-lipped silence.

He had no map, so he at once went to the staff-captain on some pretext, looked at the map by candlelight and committed it to memory. The road running through Wittmansdorf went on east-wards. A mile further on, cross a railway line ... another mile, turn off at a church, then continue until the junction of three roads ... take care not to land up in another sector of the front line ... then there was a river, and soon afterwards the village of Orlau ... there was something familiar about the name.

Sasha quickly absorbed all the necessary information and went out.

He had no more duties that night; the platoon sergeant would take care of everything. His most precious possession—a notebook containing his thoughts and jottings—was in his pocket. His idiotic sword he would throw away by the roadside as soon as possible, as well as his revolver, which he had never been able to shoot well.

It was now so quiet as to be almost peaceful. After the machine-gun fire, the few solitary rifle shots were reassuring rather than disturbing. The half-moon was setting, its light fading. The road was alive with the creak of wheels, the clatter of hooves, the crack of whips and the sound of men swearing at their horses. Obviously some people were wasting no time and were already getting out.

Without returning to his platoon, Lenartovich strode off down the road with a sense of release. Being on his own, he easily overtook the stream of traffic. If he was stopped, he would think up an excuse for his journey. But no one was checking or directing the heavily-laden ambulances and creaking ammunition waggons as they crawled along, the chains of their traces clanking against the shafts. At first there was only a single line of transport, then another stream joined it from a side-road, forming a double line which took up the entire roadway. Any vehicles coming in the opposite direction were sworn at, pushed aside and not allowed to pass, though on the whole the stream flowed peacefully enough, the drivers chatting to each other as their teams plodded side by side, cigarettes glowing here and there in the darkness.

With no one to check him, the lieutenant's legs carried him joyfully onwards. There was still time to turn back, no one would yet have noticed his absence, but he was convinced of having made the correct decision: that he had no right to run the risk of dying a senseless death in an alien cause. Having firmly turned aside from the way of the unthinking majority, he felt secure in the dignity of his refusal to be a lump of cannon-fodder.

However, following the road did not prove to be so easy as it had looked on the map, and this prevented him from giving full rein to his thoughts. There were many features of the route—hills, dips, bridges, dikes—which he had not noticed before. He found the church, but it was followed by some houses which he did not remember, and he had forgotten how far it was till he reached the main road-junction. When he did reach a junction, what appeared to be the right road turned out to be lined with trees, whereas he had been expecting a minor, cross-country road.

He did not like to ask anyone, and it was quite dark now that the moon had set. It was at this point that exhaustion caught up with him and the over-exertion of the last few days made itself felt. Sasha turned off the road and lay down in a stook. He was very thirsty, but he had no water-bottle and it was useless to try to search for water.

He woke up at dawn, shivering with cold despite the straw. Pulling himself to his feet, he was about to go back to the road when he saw on it, spaced out at intervals, several small detachments of Cossacks moving along at a walk. He went back to his stook. The reaction was innate and stronger than reason. Since childhood he had instinctively regarded a Cossack as an enemy, and a Cossack unit as a blunt weapon of repression. Even though he was now dressed as an officer (and people said the uniform suited him well), at the sight of Cossacks he still felt a rebellious student.

When the Cossacks had passed and a supply train had rumbled slowly by, Sasha returned to the road. There he stumbled against a heap of something which turned out to be loaves of army bread, already stale and mouldy. When they had been advancing they had had no bread—and now here was bread thrown away, obviously pushed off a ration-cart to make room for someone to ride.

He longed to eat, but it would look odd for an officer to be seen carrying loaves of bread under his arm. He cut one of them in half with his sword, gobbled several mouthfuls, chewed it and went on.

By sunrise, he had still not been stopped or questioned. All the people he met on the road, whether mounted or on foot, had an unfamiliar look about them to which at first it was hard to put a name. Though they might be armed and wearing full equipment, on detached duty or formed up in a unit, though it was not yet a rout and the army was still obeying orders, something was not quite right. There was an oddness in the way the men turned to look at their officers: their faces expressed a concern for themselves that was beginning to override their sense of duty.

Excellent! This meant that Sasha would be all the safer.

The road turned out to lead to Orlau after all, but just where it started to slope down towards a weir across a millstream it was joined by another, and here so many guns, ammunition waggons, carts, horsemen and troops on foot were piling up that there was no way round the bottleneck and it was somewhat risky for Sasha simply to wait his turn in the queue. Horses which had collapsed, exhausted, in their shafts were being unharnessed and shot. The nearer to the weir, the worse was the crowding, with waggons entangled with each other. Carried downhill by its own momentum, one ammunition-waggon rammed its shaft into the team in front and killed a horse. With much shouting, which almost developed into a fight, the animals were unharnessed. Soldiers and officers began to lose their tempers, and a little staff-captain with a bandaged forehead was shrieking ferociously at a tall battery commander: 'We won't let you through even if we have to use our bayonets!' To which the battery commander replied, with a threatening wave of his long arm: 'I'll crush your infantry under my wheels!'

Everyone was struggling to get his own men and vehicles through, and damn anyone else. At that moment two of the planks on the weir gave way, and a shout went up for them to be repaired. Some soldiers who were carpenters volunteered to help. From higher up on the road, people watched as officers crowded around showing the men how it should be done, until a more experienced carpenter, a paunchy old man with a bushy grey moustache and a shirt hanging out unbelted, pushed aside officers and men indiscriminately and did the job his way.

The sun was now high in the sky, beating down on the dense crowd. Horses were led down to be watered in the narrow stream, which was no more than chest-deep, and soon soldiers, and then a few officers, stripped and bathed.

At the top of the bank on the far side was, as it happened, the site of that earlier, notorious battle which had cost several thousand lives and filled the hospitals of Neidenburg. There could have been no better illustration of the senselessness of war. At one moment thousands of men had died in order to push the Germans a few miles to the north; now, thousands more, hungry and furious, were crowding into a defile, lashing their horses and threatening to punch one another just so that the Germans could push the Russians back a few miles southwards from the same spot.

But no disaster, no amount of bloodshed, is ever enough to galvanise Russians out of their passive endurance. Of the fifteen hundred-odd men crowded around the approach to that weir, not one understood the facts of the situation and there was no way of enlightening them.

Lenartovich had already heard from several men that Neidenburg had been surrendered to the Germans the night before. Where, in that case, was this stream of men to go? What of his own plans? It was difficult to decide; he had only envisaged going as far as Orlau, and had no notion of what he should do after that.

Further back in the column, waiting by the roadside to take

their places in the queue, were several ambulances, in one of which lay a likeable, wounded lieutenant-colonel. They got into conversation. The lieutenant-colonel produced a map, which he opened out above him, and they looked at it together. Sasha spun him some yarn about having been sent on a mission from his regiment, whilst he took careful note of the terrain on the map: there was a long strip of forest . . . if he could cross it by that path . . . the village of Grünfliess near Neidenburg . . . Could he just disappear into the forest and wait for the Germans to find him? Now, though, he was beginning to feel it might be a pity to let himself be captured; in all this chaos there was a chance of slipping through and getting clean away to Russia. But could he do it? The huge forest lay like a green barrier in the path of the retreating army, and beyond it, no doubt, the German machine-guns would be waiting. Already the rumour had sprung up from somewhere and was passing from man to man: encirclement.

Being unwilling to undress and wade through the marshy ground on either side of the stream, Sasha lost a great deal of time waiting at the weir.

Near Orlau he found a huge, disorderly horde of troops gathered in a field and apparently waiting for something. They were rifling the nearby kitchen-gardens and digging up whatever they could find, eating raw turnips and carrots. He had to pass through this mob in order to reach the forest he had decided to make for. Quite unafraid, he started to push his way through, certain that amidst the disorder and confusion no one would stop him or ask him where he was going.

He was wrong. Although it was no more than a mob, some senior officer appeared to be inspecting it as if this were a parade, exchanging greetings and talking to the men. Lenartovich recognised the Army Commander, whom he had seen at close quarters in Neidenburg.

There was no doubt—it was General Samsonov! A big man on a big horse, looking like a legendary knight in some oleograph, he was slowly riding around the gipsy-like horde, apparently unaware of how shamefully it differed from a body of men on parade. No one called the men to attention for him, there was no one to whom he could give permission for them to stand at ease. Now and again he lifted his hand to the peak of his cap. Instead of saluting in the military fashion, he took off his cap in a gesture of farewell. He seemed thoughtful, distraught, divested of the chief attribute of a commander—the ability to inspire fear.

As he approached, Lieutenant Lenartovich made no move to step aside. He was fascinated by a sight which gladdened his eyes. Ah, that's what the like of you need—a taste of defeat! Then see how mild and kind you suddenly become! You may be hung with medals, but give you one good crack over the head and look how you wilt! Just wait—there's more coming to you yet!

As Sasha stared at him spellbound with hatred, the Army Commander rode straight towards him and as if directing the question at him personally, although he did not address him by his rank, gazed at the lieutenant with his resigned, vacant, bovine stare and enquired paternally:

'And your men here? Which regiment are you from?'

It was an awkward situation. There was no time to think; he could not run away, everyone around him was waiting to hear what he would say. Should he tell a lie? That was no good either. The best thing was to sound as keen and brisk as possible.

'29th Chernigov Regiment, your excellency!' And at the same time, in place of a salute, he made a vague movement with his hand like the wave of a fish's fin. (One day he must tell this story to his sister Veronika and his Petersburg friends, if he ever got out alive!)

Samsonov showed no sign of surprise or of stopping to wonder what the Chernigov Regiment was doing in this area, where it had no right to be. Instead he smiled, and a warm glow of reminiscence spread across his face.

'Ah! Splendid regiment!'

(My God, now he was in a mess! Supposing the old man started asking him questions?)

'My special thanks to you, men of the Chernigov Regiment . . .'

And he gave a nod—dismissive, understanding, grateful.

He passed slowly on, his horse, too, seeming to nod in acknowledgement as it lowered its neck.

Samsonov's broad back-view made him look more than ever like the knight in the fairy tale who paused, sad and perplexed, in front of the signpost at the parting of the ways: 'Go to the left—and death awaits you. Go to the right—and death awaits you.'

46

If it had been purposely handicapped in some game, XIII Corps could not have been more awkwardly placed for a retreat. The lakes were so situated that the corps was prevented from taking the only direct escape-route. It had to start withdrawing diagonally to the south-east, but then it was immediately confronted by the three-mile-long Lake Plautziger, whose two long arms were flung out as though to stop their progress and whose blue depths glittered with the sinister warning: 'No road!' Beyond the tip of the left-hand arm was stretched the seven-foot-wide causeway of *Schlage M*, and from there on ran a string of minor lakes succeeded by a further hostile stretch of Prussian water blocking the corps' route, the two-mile expanse of Lake Maransen. Having paid dearly for the crossing of *Schlage M*, which had at least enabled it to break out to the south-east, the corps was again faced with only one possible loop-hole—the bridge and dam at Schwedrich, which it had to pass in a thin, single file. Once over that, it was not free to follow its first diagonal line of march, but was penned into a north–south corridor between two stretches of water: behind it was the chain of lakes it had just crossed, in front of it was Lake Lansker, three miles long, and a string of small lakes linked by the marshy river Alle. Having negotiated this second obstacle, the corps would find itself heading into yet a third watery embrace—two more miles of the vastly ramified, many-armed Lake Omulefoffen. Prevented from moving in the direction in which it wanted to go, it had no alternative but to push due south, getting entangled with the neighbouring XV Corps, and then move along roads that might already have been cut by the enemy. Even after looping around Lake Omulefoffen, it would come up against the limitless expanse of the Grünfliess Forest at a point where the only good, straight road in the area—the Grünfliess–Kaltenborn road—cut straight across its route at a right-angle, so that the corps was obliged to cross the forest by winding woodland paths.

In its retreat from Allenstein the wretched XIII Corps, which had advanced the furthest into German territory, was forced to cover forty miles in forty hours, without so much as a bite of hard-tack and with horses that were never once fed or unharnessed.

But a description of the state of the horses is hardly sufficient for an understanding of the peculiar nature of a retreat as a military operation. In order to make the rank and file *advance*, the leaders must devise slogans and produce convincing reasons, must offer rewards and utter threats, and above all they must themselves head the advance. *Retreat*, on the other hand, is instantly and un-questioningly grasped by everyone from top to bottom, and the private soldier is infected by it with no less immediacy than the corps commander. In a single urgent impulse every man responds, though he may have been woken up in the middle of the night, may not have eaten for three days, may be barefoot, ready to drop, unarmed, sick, wounded or slow-witted—the only ones who remain indifferent are those who can never again be roused from sleep. Whether by night or in foul weather, the stark notion of retreat is understood by all, and all are ready to make any sacrifice without reward.

The previous night, XIII Corps had been unable to go to the help of XV Corps because the men were exhausted and the supply trains had not caught up. But on the next night no one grumbled about the absence of field kitchens, no one asked about a rest-day; instead, the corps began to withdraw its bruised body with unusual speed from the forests and lakeland of Prussia.

Except, that is, the rearguard.

In the Russian army of 1914, rearguards did not save themselves by surrendering. Rearguards died.

In the low-lying basin of Hohenstein the Kashira Regiment and two battalions of the Neva Regiment were subjected to all-round attack by von Below's corps, and two Russian batteries were silenced by sixteen heavy-calibre German guns and seventy field guns. Even without artillery the Kashira Regiment fought until two o'clock in the afternoon, and then mounted a counter-attack on the railway station, after which isolated groups in houses still held out until evening. Colonel Kakhovskoy, killed beside the regimental colours, had won time—as he had been ordered to do.

On the narrow isthmus between lakes at Schwedrich the Sofia Regiment, which had so far suffered the fewest casualties, dug in and fought a bloody action until 3 p.m., thus redeeming its disgrace of two years before: since 1912 its record had been stained and it had been banned from taking part in parades, because at the centenary review held on the field of Borodino a soldier of the regiment had broken ranks and hurled himself at the Tsar's feet with a petition. Now, at Schwedrich, two out of every three companies were annihilated and of the remaining company barely a hundred men were left. But their pursuers were halted.

In this way XIII Corps escaped from all its dangerous, exposed positions.

Yet the valour of its rearguards was not enough: due to the terrain, it could no longer move back on a broad front, and was still retreating by the night of August 16th. It then had to squeeze past the rear echelons of XV Corps, which was itself under heavy pressure and retreating fast towards the same roads that XIII Corps was making for. By now XIII Corps was no longer a corps, very few regiments were up to strength and some amounted to only a few companies, although it was true that a hundred guns were still intact, as was the brigade ammunition train. Around noon Klyuev was suddenly presented with the 40th Don Cossack Regiment, whole and in fine fettle, just arrived from Russia—the very corps cavalry regiment, in fact, which he had lacked throughout the fighting.

General Klyuev was not pleased with his new burden; he had no idea what to do with this regiment of Don Cossacks. He was even less pleased by the order, brought by General Pestich, informing him that he was to take command of all three corps. Those cunning devils at Army Headquarters! They were all running away and leaving him to perish like a rat in a trap. Anyway, how was he to make contact with those three corps, when he was not even sure where all the units of his own corps were?

There was one compensation, however: up to now, Klyuev had believed that Martos had been given the more suitable westerly routes for his withdrawal, whilst he had been left with the much poorer forest terrain. Now he could re-arrange all that.

So in the late afternoon, without reconnoitring the roads, Klyuev wheeled his whole corps away from Lake Omulefoffen—not left-wards, as he had been ordered, but to the right—and cut straight across the rear of xv Corps.

In the preceding few days, xv Corps had so worn down the enemy that it had now secured for itself a moderately unimpeded withdrawal. Its only harassment was from artillery-fire, and the Germans were not seizing any localities until xv Corps had left them. But it was withdrawing without a headquarters and without many of its senior commanders, who were killed or missing, and it had started to pull back half a day earlier than had been scheduled in the 'sliding shield' plan, thereby wrecking it. Until darkness the only formation holding the 'shield', which it had done at untold cost, was the relic of xxiii Corps, while xv Corps, due to the Germans' seizure of the roads around Neidenburg, was drawn further and further towards the vast Grünfliess Forest, grim and dark long before twilight.

It was there that the two corps collided at right-angles at the fateful crossroads in the impenetrable darkness of the forest night. In a place where by daylight there was not enough room for four carts to pass in different directions, two army corps were supposed to pass through each other at night-time! If until that time the Russian Second Army could still be said to have existed, it ceased to exist after that incident.

Only someone who has been on active service can have any notion of the shouting and cursing, the grabbing of reins and shafts, the wrenching aside of waggon-teams by drivers coming from the other direction, the vehicles pushed into the ditch, the crunch of breaking branches. Naturally no senior officers were at the heads of the two columns, no one but a few junior officers, who only recognised each other after some time spent in a shouting-match, and who then devised a rough-and-ready technique to cope with the situation: they would stand at the crossroads as though rooted to the spot, seize each man by the shoulder and ask his unit, and accordingly direct the whole of xiii Corps eastwards towards Kaltenborn, and xv and xxiii Corps southwards. Thus physically sorting them was the only way to get the corps to diverge rather than cross.

The forest crossroads, where by day the sun shone gently through the silent pine-trees, seemed like a black passageway in hell. After exercising his voice hard at the crossroads, though not hard enough to make himself hoarse, Chernega fell silent only when he had counted all his wheels and made sure they were across. He did not realise that at that same crossroads five days ago they had been given a helping hand by the infantry platoon commanded by the obliging, freckle-faced Second Lieutenant Kharitonov. Nor did Kharitonov recognise in the blackness which swallowed them the same path, so cool in the heat of the day, along which they had slogged their way from Omulefoffen and back again.

After dividing, the two masses of men flowed on through the forest, groping blindly, stopping now and then. The troops, who had not eaten for two days, were staggering; their water-bottles empty, their mouths were dry as dust; having lost all faith in their generals, they refused to believe there was any reason for this forced march. Some began covering up their company numbers, so that they could not be recognised and pulled into line, others simply dropped by the wayside and fell asleep on the ground.

The cavalry, whose speed and mobility had not been utilised during the past days, were now able to make use of these characteristics. Horseman joined up with horseman (more often than not they were Don Cossacks) whenever they saw each other, and gradually formed themselves into a single cavalry column. They too had been affected by that irreversible sea-change that affects units and individuals, and causes an army to fall apart. The cavalry made for the spot where, as far as they knew, there was still a way out: the furthest point of the neck of the flask, which the Germans had not yet plugged. They had already passed by daylight over the fatal crossroads where everything was later to be reduced to chaos. Keeping ahead of the Germans, they rode through village after village, where from dawn and throughout the next day the Russian infantry would have to stand and fight. The horses soon put behind them the twelve-mile forest road leading to Willenburg, which tomorrow was to seem to the infantry as endless as the road to heaven. On their way the Don Cossacks picked up the legendary General von Torklus, who had been unable to find his division, and the dragoons came across the staff of Army Headquarters. Willenburg being already in German hands, the cavalry wheeled away from it, forced their way through the forest, left a rearguard to hold the river-crossing at Chorzele and rode on further.

It would, perhaps, have been too much to have asked them to hold off the Germans while the slower infantry and artillery pulled back to safety.

Somehow the poor old footsloggers just didn't get away fast enough.

On the morning of August 16th Second Army was a unified formation; by that evening it was a disorganised, uncontrollable rabble. On the morning of the 16th, the Don Cossacks formed a loyal part of the Russian armed forces; by evening they had discovered that Cossack blood was thicker than Russian water.

If we stick with Mother Russia we'll end up in hell! So let's stick together, Cossacks—the Don looks after her own!

They were not to be blamed, though; the attitude was far older than they were.

Thus the discharge from a schoolboy's magnetic coil may be a prophetic foretaste of a thunderstorm of incomparable magnitude in the skies.

47

A sensation of purity was seeping through his resting body. He had
no recollection of lying down to sleep or of waking up, indeed he
was not yet sure whether he had woken up. He had just enough
strength to force his eyelids apart and see some grass immediately
in front of him. Untrodden, smooth, silky, the grass was the source
of the purity that was pouring into him. Possibly he was aware that
he was lying on his side, possibly he may have had a vague glimpse
of the corner of the forest glade, but it was the grass which occupied
the whole of his feeble, blurred attention.

The grass of his childhood. Grass exactly like this, perhaps
mixed with mallow, had grown in the derelict farmyard of their
estate at Zastruzhye and in the wide village street: dense, thick-
stemmed and short, unsuitable for hay. There were not many
farmsteads in Zastruzhye, cattle were never put out to graze in the
street and it was so rarely driven over that no track ran down it and
there were not even wheel-ruts in the grass; it was a solid expanse
of turf, on which he and the village children ran around and
played games together.

He was just able to move the fingers of the hand nearest the
ground and touch the grass. Yes, it was the same sort.

He lacked the strength to do more. Some defensive mechanism
prevented him even from remembering what the date was, where
he was lying, why he was here and why everything was so quiet.
But the grass gently awakened older memories.

A chapel. A tiny stone chapel on the same village street, behind its
own fence. Hardly even a chapel, because there was not room in it
for one man to stand up straight; it was more of a roofed-in shrine.

The church services. They were held either in front of the chapel or simply out in the fields, when the procession came there from the parish church three miles away at the Feast of the Assumption, a date probably chosen because it marked the end of the harvest in the Kostroma region.

When was the Assumption? Was it over? Was it still to come? He could not remember. Everything that might have brought him back to full awakening was still veiled in protective oblivion.

The venerable, grey-haired priest never came in a carriage but always on foot and bareheaded. A pair of icons were carried before him, each one borne by two peasant women. The greater part of the voluntary members of the procession, however, consisted of the older children in the village. With a look of solemn self-importance two or three of the oldest carried the religious banners, surrounded by a crowd of shaven-headed little boys, for once not laughing or mischievous, in white or coloured Russian shirts belted at the waist, peaked caps clutched in their hands. The little girls were in long, long skirts and all of them, down to the very smallest, wore headscarves: it was not proper for a female head to be bared. They came in bast shoes or barefoot, but always in neat, clean clothes, their faces so full of naïve trust and pure faith that no trace of childish naughtiness remained. For the rest of the feast-day the two solitary banners were carried around the countryside from village to village.

Every recollection of the place where one grew up brings a twinge of nostalgia. Others may be indifferent to it or think it a very ordinary place, but to each one of us it is the best on earth—the unique sadness evoked by the memory of a country cart-track as it twists and turns to avoid the boundary posts; the rickety, lopsided coach-shed; the sundial in the middle of the yard; the bumpy, neglected, unfenced tennis-court; the roofless summer-house made of birch shingles.

When his grandfather's impoverished estate was divided among the ten children, his father had declined his share on condition that he could have the estate of Zastruzhye—for the peace of his soul, for the sake of the lonely walks he could take reflecting on his unsuccessful life, and because there were no longer any tenant farms attached to the estate; its few small fields only sufficed to feed the family of the bailiff (who was also the groom). At Christmas and Easter the bailiff sent the owners in Moscow two or three

[467]

turkeys and a crock of clarified butter. The severe, two-storey eighteenth-century manor house had been built by Yegor Vorotyntsev, a lieutenant of the Horse Guards, whose commission, written out in fine calligraphy and signed by the Empress Elisabeth, was preserved in their apartment in Moscow.

The career of Georgii Vorotyntsev derived directly from the imperial commission granted to that lieutenant of Horse Guards, for he had been the first in the family to return to the army after two generations of civilian life. (He was also vaguely convinced that his family was a branch of the extinct boyar house of the Vorotyntskys of the Ugr region, one of whom, the renowned Prince Mikhailo Vorotyntsky, had been burned at the stake by Ivan the Terrible, who saw him as a rival to the throne. But the genealogy was incomplete and it could not be proved.)

His eyes were now fully open and in the light of late afternoon took in the whole glade, fringed by a sprinkling of oaks in an otherwise unbroken sea of copper-green conifers; at that moment he suddenly pricked up his ears at the sound of a rumble of artillery, steady and not very far away. With one violent wrench the fragile cocoon of tranquillity was torn away and the hollow cauldron of his soul reverberated again, struck by returning memory like a red-hot blacksmith's hammer.

Samsonov's farewell to the army! It had all taken place today, only a few miles away. It was the end, there was nothing more to be done.

And his Estlanders were gone—men whom he had persuaded to return to the fight; had he sent them to destruction in vain?

His horse, too, was gone. Or, rather, both horses . . . Where was Arsenii?

Vorotyntsev raised his stiff body on one elbow and looked to right and left—Arsenii was not there. Twisting his neck to see behind him, feeling pain in his shoulder and jaw, he glanced round and saw Arsenii. He was lying at full length on his back, his head resting on a log. If he was asleep, he was sleeping with half-closed eyes. No, he was not asleep, but was staring ahead with the tranquil look of a dreamer.

Arsenii was the only one left. Vorotyntsev had striven to exert his influence, to help an entire army, and this single soldier was all that remained to him.

'Have we been asleep?' he enquired anxiously.

After a slight pause, military protocol forgotten, Arsenii opened his mouth in a delicious yawn.

'Aha.'

'How? We shouldn't have gone to sleep,' Vorotyntsev said in astonishment. Still lacking the strength to get up, he could only roll over on to his other side to face Arsenii. He pulled out his watch, but when he looked at it the face conveyed nothing to him.

The body has its own rhythm, its own permitted tempo. However rapidly divisions and regiments might be swept up and whirled around in the maelstrom of defeat, that lump of clay, the body, could not begin its autonomous counter-movement until some intervening stage had run its course, until it had passed through the immobility of sleep and the lazy, restful contemplation of blades of grass. In order to change from a previous tempo and direction to new ones the body was apparently obliged to traverse a phase of numbness and self-rediscovery.

How could he have gone to sleep? And for almost four hours! He had simply lain down for five minutes . . . The army had been heading towards its destruction, he might have been able to extricate some troops in those four hours, do something useful—and he had slept.

'Why didn't you wake me up? You know we shouldn't have slept.'

Arsenii smacked his lips, sighed and yawned.

'I fell asleep too, your honour. I haven't slept for three nights, and you haven't slept for five. Where's there for us to go, anyway?'

He was right, they had needed sleep; Vorotyntsev's body still lay pressed gratefully to the earth, unable to rise. But Arsenii could not know that the colonel had not thrown himself to the ground out of exhaustion, that after leaving Ostrolenka he had spent five days galloping back and forth, persuading, exhorting—and had collapsed here from despair. Never before had he known despair, and he could not forgive himself for it. He had lain here mumbling and thinking about the past—and one does not recall the past when one's mind is alert and active.

His shattered consciousness was recovering, but his memory was still unable to grasp the full extent of the catastrophe: it was boundless, irremediable. The time for saving a part of the army,

[469]

let alone the whole, was past. But could he not do *something*? Ah yes, now he remembered: his map had gone when he had lost his horse. Without a map he was blind.

Vorotyntsev groaned and beat his forehead with his fist. It was all due to the weakness of his body—though it was grateful for the rest. He pulled up his knees and clasped them with his hands. If only he had a map!

All that remained to him was his memory, which had retained an approximate idea of the lie of the land; but that was not enough.

Vorotyntsev turned round to look more closely at Arsenii, who, feeling the colonel's eyes on him, raised himself reluctantly by pushing up his body from behind with both hands, but without moving his legs. His cap had fallen to the ground, his hair was rumpled and he had a sullen look as though he had been drinking too much. He blinked.

'It's my fault that you're here,' Vorotyntsev said reflectively. 'If you'd stayed with the others, you wouldn't have been caught in the encirclement.'

'If I'd stayed with them, maybe I'd be a head shorter by now,' Arsenii countered, nodding to emphasise his point. 'The dice fell that way and there's no changing it.'

Once again Vorotyntsev was astonished at the man's dignified self-assurance, at his ability to be natural and genuine without being familiar. With none of an officer's condescension in his voice, as though speaking to an equal, Vorotyntsev said:

'But we'll get out of here, don't you think?'

'I should hope so!' Arsenii thrust out his thick lips. 'But this is some forest!'

'It's nowhere near a main road, though, and that's where the Germans are—on the roads.'

'Well, we can always sit it out here until the Germans move on.'

'Sit it out?'

'Yes, build a hut and hide in it till winter. We can always keep alive on roots and berries.'

'For three months?'

Blagodaryov frowned, peering solemnly ahead.

'People have done it. For years.'

'Who have?'

'Well, hermits in the desert.'

'You and I aren't hermits! We wouldn't last long.'

Blagodaryov looked down sideways from his raised position, and said confidently:

'You can do anything if you have to.'

'But we're not monks, we're soldiers! We'll break through. And as soon as possible, while we're still fit. Are you hungry?'

'My stomach thinks my throat's cut.' Arsenii's teeth champed on an empty mouth.

Their sleep, side by side on the ground, had done them good. The task now was not to rally troops but to get themselves through the German lines, and he, Vorotyntsev, had to get to General Headquarters in order to tell them the truth of what had happened. Then his mission would not have been in vain. That was his duty, and of all the men in this encircled army he was the only one who could perform it. There were other officers to rally the men; let them do it.

Again he pricked up his ears. Silence. The artillery had stopped firing, and there was only the occasional distant rifle-shot and a few short bursts of two or three rounds of machine-gun fire.

It could mean that it was all over.

He was about to push himself to his feet, but found that he was using the wrong arm—his shoulder was too painful. At that moment he froze, listening: Arsenii had heard something too, and, throwing off his lassitude, was staring keenly through the trees.

There was a crunch of twigs. Someone was approaching, alone and with an uncertain tread.

'One of ours,' said Arsenii confidently.

If he was alone, he would undoubtedly be a Russian.

They remained on the ground.

The figure coming towards them was an officer, staggering slightly. He was thin and very young, hardly more than a boy. Was he wounded? He seemed to be finding his sword too heavy. There was something familiar about him.

'Lieutenant!' Vorotyntsev recognised him, shouted and stood up. 'Aren't you the young fellow from Rostov I spoke to in the hospital?'

The expression on the second lieutenant's beardless, childlike face changed at once from fear to delight.

'Colonel—it's you!'

'Weren't you evacuated? Don't tell me you walked here from hospital?' Then without giving him time to answer: 'You don't happen to have a map on you, by any chance?'

The lieutenant was not wearing a sword frog, but the two leather straps with buckles running vertically down his chest from under each epaulette to his belt made him look particularly dignified. At his slim flank was an officer's knapsack of the largest size, full to bursting.

'Yes, of course!' The pale young man beamed and unfastened his knapsack. Eager for praise, he added: 'And a good one, too—it's German. I found it in Hohenstein, and I glued the sheets together while I was in hospital.'

It was obviously costing him an effort to stand and talk. Perhaps he was feeling giddy and wanted to lie down.

'Well done, lad, well done!' Vorotyntsev slapped him on the back. 'Where have you been wounded? Oh yes, I remember—concussion. Head aching? Is it getting better, though? Look—take off your greatcoat and lie down for a while, you're pale . . . Go on, do as I say—lie down!'

He was already opening up the map, folded in three double folds, and spreading it out on the ground. He hovered over it like a falcon over its prey. The fact that half an hour ago he had been asleep, or had even been capable of relaxing and lying down, now seemed inconceivable.

'Arsenii, bring me some twigs to hold the corners down. Now, Lieutenant, show me how you got here.'

Vorotyntsev knelt down in front of the map while Kharitonov lay on his stomach, his rolled-up greatcoat propping his chest. Stopping now and again to regain his breath and occasionally putting his hand over his eyes, he tried his best to give an accurate, coherent account and to sound wide awake. Pointing to the map with fingers whose nails were bitten and untrimmed, he described how he had left Neidenburg the previous evening after the Germans had already cut the main road, how he had approached the road and veered away from it, and where he had spent the night. Today he had been making for the village of Grünfliess, but the Germans . . .

'What? Grünfliess too? When did they take it?'

'As far as I know, about three hours ago.'

While they had been sleeping . . .

Kharitonov went on to say how he had hoped to find his regiment somewhere in xv Corps' area.

'And where do you reckon we are now?'

'Exactly here. If we go on further, there should be a clearing on the right, then we come to the edge of the forest and we should be able to see Orlau from there.'

'Correct. Excellent, Lieutenant. We came here from the other direction; the position tallies exactly. But it's no use trying to find your regiment now, I'm afraid.'

They had a map; they knew where they were; for the rest, he must simply use his eyes and his brain. His mind rapidly grasped the essentials, acting on the same sort of reflex with which a gun-crew springs into action or an infantry company stands to.

The Russian troops are all heading for the last gap in the encirclement; they will all be trying to get as *far* as possible from the German's western line of advance; therefore we must try and go as *close* to it as possible. The Germans in this area will have no time to spare; they will be pushing on as hard as they can go to close the ring. There are no proper roads in this vicinity, hence not much military traffic—all the better for a small group trying to slip through unnoticed. And the forest paths all run south-east, which is just what we want. We must merely make one detour of a mile or so to avoid the triangle of open country around Grünfliess village, and after that it's all forest. Then comes a railway line running through dense forest; there won't be anybody around there. More forest tracks. There are just two places half a mile apart, near the village of Moldtken, where the forest comes right up to the main road—that's the place to cross it. We must aim to keep the route as direct as possible. The less distance we have to go, the less exertion—the sooner we shall get out. To think we can sit in the forest and wait until the German troops move on and leave the main road free is a false calculation, because by then they will have put up barbed-wire road-blocks. No, we must move as quickly as possible. We won't make it tonight, though. So it must be tomorrow night. That gives us twenty-four hours to reach the main road.

There was their plan, all ready: route, timing and objective.

Vorotyntsev stared at the green expanse of Grünfliess Forest on the map spread out in front of him: it was vast, but it was neatly divided up into two hundred and fifty rectangular numbered sectors, making it easy enough to find one's way through it on foot; if the German foresters were thoroughly at home there, why shouldn't he be?

He explained some of his thoughts aloud to Kharitonov. This

concussed boy could be their weak link, but the lieutenant was so keen and showed such radiant enthusiasm as he listened to the senior officer's plan, appearing to draw strength from the very ground he was lying on, that Vorotyntsev was certain he would not weaken.

Enjoying the feel of the grass under his huge, bare feet, Blagodaryov stood upright beside the map, hopping from foot to foot. He was gazing down, as though from an aeroplane, on Prussia spread out before him: now the Germans had seized it back from them.

A few hours ago Vorotyntsev had collapsed on this spot overcome by stupefying weakness. An hour ago he had not even had the strength to think what to do. Now that his mind was clear again and he had devised a sound plan, he was eager not to waste a moment: the mainspring inside him was released and urging him forward. 'Come on! Let's get moving! Right, Arsenii, pick up the map by two corners.'

As they turned the map round and oriented it by compass, their forsaken little glade fell into precise place within the layout of the forest, and the path that crossed it showed them which way they should set off.

'Well, lads, shall we go?' Vorotyntsev said impatiently. And glancing apprehensively at the lieutenant: 'How d'you feel? Want to lie down a little longer?'

Kharitonov needed more rest, but he replied:

'I'm ready, Colonel.'

Smacking his lips loudly, Arsenii started to pull on his boots.

Vorotyntsev carefully picked up the map, deciding which part of it would be needed next, and bent it into new folds so that it would not get frayed and torn along the old creases.

Although the western edge of the forest was not far away, the sun no longer shone into the glade from that side, having set behind the thick wall of trees. The rustling, bronze-coloured woods were dark, only the seventy-foot pine-tops still tinged with gold.

'Right! Throw it away!' Vorotyntsev ordered firmly, seeing how the sick lieutenant was hindered by his sword.

'What?' said Kharitonov in uncomprehending amazement.

'Get rid of it!' Vorotyntsev said cheerfully, making a throwing movement. 'I order you to. I'll take the responsibility. I shall throw my own sword away too.'

But he did not do so.

'Then shall I . . . break it, Colonel?'

'Yes, if you feel strong enough. You go last, Arsenii. Take the lieutenant's greatcoat.' He raised a finger to forestall the lieutenant's protest.

They set off in single file. With only his leather straps and knapsack now, head firmly erect, the thin young man did his best to keep pace between the brisk, stocky colonel and the huge, slow-striding soldier. Besides two greatcoats and rifles, a pack, mess-tin and water-bottle, Blagodaryov was also carrying a heavy, sealed ammunition-box, and an entrenching-tool was bumping against his hip, all of which he managed with ease.

They passed three sectors of the forest, then turned. Halfway along the next sector, despite the premature onset of darkness in the forest, Arsenii noticed a man sitting on a stump about ten trees' distance into the wood from the path.

'Ha!' he boomed as though shouting into a barrel. 'Someone's sitting over there.'

Given the present situation, a man might be hiding behind every bush.

The officers turned and looked. The man continued to sit, without attempting to fire, run away or hide. Nor did he make any move to join his fellow-Russians.

Then he stood up and walked slowly towards them.

On the pathway there was still enough light to see that he was smeared all over with earth, but although his face was dirty, it had a proud, stern look. An ensign, also without his sword. Noticing the colonel's epaulettes, he hesitated whether to salute. He did not, nor did he come to attention; they were, after all, in the depths of a forest. He frowned. After a pause, as though in pain or trying to think, he announced himself.

'Ensign Lenartòvich, Chernigov Regiment.'

At that moment, Vorotyntsev noticed the university graduate's badge on the tunic under his open greatcoat. It being his habit to weigh up every officer and soldier as if he were serving under him in his regiment, he mentally took stock of this young man. He was wondering too how he came to be in these parts: the Chernigov Regiment ought not to have been in this area. However, one never could tell in all this chaos.

'Are you wounded?'

'No.' Sullenly and with an air of independence he added: 'But I was almost killed.'

'I don't understand.' Vorotyntsev checked him sharply. Practically everybody could claim he had been 'almost' killed. That was the sort of story you told to women after the war.

Lenartovich pointed over his shoulder.

'I was trying to make for the village, but the Germans were already there. A machine-gun pinned me down in a potato field and I just managed to crawl away.'

'Where's your platoon?' Vorotyntsev put in quickly. The moon, in its first quarter, could be seen in the grey sky, but it did not give much light in the forest. They must not waste time and lose the night. A cluster of olive-coloured clouds was strung across the sky, but they were unlikely to mean bad weather. While looking at the sky he missed the ensign's reply. He probably would not have believed his story; anyway greater things were at stake than the fate of one ensign. Nor would he have cared to have the young man in his regiment, but even so he could see how even this young student who despised military service might make a good officer yet. He was tall and good-looking and held himself well.

Hurriedly, he asked:

'Do you want to stay here? Or will you come with us? We are going to break through the lines.'

A moment of hesitation, then with more animation than before he answered readily:

'With your permission.'

Vorotyntsev said harshly:

'I warn you, we share all our duties without regard to rank. There are the fit and the wounded, that's the only difference among us.'

'Good, good,' Lenartovich agreed enthusiastically.

He liked that; it was thoroughly democratic, and he had always hated the way the army classified people into 'upper' and 'lower' grades.

With a nod Vorotyntsev gave the order to his party:

'Quick march!'

And they set off again.

Lenartovich was truly glad that he had evidently fallen into reliable hands. He had swallowed mouthfuls of earth in the potato field, been spattered with dirt from bullets that had only just missed him, and had said goodbye to life—the life he loved so much, unfulfilled, hardly even begun. Worming his way along, he had crawled out of that endless furrow, never once raising his head from the ground. He had wandered around the forest in a daze, deafened, his hands torn and bleeding, with a sprained finger, continually spitting earth from his mouth and digging it out of his nose and ears.

Surrendering had proved to be even more dangerous than fighting. This was war: there was no way to shake oneself free of it. Provided these people did not suspect him or accuse him, and since they intended to break through the lines, there was nothing for it but to go with them, to stay and fight on. If the enemy was so intent on killing him and had almost done so, he had the right to pay them back in the same coin—and may the best man win.

He noticed that the soldier had a water-bottle. His throat was parched with thirst, but for some reason he could not bring himself to ask for a drink.

48

He was being led, carried along, his body not moving of his volition; he was absorbed in thought. His world had finally collapsed; the dust had settled, the ruins were plainly visible. The time of desperate, confused movement back and forth was over; past and present now stood out with absolute clarity.

The film which had dulled his mind was removed and a great weight had fallen from him: since the moment at Orlau when he had ridden among the troops to thank them and take his leave of them, a rock had been lifted from his soul and he felt the relief. Although those few soldiers on the hill at Orlau were incapable of forgiving him for what he had done to their army and to Russia, he had longed for their forgiveness. He was not much concerned by the thought of a court of inquiry: officers of his seniority were never hauled before a tribunal. They might be reproached and relegated to the reserve, or they might be given another appointment; the shame was something that one could, after all, survive. Even if a court of inquiry were to be set up, it would find the case impossible to investigate—the events were beyond anyone's powers to unravel, and in any case it was too late. What had happened was evidently part of God's purpose, and that was something beyond the comprehension of the men of our time.

Samsonov was no longer the proud rider, high on his horse, but a passenger in a cart, jolting over tree-roots and potholes. Although he and Postovsky were bumping shoulders, the two men did not talk; Samsonov had forgotten about him, absorbed in his own reflections.

He was not thinking about Zhilinsky or about Army Group Headquarters, nor was he dwelling on the insulting and offensive treatment which had recently hurt him so deeply. He was not racking his brains for ways to prove that Zhilinsky was more to blame than he was. His mind was clearer and less heated now, he was no longer piqued by the thought that Zhilinsky might be able to wriggle out of the responsibility and emerge unscathed. It was strange that an accusation of cowardice from that insignificant man had a short while ago stung Samsonov so hard that it had influenced his decisions affecting whole army corps.

Instead, he was thinking how difficult it was for the Tsar to choose the right advisers. Evil, selfish men were more self-assertive than good and loyal ones; it was they who always tried hardest to show off the loyalty and the abilities they did not possess. No one had to deal with as many liars and flatterers as the Tsar; yet how was he, a mere man, to acquire the godlike insight needed to see into the dark corners of other men's souls? Thus it was he who had become the victim of his mistaken choices, and his self-seeking appointees were gnawing like worms at the strong tree-trunk that was Russia.

Jolting and swaying in a cart, Samsonov was still thinking as though he were a leader on horseback. Calmly absorbed in these elevated thoughts, his mind was wholly unconcerned with the present mission of the officers of his staff, which was to find a gap in the encirclement and escape through it. When interrupted in his meditations, he was slow to absorb the import of what they were telling him—that the route to Janów, which they were following, was cut off by the Germans, who were shelling the road where it emerged from the forest. The officers proposed to change their southward line of march and turn east, making a wide detour towards Willenburg, which should still be occupied by Russian troops of General Blagoveshchensky's corps. Samsonov made no objection and merely nodded.

This meant losing precious space and time in retracing their steps, and then turning aside as soon as they found a suitable escape-route to the east. Samsonov took no interest in the time-consuming business of finding a gap in the enemy lines. A protective mental wall seemed to be shielding him from every source of distress and irritation; the faster and more irrevocable became the flow of external events, the slower grew his reactions to them and the more his mind became concentrated on his private thoughts.

He had wanted only to do good, yet what he had achieved had been an unmitigated evil. If such disasters could result from decisions taken with the best intentions, what might be the outcome of actions whose motivation was base and selfish? And if there were more defeats, might not rebellion rear its head again in Russia, as had happened after the Japanese War?

The knowledge that he, General Samsonov, had served his sovereign and his country so lamentably was a terrible and painful burden to bear.

It was now nearly evening and the sun was low in the sky. The staff officers had reverted to the plan of making an attempt to turn southward again and to find a way out in that direction. The Army Commander nodded but paid little attention.

The going was beginning to get much harder. They had left the tall pine forest with its dry, firm floor and were now crossing some low-lying ground dotted with bushes, criss-crossed with sandy tracks which slowed up their progress, and full of unexpected obstacles such as streams and ditches which could only be crossed by wading.

Several times the Cossack escort rode on ahead to reconnoitre, only to return quickly, after a burst of machine-gun fire, with the news that wherever they looked the way ahead was blocked.

These Cossacks should never have been in a headquarters escort squadron; they were second- and third-grade troops, so unreliable and cowardly that they disappeared into the bushes at the first sound of firing. It was as though Russia herself was so depleted of manpower that the general who in his time had been Ataman of the Semirechiye and the Don Cossacks could not even muster a squadron of good Cossacks for his personal escort.

The Army Commander was still being forced to take frequent decisions. Postovsky or Filimonov should have been able to take over the leadership of the little headquarters group, but both men had collapsed. The wolfish look had vanished from Filimonov's face, and he now sat hunched and snivelling as though suffering from influenza. When they reached the village of Saddek, the junior staff officers had to ask the Army Commander himself for permission to send the Cossack squadron into the attack to try and make a breakthrough.

Over half a mile lay between their position on the edge of the forest and the high ground that flanked the main road, and this open terrain looked most unpromising for a cavalry attack, but the officers insisted hotly that they should at least be allowed to have one attempt at it, and Samsonov, as though in a dream and without sufficient thought, gave his permission.

Colonel Vyalov tried to persuade the surly Cossacks to go into the attack, but they hung back, refusing to leave the safety of the woods, complaining that their horses were exhausted. Only when Staff-Captain Ducimetière, shouting 'Hurrah!' and waving his sword, galloped off alone towards the German machine-gun, followed shortly by Vyalov and two more officers, did the Cossacks move. They streamed out in a disorderly mob, firing aimlessly into the air and shrieking and yelling—not so much to frighten the enemy as to bolster their own spirits. But three of them were shot from their horses, and fifty paces short of the machine-gun position they wheeled aside and turned into a nearby copse.

The sight of this disgraceful performance shocked Samsonov into decisive activity. He recalled the whole party and forbade the officers to mount a second attack, which they were now proposing to make on foot. He then ordered the headquarters group to turn back northwards and make another attempt to break through towards Willenburg in the east.

In the growing darkness they rode back into the forest, where they made rapid, unhindered progress along a metalled road towards Willenburg. Two miles short of the town, however, as they came out of the forest in the twilight, they met a Polish peasant and asked him if there were many Russian soldiers in Willenburg. Clasping his head in his hands, he replied:

'Nie, panowie, tam wcale niema Rosjan, tylko Niemcy; dużo Niemców dziś przyszło.'*

Bewildered and despairing, the staff officers sat down. Where could Blagoveshchensky's corps possibly be?

Samsonov sat on a broad tree-trunk, his beard sunk on his chest. If even the army headquarters staff had failed to break out, what fate must now await the army itself?

The officers conferred. Their last hope, it was decided, was to slip through the German lines that night. To Samsonov the news

* 'No, gentlemen, there are no Russians there at all, only Germans; many Germans came there today.'

was nothing less than a sign of divine retribution. Why had his judgment been so clouded that he had abandoned his army? The finger of God was pointing at him.

Firmly he announced:

'I release you all, gentlemen. General Postovsky, you will take command of the headquarters party and break through the German lines. I shall return to xv Corps.' (At that very moment, in the twilight seventeen miles away behind Samsonov, xiii and xv Corps had become tangled in irretrievable confusion at that fatal crossroads in the forest and had ceased to exist.)

However, as one man, all the officers of the staff gathered around the Army Commander and, each with his own argument, joined in the attempt to persuade Samsonov how wrong, how absurd, how unthinkable, how impossible his decision was. He was in command of the whole army, and even if he was out of touch with the centre corps he had a duty to the flanking corps and to Army Group Headquarters. He was the only person who could rally the remaining forces of Second Army in the few hours that remained. Only he could save the country from a German invasion. Yesterday, when opinions had been divided over whether to withdraw from Neidenburg to Nadrau, his staff would not have dared to argue with him so forcefully. But much had changed since then. Samsonov, sitting on his natural wooden throne, closed his eyes as he listened to them. He thought how disagreeable all the members of his staff were; having been selected at random, they were all, to a man, uncongenial to him in mind and spirit. The only one he liked and trusted was Krymov, and he had been sent away.

Although they sounded cogent enough, Samsonov detected a note of falsity in the staff officers' arguments. He did not openly accuse them of cowardice, but it was plain enough to him as he listened that they were not concerned about the army, but about themselves: none of them wanted to go back with him into the thick of the fighting, yet service tradition forbade them to break out of the encirclement without him. Samsonov, however, no longer had the energy to compete against the pressing arguments of a dozen of his subordinates. Worse still, he lacked the strength to set off alone with his orderly, Kupchik, on the long trek through the gathering darkness.

Curiously enough, no one suggested the other alternative—to order combatant units to move to this locality and to fight their way out. The idea simply did not occur to anyone. The problem of escape thus remained to be solved. Opinion being unanimous that the Cossack squadron was useless as a means of getting out by force, the Cossacks were released from escort duty and told to try and break through independently. The headquarters staff would go forward on foot, having persuaded themselves that without horses it would be easier to escape at night through this trackless countryside. The region was inhabited by Poles, who were regarded as pro-Russian.

Samsonov, head on chest, sat on his tree-trunk as though oblivious of the discussion. The defeated commander, calmer than the officers of his staff, sat waiting for an end to all the bustle and confusion which was distracting him from his thoughts; he was looking forward to getting on the move again; steady, regular movement would help him to think.

However, when they had dismissed the Cossacks and unbridled their horses and released them, the officers were not ready for their night march, but were still busy with preparations. As the last of the grey light of day merged into moonlight, Samsonov could just make out that they were digging a hole and putting into it things from their pockets and their uniforms, but he did not grasp its significance: he had ceased to regard himself as their commander with the power to give orders. He was simply waiting for them to take him on the next stage of the journey.

The short, officious figure of Postovsky approached and leaned towards him.

'Your excellency, allow me to point out ... We don't know what may happen to us ... If we fall into enemy hands ... All documents, all badges of rank ... There is no reason why we should make it easy for them ...'

Samsonov did not understand. Make *what* easy for them?

'Alexander Vasilich, we are burying everything that could identify us. We have made a record of this spot and we will either come back for our things later or send someone to recover them. If you have any documents, or anything likely to reveal your name ... And you should remove your epaulettes ...'

'My *epaulettes*!' Realising at last what they were doing, Samsonov gave a hoarse roar and stood up from the tree-trunk like a bear roused from its lair. As though unused to standing on two legs, leaning forward slightly, forearms dangling, he placed his hands on Postovsky's narrow shoulders. Unable to believe his eyes in the faint light of the moon shining between the pine-trees, Samsonov found that it was true: the shoulders of his Chief of Staff were devoid of epaulettes. Only a torn scrap of cloth still flapped on his coat.

With the same stooping gait, his arms hanging slightly forwards, stiff from having sat so long, he walked up to the nearest officer and put a hand on his shoulders—the epaulettes were gone. He moved on to the next man—gone too!

'Gentlemen!' Samsonov bellowed, straightening up. 'You are betraying your oath of allegiance. Who gave you permission to do this?'

Each man stood stiffly to attention, but none of them showed any regret or asked forgiveness. No one rushed to dig his epaulettes out of the hole in the ground and stick them back on his shoulders. The junior officers among them approached him and again began confidently persuading him that they must not let the enemy know *whom* they had captured, that the Germans should be led to believe that the Army Commander and his staff had escaped, that they should not allow the badges of rank of a general, alive or dead, to be mauled by unworthy hands; they would, they insisted, do the same thing with the regimental colours if a unit was cut off—the colours would be cut up, burned or buried: anything rather than let them fall into enemy hands. After all, documents and epaulettes were not weapons—they were just pieces of paper, metal and cloth . . .

Perhaps they were right . . . But how quickly everything had changed. A mere quarter of an hour ago he could still have made the choice of agreeing with them or refusing to go with them. They had begged him to stay, that was all; nothing had been said about removing their epaulettes. Had it come to this so soon?

Maybe it was a sensible precaution. But he could not bring himself to do it.

Postovsky sidled up to him, fussy and ingratiating, discreetly offering assistance.

'I'll help you, Alexander Vasilich . . . Won't take a moment . . . There we are . . . And your St Vladimir's Cross will have to go too, I'm afraid . . . That's it, that's all . . . And check through your pockets . . . There may be something . . .'

The feeling of being stripped naked, of being degraded, humiliated, punished . . . His watch? His wife's medallion? He could keep those. The Tsar's presentation sword? That he would keep till his death!

Something irretrievable seemed to have been lost in those two minutes. His shoulders and his chest no longer felt the same. He could not hold up his head as before: he was, in fact, no longer the Army Commander. That was why they did not obey him—indeed, they had ceased to obey him some hours ago. As though he were a golden idol, like savages they continued to carry the statue of their powerless god with them lest curses fall upon their heads.

And upon his.

Yet as all his badges were removed the last of his cares seemed to fall away. At last his head and chest felt free.

They set off in single file, Samsonov somewhere in the middle, followed by Kupchik carrying the saddle-cloth from the general's horse, which had been let loose. By the faint moonlight which penetrated where the woodland was thinner, it was just possible to make out tree-trunks, undergrowth, clumps of scrub or open space, but only in the immediate vicinity; human figures could not be distinguished unless they were very close. The men at the head of the file were making their way forward by compass, half-groping; whenever they stopped to check the direction, the whole party halted. It proved impossible to advance in a straight line: they were constantly forced to make detours to avoid ditches, swampy ground or thickets, and then to pick up their direction again.

Samsonov was free to think. Undisturbed, with no one to interrupt him, he could at last follow his thoughts to their conclusion. Yet there seemed no point in pursuing them any further now. What was the use? Everything had already been thought out and decided for him. The slate was wiped clean, the responsibility over. Memories were the only pleasure left to him.

The memory that kept returning was not that of his country childhood in Ekaterinoslav, nor his cadet school, nor the cavalry training depot, nor the countless events, places and brother officers of his army career; for some reason, the image which insistently came back to his mind's eye was the huge, grim cathedral of the Don Cossack Host, perched on a hilltop, with its intricate ornamental brickwork. Born in the Ukraine, he had lived in Moscow, in Petersburg, in Warsaw, in Turkestan and in the Trans-Amur territory, but although he was not a born Don Cossack his thoughts kept returning to that great hill in Novocherkassk. What bliss it would be to seek eternal rest in that cathedral—not on the upper side, the burial place of Yermak, the conqueror of Siberia, but on the lower side, on Kreshchensky Hill, where on a low granite tomb, only slightly higher than the surrounding cobblestones, there lay a cast-iron cloak and Cossack hat, as lifelike as though their owner, Baklanov, had just been there, had thrown them off and gone away.

That was where he longed to be: in the tomb in the crypt, where soldiers are buried when they have won victories which can be carved in granite . . .

He was finding it difficult to walk. His legs had grown unused to walking, but worse still was his shortness of breath, which made him wheeze asthmatically even when unburdened and moving at an ordinary pace.

When a man loses not only his eminence over other men but also his means of conveyance and his means of protection, it can be a testing time for his body. Samsonov discovered that his Achilles' heel was not the spiritual wound caused by the removal of his epaulettes, but the failure of his bodily organs: his pounding heart, the inadequacy of his lungs, as though they were two-thirds blocked up, and his weak, unreliable legs, with their clumsy gait, their proneness to stumble on tussocks and pieces of stray brush-wood, to slip on mossy ground. He began to find that his only source of relief was not the fact that the party was making good progress or that they might escape, but the chance of resting against a tree-trunk and getting his breath back whenever the column halted at an obstacle.

Although Samsonov was too ashamed to ask for a rest, out of consideration for him the group halted once an hour and sat down. Kupchik would then appear and promptly spread out the saddle-cloth for his general to sit on.

Glad though Samsonov was of the chance to stretch out and ease his aching legs, the party did not dare to rest for too long: the hours of darkness, their last chance to escape, were all too short. At midnight the moon began to set, then clouds began to cover both the moon and the stars high in the sky. It soon became quite dark, and nothing could be seen; only by the crunching of twigs under foot, by the sound of breathing, or by touch, were the links of the moving human chain aware of each other. The going, too, was getting worse—a squelch of marshy ground under foot, an impenetrable thicket blocking the route, or a dense fir plantation. It was considered too dangerous to veer in the direction of Willenburg, where they might easily bump into a German patrol. There was an equal danger that they might get lost. The officers gathered into a huddle and conferred in whispers. There were to be no more halts. Whenever they came to a ditch, Kupchik and a Cossack captain each took one of Samsonov's arms and helped to drag him across.

It was his body and nothing else which was pulling Samsonov down. It was the dead weight of his body which had dragged him down into pain, into suffering, shame and disgrace. All that was needed to release him from the burden of pain and shame was to free himself from his body. It would be a simple step to take, and one which he desired as much as he longed to draw the first full, deep breath into his congested lungs.

That evening, only a few hours ago, the officers of his staff had regarded him as a kind of talismanic idol; by midnight he had become a millstone around their necks, a mere lump of carved stone.

The only difficulty was to escape from Kupchik, who had kept close behind his general all the way, now and again reaching out to touch his back or his arm. But while skirting one of the frequent clumps of bushes, Samsonov gave his Cossack orderly the slip, stepped to one side, and hid himself.

The noise of breaking twigs and the crunch of heavy footfalls passed him by, faded into the distance and died away.

It was completely quiet. The whole world was silent, as though the clash of armies had never been; only the breath of a gentle night breeze sighed in the tops of the pine-trees. There was nothing hostile about this forest: it was not a German or a Russian forest, but simply God's forest which gave refuge to all manner of creatures.

Leaning against a trunk, Samsonov stood and listened to the sound of the forest. From nearby came the rustle of a piece of torn pine-bark, and from above the faint, soothing hum of wind-blown tree-tops.

He felt increasingly tranquil. He had lived out a long life of army service in which the risks of danger and death were inevitable; now that he had reached the moment of death and was ready for it,

[487]

he realised for the first time how easy, how great a relief it would be.

The only problem was that suicide was accounted a sin.

With a faint click, the hammer of his revolver slipped readily into the cocked position. Samsonov put it into his upturned cap, which he had laid on the ground. He took off his curved sword and kissed it, then felt for his wife's medallion and kissed it too.

He walked a few paces to a small clearing open to the sky.

It was cloudy now, and only one small star could be seen. It vanished, then appeared again. He knelt down on the warm pine-needles, and because he did not know where the east lay he prayed to the star.

He began with the set prayers, then none at all, simply breathing on his knees and looking up into the sky. Then, casting aside restraint, he groaned aloud, like any dying creature of the forest:

'O Lord, if Thou canst, forgive me and receive me. Thou seest—I could do no other, and can do no other now.'

49

(16th and 17th August)

The main road from Neidenburg to Willenburg was so smooth that it might have been specially made so that von François' mobile units could race along it and link up with von Mackensen as fast as possible. This highway, which the centre Russian corps, unaware of their impending fate, had crossed a few days before, had in the meantime been turned into a fortified barrier designed to trap them. After a short night's rest, von François' leading units set off before dawn on the 16th and made for Willenburg with all speed, occasionally shooting up supply waggons and stray Russian units. There was no opposition, and by evening they had occupied Willenburg—although the forty kilometres of road behind them was held only by isolated pickets and a few patrols, so that the encirclement was still an extremely tenuous one. It took one of von François' divisions more than a day to spread out along this highway and take up positions.

On much poorer roads, the troops of the leading brigade of von Mackensen's corps were also pressing forward on the eastern flank; to make the march less arduous they had loaded their knapsacks on to commandeered civilian carts and then climbed on top of them. Von Mackensen headed down from the north towards the same Neidenburg-Willenburg road, sending out detachments to either side as he went—to Ortelsburg and deep into the forests towards the encircled Russian centre.

Towards evening on the 16th, even though the jaws of the pincers had not quite closed, the space between them was no more than six or seven miles of trackless, impenetrable forest in an area so far from the nearest Russian unit that for any Russian force to have reached it was unthinkable. Yet as Hindenburg signed the army order that evening for the following day, he was still unsure of the success of the encircling movement: in the rest of the semi-circular ring the fighting, which had been so fierce during the day, had now died down. The pursuing Germans had been successfully held up in skirmishes on several of the narrow necks of land between lakes, and there were no reserve forces which could have been spared for defence if on the 16th the Russians had broken through the ring from the outside.

But no such attempt was made.

Samsonov's last dispatch, sent on the evening of August 15th, had succeeded in getting through a gap that the encircling forces had not yet closed and reached Bialystok on the morning of the 16th, just before Zhilinsky and Oranovsky sat down to breakfast. Ill-fated and unsuccessful, but dogged as ever, Samsonov announced that he had given his whole army the order to retreat behind the Ortelsburg-Mlawa line—that is, almost to the Russian frontier. In Zhilinsky's eyes it was a fate he had deserved—indeed, it could have been foreseen. It was a good thing that by assuming responsibility for the withdrawal without asking Army Group Headquarters Samsonov had taken the shame of it on himself. Over breakfast on that fine morning (when the doomed Kashira Regiment had already been surrounded in Hohenstein), Zhilinsky and Oranovsky decided that it had been a mistake the previous day to make Rennenkampf advance into an area which it now appeared was empty, since Samsonov had vacated it. They therefore telegraphed to Rennenkampf:

'Second Army withdrawn to frontier. Halt any further movement of your troops going to its support.'

Rennenkampf had only started to move the previous evening after dinner; even if his corps had been able to head straight for the scene of today's battle (which was impossible in that terrain), the distance for the infantry was sixty-five miles, for the cavalry forty-five. So at midday he gladly gave immediate orders to his corps to halt at once and to pull back the next day.

However, Zhilinsky and Oranovsky felt a new tremor of anxiety, and at two o'clock in the afternoon they sent Rennenkampf a contradictory telegram:

'In view of Second Army's engagement in heavy fighting, move your forward corps and cavalry to Allenstein.'

(Why to Allenstein? How could anyone in their right mind send *eight divisions* to a place where no one had needed their help for the past forty-eight hours at least?)

Anyone with military experience can judge what a happy effect these rapid counter-orders had on troop movements.

Manoeuvring such vast masses far from the field of battle, Zhilinsky and Oranovsky did not concern themselves with moving the flanking corps which were close to the fighting; it was in any case regarded as improper for Army Group Headquarters to bypass the Army Commander and interfere with the functioning of his corps. However, since Blagoveshchensky's corps was having a rest-day, there could be no harm in ordering his cavalry to attack.

So in the middle of the day General Tolpygo's cavalry division was sent into action. Its route was barred by the ill-omened town of Ortelsburg, which had been empty yesterday when Samsonov had ordered it to be held at all costs. Today, however, there had been intermittent gunfire coming from it since dawn. The cavalry division therefore skirted the town and advanced cautiously through an abandoned village on the route which it had been told to follow until it met the enemy. But the gathering darkness and the forest were unsuitable conditions for cavalry, and General Tolpygo decided that he had better rejoin his corps. Although movement at night was difficult and dangerous, by morning his division had returned. A comic incident had occurred during their ride: they had surprised a German general, a divisional commander; although he managed to escape in his car, he left behind his greatcoat, which had a map in it. The map was marked to show von Mackensen's plan for encircling the centre Russian corps. *No attention was paid to this map.* (It was much less trouble to disregard it.)

I Corps did not have such a quiet time as Blagoveshchensky's VI Corps. Despite the great distance it had retreated, on the night of the 15th/16th a captain, sent by Samsonov, managed to reach I Corps with an order to advance immediately on Neidenburg to relieve the situation of the centre corps, who were surrounded by the enemy. (If the one and a half corps which were at Mlawa *had* moved immediately to Neidenburg, then by midday on the 16th, with their overwhelming superiority in numbers, they could have entered the town without hindrance; not only would the German encirclement have been smashed, but, as happens in mobile warfare, von François' corps would have found itself gripped in a tight pincer-movement and threatened with a retaliatory encirclement.)

However, even though they had received a definite order, it was not so easy for the random collection of generals from various divisions and other units to meet together to carry it out. Nor was Colonel Krymov, whom General Dushkevich had selected as the new Chief of Staff of I Corps, able to induce the generals to agree. It was obvious that someone would have to carry out the order—but who? In the absence of any officer of undisputed seniority, each general was able to assert that *his* unit would not go as long as he was in command. All day on August 16th the generals in Mlawa haggled over the make-up of the composite detachment and who should lead it. In the end, its one wholly intact component unit was the Petrograd Regiment of Life Guards, taken from the shattered Guards Division, while the other battalions, squadrons and batteries were drawn from any units which could spare them. It therefore fell to the lot of the commander of the Warsaw Guards Division, General Sirelius from Petersburg, to lead the force on this desperate venture.

When all the arguments and preparations were over, Sirelius set out at six o'clock in the evening, and then only with the advance guard; the remaining units were to follow in an agreed order. For the rest of the evening and throughout the night, Sirelius' detachment covered the required twenty miles, and the first clash with the German screen took place on the morning of the 17th, three miles from Neidenburg.

Then a German aeroplane appeared in the sky above them.

By then General von François had spent two night in Neidenburg; he had already received two sets of daily orders from Ludendorff and had scoffed at them: Ludendorff still had not realised that the encirclement was well under way, being more concerned with taking precautions against Rennenkampf. Von François had little sleep on the night of the 16th/17th, because on his own orders a large number of captured Russian guns were hauled into the market square to be put on show. He woke up and jotted down a few felicitous remarks for his memoirs. On the morning of this 'proud and wonderful day' in his life, he leaped out of bed feeling keen and refreshed, sent a triumphant telegram to Ludendorff and, sensing that he was on the point of achieving fame in Germany

—indeed throughout Europe—as the victor of a modern Cannae, he went out on to the porch to inspect the spoils of war. Then came the hum of an engine in the sky: a reconnaissance plane had returned from a mission to observe the retreating Russians. To spare the general from suspense while he landed and delivered his message, the pilot neatly dropped the package in the roadway in front of the hotel. Von François smiled his congratulations. An aide-de-camp ran and handed the envelope to the general, who unsealed it: 'Aircraft flown by Lieutenant ... Route ... Message dropped ... Column, made up of all arms, observed ... Head of column 5 kilometres south of Neidenburg, end of column 1 kilometre north of Mlawa ...'

Just as if he had been a player in a game of chance whose piece is sent tumbling back from the finish to square one by an unlucky throw of the dice, the beaming smile on the face of the victor was at once replaced by the chastened look of a pupil who must learn his lessons all over again. He tossed the report over to his staff officers, but he needed no calculations to realise that a twenty-mile-long column was an army corps. A rapid burst of decisions followed. There was no time for written instructions; they would have to be oral. The reserve (was it two battalions?) was to advance to contact and engage the enemy. One battalion was dispersed on sentry-duty; all sentries were to be recalled. There were no artillery batteries south of the town, but two to the north; they must be transferred to the south. No troops were to be removed from the main road: the encirclement must be maintained. The Russian prisoners in the town were to be taken north. A *Landwehr* brigade had remained in Soldau; it was to be brought to Neidenburg with all speed. A report was ordered to be sent by telephone to Army Headquarters, but the town was under fire and the line had been cut. No matter, there were plenty of cars: they must be used to take dispatches. Russian shrapnel was bursting overhead, high-explosive shells falling—this was no place for Corps Headquarters. Retreat? No, advance—along the road to Willenburg!

A yellow lion was mounted on the radiator of von François' car. His son was noting down the general's thoughts. A car came towards them carrying a Russian general captured at dawn. They stopped, and the Russian was brought over. He was exhausted, his clothes snagged by branches and torn by bullets, his eyes wandering, his lips parched. Slim and light on his feet, unlike the familiar type of Russian general, he was clutching a useless cane. As he was a full general, it was not hard to guess

[493]

that he had been in command of the corps which had been harassing von Scholtz for a whole week. Von François got out to meet him, shook hands and said a few words of praise and consolation: a bold general, he said, was never safe from capture.

Sent to Neidenburg on a fruitless errand, Martos had spent a whole day lurking on the edge of Grünfliess Forest, deprived of troops with which to attack the town that he had himself captured a week ago. His Cossack escort had deserted and he had come under close shrapnel fire. That night a German searchlight had picked him out on the road; he had broken his sword and handed the pieces to a German officer.

However, Martos' hopes rose when to his amazement he heard the sound of Russian artillery firing on Neidenburg from the *south*. So it was still not certain who was encircling whom . . .

'Tell me, General,' said von François, 'what is the name of that corps commander? I shall suggest that he surrender . . .'

Until the morning of the 17th, Ludendorff restrained himself from making a premature announcement; but on that morning he reported to Supreme Headquarters that a vast encircling operation had been accomplished. Half an hour later came a telephone call from von François howling for support—then the line was cut. At once three divisions were detached from von Scholtz's pursuit of the enemy and made to march twelve, fifteen and eighteen miles respectively to the relief of Neidenburg. In the ensuing hours came a report that several of Rennenkampf's cavalry divisions were advancing further into Prussia. Another airman reported a Russian force advancing on Willenburg.

The encirclement was beginning to crack open. Faced by eight companies of second-line infantry, General Sirelius held his position for ten hours, waiting for the rest of the corps to join him. By the evening of the 17th, he had pushed the Germans out of Neidenburg, but it was too late for him to cover the remaining few miles needed to break through and link up with the main force: there were already a hundred guns ranged against him, and the Germans were being reinforced from all sides.

In distant Bialystok Zhilinsky and Oranovsky learned of these events not from airmen, nor from reconnaissance, nor from reports by the commanders of units in the field, but from a deserter—General Kondratovich. On August 15th Kondratovich had withdrawn half a dozen companies from the front line for his personal protection, fled over the Russian frontier to Chorzele and spent the 16th there anxiously awaiting the reports of dispatch-riders, to learn whether the Russians or the Germans were gaining the upper hand. Then, ingeniously concealing the fact of his desertion, he reported by telegraph that he had only just arrived, and supplied to a grateful Army Group Headquarters information about the centre corps which he could not possibly have received.

At an unseemly hour Zhilinsky and Oranovsky were roused from their beds (possibly at about the time when Samsonov was cocking his revolver to shoot himself). After a quiet day, they were now forced to spend the night trying to decide how to save the situation. Until then it had seemed to them that Samsonov was responsible for the defeat and rout of Second Army: he, after all, had given the order to retreat. In the changed circumstances it was now apparent that Zhilinsky should have ordered Second Army to retreat even before Samsonov had; in that case part of the blame for the encirclement must fall on Zhilinsky too. How was he to wriggle out of it? His solution was to make up a telegram that read: 'Commander-in-Chief has ordered Second Army to retire to line Ortelsburg-Mlawa . . .' The message was not marked with a precise time of origin and was made to look as if it had been sent in time to Samsonov; Zhilinsky would claim that it was not his fault that the telegraph line to Second Army Headquarters had been cut.

A further signal was sent to Rennenkampf ordering him to 'organise a cavalry search to clarify the position of General Samsonov's forces'. Blagoveshchensky was ordered to concentrate his corps on Willenburg (it was not thought necessary to specify that he should *capture* it). Kondratovich was told to rally all troops at his disposal (his bodyguard) in Chorzele (where he already was), whence he was to link up with Blagoveshchensky and 'act as the situation demands'. The airmen were given instructions to find the whereabouts of Second Army Headquarters, I Corps and XV Corps, which were thought to be somewhere in the region between Hohenstein and Neidenburg; all reports were to be passed on verbally and on no account in writing. Finally, I Corps was ordered to 'try to occupy Neidenburg'.

Unfortunately, it looked as though Zhilinsky was also due for a little trouble over his handling of I Corps: in a signal dated August 8th the Commander-in-Chief had given permission for I Corps to be moved beyond Soldau. Zhilinsky had ignored this, and he would be called to account for it.

50

Had it not been for the well-kept paths dividing the forest sectors, it would have been impossible to move at night; but the number and location of these paths corresponded exactly with the German map. Checking the route by the light of an occasional match and pacing out the distances to verify them, Vorotyntsev led his group in a detour around the triangle of open country, ending up at precisely the lonely homestead in the forest for which he had been aiming.

It was not a forester's cottage, as they had supposed, and in the dark it was impossible to tell exactly what it was. They stumbled across a pile of mysterious objects, flat and crumpled, soft and hard. Only later, when they found and lit a lamp, did they see that their boots and breeches, and in some cases their hands, were smeared with blood. The objects were animal skins, and someone had been slaughtering cattle here. There was a well, which enabled them to wash and drink their fill; there were stocks of dried and smoked meat, more than enough to eat and take with them, also some bread and a kitchen garden. Blagodaryov found a selection of meat-cleavers and long, straight-bladed knives, several of which he chose for himself. Vorotyntsev took a small, handy axe and stuck it under his belt. Searching for booty, they took care not to let the light show. Then, well fed, three of them lay down for a short sleep while Vorotyntsev kept guard.

Given his character, sleep was impossible for him. The break-out plan and the calculation of their chances obsessed him, and until it was accomplished he was incapable of relaxing or sleeping. His thoughts ran ahead even further—he began considering what he would say at General Headquarters if he got out, how he would say it, and what effect it might have.

His great need was not to keep himself awake but to control his impatience. He paced up and down the spacious, grassy farmyard, which nestled in an oval-shaped clearing cut from the tall, protective forest. The setting moon, still occasionally to be glimpsed through the black wall of trees, was reflected in the oval patch of sky by a strip of small, fluffy clouds, shedding a gentle, diffused light against which the lofty tops of the nearest trees stood out clearly. Neither the raggedness of the clouds nor their slow speed were likely omens of bad weather, which was all to the good. Around midnight, when the moon had set completely, the sky clouded over altogether, but it cleared again later. The night turned cold, but the dew was light.

All around a whole army was collapsing, regiments and divisions were going down to their destruction—and yet not a sound was to be heard. Near Neidenburg and along the whole German front line to the west even the rifle-fire had stopped, as though the Germans were content with what they had already achieved, and, satisfied, were not intending to pursue the Russians any further.

Few stars were left. From its deep nocturnal black the sky was slowly turning grey, and were it not for the stars it would have simply looked overcast. It was the hour when colour disappears altogether: the sky grey and everything else a uniform, neutral dark. If one had never seen the colour green, for instance, it would have been impossible to guess what it was like from looking at the trees and grass.

They could not waste much more time, and Vorotyntsev went to wake up his party. Kharitonov awoke easily, as though he had not been asleep but waiting for the sound of footsteps. Lenartovich jumped at the touch as though he had been hit, but got up without delay. Arsenii groaned, protesting in an incoherent mumble; only after being shaken by both shoulders did he wake up, and even then he lay there for a while, breathing deeply.

Laden even more heavily with meat and butchers' knives, they set off again in single file. Branches or human figures could only be seen against the sky; otherwise everything merged indistinguishably into the dense, surrounding darkness.

Although they had not slept for long, Yaroslav Kharitonov's head felt clearer and steadier than yesterday. He was feeling better every day; only his ears remained partly deafened, and in consequence he missed hearing the faint, rustling sounds of the woodland. While still in hospital he had enviously wished that he were serving under this quick-thinking colonel, with his keen, mobile glance; and he had felt a wave of relief and delight at stumbling across him again in the forest—especially as he had done him such a service by producing his map. Things were going badly for the army and for his regiment, and he had lost his platoon, but he himself could not have fallen into better hands: he would return to his own, unique, beloved life, which he would not change for any other.

As the deserted forest began to grow light with the morning, they became more alert. After careful checks they crossed two sectors and turned at the second path, which widened out into a long, winding clearing. It was rapidly getting lighter and visibility had increased to nearly four hundred yards. At that moment they noticed a group of men walking through the same clearing ahead of them. They were soldiers, in caps, not spiked helmets, so they were Russian. They were moving slowly, weighed down by a heavy load on their shoulders.

There was no other way but to catch them up. The other group had noticed them by now, and two men with rifles broke away from the party towards the cover of the trees, but Vorotyntsev raised his cap and waved, and they recognised him. The party of four quickly caught up, and the eight stretcher-bearers ahead put down their two loads on the ground.

The stretchers, made of branches plaited between two poles, with small logs lashed on as feet, had been rapidly cobbled together in the forest by skilled peasant hands. Yaroslav had never imagined that such a thing was possible.

On the rear stretcher was the large, thick-set body of a dead man. A white handkerchief, knotted at the four corners, covered his face and he wore colonel's epaulettes. On the front stretcher lay a lieutenant whose trouser-leg was cut away to reveal a heavily bandaged knee. The remaining ten men on foot were private soldiers, not a single non-commissioned officer among them, and almost all of them were middle-aged reservists. Close to, the grey-blue light was now strong enough to make out their features—haggard, hollow-cheeked, some with clots of dried blood, all with dirty, rumpled uniforms. The eight stretcher-bearers had no easy task:

they were all carrying rifles, some of them also had heavy knapsacks hanging down from their belts, while the two men not carrying stretchers were hung with more equipment.

Where had they come from? Who were they? Vorotyntsev and Lieutenant Ofrosimov introduced themselves to each other. Both of the lieutenant's arms were uninjured, as was the whole upper part of his body, so that he was able to give orders and to shoot, but could not walk. The lieutenant, coarsely-spoken and with pitch-black curly hair, had a hoarse voice and told his story incoherently and slightly unwillingly, rather as if he had been stopped and questioned all the way through the forest and was by now tired of telling it. He raised himself from his stretcher on his elbow, but as this still hardly brought him above ground level, Vorotyntsev squatted down to him on his haunches. The ten soldiers did not move away out of earshot of the conversation between officers, as was proper, but remained standing and sitting around in a tight group as equal participants in the discussion, some of them even putting in a few words. (This is good, Yaroslav thought: this is the right way to treat soldiers. If they have to share the risk of getting killed, they should be granted equality in everything else.)

They were all from the Dorogobuzh Regiment, left behind as a rearguard the day before yesterday. They had held off the Germans until dark, mostly with bayonets, as they were badly short of ammunition. (Now, having learned the lesson that ammunition was more valuable than bread, they had filled their pouches with cartridges discarded by other troops.) Their regiment had been destroyed, a dozen men or less surviving from each company.

They had decided to take their regimental commander, Colonel Kabanov, home to Russia for burial.

That was all they had to tell—a glum, wounded lieutenant and ten soldiers. The lieutenant was the type of officer Yaroslav disliked—he looked as if he might be a gambler, swore obscenely and told unfunny dirty stories. Yet these men must have loved him if they had carried him all this way, grunting and panting, with such superhuman exertion. What a fight that must have been, bayonets against machine-guns and artillery! Yaroslav could not begin to picture the reality.

When they had told their tale, they stayed silent in their tight circle for a minute or so longer before having to return to their places and pick up the stretchers—they were heading in a different direction. But they delayed their start, held back by something that inspired their confidence. (The thought occurred to Yaroslav that his favourite colonel might take these men of the Dorogobuzh Regiment under his wing too. They were all ultimately making for the same place, after all, and it would cost him no extra effort.)

Vorotyntsev himself, the bruise on his jaw suffused with blood, was not so much interested in having the men's confidence as in learning more about the recent fighting. Spreading out the map over the cones and pine-needles, he was mentally trying to recreate the situation of their distant, annihilated regiment.

'*There*—is that where you were? Which way did you come? How far was it?'

Before the lieutenant could answer, the soldiers spoke up:

'About twenty-five miles . . .'

'Maybe more . . .'

(Twenty-five miles! And carrying those stretchers! What faith, what strength was it that had sustained them?)

The lieutenant was not able to indicate much by means of the map, because he had been without a map for days; all he could remember was the village of Dereuten and a compass-march southwards towards a narrow neck of land between two lakes, which they had crossed earlier, during the advance. After that the soldiers took it in turns to describe the journey: through a mixed wood of oaks and pines, climbing hill after hill; through the German lines; a ruined farm; a long stretch of woodland; a densely overgrown isthmus; a village with a church; fording a river; then in the dark they had turned away from the mainstream of the retreating Russian troops—and that was all . . .

Somehow these survivors of the Dorogobuzh Regiment did not seem to belong to their corps any longer: having paid so dearly, they had settled accounts with it for the rest of the war. On that Day of the Assumption they had all died, as it were, and any man whose legs could still carry him now had the right to get out as best he could. They had covered the retreat of all the others with their own defenceless bodies and they owed them no further sacrifice. Although none of them expressed this idea openly—they were probably not even conscious of it—it was implied in all they said and in their silences, and in a special air of complicity with which they talked to this unknown colonel over the head of their lieutenant; it was implicit, too, in the two stretchers they had carried uncomplainingly along twenty-five miles of remote forest paths. (As the crow flies the distance was twenty miles, but the twists and turns made it more than twenty-five.) They had kept apart from their former corps, having apparently crossed its route secretly in order to follow their own line of march. No one had forced them to do it: no sergeant had given them orders and chivvied them along, and clearly they were not acting on Ofrosimov's instructions, because no officer could have commanded his men to carry him, wounded, on their shoulders for twenty-five miles. All the disruptive factors that might have existed between them up to the day before yesterday—mutual recrimination, dislike, exasperation—had been scorched out of existence by that day of death.

They had one more secret to tell, which they were so reluctant to impart that they kept it until the very end, although there was no point in concealing it: they had brought the regimental colours with them. They were wrapped around the lieutenant's body.

Yaroslav felt a lump in his throat. He envied Ofrosimov: what a way to merge oneself with the people! It was in the hope of something like this that he had joined the army. But in his platoon the soldierly-seeming Kramchatkin had turned out to be a fool who could not shoot, and Vyushkov had been revealed as a rogue and a thief. If he had dared, Yaroslav would have pulled at the colonel's sleeve and whispered quietly to him: 'Let's take them with us! They're such noble fellows!'

The colonel seemed to have guessed what was in his mind. Folding the map into a small square, he asked in a quiet voice:

'When did you last eat, lads? Would you like a bite?'

Murmurings. They would.

'Good. That means less for us to carry. Go and sit down over there, under the trees, and take the lieutenant with you. No need to sit out here in the open. Arsenii! Give them all the meat.'

Blagodaryov raised his eyebrows and coughed, looking at the colonel as though he had not understood. Then he reached for his large gipsy-like bundle, knelt down in front of it, untied it, and began slicing up the meat with his butcher's knife.

'Ye-e-es,' he said, as he handed the meat round, 'I can see you've had a hard time—very hard.'

The men were ravenously hungry, and one shoulder of beef

between them was not much of a breakfast; but there was more besides.

Vorotyntsev walked over, lifted the covering from the dead man's face and looked at it. Yaroslav would also have liked to gaze upon the face of a hero; though now far above earthly things, it might still bear some trace of the inspiration with which he had summoned his men to the last counter-attack. But feeling too embarrassed, he did not dare to intrude.

The sky above the pine-trees was turning blue and the few vaporous clouds that had not yet dispersed were tinged with pink. Another quiet, beautiful day had dawned, innocent of war. The only firing that could be heard was muffled and far away.

'I've a feeling you're from Tambov, aren't you?' an elderly soldier with a beard like a birch-broom said thoughtfully to Arsenii. 'What district?'

'Why, from Tambov district!' Still kneeling, Arsenii replied with his usual promptness.

'So am I!' the bearded soldier said with dignified surprise. He had the air of a literate peasant. 'Which parish? Which village?'

'I'm from Kamenka,' said Arsenii, delighted.

'Kamenka? What's your surname?'

'Blagodaryov.'

'Which Blagodaryov? You're not the son of Elisei Nikiforych Blagodaryov, by any chance?'

'Yes! I'm his youngest!' Arsenii beamed.

'Well, well,' his elder neighbour said approvingly, stroking his beard with leisurely, civilian dignity. 'I know you. Do you know Grigory Naumovich?'

'Of course I do!' Arsenii was almost offended. 'We all call him the boss. Got a good head on his shoulders, too. Where are you from?'

'I'm from Tugolukoye.'

'Tugolukoye!' Arsenii flung out his arms for all the world to see. 'That's where all the good horses come from. We've bought some.'

'My name's Kornei Luntsov.'

'There are five hundred farmsteads in your village—too many for me to know them all.'

Everyone broke into delighted smiles at the discovery of this link between the two groups. What was regimental comradeship compared with the bond between neighbouring villagers?

'There's another one of us from Tambov. Kachkin!' Luntsov pointed to a sullen man of about thirty with pig-like eyes, a broad head, shoulders that seemed too wide for his short arms, a vast, barrel-like torso and a chest thrust out almost as far as a woman's breasts, except that it was so obviously male that he looked as if he could easily be harnessed to a plough. 'Only he's from far away, from Inokoye.'

'Ah!' Arsenii waved his arm. 'Inokoye—isn't that near the river Vorona?'

'Yes. Listen, Averyan, here's a fellow from the next village to me.'

Kachkin scowled at him, but approvingly.

'He fed us—good lad.' He screwed up his small eyes even narrower, into two cunning slits. 'Throw me one of those knives.'

'What for?'

'To stab myself a German with.'

'I need it for that too!'

'Yes, but you've got more than one.'

It was true; Arsenii had brought several spare knives. But should he give one to a soldier he didn't know? He glanced at his colonel.

Vorotyntsev looked at Kachkin's barrel-chest and said:

'Give one to him.'

Arsenii did not get up to hand the knife over. From where he was kneeling, about eight paces away from Kachkin, he drew back his arm and threw the knife past another man's shoulder. Slicing the bark off a protruding birch-root, it plunged itself upright into the ground at Kachkin's feet.

Kachkin did not flinch or move his foot. He pulled out the knife and said:

'Not bad. You're from Tambov all right.'

He held the blade up to the light and inspected its cutting edge.

'Anyone here from Kostroma?' Vorotyntsev asked.

No, there were none; one man from Voronezh, two from Novgorod.

Slowly and attentively the colonel looked them all over. One surly devil among them did not matter. He noticed another man, keen and obliging-looking, who seemed to be eager to be questioned.

'Where are you from?'

The man leapt to his feet, beaming.

'Archangel, your honour. Pinega district. The monastery of St

Artemy the Righteous is in our village—perhaps you've heard of it?'

'Yes. Sit down, sit down.' He looked further and saw a big, round-eyed reservist with a beard that would need a harrow to comb it. 'And you?'

Without getting up, he replied casually as though chatting to a friend: 'I'm from Olonets.' He was eating slowly, and had glanced up unhurriedly.

Vorotyntsev was beginning to look worried.

'Had enough to eat? You'll find water a little further on, there's a small lake. Are your legs in good shape?' They replied that they were, but he was not thinking about their legs. 'You can come with us if you like.'

Kharitonov beamed. He had been right.

'We shall have to cross the lines at night,' Vorotyntsev explained, with increasing concern. He was not looking at the lieutenant but gazing at the soldiers' faces, particularly at the man from Olonets, Luntsov and Kachkin. 'Tonight, in fact. We shall have to cross the main road. It'll be difficult. Then after the road we shall probably have to run for it.'

On a stump some way apart sat the stiff-backed Lenartovich, looking at Vorotyntsev in horror. He had been too hasty in thinking this colonel was intelligent. Had he gone mad? If they were going to have to run for their lives after crossing the main road, how could they lug the lieutenant along on his stretcher? And take the corpse too? They would all be shot down. Sacrifice the living to the dead? Surely he wouldn't?

It was this very quality of irrational persistence which thrilled Yaroslav and touched him deeply—the fact that these men insisted on carrying the corpse with them, that they refused to leave their regimental commander behind in a foreign land even when he was dead. He also understood why Vorotyntsev was worried and hesitant: there was something odd about this group, something unmilitary. Their relationship was not based on subordination, but on trust. Lieutenant Ofrosimov was not in command of them, the group seemed to run itself, and that was why the soldiers themselves had to be asked.

Vorotyntsev looked round at the men, who said nothing.

Then it dawned on Lenartovich that there was a certain logic in the situation. It would have been difficult for Ofrosimov to have ordered the men to leave the colonel's body behind and carry only him: if he had assailed their naive superstition about the dead man, they might have left him behind as well. But Vorotyntsev had the necessary authority to order them to bury the corpse; he should also think carefully before agreeing to take the lieutenant.

The Dorogobuzh men were seated, scattered, on tree-stumps, on the ground, on rolled-up greatcoats; it was like a meeting of a village commune but for the two pyramids of piled rifles. Vorotyntsev, usually so active, confident and firm, now seemed unsure of himself, standing with his legs apart, twisting his locked fingers and staring out from under the peak of his cap. Silent, he looked at the men.

The soldiers, too, were silent, not all of them looking at the colonel; some were staring at the ground, others glancing at the stretchers.

When, after another look around the group, the colonel's glance fell on Kornei Luntsov, the latter stroked his grey, birch-twig beard, which was so full he could not grasp it in one hand, and asked significantly:

'How many miles from here to Russia, your honour?'

What idiots they were, thought Sasha; all they could think about was Russia—as if the Germans could not advance into Russia and catch them there too! Machine-guns meant nothing to them—they could only think in terms of miles. If the colonel gave in to them and agreed to go the shorter but more dangerous way, then Sasha would have to leave them.

Kachkin, with the little stubby ears, was throwing a piece of gnarled root from hand to hand: this way and that, this way and that . . .

Vorotyntsev turned again to fathom the deep waters in the eyes of the man from Olonets. Then he straightened up, hesitation gone, and said crisply:

'Right, let's go! Lieutenant!' He frowned at the proud face of Lenartovich. 'You and I will take the places of two of the men carrying the colonel's body.'

He had cleverly put Sasha on the spot. Ridiculous business, but there was no alternative: he had to obey. Sasha looked up incredulously, then shrugged his shoulders, slowly got to his feet and walked over to the stretcher. A funeral procession—the idiots!

'I'll help too, Colonel!' Kharitonov stepped forward unsteadily, but Vorotyntsev motioned him aside.

The colonel and Lenartovich stood by the front poles of the stretcher and raised them to their shoulders, coinciding more or less with the hoist by the two men at the back. Equal in height, they set off, falling into step to keep the stretcher from swaying too much. With four men it was not particularly heavy, but it was awkward and they were inclined to stumble.

Although the colonel had accepted him yesterday evening with hostility and evident distrust, since then Sasha had come to realise that he had been lucky to meet him. If anyone could get them out, this man could. The hours ahead were going to be so exhausting, their strength would be so taxed by simply keeping moving and staying out of danger, that it would be reassuring to submit to a trained mind—not to have to think or worry, but just keep going and do what one was told. What was more, this clear-headed colonel, as Sasha had readily perceived from the beginning, was an extremely rare type of officer: a genuinely intelligent and educated man. On the other hand, if he really were educated, why, since he wielded the necessary authority, was he giving in to the ridiculous obscurantist notions of these peasant reservists from the darkest corners of Russia? It was not so bad about the colours; even though they were just a scrap of government-issue dyed cloth which every sensible person jeered at, at least the rag weighed nothing, and anyway it was a good excuse for Ofrosimov to persuade them to carry him. All the same, he could not help saying to Vorotyntsev:

'Colonel, why must we carry this dead man? It's sheer superstition.'

As they were in front, walking with their heads down, swaying to the motion of the stretcher, they could only be heard by someone very close behind them.

Vorotyntsev made no attempt to contradict him.

'Surely this isn't the way to behave in modern war?' Sasha ventured boldly.

The boy looked intelligent; it was no good trying to fob him off with some routine piece of army claptrap. But the tone of Vorotyntsev's reply made even Sasha's intelligent eyes blink.

'Modern war will catch up with us soon enough, Lieutenant, when we reach the road. You'd better be worrying about what you can use to shoot with. You won't hit anything with that pop-gun of yours.'

That might be true, but it was an evasion none the less. Sasha was not one to give up so easily.

'Now you're making us carry this corpse, later you'll order us to carry that lieutenant. I can tell from his face that he's a Black Hundreder.'

Sasha was counting on making the colonel lose his temper. But no; as crisply as before, but almost absent-mindedly, he said:

'Yes, I shall. At a time like this, Ensign, party political differences are just so many ripples on the water.'

'Party politics—ripples?' Astounded, Sasha tripped and almost dropped his pole. He could think of several answers, but decided that attack was the best defence. 'What about international politics, then? Are they just ripples on the water? It's because of them that we're fighting, isn't it? In that case, what differences mean anything at all?'

'The difference between decency and swinishness, Ensign,' Vorotyntsev snapped back at him. With his free outside hand he lifted up his map-case, unbuttoned it and glanced down as he walked, now at the ground underfoot, now at the map.

Sasha was not just objecting on principle, in fact principle scarcely entered into it: the truth was that it was not easy, indeed it was extremely difficult, to carry a stretcher when the man on it weighed almost as much as two men and the pole cut into your shoulder, forcing you to bend forward. In fact the man behind was shouting at him now:

'Higher, your honour!'

All his life Sasha had cultivated his brain as being of prime importance; he had never had time to exercise his body. The recent day's fighting had exhausted him. Gritting his teeth as he carried the stretcher, he picked out a tree ahead of them which he could reach before asking to be relieved. Then he would carry on for another stretch.

Now the sun was shining on them almost directly over the tops of the distant trees, and a glade opened out to their left. Crossing it, they found themselves again on a straight path between dark, dense pine-trees. The ground started to rise and carrying became still harder work, making Sasha's heart thump. The colonel turned the party away from the path, up an even steeper slope straight into the woods. Here, though, the trees were thinner, the ground was clear of brushwood and undergrowth and the going was much easier on the soft pine-needle carpet, made uneven only by scattered cones. Feeling that it would be shameful to give out on this slope, Sasha endured. Just before reaching the top the colonel himself gave the order:

'Halt! Put it down.'

They were deep in the forest on the open, sunlit slope of a ridge. Here the surrounding pine-trees grew more sparsely, their bronze-coloured trunks occasionally wind-bent, their great, gaunt crowns supported on a scaffolding of spreading branches. The early sun was warming the trees; it would be late evening before the party could set off again. It must have been a favourite spot in spring for squirrels to take the air after their winter hibernation: here would be the first place where the snows melted, and the water would always drain away. Behind them, in the direction they had come from, the ridge fell away in a long, sweeping slope towards a broad hollow, the carpet of clean pine-needles inviting one to roll all the way down between the trees.

On the top of the ridge was a small mound, beside which they put down the stretchers.

Without a word of explanation Vorotýntsev stopped and gazed around, and the others followed his example. Unhesitatingly, no hint of entreaty in his tone, he announced firmly to the soldiers of the Dorogobuzh Regiment:

'Now, lads, we're going to bury Colonel Kabanov here. We won't find a better place. And the Germans are Christians too.'

The men exchanged looks.

Vorotýntsev added quietly:

'There's no alternative. If we don't, we'll never get through.'

The inadmissible thought, left unspoken when they had first met at the clearing in the grey dawn light, became acceptable as he uttered it on this pleasant, open ridge, where the gentle morning sunlight was starting to bring out a whiff of resinous aroma in the pines—and it was all the more easily acceptable since he himself had helped to carry the stretcher. The grim shadow on their faces—an indefinable look, perhaps of guilt at having survived when so many of their comrades had been killed—was swept away by the colonel's words, leaving no sign of protest.

The man from Olonets took off his cap and turned to the east; praying in silence, he crossed himself fervently, bowed from the waist and said gravely:

[508]

'God will forgive us.'

Several others crossed themselves.

Anxious not to waste a moment, Vorotyntsev called out: 'Arsenii, where's your spade? Start digging. Over there.' He pointed to the mound.

Fully equipped for any task and always ready, Blagodaryov uncomplainingly took out his entrenching-tool as though he had come here just for this and climbed to the top of the mound, which was large enough for the whole party to assemble on. Kneeling down, which hardly seemed to reduce his great height, he started hacking at the ground in a place free of roots.

Two of the Dorogobuzh men also had spades. Always the most active of them, Kachkin ran up the hill with surprising speed for a man of his bulk and, likewise kneeling, began thrusting and digging with savage force, never pausing for breath.

'Well done, Kachkin, you'll do it in no time,' Vorotyntsev said encouragingly.

Kachkin paused, grinning on his knees.

'Kachkin can do anything, your honour. Even this.'

Then another soldier, an ailing, elderly man, clumsily, with the last remnants of his strength, gasping for breath, began picking at the earth as best he could with the tip of his spade.

'If you can do it, so can I!' said Kachkin with a malicious glance from his little pig-like eyes as he scooped away again. Soon the soil began to get looser and easier to dig, as though his was the fairy-tale spade which could magically build palaces overnight.

Sure enough, Kachkin could do anything; he was swinging his spade this way and that, this way and that.

Luntsov and another man set off to cut down saplings to plait a cover which would transform the stretcher into a coffin.

The forest was so dense and vast that the war, raging all around it for a whole week, had not yet penetrated as far as this: there was not a slit-trench to be seen, not a shell-hole, no wheelmarks, not even a discarded cartridge-case. The peaceful morning grew warmer, bringing out the smell of the pines more strongly, and birds chirped softly or flitted among the trees in the calm, August weather. A sense of freedom and security came over the men too, as though there were no encircling Germans and after the funeral they would go home.

The grave and the cover for the stretcher were ready, but what sort of a ceremony could they hold? A fragment of the Burial Service? Vorotyntsev had heard it often enough, but he could never have recited the words or told anyone else the sort of thing to say. That was a chaplain's duty; an officer was not expected to know it.

Dubiously he glanced at Arsenii, who was getting to his feet and straightening his back. As he did so, he realised that the fellow, with his uneducated but quick-witted shrewdness, had guessed what was in his mind. In those last three, action-packed days an unspoken division of rights and duties had been mutually agreed between them, of a kind normally unthinkable between a colonel and a private soldier or between two men of such different ages. Thus, without receiving a word of command or making a suggestion himself, Arsenii, who had already shown himself so versatile, displayed yet another side of his nature.

Drawing himself up majestically to his full height, he took off his cap and threw it behind him without looking; frowning, his expression and tone taking on a dignity borrowed from some source in his past life, in a strangely exalted, authoritative voice he addressed a question to the assembled company:

'What were the names of the deceased?'

None of the soldiers knew; they had never had to call him anything but 'your honour'. They would never have known had not Ofrosimov spoken up. From his stretcher on the ground he looked up at the tall private and said:

'Vladimir Vasilievich.'

At that Blagodaryov strode up to the dead man, bent down and took the handkerchief from his face—something which five minutes ago he would not have dared to do. Chest out, head up, he turned to the rising sun and in a clear, strong voice, precisely in the style of an Orthodox deacon, intoned to the high pine-tops:

'In peace let us pray to the Lord!'

It was so powerful, so compelling and so exactly like a church service that no further invitation to join in was necessary. The man from Olonets and two more at once responded, crossing themselves, each man bowing to the east where he stood:

'Lord have mercy on us.'

Leading them, his voice rising above the others, Arsenii sang the response, changing the tone from that of deacon to choir-leader. Then after the response he reverted to his rich, powerful diaconal voice, reproducing with astounding accuracy the rhythm and intonation of ecclesiastical plain-chant. Although he could never have repeated them, Vorotyntsev recognised the verses as entirely correct:

'For the ever-memorable servant of God Vladimir, for his repose, his peace and his blessed remembrance, let us pray to the Lord!'

All of them, including the officers, had now gathered around the body, bare-headed and facing east.

'Lord have mercy on us.'

How amazingly many-sided this young peasant from the depths of the Tambov countryside was! Vorotyntsev had been through death with him for three days and afterwards might have lost sight of him without ever discovering, were it not for this incident, that he had sung in a church choir—and obviously sung in it for some time, listening attentively to the services, taking it all in; this was something important in his life which he loved and which he did well. His enunciation of every sound, his observance of every pause, was so precise that he unquestionably had a deep understanding of its meaning.

'That he may take his place without blame at the dreadful throne of the Lord of Glory, let us pray to the Lord.'

Ofrosimov was carried up to the graveside, his face to the east, and from his sitting position he crossed himself and sang. Kharitonov, having at last seen the hero's face, sang too, feeling the onset of tears—but tears of comfort and relief.

'Lord have mercy on us.'

On rolled the deacon-like voice, undisturbed by the alien surroundings of the Prussian countryside.

'That the Lord our God may take him into the place of light and plenteousness and peace, where all the righteous repose, let us pray to the Lord.'

The prayers for the man's soul were almost over; for his body they had done what they could to find the quietest, most pleasant spot.

All facing east, they could only see each other's backs; unseen behind them, never joining in the responses, with a twisted smile of condescension yet with head bared, stood Lenartovich. In front of them all, bowing from the waist and straightening again was the supple back of Blagodaryov, which because of his great height seemed much less broad than it was. Frequent and fervent were the sweeps of his great, strong arm as he crossed himself, an arm prepared with equal readiness to work and to fight for his life in the dark.

'Having besought the mercy of God, the Kingdom of Heaven and the forgiveness of sins for them and for ourselves, let us commend ourselves and one another and our whole life unto Christ our God.'

And soaring higher than the sun, higher than the sky, directly to the throne of the All-High, from fourteen men's voices the familiar chant arose, not in supplication but in sacrificial offering, in renunciation:

'To Thee, O Lord . . .'

51

————————

Having lost their commanders, now a motley collection of different arms of the service and units filling the forest paths to the verges, the Russians were able to move relatively unhindered as long as they kept to the depths of the woods. But each time they emerged into open country, such as a large glade or clearing or a village, they were met by gunfire. One burst of fire evoked another, and there were times when, mistaking each other for Germans, they fired on their own troops.

At the edge of a wood five hundred yards from the village of Kaltenborn, at dawn on August 17th, the head of a disorganised column of what yesterday had been XIII Corps was met by artillery and machine-gun fire. Although the column had not been formed into a composite unit and had no commander, by chance Colonel Pervushin was in the advance-guard, and with the help of casual volunteers from various units he deployed several guns which happened to be there. The guns opened fire, while the colonel attacked the village with a scratch company headed by the unfurled colours of the Neva Regiment. The Germans ran, leaving four guns.

The ground won at Kaltenborn, however, amounted to no more than half a mile square, and again the column had to turn back into the forest. A mile further on there was another open stretch around a village, and again a barrage of fire came down, accurately distributed over the paths and tracks coming out of the forest. Mikhail Grigorievich Pervushin, who in all his years of service had never lost his gift of leading men, was also the heart and soul of the next break-out. There was such an affinity between him and the troops that he never led them into an attack that was beyond their powers—but if he had, they would have followed him. His advance-guard was an assortment of men from the Neva, Narva, Kopor and Zvenigorod regiments. They were supported by two under-strength batteries, including Chernega's.

Again the few available machine-guns and field guns were put in position and suddenly opened up with running fire—whereupon the infantry was again launched into the attack. Once more Pervushin led them, and received a bayonet wound. Here, too, the Russians' unexpected break-out was conducted with such dash that the German screening-force, in regimental strength, took to its heels, abandoning several machine-guns and twenty pieces of artillery, some of them complete with their draught-teams.

In these feats of arms, as our forefathers would have put it, Pervushin's advance-guard was engaged all day. There were still many miles of forest to traverse before the final break-through, obstructed by one German detachment after another, by road-blocks and barbed wire; machine-guns at crossroads and artillery at defiles lay in wait for their disorderly, bunched-up prey. The Russians only had to show their faces for the Germans to greet them with every kind of enfilading fire. With each successful action, progress became harder for the Russians: fewer men, increasing hunger and thirst (the wells were blocked), dwindling supplies of rifle and artillery ammunition, more wounded, stronger opposition. Their only remaining hope was a bayonet attack.

It was late in the afternoon. The strength of the column had dwindled since morning. Unhinged by the strain, the men were less and less able to act rationally and were losing hope.

Before the last desperate push, Colonel Pervushin, now with two bayonet wounds, gave the order to the standard-bearer . . .

Screen

     = who is holding the colours, now furled.

        He is the kind of man who never gives up, but would die with the colours.

     = Pervushin, one wound bandaged, the other not, gives a wave of his unhurt arm: take down the colours!

Gunfire. Shells burst near by.

     = The colours are decorated with the St George's Cross, fastened to the ornamental fretted spike of the colour-staff.

≈ Deeply distressed, the standard-bearer crosses himself.
He unmounts the colours and hands the staff to his
deputy, who breaks off the staff below the banner
and throws away the lower part—now just a stick.
≈ Dejectedly they take a spade
≈ and start digging. Having dug a hole,
they glance at the trees for recognition-marks.
The tree-tops quiver

In the blast of shellfire. Explosions. To the sound of this music
≈ Pervushin sits down on a tree-stump,
sits and thinks.

In close-up we see
≈ him, his movements stiff from his wounds.
There is blood on his face, his neck, his tunic.
His cap is torn, and he wears it askew, at a non-regulation
angle.
His bristling moustaches are drooping. His eyes have lost
their bold, humorous sparkle—he has lost hope.
≈ He talks to no one, no one comes up to him. These moments of thought may be the last in his fifty-four years.

Explosions. Crackle of rifle-fire.
He turns his head
towards the standard-bearer, who reports that the order
has been carried out. The colours are buried. It is as
though they were a piece of his heart.
≈ With an effort (how can he drag himself to his feet?) he
shouts:

'*Staff-Captain Grokholets!*'

≈ Here comes the familiar figure of Grokholets. He has lost
his cap and is bald except for two strips of hair on
either side of the crown of his head. He is far from
young; how does he manage to be so keen and agile?
Perhaps it is because he is so thin. The ends of his
moustaches are still curled, but now perhaps they are
curling in desperation.

Pervushin says to him:

'*Well, shall we try for it? Muster
every man who can hold a rifle.
Post the machine-guns.*'

Grokholets:
> *'Very well, let's try. Right away.*
> *We'll make it.'*

Pervushin gets up. He is badly hurt. He looks grim.
He is like a father to his men; they will follow him.
Takes off his cap and waves twice
⇒ to the guns. There are two guns, ready to fire, but they
are at some distance through the trees and are manned
by over-strength crews in order to manhandle them to
the edge of the wood.

We see Chernega, stripped to the waist. His shoulder
muscles stand out so much that they look like snakes
crawling over him.

Still the same round head like a Dutch cheese and short
moustache, he is roaring:
> *'Right, boys! Heave!'*

The guns roll forward.
Crunching, crashing, tramp of feet. Then Chernega's desperate
voice, scarcely recognisable:
> *'Running – fire!'*

The guns roar. And the machine-guns open up somewhere near by.
There are not many, but they are all that are left.

From behind we see:
⇒ through the distant trees and undergrowth, through pine-
saplings,
Russian troops come running.

Junior officers in the lead, of course, waving their swords
over their heads—
helpless gesture, no threat to the enemy, but to their own
men it means: keep going, lads, we're in this with you!

Alongside the men running forward
⇒ others stumble, too weak to attack.
They shout, all that they can muster of a 'hurrah':
> *'A-a-a-a-h . . .'*

They have rifles with fixed bayonets, but can barely
carry them—how will they find the strength to lunge
and thrust?

One man turns head over heels.
Has he been killed? No, he has simply collapsed from
exhaustion under a young pine-tree: 'Go on without

me, I'm all in, I'll just wait here for what's coming to
me.'
        The officers' swords are beginning to waver, then fall.
Chatter of machine-guns.
    ⇐ Our men are falling! Falling, dropping their rifles . . .
        What's happening? One rifle with its bayonet thrust into
            the ground, the butt swaying, swaying.
    ⇐ Grokholets, with his bald head, runs forward desperately.
        Has he been hit? No, he's still running.
    ⇐ Ahead of them all is the tall Pervushin.
        His face turned grimly round
to his own men,
        moustache bristling,
        waving a rifle with fixed bayonet!
        He stumbles on an unseen trip-wire.
    ⇐ Out of the cover of a slit-trench there comes towards him
        a strapping German
        who bayonets him—
        the great, the terrible Pervushin!
        His third bayonet wound—just his luck.
        Colonel Pervushin falls.
Machine-gun fire
    ⇐ slices through the attacking Russians, who
            falter and
            turn back.
    ⇐ On the edge of the wood, Chernega, muscles rippling
            with savage exertion, sees that this is no time to go on
            firing: they must run for it.
        Jumping up on to the wheel of the gun, he
            starts unscrewing the gun-sight; at a
            sign from him
            the crews start dismantling and removing
            the breech-blocks from the guns.
    ⇐ Following him, they all take to their heels,
        running into the forest,
        running back . . .

52

General Klyuev himself was neither at the head of the corps, where Pervushin was, nor with the rearguard, where the Sofia Regiment fought the enemy to a standstill over a hundred-yard stretch of woodland; he remained in the middle of the column, where he tied it into knots by veering away from every German harassing detachment. The encircling ring seemed to him unbreakable, and there was no one to whom he could entrust a half-corps in order to make a break-out in force.

The remnants of the artillery acted on their own initiative: they changed positions, fired at the enemy over open sights whenever they saw him and, when forced to run, either towed the guns away or abandoned them. At the point where the Grünfliess Forest opens out, there is a broad marshy region criss-crossed with ditches; this barred the Russians' passage, and the artillery and supply trains sank in the swampy, low-lying hollow. Although the main road was in sight only a mile ahead, the gunners had to veer eastwards towards German-occupied Willenburg in search of a route over dry ground. The stream of men in retreat melted away, hundreds, even thousands, disappearing hourly, no one knew where. The chaotic mob around Klyuev poured out into open ground near Saddek, where it was met by shrapnel cross-fire and shied back into the woods.

At this point General Klyuev's cup of endurance ran over. '*To avoid useless bloodshed*',' the commander of the two centre corps ordered the white flag to be raised—when he had twenty batteries of guns, still intact after being dragged halfway round Prussia, against only eight German batteries, and when his tens of thousands of men dispersed through the forests were faced in this sector by no more than six German battalions.

'To avoid bloodshed'—golden words. Every human action can be disguised with a coating of gilt. 'To avoid bloodshed' sounds noble and humane; who could argue with that? One might perhaps raise the objection that the truly far-sighted way of avoiding bloodshed would have been not to become a general.

However, there turned out to be no white flags; they were not, after all, issued to units in the Table of Equipment along with the regimental colours.

The scene took place in a clearing near the edge of the forest.

Screen

≏ Everything on wheels—supply, artillery, medical—has filled the clearing in disorder: no lines, no ranks, no direction.

   In two-wheelers and ambulance waggons—wounded, nurses and doctors.

   Carts piled with random heaps of weapons, equipment, baggage, probably including goods looted from the Germans . . .

   Infantry soldiers standing, sitting, changing boots, sorting out their belongings . . .

   Mounted Cossacks in uneasy groups . . .

   Individual guns separated from their units . . .

≏ A doomed mob of soldiery.

≏ The general and his suite, on horseback and accompanied by an escort squadron of Cossacks.

≏ General Klyuev. Straining to maintain outward dignity. He must keep up appearances, must raise his eyebrows (otherwise they will cease to obey him); he calls out:

> *'Sergeant-major! Take off your shirt!*
> *Tie it to your lance and ride slowly towards*
> *the enemy.'*

≏ The sergeant-major does as he is told. He hands his lance to his neighbour, takes off his tunic and takes off his shirt . . . then

≏ dressed in his tunic again, his shirt tied to the top of his lance . . . will he ride off?

[519]

Murmur of voices.
  ⇒ The Cossacks are muttering amongst themselves.
  ⇒ The sergeant-major looks at them, freezes to the spot.
    Klyuev turns round to them.
Murmuring dies down.
    Klyuev waves his arm,
    and the sergeant-major rides away bearing the white flag.
Loud murmurs.
  ⇒ A voice from another group of Cossacks, standing
    slightly further away:
      'We'll stick it out!'
      'Cossacks don't surrender! Who ever
      heard of it?'
    And Artyukha Serga, a bulbous, cheerful rogue, his cap
    askew, shouts from behind another man's back in a
    loud, cheeky voice:
      'They can't order us to give in if we don't want to.'
  ⇒ Klyuev, with a supreme effort (but no confidence in his
    voice) shouts:
      'Who's in command over there?'
  ⇒ An officer rides up. He wears captain's epaulettes without
    stars; tall, supple, a born rider, with finely moulded
    features and black eyes. His attitude—arms akimbo,
    one hand on his sword—betrays his complete lack of
    respect. He says:
      'Captain Vedyornikov, 40th Don Cossack
      Regiment.'
    He looks at the general. Should he say anything more?
    He says no more.
More voices, exclamations.
  ⇒ Klyuev looks round
    at the infantry, at the crowded mass of humanity.
    Reactions differ. Some are exhausted and ready to
    surrender.
    But there is a soldier, one hand clasping the nape of his
    neck, his cap knocked off—what has become of the
    troops' discipline?—who shouts:
      'What's that? Surrender? We won't let 'em!'

Chorus of approval

> from the troops around him.
>
> Their commanding officer, a lieutenant-colonel,
>   marches up, cutting his way through the crowd,
>   avoiding waggons,
> towards the mounted general.

Change of angle:

≈ Klyuev viewed from below. The lieutenant-colonel looks
    like an assassin about to make an attempt on the Tsar.
    His arm makes a flourish—but he is merely saluting.
He says:

> *'Lieutenant-Colonel Sukhachevsky, Alexeyev Regi-
> ment. You have taken command of XV Corps as well.
> It is your duty to lead us out of this . . . General!'*

Looks up at him with piercing contempt.

≈ He has failed to address him as 'your excellency', but
    Klyuev lacks the courage to object. His head swims.
    He closes his eyes, opens them again.
Sukhachevsky is still there.
Of course he knows his duty! Does Sukhachevsky think
    he finds it easy? And he gave his reason: 'To avoid
    bloodshed' . . . But he is incapable of insisting on any-
    thing. Weakly, he says:

> *'Very well . . . anyone who wants to may try to escape
> as best he can.'*

He takes out a handkerchief to mop his brow. He looks
    at it:
A handkerchief! It's white and large, a general's hand-
    kerchief.

≈ Holding it in front of him, waving it as a talisman of
    safety—anything to avoid any further scenes with his
    mutinous subordinates—
he walks his horse towards the edge of the wood to sur-
    render, following the sergeant-major and his white shirt.

≈ His staff follows him in a cavalcade.
Everyone else who wants a quick end to the agony starts
    to follow him . . .

≈ Near the crowd of ambulance waggons a doctor on horse-
    back gives the order:

> *'Listen! The corps commander has declared*

a surrender. Everyone near my field hospital
must lay down his arms. Go on—throw them
away!'

⇐ Baffled, nursing his rifle in his arms, a little soldier says:
'Where shall we throw them?'
'Under the trees, over there!'

A wounded man, bandaged and wearing nothing but his
underwear, emerges from an ambulance and shouts:
'Never! Give me your rifle, chum!'

Takes it from the little soldier and stalks off in his underpants.

⇐ Others take their rifles and
throw them
on to the ground
under the trees.

A soldierly voice rings out:
'Hey, Cossacks!'

⇐ It is Captain Vedyornikov, turning his horse to face the
men.
'This is no place for us!'

⇐ His Don Cossacks will stand with him. They won't
surrender.

Rumble of approving voices.

Artyukha Serga grins. Do we notice something attractive
about him now that we can see him?

⇐ Vedyornikov gives the order:
'Detachment—mount! By the right,
in column of threes at the trot—march!'

A wave of his arm and they move off. Following him, the
Cossacks fall into line by threes.

⇐ Lieutenant-Colonel Sukhachevsky (he is short and cannot
see over the men's heads so easily) shouts:
'Men of the Alexeyev Regiment! Shall we
surrender—or break through?'

The troops shout back:
'Break through! Break through!'

Not all the men shout it, so Sukhachevsky adds in a loud
voice:
'No one is forced to go. Anyone who wants
to volunteer . . .'

he thrusts out his arm

'. . . *fall in over there in four ranks!*'

The men jostle their way forward and sort themselves out into four ranks.

Some of them would prefer to stay, some can hardly walk, but the urge to stick with their comrades is stronger.

← Some men from another regiment come up to him and ask:

'*We're from the Kremenchug Regiment—can we come too, your honour?*'

Grim but pleased, Sukhachevsky replies:

'*Good lads! Yes, come on and join us.*'

screen fades out

General Klyuev surrendered nearly thirty thousand men, most of them unwounded, although the majority were stragglers who had lost their units.

Lieutenant-Colonel Sukhachevsky successfully broke out with two thousand men.

Captain Vedyornikov's cavalry detachment charged the Germans and captured two guns.

53

General Blagoveshchensky had read about Kutuzov in Tolstoy's *War and Peace* and at sixty years of age, grey-haired, fat and stiff, he felt himself to be just like Kutuzov, except that he still had the sight of both eyes. Like Kutuzov he was wary, cautious and cunning. And like Tolstoy's Kutuzov he realised that one should never issue sharp, decisive instructions; that 'nothing but confusion could result from a battle started against one's will'; that 'military matters go their own way, which they are fated to follow whether or not it corresponds to what men propose'; that 'there is an inevitable course of events', and that the best general is the one who 'declines to participate in those events'. His long military service had convinced the general of the correctness of Tolstoy's views; there was nothing worse than sticking one's neck out by using one's initiative—people who did so always got into trouble.

For three days VI Corps had been happily resting in a quiet, deserted spot right on the Russian frontier. The Corps Commander had billeted himself, separately from his staff, in a little country cottage whose very lack of space he found comforting. The distant sounds of artillery, merged into an indistinct rumble, could only occasionally be heard, and there were grounds for hoping that the major events of the Prussian campaign would pass by without involving Blagoveshchensky's corps.

Resting, the corps did not know that it owed its well-being to the skilfully contrived dispatches written by its commander. Tolstoy neglected to point out that if a general refrains from taking decisions it is all the more important for him to be able to compose the right sort of dispatches; that without carefully drafted, decisive-sounding dispatches which can make inaction sound like hard fighting one cannot extricate one's troops from a bad thrashing; that in the absence of such reports a general cannot, as Tolstoy's Kutuzov could, 'direct his efforts not towards killing and destroying men but towards saving them and caring for them'.

Thus in his report for August 16th Blagoveshchensky honestly described how General Richter's division, at last brought up to strength by the belated arrival of a regiment, had moved off to seize the town of Ortelsburg on the following day (abandoned in panic only two days ago to a non-existent enemy), where there were said to be strong enemy forces in divisional strength (in fact, two companies and two squadrons), while General Komarov's division was holding its ground to the left 'in echelon' (an important, modish expression in Russian strategic terminology, without which no military document looked convincing). The many moves of General Tolpygo's division, too, were a great embellishment to the report, and Blagoveshchensky felt quite justified in expecting to survive August 17th without excitement.

On the morning of the 17th Richter's division, which had so far not once been in action, deployed itself outside the half-empty town of Ortelsburg according to all the rules of the art of war. The artillery preparation having already opened up, it was advancing to the assault and the town was bound to be taken—when suddenly at eleven o'clock, after a five-hour delay, the morning's directive from Army Group Headquarters descended upon them. It stated that Blagoveshchensky's corps must go to the rescue of the disintegrating centre corps, and should therefore not advance on Ortelsburg, which was almost due north, but on Willenburg, almost due west. It concluded: 'The Commander-in-Chief insists that this task be energetically carried out and that communications be established with General Samsonov as rapidly as possible.'

This was just what General Blagoveshchensky had been afraid of. In its final phase, the edge of the tornado had caught him up— but it was still not too late for this final phase to bring about his destruction.

The operational task, however, allowed for a certain freedom of interpretation. Relatively, it was as if the forces had been advancing from Ryazan north-north-west towards Moscow and had then been ordered to go west to Kaluga. What solution could be neater and more convenient than to make them go back to Ryazan and then set off again for Kaluga? Blagoveshchensky ordered Richter's division, which had already forced a successful entry into Ortelsburg, to leave the captured town and, instead of wheeling leftwards to Willenburg, to retire nine miles and only then, without losing momentum, to make for Willenburg.

Even before executing these manoeuvres Blagoveshchensky had sent a briskly worded message to Army Group Headquarters, which read:

'To find and contact General Samsonov have dispatched *patrol* to Neidenburg; to establish communications with XXIII Corps have dispatched *patrol* to Chorzele. No information *so far*. Am engaging enemy at Ortelsburg. Intend to withdraw headquarters via route — to —' (after all, the new situation required the Corps Headquarters to pull back further still) '... in order to conduct operations towards Willenburg.'

It was natural, also, to employ Tolpygo's cavalry division for the advance—even though this meant their simply going back to the same place from which they had returned on their own initiative that morning. General Tolpygo, however, in a lengthy report which matched Blagoveshchensky's in skill, explained in detail that his exhausted division had just unsaddled its horses and could not move off to repeat the difficult task required of it. Blagoveshchensky sent him a second written order, which Tolpygo also answered in writing. Only at the third time of asking, which was accompanied by threats, was the order obeyed and the division made to saddle up.

Now that the more complex part of the manoeuvre had been satisfactorily accomplished, it was thought proper to send someone straight to Willenburg. A suitable unit for this purpose was the composite detachment commanded by General Nechvolodov. Yesterday, during the calm of a rest-day, by the most reprehensible 'creeping' tactics, of which Blagoveshchensky thoroughly disapproved, Nechvolodov had already carried out a raid of this kind, but now he was told to wait for instructions. It was men like Nechvolodov whom Blagoveshchensky found intolerable as subordinates, and he punished them by contriving to make their lives as difficult as possible. What was worse, Nechvolodov was a *writer* and had pretensions to holding opinions on all sorts of matters apart from the service. He was therefore the obvious choice for this dangerous advance-guard mission.

After midday on August 17th he was dispatched with the Ladoga Regiment and two batteries of guns. He was ordered to move *with speed*; the main body of the division would leave later.

Nechvolodov's chief attribute, however, was not speed but dogged persistence. He had observed more than once in his lifetime that with persistence one reaches one's goal in no less time than by hasty, unsteady advance along a wavering course.

Unconcerned with personal advancement, his goal was a selfless one. Still a bachelor at fifty, having without undue strain brought up one adopted son, he had the leisure, the private means and the personal freedom to devote himself to other, higher interests. Since entering a military high school in an access of boyish enthusiasm and first taking the oath of allegiance as a cadet in the year that Alexander II, the Tsar Liberator, was basely assassinated, his aim had been to serve the throne and Russia. And for forty years his devotion to that aim had not weakened, had remained undivided and unshaken; only the rhythm of his life of service had changed. As a youth, striving impetuously to move mountains with his own two hands, he had finished the routine course of an officer's training well ahead of the scheduled time and, having barely graduated from the Military Academy, had written a paper proposing the reform of the General Staff and the Ministry of War. That, however, marked the end of his remarkable progress in his military career. For the first of many times he came up against the united ill-will of the senior officers, the generals and the Guards. Nechvolodov expected all of them to be ready to make certain sacrifices necessary to strengthen the Russian army and—as a consequence—the Russian monarchy. But it transpired that even in these circles, although it was customary to *talk* about the monarchy in resounding tones, to be genuinely devoted to it was 'not done'. The higher they were in rank, the more thoroughly they were imbued with an ardour that was not patriotic but self-seeking; they were not serving the Tsar because he was the Lord's anointed, but because he was the source of patronage. And before Nechvolodov had summed them up, they had summed *him* up—as an alien and dangerous presence for the very reason that he was not seeking personal advantage and that his actions might therefore prove ruinous to his fellow-officers. From then on Nechvolodov was kept firmly within the slow, tedious system of promotion by seniority and of precise conformity to orders without scope for individual initiative. Prevented thus from serving the throne by dash or speed, there remained only persistence, and, on occasion, bravery.

In searching for an outlet for his surplus mental energy, Nechvolodov had occupied himself with his unsuccessful text-book of Russian history, written for simple peasants. He perceived Russian history as nothing less than service to a cause, a national tradition, within which he also found the sole justification for his present service as an army officer. For himself he sought in history the vitalising, refreshing effects of contemplating another age, an age in which Russians had had a different attitude to their monarchs; as for his readers, he sought to reconvert them to the old ways and thereby lend even greater scope and durability to the achievement of his unchanging aim. But although this history-book was accorded the Tsar's approval and recommended for inclusion in army and public libraries, the author found no evidence either that it was widely and eagerly read or that it was changing people's attitudes. Nechvolodov's devoted monarchism, which had alarmed the generals because it was so extreme, now aroused the derision of people in 'educated' circles who were convinced that Russian history could only evoke laughter or repugnance; they even questioned whether there *was* such a thing as Russian history. What they found most reactionary of all was Nechvolodov's conviction that for Russia the monarchy was not a set of shackles, but a clamp: that it did not fetter the country, but preserved it from disaster by binding it together. Because of his loyalty to the dynasty he was powerless to argue with his critics; whatever might happen in Russia, he would never presume to condemn either the Tsar or those around him; he could only defend them and point out the good in what educated society found bad.

Obliged to be silent and forbearing, he was once more thrown back on his rock-like devotion to the monarchy. It was because of this, for instance, that he had a special affection for the Ladoga Regiment: it had proved to be loyal to the throne during the Moscow uprising of 1905. Although Nechvolodov himself had never served in it and almost the whole complement of the regiment had changed since then, he still knew a few of the long-service men and singled them out for his regard.

Silence and forbearance had also been Nechvolodov's lot during the lull which VI Corps had been experiencing during the last few days. The resolution with which he had conducted his rearguard actions had inspired no one else. He found inactivity painful at a time when the all-important battle was being fought fifteen miles away and when, by all accounts, it was going none too well. He rode to a hilltop a mile or so away, listened to the sound of the guns and gazed helplessly through his binoculars.

After wasting two whole days, Corps Headquarters had ordered Nechvolodov to move 'with speed'. He did not move with speed but simply set off at once without fuss, having made all the necessary preparations two days ago. He would not make up for the negligence of the staff by over-exerting his troops, and in any case it would take the main body some time to catch up. Only his cavalry—consisting of no more than a half-troop commanded by Cornet Zhukovsky—did he send on ahead.

During the two days in which he was not allowed to go into action, Nechvolodov was sick, listless and morose; but no sooner did he get the order to move than his health recovered in a matter of minutes. He smiled at his men of the Ladoga Regiment—the only men in the corps permitted to fight—and shouted encouragingly to the gunners that they were off to help their comrades out of a tight corner.

The morale-raising awareness that they were going on a rescue operation gave one regiment the strength of two and made two batteries worth four. Unfortunately they were given no spare ammunition; but there was compensation in being spared the irritating attentions of the higher-ups. Nechvolodov had a free hand, and his head was clear.

Mounted as always on his powerful stallion, his stirrup-leathers fully extended, the lanky, taciturn Nechvolodov rode ahead of his composite detachment, now the advance-guard, while a horse's length behind him and to one side rode his keen, dumpling-fed aide-de-camp from the Ukraine, Roshko, his round face glowing like a burnished copper kettle.

As they neared Willenburg their route passed through a dense, well-kept pine-forest. All the dead branches had been lopped from the sleek, copper-coloured trunks, and the tops of the sixty-foot trees were gently waving in the clear, summery sky. Twilight set in early in the forest.

In the last few miles of their journey the sound of rifles and machine-guns could be heard more and more clearly, whereas gunfire was rarer. What could this mean? It meant that the Russians were attempting to break through and were firing at the Germans. Willenburg was obviously the outer pivotal point of the encircling movement, and the Russian troops might be—indeed were bound to be—located just beyond it. Nechvolodov's stallion quickened its pace, until it was moving too fast for the infantry.

The woods concealed the approach of Nechvolodov's detachment almost as far as Willenburg itself. In any case there were no Germans to be seen; they were so confident that they had dispersed their forces, leaving this side of the town unprotected. At the edge of the forest Nechvolodov ordered the detachment to turn aside and rest, while he rode out through the last of the trees. There stood several troopers, holding the horses of the reconnaissance detachment which the cornet had led forward on foot. The yellow sun, as it set behind the town, blinded them with its light. Even so they could see in front of them a low-lying meadow leading down to a small river and traversed by a solitary raised road—clear and running straight ahead to an undamaged bridge; no doubt the Germans had thought it would be a shame to blow up a good German bridge. There was no road-block on this side of the bridge either—the Germans must take them for absolute fools! In fact, on the far side of the bridge, among the first few houses of the town, the cornet and his scouts were already in position and firing. Nechvolodov decided that he had better send them a squad with two machine-guns.

Beyond that the houses were denser, then came the railway station and the town proper. They could not outflank the town to the right—there was a swampy meadow. Nor could they go round it to the left—the route was cut by a second small river, which flowed into the other. If there were no artillery opposition the whole regiment, moving in line of march, could be across the bridge in an hour, and then deploy to attack the town.

Nechvolodov ordered both batteries to take up positions at the edge of the forest, to right and left of the road.

There was firing on the near outskirts of Willenburg. There was also firing on the far side. No doubt about it, the Germans in this town were in a shaky position. Their situation was even worse than if they had been caught in a pincer-movement: they had posted their 'guns' facing westwards, unaware that the 'beaters' were creeping up on them from the east.

The general's heart beat faster and his calm, swarthy face lit up with expectant joy at the prospect of the brief, easy victory already in his grasp. He called up the battalion and battery commanders and discussed with them how to cross the bridge and which tasks should be allotted to the various units once they were over it.

That moment a dismounted dragoon came running up with a message from Cornet Zhukovsky reporting that several men had joined him on *this* side of the town after breaking through from the far side: they included two men of his own regiment, the 6th Dragoons, who had been cut off, four infantrymen from the Poltava Regiment and one Cossack from the Army Commander's escort. The latter had assured him that General Samsonov had been caught in some cross-fire and killed.

Without paying much attention to the news about Samsonov, which might be mere rumour, Nechvolodov seized on what was most important in the message—namely that individual soldiers were already passing through Willenburg as though through a sieve. He only had to reach out for it and the place was his! The moment had come to smash into it like a battering-ram going through a barrel riddled with holes. And the sooner the better, because the Russian troops on the far side must be in a state of perilous disorder if the Poltava Regiment was there (its rightful place being on the *furthest* flank of the army) and if men from it were breaking out in this direction.

He sent word to the Ladoga Regiment that our troops were already breaking through and had arrived. Then he sat down to write a message to Divisional Headquarters, saying that he was starting the assault on the town, requesting support from the commander of the division's leading column, urgent delivery of more ammunition and the addition to his force of at least another battery.

The sun had set, but it would be a long time before it was dark. Two houses could be seen burning at the spot where the cornet and his dragoons were in action. He ordered the first battalion to follow him across the bridge, the second to come behind them after an agreed interval.

The first battalion got across without being shelled, but it had been spotted, and the second battalion was fired on by a small battery from a clump of trees on the far side of the left-hand river. Another German battery opened up. Meanwhile the second battalion ran across the bridge by companies.

The evening was turning greyer. The fires in the town stood out more brightly.

Nechvolodov reached Cornet Zhukovsky and saw the Poltava men and the Cossack from Samsonov's escort, who looked a dirty, shifty type. The first battalion took up positions opposite the railway station, from which the Germans were firing with some determination, and waited for the rest of the Ladoga Regiment. As it was now dark, the third and fourth battalions would be able to cross the bridge more easily.

The twilight thickened into night. The artillery fell silent. The burning buildings shone a lurid red. There was no lighting in the town other than a few weak flickers, as the electricity supply had been damaged. High above, the moon, waxing towards the second quarter, was beginning to cast a stronger light—just enough, in fact, to enable the Russians to see each other as they attacked, but not enough to allow the Germans to see them at a distance. Everything was combining in their favour. In an hour the battalions would be in position, would make ready—and at a crouching run the first two would assault the town without firing, the third would make a flanking attack on the sawmill while the fourth stayed in reserve. Meanwhile Nechvolodov, Roshko and several other officers, bending double as they ran, reconnoitred leftwards to the river and then up the slope of a firm, dry stretch of pasture to the right. Nechvolodov showed them where to take the battalions.

The firing on the far side of the town had still not died down, but it was getting sparser. A mile or two divided them from the other Russians; here they felt strong and united, while over there the others were dispersed, surrounded, abandoned and about to perish.

Moving freely now at his full, magnificent height, Nechvolodov strode back and forth in the milky, moonlit night, waving his long arms as he gave directions.

He was certain of success. He had adequate forces for a night attack on a town, the main body was coming to back him up and by morning the German ring would be broken. They only had to hold the breach for a day and the encirclement would collapse, allowing the Russians to pour out through this gap.

Nechvolodov was shaken by a sudden surge of expectant joy; he could not remember feeling such elation in all the weeks of war, in all the years of peace.

There were fifteen minutes to go before the attack was due to start.

He turned back to the road.

At that moment a messenger from Divisional Headquarters arrived looking for him. Taking from his greatcoat pocket his reliable, oblong German torch, Nechvolodov shone it on the piece of paper, screening himself from the town behind a telegraph-pole.

He read:

'To Advance-Guard Commander,
General Nechvolodov:

In view of absence of significant enemy forces the main body has been recalled. Do not engage enemy at Willenburg. We shall not give support, since we are expecting orders to send the whole corps back into Russian territory. Await further orders.

Colonel Serbinovich.'

Roshko gave a shriek; his general groaned as though he had been stabbed between the ribs, staggered back and sank his teeth into the dry, splintery wood of the telegraph-pole.

54

On the ridge where they had buried the commanding officer of the
Dorogobuzh Regiment, a moment occurred when they almost
changed their plans. A burst of firing came from the direction of
the hitherto dormant Neidenburg, and it was obvious from the
sound that someone was firing into the town from outside it—that
Russian artillery, in fact, was bombarding Neidenburg and the
Germans were not replying. Vorotyntsev was already prepared to
turn round and head in that direction when the gunfire stopped,
followed only by a desultory exchange of rifle-shots.

Although his plan was fully worked out, throughout the rest of
the day, every quarter of an hour or so, Vorotyntsev constantly had
to listen, look, study the map, check the terrain, watch his men for
signs of fatigue, take decisions and give orders. Preoccupied with
military matters, one might have thought there could be no room in
his mind for anything else.

Yet there seemed to be two parallel corridors in his head, divided as though by a glass partition, each visible though inaudible
to the other. Down one corridor practical thoughts streamed un-
interruptedly—about how this party of fourteen and one wounded
man would break out; down the other, unprompted, unhurried,
disconnected, there drifted a series of quite different, independent
musings. They were largely about the past, unexpected memories,
mistakes he had made in his time. The first kind was straining towards life; the other looked ahead to the possibility of death.

He could not get rid of the thought of those Estlanders. They
had not left their posts, had not run away or demanded their right
to escape. (Or so it had been for the first day; had the pressures on

them increased later?) It had happened such a short while ago, and now everything had irrevocably changed: those who preferred capture were probably prisoners of war by now, the ones who wanted to try and break out would have had to do so on their own initiative, while the men who were fated to be killed would already be dead. Thinking about it did no good. Vorotyntsev, after all, had not deceived them in any way; yet it was with reproach on their faces that they dragged themselves along the second, silent corridor —starting with the black-bearded peasant with the scarred cheek who had been the right marker. No, he had not deceived them— but would he ever be rid of that reproach? He had not deceived them: he had explained everything to them frankly, and for twenty hours they had held a vital sector of the line; if others had only done their job properly it might have been of help to the entire army, but the others had failed.

Therefore he *had* deceived them.

What was the right thing to do? Surely it was right to push oneself, to exert one's faculties to the utmost, to drive oneself to exhaustion? If not, there was no point in being a regular officer—no point in living, even. Yet whenever one used one's brain or did anything constructive, it was inevitably ruined by some stupid, blundering fool in the high command.

When everything was crumbling around one, which was right— to act, or not to act?

What went on in the second corridor did not interfere with the first in any way; moving at their own pace, the thoughts in it were no disturbance to the others. Their pace allowed room, too, for memories and regrets. Alina; unexpectedly, incoherently, he thought of Alina.

He suddenly remembered how in Petersburg she had cleaned every speck of dust from his desk without moving a single pencil; how she had kept silent for hours, moving past his room without a sound when there was a special need for quiet; how, though she loved having company at home and visiting friends, she had refused invitations and had never begged to go out, so as not to let him see how disappointed she was. Suddenly he remembered everything good about her: although she made demands on him she was above all capable of great sacrifice.

How could he have been glad to leave her? How could he have felt relief at not having to see her? It had all been some strange misunderstanding; somehow he had grown stale. When he came home from this war everything would fall into place again and their life would be as full of happiness as it had been after his return from the Japanese War.

The thoughts faded away; no doubt they had been summoned by the imminent possibility of death. But I . . .

'But I'm quite safe, you see, I'm bound to come out of this alive,' Vorotyntsev said with a smile at Kharitonov as they lay side by side on their stomachs, sharing a greatcoat.

'Really? Why?' the freckled boy said delightedly, taking him quite seriously.

'An old Chinaman told my fortune in Manchuria.'

'What did he say?' Yaroslav enquired eagerly, gazing at the colonel with hero-worship.

'He predicted that I wouldn't be killed in the Japanese War and that I wouldn't be killed in any other war in which I might fight, but that I should die a soldier's death all the same at the age of sixty-nine. As a professional officer, could one ask for a better prophecy?'

'Magnificent! But wait—when will that be?'

'One hardly even dares to say it aloud: it will be in 1945.'

He was right; mentioning a date so far ahead was uncanny, like something from H. G. Wells.

They were lying in a dense thicket of green-tipped young firs, the kind of place where hares like to play in the sunshine in winter. Vorotyntsev had chosen the spot because somebody could have passed five paces away without noticing them there. It was only a kilometre and a half to the main road; they could already hear the unmistakable hum of cars and motor-cycles moving in both directions. If the Germans had been here in strength they would have sent patrols into the wood to comb it. Obviously they lacked the forces to do so, but even so the party dared not move out prematurely: ahead of them there was only a narrow promontory of woodland in which other groups of Russians might have collected, and the Germans could easily send out search-parties in daylight from the nearby village of Moldtken. Placing the bulk of his party in the middle of the thicket, Vorotyntsev had posted three pairs of men to lie further forward as look-outs. They had arrived here in the heat of the afternoon; the place was heavy with scorching-hot, stagnant air which drained their strength and made them thirsty—and not every man had a water-bottle. But no one wanted to pull back to a cooler spot now. It had been hard enough getting here; they had had to come into the open to cross a railway-track which the Germans could easily have kept under fire from hand-trolleys. However, they had apparently been too short of troops to do this; something had been afoot all day around Neidenburg; there had been frequent bursts of firing, although they came no nearer. Today was the right day to break out; tomorrow would be too late.

The catastrophe that had overtaken the army obsessed Vorotyntsev. He was much more concerned about the outcome of the fighting around Neidenburg, about what was going on at 1 Corps and where Krymov was than about the break-out of his detachment. However, during all the hours that he had been holding the map open in front of him he had forced himself not to look at the wider scene of battle but to imprint on his memory while it was still daylight every twist and turn of the nearby forest's edge, so that wherever they might emerge in the dark he would have a precise idea of distances; otherwise he would be bound to miss some feature, and then, if he became unsure of himself, he would have to study the map under his greatcoat by the light of matches.

Vorotyntsev did not explain his carefully devised plan to a gathering of the officers, as was normal, but in view of the semi-guerilla nature of their operation he gave out the details to the men who would have to carry it out: Blagodaryov, Kachkin, the two best shots among the Dorogobuzh men, whom they had themselves selected—a tough, slow-moving hunter from Vyatka and a young man called Yevgrafov from Ryazan, who had been a salesman in a draper's shop—and Lieutenant Kharitonov, who turned out to have been one of the best marksmen at his cadet school and who asked to be given the most distant targets to cover. Vorotyntsev made these five stretch out around him on the sandy ground under the low branches of the pine-saplings, six heads huddled together, six pairs of legs fanning out in a circle. The spot was chosen so that Lieutenant Ofrosimov, too, was within earshot on his stretcher. He had a fever, his wound was starting to give him pain, and there was nothing they could do for him; but there was one thing he alone could say to ease their lot—and Vorotyntsev had put him in a position to say it.

They were to start moving after dark, when the moon was up.

They would begin by running at a crouch, and at the first sign of danger they would have to restrict their movement to crawling. The leading group would be made up of Blagodaryov and Kachkin, armed with knives. They were to edge forward very slowly without breaking a single twig. They had half the night for this first phase; the main party would cross the road nearer dawn, because during the early part of the night the Germans would be more alert. Having covered two hundred yards in safety, one of them was to come back and call the second group, the marksmen, forward. When the latter had also covered two hundred yards, they were to send back a runner to fetch the third group, consisting of the remainder and the stretcher. If the first group met a German sentry or a sniper they were to dispatch him silently with their knives.

'Understood?' he queried, staring closely at the broad-lipped Blagodaryov and the close-cropped, bullet-headed Kachkin.

'Oh Lord,' Arsenii sighed like a blacksmith's bellows. 'They'll never let us get home!'

Kachkin gave a twitch of his stubbly black cheek.

'I can kill enough cattle for half a village.'

There were to be four marksmen, including Vorotyntsev. Lieutenant Kharitonov was to take Blagodaryov's well-tested rifle. The ammunition amounted to three pouchfuls. They were unlikely to have to open fire in the wood, it would probably be from the edge of the forest towards the road; then, from the far side of the road, they would give covering fire to the others as they crossed over.

He explained what type of fire to give to different targets—when to fire in volleys and when in their own time. At that moment he heard Lieutenant Ofrosimov say the words which showed that he knew his duty. Unshaven, dirty, limp, eyes swivelling, he raised himself on one elbow from his detested stretcher.

'May I say something, Colonel? Please . . . don't think you have to take me. It might not be . . . convenient. Let's unwind the colours now, and I'll hand them over to someone else. Just put me in a comfortable position and give me a few more rounds of ammunition.'

'Agreed,' Vorotyntsev responded at once. 'Thank you, Lieutenant. Yevgrafov, take the standard.'

The quick-witted Yevgrafov, who like Kachkin recovered from a shock quicker than any of the other Dorogobuzh men, jumped into action.

'Very good, your honour! Will you wind it round me?'

'Lie down.'

It had worked out so that Lenartovich had been the only officer not summoned to the council of war. It was not quite clear whether he was offended or not, but he was sitting close to Ofrosimov and listening. He now asked:

'Colonel, please explain to me: supposing it proves to be quite impossible to cross the road?'

'What do you mean—impossible?' Vorotyntsev looked at him sternly and sadly; the boy had good potential, but there was no time to make an officer out of him now. 'They won't be standing shoulder to shoulder, you know. You can imagine a fox running across the road, can't you? Well, that's how we shall cross it. Have you thought of what it must be like for the *Germans* along the road? They are strung out in a very thin line, so it's more frightening for them. They don't know when they may be attacked from the forest.'

'There's no such thing as "impossible" in the army,' said Ofrosimov didactically. 'Everything's possible in the army.'

Lenartovich did not reply; he was thinking. That was the worst about these people: they had grown used to thinking that they could do anything. Another reason for disbanding all the armies in the world.

The council was over, the colours had been handed over, the ammunition issued. Vorotyntsev insisted on Lenartovich taking his little hatchet.

'You're empty-handed, what will you use for a weapon?' Seeing the young man hesitate because he thought the others might laugh at him, he went on: 'Go on, take it. Man's first weapon was the axe!'

The colonel spent a long time instructing the men with the knives and the marksmen what their route would look like and how many paces they would have to take. Then he made them reproduce the instructions by drawing diagrams in the sand to show that they had understood.

After that the only thing to do was to lie down, head on arms, face down in the sand, waiting anxiously. Everyone longed for the night to come quickly: they could not relax for a moment during these next few hours. No one talked of the war or the fighting. The older men discussed cattle-feed and the difference between the black-and-white cows in Prussia and their own breeds at home. Then conversation died away and stopped altogether.

As the sun began to go down, its heat lessened, although it still penetrated the short growth in their thicket, and the purple-red glow reached them in fitful gleams through the trunks of the mature forest around them. Clouds spread outwards from the setting sun, pink at first, then darkening to mauve-blue; did this herald a change in the two weeks of unremitting fine weather which had witnessed both the arrival and the destruction of the Russian army?

Never before had Sasha faced so many grim questions. Would he be alive by the morning? Was this his last sunset? Where would he find himself tomorrow? Lying face down in the sand, arms outstretched? Under escort as a prisoner of war? Or would he be writing ecstatically on a scrap of paper: 'Dearest ones! I got out! I'm alive!' And: 'Veronika, kiss Yolya for me!' Here, these thoughts did not seem like incoherent babblings or bad taste; they were deeply felt.

He turned over the hatchet in his hand. It was small and light and honed to such a sharpness that it was easy to imagine it crunching into a skull. But could he strike a man down with it? Sasha had never known himself show the kind of determination needed for that. No, it was disgusting—it was murder. In principle, he reasoned, an axe was no worse than a bullet. Yesterday the enemy had done their best to kill him and had almost succeeded; and if tonight there proved to be no alternative, and Kachkin and Blagodaryov had to knife some Germans in silence or that calf-faced young lieutenant had to shoot a few of them, there was no point in regretting it. But to do it himself, with an axe, seeing the man's very face—no, he couldn't bring himself to it.

Events were taking their inexorable course. The Germans were moving noisily up and down the road. Among them were social democrats, forcibly enlisted to take part in the slaughter. In different circumstances Sasha would have been glad to shake them by the hand, to greet them at a political meeting. Yet today, as a child depends on his father, he depended for his survival on this colonel, this servant of the Crown.

Twilight drew in. The whole forest was dark, though the moon, slightly fuller than half, shone more brightly in their plantation of young trees. Across the western sky dark bands of cloud were stretching towards the moon, threatening to blot it out.

Vorotyntsev gave the order: 'Move off, without making the tree-tops sway as you go.

They passed into the forest. Here it was much darker, although the moon occasionally shone through. The men with knives set off. The riflemen assembled. Suddenly a terrifying light flared, brilliant, phosphorescent. Alarmed, they glanced back at the thicket: it was a searchlight positioned somewhere close to the main road, near the village. It was not shining in their direction but to right and left in front of them, along the road; from the narrow source of light only a vague, diffused gleam penetrated to where they were. So much for their chances of getting across! It just showed how little one could rely on being able to calculate all the factors in war.

'That's done it!' Sasha gasped. 'If only it wasn't shining just where we want to cross, but further on.'

'It's a good thing it's close,' Vorotyntsev reasoned. 'What you should say is, let's hope there isn't another searchlight as well. As it's close, we can shoot it out of action; it's well within range.'

The marksmen set off.

Clouds covered the moon. The beam did not move, its diffused light revealing only black silhouettes. Now everything that happened was expressed in sound. A few bursts of machine-gun fire could be heard along the road, either intended as a threat or because some Russians had already emerged from the forest. Then a rustling approached. Every sound might be an enemy, but it was one of the sharpshooters returning—the next stage of the journey was clear. They carried Ofrosimov with lowered arms, stepping slowly and carefully as though not to waken a sleeper. This meant carrying the stretcher for a longer time, which was a strain on the arms. The forest floor had looked smooth, but it was full of obstacles such as piles of fir-cones (the Germans tidied them up as though they were indoors), ditches or pot-holes. After two halts, they waited a long time for the call from the advance-party, beginning to think the attempt might fail. It turned out that the men in front had dropped their compass and had been looking for it in the dark. Instead of groaning, Ofrosimov swore in a vicious whisper, and Sasha told him to stop it. This was very careless of him, as just then voices were heard close by. They were probably not from their group— but who were they? It was impossible to tell which language they were speaking. The men froze and drew their bayonets. The sound faded. Then came a faint noise as though a dog were growling not far away, but it was not a dog and it, too, faded. They had come about half a mile like this, if not more; whenever the noise of traffic or a machine-gun burst was heard from the road, it sounded right beside them. And it was growing brighter, because they were closer to the light diffused sideways from the searchlight beam; fortunately it remained motionless. About three hours passed like this. Nothing had changed in their favour, and it might be that they had walked into a trap from which there was no escape either forwards or backwards. The Germans only had to swing the searchlight and send a skirmishing party to flush them out. Sasha was not exactly frightened; what he felt was more like hopelessness, despair. Clutching the axe-handle, he realised that if he had to he would bring it crashing down on a skull.

Suddenly, from nearby on the right, the marksmen opened fire—four rifles firing rapid, as though competing with other each in speed—and after a dozen or so shots the searchlight went out. As it did so the entire world was extinguished, plunged into total darkness. The four men stopped firing.

What of the main party? Where were they to go now?

A machine-gun, followed by another, opened fire along the road, but they were shooting wildly, at random.

Then, snorting and crashing through the wood like a wild boar, something loomed up ahead of them—what, who was it? It was Kachkin, who said:

'Where's the lieutenant? Forget the stretcher—I'll carry him across my shoulder. Come on, you lazy sods—let's go!'

55

On the morning of the 17th a sudden burst of gunfire came down on Neidenburg from the south. In the hospital, the Russian wounded perked up and with arms akimbo looked out of the windows from their beds, while the nurses ran outside, delighted at the puffs of Russian shrapnel and the fountains of earth thrown up by Russian high-explosive, as if their own men might not be killed by them too. The German doctor and his assistants smiled, convinced that their side would not withdraw. The firing went on around them all day, but there was no fighting, and although the town contained practically no German troops, the Russians did not enter it. Not until that evening did the German sentries abandon the hospital, leaving their wounded in the wards. The new Russian occupying forces seemed in no hurry to put in an appearance, to enquire about the hospital or to evacuate their wounded to the rear.

In the dark, Russian horsed transport, foot soldiers and horsemen moved about the town. Several buildings, set on fire during the day, became the sole and menacing illumination in Neidenburg that night. In Tanya's ward one window opened on to a view of the town and the fires; she threw open the shutters and stood gazing out, occasionally replying to questions from the wounded men. Against the ruddy background of the fire, the architectural peculiarities of the German houses stood out—statues mounted above façades, patterned and crenellated ornamental brickwork, wrought-iron balconies.

Tanya was in a state of mind in which the shelling, the fires, the departure and arrival of troops did not frighten her but rather gave her a feeling of relief. In the stuffy wards, amidst the glare of fires and explosions, she felt completely cool; she did not know ordinary fear. On the contrary, she actually felt better and the pain in her heart was eased. Although she realised that something terrible was happening, she saw it all through a veil of private suffering; but her heart felt lightened, and from this she drew great strength, so that she hardly needed to sleep or eat and gave herself up entirely to her duties.

No reliable information was available at the hospital, but there was an abundance of rumours. Even while the Germans had been there more Russian wounded had come in from various units and had reported that all the senior commanders had been killed, the Russian forces were in complete disarray, and the Germans were firing at them from all sides, cutting them to pieces and taking them prisoner. One of the new admissions to Tanya's ward was a Cossack sergeant, a man with a curled forelock, from General Martos' escort (he was in the corner bed previously occupied by the lieutenant from Rostov, who had left on foot in the last hour before the Germans arrived). Though not severely wounded, he was in a highly excitable state and disturbed everyone with his loud, confused stories about the destruction of xv Corps and the death of their general. Unstoppable, he described his adventures with great gusto, as though talking about the disastrous situation and the ruinous casualties gave him pleasure. News of the sergeant spread all over the hospital, and even the doctors came to listen to him.

As night fell waggons were expected to arrive to evacuate the patients. A visit from a senior officer was also expected. Sure enough, at midnight, by the murky red glare of a distant fire, a car drove into the square in front of the hospital and out of it stepped the Medical Director, a general and his aide-de-camp. Two minutes later they were in Tanya's ward and went to see the Cossack sergeant. Tanya brought a kerosene lamp from her table over to them in the corner.

The shock-headed, dishevelled sergeant was seething with expectation as the general approached his bed, as though he had been waiting for him and his whole story was being kept for the general's ears alone. His face very pale and sleek, with well-groomed moustaches and a disdainful Petersburg air, the general likewise seemed to have been looking for the sergeant. His questions were by no means hurried or off-hand; he sat down on the man's unwholesome bed, gave him an imposing stare and ordered his aide-de-camp to note everything down, beginning with his name, rank and unit.

With an unfaltering hand Tanya held the tall yellow-and-green lamp above the aide-de-camp's notebook, between the heads of the sergeant and the general, and watched them with a searching, penetrating gaze.

For what must have been at least the twenty-fifth time the sergeant repeated his story, which everyone else knew by now, embellishing it with fresh details, some of which did not actually contradict his previous versions. He described how the whole corps, though badly shattered, had remained in its positions when General Samsonov had sent General Martos to occupy Neidenburg, how they had ridden to Neidenburg only yesterday morning, but had learned from some dragoons that it was already in German hands. On their way to select a position they had come under artillery fire from a range of six hundred yards; the Corps Chief of Staff and a divisional commander, General Torklus, had been killed, as had numerous Cossacks. The remaining Cossacks had loyally stayed with Martos and retreated with him into a wood. Martos' aide-de-camp had disappeared with his knapsack containing his food, cigarettes, compass and maps, so that the general was left hungry and disoriented. Their horses having been shot from under them, they had wandered about in the wood on foot, but whichever way they went they found Germans already there. Martos had ordered this same sergeant to break through to the town and report the disaster; he had embraced him in farewell, and then and there, in front of the man's eyes, had shot himself, unable to bear the shame.

With a head whose white, tightly stretched skin made it look like a huge chicken's egg, the general nodded and asked:

'In fact, you confirm that General Martos shot himself in your presence?'

'That's God's truth, your excellency!'

The aide-de-camp made a note.

Stern and grieved, but with no sign of surprise, the Guards general nodded: he had expected, indeed had foreseen this. He was, however, surprised and irritated by the look on the nurse's face, with its disagreeably suspicious, burning, piercing look directed past the lamp and fastened on him. Because of it he twitched his neck several times and tried not to look at her again.

It was as if Tanya had woken up. For the first time since her fiancé had jilted her she had forgotten about herself and given her complete attention to an incident in the external world, in this case taking place two feet away from the clean, bright, soot-free glass chimney of the lamp which she was holding. She had no evidence, she could not prove it, but with her remorseless gaze she had uncovered the reason why the sergeant felt this urgent, passionate compulsion to tell his story to everyone at such length: it was because he had to conceal the sinful fact that in reality he had deserted General Martos when he was in danger and had run away. And this smooth, pompous general was all too willing to believe the man; he had not tried to catch him out or confuse him because for some reason he *wanted* to hear this version of events and it suited his book.

Like the Maiden of Light she had carried the lamp over to that dark triangle of three heads and fearlessly cast her light upon it.

Until then she had regarded war as an inevitable, ungovernable, natural disaster in which soldiers are doomed to be wounded and to die and whose malign force no human power can control. Even while watching and alleviating the sufferings of the wounded around her, it had not once occurred to her to regard her own heartache as of less account than their wounds: all their sufferings were the result of an elemental force which it was useless to blame, whereas hers sprang from injustice, meanness and betrayal.

Now, however, from that dark triangle of men, questioning, answering and taking notes, Tanya felt the undeniable breath of an evil will upon her—and felt it so strongly that she knew that on that evil will depended the fate of their hospital, of all the men already wounded and especially of all those who might be wounded tomorrow. For the first time the pain of others burst in, pushed aside and trampled her own sense of humiliation and betrayal, which suddenly no longer seemed the worst form of suffering in the world—seemed, indeed, quite a minor affliction.

With an obstinate, challenging look she kept the light of truth burning, aware of how it hurt the general's eyes and how unpleasant he found it.

Pushing his boldness to the limit, the garrulous sergeant said persuasively to the general:

'Your excellency, the Germans had a reason for letting you take this town. It's a trap. There were lots of them here, and now they're out of it they're making a circle round the town. See that they don't close it on you!'

Yes, that was just what General Sirelius was afraid of. He, too, had been amazed that the Germans had given this key town away to him so easily. They were stronger than us—why should they give it up? His division's isolated stand here was becoming more and more dangerous. There was no knowing when the reinforcements being brought up from Mlawa would arrive, and the trap might be sprung at any moment, particularly at dawn. Although the encircled centre corps might not be far away, perhaps six miles or so, it was impossible to try and join them at night when he had no idea where they were and would have to move through the thick of the German lines. In any case, what sort of a state were those corps in now if eye-witnesses like this man reported that generals had been killed and units dispersed? They were ruined anyway, and there was no point in adding to the dimensions of the defeat by offering up a fresh crop of victims—Sirelius' Guardsmen. Furthermore, the orders on which his detachment had been sent here were not wholly binding: Sirelius belonged to XXIII Corps and was a distinguished Guards officer; he was not obliged to take orders from I Corps, which was commanded by mere officers of the line. The eye-witness testimony of this sergeant gave him a good excuse to re-interpret his orders.

Craning his neck forward like a goose to avoid the probing, hate-filled glance of the tall, dark-eyed nurse, keeping his eyes away from her bright lamp, Sirelius stood up and went out with his aide-de-camp.

Soon afterwards the car started up with a snort and drove out of the square.

No one knows what the general thought or what he decided. But everyone in that ward had been awake and listening, and they understood what the conversation meant. It meant that they were never going to be evacuated, that they would stay and be captured.

Tanya ran to look for the doctor, Valerian Akimovich; he had never believed the sergeant's story from the first, but what could he do? Go to the Medical Director? The latter carried no weight outside the hospital; compared with a general he was very small beer. And what evidence had she, apart from her intuition?

As never before, she wanted to be useful, but she had no idea what to do. She felt ashamed for having so long put her own unhappiness before the misfortunes of others.

The rest of the night passed without artillery fire. Unattended, the fires burnt themselves out. Gun-teams galloped through the town, but in the opposite direction to those of yesterday evening. The infantry turned about and marched away down another street. At dawn everything was quiet and deserted. Earlier than usual, before sunrise, the civilian inhabitants began to come out of doors —they had not been asleep behind their windows either. Soon there was a joyful hubbub of shouting and congratulation as they waved their hats to greet the first German troops marching into the town.

The wounded lay there, clutching their heads, and the nurses wept as they went on their rounds.

German sentries came and stood in every corridor.

It was after the Germans' arrival that an elderly, fussy, snub-nosed nurse came running in from the abdominal ward and whispered, panting:

'Tanya! A new patient has just come in . . . he's in my ward . . . he was hardly able to get here, he'll die any minute. He has the regimental colours of the Libau Regiment wrapped around his chest. What are we to do?'

Without a moment's hesitation, her eyes sparkling, delighted even, Tanya replied:

'Come on—I'll wrap it round my body!'

'But there are Germans in the corridor,' clucked the snub-nosed nurse. 'You'll have to do it in the ward—and quickly.'

'Well, let's go to the ward then.' Confidently, Tanya strode off ahead of her.

'But how can you—in front of all those men? You'll have to put it under your shift, it means taking off all your clothes!'

'All right, then I'll take them off.' Tanya had already reached the other ward.

She had always avoided undressing even in front of other women, because she was ashamed of her breasts, which were big and over-generous even for a girl of her build. When she was younger she had cried about it, thinking it was a deformity.

'Shall we fasten it with pins?'

'No, we'll sew it. One of you wind it round me and sew it up, and the other keep watch on the door to make sure the Germans don't come in.'

*

It is true, of course, that even if Sirelius had not lost his nerve that night he would have been unable to hold the town. Quick off the mark as ever, by the very early morning von François had three divisions surrounding the town and two on the way to it. Although von François himself, like a tightrope-walker on a wire, was sitting on the narrow strip of road at the village of Moldtken with no supporting troops, while groups of Russians were breaking through from the north around the village itself (some of whom put his searchlight out of action with rifle-fire) and might even have reached his headquarters, he spent his time drafting the orders instructing his five divisions how to take Neidenburg by a concentric attack. And with its usual malleable compliance the Russian high command obliged: on the very evening of August 17th, at the high point of Nechvolodov's and Sirelius' success in counter-attacking, when many large groups of Russians (e.g. fifteen thousand men at Willenburg) were preparing to break out of the ring that night and the next morning, Zhilinsky and Oranovsky ordered the flank corps not to attempt to rescue the encircled men in the centre but to *retreat*.

And what a retreat it was! Blagoveshchensky was told to withdraw twelve miles if the enemy did not press him, and to move back as far as Ostrolenka (a further twenty miles) 'if the enemy presses'. Dushkevich received orders to retire eighteen miles and, if necessary, to Novo-Georgievsk (a further thirty-six miles). How wise Kondratovich had been to retire the same distance in good time!

Next morning fear was even more rampant. When on August 18th Postovsky, on his own initiative, withdrew Army Headquarters (having been rescued by some dragoons) and set it up twenty-five miles behind its previous site at Ostrolenka, Army Group Headquarters sent him a message stating: 'Agree to your change of location.' After all, it was so convenient: with telephone and telegraph communications re-estab-lished with Army Headquarters, they could start a normal exchange of messages. It was then that Second Army Headquarters received written permission from Army Group Headquarters 'to move General Arta-monov's I Corps beyond Soldau if necessary'!

Meanwhile what of Rennenkampf? 'General Samsonov has suffered a complete reverse, and the enemy is now free to operate against you.' After all the delays, his cavalry had just begun to penetrate deep into

German territory: General Khan Nakhichevansky's cavalry corps was already poised above Allenstein, while General Gurko's cavalry division was advancing to cut the weakest—the eastern—arc of the encircling ring! But this move was thought to be too risky, too dangerous. 'Forward cavalry formations are to concentrate with the main body of the army . . .' (a wording devised to avoid using the word 'backwards'). Whereupon the whole of First Army began to retreat.

(Rennenkampf was dilatory about even this, perhaps out of pride. A week later, having escaped from an encircling movement similar to that which had engulfed Second Army, his army was to be caught up in a marathon rout—*Rennen ohne Kampf*.)*

Oh yes, one more thing: as a worthy replacement for the deceased Samsonov, a corps commander was promoted to command Second Army—General Scheidemann.

A future bolshevik.

Document No. 3

August 18th

REFUTATION
ISSUED BY THE CHIEF DIRECTORATE
OF THE GENERAL STAFF

In their communiqués on the situation in the theatre of military operations, the German and Austrian general staffs continue to maintain the system they have adopted: according to Wolff's Telegraph Agency 'the German army has won a complete victory over the Russian forces in East Prussia and has thrown them back across the frontier . . .'

No comment on the accuracy and value of this statement is needed.

---

*

'You won't get away from fire by hiding it under your coat!'

---

* Literally 'running without a fight', a pun on the general's name.

56

Screen

A horse's muzzle;
no thoroughbred, just an ordinary Russian bay horse. A
    gentle, helpless-looking muzzle.
No less than a human face, it can express despair: What's
    happened? Where am I? I've seen so many others die
    —and I'm nearly dead myself.
The horse's collar has not been removed or loosened.
Exhausted, its legs can hardly support it. It has not been
    fed or unharnessed, but only whipped and whipped:
    'Giddup! Pull! Save us!' The traces are broken, the
    horse has dragged itself free.
Ears pricked up, it wanders hopelessly until
a leg gets caught in a
gurgling
    patch of swamp.
The horse jerks violently to pull itself out of danger,
then roams off again, treading on the traces which are
    dragging along the ground;
its head is hanging down, although it is not looking for
    grass because there is none here . . .
It nervously skirts
the corpses of other horses lying with all four legs point-
    ing stiffly into the air and bellies distended.
They are terribly swollen—how hugely horses swell when
    they are dead!

Whereas a man shrinks. He lies face down, shrivelled, so
small that it seems incredible that all this thunder and
gunfire, the movement of all these masses stemmed
from him,
masses that are now abandoned, shattered. A waggon lies
on its side in a ditch,
its back wheel sticking up like a rudder . . .
Another, lying on its back as though in horror, its
draught-bar upwards . . .
a cart that seems to have gone mad, rearing up on its
end . . .
tangled, torn, discarded harness . . .
a whip . . .
rifles, loose bayonets and smashed rifle-stocks . . .
first-aid bags . . .
officers' suitcases . . .
caps . . . belts . . . boots . . . swords . . . officers' knapsacks . . .
soldiers' packs . . . some of them still
on corpses . . .
Barrels—some whole, some smashed, some empty . . .
sacks—full, half-empty, tied, untied . . .
a German bicycle which did not get taken back to
Russia . . .
newspapers . . . *Russkoye Slovo* . . .
orderly-room documents fluttering in the breeze . . .
corpses of those two-legged creatures who harness us,
drive us, whip us . . .
and more of our kind—dead horses.
If a dead horse has been disembowelled, then—

Close-up:
flies, gadflies and mosquitoes
buzz greedily
over the rotting entrails.

Higher in the sky
birds are circling, swooping down on the carrion
and crying excitedly in a dozen different voices.
⇌ Our horse will never forget this.
and it is

Normal screen expands to wide screen

= not alone! Countless more are roving about the battlefield
in this low-lying, accursed, marshy place

where all these things have been thrown away, abandoned,

among so many corpses.

= Scores, hundreds of horses are wandering around,
gathering into herds

and into twos and threes,

lost, exhausted, bony, but still alive where they have been
able to wrench themselves free from a team whose
other horses have been killed;

some, like our horse, are still in harness,

or dragging a shaft with them,

or there is a pair with a broken draught-bar between
them . . .

and there are wounded horses . . .

the undecorated, unnamed heroes of the battle who for a
hundred, two hundred miles have hauled

this artillery, now dead and drowning in the swamp . . .

and all that ammunition, ammunition-limbers with their
chains . . .

= The fate of those who failed to drag themselves clear:
two complete teams, all dead, lying across one another,
three limbers and three teams . . .

having trampled and crushed each other to death, they
lie where they fell . . .

though perhaps some of them are not dead and may be
pulled out and saved.

= Or else like those dead teams over there, hit by shellfire

as they rode up to haul a battery away from its position.
The battery kept firing to the last round: smashed
guns,

· surrounded by dead crews

and a colonel, six-foot body flung to one side, who was
obviously in command in place of a troop-leader . . .

But the field in front of the battery is also scattered with
the corpses of Germans who died in the attack.

= The horses are being rounded up. They are chasing us,
catching us,

and we horses shy and bolt . . .
but they grab us and tie us up . . .
It is being done by German soldiers.
Not an enviable job, chasing horses.
Thousands of captured horses slip through their hands.
= They are not only chasing horses. Over there, on the edge
  of the wood, they are lining up a column of
Russian prisoners
and men with unbandaged wounds.
Deeper
and deeper in the forest,
many more are lying on the ground, exhausted, asleep
or wounded.
The Germans have formed a line to comb the forest
and are flushing them out
like animals.
They pick them up
and if they are badly wounded
they shoot them
to put them out of their misery.
= Here comes a column of prisoners, virtually unescorted.
Prisoners' faces. Terrible fate—only those who have
  experienced it know what it means.
Prisoners' faces . . . Capture does not mean being saved
  from death; it means the beginning of suffering.
They are already swaying and stumbling;
it is worst of all for those with leg-wounds.
You are lucky if you have a faithful comrade so that you
  can put an arm round his neck and he
can half-lead, half-carry you.
= For other prisoners it is even worse: they are not allowed
  to march away but are harnessed instead of horses
to their own Russian guns, which are now trophies
of war, and have to drag them,
pull them and push them up to where the
victors are patrolling the main road in armoured cars,
with armed cyclists and
machine-gunners ready to open fire.
= Large numbers of Russian guns, howitzers and machine-
  guns are lined up.

[554]

= Along the road a team of powerful cart-horses is pulling
    a large civilian cart with extra sides made of staves—
    a tumbril, used for carting hay. Its load consists of—
close-up
    Russian generals!
    Nothing but generals—nine of them.
    They are sitting quietly on a bench, legs crossed,
    all of them facing one way, all of them looking dejectedly
        towards the prisoners,
    resigned to their fate. Some look grim, some actually look
        relieved: their fighting days are over, and with them
        their worries.
= The cart is stopped by
    a German general standing beside his car; he is short,
        keen-eyed, slightly tense, perhaps with triumph. It is
    General von François, with the frown of a victor.
    He does not feel sorry for these generals, but he finds
        their wretchedness intolerable. With a gesture
    he invites them to get down—why are they riding in a
        cart? He has enough cars for
    the generals: there are four standing over there.
= Stretching their stiff legs, the Russian generals get down
        from the cart, mostly shamefaced, though some are
        gratified at the honour done to them, and they
    take their seats in the German cars.
= The column of men on foot is led
    into a cage for people, fenced in
    with barbed wire, so makeshift as to be little more than
        symbolic,
    on temporary poles stuck into the ground.
    Here the prisoners are strewn about on the bare earth,
    lying, sitting, clasping their heads,
    standing, walking,
    exhausted, some with their arms in slings, some ban-
        daged, some unbandaged, some bruised, some with
        open wounds and
    others, for some reason, in nothing but their underwear;
    some are barefoot
    and none of them, of course, have been fed.
    Mournful, forsaken, they look at us through the barbed
        wire.

[555]

- A novel problem—how to hold so many people in an open field and prevent them from running away?
  Where are they to be put?
- The novel solution—a *concentration* camp!
- The fate of men for decades to come.
- The herald of the twentieth century.

Document No. 4

FROM THE HEADQUARTERS OF THE COMMANDER-IN-CHIEF

August 19th, 1914

Having been strengthened by reinforcements drawn from the whole front by means of the highly developed rail network, the Germans, with superior numbers, attacked our forces of approximately two army corps after subjecting them to an intense bombardment by heavy artillery, from which we suffered heavy losses. According to the available information the troops fought heroically; Generals Samsonov, Martos, Pestich and a number of staff officers perished. The necessary steps to counter this unfortunate reverse are being taken with the utmost vigour and firmness. The Commander-in-Chief continues to believe firmly that God will help us to carry them to a successful conclusion.

57

Some children take after their parents, others grow to be quite different from them. Some assume our views and habits as though they could wish for none better. Others, though apparently given all the right guidance at every step and outwardly obedient, evolve, with the unswerving persistence of a tree-trunk, in a direction which is wholly theirs and not ours.

Both examples were experienced by Agnessa Martynovna Lenartovich when, after being widowed, together with her sister Adalia she brought up a son and a daughter.

Sasha grew up to be typical of a family in which the portrait of Uncle Alexander, who had been executed as a revolutionary, was held sacred. Social and political problems absorbed him completely, and he could not imagine a life, still less a career, that was not bound up with them. Sasha measured people, events, books by one yardstick: did they contribute to the emancipation of the people or to the consolidation of the state?

Naturally a woman cannot always be expected to be so consistent; nevertheless in their day, when Agnessa and Adalia had been young, it was not unusual to find girls who regarded service to the social cause—and if necessary, self-sacrifice in the interests of the people—as of incomparably greater importance than their personal happiness as women. Veronika, however, did not grow up like that.

Year by year the child questions the values of his elders by which he comes to maturity; year by year the future adult emerges within him. (How long it takes to bring him up; how little time to kill him in war!) When Veronika was nine—fair hair parted down the middle into two plaits, fair eyebrows over two bright, clear eyes, placid mouth with two rather thick little lips—no one could have foreseen how much she would change in four years, and change even more over the following four: how her hair would darken, her eyes darken and take on a sly look; how those lips would set into quite a new shape, how much new meaning would be found in her smile; how, in fact, the triumphant progress of beauty—or rather the incursion of beauty, because its power is complete and long-lived—would capture her features.

Striking beauty can be as dangerous for a woman as keen intellect for a man: neither, more often than not, has a favourable effect on the development of a person's character. The dangers of beauty are well-known: narcissism, irresponsibility, selfishness. When they detect that perilous flame burning in a girl's face, her mentors should beware. Agnessa and Adalia Martynovna did their best to belittle the significance of beauty in Veronika's eyes and to stress the importance of character; they surrounded the girl with examples of heroic womanhood of the *narodnik* movement—serious-minded women who looked you straight in the eye, whose lives were dedicated to achievement and sacrifice, and whose distracting beauty, if they possessed it, was hidden beneath clumsy dark-brown dresses and headscarves worn peasant-fashion.

All this was firmly impressed on Veronika and to some degree it was her salvation. At the age of greatest frivolity, when nature asserted itself in an instinctive display of flirtatiousness, and in strong contrast to those exemplary traditions, *ad-mir-ers* began to hover around the girl, she reacted to them with such innocent purity that neither by touch, word or look were they able to gain their ends; everything was transmuted into friendship and earnest discussion, even on summer excursions to admire the famous Petersburg dawn. It was instilled into Veronika that one must see and awaken the good in people—and that she did.

In this, as her mother and aunt saw it, another innate element played its part: her temperament. With her melting glance and beautiful hair piled above a majestic forehead, Veronika would have succumbed at an early stage were it not for the solid ballast of imperturbability and the calm, relaxed attitude to the outer world which marked her character.

Her temperament kept her away from the dangerous paths that beckoned to a beautiful girl and it seemed to abet the educative efforts of her elders, although that temperament of hers also hindered their success. Veronika was sincerely moved by the miseries of others—but her feelings never grew into an urge to become involved in the struggle or into hatred of the oppressors. Her immense but nebulous compassion was innocent of the categorical bounds which divide the victims of social oppression from those who suffer from inborn defects, from failings of character, from emotional disasters—even from toothache.

Recently, for example, there had been a discussion at home about the behaviour of the socialist deputies in the State Duma and the tragi-comedy of the one-day session at the outbreak of war. The socialist deputies had not behaved in a cowardly fashion and had not let themselves be taken in by the wave of patriotic hysteria. Khaustov had predicted that the forces of socialism in every country would turn the present war into the last flare-up of capitalism.' And Kerensky, in a bold and extremely adroit speech, had managed to hurl a series of accusations at the government: it was gagging the voice of democracy, even now it had not accorded a real amnesty to political prisoners, it had no intention of seeking reconciliation with the oppressed national minorities of the empire, and the burden of military expenditure was being placed on the workers. He had bravely said all this, unaffected by the patriotic uproar about him, not omitting the charge of 'inescapable responsibility' for the war, and in a brilliant peroration he had hinted at the advent of revolution: the peasants and workers, he had declared, would defend their country—and *then* liberate it! The newspapers, however, had scandalously misreported him by quoting him as having urged the peasants and workers 'to defend their country and liberate it', thereby implying that he had called upon them to liberate it from the Germans. Only in Russia could newspapers get away with such barefaced distortion!

And what of Veronika? While this conversation had been going on she had been sitting beside them and calmly looking through the current issue of *Apollon*. 'Veronya!' Adalia had exclaimed in a pained voice. 'Don't you think it's outrageous?' Veronika had put on a sympathetic look. 'It's most vexing, Aunt Adalia. But what am I supposed to do about it?' 'Vexing?' One should not merely be vexed by such things; they should arouse such indignation that one's feelings are converted into positive action.

It was around that time that the Council of St Petersburg University had sent a 'loyal telegram' to the Tsar, which had begun:

'Be assured, great Sovereign ... that *your* university is afire with the urge to devote its powers to the service of you and the Fatherland'. Surely they could have been spared that sort of boot-licking.

'Veronya! What do you think of that? Why haven't you reacted to it?'

'Mama, it wasn't the students who sent it; after all, it was the professors. In any case, the professors in our college didn't sign it.'

'But supposing they had—would you have protested? Would your friends have protested?'

Nor did Veronika share their satisfaction over the slight political consolation they were able to extract from the little news which filtered through when the Russian forces were defeated (a delight clouded by the fact that Sasha and many other worthy young men were at the front too): she could only see the obvious, superficial fact that people were being killed and posted missing, leaving widows and orphans.

In the past Sasha had been a very good influence on her, had in fact influenced her more strongly than her mother or her aunt. Being five years older than his sister, a time-span equal to half the high school course and the whole university course, and being a person of decisive opinions who never allowed an objection to his arguments to remain unrefuted, the effect of his intellectual and moral influence on Veronika was to make her feel ashamed of the waywardness of her ideas, so that she tried to throw them off, or at least conceal them, and to be worthy of her brother. But a year ago the voracious machine of the army had swallowed Sasha, and for his sister that year had been the most important one—her first year at university. Whilst she had been at home and alone, Veronika had been more receptive to the inculcation of civic ideals than she was when she was with her student friends.

Quite probably the atmosphere which had dominated student circles ten or twenty years ago would have guided Veronika's sympathies and antipathies into the proper channels. But—and this could only happen in submissive, long-suffering Russia!—during the repressive period after the 1905 revolution the students had not been fired to greater efforts, had not steeled themselves for the struggle, but had given way to the general trend of lassitude, doubt, the doctrines of dubious prophets, and many of them were now of quite a new breed—politically apathetic and inclined to mysticism, in fact the complete reverse of the accepted image of a Russian student. If it went on like this for a few more years, the great tradition of half a century would break down and collapse ingloriously, to the ruin of all those libertarian ideals by which the previous generations of students had been inspired.

Among Veronika's first-year friendships was one, with a girl called Yolya, which was most unfortunate. It was very hurtful that the first student friend Veronika brought home should turn out to be from a completely different world— a creature with a frail, thin figure, always playing with her shawl, whose head was stuffed full of Symbolist rubbish. Now and again, at moments suitable and unsuitable, she would recite the obscure gibberish of her modish poets:

> The builder of the tower shall take wing,
> Dreadful his urgent flight;
> From the depths of the well of the world
> He shall curse his madman's plight.

From the inflection of her voice, but much more from the play of her glance and her eyelashes, by the remote look in her beautiful eyes, expressive of some esoteric significance, one was immediately made aware that her apprehension of the world around her differed from that of everyone else. Yolya had a habit of turning her head with a slow perplexity, and her hair fell loosely down to her shoulders in the manner of a beautiful courtesan. Sometimes she had a ribbon in her hair, always she had a shawl on her shoulders which she was constantly pulling around her slim, almost hipless figure, very fashionable at the time, which she emphasised by wearing straight, smooth, tight dresses without a belt.

'Yolya' was her way of disguising her obscure name of Yelikonida, which betrayed her merchant-class origins. Veronika, though, called her 'Likonya' to rhyme with Veronya. The two were alike in more than the sound of their names: they had the same thick, dark hair—Likonya's being quite black—the same placidity and the same piercing stare, except that everything about Veronya was more robust, more solid, steadier.

What could be lurking inside the head of this girl whose mannerisms were so charged with enigmatic significance? She was obviously not guided by the bright light of reason. At the tea-table, and casually on every possible occasion, by question and argument the two ageing sisters tried to discover just what there was inside that little head beneath its cascade of hair.

But Likonya did not reveal herself under questioning, and when her friend was there Veronya became dull and taciturn, and there was no way of making them talk. They simply listened, Veronya with gentle patience, Likonya with distracted perplexity, stirring the jam in the jam-dish, glancing up at the clock. They never objected or argued; instead they were always in a hurry to go somewhere, not to teach workers at evening classes, not to spread enlightenment, but simply for their own passive enjoyment and pleasure: to an art exhibition, or a lecture on the values of life (as if they needed explanation!), or a discussion on 'The Problems of Sex', or another novelty—the cinematograph.

If they stayed at home, the result was sometimes even more shocking. In the very dining-room where Uncle Alexander's portrait hung in its dark frame, the features so expressive of a presentiment of his doom, Veronya would sit down on the divan, tucking up her legs beneath her, and little Yolya, the tips of her fingers wrapped in her shawl and pressed against the wall behind her, would sway her body and head, a look of wonder on her face, her small, questioning, childish mouth giving voice to her feelings in the borrowed words of the sacrilegious verses:

> *The breaker of the tower shall be crushed,*
> *Cast down midst shattered stones,*
> *Forsaken by all-seeing God,*
> *To mourn his death with moans.*

58

The notion may have been copied from the English, or it may have arisen spontaneously in the capital, that in times like these it was shameful to be idle, that everybody should *do* something. But nobody knew what. On August 19th, long before the start of term, when usually there was no one about in the college corridors, the girl students were already standing about in groups or walking up and down in the warm sunny weather wearing only summer dresses.

No specific matter had arisen; the administration had issued no call or notice to summon the students. But the girls themselves were discussing the 'flag day' which it had been announced everywhere would be held tomorrow, and many of them had already enrolled as flag-sellers; others were hesitating, wondering whether it was a good thing to do; a third opinion held that to hand round the collecting-box for one day was absurdly insignificant when so many young women had given up everything to volunteer as sisters of mercy. Of course it would have been stupid to leave the university to go and be a nurse, but the war was so hugely, blunderingly implacable, thrusting itself into everyday life, that some students did seriously discuss the possibility of becoming nurses and no one openly scoffed at them. Things which had been unmentionable or would have sounded false a month ago were no longer laughed at now: in one group a tall, resolute student, waving her arms in mannish fashion, was saying at the top of her voice, as though making an announcement to all near her or passing by:

'Yes, we needed it! We *needed* the war! Not for the Serbs' sake, but for our own salvation! Because we have lost confidence in ourselves, we've become decrepit, we've sunk so low that we can't go any lower—we've sunk to the *Blue Journal* and the tango! We need some great *exploit*, so that we can renew ourselves! We need victory, to freshen the atmosphere—we're stifling!'

No one hushed her or cried 'Shame!'. Only one bright little girl in grey protested in a shrill, sharp voice:

'Stifling? Yes, we are being stifled—by rotten government. We don't need a war—we need a long peace!'

Everyone around her, however, seemed to be on the side of the tall girl, who went on insistently, her heavy, striking features animated with lively expressiveness:

'A long peace breeds cowardice and egotism!'

Others protested, though their remarks represented differences of attitude rather than objections:

'It's not a question of patriotism, it's a chance to merge ourselves with the people, to march alongside them as equals—the very opportunity we've been dreaming about for decades . . .'

The girls who would be entering their second year in the coming term, still feeling themselves to be the most junior, were not talking so loudly. Nevertheless Veronika joined the group and said very coolly, as though thinking aloud:

'What is the point of this war, after all? Supposing we hadn't joined in?'

The people standing near by heard her, and a student with straight hair and a drawn face, who was considerably older than all the others, turned on her almost scoldingly.

'You have to think in terms of our national existence. A clash was inevitable. If we hadn't supported France, Germany would have defeated her by now and would have turned on us—and we should have had to face Germany alone!'

This made Veronika think.

They also argued about the change in the city's name from Petersburg to Petrograd, which had taken place the day before. No one called this ridiculous either, or a piece of cheap chauvinism, but they objected to having lost the 'Saint' in St Petersburg, and to the fact that they had changed the patronal name from the apostle's to the emperor's without seeing that the new name should have been St Petrograd. Others recalled that the city had originally been given the Dutch name of Piterburgh, that Petersburg had been imposed on them by the Germans, which was a symbol of their eternal subjection, and that it was therefore a good thing that it had been discarded.

Someone said that the lecture-list had already been posted. So long before the beginning of term? Yes, the challenging mood of the times had apparently made itself felt in the faculty offices too. The second-year girls went to look, among them Veronya and Likonya, the hawk-nosed Varya from Pyatigorsk, another Varya, a blonde from Velikie Luki, and some others. They discussed the list.

Its most notable feature was that the lectures on Medieval History would be given by Professor Andozerskaya—a woman and a professor! It was true, of course, that she had gained her doctorate in France and not in Russia, but things were changing even in Russia, where she had recently been granted her master's degree. In the lecture-list she was still referred to as 'lecturer', but in university circles her new status was already accepted and it was known to the students that she was a 'prof'. Apart from teaching Medieval History to the second year, she would also hold seminars with the senior years on the 'The Use of Sources'.

This was most interesting. The little flock of second-year girls drifted over to the window and started telling each other what they had heard about Andozerskaya. This undoubted victory for women's emancipation was an achievement, a step forward for all the oppressed. Andozerskaya had helped raise funds for a dining-hall, a hostel and scholarships. Yet at her seminar, begun last spring, she had proposed to the students that they should pore over eleventh-century papal bulls written in Latin. It was the same with her published works, which were about ecclesiastical society in the Middle Ages, pilgrimages to the Holy Land . . . This caused some perplexity. The girls felt they would like to have a look at their professor today and form an opinion about her. This they were able to do. They found out in the faculty office that Andozerskaya was with the dean at the moment. They waited for her.

She soon came out. She was quite short, and if she seemed taller than Likonya it was only because she wore her hair piled on her head. She was far from negligently dressed, although her frock, apart from being an attractive grey with a slightly shot-silk effect, was devoid of any adornment and was designed not to show off her figure too much.

She walked past with a modest air, holding a small book rather like a prayerbook, in a very old binding but with a gay pink book-marker. She was young, not only for a woman professor but for any professor; perhaps a little over thirty.

This made it all the easier for them to gather round her and question her all at once:

'Excuse me, please . . .'

'Will *that* be one of your texts . . .?'

'What are we to call you?'

'Olda Orestovna.'

'Olga?'

'No, Olda.'

'Is that a Scandinavian name?'

'Perhaps. It was a fancy of my father's.'

Glad to stop and talk, Andozerskaya gave a charmingly natural smile.

(It was, of course, the case that even the most distinguished pro-fessors willingly talked to both men and women students. It was an unwritten law of Russian higher education that the fame and standing of a professor was determined by student opinion and not by the good-will or otherwise of the university authorities. A pro-fessor who was disliked by the governing body had gone on teach-ing for a long time and had been the students' favourite; even after being dismissed he did not lose his halo in their eyes. But woe to a professor whom the students regarded as reactionary: contempt, boycott of his lectures and books and an inevitable, inglorious departure were his fate.)

'Is that why you specialised in medieval Western Europe?' An-other, more intelligent girl said: 'Don't be silly. Where else but in Western Europe can a woman get a higher degree? And they don't study Russian history there.' But some said dubiously: 'Of course it's a good thing that a woman should get a professorship, but. . .' Varya from Velikie Luki put in: 'But isn't it too high a price to pay? I mean, burying yourself in the useless old Middle Ages?' Veronika answered her: 'Why? What about Kareyev? What about Grews?'

After the light, even pace with which she had just glided past them, Olda Orestovna readily planted her high heels where she stood on the parquet floor; the pseudo-prayerbook did not prevent her left hand from backing up her right as she gestured and the expression on her face showed readiness to conduct a seminar or an argument there and then.

'It isn't "paying a price" at all. If you reject the Middle Ages, the history of the West collapses, and then the rest of modern history becomes incomprehensible.'

She gave a special glance at Veronika's calm, dark-eyed face.

Varya from Velikie Luki: 'But, practically speaking, the history of the West, and everything we need to know about it, begins with the French Revolution . . .'

Varya from Pyatigorsk: 'With the Age of Enlightenment.'

'Well, yes, with the Enlightenment. What on earth have pilgrimages to Jerusalem got to do with it? What use is paleography?'

Her lips slightly pursed, Olda Orestovna listened to all these objections as though they were familiar.

'That's an error of over-hasty thinking—to point to a branch and claim that it's the whole tree. The Enlightenment is only one branch of western culture and perhaps by no means the most fruitful. It grows out of the trunk, not from the root.'

'Which branch is more important, then?'

'Well, if you like, the spiritual life of the Middle Ages is more important. Mankind has never known a time, before or since, when there was such an intense spiritual life predominating over material existence.'

(Could she mean it? What about obscurantism, Roman Catholicism, the Inquisition?)

Both Varyas: 'But really! How can we in the present day spend our time on the Western Middle Ages? How is it going to help to emancipate our people? How will it help progress in general? Do you expect us in Russia *today* to study papal bulls? And in Latin, too!'

Olda Orestovna flicked the edges of the pages of her pseudo-prayerbook in a gentle *glissando*. It was a rare Latin edition. She smiled, unabashed.

'History, my dears, is not politics, where one chatterbox repeats or contests what some other chatterbox has said. The stuff of history is *not opinions* but *sources*. And your conclusions are determined by the source materials, even if they contradict your preconceived views. Independent scholarship should rise above . . .'

Now this was really getting nowhere! This was too much! Here the two Varyas were not the only ones to exclaim:

'But what if your conclusions conflict with the needs of present-day society?'

'Surely for practical purposes all we need today is an analysis of

[567]

the contemporary social environment and material conditions? What can the Middle Ages add to that?'

Invisible among her group of questioners due to her small stature, Andozerskaya tilted her head slightly to one side and gave a very confident, meaningful smile.

'That would be so if the life of the individual really were determined by his material environment. It would be much easier then: the environment is always at fault, so all you have to do is to change it. But apart from the environment there is also a spiritual tradition, hundreds of spiritual traditions! There is, too, the spiritual life of the *individual*, and therefore each individual has, perhaps in spite of his environment, a *personal* responsibility—for what he does and for what other people around him do.'

Veronika emerged from her pensive mood as though she were a fresco coming alive.

'For other people too?'

Again Olda Orestovna's glance singled her out.

'Yes, for other people too. After all, you can choose to help, you can hinder, or you can wash your hands of it all.'

Finding no further sympathy, she smiled, gave a slight bow as a dignified way of dismissing them—or herself—and set off, a small, slim, unbending figure, looking from the back almost like a student except for a certain added elegance which was rather unusual for a member of the intelligentsia.

The students began to buzz with talk, both Varyas reacting indignantly. Did she mean that the spiritual life of the Middle Ages wasn't an outcome of the socio-economic conditions of the time? If she dared say anything of the kind in her lectures . . .! Others protested: all that old stuff about deriving everything from economics was so boring.

With a catch in her voice Varya from Pyatigorsk said:

'Oh, how things are changing! I have a friend, I've told you about him . . . Well, a week ago I met him at the station . . .'

Stimulated, pressing her point, Veronika went on defending the professor:

'Surely the personal responsibility of the individual is an admirable idea? If nothing matters at any given time but the environment, then what are we all? Just a lot of zeros?'

'We are molecules of the environment,' Varya from Velikie Luki said aggressively. 'And that's that!'

Likonya, meanwhile, had wandered away and was looking out of the window. No one asked her opinion. She raised her eyebrows, turned her neck, shrugged her shoulders one at a time.

'I liked her very much. Especially her voice. As though she was singing an aria. But such a complicated one that you couldn't make out the tune.'

Her friends laughed.

'And what was the meaning?'

Likonya's little forehead wrinkled into a frown, but there was a smile on her plump lips as she said:

'The meaning? I didn't notice.'

*

You shouldn't have searched in the village, but in yourself.

59

Aglaida Fedoseyevna Kharitonova was a hard woman who was used to being in a position of power, and power suited her. The concession she had made to Tomchak over his daughter was one of the rare concessions of her life. Her late husband, a good man, was afraid of her from the start of his courtship to his dying breath. In his work as an inspector of high schools he constantly asked her advice, while outside his professional life he submitted to her completely; the children knew that in all serious matters only Mama could permit or forbid. The municipal authorities took great account of Kharitonova, and no one dared to put pressure on her or to warn her about the 'left-wing liberal' views which predominated in her school. (This being the Don Cossack capital, the whole of educated society in Rostov was in duty bound to assume a left-wing liberal stance.) At Kharitonova's school history was taught by the wife of a revolutionary who had been imprisoned and was said to have escaped and to be active in the political underground in Rostov itself, and the school's entire history course had an overt revolutionary bias. The teaching of Russian literature was informed by similar sympathies. Naturally she could not avoid giving the obligatory lessons in scripture, but the priest who came to teach was not an obscurantist or a fanatic and in any case more than half the pupils were excused as being of the Jewish faith. On special occasions, too, the girls had to sing 'God Save the Tsar' in the assembly hall, but it was done with an obvious lack of enthusiasm. However, Aglaida Fedoseyevna did not allow this ironic lack of respect for the powers that be to extend to her own authority within the school walls, which she exerted inflexibly without allowing it to be undermined in any way. Not only did all the students tremble before her, but the high-school boys or cadets from the nautical college invited for social occasions would mount the staircase with trepidation, knowing that the stony headmistress was standing at the top to give each of them a piercing stare and that she would instantly turn anyone away for the most trivial incorrectness of attire. The morals of Kharitonova's high school were beyond praise. In view of the high fees (without which no school can keep up high standards) the pupils all came from well-to-do families and only two girls in each class were maintained free.

Ruling the school with an iron hand, her own small, docile family was the last place where Aglaida Fedoseyevna would have expected to encounter rebellion. It was not her husband but, after his death, her eldest son—christened Vyacheslav but called Yaroslav on his mother's whim—who had shown recalcitrance. Apparently imbued with the spirit of enlightenment from his earliest years, at the age of twelve he had suddenly conceived an urge to enrol in the Cadet Corps. A mother so domineering and self-assured could not lightly tolerate any straying on the part of her son, but she found this deviation particularly insulting: behind the irrational, boyish impulse lurked the grey outline of *betrayal*. Her eldest son wanted to enter the obtuse, reactionary officer caste, which was untouched by the spirit of critical thinking. The healthy love for the people instilled into Yaroslav had become unexpectedly distorted: instead of trying to help the emancipated peasants, he wanted to identify himself directly with their earthy strength, which he regarded with an almost religious awe. Yaroslav was a pliable boy, but this aberration of his proved stubborn. For three years his mother fought him and put pressure on him, but after high school her maternal authority, her logic, her anger were all insufficient; Yaroslav went to Moscow and entered the Alexandrov Military Academy.

She might have continued the struggle over her son, for liberal thought had been known to penetrate even the officer class—after all, Prince Kropotkin, the anarchist, had graduated from the Imperial Corps of Pages and the revolutionary writer Chernyshevsky had taught at a cadet school—had she not been struck a second blow by her daughter Zhenya, and in the same year.

For all her great devotion to freedom in social relations, to equal rights for women (even to the primacy of women), Aglaida Fedoseyevna persisted in adhering to the rule that a girl ought to marry more than nine months before having a baby. Zhenya had broken that rule, and, being obliged to get married, had not waited for her mother's blessing. Her studies at a teachers' training college had been brought to an end by the birth of the child. To crown it all, Zhenya's husband, Dmitry Filomatinsky, the son of a deacon and still only a final-year student, was far from being the powerful, virile man Aglaida Fedoseyevna would have expected for her lively, vigorous, well-bred daughter. She implacably refused to recognise the marriage, regarding it as not having taken place and her grand-daughter as never having been born, and placed all three of them under her ban, refusing to allow them to come to Rostov. So, in an attic somewhere in Moscow's Kozikhinsky Street, Zhenya rocked little Lyalka in her cradle while her husband studied for his final examinations and his diploma thesis.

For the past year Xenia Tomchak had visited them frequently; she felt extremely sorry for the banished Zhenya and became her staunch defender, by letter and during her visits to Rostov. She actually succeeded in making Aglaida Fedoseyevna change her mind, and the headmistress allowed the outcasts to come home that spring.

Although she had been very angry, she was also just. She had to admit that Zhenya's errors, if errors they were, had been redeemed. Although her son-in-law had proved to be puny and ugly, little Lyalka was a splendid, healthy baby, just like her mother. Having almost broken up the family by being born, Lyalka now became its shining, gurgling focus, usurping this place from her uncle, the eleven-year-old Yurik. After taking one look at her, her grand-mother never wanted to be parted from her again. What's more, her son-in-law turned out to be both intelligent and efficient. He was not just an ordinary engineer, but had kept up with the times by specialising in calorific engineering, and there happened to be plenty of work for a young graduate, both in high-temperature and refrigeration technology, in Rostov and in Alexandro-Gru-shevsk; he was also offered laboratory work at the Don Polytechnic. He was not dazzled by false glamour—so much more sensible than poor, silly Yaroslav! The engineer's crossed hammer and spanner were becoming the badge of the new age in place of crossed swords or flags. Realising this, her son-in-law behaved with modesty backed by a strength of mind that was not obvious on the surface. At table he was occasionally overwhelmed by the presence of his mother-in-law, but not by her caustic jibes, which he turned aside, it had to be admitted, with a wit that was devoid of malice. His professional success, his wife and his baby kept him in a constant state of brimming happiness. Zhenya was borne along on a flood-tide of even greater happiness. Happiness, like a rosy mist, enveloped the whole Kharitonov apartment, and no one who breathed it could fail to be infected by it. And Aglaida Fedoseyevna, as she passed through the school corridor into her apartment three times a day, could not for all her obstinacy avoid giving way to the magic of that rosy mist. Lyalka's crying, her daughter's singing, Dmitry's quiet laugh, Yurik's increasingly grown-up talk at table—all this began to heal the old wound of her husband's death and the new wound of her eldest son's self-willed behaviour.

This was how Xenia had seen the Kharitonov family in July, before the outbreak of war, when she had gone south from Moscow. She always liked being with these people, but never before had she been moved to tears by such happiness. Zhenya's letters sent to Xenia at the Tomchaks' family estate were full of the same bubbling, incredulous joy, and the war had cast practically no shadow on their lives. Returning to Rostov with anticipatory delight at the prospect of plunging into the rosy mist of their happiness, Xenia got out at the station and took a cab, having counted her six pieces of luggage.

It was true that although she had flown to Moscow as joyfully as a bird, she was returning with a burden of anguish. Where else than to the Kharitonovs should she go to seek help, protection and advice? Her father's grim command had come crashing down like a slab of black stone: it was not his refusal to let her be a dancer which so distressed her—there was no point in regretting that—but he had now ordered her to give up her studies and get married! With Orya's help she had postponed her return until Christmas, because of the war. At home, apparently, there would be no getting out of it: how could she argue with her father? But no sooner did she wake up in the morning in the sleeping-car at Bataisk station and see the terraced streets of Rostov on the long ridge above the river—the huge, carefree, gay city where she had first known free-dom and joy, where her interests had developed—than the crushing weight of the threat began to roll away and her big-nosed, loud-mouthed father ceased to be the sole, terrible, incontestable arbiter of her life.

Her heart always beat faster whenever she returned to Rostov, especially, as now, in the early morning, when Sadovaya Street was fresh and clean in the deep shade of trees as it climbed the hill towards Dolomanovsky, and the cab-driver furiously put on speed so as not to be overtaken by the tram. The trams were not at all like the ones in Moscow; they were slower at picking up speed, they had long arms with runners instead of hoop-shaped pick-ups, there were special cars for summertime with airy, open sides, and on the coupling-hook at the back, called a 'sausage', in true Rostov fashion all the small boys would sneak a free ride as far as the policeman at the next crossroads. Typical, too, were the special mobile lattice-work bridges, arc-shaped with hand-rails, which were put across flooded streets in the southern rainstorms and were kept on the pavements when the weather was dry. From Nikolsky Street onward the Bolshaya Sadovaya straightened out and ran like a mile-long arrow to the city limits at the suburb of Nakhi-chevani. There were the first-floor windows of the Arkhangorod-skys' apartment, the corner balcony of their drawing-room shaded by a linen awning, and that might even be Zoya Lvovna herself arranging flowers, but Xenia could not see properly through the thick foliage and in any case she would certainly be calling on the Arkhangorodskys tomorrow. Over there, on the sunny side of Sadovaya, was the fashionable Chyorny's, a two-storey shop with a rough-cast façade and a striped, fringed awning above each shining glass show-window. The driver wanted to turn along the Tagan-rogsky Prospekt—no, go straight on, up to Soborny Prospekt. (If they had gone along Taganrogsky, they would have passed the Old Bazaar and the fish-stalls with their eternal reek from the huge bream, carp and *suly* which were abundantly displayed right on the pavement, and it was at this time, in the morning, that the whole of the night's catch, as yet unsold, was lying still alive, silvery, twitching and splashing across the counters.) On the corner of the Taganrogsky was a modern building of a kind that was rare enough even in Moscow—the walls of its upper floors almost en-tirely of glass. The Grand Hotel ... the Merchants' Garden ... the San Remo ... There was so much of Rostov, yet it was such a friendly place. Advertisements ... What's on? Someone's benefit-night at the Makoshinsky Theatre ... Truzzi's Circus ... The French 'Théâtre des Miniatures' ... at the Soleil cinema, a heavy drama and one of Max Linder's very funny pictures ... she really must go and see them while she was here. From the Municipal Gardens they turned into the Soborny Prospekt with its rather uneven cobbles. There was the Modern Secondary School where Yurik was a pupil. The Post Office. Glimpsed down a side-street, the Old Cathedral, a heavy, ugly carcass of a building, and nearer, in a neat little square, the memorial to Alexander II, surrounded by an octagonal railing. There was the gay, seductive Moskovskaya Street, one long row of shops, with more shades over the shop-windows; in Rostov's Moskovskaya Street you could dress yourself quite as well as in Moscow! Then a diagonal turn, past the side of the market delivery-yard and there was the Kharitonovs' school . . . No, this is the main entrance, take me round to the other side please, to the headmistress's apartments.

That dear staircase, and every door a familiar old friend! As soon as she crossed the threshold she sensed the intellectual freedom and the ease in personal relationships which were always to be found in this family. And Zhenya, darling Zhenya, who flew into their embrace like a whirlwind, as though she were younger than Xenia. Her mobile, determined features were alight. 'How lovely! We weren't expecting you so soon. Why have you come so early? Trouble? . . . You must break with your father! Do as I did! They'll change their minds afterwards! . . . But listen: Lyalka— she's a marvel! She's musical—I swear it! She burbles a sort of improvised recitative the whole time! She almost sings! Come on, come and hear her! No, right now she's just talking. She talks endlessly, though I'm the only one who understands it all . . . and she hides under the blanket and says from underneath: "Come and find me!" And she has such a tender little skin, feel it and see—it's absolutely lovely!'

Gay, lissom Zhenya, with her happy, full-throated laugh, was so brimming with happiness that she had more than enough for herself and scattered the surplus around her. The two girls had never lived together here: Zhenya had been away at university when Xenia had occupied her room. There was a difference of five years in age between the girl student in Moscow and the little tomboy from the steppes. Zhenya had snorted at first, wondering whether this rich little girl would put on haughty airs; she would not have tolerated that and was quite prepared to take her down a peg or two. But Xenia had no such airs; she was a receptive, hardworking pupil. Later she had acted as the emissary from Moscow and their difference in years had been ironed out. Now there was another difference between them: the one a mother, the other still a girl . . . (Will I have children? I shall! I shall! Otherwise, what is it all for? Fulfilment is good, but expectation can be good too. After all, I can go one better—I can have a son. Dmitry Ivanych is a splendid man, but I—I shall find myself *such* a husband . . .!)

If she could forget her father's threat, or rather if she disobeyed it (though that would be terrible, quite terrible!) she could have such a happy life and everything would be wonderful!

They had a new hobby now—photography. They had a Kodak, Mitya often took snaps, and by the red light of the darkroom lamp they would develop them and Zhenya herself would frame them. The walls were covered with photographs—square, round, oval, diamond-shaped, some against natural backgrounds, some with an artificial white one: Lyalka in a little bonnet, Lyalka naked, Lyalka in the bath, Lyalka with a doll, Mama with Lyalka, Papa with Lyalka, Granny with Lyalka, Zhenya and Mitya at the seaside. 'That was on the Sea of Azov, lovely bathing, so near and so cheap, we're going to go there every summer!'

But it was not all so happy. She must go and say how do you do to Aglaida Fedoseyevna. 'All is not well, you see—Yaroslav . . .' 'Wha-a-at?' 'No, he's all right, but two army corps have been smashed up and in the very sector where . . . Go in and see Mama.'

For Xenia, Aglaida Fedoseyevna was not 'Mama' but 'the head-mistress'. To the end of her days she would be the headmistress. Feeling timid, she smoothed down her hair—meeting her was always slightly awe-inspiring and one could never argue with her or contradict anything she said.

Aglaida Fedoseyevna was sitting motionless in a twin-backed chair draped in a loose cover, at a little round table with a cloth, laying out a patience called 'Cross beats Crescent'. As Xenia entered, she gave a slight turn of her majestic head and held out her cheek, by now remarkably wrinkled and even slightly pendulous. (Only when Xenia had left the school had she granted her a daughter's right to kiss her.) As she bent close to her, Xenia noticed how grey the headmistress had grown at the temples and in the circlet of hair above her forehead, which had never been noticeable before.

In the past, too, she had only played patience in her blessed hours of evening leisure, never in the morning: Aglaida Fedoseyevna had always been up and about early every morning to cope with the affairs of her busy life. Now she was seated heavily in an armchair, her elbows on the table, disinclined to move.

Attentive, as always, to a visitor, as though she could have no news of her own, her usual cool reserve hiding any hint of gentleness or simplicity in her voice, Aglaida Fedoseyevna asked Xenia the usual questions across the table. How had she spent the summer? Were they all well at home? Why had she come so soon? When was she going back to Moscow? Yet she was looking not at Xenia but at the cards laid out in nine piles for the crescent and four piles for the cross, moving them from pile to pile slowly and reflectively.

It was a suitable moment for Xenia to talk about her troubles and beg for protection from her obstinate father. She began telling her story. What a stupid, nightmarish business it was! After all, it was difficult enough to get a place at the Golitsyn Academy of Agricultural Science, they accepted practically no one but gold medallists—and now she was supposed to leave and give it all up . . .

The headmistress frowned with strain. Yes, she understood; yes, Xenia was right; yes, she would have to write to Zakhar Ferapontovich . . .

But behind the pince-nez there were dark rings under her eyes. The set of her lips showed strong displeasure, as when she gave the whole class a dressing-down. Pressed under a vase lay an envelope with a bit of Yaroslav's handwriting visible. Xenia blushed with shame and exclaimed sympathetically:

'Aglaida Fedoseyevna! What is the date of your letter from Yarik? I've had one too! Such a joyful letter, I'll read you some of it later . . .'

The headmistress sharply raised her head, and one eyebrow.

'When was it sent?'

'August 5th. It's franked from Ostrolenka and marked XIII Corps . . .'

That accursed Thirteen again.

Aglaida Fodoseyevna returned to her patience.

Her letter, too, was dated August 5th. Today was the 19th. And today a letter might come from 'General Headquarters of the Commander-in-Chief'.

She turned over a card. She looked at Xenia. The girl was sun-burnt, her hair almost blonde. Cheerful a moment ago, her face was now not far from tears.

She and Yarik had been like brother and sister. She had been even closer to Yarik than Zhenya had.

'Bring it here!' Aglaida Fedoseyevna pointed to a photograph on the other table, mounted, held upright by a glued-on support—Yaroslav in his ensign's uniform after being commissioned.

Xenia seized it. They looked at it together.

My God—under that enormous peaked cap, above that high collar, he looked more of a boy than when he was wearing a shirt at home! And how straight he stood in those vertical leather straps, and what a look of content! And that great heavy revolver at his wide belt . . .

Relaxing her habitually straight back and firm shoulders, Aglaida Fedoseyevna said to Xenia as though to a daughter:

'You can see for yourself, he has taken obstinacy beyond its limit . . . He would have been a third-year student now, and he wouldn't have been touched by the call-up . . . The newspaper reports are purposely written so that no one can understand any-thing . . . Where is that corps of his? Where is the Narva Regi-ment? And the Ostrolenka postmark means that he's in the south-ern detachment, Samsonov's army . . . He's out there . . .'

On the seven of hearts was a single teardrop.

Suddenly—for the first time!—Xenia embraced the frail, ageing neck with her warm, young arms—Aglaida Fedoseyevna was a mother to her, even more than a mother!

'Dear Aglaida Fedoseyevna, he must be alive! I'm certain he's alive, my heart tells me so! And I can guess from the tone of his letter that he's happy! People like that don't die early! He has a happy fate in store for him! You'll see! We'll get another letter soon!'

The headmistress removed the teardrop from the seven.

Fate? All she wanted to know about his fate, his life, his letter, was—would there be that one final letter? But Aglaida Fedoseyevna knew no way of communicating with the mysterious forces which governed these things—fate, life, letters.

Except by playing patience . . .

She pulled herself back into her habitual pose and frowned, re-erecting the barrier of reserve with a movement of her eyebrows. But her voice choked as she burst out:

'Have you seen Yuk yet? Go and have a word with him. When the army volunteers marched along the Sadovaya, he was there on the pavement the whole time. Then some Cossacks came in from the villages, it was some kind of patriotic demonstration with religious banners—and he was there again. Some schoolchildren were sent there with flags to sing "Save, O Lord"—but he went of his own accord.'

He was called 'Yuk' at home because as a young child, when he had tried to say 'Yurik', he could not pronounce the 'r'.

What had once been the boys' room had been given to Dmitry Ivanovich as a study, but a corner of the big room had been screened off with cupboards for Yurik. He was not there, but was lying on his stomach on the balcony over a quiet side-street and, with great deliberation, drawing crooked lines with black crayons on the smooth, green-coloured paper of a big Marx's atlas.

'Well?' Xenia called out to him cheerfully and squatted down beside him on the ground, her skirts raising a little breeze. 'Hullo, Yuk!'

She poked the crown of his head and scratched it with her fingers. His hair was not cut short, and bristly tufts, snipped off at various lengths, stuck up in different places. Out of politeness Yurik rolled over on to his side to look at her, but he did not put down his pencils and the expression on his face remained absorbed.

'What are you doing? Why are you scribbling all over that beautiful atlas?'

'It's mine. And I'll rub it out afterwards.' Yurik made no effort to distract himself from his occupation.

'What do those lines mean?' Xenia asked in a jolly, wheedling tone, still squatting, her skirt covering half the balcony.

Yurik looked gravely at her with his greenish eyes. She had never given away any of Yarik's or his secrets and they trusted her.

'But don't tell any of the family!' He wrinkled his nose, again with a serious look on his long, fine-drawn, sunburnt face. 'That's the front line. When somebody wins a battle I rub it out and move it forward.'

He had been rubbing out when she had found him: one flag had given way, but the centre was holding out well.

'But that's Southern Russia—why are you marking it there? You've made the Germans capture Kharkov—and Lugansk!' She did not want to hurt the boy's feelings, but could not help laughing.

'You ought to use another map; the war will never come as far as this, Yurik.'

Yuk gave her a superior, sideways glance.

'Don't worry. We'll never surrender Rostov.'

He turned over on to his stomach again and began moving the front line northwards from Taganrog.

60

_____

(A Random Selection from the Newspapers)

MUST WIN!

Disorders in the German army . . . After Gumbinnen, a battered Germany . . . transfer of a significant force of cavalry from Belgium . . .

German subsidies to the Turks . . . a quarter of the war-indemnity . . .

GERMANS DESECRATE ORTHODOX ICONS

In Brussels the Germans have been killing wounded men . . . the Austrians are murdering peaceful Serbs without regard to age or sex . . .

The Emperor Wilhelm's sleepless nights. In the grip of his blood-stained fantasy . . .

. . . the prophetic words of Knut Hamsun: 'The Slavs are a turbulent people and will be the conquerors of the world after the Germans.'

THE WAR HASN'T STOPPED US WORKING
As before, we are selling
'Viktoria'
rapid-knitting machines . . .

DOUBLE YOUR INCOME!
Buy a Mandel's photographic camera

RACING *today.*

The news of the glorious feat of Kozma Kryuchkov has spread all over Russia . . . We, a group of schoolchildren . . . modest mite, all we can afford . . . enclose five roubles . . .

Be sober, be wide awake! Everywhere, mobilisation . . . inspired by tremendous national enthusiasm. Apart from the profound motives concealed deep within the secret places of the glorious Russian spirit . . . the closing of **liquor shops** . . .

The German schools in Petersburg . . . Harsh treatment of the pupils . . .

The crime-rate in Petersburg has been reduced by 70%.

The Nizhni-Novgorod fair . . . the dealers in Siberian squirrel-fur are in a state of dejection . . .

. . . one of the wounded described how for days the Russian troops did not meet a single German. Often an accordionist marches in front of a detachment and plays as the soldiers sing . . . You forget you are at war . . .

We who have not been called to the Tsar's colours must do the work both for ourselves and for those who have gone . . . The whole commune should plough and sow the fields of the men who have been called up, carry away the wheat of those without horses. In case of doubt refer to your Land Captains.

A well-known Russian socialist in Paris, Burtsev, has issued a call to all political parties in Russia: forget your quarrels, rally round the government, stand up for your Russian nationality ...

... from words to deeds. The strength of the Germans lies in their astounding cohesion, efficient organisation and capacity for hard work ... The time has come when every one of us must work ...

The Russian army has occupied the towns of Soldau, Neidenburg, Willenburg, Ortelsburg, and is marching to cut off the retreat of the shattered German forces ... The German corps are running the risk of finding themselves in captivity ...

RACING *today*

EXCHANGE WAGE-SLAVERY
for the chance to run
your own business with
an income of between 2 and 6
thousand roubles a year.
Buy the translation of the
famous book by
Prince Kropotkin!

Special braces which lend the wearer
a magnificent military bearing ...

MUST WIN!

Will Germany Perish from Hunger
or on the Field of Battle?
AN ARTICLE BY AN ECONOMIST

GERMAN ATROCITIES

The cruellest tortures and horrors of the Inquisition pale before . . . One of the wounded officers, who took part in the battle of ░░░░░ informed the correspondent of the *Stock Exchange Gazette* of the following method, widely practised by the Germans. Lightly wounded Russian soldiers who are taken prisoner are subjected to an operation to sever the tendons in their arms. After this the Germans are assured that the wounded man will never again handle a rifle . . .

Attempted Advance by the Germans in East Prussia

Transfer of German troops from the French frontier . . .

Turkey hardly conceals her hostility to Russia; let us hope that Turkey will not escape the consequences. The Greeks cannot refrain from the temptation of settling accounts . . . the Arabs, who are obedient to the orders of England, the Armenians of the Caucasus, who want more than has been granted them . . . It is hard to say what will be left of the Ottoman Empire if it risks . . .

CHOLERA AMONG TURKISH TROOPS

Refugees from Adrianople describe . . . the unheard-of atrocities of the Germans of the homeland . . . profound indignation among the German colonists in Russia . . . With the aim of dissociating themselves from German barbarity, many colonists, especially in Kherson Province, have decided to petition to be allowed to change their surnames and even their Christian names to Russian ones . . .

Latvian soldiers! Together with the heroic Russian army you are approaching the ancient capital of the Knights of the Teutonic Order, Marienburg. From there the rapacious horde of the Teutonic Knights kept our motherland in their iron grip . . . Latvian girls taken hostage . . . Latvian brides will welcome home none but heroes . . .

WHEEL CHAIRS
for the war-wounded

FOR LOVERS OF MUSIC

*A selection of difficult
pieces in easy arrangements* ...

DEBILITY

in all its forms gives way
to the successful treatment
provided by the stimulant ...

BULLETPROOF VESTS

MUST WIN!!

The War and Vodka

In the times we are living through, the population experiences so much personal grief and so much national joy that there is no serious psychological need for vodka ...

DRAYMEN'S PETITION

Without liquor the customary rudeness has been mitigated ... work has been done faster, more efficiently ... prolong this happy time at least until the end of the war ... The police, relieved of the need to pick up drunkards on the street, has begun to be more vigilant in its pursuit of thieves ...

Issue of rations to the families of reservists. For each member of the family of a man called to the colours: per month, 68 pounds of flour, 10 pounds of barley, 1 pound of sunflower seeds ...

The need for strict observation of military secrecy obliges the Commander-in-Chief to be extremely sparing of information on the progress of military operations. Whereas the German military authorities in their communiqués may describe victories which did not take place, our General Staff sometimes remains silent over victories that have been won ... Only on the frontage of our southern detachment have the Germans been able temporarily to check the encircling movement of General Samsonov's columns, in the course of which the Army Commander himself and Generals Pestich and Martos have been killed, the staff has suffered fearfully under artillery fire and heavy losses have been inflicted on the Russian regiments.

However, our strategic position has in no way been affected by this unfortunate occurrence ... The uninterrupted flow of reinforcements from Russia has changed the balance of forces in our favour ... In order to halt Samsonov the Germans were obliged to transfer two corps from Belgium.

Thus General Samsonov's vigorous action was, as it were, a blood-sacrifice upon the altar of brotherhood in arms ...

In Memoriam A. V. Samsonov

Your watch you kept with eagle eye,
O'er storming men, o'er victory's gain;
Far, far above you in the sky,
All but unseen, an aeroplane ...

According to persons who knew the deceased well, he was held in a rare degree of affection by his subordinates. A calm, exceptionally competent officer, he was always quick to grasp and weigh up the circumstances ...

His Majesty has been graciously pleased to award General-of-Cavalry P. K. Rennenkampf the Order of St Vladimir, Second Class with Swords, for distinguished service ...

No one expected a triumphant march on Berlin or Vienna, because the maddened enemies of the peaceful nations have staked everything on one card and war against them will inevitably be a fierce struggle. Recently our forces smashed three German corps at Gumbinnen and now we learn that, having hurled himself on our two corps with overwhelming strength, the enemy has struck us a great blow. Among the dead is General Samsonov. Naturally, no one will be downhearted at this news and no one will respond with despair at the death of these brave men. Their blood will temper our courage even further . . .

We have been stricken by misfortune and this news will indisputably have a depressing effect on everyone. At the same time, however, it is quite natural that together with this sense of grief there should be another feeling, a feeling of joy. We rejoice in the frankness of the official announcement . . . He who fears not to speak the truth, however bitter it may be, is strong. It is the weak who lie!

> *Once more, as of old, millions of voices*
> *Shall answer for Russia as one.*
> *Once more, we shall stand, shoulder to shoulder,*
> *To face and repel the Hun.*
>
> *Until the arrogant Swabian devil*
> *Has laid down his arms again,*
> *Let each of us fight, every man with his weapon—*
> *The bayonet or the pen!*

The Chief Directorate of the General Staff is being inundated by a flood of reply-paid telegrams containing petitions and requests for the release from service of mobilised persons, for their deferment and other exemptions.

The C.D.G.S. announces through the press that for those called up for active service there exists a statutory definition of their rights; requests on their behalf by relatives, therefore, will not be considered.

MANIFESTO
BY THE PRESIDENT AND GOVERNMENT
OF THE FRENCH REPUBLIC

Frenchmen! By the brave efforts of our
gallant soldiers . . . under the pressure of superior
enemy forces . . . Out of concern for the national
welfare, governmental and political institutions
will temporarily be removed from Paris . . .

THE SITUATION IN EAST PRUSSIA

We are informed from wholly reliable sources that the situation in
East Prussia is not causing any alarm. The extent of the losses in
the two corps is explained by the use of long-range heavy artillery
and the wide blast-area of the shells. This event cannot have a
significant effect on the general course of military operations in
East Prussia.

FRENCH SUCCESSES!

The French army, having reached Paris, has gone over to the
attack . . . The French government has moved to Bordeaux . . .

OUR GREAT VICTORY OVER THE AUSTRIANS
Advance along 100-mile front!

August 21st, the first 'Flag Day'. Hardly had the grey autumn day
dawned than there poured through the streets of Moscow a whole
army of volunteers selling the flags of the Allies 'in aid of the victims of war' . . . In restaurants . . . in clubs . . .

NOW IS THE TIME
TO BE THINKING OF A MUSEUM
DEVOTED TO THE
SECOND WAR FOR THE FATHERLAND!

Our advance deep into East Prussia continues. The constant flow of fresh forces from Russia enables us to continue the penetration . . . It is also further weakening Germany's Western Front . . .

WAR TO THE END

A treaty by which the parties agree not to make a separate peace with Germany is an act of mutual insurance against a desire for peace. History knows of many examples of unexpected outbursts of magnanimity which have destroyed what has been achieved at great price . . . The universal moral significance . . . diplomatic oath, sworn on blood-stained swords . . . noble fidelity of the three Powers . . .

61

For several weeks Ilya Isakovich had been warned by his engineer friends from Kharkov, Petersburg and the Kolomna Engineering Works, one of the many firms which he represented in south-east Russia, that he must be sure to meet and get to know a brilliant engineer called Obodovsky who was coming to Rostov. So far the man was only known in Russian engineering circles for his books written in German: on general economics, on the lay-out of ports, on methods of industrial concentration, on the prospects of trade between Russia and Western Europe, on price-fluctuation—quite apart from his specialised works on the mining industry which were of interest only to mining engineers. There were anecdotes about him, such as the story of how when he had been wandering penniless through the streets of Milan he had worked out how the tramway traffic could be more efficiently planned, sketched out a project—and sold it for a good price to the city council. Yesterday Obodovsky had been an émigré; before that he had been a political criminal wanted for revolutionary activities, but he had been pardoned under the 1912 political amnesty declared in honour of the three-hundredth anniversary of the Romanov dynasty. For a further political offence he had then been 'freed of the charge and subject to no further investigation'. For the past three months he had been making an unofficial but triumphal tour of all the centres of the engineering industry in Russia, during which he had been greeted with particular warmth on account of both his outstanding talents and his political past. The war had broken out when Obodovsky was visiting the Donets Basin, the main object of his tour, but he had spent a whole month there as planned; now he had arrived in

Rostov-on-Don, and one of his introductions was to Arkhango-rodsky. They arranged by telephone to spend the first half of August 20th together and to have lunch at home with Ilya Isakovich. They met in the morning at his office (which was also the south-eastern branch of Erlanger & Co., a company which made milling machinery), where they looked through drawings and catalogues, then went to inspect Arkhangorodsky's two favourite achievements in Rostov—the new municipal grain-elevator and the Paramonov mill, which had an annual turnover of a million.

Despite the many differences between them, they took to each other from the first. Ilya Isakovich was about ten years older, short, on the fat side, laconic and not given to gesture, extremely fastidious both in dress (all his clothes were made by the best tailor in Rostov, an Armenian) and in the sleekness of his dark moustache, eyebrows and hair. The thirty-six-year-old Obodovsky was tall and fair. Dressed rather untidily, indeed carelessly, he would occasionally wave his arms with such violence as he walked along that he staggered; he had a permanently dazed air, as though he had been overtaken by some important thought while in the midst of dealing with another. He was bursting with surplus energy. Soon after they had met he announced:

'You know, during this trip I have felt like a samovar with several taps. And I'm always grateful to someone who can turn on one or two of the taps and let out a little of the boiling water. If I had stayed abroad I should have exploded with the amount of material that was accumulating inside me. I've made this journey in order to discharge it all—and I'm hurrying, as Gorky puts it, to stir up the sediment of life. Abroad, I made the mistake of writing all sorts of instructive books that Russia can't read. How I pined for home when I was abroad! I want to shape the life of Russia with my own two hands! I can do with four hours sleep in twenty-four. I shan't sleep any more than that on this journey . . .'

His smile was frank, the smile of a man with nothing to hide. In conversation his features were ceaselessly mobile and his forehead was alive with frequent ripples of thought. His soft hair, which was cut evenly *en brosse*, covered his head lightly and loosely.

His answers to questions were interesting and given readily. Whenever he was speaking he was liable to be fascinated by some urgent, elusive thought which he would hasten to pursue in all its ramifications, even if irrelevant, following each one up, as people did in the West but not in Russia.

To an outsider their day would have seemed boring, but for them it passed in an exciting cascade of ideas, information and suggestions. They kept up their conversation wherever they went, by cab and walking across yards, up and down staircases and through workshops, the talk sandwiched in between discussions of the machinery and processes which they had come to look at. To show one's work to someone who understands it is always satisfying, and disposes one well towards him. Obodovsky missed nothing important—the use of Swiss-made rolling-presses, the technique for washing grain—and everything he saw he praised in terms that reflected its precise value, no more. Apart from this, though, he had a remarkable breadth of outlook: he would assign each process, each solution of a problem, its correct place in the Russian economy as a whole and in future trade (without the war it would have been current trade) with the West.

Although there was no similarity or even contact between the lives, experience and specialised interests of the two men, they shared a common engineer's spirit which like some powerful, invisible wing lifted them, bore them onwards and made them kin.

They also found time to talk of more general matters. Drawn out by his guest's questioning, Arkhangorodsky described how he had been in the first class to graduate in milling engineering from the Kharkov Technological Institute; there had been only five of them, and a wide choice of highly-placed, well-paid jobs had been available to each graduate. Arkhangorodsky, however, had not gone straight into a senior post; to the indignation of his father, a small-time broker, he had signed on as a labourer in a mill, where he worked for a year before becoming the miller's assistant, and only after two years in that job did he become a miller himself, considering that this was the only way to find out how mills really worked and what their requirements were.

They went out and looked at the town—or rather the guest asked to see the steep place where Taganrog Hill sloped down to the Don and where Rostov City Council was thinking of installing an escalator to carry people up from the embankment. In Moscow, according to Obodovsky, the war had put paid to the plans for an underground railway—a 'metro': a generating station to power the trains was already being built, and in 1915 the first line was to be run from the Bolshoi Theatre to Khodinskoye Field. In general, construction in Moscow was going ahead at an insane rate and countless new buildings were being put up.

With his cool, appraising gaze, Ilya Isakovich studied the nervous Obodovsky. Just as Ilya Isakovich's life was serious, steady and consistent, Obodovsky's had been made up of twists, starts and stops; he actually breathed unevenly, as though wanting to take in enough air for ten lungs, and although he cursed the war he seemed to find peacetime life insufficiently rich in incidents, which was why he had always done his best to stir things up.

He made no reference to his distant, anarchist past, during which he had twice been convicted, had been imprisoned and exiled, and had fled the country. He spoke rather of his recent impressions gained abroad: he had been to America, had studied the mining industry in Germany, had been involved in workmen's insurance in Austria and written a book about it (a book meant for Russia, although its publication in Kharkov was still held up after months of delay—at one moment, apparently, they had lacked the right typeface, then the publishers had lost the preface). The most fascinating experience, however, was his present journey: the Russian coal and ore mines had been wide open to a graduate of the Institute of Mines, but in those days his chief aim had been revolution and he had almost ended up in the Siberian mines as a convict in fetters. Afterwards, during his emigration, he had longed to get back to the Donets Basin and turn his hand to practical work. Now he was describing enthusiastically just how much could be achieved here in ten years, and how much in twenty, by the application of a single, integrated plan in which each step was related to future developments. Take the underground gasification of coal . . .

'The great thing is—we're out of the doldrums! The doldrums are over for Russia! And when the wind blows we can even make up our leeway!' Obodovsky exclaimed enthusiastically.

Everywhere he had met his contemporaries, mining engineers who had graduated in the same year, 1902, or thereabouts, who had welcomed him with a warmth which had brought a lump to his throat, had offered him engineering jobs, consultancy posts, lectureships, even the directorship of the entire Department of Mines!

'The fact is, we haven't enough people to fill the jobs!' Obodovsky said in half-mock horror, laughing. 'No sooner do they spot someone who's even mildly competent than they grab him and offer him every kind of inducement. What a country this is! Full of stuffed shirts, full of civil servants, full of idlers—and yet there's no one who can do a job of work!'

'And which offers have you accepted?'

'I turned down all the best ones. For the time being I shall give some lectures at the Institute of Mines and do various other things in Petersburg. Really, I can't decide which is the most important —teaching, insurance, labour bureaux, ports, trade, banking, technical associations—Russia needs them all and it's impossible to be everywhere at once. Speaking in general, we have two main tasks of equal importance and both of them need to be given maximum priority: the development of productive forces and the development of voluntary social institutions.'

'Yes, if it weren't for the war.'

'If only they could even run a war properly! The machine's like a rusty old spring, and all the wrong people are in charge—a bunch of doddering fools! Everything they touch withers and dies, and they touch everything. They don't understand a single thing they're doing, they don't understand this century! They look upon this amazing country as though it were their personal fief: if they feel like it, they'll make peace; if they feel like it, they'll make war— just as they behaved towards Turkey in the last century. And they imagine they'll always be able to get away with it. Why, not one of the grand-dukes even knows what the words 'productive forces' mean! The people at Court are supplied with whatever they need, and that's as far as their interests extend. They're much more concerned about things like anniversaries: at the moment they're celebrating what Ivan Susanin did three hundred years ago, or holding some festival in Kostroma, or striking a medal . . .'

'Still,' Arkhangorodsky said with a sly dig at his companion, 'if it hadn't been for the political amnesty issued for the tercentenary you wouldn't have been able to come home and your samovar would have exploded somewhere in the Ruhr.'

'Yes, that's true enough!' Obodovsky laughed. 'No, seriously, give us ten years of peaceful development and you won't recognise Russian industry—or Russian agriculture for that matter. And what a trade treaty we could have made with Germany! We stood to gain so much from it. It's astounding, I'll tell you all about it in detail later . . .'

They had arrived home, and Ilya Isakovich rang the bell. They were seen from the first floor and the door opened automatically; their house was designed to do without a porter. Their apartment had many rooms, all opening off a dark passage. Ilya Isakovich had brought his guest home ten minutes before the time arranged for lunch, and he was embarrassed and nervous lest his wife Zoya Lvovna might not be ready and thus put him in an awkward position. They had a cook who, if she were not disturbed, normally had lunch ready strictly on time. But her cooking was not subtle enough—it would have been all too obvious what each dish had been made from and what ingredients had gone into it. So for the distinguished guest 'Madame Volcano' (as Zoya Lvovna was known) had insisted on taking a hand. On occasions like this her somewhat erratic culinary enthusiasm rose to the challenge and she produced a meal with the aid of Malakhov's cookery book.

From the corridor leading to the kitchen, hot from the stove and in a breathless whisper, Zoya Lvovna announced that lunch would be half an hour late. So the compliant Ilya Isakovich had to fetch a decanter on a tray from the dining-room, together with some cold salmon and slices of bread and butter, and take them into the study.

'Ah, yes—and there's the Union of Engineers,' Obodovsky greeted him indefatigably. 'How is it down here?'

'Rather feeble, I'm afraid.'

'In many places the branches are big and lively. I believe the Union of Engineers could easily become one of the leading forces in Russia. It's more important and more constructive than any political party.'

'You mean—take part in government administration?'

'Not in government, we don't need power; in that respect I'm still faithful to Pyotr Alexeyevich . . .'

'Who's that?'

'Kropotkin.'

'Do you know him?'

'Yes, well. When I was abroad. Intelligent, practical men don't govern—they create and transform; governmental power is a dead horse. But if the government hinders the development of the country, then we might have to take power.'

The first glass warmed them, the second even more, and their talk grew more and more expansive. From the depths of the blue plush divan Obodovsky flung out a thin arm and, going off, as usual, at a tangent, protested:

'What I'd like to know is why are all your agencies referred to as being the "south-eastern" branch? Do you think you're in the south-east of Russia? You're in the *south-west*!'

'The south-west is the Ukraine. Even our railway is called the South-Eastern.'

'It all depends on your point of view. Where are you looking from? From what you say, I can tell you can't see Russia as it really is. Russia, my dear chap, needs to be looked at from far, far away—almost from the moon! Then you would see the Northern Caucasus lying at the extreme south-west of this great mass. Everything in Russia that's vast and rich, our entire hope for the future, lies in the *north-east*! All this fuss about the Straits, a gateway to the Mediterranean and so on, is just so much rubbish— we must look to the north-east! I mean from the Pechora to Kamchatka, the whole of northern Siberia. God, what potential! Lay a radial and diagonal network of railways and roads, heat the tundra and drain it—then see what minerals we could dig out, what we could plant, cultivate, build, how many people we could settle there!'

'Yes, yes. Didn't you almost set up a Siberian republic? Didn't you want to secede?'

'Not secede.' Obodovsky waved the idea away cheerfully. 'But we did want to use it as a base from which to liberate Russia.'

Arkhangorodsky sighed.

'All the same it's chilly out there. I wouldn't much like to go there. It's better here.'

'People ought to want to go, Ilya Isakovich! Well, maybe not at your age, but young people should. The way the world is going, very soon it will be impossible to keep those regions empty. Mankind won't allow us to—we shall be in the position of a dog in the manger. Either make use of them or give them up. The real conquest of Siberia was not Yermak's expedition—the real conquest is yet to come. Russia's centre of gravity will shift to the north-east: that's a prophecy that's bound to come true. Incidentally, Dostoyevsky came to the same conclusion towards the end of his life; he gave up his ideas about Constantinople—read his last essay in *The Diary of a Writer*. It's no good frowning—we have no alternative. Do you know what Mendeleyev calculated? He worked out that by the middle of the twentieth century the population of Russia would be well over three hundred million, and a Frenchman predicted that by 1950 we should have three hundred and fifty million!'

Small, neat and cautious, Arkhangorodsky sat in his round, revolving, leather arm-chair, his short arms folded over his protruding stomach.

'Always provided, Svyatoslav Iakinfovich, that we don't decide to rip each other's guts out in the meantime.'

62

Ilya Isakovich knew, and reasonable people had often told him
the same, that marrying a beautiful woman is not the best way to
wedded bliss, that beautiful women, especially if they are tempera-
mental, are very uncomfortable to live with; even so, he had not
been able to resist the temptation of marrying the golden-haired
Zoya, with her volatile moods, her 'all or nothing' attitude—either
she wore a dress whose collar came right up to her ears or one with
the most revealing décolleté; if she did not like her face on a photograph she would blot it out. Then there was her failed attempt to
go on the stage (her parents would not let her) and her unfinished
course at the Warsaw Conservatoire; at home it was either drama-
tised readings from Schiller or musical evenings. She had a passion
for vases, rings, brooches, and she despised the needle and the
duster. Jewellery, it is true, greatly suited her—either entwined in
her hair or worn on her neck, her breast or her fingers, but when
they had married Ilya Isakovich had warned her, and had subsequently repeated his warning several times: 'I'm an engineer, not
a businessman.' (While still constructing mills, he could have
switched the emphasis of his work and bought up buildings and
land, but that would have meant giving up the purely engineering
side.) On the other hand, his wife's way of life provided her husband with a complete change and a relaxation from his daytime
occupation, although among the numerous draperies, curtains and
satin frills that filled the apartment an outsider felt that something
was lacking: light, perhaps, from the windows and lamps, or heat
from the radiators, or the fact that the corners had not been properly
swept and not quite all the crumbs brushed from the sideboard.

Although late, lunch was eventually served. The table was covered with a whiter and grander tablecloth than usual in the dark but very spacious dining-room, which could have seated forty people, and at this moment the tall, good-looking housemaid was laying the final pieces of cutlery, taken from the huge, old-fashioned sideboard, for seven places at table. (Devoted to beauty in all things, Zoya Lvovna kept only pretty housemaids, even though they made her jealous.)

Having taken off her apron, Zoya Lvovna went round the rooms and called everyone to table. Apart from the principal guest, the others were all members of the family, or almost: her son was not at home, but there was her daughter, Sonya, her schoolfriend Xenia, and a young man called Naum Galperin, the son of a well-known Rostov social-democrat whom the Arkhangorodskys had hidden in their home in 1905 and who had been a close friend ever since; finally there was Mademoiselle, Sonya's governess since early childhood, who counted as one of the family.

Naum and Sonya could scarcely have been wholly alike, but in some ways they were: both had masses of black hair (Naum's was not very well combed) and shining, dark eyes, and both were aggressively argumentative. They had already agreed to have an earnest and edifying talk with her father on the subject of his participation in the shameful, so-called patriotic demonstration that had been held by the Rostov Jews. The demonstration had taken place at the end of July and had begun in the choral synagogue, where Ilya Isakovich only put in an appearance on festivals and where by tradition he had a place of honour on the east side; however, he was not a believer and could easily have avoided going on the demonstration—yet he had gone all the same. The synagogue had been decorated with Russian national flags and a portrait of the Tsar. It had begun with a service of intercession for the victory of Russian arms in the presence of army officers. The rabbi had read a speech, followed by the chief of police, and they had sung 'God Save the Tsar'. Then about twenty thousand Jews with flags and with placards inscribed 'Long live one great, united Russia', together with a separate detachment of men who had volunteered for the army, had processed round the streets, held a meeting at the Alexander II memorial, called on the city governor and sent a loyal telegram to the Tsar—to mention only some of the disgusting things they had done. However, soon afterwards Ilya

Isakovich had gone away, and so had Sonya. Now the family was assembled again, and her fury had been increased only yesterday because in two cinemas they had shown a newsreel of the demonstration which was so mawkish, so false, so intolerable that she had come away burning to have it out with her father.

It was only just before lunch that Sonya and Naum learned that there would be a guest—a man who had once been a famous leading anarchist, but who had now renounced the cause. At first they were undecided whether to postpone attacking her father, but then they agreed that it would be better to go for him straight away: if this anarchist had preserved a scrap of his revolutionary conscience, he would support them; if he proved to be a thorough-going renegade, then the battle would be all the more furious and interesting. So they sat down to table on the look-out for the first excuse to get their claws out, preferably no later than the soup.

The hors-d'oeuvre had been standing too long because of the delay, so by telephone (there was a telephone from the dining-room to the kitchen, separated only by the length of the corridor) Zoya Lvovna called up the rather strange soup—it was supposed to have been borsch, but there was practically no beetroot in it, though it was served with some delicious puff-pastry curd-cakes. The hostess was seated at the head of the table, the guest beside her. He at once complimented her on her cookery, then told her where he had come from and where he was going, and announced that he was taking on a number of professional commitments in industry ... Here, surely, was an opening to launch the attack? Yes, a perfect opening! Turning a threatening stare on the erstwhile anarchist, the shaggy-haired Naum asked tensely:

'But *what* industry are you going to develop? Capitalist industry?'

Ilya Isakovich glowered, guessing that the youngsters were preparing to make a scene. He would have liked to put a stop to their cheek at once.

Obodovsky guessed it too. He had a dozen more business calls to make after lunch and had hoped to be able to eat his meal in peace. The samovar-taps of his loquacity were for use with like-thinkers and in order to get through his business as quickly as possible; to indulge in arguments with hostile, half-baked youth struck him as *vieux jeu* and boring. However, being a guest, he made an effort (not a very big one, given the unfettered ease with which he spoke) and gave a detailed and amiable reply:

[600]

'I've been hearing that question for twenty years! At student meetings in the late 'nineties that was exactly what we asked each other. Even in those days the students were split between the revolutionaries and the engineers—the destroyers and the builders. In those days I, too, thought that to build was impossible. But one only had to spend some time in the West to be amazed at how peacefully the anarchists lived there and how hard they worked. As for industry, anyone who has created something with his own hands knows that production is neither capitalist or socialist, but *one* thing only: it is what creates national wealth, the common material basis without which no country can exist.'

Naum's burning, black eyes were not to be dazzled by such charming eloquence.

'Under capitalism the people never see any of that "national wealth" and never will see it. It just floats past them—and all goes to the exploiters!'

Obodovsky smiled gently.

'What is an *exploiter*?'

Naum shrugged his shoulders.

'To my mind, it's only too obvious. *You* ought to be ashamed at asking a question like that.'

'No one who earns his living in industry is ashamed to ask such a question, young man. The person who sits with his arms folded and pronounces judgment from a distance is the one who ought to be ashamed. Today, for instance, we were looking at a grain-elevator, where not long ago there was nothing but long grass growing, and then we looked at a modern mill. I can't begin to convey to you how much intelligence, education, foresight, experience and organisation have gone into that mill. Do you know what it all costs? Altogether, it costs *ninety per cent* of the future earnings! The labour of the workers who laid the bricks and hauled the machines costs ten per cent—and even that could have been largely replaced by cranes. And they got their ten per cent. But then along come some young men, arts students . . . you are reading an arts subject, aren't you?'

'What difference does it make? Well, yes.'

'Along comes a bunch of arts students and they explain to the workers that they are earning too little, and that that little engineer over there in spectacles is earning God knows how much, and that it's sheer bribery. And these simple, uneducated people believe it and get indignant: they can understand the value of their own work, but they're incapable of understanding or putting a price on somebody else's.'

'But why should Paramonov, the mill-owner, make all that profit?' Sonya shouted.

'He doesn't get it all for nothing, believe me. Remember, I said "organisation". He works for his share too. And if anybody does get something for doing nothing, then we must gradually see to it that that money is channelled elsewhere, by rational political measures. We mustn't try to take it away by throwing bombs, as we did.'

He could not have expressed his backsliding and apostasy more openly. Naum gave a scornful sneer and exchanged glances with Sonya.

'Does that mean you have rejected revolutionary methods for ever?'

Contempt and nervous tension had made Naum and Sonya forget their food. Meanwhile the tall parlourmaid had brought in the second course and the hostess made the guest admit that he had no idea what the dish was or what it was made of. She was the same age as Obodovsky and was attractive even when paid no compliments, but when praised she positively glowed. He obviously preferred talking to her, but four fiery black eyes were still searing the renegade across the table. He gave his concluding reply:

'I would put it rather differently. Before, I was most concerned about how to *distribute* everything that other people had created without my help. Now my main preoccupation is how to *create*. The best brains and hands in the country should concentrate on doing that; we can safely leave distribution to the second-raters. When enough has been built and made, then even if distribution is less than perfect no one will be left completely without his share.'

Naum and Sonya were sitting next to each other on the long side of the table, immediately opposite the engineers. They looked at each other and snorted.

'Create! Tsarism is preventing you from even doing that!' With this, they decided to change the topic for the main one, which they had been keeping in reserve. But at this point Obodovsky wanted to know something.

'Tell me, please, which party do you belong to?'

Naum had to reply, and did so modestly and quietly; it was not the sort of thing one shouted from the rooftops.

'I am a social-revolutionary.'

He had not followed in the footsteps of his menshevik father, because he regarded the menshevik brand of social democracy as too milk-and-waterish.

Even when he was delivering his opinion emphatically on the most important matters, Ilya Isakovich never raised his voice. His reprimands to his children were accompanied by no more than a faint tap of his fingernail on the table, which was always completely audible. Now, from under his thick black eyebrows, he gave Naum a look that was almost affectionate.

'May one ask where your party gets its funds from? After all, it has to pay for things like false passports, rented apartments, disguises, bombs, travel, escapes, pamphlets. Where does the money come from?'

Naum gave a short, dismissive twist of his head.

'I thought it wasn't done to ask questions like that . . . In any case, I believe the public at large knows perfectly well.'

'That's just what I mean.' Ilya Isakovich polished his nail on the tablecloth. 'There are thousands of you, none of you has done any work for a long time, it's not done to ask where your money comes from, and you are not exploiters. But you go on consuming the national product, claiming that the revolution will redeem all that.'

'Papa!' his daughter exclaimed in a voice ringing with indignation. 'You may not have done anything for the revolution' (she, of course, had not done anything for it either) 'but to talk about it like that is an outrage! It's disgusting!'

She was sitting diagonally across the table from her father, as was Naum from Obodovsky. The furious glances of the two young people crossed like arrows in mid-air over the table.

Meanwhile a telephone-call had summoned the fish, chopped up and served in large scallop-shells. Once more the guest expressed his complimentary astonishment and Zoya Lvovna prattled on in reply, making play with a finger adorned with a large platinum-set diamond. This talk of politics bored her; if there was one thing she really hated, it was politics.

At the far end of the table, facing the hostess, equally bored by politics, sat Mademoiselle; she found it even more tedious, as there was simply no one for her to talk to; all she could do was thank the maid. Fifteen years ago, when the chief magistrate of Rostov had made her acquaintance in a gay Parisian café and brought her back to Russia, she had not known a word of Russian, and on the assumption that her first Russian charges were too small to know French she had lulled them to sleep with little songs about who had crept into whose bed. Since then she had learned enough of the language and customs to understand and detest these eternal conversations about politics. Since then, too, her collection of admirers had aged; she had taken to good works, and in the past year she had been going out to visit a lonely street-hawker to give him French lessons—Zoya Lvovna had known that Mademoiselle would marry him soon, but then he had been taken off to the war.

Near Mademoiselle and beside the infuriated Sonya sat Xenia, modest and well behaved, her eyes glittering. At high school she and Sonya had been the star pupils of their class: invariably side by side on the front bench, they had always put their hands up simultaneously and matched each other in getting top marks. But at school the correct answers had always been obvious: everything one needed to know, then and for ever, had either been told one before or could be found in text-books, incontrovertibly stated. Now, however, Xenia found that she had nothing to contribute to the conversation and that she was terrified of saying something stupid or tactless. All these clever people round the table had different points of view, and it was impossible to say who was right. But living with the Kharitonov family had long since taught the unsophisticated country girl that on such occasions she should not reveal how boring and incomprehensible she found the table-talk by staring blankly or yawning, but instead put on a convincing show of being interested and understanding the arguments by means of a few little tricks: turning to face the person who was talking, occasionally nodding approval, giving an attentive smile or an astonished lift of the eyebrows. Without actually listening to what was being said, Xenia was now assiduously going through the whole performance, at the same time trying hard to use the right knives, forks and spoons from the varied selection. But she was thinking about her own affairs.

She was contemplating her life, intoxicated by something too great to be expressed in words. Every day, every step she took, was bringing her, imperceptibly and inevitably, nearer to that supreme happiness which is the only reason for which we enter this world.

And that longed-for happiness of hers would depend neither on wars and revolutions, nor on revolutionaries and engineers: it was simply bound to come.

Ilya Isakovich gave the appearance not so much of arguing as of thinking aloud over his plate.

'How impatient you are for this revolution! Of course, it's easier to shout and it's more fun to make a revolution than to build Russia up. That's too much like hard work. If you were older and could remember 1905 and how it all looked at the time . . .'

No, Father was not going to get away with it so easily today; they had a showdown in store for him.

'You ought to be ashamed of yourself, Papa! All the intelligentsia are for the revolution!'

In the same calm, reflective tone her father went on:

'Don't we belong to the intelligentsia? We, the engineers, who make and build everything that's really important—aren't we the intelligentsia too? A reasonable man cannot be in favour of revolution, because revolution is a long and insane process of destruction. Above all, no revolution ever strengthens a country: it tears it apart, and for a long, long time. What's more, the bloodier and longer-drawn-out it is, and the dearer the country pays for it— the more likely the revolution is to be given the title of "great".'

'But we can't go on living as we are at present either!' cried Sonya in an agonised voice. 'Life is impossible with this stinking monarchy, and it won't just bow out of its own accord. Just you try telling the *monarchy* that it's ruining the country and that it's time for it to abdicate voluntarily!'

In a firm voice, the pot-bellied Ilya Isakovich continued to polish his fingernail on the same piece of tablecloth.

'Don't run away with the idea that everything would suddenly improve if you abolished the monarchy. Something different, and no better, would take its place. Don't imagine that a republic automatically means bread and circuses for all. What would happen? A hundred ambitious lawyers would assemble—and who talks more hot air than lawyers do?—and shout each other down. The people will never be able to govern themselves, in any case.'

The parlourmaid, who was treated by the Arkhangorodskys with more politeness than most people showed to their servants, was handing round the dessert, made up in the shape of little baskets. Zoya Lvovna was telling Obodovsky how last summer she and Mademoiselle had taken a trip with the children around southern Europe..

'They will! They will!' Two voices shouted in unison, two confident young fists banged the table. And with a last, black glance of fierce hope they looked again at the former anarchist: surely no one could fall so low and so irretrievably?

No, he was not wholly ruined: he appeared to be in agreement with them, but although he looked as if he would like to contradict the host, he was listening to his hostess.

Ilya Isakovich began talking with greater insistence; he was starting to get excited, which he betrayed by a slight twitching of his eyebrows and moustache.

' "Arise, ye starvelings from your slumbers", eh? That is pure irresponsibility. I have built two hundred mills, steam and electric, in southern Russia, and if those starvelings really do arise and start lashing out, how many of those mills will be left to grind the corn? And what will we have to eat—even at this table?'

He had laid himself open, he had offered them the ideal moment to strike! Scarcely able to hold back her tears of outrage and shame, Sonya almost exploded as she shouted:

'And that's why you and the rabbi *demonstrated* your loyalty to the monarchy and the city governor, is it? How *could* you? What came over you?'

Ilya Isakovitch smoothed down the table-napkin on his chest. He did not allow his voice to rise or to crack as he said:

'The process of history is much more complex than you, with your crude plans to lay violent hands on it, can imagine. The country one lives in is in trouble. So which is right: to say, "Go to hell, I'll have none of you" or to say, "I want to help you, I belong here"? Living in this country, one must make up one's mind once and for all and stick to one's decision. Do I really belong to it heart and soul? Or don't I? If I don't, then I can smash it or leave it, it makes no difference which I do . . . But if I *do* belong to it, then I must adapt myself to the slow process of history, by work, by persuasion and gradual change . . .'

Zoya Lvovna was listening too. She had resolved this problem in her own way. At Passover they ate matzos and then, at the Orthodox Easter, they baked Easter-cakes and painted eggs. Broadminded people should be able to accept and understand all viewpoints.

Naum wanted to cut him off sharply, but out of respect and gratitude for what the Arkhangorodskys had done for his father he thought better of it. Sonya, however, screamed out everything that had been building up inside her:

'Living in this country? You call it *living*? You live in Rostov by grace of the fact that you're an honorary citizen—but anybody who hasn't managed to get an education can rot in the Pale of Settlement! Because you've called your daughter Sofia and your son Vladimir, do you really think they take you for a Russian? It's an absurd, humiliating, slavish position—but at least you don't have to emphasise your loyalty to the slave-master! You're a city councillor! What kind of Russia do you think you're supporting "in trouble"? What kind of Russia are you proposing to build? Have you seen the notices advertising training-courses for nurses? "Only those of the Christian faith will be accepted"! I suppose Jewish girls are going to put poison in the wounded men's food, are they? And in the Rostov hospital there's a plaque over a bed which reads: "In honour of P. A. Stolypin"! And another "In honour of the Governor of the City, Major-General Zvorykin"! What lunacy! Is there any limit to such absurdity? The colossal city of Rostov, so full of educated people and with all your mills and your city council—yet by a stroke of the pen it's put under the jurisdiction of the Ataman of those same Cossacks who ride us down with whips! Do you really have to go and sing "God Save the Tsar" at a tsarist monument?'

Ilya Isakovich bit his lips, and his table-napkin fell out of his tight collar.

'All the same . . . all the same . . . one must rise above it, and one must be able to see that there is more to Russia than the "Union of the Russian People", that there is also . . .'

He was either out of breath or deeply hurt, and Obodovsky gently filled in the pause by remarking:

'There is also the Union of Russian Engineers, for example.'

And he turned his keen eyes on the young people.

'Yes!' Arkhangorodsky pulled himself together and leaned his arm on the table. 'The Union of Russian Engineers—does that count for less?'

'The Black Hundreds,' Sonya shouted, attacking her dessert, 'that's what counts! You went to pay your respects to the Black Hundreds, not to your country! I'm ashamed of you!'

Now she really had gone too far. In a shaking voice, both palms on his chest, Ilya Isakovich mimed his feelings.

'On one side—the Black Hundreds, on the other—the Red Hundreds! And in the middle'—he formed his hands into the shape of a ship's keel—'a dozen people who want to pass through to get on with a job of work! Impossible!' He opened his hands and clapped them together. 'They are crushed—flattened!'

63

During the reign of Alexander III the Grand-Duke Nikolai Nikolaevich was in disfavour, and was not included in the Tsar's entourage. Under Nicholas II he was given preferment over the swarm of other grand-dukes, among whom he stood out head and shoulders, both physically and intellectually. Yet his position was not secure. At times he exerted a strong influence on the Tsar and bent him to his will. It was said, for instance, that it was the Grand-Duke Nikolai Nikolaevich who, by threatening to shoot himself in the Tsar's study, had forced Nicholas II to issue the constitutional manifesto of October 17th 1905 and to convoke the Duma. The Grand-Duke was in touch with public opinion; he did not turn away in fear from the demands of the various political parties, but listened to them. There were occasions, in his hopeless behind-the-scenes struggle against the Empress, when he lost appointments, influence and support, and relapsed into the shadows. Thus the dissolution of the Council of State Defence in 1908 was motivated by sheer jealousy, the aim being to deprive the Grand-Duke Nikolai Nikolaevich of his chairmanship of the Council, a move which also had the effect of putting a stop to all the work of re-forming the Russian army which he and General Palitsyn had inaugurated after the Russo-Japanese War. Since then Nikolai Nikolaevich had been excluded from all participation in strategic planning and the general formulation of army policy, merely retaining the rank of general and the post of Commander of the St Petersburg Military District.

As the likelihood of war grew, the Emperor was persuaded that only he himself had the right and the ability to command the

Russian army; consequently, in his own peculiar, arbitrary and to a trained military mind incomprehensible fashion, he set about choosing his close advisers and subordinates. As Chief of Staff to the Commander-in-Chief he appointed Yanushkevich, well known as an office-bound pen-pusher. He was, in fact, a professor at the General Staff Academy, but he was only the Professor of Military Administration; although well versed in the organisation, logistics and accounting procedures of the army, he had not the faintest conception of the command of troops in the field. This lack might have been made up by the appointment of a strong, competent Quartermaster-General, but instead the Tsar selected for the post the plodding, slow-witted and narrow-minded General Danilov.

When war came, however, the Emperor, either through failure of nerve, or on constitutional grounds, or from awareness of the public mood, changed his mind. Despite his previous decision, and against Court opposition, he appointed the Grand-Duke Nikolai Nikolaevich as Commander-in-Chief. And in his usual charming, unbusinesslike manner, he asked the Grand-Duke, as a personal favour, not to change the staff of General Headquarters but to leave his appointees in their posts.

Nikolai Nikolaevich had always regarded the will of the Lord's Anointed as sacred. He had been brought up to regard his nephew as his ruler; otherwise the monarchical principle was meaningless. Previously, in anticipation of his appointment as Commander-in-Chief, Nikolai Nikolaevich had intended to make a clean sweep of Headquarters and to staff it with efficient and deserving men; he had enjoyed the thought of how he would astonish Russia and shock the Court by appointing General Palitsyn as Chief of Staff, and as Quartermaster-General the modest, unassuming General Alexeyev, a man with an amazingly clear military mind, whose talents the Grand-Duke had been the first to discover at a conference held to discuss the annual manoeuvres. Obliged to accede to the Tsar's request, he had to start work with a headquarters staff made up of incompetent men who had been wished upon him and who were more of a hindrance than a help; he also had to accept a war plan which he had not drawn up, which was at odds with his own thinking, and of which, indeed, he knew nothing when he took over his appointment.

He was, however, surprised, delighted and encouraged by a divine omen. On arrival at General Headquarters at Baranovichi

the Grand-Duke received a sudden premonition that his tenure of
the supreme command would be a fortunate one and that Russia
would therefore be victorious. This was vouchsafed to him through
an extraordinary, almost impossible and hence mystic coincidence.
In the small town of Baranovichi (which was little more than a railway junction, and to which General Headquarters had been transferred from St Petersburg), the church turned out to be dedicated to
St Nicholas—not St Nicholas of Myra, whose shrines were to be
found all over Holy Russia—that would have been quite unremarkable—but the Blessed Nikolai Kochan, a fool-in-Christ and miracle-
worker from Novgorod, whose feast-day was July 27th (almost the
day of their arrival at Baranovichi); this was the Commander-in-
Chief's own name-day and the Blessed Nicholas was, therefore, his
patron saint. There were practically no other churches dedicated to
him in the whole of Russia. This coincidence could not be mere
chance; it was a mystic sign. In order to have time to meditate upon
the full, true significance of this heavenly portent the Grand-Duke
clearly ought not to absent himself long from this place of good
omen. Rather than spend his time among the regiments and
divisions in the front line, he should remain at Baranovichi, where
all the railway lines intersected; it was here that fate intended him
to bring about a Russian victory!

The decision to keep General Headquarters permanently at one
site resulted in a steady, comfortable routine in which duty and
leisure alternated in measured sequence. The two trains comprising
General Headquarters were drawn up at the edge of a forest;
the Commander-in-Chief's personal train was stationed almost in
the middle of it. The Quartermaster-General's Department, where
all operational and strategic matters were dealt with, was billeted in
a little house chosen because it was a mere twenty paces from the
coach in which were the Grand-Duke's sleeping quarters. If any
signals or other news arrived at night the Commander-in-Chief was
not disturbed; only after he had risen at nine o'clock in the morning, had washed and said his prayers, were messages brought for
him to study over his morning tea. After tea the Chief of Staff came
to make his report. Two hours were spent in discussing operational
matters, followed by lunch at noon. The Grand-Duke then lay
down to rest, and afterwards went for a drive in his car (never
faster than fifteen miles per hour, for fear of accidents); it was by
then time for afternoon tea, after which there were no further

serious duties, the rest of the day being taken up with minor matters such as the affairs of his personal suite, or with private talks. Before dinner the Grand-Duke would sit down in his coach to write his daily letter to his wife in Kiev, in which he gave a minute account of the events of the day. He found life impossible without mental communion with his beloved wife: this was one thing which he would have to forgo if he were to spend time visiting the front-line units; as it was, the permanence of his location at General Headquarters enabled the Commander-in-Chief to receive his wife's letters with absolute regularity. At half-past seven in the evening, as in Petersburg, dinner for all officers of the staff was served in the dining-car, always with vodka and wine; later there was tea again, although attendance at this was not obligatory.

Daily at vespers and at the liturgy on feast-days the Commander-in-Chief attended his own church, where the choir consisted of specially chosen singers from the Court chapel in St Petersburg and the Kazan Cathedral. When alone, the Grand-Duke always felt himself to be in the presence of God; he never sat down to a meal without saying grace, and every night he used to pray for a long time on his knees, bowing his forehead to the ground, completely absorbed in his devotions, convinced that they were of the greatest practical help.

However, no victories came. Even on the Austrian front things were not going well, whilst in East Prussia the battle of Gumbinnen was not followed by a second, culminating success: the Russian armies were not pushing the enemy either into the sea or across the Vistula. Samsonov began by capturing several towns, then communications were broken off. The next news was of Artamonov's dismissal; in the Grand-Duke's opinion this had been done much too hastily—removing one's corps commanders in that fashion was no way to fight a war. Then came general silence. On the 16th Zhilinsky arrived in Baranovichi, complaining that Samsonov had arbitrarily broken off communications and was now completely out of touch. Colonel Vorotyntsev, who had been sent to Second Army, had for some reason not yet returned. This prolonged lack of information was most unsettling. All day long on the 17th there was still no news. On the night of the 18th the Grand-Duke was woken on the receipt of a strange, dubious and alarming telegram: although enciphered in the correct military code, it had been sent by the normal civilian telegraph service, bypassing Army Group

Headquarters, and read as follows: 'After five-day battle region Neidenburg-Hohenstein-Bischofsburg greater part Second Army destroyed. Army Commander shot himself. Remnants of army fleeing across Russian frontier.' It was signed only by the Chief of Signals of Second Army. Why had it not been signed by a more senior officer? Why not by the Chief of Staff? What was the answer to this mystery? Was it a mistake made under stress by some nervous officer? Why had nothing been heard from Zhilinsky and Oranovsky at North-Western Army Group Headquarters, who should be able to provide more information?

Yet the only communication received from Zhilinsky and Oranovsky throughout August 18th was a statement attributing all blame to Samsonov and an account, which read like a boys' adventure story, of how the headquarters staff of Second Army had escaped encirclement. The report ended: 'No information to hand concerning situation of corps of Second Army. Can be assumed that I Corps is still engaged around Neidenburg... Large numbers of stragglers from xv Corps arriving in Ostrolenka.'

This was too little to clarify the situation, but enough to cause disquiet.

Nevertheless Danilov and Yanushkevich were still combining to persuade the Grand-Duke that the situation did not amount to an irretrievable disaster and that it might yet turn out favourably. All the same, the Commander-in-Chief felt a twinge of unease: if nothing more precise than Zhilinsky's vague assumption was known about I Corps, which was relatively close and accessible, then what of those corps which were further away? He sensed the onset of a catastrophe in which human forces were powerless to intervene and only Heaven itself could save them. He went to vespers as usual and later, in his private compartment on the train, he remained alone for a long time, praying on his narrow, bony knees in front of the lighted icon-lamps, a tall figure even in this posture.

So far there was still no formal, written report from Zhilinsky on the rout of Second Army, and consequently the Grand-Duke was not justified in submitting a similar official report to the Tsar. However, for the next few days he went through his daily routine dully and mechanically: tall and stately as a poplar, stiffly erect, shoulders squared, he strode about the site of General Headquarters or walked up and down the little garden that had been laid out alongside the railway track. The keen, soldierly expression which made him look so much younger than his age had vanished from his face; he was now patently almost an old man. With his usual reserved courtesy he chatted with members of his personal suite and with officers of the staff, although, according to the tacit rules of security observed at Headquarters, operational matters were never discussed anywhere except in the building occupied by the Quartermaster-General's staff. It was particularly important to conceal the news from the representatives of the Allies—the Frenchman, the Englishman, the Belgian, the Serb, and the Montenegrin—who were living in the same train and always dined with the Russian officers; there was no need for them to know the bad news until it had to be publicly admitted. And although the disquieting rumours passed to and fro in whispers and faces began to look grim, they all followed the Grand-Duke's example, and life at General Headquarters outwardly maintained its unbroken routine. Apparently nonchalant, Count Mengden of the Chevalier Guards, the Grand-Duke's aide-de-camp, still walked up and down between the Grand-Duke's coach and the Quartermaster-General's house giving his piercing whistle to summon and dispatch his carrier-pigeons, and continued to train his pet badger.

By the 19th, however, the time had come not only to report the catastrophe to the Tsar, but to release a statement to the newspapers, for rumours were already filtering through to the press.

The Grand-Duke took refuge in uncommunicative gloom; he could not predict how the Tsar, who was notoriously fickle in his attitude towards his favourites, would react to the news. His reply to reports never came quickly, so they would have to wait for two or three days. Of course the Empress, together with the Rasputin party at Court and Sukhomlinov, would inevitably try to use the defeat in East Prussia as a weapon against the Grand-Duke and might even succeed in having him dismissed without being given a chance to justify himself. Seen from Petersburg, the vast distances which separated Neidenburg or Bialystok from Baranovichi shrank to nothing; they would have little difficulty in convincing the Tsar that the whole affair was the fault of the Commander-in-Chief.

But even more oppressive than waiting for the monarch's reply was the Grand-Duke's nagging awareness of his own ignorance of the events for which he expected to be punished. What had happened? How had it happened? What was the extent of the disaster? It was all still confused or unknown. Zhilinsky had powerful connections at Court, and the Grand-Duke was not in a position simply to order him to give a rapid and complete account of what had happened as he would have done with any other subordinate. It might be that he knew the answers but was concealing them, while the Commander-in-Chief bore the ultimate responsibility.

On the night of the 20th General Headquarters again demanded a detailed report from North-Western Army Group Headquarters, but Oranovsky replied that he too was still unable to obtain enough information for a comprehensive statement.

Until then, although the nights had been cold, the days had been regularly and oppressively hot. On the morning of the 20th, however, the sun had not shone in its full splendour, the weather had been overcast since dawn, and the sky had grown imperceptibly hazier hour by hour. There were no clouds and only a very light wind, but it was chilly. Then a mist had arisen in the west and by noon the whole sky was lowering and grey.

Although heavy-hearted, the Grand-Duke did his best to keep to the usual routine. At the appointed time he came out of his coach dressed for his daily airing, which today was to be on horseback. Then he saw the Chief of Army Communications, a ponderous, slow-moving but kind-hearted man who collected cigar-labels. The Commander-in-Chief remembered that he had some labels from a new brand of cigars, told his colleague to wait and went back into his coach to fetch them.

As he came out of the coach again he saw coming towards him, striding out of the forest, none other than Colonel Vorotyntsev. Could he be dreaming? Was this Vorotyntsev, alive and well? Here was the man he needed more than anyone else.

Vorotyntsev was walking swiftly, glancing around as though trying to overtake someone in order to be the first to arrive. But there was no one else apart from the Chief of Communications (delighted with his cigar-labels), an aide-de-camp and the general-in-waiting, who was standing a little further away. Vorotyntsev was wearing no greatcoat, only his tunic, as though he had been at Headquarters all the time. Although his was the unmistakable stride of a regimental officer, it betrayed a slight stiffness which almost amounted to a limp. One of his shoulders was noticeably higher than the other, there was a scab of clotted blood on his jaw and his cheeks were unevenly shaven.

'Vorotyntsev!' the Grand-Duke was the first to exclaim with pleasure before the colonel had time to approach and make his report. 'You're back! Why hasn't anyone told me?'

Vorotyntsev saluted with rather less smartness than was normal at General Headquarters and with a trace of the same stiffness that was in his gait, as though his arm was heavier than usual.

'Your Highness! I've only just arrived—about ten minutes ago.'

(He had not 'only just' arrived, but had been lurking in the forest for several hours, where he had left Blagodaryov with his greatcoat and knapsack. Knowing how things worked at Headquarters, he had purposely arranged this direct meeting with the Grand-Duke, so as to avoid seeing Yanushkevich and Danilov.)

'Are you wounded?' With a rapid, expressive movement of his eyebrows the Commander-in-Chief indicated that he had guessed at Vorotyntsev's bandaged shoulder under his tunic.

'Oh, it's nothing.'

With urgent entreaty in his eyes he stared at the Grand-Duke. The latter's strong, angular features had at once taken on a more youthful look, although the change was provoked by a sense of alarm.

'Well,' he said, 'what's been happening out there? Tell me!'

Vorotyntsev was standing stiffly to attention in the regulation manner required when reporting to a senior officer, but his eyes were watching the aide-de-camp and the general who was approaching from the opposite direction. If only he could gain the Grand-Duke's attention before all these others bore down on him!

'Your Highness, I request your permission to be heard in confidence.'

'Yes, of course.' The Grand-Duke gave a decisive nod and with a characteristically abrupt movement turned sharply on his heel. His long, thin, booted legs were already mounting the steps of his railway coach as he ordered his aide-de-camp not to admit anyone.

The interior of the coach had been converted into a study. Carpeted from wall to wall, it contained a desk, a large icon of Christ and a portrait of the Tsar; a presentation sword, crossed with its scabbard, hung on the wall.

The Supreme Commander-in-Chief of all the armed forces of

mighty Russia—serious, intelligent and accessible to rational argument—was now facing the colonel tête-à-tête across the desk, undisturbed by advisers, eager to hear the news which Vorotyntsev alone could give him.

In all Vorotyntsev's military career he had never been in such a situation before—and never would be again. It was a unique, unrepeatable encounter: a chance for a clear-thinking combatant officer to exert a direct influence on the functioning of the entire military machine. All his previous service had been a prelude to this culminating moment: his thoughts were ordered and purposeful, his mind keyed up to full pitch. He had slept like a log for almost two nights and a day, and although his body still ached and throbbed, his head was clear. The fortunate start to the interview increased his mental alertness.

He began his account, talking with ease and fluency; never overawed in any company, he was unaffected by the august presence of the Grand-Duke. In crisp, summary terms he described the inadequacy of the preparations for Second Army's advance: how it had been forced ahead too hard and too fast; how Samsonov had intended the operation to go, and how it had actually gone; how the Germans had reacted; how many major opportunities had been lost and what had occurred as a result. Throughout the period of Second Army's encirclement by the Germans, and afterwards among the survivors, Vorotyntsev had asked questions and collected data whenever possible, and all this information now helped him to re-interpret the clear mental picture of the battle-front with which he had so boldly strode into Samsonov's headquarters only nine days ago. But more than that, he brought with him into the Commander-in-Chief's private quarters the scorching breath of battle which he had inhaled during the ebb and flow of the fighting around Usdau and the hopeless attempt to defend Neidenburg with a few companies of the Estland Regiment. He brought with him, too, that passionate sense of conviction which inspires belief less by its veracity than by its origin in personal suffering. He spoke with the special insight of one who had witnessed Yaroslav Kharitonov's boyish delight when on discovering that the troops ahead of them were Russians he had said:

'You mean . . . you haven't been surrounded? And the people behind you are Russians too, not Germans?'

Graven equally on his memory were the words of Arsenii

Blagodaryov as he gave a sigh of relief like a blast from a blacksmith's bellows:

'Is that Russia ahead of us? Whew, thank God—we thought we'd
never drag ourselves that far . . .'

Then, collapsing like an empty sack, he had rammed his now
unnecessary butcher's knife into the ground.

Everything which the Commander-in-Chief, unable to see or
imagine the reality, had summoned into motion from a great
distance was now being brought back by Vorotyntsev and dumped
in the middle of his desk.

As far as he knew it, the colonel undertook to describe the fate of
each battalion of almost every regiment—which ones had been
destroyed while fighting rearguard actions, which ones had escaped.
The artillery had been completely wiped out and no less than
seventy thousand men had been caught in the ring of encirclement,
though there remained the consolation that the remarkable number
of between ten and fifteen thousand had managed to get away,
without the benefit of leadership from their generals.

Didn't the Commander-in-Chief know any of this already? Had
North-Western Army Group Headquarters told him nothing?

The Commander-in-Chief's long, thin, well-bred features had
taken on the intent look of a hunter. He hardly interrupted or asked
questions (Vorotyntsev's account was in any case fluent and
articulate), only occasionally picking up his fountain pen with a
mechanical gesture, but without taking notes. He chewed on his
cigar and smoked it furiously, as though its very length was keeping
him from reaching the truth. To say that he sympathised with the
men of Samsonov's army was an understatement: he was absorbed
in the story, was himself transformed into one of the wretched
participants in that disastrous battle.

The hope grew in Vorotyntsev that he had not plunged in vain
into that hell-fire, had not wasted his time there as a mere onlooker,
and that he would soon justify himself by causing the heavy hand of
the Grand-Duke to be raised in retribution against all those block-
headed fools. Vorotyntsev had never been guilty of overmuch
respect for his superiors in rank, and was now less so than ever.
He discussed corps commanders as though they were inefficient
platoon leaders whom he himself could dismiss.

Suddenly, while talking about Artamonov, who more than any
other commander had aroused his anger, he sensed a cooling of

the Commander-in-Chief's attitude and a hostility in his glance. For all the dissimilarity between the two men, he could not help being reminded of the look of blank impenetrability which he had seen in the eyes of Artamonov.

The Grand-Duke agreed that the story about the fatal order was incomprehensible; but it might, of course, have been due to a mistake made by a junior officer.

It was a weakness of the Grand-Duke's that he tended to accept and overlook the failings of his subordinates. Unlike the Tsar, who, while smiling his habitual shy smile, was quite capable of casting his favourite of yesterday into outer darkness, the Grand-Duke was proud of his positively quixotic loyalty: he would always defend anyone whom he had once liked.

Even if the man were an incompetent clown.

As a way of testing the Grand-Duke's reactions, Vorotyntsev listed the names of the brave regiments who had been annihilated at Usdau by Artamonov's act of criminal foolishness, taking care to mention the Yenisei Regiment at whose head the Grand-Duke himself had so recently led the ceremonial parade at Peterhof. At this the Commander-in-Chief said:

'Of course, there will be the most rigorous enquiry. But he is a brave general and a deeply religious man.'

At this moment his interest in Vorotyntsev's story, all his sympathetic attention, seemed to undergo an eclipse by a vaporous cloud of grand-ducal solemnity.

Vorotyntsev fell silent. If the order to retreat from Usdau was not absolute folly, if it was not a crime to pull back troops who after hours of bombardment had spontaneously gone over to the attack, if the decision to cause a thoroughly battle-worthy corps to withdraw twenty-five miles, thereby destroying an army, was not treachery; if all this was not good reason to call Artamonov to account and tear the general's epaulettes from his shoulders—what was the point of mobilising an army at all? What indeed was the point of declaring war?

Why, the Grand-Duke's very coach should have reared up in horror at Vorotyntsev's account! The whole train ought to have shuddered and jumped the rails! But it stayed unshaken and the remains of some tea, cooling in a glass, did not so much as tremble. The Commander-in-Chief's strong right hand was not going to be raised in punishment and redress, and Vorotyntsev's superhuman efforts had been made in vain. He had accumulated all the initial impetus needed to move a vast mass, he had been utterly convinced that he was about to jolt it into motion—yet after all the mass had proved smoothly resistant, and his outstretched arms had slithered ineffectually off its rounded surface.

He had attempted to move the immovable.

His strength had not failed him while he was giving his report, although he had talked long and hard. Now he was spent; he needed to rest and draw breath.

The Commander-in-Chief, too, sat there like a beaten man, shoulders slumped, his martial bearing gone.

'I thank you, Colonel. What you have said will not be forgotten. General Zhilinsky arrives here tomorrow, and we will arrange a conference in the Operations Section. You will attend and make your report.'

Hope revived in Vorotyntsev as he stared across the desk at the sad, thin, old man with the long, horse-like face. Perhaps tomorrow the whole affair might be dragged into the open; perhaps the right steps would be taken after all. In fact, Artamonov was not important; what was important was that the appropriate lessons should be learnt.

The Grand-Duke made a gesture indicating that the audience was over. Vorotyntsev stood up and requested permission to go. Only now did he realise that he had been sitting there for two hours.

Nikolai Nikolaevich's strong mouth was twisted into a deep grimace of pain: Vorotyntsev believed his report had not been entirely useless.

There was a knock at the door, and Derfelden, an aide-de-camp, hurried in with a sealed telegram. Leaning forward respectfully, the tall Horse Guard announced as he handed it over:

'From His Majesty!'

He turned on his heel and started to leave.

The Commander-in-Chief rose and read the telegram standing up.

Vorotyntsev's mind was still in such a whirl that he failed to realise that he had no right to be present during the reading of a telegram from the Tsar. He had a confused impression that something still remained to be said.

By the fading daylight (the weather outside was becoming more and more dull and overcast) he saw the noble features of the

Grand-Duke lighten, grow calmer and younger. The crooked line of grief which Vorotyntsev's story had just chiselled around his mouth smoothed out and vanished.

The Commander-in-Chief stretched out his long arm after the retiring Derfelden.

'Captain! Ask the archpriest to come and see me—I saw him pass by a moment ago.'

All his erect dignity of bearing had returned to the resilient, wiry old man. He took up a majestic stance in front of the portrait of the man who was the ruler of all Russia by the mandate of Heaven: his sovereign.

Vorotyntsev stood half a head shorter than the Grand-Duke. Once again he saluted and asked leave to go, but the Commander-in-Chief replied solemnly:

'No, Colonel, since you are here, and since you have not shirked your duty in telling me your unhappy story, you have earned the right to be the first to hear our consolation for it. Listen to the comfort His Majesty offers us, hear how graciously he has responded to the report of the catastrophe!'

' And he read out the telegram in a clear voice, savouring every word of the text more than if he had composed it himself:

' "Dear Uncle Nick, I grieve deeply with you over the loss of our gallant Russian soldiers. But we must submit to the will of God. He who endures to the end shall be saved. Yours, Nicky."

' "He who endures to the end . . . shall be saved!" ' Entranced, the handsome, erect old campaigner repeated the phrase in a reverent tone as though reporting to some invisible senior officer. Relishing the old-fashioned, biblical words, he seemed to find new meaning in their repetition.

There was a knock and the archpriest entered, a man with a thin, gentle, intelligent face.

'Listen, Father Georgii. Hear how kind His Majesty has been to us, what joy he sends us! "Dear Uncle Nick, I grieve deeply with you over the loss of our gallant Russian soldiers. But we must submit to the will of God. He who endures to the end shall be saved. Yours, Nicky." '

Composing his features into a suitable expression, the archpriest crossed himself towards the icon.

'And there is another message as well,' the Grand-Duke went on. 'The Tsar informs us that he has ordered the icon "The

Blessed Virgin Appearing in a Vision to the Holy Father Sergius"
to be dispatched immediately to General Headquarters from the
Monastery of the Trinity and St Sergius. What a joy this is!'

'That is splendid news, Your Highness!' said the archpriest,
stressing his remark with a dignified bow. 'This exceptional icon
was painted on a piece of wood from the coffin of the Holy Father
Sergius himself. For three centuries it has accompanied our armies
into battle. It was with Tsar Alexei Mikhailovich on his Lithuanian
campaign; it was with Peter the Great at the battle of Poltava, and
with Tsar Alexander the Blessed on his European campaign. It
was also . . . at the Commander-in-Chief's Headquarters in the
war against Japan.'

'This is wonderful! It is a sign of God's grace!' The Grand-
Duke strode excitedly across the floor, covering the distance in two
of his long strides. 'This icon will bring us the aid of the Mother of
God!'

*

"Praying kneads no dough"

*

Document No. 5

AUGUST 20TH 1914, TO THE EMPEROR NICHOLAS II:

*Happy inform Your Majesty good news. Victory won by
General Russky's army at Lvov after week's uninterrupted
fighting. Austrians retreating in complete disorder, some
in headlong flight, abandoning light and heavy weapons,
artillery and transport. Enemy suffered huge losses, large
numbers of prisoners taken . . .*

(Signed) **Nikolai,**
Adjutant-General,
Commander-in-Chief.

Document No. 6
German leaflet dropped from aircraft

RUSSIAN SOLDIERS!
THE TRUTH IS BEING KEPT FROM YOU.
THE RUSSIAN SECOND ARMY IS DESTROYED!
300 GUNS, ALL TRANSPORT, 93 THOUSAND
MEN TAKEN PRISONER . . . THE RUSSIAN
PRISONERS OF WAR ARE VERY SATISFIED
WITH THEIR TREATMENT AND DO NOT WANT
TO RETURN TO RUSSIA, AS THEIR LIVING
CONDITIONS IN GERMANY ARE GOOD.
BELGIUM IS BEATEN. OUR TROOPS ARE ON
THE OUTSKIRTS OF PARIS . . . .

64

The season had turned to autumn so quickly, it seemed incredible that only two days ago it had been hot summer weather and a greatcoat had been a burden to one's shoulders. Today, though, a coat was just right. An autumn wind was blowing gustily through the sparse pine forest and now and again a shower would fall from the cloudy, changeable, sky. In weather like this it was good not to have to crawl about in the swamps.

The two men, Vorotyntsev and Svechin, had turned up the collars of their greatcoats, thrust their hands into their pockets and were walking, without swords, almost as if strolling about off duty. Around them stood the tall, bare pine-trees, only their tops moving slightly in the wind.

'No!' Vorotyntsev shook his head. The two days he had spent at General Headquarters had not succeeded in calming his feelings. 'To speak out once and for all and say what one really thinks—it's more than a pleasure, it's a sacred duty! One ought to get it all off one's chest and then die afterwards if necessary.'

All Svechin's features—ears, nose, mouth, flashing eyes—were built on the generous scale which denotes a man of passion, yet he was grimly imperturbable and unconvinced by Vorotyntsev's outburst.

'Have you ever seen a junior officer in the Russian army induce his seniors to change their minds by making passionate speeches at them? On a minor issue a well-argued case or a well-written document can sometimes be effective, but never in a big thing like this. You don't really believe that you're going to shake them up and make them see reason all at once, do you? I warn you: you're standing on the edge of a bottomless pool—and not a pool of water either, but pitch. There won't even be a ripple to show where you fell in. You'll only destroy yourself.'

'What if I do? "He who endures to the end shall be saved"! They can't do any more than send me to command a regiment. And I wasn't a bad regimental commander in my time.'

Svechin was two years younger than Vorotyntsev, but it was impossible to tell this from his manner of speaking.

'Fine—except that there will be a bunch of thick-headed fools above you, hindering you at every step. They'll give you idiotic orders, you'll have to carry them out and you'll pay for it in soldiers' lives. You'll end by sending me a telegram at General Headquarters begging me to save you from these imbeciles and get you out of an impossible position! No, my dear fellow, the people who get things done around here are not the rebels but the doers. They go about it discreetly and they don't make a lot of fuss, but they get things done. For instance, if in one day I manage to alter a couple of stupid orders so that they make sense, and by doing so justify a decision made by a brave regimental commander or save a battalion of sappers from being needlessly sent to their deaths, then I reckon my day hasn't been wasted. And with you working alongside me we could probably see to it that two more orders were redrafted on the right lines—perhaps even four! It's senseless to try and fight the authorities; the way to deal with them is to steer them discreetly in the right direction. You can be more use to Russia here than anywhere else. If you get yourself kicked out of Headquarters they'll simply send in someone else worse. Why let that happen?'

Of all the officers in the Operations Section, indeed in the whole Quartermaster-General's Department and, for that matter, in the entire General Headquarters, Svechin was the only man Vorotyntsev trusted, and Svechin felt the same about Vorotyntsev. But trust between individuals is not enough; if there is to be trust, it should not be kept in compartments. The previous evening, after his interview with the Commander-in-Chief, Vorotyntsev had made his report to Yanushkevich and Danilov, but it had been an extremely superficial affair: they had made no attempt to go into detail and would have preferred no report at all. With Svechin, however, he had discussed the subject at length late into the night, and the latter had supplied him with certain extra details only available to someone at General Headquarters. Today, from early morning right up to the last minutes before the conference, they had continued to thrash the matter out.

'No doubt you're right,' Vorotyntsev replied with an obstinate grin on his emaciated but still keen and lively face. 'But if only you had been through what I've just been through . . . Even your common sense and mine put together wouldn't . . . No, I'm sure this is a state of mind which only comes to us once or twice in a lifetime. I'm determined to see to it that, come what may, the truth and nothing but the truth gets hammered out today. If only the Grand-Duke had reacted differently yesterday . . .'

'You must realise that the Grand-Duke is simply waiting for the arrival of the telegram announcing the capture of Lvov. They're *all* waiting for that telegram,' Svechin went on insistently, unsmilingly, with irrefutable logic, his eyes glaring ferociously as he pressed the point home. 'And that telegram will simply be used to obliterate the whole Samsonov affair. They'll set the bells ringing all over Russia to celebrate our own incompetence—because the truth is, we had the Austrian army in the grip of a pincer-movement and let it go, so that when we captured Lvov it was empty.'

But Vorotyntsev was incapable of grasping the significance of the Austrian front; his mind was obsessed by the German encircling movement at Neidenburg. He replied heatedly:

'You might have convinced me and I might have kept my mouth shut if this were a purely military matter. I agree that a defeat in one sector can be counterbalanced by success somewhere else. But this isn't just a military problem any longer, don't you see? It's a *moral* issue. To drive one's people unprepared to the slaughter is something far beyond the considerations of mere strategy. "He who endures to the end . . . !" Thanks to them, *we* are the ones who have to suffer and endure—to the bitter end! And none of *them* even go to the front line to see for themselves! They're quite ready to endure four or five more massive defeats on this scale—but by then only the Lord above will be able to help them!'

'Even so, you won't do any good,' Svechin insisted firmly, hissing the words through clenched teeth. 'Nothing would be changed and you'd simply get a bloody nose. Russia is doomed to be governed by fools; she knows no other way. I know what I'm talking about. The only thing to do is keep your head down and get on with the job.'

'But I can't sit quietly and keep my head down! I won't be able to sit through this conference without getting up to say what I think. Look—don't you see?—it's like an arrow in my chest, burning and throbbing, and I've got to pull it out. How can I settle down to work again until I've done that?'

'I'm afraid you'll do something stupid. Keep an eye open in my direction during the conference.'

They had come back to the cluster of buildings beside the Headquarters train at the edge of the forest. It was five minutes to ten, and other officers were starting to converge on the cottage that housed the Quartermaster-General's Department.

Just then, on a path at the edge of the wood skirting the senior officers' quarters, waddling like a duck in his haste, a fussy little army clerk came towards them. He was followed by Arsenii Blagodaryov striding along at one pace to the other man's two, with his naturally straight-backed carriage which owed nothing to military training. Chest out, arms swinging freely as though he had cast all his burdens from his shoulders, Blagodaryov looked around him with an uninhibited curiosity that was quite unaffected by the exalted atmosphere of the Headquarters and the proximity of any number of grand-dukes.

At once Vorotyntsev's tension and irritation seemed to vanish. He held out his hand to stop the clerk.

Preoccupied but quick-witted, the man saluted without touching his temple and without holding his elbow fully extended (like all the rankers at Headquarters, he was well aware of the exact pecking order among all these senior officers) and spoke first without waiting to be questioned.

'Yes, we're going to take a complete record of the conference, your honour; every word will be noted down.'

'H'mm.' Vorotyntsev let him go and turned affectionately towards Arsenii.

Blagodaryov saluted the two officers, 'his' colonel and the other, his elbow well out and his head held straight, but without any hint of servility and almost as if the gesture were part of a game.

'Well, Arsenii, are you being posted to the artillery?'

'Seems so,' said Arsenii with a condescending smile.

'Built like a grenadier, isn't he?' said Vorotyntsev to Svechin, as he clenched his fist and gave Arsenii a friendly, admiring punch in the chest. 'I've arranged for you to be posted to an artillery brigade.'

'Well, that's fine . . .' said Blagodaryov, grinning and running his

tongue round the inside of his cheek. Then he pulled himself up
with a jerk, remembering that this was not the way to behave here;
they weren't in the front line now. 'Thank you very much indeed!'
He saluted again, his large underlip jutting out in what was almost
a smile.

His attitude was not an acquisition dating from the terrible days
of the encirclement and retreat; he had been just the same when
Vorotyntsev had found him at Usdau. Even then he had had the
ability to strike the right note, not only with 'his' colonel but with
every officer. He unfailingly used the correct military expressions,
one felt certain that he would never overstep the bounds of the prescribed relationship, and yet there were times when his tone implied that it was all a game. Although quite unschooled, Arsenii
gave the impression of knowing all there was to know about military science and a great deal more.

'Supposing I'm sent to command a regiment—would you like to
come and join me there?'

'Infantry?' Arsenii pushed out his lower lip.

'Yes.'

Blagodaryov put on an expression as though he were thinking.

'No-o-o,' he drawled. 'I'd still prefer the artillery.' But then he
pretended to check himself. 'But of course—anything you say!'

Vorotyntsev laughed in the way one laughs at children. He put
both his hands on Blagodaryov's shoulders, which meant raising
them well above the height of his own; the epaulettes were no longer
crumpled but had been smoothed out and stiffened with cardboard.

'I'm not going to give you any more orders, Arsenii. You're not
angry with me for having taken you away from the Vyborg Regiment, are you? And for having dragged you into the trap set by the
Germans?'

''Course not,' Arsenii replied quietly and naturally, as though to
a friend from his own village. His nose twitched.

While they had been fighting their way out of the German encirclement, there had been no time to talk, and after that they had
both needed a good long sleep to recuperate. Now each had to go
his separate way in the service, and in any case there was too much
difference in their ranks for a real talk. Somehow the opportunity
had passed.

Vorotyntsev felt a lump in his throat and had to swallow. His
squashed-potato nose still twitching slightly, Arsenii ran his

tongue round the inside of his mouth; his tongue felt as if it was slightly too big.

'Well, who knows . . . perhaps one of these days . . . we can . . . Do your duty, Arsenii . . . I expect you'll be a colonel too one day.'

They both laughed.

'And make sure you go home in one piece.'

'You too!'

Vorotyntsev took off his cap, and Arsenii snatched off his own. A cold wind blew around them, and there was a slight drizzle.

They kissed on the lips. Arsenii had a hug like a bear.

Vorotyntsev turned and ran after Svechin to catch him up. Blagodaryov strode on after the fussy, ill-tempered little clerk.

In the cottage occupied by the Quartermaster-General's Department there were no large rooms; the biggest could just take twenty people sitting closely packed. There were not, on paper, as many as twenty key senior officers in the whole of General Headquarters, but twenty were now assembled, all of them obviously men whose opinions were important.

Two small tables were placed at right angles to each other. At one end was the Commander-in-Chief, the tallest man in the room even when sitting down. Beside him, inseparable as ever, was his brother the Grand-Duke Pyotr Nikolaevich, wearing an expression of diligent attention (although everyone knew that for years he had been engaged not in military affairs but ecclesiastical architecture). Next to him was their cousin, Prince Pyotr Oldenbourg (a charming man). Then came His Serene Highness Adjutant-General Prince Dmitry Golitsyn (who in recent years had been in charge of the imperial hunting estates). The rest included the general-in-waiting, General Petrovo-Solovovo (a most delightful person, the Marshal of Nobility of Ryazan Province), the Commander-in-Chief's Chief of Staff, Lieutenant-General Yanushkevich, the Quartermaster-General, Lieutenant-General Danilov, and the duty general officer of the Headquarters. Immediately opposite the Commander-in-Chief, with his back to the wall at the angle of the tables, sat the General Officer Commanding the North-Western Army Group, General-of-Cavalry Zhilinsky. Next came the representative at Headquarters of the Foreign Office, the representative of the Admiralty and the Chief of Army Communications.

'Those for whom there was not room around the tables included several senior officers from the Operations Section, the Commander-in-Chief's duty aide-de-camp, a Kalmuck prince who was Yanushkevich's ADC, and Zhilinsky's ADC; these had to sit where they could, on chairs by the window or the stove, and, when necessary, wrote in note-pads held on their knees.

The stove had been lit since early morning and its heat was needed. More and more often the window-panes were spattered with showers of chilly rain. Outside it was so dull that it was almost dark enough to switch on the electric light.

As there was so little room to spare for standing up, it was agreed that officers would speak sitting down. This gave the meeting the less formal and more businesslike air of an exchange of opinions rather than an affair of set speeches.

At the invitation of the Grand-Duke, the conference was opened by Zhilinsky. Feeling it unnecessary to look at more than a few of those present, he only half-raised his grey eyebrows and either looked down at his papers or up at the Grand-Duke, occasionally extending his field of vision by moving his head. As usual, he spoke with no attempt to colour his words with emotion. He did not accept that anyone present might regard him as the accused. He spoke in a harsh, didactic tone, as the equal of the Commander-in-Chief who had been summoned on terms of parity to discuss an event which was unpleasant but not of major significance.

The dire catastrophe which had befallen Second Army was wholly the fault of the late General Samsonov. It had begun with Samsonov's failure to carry out the Army Group's initial directive concerning the main axis of advance. (This was then described in detail.) Arbitrarily deviating from the prescribed axis, he had inadmissibly allowed the frontage of his army to become overstretched, had made his army corps march too far and had thereby over-extended the lines of communication and supply. What was worse, he had allowed a gap to open up between First Army and Second Army which had hindered their mutual co-operation. Unlike the punctilious General Rennenkampf, Samsonov had furthermore taken an excessively independent attitude towards many other orders issued to him. (There followed a detailed list of what these were.) Particularly incomprehensible to a normal mind was Samsonov's order of August 14th/15th to his centre corps to continue advancing, when he already knew that both his flanking

[630]

corps had veered outwards from their given axes. This crass error was compounded by Samsonov's impetuous decision to cut off telegraph communication from Neidenburg, thus depriving Army Group Headquarters of any chance of preventing the defeat of Second Army. When, after some delay, Army Group Headquarters discovered the state of affairs, it immediately telegraphed to all the corps of Second Army to retire to their starting lines, and it was entirely the fault of General Samsonov that the centre corps did not receive these signals.

The Army Group Commander did not raise his grating voice in the passages where he accused Samsonov; this served to reinforce the impression of events that he was attempting to convey to the conference, namely that everything was, quite simply, Samsonov's fault—a view which naturally lessened the feelings of guilt and unease of all present.

No one interrupted, no one whispered or even coughed. Only the flies, brought to life by the heat of the stove, buzzed about the room and settled in black clusters on the whitewashed stove-chimney and the ceiling.

Inwardly, Vorotyntsev writhed in agony. At that moment, there was no one in Russia, indeed in all war-torn Europe, whom he hated more than this man who was nicknamed 'the living corpse'. He hated his voice, his mud-coloured face, his long, dyed moustaches with their ends turned up in an attempt to look impressive. But it was not merely for his performance today that he hated this grave-digger: forged link by link ever since his appointment as Chief of the General Staff, the chain of his incompetence had been hung around the neck of the Russian army and was dragging it down to destruction. Now he was deliberately exculpating himself without fear of being contradicted or that there might be any other interpretation of events, least of all that he might be called to account or dismissed from his post, though even if this should happen there would always be another, eminently suitable job waiting for him somewhere else. He had, after all, fulfilled his chief duty, which was to assist General Joffre and Russia's ally France. At the very least he would be invited to Paris to accept bouquets of flowers from grateful French ladies and to lunch with the President of the Republic.

However, notwithstanding the legacy of the cowardly Samsonov, General Zhilinsky was not going to leave his listeners without hope.

He suggested some bold plans for retrieving the situation, namely to stage an immediate repeat performance of the combined manoeuvre of First Army and Second Army around the Masurian Lakes! Rennenkampf was already excellently placed to carry out this operation, having pushed deep into East Prussia, and it only remained to bring Second Army up to strength again with reinforcements, to re-form some of its army corps and to send its new commander, General Scheidemann, into the advance on the same axis as that chosen before the outbreak of hostilities.

Although Zhilinsky's report had covered everything of importance, it was now the turn of General Danilov to speak. The occasion would not be complete without a word from the man whom everyone present regarded as the leading strategist of the Russian army. As such, it was incumbent upon him not only to speak but to utter some profound thoughts, to make it clear that behind that domed forehead his great mind was ceaselessly at work on a whole host of brilliant strategic concepts. The truth was that his forehead was solid bone, his mind moved at a snail's pace, and the thoughts which passed through it were worthless. This being the case, the Quartermaster-General launched on his speech with all the smug self-confidence of a limited, second-class intellect.

He fully agreed, he declared, with all the points that the Army Group Commander had just made. (There followed a detailed recapitulation of what they were.) But certain important observations should be added to that account. If Samsonov had not been so far behind schedule but had crossed the German frontier on August 6th according to plan, and if he had struck a blow at the enemy's flank in the area of the Masurian Lakes as he had been instructed instead of waiting until the Germans had been given time to wheel and make a frontal attack, then the enemy would undoubtedly have been caught off balance and we should today be celebrating a major victory. Furthermore, the disaster had been in no small part due to the fact that the men of Second Army were exhausted, for which General Samsonov was to blame through his failure to give his troops their proper rest-days as laid down in the Manual of Infantry Regulations. He was also guilty of many other errors of lesser significance.

Even worse than what he said was the stupefying air of self-importance which the Quartermaster-General assumed when he had finished speaking. His very face, with its timid eyes, flat, shapeless little ears and thin, spindly moustaches so incongruous that they seemed glued on, was stamped with the blinkered dullness and inertia of some minor provincial official. Yet the airs the man gave himself! When he stopped talking it was as though he dared not go further because it would mean touching on some profound secret which he could not divulge because the present assembly was not select enough. Deliberately he was creating the impression of martyrdom: he, Danilov, must guard the secret and carry on his narrow shoulders the full weight of military responsibility in all its complexity; onerous though the burden was, he, the expert, would solve all their problems for them. He alone, he implied, was the key figure in Russian strategy: officers junior to him could not hope to be so well informed or so capable, whilst above him were only the active but inexperienced Yanushkevich and the Grand-Duke, who, though brave and keen, was quite untrained as a strategist.

Now the floor passed to the Commander-in-Chief's Chief of Staff. How he wished that he could miss his turn! Dark-eyed and bushy-moustached, Yanushkevich was a small man with a puffy face, an insinuating manner and a deep affection for paper and files. Appointed in a fortunate moment by the good-natured Tsar, faced with strategic operational matters the affable Yanushkevich had felt as frightened and lost as Little Red Riding Hood in the dark forest. But it was flattering to occupy such an exalted post, and his delight in being offered it overcame his fears; in any case, how could he disappoint the charming, blue-eyed Emperor, who was as shy as Yanushkevich himself, and admit that he knew nothing at all about the job? Whenever he went driving in a carriage or walked across the parquet-floored expanses of the palaces of St Petersburg, he could not help watching himself from the wings and repeating with fearful delight: 'Lieutenant-General Yanushkevich, Chief of the Russian Imperial General Staff!' As he owed his promotion to the Minister for War, he did express certain doubts to him, but Sukhomlinov brushed them aside in his usual hearty, optimistic manner: 'You'll soon learn the ropes, my dear fellow!' From his first day of appointment, Yanushkevich found himself the prisoner of Danilov, who was the only man who knew anything about operational matters and whose tone of voice never failed to convey reproach that Yanushkevich rather than he had been made Chief of Staff. Yanushkevich, on the other hand, did at least know one thing: that there were several officers in the Russian army who were much greater strategists than Danilov. But the latter was Sukhomlinov's nominee, and Yanushkevich, having privately admitted to Danilov that he regarded him as his superior in military thinking and having promised to make sure that the latter was given exactly the same decorations and promotions as himself, had come to the conclusion that it was after all better to leave Danilov in the job. The only way that these two men could survive the war was to remain lashed together like a pair of boats: Yanushkevich would look after the administrative side, Danilov the strategy.

Yanushkevich went through agonies every morning during the inevitable conferences on operational matters, but he was obliged to look as if he knew what he was talking about. But now the effort required was far greater: he had to maintain sufficient dignity so that no one should suspect how terrified he was of tripping up and how desperately inadequate he felt. How could he possibly criticise Zhilinsky, when the latter was a full general and, although formally his subordinate, in fact senior to him in the General Staff list, and when he himself had been promoted to lieutenant-general ahead of his proper seniority?

In carefully rounded phrases, delivered in a respectful tone of voice, Yanushkevich repeated everything that the others had said before him, adding nothing and missing nothing out, simply altering the sequence of their remarks.

And so it became increasingly clear to the conference just how deeply the late General Samsonov was to blame for the destruction of Second Army. What a relief that he had removed himself by committing suicide! The other generals, of course, would never have made the same mistakes. Consequently the meeting had lost much of its tenseness; everything had been exhaustively discussed, every point covered.

Meanwhile Vorotyntsev, his pencil racing nervously across a sheet of paper on his map-board, had been noting down their excuses and evasions, together with a shattering series of counter-arguments. Higher up on the same sheet of paper, in a steadier and more even hand written the night before in black ink with a Japanese fountain-pen, he had listed the main points of his case. When Yanushkevich spoke he did not even bother to make notes; scarcely listening, he half closed his eyes to avoid the sight of them all and in their place summoned up a mental picture of Samsonov's frank, guileless features—not as they must be now, lying in some unknown forest thicket, nor as they were at Orlau when he had said farewell to his men, but as they had been at Ostrolenka, when he was still fully in charge, still capable of saving the battle (though even then there had been something helpless about his expression). And Vorotyntsev remembered how they had crashed their way through the undergrowth like wild boars as they escaped, remembered Kachkin's boarish snarl as he carried Ofrosimov on his shoulders, and how Blagodaryov had collapsed when they reached the Russian lines as though he had just ploughed two or three hundred acres, and how as a final gesture he had thrust the point of his knife into the ground with his remaining strength.

Vorotyntsev started up from his chair as though about to stand and speak without permission, but Svechin, who was beside him, squeezed his elbow to advise caution. The Grand-Duke did not look in his direction.

With one thin cavalryman's leg crossed over the other, unbending, unapproachable, the ends of his moustaches turned slightly downwards, the Grand-Duke stared ahead, and if he did look at anyone in particular he glared straight down the table into the greyish-yellow face of Zhilinsky with its idiotically raised eyebrows. Only recently, in response to complaints, he had personally empowered Zhilinsky to dismiss Samsonov if it proved necessary, but since yesterday it had become more and more obvious to him that it was Zhilinsky who was chiefly to blame for the catastrophe; his immediate dismissal would be a most suitable demonstration of the Commander-in-Chief's powers and the best possible lesson to the other generals. It would, however, be a pointless move: Zhilinsky's post as Commander of North-Western Army Group was too low for a man of his seniority, and he would be glad to be rid of it. He would immediately rush to Petersburg to complain to the Empress Dowager and the Tsarina, to whisper in corners with Sukhomlinov and to smile at Rasputin. In the overheated atmosphere of court politics anything was likely to be seized upon and turned against Nikolai Nikolaevich: if the war was going badly it was because he lacked the qualities of a Supreme Commander; if things were going well, it was because he was ambitious, because he was a threat to the imperial family and was acting the part of 'Nicholas III'.

The Lord above knew how deeply the Grand-Duke grieved over the loss of the flower of his officer corps and the desperate sufferings of his troops caught in the German encirclement. But even the loss of seventy thousand men as casualties and prisoners of war was not the loss of Russia; Russia was a hundred and seventy million people. And to save them *all* one must win not merely a battle or two at the front, but first and foremost the much more serious battle going on at Court to gain the heart of his beloved Emperor. To do this he would have liked to get rid of the odious Sukhomlinov, banish the filthy Rasputin (or, better still, hang him), and finally and most important of all, have the Empress shut up in a nunnery. (This was of course impossible; the Tsar would never agree to it and the Grand-Duke was incapable of acting against the Tsar's wishes, and yet … for Russia's sake … he could still dream of it.) In order not to spoil the chances of carrying out this plan, it was important for the time being not to strengthen the hand of the Court party by provoking the ill-will of Zhilinsky. Out of love for Greater Russia the Grand-Duke had to stifle his feelings of pity and affection for that microcosm of Russia represented by Samsonov's army, which by now was in any case annihilated.

Nevertheless, it was necessary to shock Zhilinsky, to give him a thorough fright by letting Vorotyntsev loose on him. The Grand-Duke had not forgotten Vorotyntsev all this time; he had been watching the man's unease and suppressed fury out of the corner of his eye.

Outside the weather was as gloomy as ever, the rain still pattered on the panes and it was by now so dark that they turned on the electric light. The whitewashed walls made the room appear very bright and everything stood out in the sharpest detail.

It was now the turn to speak of the diplomat who represented the Foreign Office at General Headquarters. He asked the generals not to forget Russia's relations with foreign states, her obligations and other factors of external policy. France was convinced that Russia was capable of making an enormous contribution to the common cause. The French government had been making representations to the Russian government suggesting that Russia had so far failed to put her full military potential into the field; that the advance into East Prussia was a half-hearted measure; that according to French intelligence—which admittedly contradicted the information available to the Russians—far from having transferred two army corps from the Western to the Eastern front, the Germans had transferred them *from* the Russian front to the West, and that as an ally France had the right to remind Russia of her promise to launch an energetic advance on . . . Berlin.

Just as etiquette demands that one take no notice of a tactless or improper word spoken in polite society, so all the grand-dukes and generals now ignored that last embarrassing word, some by gazing out of the window, some by looking at the wall opposite them, others by staring down at their papers.

In actual fact the word 'Berlin' had not been uttered. But the diplomat's implication had been uncomfortably accurate: everyone knew that it was the Tsar's wish that they should come to the aid of their French ally at all costs and with all possible speed. Naturally, the Russian losses were painful to bear, but the important thing was not to let the Allies down.

The Chief of Army Communications then reported that the German front was being reinforced at full pressure, for which purpose a steady stream of troops was being transferred from the military districts of Asiatic Russia. At this moment three Caucasian army corps—one from Turkestan and two from Siberia—were on their way or were already de-training in the west, and three more Siberian corps would arrive soon. Thus the material preparations for an immediate Russian counter-attack, so essential from a morale point of view, were already well under way.

This was the reason, said Zhilinsky, why he was asking those present at the conference to give him permission to repeat the operation around the Masurian Lakes.

Vorotyntsev knew that if he jumped to his feet now not only would he lose everything—his rank, his seniority, his whole army career —but the top of his own head was likely to explode with the sheer pent-up pressure of frustration. Lies, lies, lies! Were there no limits to this man's falsehood? Wrenching his elbow out of Svechin's grip and forgetting that speakers were not supposed to stand up at this conference, he rose in fury. His wrath was so great that he had forgotten how he had intended to start his speech. Then he heard the firm voice of the Grand-Duke:

'I shall now ask Colonel Vorotyntsev to give a report on his personal impressions. He has been with Second Army.'

Vorotyntsev's headlong, passionate, overmastering anger was only too visible; then discretion gained the upper hand and he took a grip on his pounding heart as he remembered the proverb, 'Master of your own anger—master of all'.

'This conference is all the more necessary, Your Imperial Highness, since Rennenkampf's army is at this very moment under threat and may suffer an even worse fate than Samsonov's.'

(Too loud; keep it quieter, don't show your feelings so openly.)

Everyone present, including the Grand-Duke, shuddered and stirred uneasily as though someone had smashed a window-pane and the cold, wet wind was raging in from outside. His self-control increasing from sentence to sentence, Vorotyntsev gave what appeared to be a carefully prepared speech in which all viewpoints were judiciously weighed.

'Gentlemen! No one from Second Army has been invited to this conference, indeed there is practically no one left to invite. But I was there during the last few days and I hope I may be allowed to put forward the views which would have been expressed by men who are now dead or have been taken prisoner. I shall speak with the frankness which soldiers are taught to use and for which the dead may be forgiven . . .'

(He must keep his voice from breaking, must not gulp for breath.)

'. . . I shall not speak of the gallantry shown by the men and their officers—no one at this meeting has cast any doubt on that. The names of certain regimental commanders—Pervushin, Alexeyev, Kabanov, Kakhovskoy—deserve to be recorded in the annals of bravery. The fact that upwards of fifteen thousand men escaped from encirclement is due to the efforts of a few men at the level of colonel and staff-captain, and to no one seated here. Whenever the Germans had less than a twofold superiority in artillery, and sometimes even when they did, our units won the tactical battle. Under the heaviest possible bombardment they held their defensive lines for hours, as did the Vyborg Regiment at Usdau. Yet in spite of this the battle as it was fought at army level resulted not merely in failure, as has been suggested here, but in total destruction!' He stressed the word so violently that the whole room almost exploded. The blast of it lashed across the generals' faces.

The word 'destruction' was a challenge even to the Commander-in-Chief. He could not admit that much to the Tsar, despite his intention to hang his head in shame before His Majesty. He could not admit it, but he did not interrupt Vorotyntsev. Dignified, stern, aristocratic, he sat proud and stiff, so close by birth yet still so far from the seat of monarchy.

'. . . I have heard today how all the blame lies with General Samsonov. How convenient; the dead, after all, cannot answer back. It is particularly convenient since it absolves all of us here from any need to make amends. Convenient it may be, but if no changes are made—if you will forgive me for assuming the self-imposed role of prophet—then catastrophes like this will be repeated and we shall lose the whole war!'

There was a rustle of indignation. Zhilinsky raised his dull eyes to the Commander-in-Chief with a look which said it was high time to make this impertinent colonel stop talking and sit down.

But the Grand-Duke, who could act sharply enough when he wanted to, did not move his stiffly upright head. He showed only that he was master of the situation.

'. . . Furthermore, on behalf of the late Alexander Vasiliech Samsonov I feel obliged to object to those who have already spoken. When he arrived at Bialystok from Turkestan, it was his opinion that the plan prepared in advance ordering him to move his army forward into the depths of the Masurian Lakes region, into an obvious geographical vacuum, was absurd. He wrote his alternative operational proposals in a detailed report to the Commander-in-Chief, and on July 29th he handed it to Lieutenant-General Oranovsky, Chief of Staff of the Army Group.'

(Your voice is getting shriller—keep it down, keep it down.)

'. . . Days passed and he grew uneasy. No reply to his report was forthcoming. He asked me specifically to clarify the matter at General Headquarters and only yesterday I discovered that the Grand-Duke had never been given the report!'

Zhilinsky, the 'living corpse', gave Vorotyntsev a deathly stare. As the Commander-in-Chief himself said nothing, he felt the moment had come to intervene.

'I know nothing of this report.'

'So much the worse for you, your excellency!' Vorotyntsev seemed positively pleased at this interruption, which gave him the opportunity to turn on Zhilinsky. 'That means that the truth cannot be discovered without a court of inquiry! And if one is held, I shall request the court to *find* that paper!'

Once again a shiver of horror crossed the generals' faces. It was already clear what kind of a court of inquiry this impudent colonel . . . Everyone stared at the Commander-in-Chief: this lunatic must be stopped!

But the Grand-Duke kept his unwavering gaze riveted at a point above Zhilinsky's head.

His voice for once losing its characteristic dryness, Zhilinsky strongly protested:

'Most probably General Samsonov withdrew his report and took it back.'

Vorotyntsev, as if he had been waiting for this objection, retaliated hotly:

'No, he did not take it back, that has been verified!' And he stared unwaveringly back at Zhilinsky, the Zhilinsky who at Ostrolenka, at Neidenburg, at Orlau, had been an invisible presence, but was now sitting an arm's length away—a deathly grey, bony old man with a stiff back who suffered from a continual need to go to the lavatory. 'The variation in the axis of advance which General Samsonov proposed and which he partially put into effect was a correct one, because it meant outflanking the enemy far more deeply than was proposed by Army Group Headquarters; its only defect was that it did not go deep enough. And the over-extension of the army's frontage was due in no less a degree to the Army Group Commander's incomprehensible obstinacy in refusing to send troops to fill the gap beyond the Masurian Lakes.'

'That was not a gap—that terrain was the link between the two armies!' Zhilinsky interrupted in a firmer and sharper voice than before.

By now Vorotyntsev was aware of a tacit agreement between himself and the Commander-in-Chief: the latter was not going to interrupt him. And none of the other generals, singly or together, was in a position to contradict him. He had made the breakthrough. His mission had not been in vain. Cooler now, his tone more judicious and his lips twisted in sarcasm, he mercilessly thrashed Zhilinsky with sentence after sentence, each one curling like a whiplash:

'How could the two armies link up, when one of them was being made to advance by forced marches and the other had practically been sent on leave? How could they link up, when after the battle of Gumbinnen *five* of General Rennenkampf's cavalry divisions had failed to set off in pursuit of the enemy and were not sent to the rescue of Second Army at the time when it was in crucial trouble? It almost seems as if Army Group Headquarters purposely made it impossible to co-ordinate the actions of the two armies by ordering

First Army to advance a week earlier than Second Army. Why was this so? Or was the linking up of the two armies intended by transferring General Scheidemann's corps to Rennenkampf on August 10th, and then on the 14th ordering it to go to Warsaw? Apparently it was not needed in East Prussia on the very day when the decisive battle was being fought that was to seal the fate of Second Army.'

How on earth did Vorotyntsev know about that particular episode? Here was an error of which General Headquarters itself was guilty. Danilov glanced suspiciously at Svechin and said uneasily:

'That was done for strategic considerations. Ninth Army was being prepared to advance on Berlin . . .'

'Meanwhile Second Army could be thrown to the wolves, I suppose?' Vorotyntsev rudely cut him off. 'All the same, Scheidemann's corps was sent to help Second Army on August 15th, and yet Army Group Headquarters ordered it to march *in the wrong direction*! But on the 16th that corps was ordered back to Warsaw, and on the 17th General Rennenkampf redirected it northwards—was that the link-up of the two armies? And yet North-Western Army Group was created solely in order to co-ordinate the actions of First and Second Armies. General Samsonov has been accused of showing a lack of decisiveness, but what more crass example of indecision could there be than the Army Group Commander's, when, on the grounds of 'security', 'guarding the lines of communication', 'covering the rear', etcetera, he refused to allow *half the army* to move further forward than Bischofsburg and Soldau?'

Vorotyntsev had pressed home his point with such vehemence that Zhilinsky's moustaches, which were already trembling with fury, looked as if they might go up in smoke at any moment.

'Half the army? What do you mean—half the army?' There was a buzz of objection, not only from Danilov but from his stupid protégé, a colonel who went by the nickname of 'Brother Cain'.

'Just count, gentlemen. Two army corps, one on the right flank and one on the left, and three cavalry divisions—that makes up exactly half the army. And with the other half Samsonov was ordered to advance and win a victory. And if Army Group *had* to keep control of the flanking corps, then the very least it should have done was to move them in to help out the centre corps when they were in trouble. Yes, I agree that General Samsonov made mistakes, but they were tactical mistakes. The strategic mistakes must be laid at the door of Army Group Headquarters. Samsonov on his own did not have numerical superiority over the enemy, but Army Group did, and in spite of that the battle was lost. We must draw our conclusions, gentlemen—otherwise what is the point of this conference? What, in the end, is the point of having a staff and General Headquarters at all? *We are incapable of deploying units bigger than a regiment*—that is the conclusion!'

'Your Highness, I request you to put an end to this colonel's idiotic remarks!' Zhilinsky demanded, thumping the table to show that he was not yet quite a 'corpse'.

The Grand-Duke stared coldly at Zhilinsky with his large, expressive, oval eyes. Then he said firmly and quietly:

'Colonel Vorotyntsev is talking sense. I myself have learnt much from what he has said. In my opinion General Headquarters'—here he looked at Danilov, who lowered his bovine forehead, a movement politely imitated by Yanushkevich—'exerted practically no direction over this operation at all, entrusting it entirely to North-Western Army Group.'

He knew quite well how worthless Danilov was. Often, when reading reports that Danilov had himself prepared, the Grand-Duke was far quicker at grasping the gist than the slow-witted general.

'And if the colonel commits an error, you are always at liberty to correct him.'

Groaning, Zhilinsky rose and went out to answer the call of nature.

The Commander-in-Chief felt greatly tempted. The facts of the case had all been given. They should be studied further, and a court of inquiry set up. Zhilinsky should be dismissed with ignominy, and General Headquarters would be in the clear.

However, by his gracious telegram of the day before the Tsar had shown the Grand-Duke an alternative way out: the way of forgiveness, of letting bygones be bygones. Also, another imperial edict, as yet unannounced, had just arrived, authorising Oranovsky's promotion to the rank of full general; matters concerning promotion took their course independently of the progress of war, and there was no holding them up.

Just as the cavalry, having broken through a defensive position with some losses, has a free hand to ravage the enemy's rear, so Vorotyntsev now had a chance to gallop around and deal out a few more sabre-blows. The real conference, in fact, was only just beginning!

'. . . However, I had intended to deal with broader issues. What was it that sapped the strength of Second Army? It was having to march on foot across our own deserted, trackless Russian territory. Before even reaching the frontier, before even making contact with the enemy, the troops had to spend five or six days slogging their way through sand! And then we had to transport ammunition, guns, food, supplies, across that same expanse—and what with? With inadequate transport. Why were no supplies built up in readiness along the frontier before the war began?'

Yanushkevich frowned. It was positively painful to have to listen to this unrepentant 'young Turk' from Golovin's class at the General Staff Academy. Why was the Grand-Duke subjecting them to this torture?

'If we had done so, the enemy might have seized those supplies,' he explained cuttingly from under his bushy moustache.

'But surely,' Vorotyntsev remonstrated, his jaw mottled purple with anger, 'you don't think it's preferable to lose twenty thousand men killed and seventy thousand prisoners rather than a few dozen military storage depots?'

'The storage depots were not built near the frontier,' Danilov confidently insisted, 'because we had not planned to conduct an offensive on that front, but to defend it.'

This was true. In mentioning it, however, he had touched on the fact that the whole war-plan had been hastily altered—altered, indeed, by none other than Zhilinsky himself during his time as Chief of the General Staff, an action which had been approved not only by the Minister for War, but by the Tsar himself. This was the new plan which the Grand-Duke had been forced to accept a month ago. Here Vorotyntsev was on thin ice and could venture no further. He was just about to make another pointed remark when the door opened and Zhilinsky waddled back to his seat.

'. . . But the chief reason why Samsonov's army was destroyed was because it, like the rest of the Russian army, was not ready to advance so soon. Everyone here is aware that full readiness was calculated as being attainable two months after the date of mobilisation. A month at the very least was needed to enable any sort of advance to take place.'

Zhilinsky had reached his seat, but he did not sit down. The discussion was getting too near the bone, so he remained standing, facing Vorotyntsev, his fists resting on the table. Throwing out his chest like a boxer, purple in the face with tension, Vorotyntsev aimed his remarks at Zhilinsky alone:

'The fatal decision was taken when, out of a desire to please the French, we gave that light-hearted promise to begin war operations on the *fifteenth* day of mobilisation, a date on which the Russian army would be at *one-third* readiness! What incompetence—to promise to send our forces into battle only partly mobilised and wholly unprepared!'

'Your Highness!' Zhilinsky exclaimed to the Grand-Duke. 'This is an insult to Russia's national honour! The decision was approved by the Tsar. By the convention signed with our ally France . . .'

Seizing the last second of the Commander-in-Chief's patience with him, Vorotyntsev hurled back an answer vivid with hatred:

'According to that convention Russia promised "decisive help", not suicide! It was your signature which committed Russia to suicide, your excellency!'

(Yanushkevich, his head lowered cravenly, was forgotten. It was he who had demanded of North-Western Army Group that the advance should start four days earlier than planned.)

'It was signed by the Minister for War too!' shouted Zhilinsky, but in a voice that was beginning to crack and had lost its force. 'And approved by His Majesty. An officer like you has no business to be at General Headquarters! And no business to be in the Russian army either! Your Imperial Highness . . . !'

Handsome and dignified as ever, the Grand-Duke sat as though carved in stone, half-turned from the table, one leg crossed over the other. To Vorotyntsev he said sadly, but with stony insistence:

'Yes, Colonel. You have overstepped the bounds of what is permissible. It was not for this that I allowed you to speak.'

His speech was over—the last words, perhaps, of his whole military career. Yet it pained him not to be able to say one final thing: not to speak what he knew to be true was unbearable. Knowing that all was lost, having nothing more to fear, free of all inhibitions, seeing with his mind's eye the men of the Dorogobuzh Regiment bearing their dead colonel on their shoulders, carrying the wounded lieutenant, seeing Staff-Captain Semechkin, that bold, cheerful, little turkey-cock of a man, breaking his way through the German lines with two companies of the Zvenigorod Regiment,

Vorotyntsev turned and gave a ringing reply to the Commander-in-Chief:

'Your Imperial Highness! Like you and like General Zhilinsky I too am an officer of this army, and all we Russian officers bear a responsibility for the history of Russia. We simply cannot be allowed to go on losing campaign after campaign. Tomorrow it will be the turn of the French to despise us!'

Suddenly the Grand-Duke flared up in one of his rare bursts of anger and cut him short:

'Colonel! Leave this conference!'

But Vorotyntsev felt a great sense of relief and freedom: the burning arrow had been wrenched out of his chest. Yet it had taken some flesh with it too. He said no more. He sprang to attention, his hands down the seams of his trousers. He turned about with a click of the heels and marched towards the door.

Through the door, towards him, came an aide-de-camp, beaming with delight.

'Your Imperial Highness! A telegram from the South-Western front!'

This was it. This was what they had been waiting for. Turning, the Grand-Duke stood up. All the others rose.

'Gentlemen! The Mother of God has not abandoned our Russia! The city of Lvov has been captured. A colossal victory. We must give the news to the press.'

*

*Untruth did not begin with us;
nor will it end with us.*

1969–1970

Maps

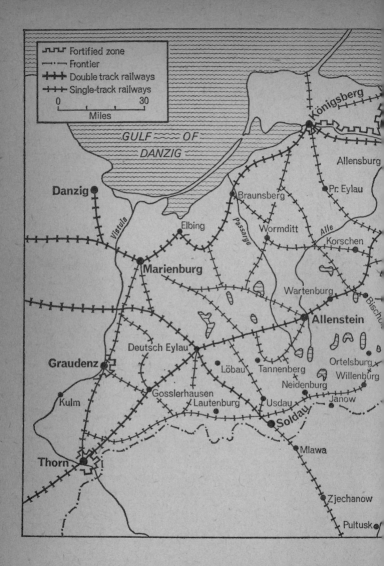

Legend:
- ⌐⌐⌐ Fortified zone
- —·—· Frontier
- +++ Double track railways
- +++ Single-track railways

0 ____ 30
Miles

GULF OF DANZIG

Königsberg

Allensburg

Danzig

Braunsberg

Pr. Eylau

Elbing

Passarge

Wormditt

Alle

Korschen

Marienburg

Wartenburg

Bischo...

Allenstein

Deutsch Eylau

Graudenz

Löbau

Tannenberg

Ortelsburg

Willenburg

Neidenburg

Kulm

Gosslerhausen

Lautenburg

Usdau

Janow

Soldau

Thorn

Mlawa

Zjechanow

Pultusk

Vistula

MAP 1

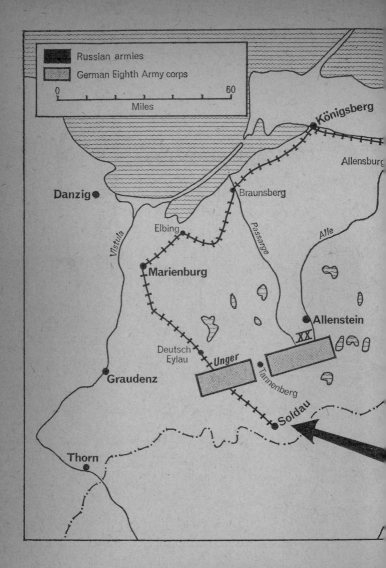

MAP 2

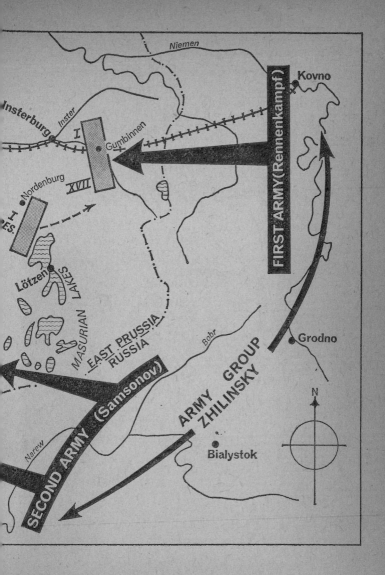

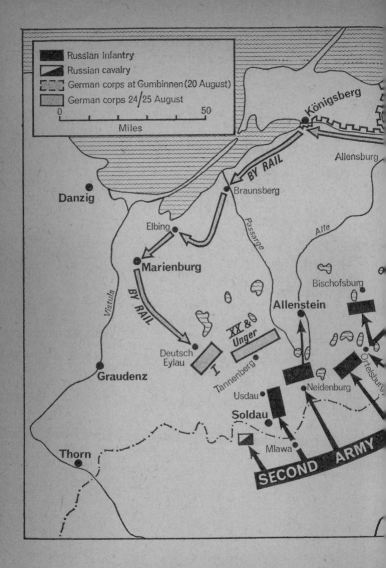

Russian infantry
Russian cavalry
German corps at Gumbinnen (20 August)
German corps 24/25 August

0   50
                    Miles

Königsberg

Allensburg

BY RAIL

Danzig

Braunsberg

Elbing

Passarge

Alle

Marienburg

BY RAIL

Bischofsburg

Allenstein

Vistula

XX & Unger

Deutsch Eylau

I

Tannenberg

Ortelsburg

Graudenz

Usdau

Neidenburg

Soldau

Mlawa

Thorn

SECOND ARMY

MAP 3

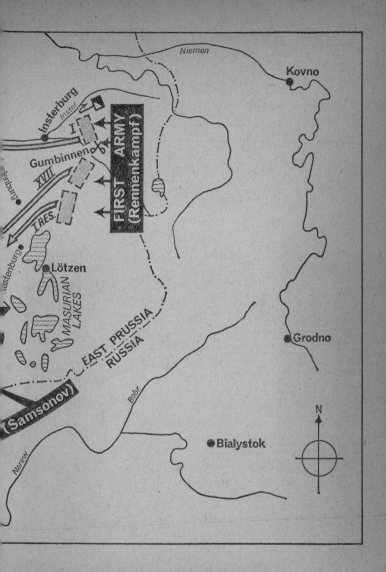

Niemen

Kovno

Insterburg

Inster

I

Gumbinnen

enburg

XVII

FIRST ARMY (Rennenkampf)

I RES.

enburg

Lötzen

MASURIAN LAKES

EAST PRUSSIA
RUSSIA

Grodno

(Samsonov)

Bobr

Narew

Bialystok

N

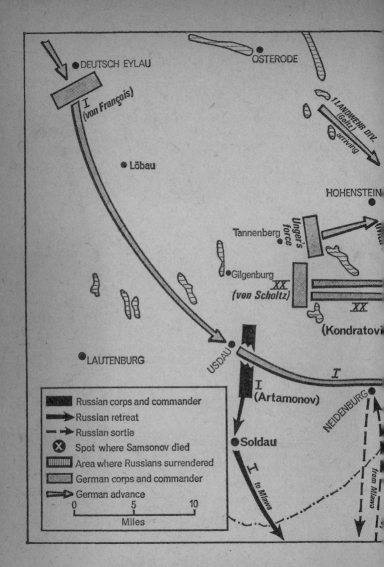

DEUTSCH EYLAU

OSTERODE

I
(von François)

1 LANDWEHR DIV.
(Goltz)
arriving

● Löbau

HOHENSTEIN

Tannenberg ●

Unger's
force

● Gilgenburg

XX
(von Scholtz)

XX

(Kondratovi

● LAUTENBURG

USDAU

I

I
(Artamonov)

NEIDENBURG

from Mlawa

Russian corps and commander
Russian retreat
Russian sortie
Spot where Samsonov died
Area where Russians surrendered
German corps and commander
German advance

0   5   10
Miles

● Soldau

II
to Mlawa

MAP 4

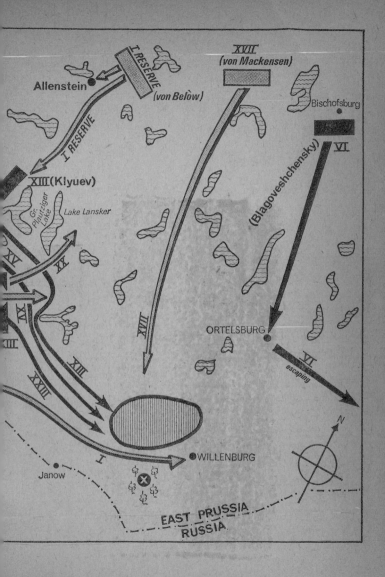

Allenstein

I. RESERVE
(von Below)

XVII
(von Mackensen)

Bischofsburg

I. RESERVE

VI

XIII (Klyuev)

Gr.
Plautziger
Lake

Lake Lansker

(Blagoveshchensky)

XV

IX

XVIII

XXIII

ORTELSBURG

VI
escaping

XIII

XXIII

N

I

WILLENBURG

Janow

⊗

EAST PRUSSIA

RUSSIA

750397

F   Solzhenitsyn,
Sol   Aleksandr
          Isaevich
          August 1914